THE

CHILD OF TWO FATHERS;

OR,

THE MYSTERIES OF THE DAYS OF OLD.

————————

A ROMANCE OF DEEP INTEREST.

————————

LONDON:

PUBLISHED BY E. LLOYD, 12, SALISBURY-SQUARE,
FLEET-STREET.

THE
CHILD OF TWO FATHERS·
OR, MYSTERIES OF THE DAYS OF OLD.

CHAPTER I

Beneath these battlements, within those walls,
Power dwelt amidst her passions; in proud state,
Each robber chief upheld his armed halls,
Doing his evil will.—BYRON.

Two roofless towers, and a ruined wall, upon which many winters have shed their storms, and from whose crumbling summit the ivy hangs in wreaths of glossy green, is all that now remains of a once spacious castle, which in former times belonged to Geoffrey de Albini, a wealthy and powerful baron, who, during the unsettled reign of Henry I., had fortified, at considerable trouble and expense, his dwelling-place. The castle was situated upon the bank of a winding river; the ground rose precipitously behind it, and at a little distance, upon a meadow which also skirted the stream, stood the venerable building appropriated to a family of nuns of the order of St. Bridget. The contrast between the castle and the nunnery was equally striking in the domains which belonged to each building, as in its inhabitants. The castle walls, built partly of flint stones curiously cut, and laid together without any discernible cement, enclosed a large space of ground which served as a place of military exercise rather than as a garden, for flowers, even herbs, it had none; a small grove of trees, however, sloped down to the river, affording a shady walk to the females of the family. Very different was the tasteful flower garden of the neighbouring convent. Its walls, built like those of the castle with a due regard to the security of the inmates, enclosed a verdant lawn, upon which the yew and the cypress cast their dark shade; while in various sunny nooks, the earliest spring flowers put forth their welcome buds, and culinary herbs were carefully reared to vary the plain fare of the convent table. Peace seemed to have taken refuge in the holy abode from the storms and disquietudes of the world, and peace also reigned in the castle, although under a different guise. There it took the form of active duty and connubial happiness, alas! too soon to be interrupted.

Love had united Geoffrey de Albini and the Lady Elfrida in early life, and a lovely little girl cemented their union. Albini at first repined that a son had not been given to him, whom he might train up to be a loyal and brave warrior, as he himself was; but when on his return to Thornbury Castle, fatigued, and perhaps disheartened by the course of public affairs, the little babe met him with laughing eyes and attempted words of affection, the chieftain no longer regretted that he had not a son. A daughter might be a treasure and a consolation in his old age, a son must be given to his country.

One winter's evening, the inhabitants of the convent were startled at their devotions by a loud ringing at the door-bell, and a man impetuously demanded to see the abbess. Upon being told that she was engaged at vespers, he reluctantly consented to await her leisure, delivering to the attendant a signet which he desired might be given to the abbess immediately upon her return from the chapel. His request was complied with; and by the abbess' orders he was ushered into the parlour, where, placing a basket upon the table, he gave a sealed packet to the abbess, and immediately withdrew. His abrupt actions and departure startled the abbess, but the signet roused her attention, and a low moan which proceeded from the basket made her hasten to uncover it, when an infant of about three months' old met her astonished gaze. The child was richly and delicately clothed, and attached to its robe was a ticket bearing the words, "Cordelia, December, 3rd." The abbess knew but too well the history of the little stranger, and without waiting to open the packet she summoned to her presence one of the elder nuns of the convent, a person of discretion and feeling.

"See, Sister Maria, the gift which has been bestowed upon us to-night," said the abbess; "to your care I commit this lovely babe until I can make arrangements for its comfort. I wish now to be alone for a time; see that it be fed carefully, and I will ring the bell when I wish you to bring it to me again. But I charge you let no idle gossip arise from this occurrence; you see the name which the poor outcast bears, further than that, it is not probable that any under this roof will ever know; therefore warn your younger companions from any absurd surmises or reports."

Sister Maria promised obedience to the injunctions given her, and with many exclamations of wonder, which she could not repress, intermixed with epithets of admiration of the infant, and its equipments, she left the room, to excite in her fellow inmates the feelings which she herself experienced.

We must not intrude upon the privacy of the lady abbess, nor inquire into the secrets which the packet unveiled to her; it is enough to say, that after the space of two hours, Sister Maria was again summoned to the parlour, where she found the abbess with eyes red with weeping; but with her usual air of composure, she gave the orders requisite for the attendance upon her new charge.

The news of the occurrence at the abbey speedily flew to the castle, and brought the Lady Elfrida to see the little stranger, whom she at once recognised as the offspring of noble parents. Of course her curiosity was excited to learn its parentage, and the cause of its being thus placed in the hands of strangers, but a few words from the abbess checked her inquiries, which she at once saw it was in vain to push any further.

" If I may know nothing," said the lady, " of this poor infant's past life, at least I may take an interest in its future welfare. She will be a playfellow for my child, and as her clothing betokens her of noble birth, she may visit the castle as an equal."

The abbess expressed a disinclination to allow the infant to leave the convent, and seemed rather to draw back from the offered attention of Lady Elfrida.

" We know not," she said, " what the destiny of this child may hereafter be; and if she be intended to enter our society as a sister, it would be extremely unwise and unnecessary to expose her to the allurements of the world. Although nobly born, she may yet be happier in seclusion, than in assuming the place and dignity of her birth. Nevertheless, whatever the Lady Elfrida may wish, shall be acceded to if possible by me."

Twelve months passed away; the young heiress had accomplished her third year, and the little stranger, Cordelia, her first. Each promised to be beautiful, and each was the petted plaything of those around.

Near the brink of the river, in the grove which was the place of recreation to the female inhabitants of the castle, stood a low tower, probably originally intended for a banqueting-room; but as Albini had never used it as such, preferring the spacious hall, where he might have his retainers about him more commodiously, Lady Elfrida had appropriated the garden tower to her own use, and had furnished it according to her own taste, exchanging the warlike implements which had decorated its walls, for the more harmless ones which belonged to the female employment; and here, in the " Lady"s Tower," as it was called, Elfrida passed much of her time in company with her attendants. Here, too, the young heiress of Thornbury Castle pursued her childish amusements, and upon the smooth green terrace, which, raised a little above the river, communicated with the other part of the domain, her infant steps first ventured alone. Many hours in the day did the Lady Elfrida pass in laying plans for the future prosperity and happiness of her darling child, upon whose destiny it seemed to her that a cloud could never rest.

That tower is now in ruins, and of the castle but little remains; the banqueting hall, the armoury, the drawbridge, and the keep have fallen; the lonely owl now sings her nightsong where formerly was heard the hum of many tongues; the bat flaps her wings upon the walls from which the archers were wont to bend their bows, and send destruction among their foes.

One lovely summer's evening the Lady Elfrida was seated at the window of the tower, watching the deepening shadows as they stole gradually upon a grove of majestic oaks which clothed the side of an opposite hill, and from time to time, remarking to her attendant the hues which the setting sun cast upon the river beneath, when her attention was attracted by a small white object on the surface of the water. It first caught her view just below the abbey garden, and as it approached nearer to the tower, she said to her attendant,—

" Alice, do you see that small speck of white upon the river below? my curiosity is excited, go down to the terrace, and bring me back word what it is."

Alice obeyed her lady, and was absent for some time, till the lady becoming impatient, she was proceeding herself to the steps of the terrace, when Alice returned saying—

" My lady, it seems to me to be the bonnet which the sisters of the abbey embroidered for little Cordelia, like the one they presented to our young lady. I endeavoured long in vain to reach it, but I will go to the castle and obtain help; the sisters will be sorry to lose it."

"Go, Alice," said her mistress, "I will remain here till your return. It is a strange accident, but the wind was very gusty this afternoon, and no doubt Cordelia was with her nurse in the lawn when it was blown away from her head. But be quick, as your young lady will expect me as usual to attend upon her undressing for repose."

When Alice went down to the castle, the first person whom she met was the nurse.

"Why does my lady keep my child so long out in the evening air ?" she said to Alice. "The sweet little angel coughed this morning, and my lady will kill her by letting her breathe the damp fog which is now rising from the meadows."

"She is not with my lady," replied Alice ; "my lady is coming presently to see her before she goes to bed."

"Then," replied the nurse, in a low tone of alarm, "I do not know where she is. The girl, Ursula, took her as she said to the terrace. What shall we do ?"

"Oh," replied Alice, "no doubt Ursula changed her mind, and she is in my lady's dressing-room ; I dare say, I cannot stay now, I want some one to help me to get little Cordelia's bonnet out of the river; it is just at the terrace steps, and my lady desired me to have it got out, as she thinks the sisters would be sorry to lose it."

"Here is Ambrose coming," said the nurse, "and I will go with you."

Accordingly the three servants proceeded to the edge of the river, and Ambrose having, with considerable difficulty, obtained the bonnet, Alice was going to take it to the castle, when the nurse screamed out,—

"It is hers !—it is not Cordelia's ! Here is the ribbon which I sewed on myself this morning—where is my darling ? I am sure she is drowned !"

"Nonsense, nonsense," said Ambrose ; "this bonnet fell from the bank of the abbey garden, I dare say."

"I am sure it is hers !" replied the nurse, hastening towards the lady's tower with the bonnet in her hand.

"Where are you going, foolish woman?" said Ambrose, catching hold of her arm; "you will kill our lady, go back to the castle, you will find the child there, no doubt."

"But she is not there; I told Alice just now I had lost her."

"Lost her !—what do you mean?"

"Oh, I am sure she is drowned !" exclaimed Alice, having caught the nurse's fears.

"Then I will not go with you to tell my lady," said Ambrose ; "let us all go to the castle."

They went to the castle, and after making inquiry of the rest of the domestics for Ursula, and searching everywhere for the little girl, without the slightest prospect of success in learning tidings of either, the servants drew together, and were conversing about the mysterious disappearance, when their lady approached.

"Alice," said Lady Elfrida, "I desired you to return to the tower when you rescued the bonnet, why did you not do so? Let the bonnet be carried down to the abbey this evening."

"My lady," sobbed the nurse, "it is not Miss Cordelia's bonnet, it is my young lady's."

"Well, do not afflict yourself, nurse," said her lady, "it is an accident of little importance, except that the sisters will be sorry their work should be spoiled. Bring the child to my dressing room, it is late."

"Oh, my lady ! my lady !" cried the nurse, catching hold of Lady Elfrida's dress, "pray forgive me."

"Yes, yes," answered her lady ; then observing for the first time the sorrowful countenances around her, "what is the matter ?—tell me quickly where is my child ?"

No one answered.

"Speak! I command you, speak?" cried the lady, vehemently, "has any harm befallen my sweet babe? Nurse, you had the charge of her, tell me what is the matter?"

The nurse at last murmered out that she had given the child to Ursula's care to carry her to the Lady's Tower, and that neither of them had been seen since.

The lady heard no more; she fell into a swoon, from which she was recovered only to fall into another; and in this state, between life and death, she continued during the whole night, and upon the return of Albina the next day great fear was entertained lest her strength should entirely sink under the vehemence of her maternal feelings. At length, however, she became more calm, and a flood of tears relieved her overcharged heart.

Albini was no less afflicted than his wife, but his sorrow showed itself in making an active search for any circumstance that might decide the fate which had so mysteriously befallen his child. Vain were all attempts to unravel the cause of the accident; no other vestige of either nurse or child was discovered, and at last it was agreed by the inhabitants of the castle, that Ursula having by accident lost the child in the river, had gone immediately away through fear of the consequences of her carelessness.

To the Lady Elfrida the blow was overwhelming; her only child had been the idol of her heart and her hopes; she could not, like Albini, forget for a time in the stirring pleasures of the chase, the desolation which made her once happy home a scene of misery; and after struggling for a few months in a state which gave additional pain to her attached husband, she acquiesced in his proposal to leave Thornbury, and take up their residence at another castle which he possessed in a distant part of the kingdom. Albini urged this step with the more earnestness, as a stranger baron had applied to him to hire the castle of Thornbury, and he was not sorry to have such an excuse for leaving a spot which recalled such bitter associations.

One person alone endeavoured to change the purpose of Albini; this was the prior of a neighbouring monastery, a man of austere virtue, and one who, having through remorse at early vices withdrawn himself from the world, had no longer any sympathy with human weakness. His early feelings hardened by folly and dissipation, his manhood stained by vice, Father Augustine sought by repeated and painful penances to atone for former sin; and while his awakened soul acknowledged and admired the stainless character of Albini, he morosely endeavoured to impress upon his noble penitent the conviction that this world is one of misfortune and suffering solely, and that in flying from the scene of his misery, he was rebelling against the hand which had so grievously chastened him. But his exhortations were in vain; the life of his lady was dearer to Albini than anything now left to him, and, although honouring the stern virtue of Father Augustine, he could not submit to his control.

A trial awaited the lady in parting with the infant at the convent. She had loved Cordelia, as well as a bereaved mother could love her, and the mystery which hung over the child strengthened her love. She had even hinted a wish to take the child entirely herself, but the abbess had so decidedly and firmly given a refusal to this request, that Lady Elfrida was obliged to content herself with a daily visit to the convent, for the purpose of weeping over an object which reminded her so powerfully of the treasure which she had lost.

On the morning preceding the departure of Albini and his lady from Thornbury Castle, the latter went to the convent, and after caressing the infant she said to the abbess,—

"You will not allow me to replace my lost darling, by taking away with me this little treasure; but you cannot, you must not, deny me one request. If ever sickness or misfortune should deprive Cordelia of your protection, will you send her to me as a mother? I will endeavour to be such an one to her."

"Alas," replied the abbess, "would that I dared to promise this; but they are yet living who have a right to Cordelia's love, and to them I might be called on to resign her, although fervently I hope such a duty may not be forced upon me."

"You know then the history of this child, and her family?" said the lady.

"But too well," replied the abbess. "Cordelia is nobly born; her mother was beautiful, and of high rank; but she threw away the gifts of nature and of fortune, and became an outcast. The last, best act of her life was to save her unhappy child from a like fate, by placing it under my roof. But times may change, and my Cordelia may yet shine in the situation to which she was born. I dare not say more, or to no one would I so unreluctantly trust the secret of her history as to yourself; therefore, I pray you, ask no further questions; and above all, do not hint to Father Augustine, that I have said a word about my child."

The lady promised circumspection, and taking a respectful farewell of the abbess, and a tender adieu of Cordelia, she left the convent, and shortly after departed with her husband to a distant country.

Years passed on; the young Cordelia grew up, beloved by the inmates of the convent, and deserving their love. Tidings had arrived of the birth of a son to Albini, about a twelvemonth after he had left Thornbury; but neither himself nor the Lady Elfrida had ever felt sufficient fortitude to revisit the scene of their affliction.

Who, then, is the inhabitant of Thornbury? Whose vassals are they that almost in countless numbers sit in the hall? Who is the chief to whom they bow? Look at him at the festive board surrounded by friends and dependents; his fine features wear a deep, stern look, save when he turns to the fair being seated by his side; then does a smile of exquisite tenderness, tinctured with melancholy play around his lip, and his dark and penetrating eyes beam with a joy never awakened in his heart, except in the presence of the gentle creature. Yet it is not that the heart of Ralph de Fougeres was cold, trials and sorrows in early life had thrown a reserve over his demeanour, but gentle and kind feelings still throbbed in the secret recesses of his bosom; his bearing was lofty as suited his rank, but it spoke not of haughtiness; his vassals loved him while they feared him, and were ready to yield their lives in the service of their lord.

And who is the golden-haired creature by his side? 'Tis Edith, his only child, the pride of his home, the joy of his heart; love beamed from his eyes when she appeared, and tenderness dwelt in the tones of his deep voice, when in his discourse with her. And Edith loved her father; for him she wove bright banners; but when she saw them unfurled, and borne at the head of his vassals, tears would chase each other down her pale cheeks, and retiring to the Lady's Tower she fervently prayed that her beloved parent might be shielded from danger in the battle-field. Upon such occasions Edith did not indulge her fears without sympathy. Cordelia had from childhood been her companion—she was now her bosom friend. By nature of a lively disposition, the dull routine of a convent life had failed in checking a vivacity which found, even in the sombre dress and precise manners of those by whom she had been brought up, food for its exercise. The abbess, who was tenderly attached to her charge, saw this with extreme pain; she dreaded lest it should be the fate of Cordelia to take the veil, and she saw how totally unfitted her child was for a life of seclusion. If at any time she hinted these fears to Cordelia, they were met by a decided, although a respectful, avowal of her determination never to become a nun; and when the abbess referred to her declining health, and asked Cordelia what must then be her destiny, the poor girl was so completely overwhelmed with grief at the mere supposition of danger to her benefactress, that her own situation and uncertain fortune seemed entirely forgotten by her. The Lady Edith had indeed said repeatedly, that while she had a home, Cordelia should share it with her; but this was dependent upon the pleasure of De Fougeres, and Cordelia did not like him, except as the father of her friend. He was stern towards her, and regarded as low-bred levity those sallies of youthful spirit which the convent girl could not always repress. The period to which the abbess had referred, arrived. She was naturally of delicate habit, and an accidental illness threatened to bring her to an early grave. Who shall describe the affliction of Cordelia? Not allowed to be always with her dear mother, as she had been accustomed to call her, she used to repair to the Lady's Tower, and to Edith tell all her fears.

One evening Edith had been awaiting the arrival of her friend at the accustomed time, but more than an hour had elapsed, and she did not come. Edith, who had heard from the domestics of the castle that the abbess was rapidly becoming worse, feared that the last moment had indeed arrived; and she was leaving the tower to order that some inquiry should be made, when she perceived Cordelia slowly approaching. Upon seeing her the afflicted girl ran forward, and throwing herself into Edith's arms, sobbed out,—

"I must leave you, they are going to send me away."

"Away!" exclaimed Edith; "why is that?"

"Our mother is dying; Father Augustine has been at the convent to-day, and he talked a long while with her; and afterwards he sent for me, and he says he is afraid I must go."

"And what did you say, Cordelia?"

"I told him I would not go; I said I had no other home, no other friends, and that if they did take me away, I would watch for an opportunity and run back to you."

"Did you really tell Father Augustine this? How dared you speak so to him?"

"I could not help it; at last he seemed sorry for me, and he asked me if I would not like to live in a grand castle, and wait upon a noble lady, to hold her mantle for her, and thread the needles for her embroidery."

"And what answer did you give the father?"

"I said I would not wait upon any one except my good mother; and as to a grand castle, if it were my own, I should be very happy in it, but I would never be a menial. Father Augustine looked very severely at me, and sighed. 'You have not been taught humility, I find,' said he; 'the spirit of your race is unbroken in you.'"

"What did he mean, Cordelia?"

"Indeed, I know not. I begged him to explain what he said; I told him I would do anything if he would but tell me who I am, and who I belong to; but he said he dared not yet do so. However, he promised me that I shou'd not be sent away directly, and he is coming again to-morrow to talk with the abbess about me."

"I am very much afraid of Father Augustine," said Edith; "my father is always unhappy for hours after he has been with him, and he speaks so gloomily that he frightens me. What can he have to do with you?"

"I do not know; he never took any notice of me till lately, and now he seems as if he had authority over me. I dread to-morrow."

After many words of condolence and sympathy, the friends separated. Edith sought her father, whom she found in earnest conversation with the dreaded Father Augustine. At first she hesitated to make known the errand which brought her to him, but his entreaties and expressions of kindness drew it from her.

"Father," she said, "the lady abbess is dying; may I offer my friend Cordelia a home in this castle?"

Fougeres and the monk looked at each other for a minute in silence, till the former said,—

"I scarcely know how to answer your request, Edith; I do not like to deny you anything, but this is a matter that requires consideration. What do you say to it, Father Augustine?"

"I say, Ralph de Fougeres, beware how you interfere again with the offspring of others; you have had one warning, and years of misery must have made you feel that you have no right to indulge your feelings at the expense of others. I take some interest in this child of the convent, and I must protest against having her fortune linked in any way with yours. Punishment must one day overtake the revengeful and malicious, even although his castle walls be strong, and those who defend them be numerous. I again say, Ralph de Fougeres, make restitution before it is too late."

Edith had stood an amazed spectator of the vehemence of the father, comprehending only in part what he had said ; but what she did understand deemed like a threat to her beloved parent, and throwing herself on her knees before him, she exclaimed,—

"Oh father, do as he wishes, whatever it may be !"

"Can he ask me now ?" said Fougeres.

"Yes, now, and at all times ; in love, and in grief ;" replied Father Augustine.

"Then I now tell you, hard-hearted monk, that never till my Edith shall own a protector in a husband, will I do that which you wish to drive me to. Edith, what say you to this, are you willing to leave me ?"

"Never, never, my dear father," replied the trembling maiden, as she threw herself into her father's arms.

"Obstinate man," exclaimed Father Augustine, leaving the room, "but remember the punishment will come when you are least prepared for it."

"Edith, my child, retire," said Fougeres ; "you are agitated by this monk's effrontery ; I have many times resolved not to admit him again to my confidence, but he has been accustomed to this castle, and I believe his intentions are good."

"But what does he mean by punishment, father?" asked Edith ; "you have no faults except that you love me too well, and humour my fancies. Pray, pray, do not think of marrying me," continued she, holding down her head.

"Well, well, compose yourself, my sweet Edith ; remember you must preside at the banquet this evening ; you know that I have no delight in such scenes without you by my side."

Edith retired to her apartment in order to arrange her apparel for the evening banquet, but her thoughts were occupied less upon her toilet, than upon the mysterious words and conduct of Father Augustine. She saw with grief that it was in vain to hope that Cordelia should become an inmate of the castle, and she wept long and bitterly over the disappointment of hopes which she was not aware of having cherished until they were thus rudely broken off by the monk. She descended to the hall in a mood little calculated to enjoy the company of those assembled there.

Ralph de Fougeres loved festivity ; he filled his castle with noble friends, and provided for them every species of amusement ; the tournament, the chase, and parties upon the water were had recourse to ; every day brought some fresh pleasure, and every evening a sumptuous repast was prepared ; the meats smoked upon the board, and the goblet was liberally filled. Of these parties Edith was the star ; many a fair maiden was beside her, but she outshone them all ; her father's eyes rested upon her in proud delight, and he listened with pleasure to the praises his guests bestowed upon her. Among these guests were many who might have aspired to win the hand of Edith, and some did endeavour to gain her favour ; but, happy and open-hearted, she gave encouragement to none, and while they admired her frankness, they acknowledged that it deprived them of all hope. Once indeed Fougeres had spoken to his daughter in favour of a neighbouring baron, but his appeal gave her pain, and he never again adverted to the subject of her marriage.

On this evening, Edith was more than usually reserved and thoughtful ; she replied only by monosyllables to the remaks addressed to her, till her father observing her abstraction, said,—

"Where is Cuthred, your merry little page, my Edith ? Shall he be summoned to sing to us ?"

Edith rejoiced in the proposal ; the page was ordered to attend, and, with a sweet voice, he sang of battles and of love. Afterwards others sang lays of merriment or of sadness, as the feeling of the moment prompted. A handsome youth took his turn, and, as he leaned against a huge pillar opposite to where the Lady Edith was seated, he boldly touched the strings of his harp, and his sounding prelude gradually softened into a sweet but melancholy air which he accompanied by his rich and mellow voice.

SONG.

Oh! turn from me those eyes so bright,
    That beam with heaven's own blue;
I dare not gaze upon their light,
    So deep and tender too:

Or do they think a frowning look,
    My ardent love can kill?
Their fiercest anger I will brook,
    And e'en in wrath love still.

Oh! turn from me those coral lips,
    Whose accents flow as sweet
As honey that the queen-bee sips,
    When on her wing so fleet.

Oh! do not think a scornful sneer,
    Can bow my spirit free;
E'en that with patience I will bear,
    If it proceed from thee.

Oh! turn from me thy cheek's soft glow,
    And hide those tresses fair,
That in such gentle ringlets flow,
    And float upon the air.

Or if those cheeks should paler grow,
    And lose their soft'ning red,
I'll love them as the driven snow,
    Or a sweet lily bed.

Or if those tresses should turn grey,
    And lose their golden hue,
I still will love them many a day,
    As well as now I do.

I durst not hope—but I can love,
    And that my bliss must be,
While time and trials only prove,
    My constancy to thee.

Why has the colour mantled in the cheek and forehead of the Lady Edith? Why does she stoop to caress the faithful bloodhound crouched at her feet? Did she hear the sigh of the minstrel? No; it was hushed in its birth. Did she mark the deep passion of his eyes while singing? No; hers were cast upon the ground. Then what caused that brilliant blush? Why did her father speak twice to her ere she heard him? It was Eustace Mowbray, the playmate of her child-hood, the frequent companion of her older years, who had so feelingly sung. And she rejoiced much more than he did in the plaudits bestowed upon his minstrelsy; she did not applaud, she spoke not her thanks, but the sweet smile she bestowed at parting that evening, told Eustace that she had heard his words, and disliked them no:

Love builds with straws, and Hope rides upon a feather; Eustace returned to his home with a deepened love and increased hope; while Edith retired to her chamber, with the conviction that her father would yield his consent to her union with —— she did not finish the mental sentence, but gave a hurried glance at a castle dimly seen in the distance.

CHAPTER II.

These shall the fury passions tear,—
The vultures of the mind,
Disdainful anger, pallid fear,
And shame that skulks behind,
Or pining love shall waste their youth,
Or jealousy with rankling tooth,
That inly gnaws the secret heart;
And envy wan, and faded care,
Grim-visag'd, comfortless despair,
And sorrow's piercing heart.—GRAY.

WHILE the lovely Edith was bestowing the graces of her conversation upon the noble and renowned guests in her father's hall, and holding more familiar intercourse with the fair ladies assembled around his hospitable board, a very different scene presented itself at the neighbouring convent. Mirth, even that quiet, holy mirth, which was not unsuited to the hallowed spot, was now hushed there; every eye was tearful, every step was heavy, for the beloved abbess was supposed to be dying. Among many who had dwelt under her gentle rule, many of them from tender infancy, there were none who did not deeply grieve for their expected loss. Spotless in temper and in mind herself, she could yet make an allowance for the frailties of those around her; and her calm and gentle rebuke was felt eve by th hardened sinner.

Sister Maria and Cordelia were on this evening sitting by the bedside of their friend, engaged in pious conversation, disturbed occasionally by the deep-drawn sigh of Sister Maria, or the more irrepressible sob of Cordelia, when one of the nuns announced that Father Augustine was below, and requested the promised audience.

The invalid desired that he should be immediately admitted.

" Surely not to-night, dear mother," said Cordelia; " defer it till to-morrow, I pray you."

" Yes, even to-night, my child," replied the abbess; "I have much to converse upon with the father, and to-morrow may never come to me."

Cordelia burst into a passion of tears, and taking the hand of the abbess, she said,—

" Oh, my dearest mother! let us hope that this medicine, which is so highly recommended to us, will give the improvement that is promised; for my sake, for your poor Cordelia, who is broken-hearted to see you agitated, defer the father's visit till to-morrow; a night of refreshing sleep will enable you to talk with him with less discomposure."

" Alas! my child, you must not counsel delay; it is for your sake that I must see him to-night; as I have said, there may be no to-morrow for me. Bring me the casket, which you will find in the closet of my oratory, carefully unlock the closet, there are secrets there.

Cordelia took the keys from the hand of her friend, and went into the oratory. With a trembling touch she unlocked the door of the closet, and bringing out the casket, she placed it upon a small table which stood by the bedside. A strong feeling of curiosity pervaded her mind as she said to the abbess,—

" Is it then respecting me that Father Augustine comes to-night?"

" Why do you imagine that, my child?" inquired the abbess.

" Can you think, dear mother," replied Cordelia, " that I have forgotten the day when you tied round my neck this chain of gold, desiring me to keep it as my most valuable possession? You then said, that not even the rosary which was your own gift to me, was of so much importance to my welfare as this slender chain, and when will you give me the locket which you promised me?"

"To-morrow,—to-night,—my child, if the father advise so," replied the abbess.

"And may I then know who I am?" asked Cordelia, vehemently. "Oh! do not tell me that I belong to that harsh man! tell me anything but that."

"You must leave me now, my child; depend upon my love; and that thy life shall be made as smooth to thee as my care can render it," murmured the abbess.

"Alas, it is cruelly sown with briers at its commencement."

Cordelia reluctantly left the room, and Father Augustine entered.

"Sister," he said, "I am here at thy bidding; our businss, however painful, must be completed."

"I know it,—I know it, father," said the abbess, sobbing; "oh, do not blame me if I have delayed the task to almost the latest moment of my life. I am ready now; take the key, and let me once more look upon the likeness of her whom I have mourned and prayed for during many a heavy hour. But once have I opened that casket."

"And why that once?" asked the monk.

"But to give my child, Cordelia, a memorial of her unhappy parent," replied the abbess.

"And were you so unwise as to communicate to the girl the particulars of her birth?" asked Father Augustine, angrily.

"Nay, good father, I have not broken our compact; I merely placed round her neck the golden chain which was in the casket, telling her to value it as her life. This I did when she had arrived at her twelfth year; I have now promised to add to it the locket which contains her mother's and her father's hair.'

"An unwise promise, and one better broken than kept," replied the monk. 'However, it matters little now he is dead."

"Dead!" exclaimed the abbess. "Oh, father! tell me when?—how?"

"In Palestine, by the hand of thy injured brother," replied the monk sternly.

The abbess screamed, and fell senseless upon the pillow. Restoratives were fortunately at hand, and the monk was too much accustomed to scenes of sickness and of death to be ignorant of the manner of administering them; his attention speedily restored the invalid to her senses, and she eagerly desired him to acquaint her with the particulars of that which she was so much overcome at hearing had occurred.

"Perhaps it is time that I should break my silence," said Father Augustine. "I have hitherto pertinaciously refused to converse upon this subject, and have kept you, my sister, in ignorance of events which materially concern our present determinations. You know that when, during the absence of Robert de Hesling in the Holy Land, your unhappy sister Eleanor, betrayed her wifely duty, and fled with Walter de Dunstanville; the young couple took refuge in his castle among the mountains of Cumberland. It so chanced that one of our brotherhood resided in a convent near, and through his means I gained information of the illness of your sister, and of her unhappy state of mind with respect to her infant child. With such cruelty was she treated by De Dunstanville—by him, for whose love she had sacrificed husband, home, and happiness, that she resolved not to leave his child in his power. I knew the traitor; I knew his hard and sinful heart in times of old, before I was called from the world to a life of peace and piety; I knew De Dunstanville; and I readily acquiesced in a plan to remove the young Cordelia to a safe asylum, and to place her far away from the contagion of her mother's vicious example."

"Oh, father!" interrupted the abbess, "speak not so of her who was once spotless and innocent as the child she has left to me. You know not—you cannot know, how fervently I loved my young and beautiful sister; and when my doom was announced, that in compliance with a vow of my mother I was to take the veil, I grieved only at leaving my beloved Eleanor. Alas! had she not been left in solitude by her husband, she had never deserted her duty.'

"Hush—hush; my sister—can you speak irreverently of that holy call which has been given to so many of our noblest names to venture their earthly safety, and even to lose their lives, for the blessed land of Palestine. Hardly, have they earned the pardon of their former sins by the saving virtue of bearing the cross; and their wives and relatives should glory in their devotedness. Even I, did not age prevent me, would join the faithful band, fearless of death or disaster. Well was it for Robert de Hesling that he saw not the dishonomr of his house; well that seas rolled and mountains rose between him and the deceitful being whose guilt has tarnished his shield, hitherto so glorious. But she paid the penalty in shame and in misery; she yielded up the life which she had stained, and it would gladden my spirit could I believe that her child does not inherit her mother's faults. But much I fear that Cordelia is too ready to follow the example as soon as it shall be pointed out to her."

The abbess, weak and exhausted as she was, was roused to anger at this insinuation against her niece; she knew the temper of Cordelia to be quick, and her spirits buoyant, but she knew her also to be single-hearted and ingenuous; unconscious that evil existed, and seeking out good in everything. Expressing her sentiments with vivacity, without always duly weighing her expressions in the scale of prudence, Cardelia had repeatedly drawn upon herself the reprimands of Father Augustine; and by degrees a sort of dislike had grown up between them, which pained the good abbess, who vainly endeavoured to alleviate it. Now, however, when the child whom she had adopted and educated was thus vilified, the anger of the abbess burst its accustomed bounds, and she intimated to her companion that his dislike to the parents had been most unwarrantably extended to their innocent offspring.

"I did dislike her parents! De Dunstanville had been my friend—he became my enemy—he had earned my hatred; and for her whom he vainly endeavoured to make his wife, can virtue make companionship with vice?"

"What do you say? vainly endeavoured to make his wife?" exclaimed the abbess.

"Yes—De Dunstanville applied to the pope for a dispensation in order to wed your sister, alleging her too near relationship to De Hesling. He did this, not through love for her; do not think so; she knew it to be only to obtain her lands, and she resisted his application by means of her kindred. This raised his anger; he became her gaoler and her tyrant, and she pined beneath his cruelty; till upon the birth of her infant, she repented her discouragement of the effort which, if successful, would have legitimatised her child; but it was too late: she died ere the step could be completed, and Cordelia is an outcast."

"Not while I have life or power to bequeath a home to her," cried the abbess. "But proceed, father, tell me of the after years of her more guilty parent.'

"You may remember that a short time after Cordelia's arrival here, I was absent for a few weeks upon especial business. I went to Eden Castle; I saw your beloved Eleanor; I received her confession, and with her I concerted measures for the future guidance of her infant. She was imperative respecting any communication with you, and it was only by promising to conceal all knowledge of the circumstances from you, that I obtained her confidence. Ask not my motives—I have said that I hated De Dunstanville— yet I urged Eleanor's compliance with his wish to make her his wife—she yielded to my advice; but when at lengtht the messenger returned from Rome with the dispensation which would have made her the wife, but the hated wife, of De Dunstanville—she was a corpse. Death had even outstripped Avarice."

"But you know there was a previous betrothment, if so it may be called; that now is valid to secure my Cordelia from shame and beggary."

"A pervious botrothment? what can you mean?" cried the monk hastily. "I know of no such act.'

"Before my wretched sister could be prevailed upon to leave her husband's house, she required of De Dunstanville a solemn promise in writing and properly attested, that if at any future time her present tie to her husband De Hesling should cease or be broken, he would acknowledge her as his lawful wife, by virtue of a ceremony which had been performed before she eloped. That paper is in existence, and shall now be acted upon.''

" Stay—stay—rash woman : it may be valid, or it may be worthless ; we cannot judge of this. Where is it? let me have it ; I will ask the opinion of those more learned than myself in such matters."

" Never will I yield it up, except to the rightful owner," replied the abbess.

" And who is the rightful owner? De Dunstanville is dead, and could you recal him, you would scarcely give it to his keeping? To whom then will you relinquish it ?"

" To Cordelia—to my child.''

" Madness, or worse than madness ! It must not, it shall not be !''

A gloomy silence of a few minutes ensued, which at length was broken by the monk, who said,—

" Let us leave the discussion of this subject for the present. I said that De Dunstanville is dead, you have yet more to learn—he died by the hand of Robert de Hesling. After the death of his wife, for he so affected to call her, he claimed her lands, and being a favourite with the king he obtained them. He feasted—he revelled—but the worm was at his heart—that worm which never dies. He sent for me—he confessed his many heinous sins, not knowing that with many of them I was too familiar; but let that pass. He demanded absolution—I refused it. The church, you know, my daughter, is poor through her virtues of charity and beneficence; she cannot give absolution without receiving wherewith to exercise those virtues. I required his lands, his riches ; the despairing penitent at length yielded there ; I demanded of him his aid in the holy war against the infidels, and he departed. Thus hath the church power over a repentant son. De Dunstanville departed for Palestine, to meet the man whom he had so deeply injured, and he did meet him. Robert de Hesling had earned glory upon the fervid plains Syria; his heart had become as seared as her deserts, no well spring of mercy or love flowed from it ; he hated his fellow-creatures, because one had injured him ; and well and praiseworthy was it that he wreaked upon the infidels the wrongs his countryman had inflicted on him. His valour was applauded, his presence was necessary to lead others in the same path, he only knew that his home was desolate, and that glory and renown awaited him on the battle field.

When, therefore, De Hesling heard of the arrival of his enemy, to thwart, perhaps to eclipse, him in the path which had hitherto been his solely, he resolved upon vengeance, and he found it. An opportunity of quarrel soon presented itself. Among so many brave spirits, all eager to obtain the wreath of conquest, or the cypress crown of martyrdom, temper was not always unruffled ; and it needed not the determination to seek a quarrel, it was found without an effort. I know not the immediate cause, but they fought, and De Dunstanville fell. De Hesling, the idol of his soldiers, and the honoured of his brother barons, was held exonerated from all blame ; he continued his career of glory, and, although by news lately arrived from Palestine, I find that his views are somewhat altered, I doubt not he has chosen a wise and pious part.''

" Your tale has astonished as well as interested me. I knew not De Hesling personally, but I honour his courage and fame. What mean your latter words ?"

" You have heard of the institution of the noble and sacred order of Knights Templars, appointed by our pious king solely to defend and protect the Christian pilgrims in their devotion at Jerusalem. De Hesling has enrolled himself one of these; his wealth he has given to the church ; and I doubt not that the death of De Dunstanville has given to our community a worthy member in his repentant murderer.''

" Then my Cordelia must not look to earthly protectors. Her lands bestowed upon the church, by him who had no right to appropriate them, and I, her only friend and guardian, upon the bed of death. Alas, alas ! poor child.''

" Say not her only friend ; the church will receive her willingly and gladly, dowerless though she be.''

" But no," exclaimed the abbess, after a moment's reflection, " she is not dowerless : it shall be so, I will give her a protector."

" What mean you ?" asked the monk, in a tone of alarm.

" Leave me now, good father, I pray you ; I am exhausted, but this conversation has aroused my strength. I may yet live to see my child in the station to which she was born."

" The illegitimate and beggared daughter of a villain, a desirable station, truly ! No, my hatred to the parent does not extend to this. Let Cordelia enter the holy profession, that were a more fitting destiny. And the casket—where is the key? time passes quickly."

" Not to night, good father, leave me now ; rest and thought are needful to me. To-morrow after matins I will see you, aed we will then fix our determination respecting my beloved child. After matins, father," added the abbess faintly.

The monk saw it was vain to press the subject, and, summoning Sister Maria to the bed-side of the abbess, he withdrew, with a promise to keep the appointment on the following morning.

Sister Maria found the invalid considerably exhausted ; but, after taking a restorative medicine, she declared herself better than she had been for many days previously ; and, having given Cordelia her blessing, as usual, and dismissed her to rest, the abbess desired a trusty servant of the convent to repair to the castle, and to desire the presence of Ralph de Fougeres early on the following morning, as she had business of importance to communicate to him.

CHAPTER III.

> And greedy Avarice by him did ride
>   Upon a camel loaden all with gold;
> Two iron coffers hung on either side,
>   With precious metal full as they might hold;
> And in his lap a heap of coin he told;
>   For of his wicked pelf a god he made,
>   And unto hell himself for money sold ;
> Accursed usury was all his trade,
> And right and wrong alike in equal balance weighed.—SPENSER.

THE abbess, although a gentle, and in some respects a timid woman, possessed a considerable share of firmness in pursuing that which she felt to be right. Totally ignorant of the world, its ways, and its everchanging properties, she had governed for many years, a little world within her convent, and she had there seen and studied the same passions as agitate the large sphere of society. She well knew that, although cramped and confined by conventional restraint, the springs of action and of feeling in a convent, and in the great world, were ever the same ; and her experience of human nature, although limited, gave her a sufficient clue to unravel the intricate and dark mind of Father Augustine. His story had strongly agitated her ; but her agitation had not obscured her perception ; and she saw that she was placed, as regarded Cordelia, in a state of somewhat resembling hostility to the father. Nor had the abbess been wholly blind to the peculiarities of disposition which, from time to time, had been exhibited by the monk, when consulted upon other affairs respecting the regulation of the convent. His reputation for extreme sanctity and self-mortification had not hidden from her the stain of worldliness which still lay upon him ; and, in the recent conference, the bad qualities of the monk had stood forth in bold relief from his assumed piety. The abbess judged him rightly.

Father Augustine was nobly born ; and educated, like all others of his rank, to the profession, or rather trade, of arms. Ambitious, haughty, licentious, and giving full scope to his various passions, he was feared, while he seemed to stand superior to hatred ; but a reverse of fortune came. Together with some other daring and vicious youths, of whom De Dunstanville was one, a deed of more than usual atrocity was committed; Father Augustine, then the youthful Lord of Scrivelby, was identified as the chief actor, and he was obliged to fly the kingdom. His ill-gotten wealth was confiscated or rather seized by the crown, and after years of poverty, during which every scheme of foreign aggrandisement which disappointed ambition could suggest, had been tried by him, and had failed, the haughty baron returned to England a dejected, but not an humbled priest. Ambition was not quenched; the flame had but taken a new direction. Partly in order to atone for former sins, according to the mistaken notion of that day, and partly to give loose to his pent-up propensities, Father Augustine acted with the part of a sanctified penitent; and by this means, gaining considerable influence among his order, he became at length to be regarded as one of its chief ornaments. He had regarded De Dunstanville as the principal cause of his former disgrace and ruin, and he had vowed to be revenged upon him. How he had in part executed his determination we have seen; but that such hostility and desire of revenge, should extend itself from the guilty parent to the innocent child, can only be imagined by a mind regulated by that vindictiveness which was the prominent feature in Father Augustine's character.

At the castle, Father Augustine had acquired considerable influence. As the confessor of Fougeres, he had became acquainted with a mysterious and reprehensible act of the baron's early life, and thus he gained a stronghold upon him. Known to De Fougeres as Father Augustine only, he was revered for his sanctity, and consulted for his worldly wisdom, and if, as he sometimes did, he allowed his arguments and exhortations to outship his general moderation, De Fougeres readily attributed the inadvertency to a hatred of vice and weakness.

Such was the character of the man from whose toils the abbess must endeavour to rescue Cordelia. She saw that he placed full confidence in the validity of the marriage paper which she mentioned; she had marked the changes of his countenance when she informed him of its existence, and she saw that his present hope was, by persuading Cordelia to embrace the monastic life, to secure her fortune to the church. Perhaps in any other case the abbess would have aided his efforts, but she knew the disposition of her charge too well to hope that such a measure would secure either her peace or her happiness. Cordelia possessed not only a high spirit, but a determined mind; she had been early thrown upon her own resources for amusement and mental nourishment, and although these had been but sparingly afforded to her, she had extracted all their good. She disliked the idea of becoming a nun; she had seen that such a life had not made her best and dearest friend the abbess, happy; and she had seen also the petty rivalries and jealousies of the sisters too unreservedly not to despise them. Her entreaties had been incessant to be spared from taking the veil, and they had hitherto been effectual.

Under all these circumstances the abbess had determined upon confiding to De Fougeres, the history of Cordelia's birth and circumstances, and she hoped that his powerful influence would not only secure her a safe asylum, either in the convent, or at the castle, but would be instrumental in proving her right to the rich dowry which had been her unhappy mother's. Had she known all his history, she might not have selected such a guardian.

But how many an indifferent action or event disconcert our wisest schemes! Early in the morning, the abbess was roused by Sister Maria, who, with a countenance and accent of alarm, informed her that the Baron de Fougeres had been summoned in the dead of the preceding night to London, in consequence of the dangerous illness of King Henry, and the troubled state of affairs, which would inevitably ensue upon his dissolution.

The abbess was appalled at this overthrow of her intentions.

"When is the baron expected to return?" she exclaimed.

"His followers knew nothing of his movements; the baron departed with two of his retainers only."

This discourse was interrupted by a message from Father Augustine, to say that he awaited a conference with the abbess.

"Desire Cordelia to attend me," said the invalid. "But no; let her come when I ring my bell."

"Our child is at the castle," replied Sister Maria, "the Lady Edith sent for her early this morning, to bear her company during the baron's unexpected absence."

"It is well," answered the abbess, "she will hear the tidings in too much haste. Now place my medicine by my side, good sister, and let Father Augustine be admitted."

The wily monk entered the chamber in his most obsequious manner; he had a point to gain, and he resolved to try flattery and smoothness before he proceeded to authority. He had heard of the message which the abbess had sent to De Fougeres, and he rejoiced in its discomfiture; but it awakened him to the necessity of at once securing the treasure which he coveted so much.

"I understand, my sister," he said, when Sister Maria had left the room, "that you have attempted to gain an interview with the Baron de Fougeres; if it be your intention to disown your holy connection with our church, by entrusting its concerns to such a man, it is needless to open the casket. Send your charge up to London to your new adviser, and see what safety you will gain for her and her lands."

The abbess attempted to excuse herself, but the father interrupted her.

" No, I spoke but in raillery; you are too prudent to take such a course. You know not the baron as I know him; a word from me would drive him from the castle which he calls his, would send him forth an outcast from society, even as I was sent forth, to disgrace and poverty. And to such a man would you bequeath your sister's child?"

"I know nothing of the baron," replied the abbess, "which can prevent his being a proper guardian to Cordelia; he is a tender father to his own child."

"His own child, indeed!" said the monk scornfully, "wait awhile, and see whether his affection will be a blessing or a curse."

"But as the baron is now far away, nor likely to be soon returned, we cannot refer to his advice or assistance. I am better than yesterday, but I feel that my life is spared only to place this dear child under safe guardianship, and my existence hangs by a very slender thread. This is the key, unlock the casket, father, and place it upon my couch."

Father Augustine did as he was desired. The first thing which met his view was the painting of a beautiful female face.

"How changed when I saw her," he exclaimed, "if she ever resembled this."

"She did resemble it, and excelled it," replied the abbess. "Eleanor was beautiful, and her daughter has the fatal gift of beauty also; she is very like this picture."

"And does not the resemblance which Cordelia bears to her mother influence you to place her where beauty may be no longer a misfortune to its possessor?"

The abbess answered not; she bent in fearful silence over the picture, and seemed absorbed in recollections of early years. The moment was not lost to the monk; he gently drew from the casket a sealed packet, inscribed, "The warrant of my marriage and my fortune," and hiding it in a fold of his garment he proceeded to search deeper into the casket, as if in disappointment at not finding something that he expected. Presently, observing that the abbess had awakened from her reverie to a knowledge of his presence, he said,—

"You are better acquainted with the contents of this casket than I am, sister; make the search yourself, it is not for me to pry into any concerns which you may wish concealed from me."

This was said in a humble tone, and it completely threw the abbess off her guard, as it was intended to do. She took out of the casket two small packets, and handing them to the monk said,—

"Neither of these is the paper of which I spoke, respecting my poor Eleanor's marriage; that is doubtless at the bottom of the casket, and is of no immediate importance to us. Let us examine this packet, which appears to be in her handwriting."

The abbess untied a small paper, upon which was some feeble handwriting almost illegible, and bearing evident traces of tears. The father read as follows:—

"I am dying—I do not deserve to live—I am guilty, but I am penitent. I have been already severely punished, may I hope that my sufferings may be received in mitigation of the punishment I so deeply deserve? My great misery is, that I leave exposed to the trials and contamination of the world, one who is innocent, but alas! helpless. She must not be given to the care of her natural guardian, and I implore my beloved sister, Leftalina, abbess of Thornbury, to take the charge of my infant Cordelia; to bring her up in security from the snares of the world, and in ignorance of the sins of those to whom she owes her existence. Not by any tie of love—for of that I am unworthy—but by the remembrance of early days of peace and happiness—I ask this of my holy sister; and if, in the course of those events which we can neither foresee nor regulate, the abbess be removed from her charge, I trust her to provide a fitting guardian to my child, enjoining her then to disclose to Cordelia so much of her history as may suffice to assist her in regulating her after conduct. Fully relying upon my beloved sister in all tha regards my child's welfare, I beg her forgiveness and prayers.

"ELEANOR DE DUNSTANVILLE."

The abbess wept abundantly during the perusal of this letter, nor was the monk wholly unmoved. His heart was not utterly hardened; and besides the extinguishment of his hopes, through any declaration of her mother, he felt considerable difficulty as to Cordelia herself. The abbess was the first to break the painful silence.

"The path now lies clear before me," she said, "Cordelia must be made acquainted with her birth and prospects; and she must be placed in some family of station befitting her own, where she may perfect herself in the accomplishments necessary to her rank. This cannot be in Thornbury Castle, but Cordelia has yet another friend, and to her I must apply."

"Whom do you mean?" asked the monk.

"The Lady Elfrida de Albini," replied the abbess. "When that unfortunate lady left the castle fourteen years ago, in grief for the loss of her only child, I promised her that should Cordelia ever need a protectress I would apply to her, assured that she would then receive her as a daughter in the place of the one whom she had lost."

The monk was silent for a short time. His good and his bad feelings were at war. He knew that one word of his would make the sorrowful heart glad, and give peace to the last moments of the abbess. But he could not, he durst not, betray the secrets of the confessional; and he was silent. But he must not lose Cordelia.

"But how can you affirm that Cordelia is the legitimate child of De Dunstanville, or the undoubted heiress of her mother? this letter does not warrant either conclusion," observed the monk, "and will a lady like the wife of Geoffry de Albini, receive into her family an orphan, who has no right to either name or dower? No! Cordelia must remain here; she must become a child of the Church; she will soon be reconciled to her fate. You see that the paper of which you spoke, as witnessing the marriage of your sister, is not here. Much I fear it exists in your imagination only."

"It is not here—I see it is not, yet I know that it exists; and I much mistake if, when I last opened this casket in order to give my child her mother's bridal ornament, I did find three sealed packets—here are now but two."

"It was easy to be deceived in such a matter," observed the monk carelessly.

"No—it was not easy for me to be deceived," quickly replied the abbess, "and were it not that this casket has been carefully secured in the closet of my oratory I should suspect that the paper had been purloined from it."

No. 3.

"That is impossible," said the monk. "It is more likely that the sinner, in the last moments of her repentance, destroyed the record of her worldly vanity, if indeed such a paper ever did exist. Of course you will make no mention to your niece of this matter."

"I scarcely know what I ought to do," said the abbess hesitatingly.

"Why raise Cordelia's hopes of rank and fortune, when you have not wherewith to build them upon? better let her think herself poor and humble; her mother's example surely must show you the vanity of wordly advantages."

"You know not my child, father," replied the abbess, "she is worthy of the race whence she springs, and until my poor sister's forfeiture of virtue, there never was a stain upon the name of Tunstall. Oh! that Cordelia may indeed inherit the virtues of her maternal ancestors!"

"I would secure her in those virtues by the retirement of the cloisters," said the monk. "Leave it to me to inform Cordelia of the little that it is necessary she should know respecting her unhappy parents, and believe me that I will now, and in future, be her safest, her most trusty friend."

To this proposal the abbess gave a decided negative. The loss of the paper had recalled her prudence and forethought; and although she was perfectly convinced that such a document was in existence, yet its not being now at hand only rendered it more imperatively her duty to disclose to Cordelia every circumstance of her situation, however painful such a revelation might be to both of them. Besides, she thought she might have deceived herself in her recollection of having seen the paper; and she fancied that her sister might have deposited it for a greater safety in the hands of the abbot of a convent which was situated near her residence. In this case, it might be reclaimed when Cordelia should arrive at such an age as to be her own mistress; and she resolved to enjoin upon the friendless girl a strict and unfailing endeavour to search out this record. As regarded her future residence, she intended to consult the feelings of her charge upon that point; the apprehended death of the king would probably throw the country into a state of confusion, and perhaps in a period of civil war a convent was a more secure residence than a castle.

The monk left the room of the invalid, in imagination a richer man than he entered it. He held that under his robe which added broad and fair lands to the possessions of his convent, could such a claim be substantiated; and of this he could not doubt, the church was too powerful to be denied that which she claimed. Was it indeed for the welfare of the Church that Father Augustine was so solicitous? Was it in order to feed the hungry, and to clothe the naked, that he coveted gold and lands? Was self entirely rooted from his heart? Alas! no—he could not so far delude himself as to think this, although by his exterior appearance of mortification and disinterestedness, he could deceive others. Visions of pomp and grandeur flitted before his eyes. In his younger days, perhaps in his better days, wealth would have brought to him riot, pleasure, debauchery; he would have spent the substance of which he robbed the orphan, amidst companions like himself; the social wine-cup would have been unsparingly filled; the far-famed steed would have been purchased, and bestowed; the gaudiest of foreign toys would have been flung to those who scarcely returned an acknowledgment, but how was it now? Ambition, power, luxury, these were his aim; they were the idols of his declining years. Ambition, to be the adviser of kings; to wear the purple robe, and to step upon the neck of the prostrate worshippers. Power, to crush those who thwarted his views; to say to the monarch, "Descend thou from thy throne!" and to the prince, "Be thou cast out from the fellowship of thy species!" Luxury, a life of sloth, ministered to by slaves, every half-expressed wish anticipated—for these he now became a robber. And as he slowly wended his way to the river-side, where his well-appointed barge was waiting to waft him to his monastery, his active fancy pictured to him such scenes of pomp and grandeur, that he lost sight of the means by which they were to be acquired; and not until the arrival of the boat at its landing place did he awaken to a sense of the total inadequacy of those means to supply his pampered wishes. The shock to his mental faculties was great, and laying his hand upon the concealed packet, he sullenly repaired to his cell, to meditate in secret upon the accomplishment of his designs.

CHAPTER IV.

It is not the tear at this moment shed,
   When the cold turf has just been laid o'er him,
That can tell how belov'd was the soul that's fled,
   Or how deep in our hearts we deplore him;
'Tis the tear thro' many a long day wept,
   In a life by his loss all shaded,
'Tis the sad remembrance fondly kept,
   When all lighter griefs have faded.

Oh! thus shall we mourn, and his memory's light,
   While it shines thro' our hearts, shall improve them,
And worth shall look fairer, and truth more bright,
   When we think how he lived but to love them;
And as buried saints the graves perfume
   Where fadeless they've long been lying,
So our hearts shall borrow sweet'ning bloom,
   From the image he left there no dying.—MOORE.

AFTER the departure of the Father Augustine, Cordelia was summoned to the bed-side of the abbess. Having heard that the monk was expected at the convent, she had willingly obeyed the request of Edith, that she would pass a few hours of the morning with her, Edith being more than usually anxious respecting her father's absence on account of the state of affairs in which the kingdom would be left by the death of the king. When, however, Cordelia saw the Father Augustine pass by in his boat by the Lady's Tower where she was sitting with her friend, she started up, and bidding Edith a hasty " good morning," returned quickly to the convent, at the gate of which she met the messenger sent by the abbess.

Cordelia found her friend exhausted, but cheerful; the casket was placed by her pillow; and the abbess, noticing the anxious look which her child cast upon it as she entered the room, said,

" Yes, Cordelia; you must now learn the particulars of your early history. Prepare your mind to listen with calmness and self-control; you must in future be in a great measure dependant upon these qualities for your well-being, and even your safety."

"Oh, my dear mother!" replied the agitated girl, " I will be anything you wish; only tell me that the Father Augustine has no real right to direct or govern me. Oh! tell me that I owe him not the obedience of a relative!"

" Not in the slightest degree," replied the abbess. " You owe him some gratitude for good offices done to one of your parents; but even *I* cannot advise you to confide your conduct to that man. Now hearken to my story."

The abbess unfolded to Cordelia the circumstances of her birth and parentage; she told her how her mother had sinned; and she did not disguise from her the bad character of her father.

" I know not," she continued, " wherefore Father Augustine expresses such deadly hatred to the name of De Dunstanville, but I imagine it arises from some injury in early life which your father inflicted upon him; both were lawless and unprincipled men, and among such a broken friendship is usually succeeded by hatred."

She then related the father's description of the last days of the unhappy Eleanor, dwelling minutely upon every circumstance relating to the acknowledgment of her marriage to De Dunstanville, and expressing her firm conviction of the existence of the document respecting it, which she had expected to find in the casket; and urging upon Cordelia a constant attention to every endeavour to ascertain the fate of the paper.

"But, my dearest aunt and friend, of what use can this paper be to me, even if I ever possess it? my father gave his lands to the Church, will they ever be restored?" asked Cordelia.

"Remember that the same document proves the marriage of your parents," replied the abbess, "that is motive sufficient for your wishing to discover and possess it; and should Matilda succeed to the throne of this realm, surely an orphan and an injured maiden will not sue in vain for justice. Remember, my child, whose daughter you are; and although your life may be obscured by poverty and seclusion, still retain in your heart the sentiments which befit your birth. You are not utterly friendless; although your kindred by your mother's side are unable and unwilling to protect you, and to the relatives of De Dunstanville you *must not* apply; you have yet a friend. The Lady de Albini would, were it practicable to convey you to her, receive you, and treat you as a daughter."

"Oh! no, dear mother, let me stay here. I have never known any other home, and I cannot bend to humour the fancies, or bear with the pride of a great lady. And I cannot leave the Lady Edith."

"It is the consideration of that friendship which determines me to desire that you remain here. But Edith will marry; whenever that occurs, I charge you to seek the Lady de Albini. She can never seek you here."

"Then is it not your wish, dear mother, that I should take the vows?" asked Cordelia anxiously.

"Certainly not. An effort will be made by Father Augustine to induce you to do so; but remember my advice: make no resolutions or promises of the kind, until a few years more have passed away, your kindred may return from Palestine, and you may be elevated to the rank to which you are rightfully entitled. Take that casket, never let it leave you; even although the most precious document be missing, there are yet those remaining in it which are of great importance to you. Let no one cajole you to part with this treasure, even for a day. One word more. Cordelia, come nearer to me, child; I am exhausted, and have not long to live. Hear my last and most important words."

The weeping girl drew nearer to the pillow of her friend, and taking her hand, the abbess said in a low voice,

"Beware of that monk. If at any time you need advice, ask it of the Baron de Fougeres; he knows, or will soon know, your history. Trust him."

"Oh! my mother, the baron is so stern! he terrifies me; I cannot speak in his presence," exclaimed Cordelia.

"He will be less stern towards you in future," answered the abbess; "he is honourable, and has no motive to be insincere; but remember that your claim to your mother's fortune would set aside that of the Church, and Father Augustine is interested for his order, therefore trust him not."

The abbess was now quite overcome by the exertion of speaking, and required some more experienced attendant than Cordelia, who however was permitted to remain by her bedside. A succession of fainting fits ensued, and life was evidently fast ebbing. Serene and composed, but unable to speak, she lay until the evening, when her peaceful and just spirit was released.

There was weeping throughout the convent when the abbess died; and the bell which announced her decease to the neighbourhood, gave a pang to many a grateful heart. Edith especially, was grieved for her young friend, as well as for herself. The abbess had been kind and affectionate to her, and the inmates of the convent she owed relief in many of those tedious hours of her father's absence, which must, but for the sisters, have been passed in solitude. Edith had never known her mother; all allusion to the subject was studiously shunned by De Fougeres; and had Edith been less happy in a father's love, the mystery which hung over the name of her mother might have made her miserable. But except when she needed guidance upon some trifling subject of female etiquette, Edith could not fancy that she had a wish ungratified. Now, indeed, permitted by De Fougeres to be happy in the acknowledged attachment of Eustace Mowbray, the question would sometimes cross her mind, "Would my mother have loved him?" The answer was an undoubting assent; and Edith again turned to the future.

That future was now to be partially clouded. Intelligence arrived at Thornbury Castle that King Henry had died in Normandy; and this was confirmed by messengers from De Fougeres, who also brought the tidings of Stephen's landing in England, and of his being received as king in London, with every demonstration of joy and popularity. Still there was a powerful rival to dread in the Empress Maud; and de Fougeres dispatched a summons to his vassals to hold themselves in readiness to take the field at a moment's warning, adding that he should himself speedily return to Thornbury, to superintend the preparations for the civil war.

This intelligence brought unhappiness to the peaceful bosom of Edith. She deeply loved and reverenced her father, and she dreaded his departure for the battle-field; but she had still a deeper dread, one with which no visions of glory were entwined,—Eustace Mowbray would also be called upon to join the royal forces; and however Edith might place undoubting confidence in the courage of her lover, she dreaded lest that very courage should prove her misfortune.

On the morning succeeding the death of the abbess, Edith retired to the Lady's Tower, there to ruminate upon her anxieties, and the melancholy prospect of separation from those whom she best loved, which she had but too much reason to apprehend lay before her. Vainly did she endeavour to bend her thoughts to reading, and still more vainly did she apply to her embroidery for a solace to her uneasiness; she found not the relief she sought; and in weariness of spirit she took up her lute, and accompanying her voice with it, sang the following song, which had been taught her at the convent:—

Far, far o'er hill and dell,
    On the winds stealing,
List to the convent bell,
    Mournfully pealing.
Hark! hark! it seems to say,
As melt those sounds away,
So life's best joys decay,
    While new their feeling.

Now thro' the charmed air,
    Slowly ascending,
List to the chaunted prayer,
    Solemnly blending.
Hark! hark! it seems to say,
Turn from those joys away,
To those which ne'er decay,
    Tho' life is ending.

Oh! then in Heav'n confide,
    Humbly depending,
That grief which thy heart hath tried,
    To joy is tending.
Hark! hark! soft whispers say,
Seek thou that blessed way
Where grief shall flee away,
    Joy thy path attending.

Ere Edith had finished singing the last line of her mournful song, she was aware of a slight rustling among the branches of an acacia tree which fringed the edge of the grass walk leading from the castle to the Lady's tower ; and lifting up her head, she saw Eustace Mowbray standing before her. A brilliant smile of joy overspread her countenance, but her first impulse of recognition was checked by a sudden fear, and she sunk powerless upon the couch.

"Edith," exclaimed the youth, approaching her, "what aileth thee, that thou comest not forth with thy wonted readiness to meet Eustace ?"

"Alas !" replied Edith, "much I fear the purport of this visit. Tell me, is it to bid adieu ?"

"No—no—dearest ; though such a word my unwilling tongue may be obliged to speak ere long ; but as yet I am ordered to remain at Mowbray Castle. You have then heard the news of our king's death, and of the landing of our future sovereign ?"

"Yes," replied his beloved, "my father will speedily return to Thornbury, to arouse his neighbours, and to marshal his vassals. And your father, Eustace, does he too follow Stephen ?"

"Undoubtedly. Can our Norman blood submit to be ruled by a woman ? Are we, the descendants of Rolla and of William, to curb our spirits, under the dominion of a female ? Nay—nay—dearest, shake not those golden locks ; we willingly submit to the power of beauty, and are her devoted slaves in the bower and in the hall, but we will never own a woman for our royal sovereign."

"And yet," said Edith, sighing, "how many have sworn fealty to Matilda, even of the bravest of the land ; the bravest and the loftiest ; David of Scotland, Robert of Gloucester, the holy William of Canterbury, and your own Stephen ? Is it thus that fealty is to be kept towards a poor helpless woman ?"

"Why Edith, my pretty traitress ! What would De Fougeres say to this ?" asked Eustace.

"I know not indeed," replied Edith, sighing ; "but I think, at least, he would allow me to pity the Empress Matilda ; truly it is a riotous and distracted people that she seeks to govern,—er she willing to leave the cares of royalty to this Stephen, who seems to have exercised a charm over those who had sworn to defend his rival."

"You say truly, Edith, it is indeed a charm ; and surely Stephen ought to rule over his fair subjects more despotically ; his figure, his address, his countenance, all betoken his princely birth ; bravery and beauty seem to contend which most shall favour him. But a truce to politics, Edith ; what mournful ditty were you singing when I approached ? Methinks it were more fitted to the nuns of yonder convent than to the lady of the castle ?"

"Indeed, Eustace, I cannot be otherwise than mournful. My dear father preparing for the battle-field, and you——" said Edith, sighing deeply.

"Well—well—I will allow that we have some cause for apprehension."

"And our poor abbess too. Know you not that she died yesterday morning ?" asked Edith.

"I feared it," replied her lover, "news of her state were brought to Mowbray, and I feared that it was all over. What will become of your friend, Cordelia ?"

"Alas ! poor girl, I cannot say. Would that my father would give her a home in this castle ; but we know not who she is, and De Fougeres will not allow one of inferior birth to be the constant companion of his daughter. Yet, Eustace, I am sure that Cordelia is of noble blood, the abbess never denied it when I asked her. But the future abbess will be kind to the poor girl, for her friend's sake, and much, I hope, that Cordelia will not be obliged to take the veil."

"And who wishes her to take the veil?" asked Eustace.

"Father Augustine does," replied Edith. "He has persuaded my father to refuse all interference with Cordelia, and has repeatedly endeavoured to sow dissension-between us on this subject, happily without effect."

"I like not that Father Augustine," said Eustace.

"Nor I," said Edith, hesitatingly. "My dear father fears him; why, I know not; but I know he does not like him, and I have many times found my dear parent in a terrible state of agitation after one of his interviews with the father. De Fougeres seems to love me less when Father Augustine has been talking to him."

"Does the monk disapprove of our affection, dearest Edith?" asked Eustace.

"Not openly," answered Edith, "but he holds out heart-breaking denunciations, if my father gives us his full consent. Oh Eustace! it is not this war alone which we have to dread. There is a cloud over the future from some other cause, more mysterious, and therefore more to be feared."

"You alarm yourself needlessly, dearest," said Eustace, and taking up the lute, he said, "shall I try to sing away your melancholy? I will not choose such a ditty as I heard you sing, I will sing of a dearer theme."

Edith smiled lovingly upon the youth, who thus sang,—

> Nay, tell me not of jewels rare,
>   They match not Edith's eyes:
> The turquoise blue I gaze on there,
>   And there my jewel is.
>
> Nay, do not praise the lilies white,
>   'Tis Edith's brow I see;
> On that I gaze with fond delight,
>   The fairest flower to me.
>
> Nay, do not think the cherry red,
>   The best of fruit to be;
> On Edith's cheek its tint is shed,
>   The sweetest fruit to me.
>
> Search earth and sky, and sea and air,
>   For what they best can give;
> Then look on Edith's form, and there
>   See all their beauties live.

"Am I not a better minstrel than the sisters of the convent?" said Eustace, tenderly.

"Hush! hush!" said the blushing Edith, "see, Father Augustine and Cordelia are in yonder path; they are just come from the convent."

"Then adieu, dearest," said Eustace rising, "I am in no humour to bear the exhortations of the father to-day. He also is among those who talk of honour towards Matilda, while they seek only their own advancement. Farewell!"

"Oh! do not leave me," said Edith, imploringly, "the father will not remain long here, if indeed he come to the bower at all. See, Cordelia is weeping; oh, do not leave us now."

Eustace could not resist the appeal of his beloved, and seating himself by her, he again took up the lute, and was preluding his song, when the monk entered.

"It is well," said the Father Augustine, "such occupations become one who would laugh at the oath which he vowed before his sovereign; would that all the betrayers of their rightful queen were as harmlessly employed!"

"I never took an oath to Matilda, good father," replied Eustace, "and if we are unhappily to go to war, surely I may amuse myself thus, until I am called upon to buckle on my armour, and follow my father to the battle-field. But we talk not of war and battle in a lady's bower."

"Whether ye talk of them or not," said the monk, sternly, "they will come, and to the lady's bower, too; this devoted country will yet reek with the blood of the bravest of her sons, fire shall waste our vineyards, and famine depopulate our towns, man must pay the price of his perfidy. The young and the thoughtless may sing, the old must weep. Oh! that my arm were strong as in earlier days, when its prowess was felt in many a well-foughten field, Matilda should not then need a champion. But she needs not my arm; even as it is, the brave, the honourable of her father's nobles, are ready to shed the last drop of blood in support of her cause; a thousand swords will leap from their scabbards to avenge even a look which should threaten her with injury. But for you, ye dastards, who cling to the usurper, look to yourselves, ye may fear even a woman."

Eustace was about to answer this vehement speech in a manner that would have provoked yet more the angry Churchman, but Edith interposed, saying,—

"Farewell De Mowbray, my father's return will recal you to the castle shortly."

"Farewell now, Edith! think not that the spirit of a Mowbray is to be insulted with impunity. We shall meet again, father."

CHAPTER V.

Youth comes; the toils and cares of life
    Torment the restless mind;
Where shall the tired and harassed heart ;
    Its consolation find?
Then is not youth, as fancy tells
    Life's summer's primed of joy?
Ah no! for hopes too long delayed
And feelings blasted or betrayed,
    The fabled bliss astray,
And he remembers with a sigh
The careless days of infancy.—SOUTHEY.

'A SILENCE ensued upon the departure of Eustace Mowbray; Edith was agitated and depressed; Cordelia stood in forlorn despondency, gazing upon the river, whose peaceful and unruffled current seemed in its gentle flow to mock at the thoughts which disturbed her harassed mind; while the monk was resolving with no feelings of complacency the scene which had just passed. Its possible consequences were but too apparent to him. He knew the temper of Eustace Mowbray to be honourable, although placable, and he was fearful that he would repeat to his kindred what Father Augustine had so insultingly said. Mowbray's family were of high rank and consideration; and the monk was too politic, willingly to offend them; besides which, De Fougeres also was of the party of Stephen, and here again the monk feared the effects of his intemperate language. Oh! if he could indeed throw away the cowl, and resume the helmet! He knew the party of Matilda to be strong in names and renown, and self-interest urged him to support her cause; more was to be gained, should she succeed than he could hope for under Stephen; the monk loved power as well as riches and for the attainment of this, he would not hesitate to throw the kingdom into war and anarchy. But every thing must not be risked at once; and Father Augustine resolved to dissemble his feelings until the return of De Fougeres should be the means of informing him which party was the most likely to gain predominance in the kingdom.

The silence was broken by Edith, who taking Cordelia by the hand, said, "I was sure, my dear Cordelia, that you would not forsake me during this prolonged absence of my father."

"Forsake you! Oh no!" Cordelia replied; "indeed. dear Edith, I would die sooner than leave you,—unless——"

"Unless what?" asked her friend hastily.

"I know not, my fate is hidden from me," replied Cordelia.

"Why is it hidden from you?" said the monk, with earnestness, "because you are wilful and see not—*will* not see the path which is evenly and peacefully before you. The Church opens her arms to receive you, and you shun her embraces; what but unhappiness can be your destiny?"

"Father, I pray you try me no further; my dearest, my truest friend is not yet laid in her quiet grave; I cannot yet disobey her; give me but a few days, I beseech," cried Cordelia, sobbing.

"Why may not Cordelia remain as she has hitherto done at the abbey?" asked Edith.

"I do not urge her removal," said the father.

"I can be very happy there," said Cordelia, "I have never known any other home. The new abbess loves me, and has promised me her protection and care; why must I be persecuted to do that which no one has a right to force upon me?"

No. 4.

"Well mayst thou say *that*, poor forlorn outcast," said the monk scornfully. "No friends, no kindred—poor, deserted, despised; yet this miserable girl loves the world and its allurements."

"No, father; not friendless, not forlorn, and if right were done to her not poor," cried Cordelia, proudly. "The orphan may for a time be despoiled of her rightful inheritance, but friends will be raised up from her very wrongs, and the oppressor will ere long be obliged to yield his ill-gotten gains. You know it will be so."

"*I* know nothing of possessions or riches, *I* am sworn to poverty and meekness," retorted the monk. "It were well that penance and fasting should bring down that proud spirit. Go to your cell, there meditate upon the sin of disobeying the call vouchsafed to you, and when you are thoroughly purified and repentant I will visit you."

"I would not be presumptuous," interposed Edith, "but surely Cordelia is not obliged to profess herself; she is my friend, I will again ask my father to receive her here, until a more happy home be offered to her."

"Ask it at your peril!" cried the monk; "remember you have asked, and have been refused, and how refused?"

"Dearest Edith," said Cordelia, embracing her, "be not unhappy about me. I wait but the return of the baron, he will advise me whether to remain here or to accept the protection which was offered to me in my infancy by the Lady de Albini."

"Albini!" said Edith, "is not that the name of the lady whose picture hangs in the western turret?"

"How! have you dared to approach that turret?—much more to learn the name of her whose picture hangs there?" asked the monk.

"I love to look at that sweet face," replied Edith; "it is to me like a vision of some kind angel that used to visit me in my dreams of infancy."

"Tell De Fougeres this, and wring his heart to its core," exclaimed the monk, in a tone of bitterness which made his companions tremble. "Tell it to him! descant upon your love for that picture! speak to him of its innocent beauty! and then see him writhe in death at your feet. Do this, and I am a second time avenged."

Edith and Cordelia gazed on each other in terrified astonishment. Clinging around her friend, Cordelia wept loudly and passionately, exclaiming,

"Oh! I will do all you ask! but let me not bring misery upon my dearest Edith."

"Then give me up the casket, and all will be right," asked the monk.

"I have solemnly sworn never to resign it—I have sworn it by the bedside of her who was my dearest friend—my mother's sister—and you, father, ought to be the last to urge me to break my vow," said Cordelia, imploringly, to Father Augustine.

The monk was confounded; he saw the position in which he was placed, too clearly to attempt further coercion; and he began to think that it would be better to allow Cordelia to go to the Lady de Albini as soon as the funeral of the abbess had taken place. But he must first ascertain to what extent her vow reached, respecting the contents of the casket.

Assuming therefore his most gentle and courteous manner, he said,

"It is well that the casket remain with you, my child; its contents are for your eyes alone; it would not be fitting that others should know its secrets. Guard it carefully from all curiosity. Such doubtless was the command of the late abbess?" asked the monk anxiously.

"If the Baron De Fougeres should wish to examine the documents it contains, I had injunctions not to refuse it to him," replied Cordelia.

"De Fougeres!" exclaimed Father Augustine in a tone of surprise. "But no! the trifling casket which may well serve a vain and gaudy damsel as a safeguard for her insignificant and valueless trinkets, is beneath the notice of a brave knight like De Fougeres; he cares little for the decorations which a nameless orphan accounts valuable." Then observing Edith's air of excitement and interest, he added, " The most valuable treasure in that casket is, I believe, a lock of hair imposed upon you as your mother's."

Cordelia was stung to the quick, and repressing her tears, she said proudly, " No, father ! I am not nameless to De Fougeres ; ere this, he knows every particular of my history ; and if the name of De Dunstanville be one of shame to him, that of Tunstall is stainless, and he will acknowledge it so in me."

" Atrocious woman ! can she have done this ?" cried the monk. " And the Lady de Albini—does she too know all this shameless history ?"

" She does, or she will ;" answered Cordelia boldly, as marking the ashy paleness of the monk's face, and the dismay apparent in his manner, the warning of the abbess rushed with its full force upon her memory. " The Baron de Fougeres will protect the orphan. Hear me, father ! not unless he counsel it will I ever enter the convent as a nun. That the last documents still exist, and will be found ere long, I know ; I feel that brighter days are in store for me, the orphan will have her rights ; and he who withholds them will be brought to shame. Even had I no other friend, Robert de Hesling still lives, and to him—to the husband of my mother—I would apply."

" A pretty idea truly !" said the monk in a tone of scornful derision. But he recollected, that the expected civil war in England would probably recal many of the soldiers who had carried their arms to the Holy Land ; and he knew also, that however great might be the engrafted love for the Church in the breast of De Hesling, an uncontrollable hatred of De Dunstanville would lead him to uphold the rights of Cordelia, in order to insult even his memory. On every side an abyss of trouble was opened to him, and Father Augustine saw no escape. Still there was safety in dissimulation ; the storm might yet leave him unscathed ; and in case of the worst, the field of battle was one of renown to a spirit like that of the monk.

" Let us go to the castle, Cordelia," said Edith ; " I will show you the picture which I mentioned. Oh ! if my father would let me accompany you to the Lady Albini ? I dread his absence now more than ever. and if you are away——"

This was said in a low tone, but the monk heard it, and exclaimed, " Ask the wolf to restore the lamb to the fold—ask the hawk to loosen his gripe of the dove which he bears aloft from her nest—ask the murderer to spare the victim who writhes beneath his knife—then ask De Fougeres to yield his Edith to De Albina. Do it ! and I say again be the murderer of him who calls himself thy father !"

Saying this, Father Augustine left the Tower. His victims, for such indeed his passion rendered them, burst into a flood of tears, the more violent from having been with considerable difficulty restrained in his presence.

" What means he ?" asked Cordelia at length.

" I know not ; oh, that my dear father were here !" answered Edith. " And yet this man almost makes me dread seeing him. And Eustace, too, he left us in anger ; I fear he will not return until after my father's arrival. Oh, Cordelia ! how sad is this war ! and if you leave me I shall indeed be desolate."

" I shall not leave you, dearest Edith, unless Father Augustine force me to it. To-morrow evening my dear aunt is to be interred, and I am sure that our sister Mary, now our abbess, will be my friend ; although never can I have such a friend as I have lost."

Hours passed unheeded away while the friends were thus conversing. Anxiety and uncertainty bound them to each other more friendly than ever ; and in the midst of all their unhappiness, there was a secret feeling which prevented their being utterly dejected.

Far different were the emotions of Father Augustine. He had, as he thought, laid down for himself a line by which to act, and he had been annoyed by a stripling and thwarted by a girl. Yet still he possessed the document. He carefully shut himself into his cell, desiring that he might not be disturbed ; alleging as a reason for his seclusion that he wished to prepare his mind for the approaching ceremonial of the interment of the abbess, at which he was expected to attend.

Seating himself at his little table, which had witnessed so many of his ambitious heartburnings and jealousies, he reflected deeply, and, as far as it was possible to him, dispassionately, upon the prospects of the future. Now sincerely regretting his assumption of the monastic order, he mourned his banishment from those scenes of war and military excitement which were far more consonant to his disposition than the inactive peace of a convent life. He had been driven from society, and now, after the lapse of years, he fancied that he had done unwisely and rashly in yielding to the passing storm, he longed to escape, but feared that escape was impossible.

"I am known here but as Father Augustine, could I but once emerge from this monastery and this habit I might with impunity resume my former station and occupations. Any tale will pass credence with the multitude, and then—but stay, let me examine this paper; will the prize be worth the risk?"

Thus speaking he broke the seal of the paper, which he carried carefully concealed in his robe, and unfolding it he read the contents as follows:—

"I promise Eleanor de Hesling, in virtue of a ceremony which has taken place between us here, in the chapel belonging to the abbey of Edendale, and in presence of the abbot and certain monks of that abbey, that in case of the decease of Robert de Hesling, or in the event of my obtaining a dispensation from the holy Father at Rome, annulling the marriage between Robert de Hesling and Eleanor Tunstall, that I will openly and unreservedly acknowledge Eleanor my lawful wife; reserving to her use the lands to which she is entitled, and relinquishing all claim upon them during my life, and denying any power to bequeath them at my decease; leaving them to her, and to any person to whom she may wish they should descend —I call upon her brother, Henry Tunstall, to be her protector in case of my death before her.—Signed in presence of the abbot of Edendale,

"DE DUNSTANVILLE."

Such was the tenor of the document which it had cost Father Augustine so much crime to obtain. His first impulse was to tear it into shreds, and thus destroy all vestige of that which stood between him and his hopes; but on turning the paper, he found on the back of it a memorandum signed by the abbot of Edendale, acknowledging the possession of a document to the same effect, and promising not to deliver it up to any except Henry Tunstall, or persons deputed by him. Father Augustine knew that Henry Tunstall was a renowned baron, and powerful as well as honoured; also that he was an active partisan of Stephen; to support whom he had left Palestine, and was on his way to England. Although Cordelia had been apparently deserted by her kindred, it was probable that upon her existence being ascertained, and her right to a large dowry acknowledged, kindred and friends would flock around her; and whether as a monk or as a baron it might materially aid his views of advancement were he known as the protector of the orphan heiress. Long did the father study the part which he was to act, and deeply did he regret his precipitancy in taking the monastic habit. His assumed sanctity was such, that he felt assured that were he to escape from the convent his brethren would at once declare him a saint, and affirm that he had miraculously left this lower world, and had been received into a better; but then he had no resources, no riches, to support him.

To yield up the paper crossed the mind of the scheming monk but once; the idea was immediately dismissed. Even could he have extorted such a sum of money as would have supplied his longings for pleasure and luxury, still he was a monk, and vowed to poverty. While thus ruminating, a slight knock at the door of his cell startled him, and rising hastily, and concealing the paper in its accustomed hiding-place, the bosom of his habit, he asked angrily who was there.

"A messenger from Thornbury Castle," was the answer. "The Baron de Fougeres arrived there two hours ago, and desires the presence of Father Augustine without delay."

"I come instantly," replied the father; "let my barge be made ready."

This was the crisis of fate to Father Augustine; dissimulation must be the part for him to play. Ambition, and a still stronger feeling, which he dared not own even to himself, must be hidden under the mask of moderation, and zeal for the church; he knew De Fougeres to possess considerable discernment, but he had hitherto blinded his penetration, and he doubted not of being able to do so again.

Let us return to the castle, where the sudden arrival of De Fougeres had caused bustle and preparation. The delight of Edith was irrepressible; she hung upon her father, half in tears and half in smiles, while the baron gazed with rapture on her countenance.

"Trust me, Edith, I have not seen a face so lovely as thine in all the beauty of the court," said De Fougeres. "Let us see Stephen but firmly seated on the throne of England, and my Edith shall go with me there, she will eclipse all other dames."

"I am well content here, dear father," replied Edith, blushing, "but this war, father?"

"I trust we need only show our strength, my child; but at such a time it becomes all loyal barons to gather around the Sovereign," replied De Fougeres.

"Father Augustine talks of treachery, and of Matilda's rights," said Edith.

"Ha! dares the monk to speak so, and to my child?" cried the baron angrily; "we must understand each other better before I again leave home."

"And when will that be, dear father?" asked Edith, tremulously.

"In four short days, my child, too short a time for both of us; for you to show me your love and duty, and for me to collect my vassals in due equipment. But the king has ordered it so. Matilda has powerful and active friends, whom an early and vigorous blow may entirely disable. The presence of his barons is likewise necessary at the coronation of the king. But Edith, where is your young friend Cordelia?"

"She is at the convent; the abbess is to be interred to-night," replied Edith, rather surprised; as her father had never inquired after Cordelia before, and never encouraged her presence at the castle.

"Let her be sent for; I wish to converse with her," said the baron.

The order was immediately obeyed; and Cordelia entered the presence of the baron, who, taking her hand kindly, said—

"My child, you shall never want a friend while I am alive to protect you. I have received the packet from your late relative; I know your history, and I feel for your situation. Nor is your family unknown to me. Tunstall is indeed a name of renown; nor is De Hesling much less so; trust in the future, and hope for brighter days. Meanwhile I beg of you to make this castle your home, and bear my Edith company during my absence."

At these words Edith flung her arms around her father's neck, while Cordelia threw herself at the baron's feet.

"My dear, dear father," exclaimed Edith. "Father Augustine promised us unhappiness when you returned, but you have brought us happiness."

"And why did the father say I should make you unhappy?" asked De Fougeres.

"He said that you would send away Cordelia to the Lady de Albini," replied Edith.

The baron started as if a spectre had appeared before him.

"Has the meddling monk then dared to mention the name of Albini to my child? What said the traitor?" exclaimed De Fougeres; "it seems that I have more than one account to settle with him."

"The late abbess desired that I should ask your opinion respecting my conduct," said Cordelia, "whether I should remain at the convent, or seek the protection of the Lady de Albini, who in my infancy promised to be my friend, if I ever needed one. This is all, but——"

"But what?" asked De Fougeres, hastily.

"I had rather stay with Edith," answered Cordelia timidly.

The baron turned from the friends, and walked up and down the hall in silence; at last he said,—

"Let Father Augustine be summoned instantly. Children, you may return."

Edith kissed her father's forehead, but he spoke not; he seemed lost in troubled thought.

Father Augustine was announced, he saw immediately that some occurrence had disturbed the mind of the baron, and concluding it to be the state of public affairs, he said,

"You left the court in peace, my son?"

"Yes," replied Fougeres abruptly, "but I find not my home in peace; a traitor has betrayed his trust, and brought trouble to my household."

"What mean you?" asked the father; "has Eustace Mowbray offended you? he is a headstrong and wilful youth, and I have discouraged his visits—but in vain."

"No—thyself—thou art the traitor!" exclaimed the baron vehemently.

"Hold, De Fougeres! apply not that word to me," cried the monk, "it better befits thyself, remember thy oath to Matilda."

"We will talk of that hereafter," answered the baron. "But, traitor-monk, for so thou knowest thou art, thou hast betrayed the secrets of the confessional, thou hast dared to speak the name of De Albini to my Edith."

A sneer passed across the face of the monk, as he answered, "No, no, De Fougeres, I love not human kind well enough to add to their happiness, and I know my own part too well to betray the confessional. Your secret is yet undisclosed by me; but beware how you exasperate me, I could disclose it, and yet not betray my sacred trust. I have dearer interests at stake than mere truth; and could it further my plans, I might speak the one word which should reveal the whole; but," added he carelessly, "it is not my interest to betray you just now."

The baron looked at the monk in utter amazement. He had long fancied Father Augustine to be a hypocrite, and had regretted having confided his troubles and sorrows to his keeping, but not until this moment did he see the whole atrocity of the father's character. He now shrank in contempt and horror from the monk, as he said,—

"This is not all, Father Augustine; you are a partisan of Matilda, and you have dared to infuse your opinions into the innocent ear of my child."

"Your child? But I deny the accusation. That I do warmly and heartily espouse the cause of the injured and betrayed empress, I triumphantly acknowledge; and I hope ere long to see all her enemies trodden down in the land. Yes, Ralph de Fougeres! the day may come, and speedily too, when you may bitterly repent having offended him who is now but Father Augustine."

"Let the day come as speedily as it will," replied the baron, "I care not; my castle walls are strong enough, and my vassals numerous enough to repel a monk."

"Your castle! Restore the treasure you hold, and then show yourself undaunted to your enemies; but now, a robber, it may be, a murderer!"

"Hold, hold; you try me too far, I will bear it no longer. Leave my presence, base monk, nor enter it again without especial permission," exclaimed the baron, raising his hand.

"Then adieu, Ralph de Fougeres, we shall meet again on more equal terms; then beware of Father Augustine."

Thus saying the monk left the castle; and the baron, after having ascertained that he was indeed on his way to his monastery, summoned his retainers, in order to make arrangements for the ensuing muster and march. In the examination of weapons and burnishing of arms, De Fougeres in some degree regained his tranquillity; but the last words of the monk rang in his ears, and he avoided the company of Edith and her friend, who had now taken up her residence in the castle.

CHAPTER VI.

I love to see, all scattered around,
Pavilions, tents, on the martial ground ;
    And my spirit finds it good,
To see, on the level plains beyond,
Gay knights and steeds caparison'd.
It pleases me when the lancers bold
    Set men and armies flying ;
And it pleases me to hear around
    The voice of the soldiers crying.
        And joy is mine
When the castle strong, besieged, shake,
And walls uprooted, totter and crack ;
    And I see the foemen join,
On the moated shore all compassed round
With the palisade and guarded mound.
Lances and swords, and stained helms
    And shields dismantled and broken,
On the verge of the bloody battle scene,
    The field of wrath betoken.
    And the vassals are there,
And there fly the steeds of the dying and dead ;
And where the mingled strife is spread,
    The warrior's noblest care,
Is to cleave the foeman's limbs and head,
The conqueror less of the living than dead.—BERTRAND DE BORN.

THE interment of the abbess was conducted with the solemnity which such an event deserved. The procession passed at midnight into the dark chapel, whose wainscoted walls now reflected the glare of the funeral torches. The mass was said ; the requiem was chaunted ; and the corpse of the departed was again carried forth into the burial-ground of the convent, and there consigned to its peaceful home. The torches, as they flung their lurid glare upon the vivid walls and narrow windows of the building, cast also a brighter light upon the smooth green-sward around, showing, as in a dark picture, the sombre habits and pale faces of the mourners. All were mourners—all but one—and he too was impressed by the awe of the scene, although his soul, more gloomy than the dark yew tree which flung its baleful shadow over him, felt not the tender emotion experienced by those around him.

The thoughts of Father Augustine were far away from the scene of grief ; they were in the halls of royalty ; and on the field of battle. The trumpet of war had saluted his ear more willingly than the chaunted hymn , and the mailed vest had been more fitting to the thoughts of his soul than the monkish stole. Dark and bitter were his feelings, as he stood beside the grave of her whose pure spirit had unveiled his ambitious designs, and his recent quarrel with De Fougeres added another incentive to awaken the slumbering fire of revenge. But the time was not yet come when it might be allowed to blaze in all its fury ; a few short weeks more of disguise and concealment ; let but the partisans of Matilda lead forth her victorious knights, and Father Augustine would again lace on the corslet. That time was speedily to arrive.

The fair and fertile lands of England became the scene of violence and devastation ; private animosities also, which had with difficulty been restrained by law, broke out, and wars between the nobles were carried on with the utmost fury. Ralph de Fougeres smothered individual hatred, and fought only for his king. All now was bustle in the Castle of Thornbury ; a sufficient number of retainers were left to guard it, and the remainder marched with their lord to join the king's forces,

Melancholy and painful was the parting between De Fougeres and his daughter; it was vain that he attempted to arouse in her some of the chivalry which animated and warmed his own breast; she thought only of the danger to which he was about to be exposed, and she clung fondly to him, while the tears fell from her sweet eyes upon the steel armour in which the baron was clad.

"Nay, Edith, thou showest thyself to be but a weak maiden thus to weep; thou art but a poor soldier's child, my girl. Come, dry those blue eyes; I leave you under the care of our sick friend, Sir Robert L'Espee, who repines that he cannot be my companion. Heaven will guard me, and a short time hence I shall return to thee. In the meanwhile," continued the baron, with something of meaning in his look and smile, "Eustace will visit thee, and cheer thy heart with his songs."

Edith heard her father, but even his gentle raillery raised no answering smile upon her countenance; once more she embraced her parent, and received his blessing, then retired to the Lady's Tower. there to weep andlpray in company with Cordelia only.

A goodly company of warriors wound round the hill upon which the castle of Thornbury was situated. First rode Ralph de Fougeres upon his grey charger, his armour glittering in the sunbeam, and his crest waving in the breeze; upon him the eye might be well satisfied to rest; although youth no more lent elasticity to his limbs, and his eye had lost somewhat of its fire, yet his countenance told of valour, of resolution, and of matured thought, and the firmness and strength with which he managed and curbed his nettlesome steed might well gain the praises of knighthood.

Behind De Fougeres rode two esquires of noble parentage and education, accomplished in all the graces of knightly life, and now burning to earn the gilded spurs upon the field of battle. And well might they thirst for the fight; for accustomed to train the fiercest war-horse, to sway the heavy sword, and to wield the lance, their prowess needed only opportunity—that opportunity unhappily was at hand.

The esquires were followed by four men-at-arms, bearing the lance of De Fougeres, and leading the horses laden with equipments and conveniences for travelling. One of them led by a silken rein a black palfrey, for the use of the baron when he should wish to give some ease to his battle steed. The fourth of these followers bore the standard of his lord, on which had been embroidered by the delicate hand of Edith, the well-known crest, the eagle holding a thunderbolt in his talons. Many tears had the unhappy girl shed over this, her work; tears that such a work should be necessary; and many times did she wish that she had been born the daughter of a humble herdsman, rather than a powerful baron.

The well armed and handsomely accoutred retainers of the Baron de Fougeres followed his standard; they were attached to their lord, whose heart was kind, though his manner was stern; even in a less stirring cause they would have followed his steps to the field of battle; and now they did so with greater alacrity, because Stephen had already, by his liberality and courteousness, won the hearts of the people. Joyfully, therefore, did the martial band set forth from the castle of Thornbury.

But joy was not with the fair mistress of the castle. The duties of Edith's situation, which were increased by the absence of her father, and the attention which her sick guest required, would, however, soon have dispelled somewhat of the gloom which hung over her mind, even if she had not occasionally enjoyed the society of the noble youth, Eustace Mowbray. Although thirsting to distinguish himself, and to gain military renown, the youth had not murmured at the arrangement which ordered him to remain at home, in order to bring up additional troops should they be necessary. He did not neglect any of the cares and duties assigned to him, and he rejoiced in the close of the day, for it brought him liberty to visit Thornbury Castle. He soon found an opportunity of expressing all he felt, and Edith did not refuse to listen to him, but, in the absence of her father, she would not pledge herself.

Edith's eye did not now seek the ground when the youth sang, though the blush

yet deepened on her cheek as she listened to him. The music of his rowers they brought him to the grassy terrace, gave joy to Edith, and sometimes she could distinguish the voice of the youth as he sang the following song :—

> The moon shines bright from the sky above,
>   'Mid fleecy clouds of white;
> And the murmuring trees of yonder grove,
>   Tipt with her silvery light;
>
> The smooth waters smile beneath her beam,
>   And on the oar their sprays
> Like brightest and purest diamonds seem,
>   As her light upon them plays.

No. 5.

Oh! 'tis sweet on such a night as this,
    When Nature is so fair,
Of a deep, fond love to taste the bliss,
    And feel the heaven that's there.
Such bliss is mine, my Edith sweet,
    Where, in the silent grove,
At this still hour we joy to meet,
    And whisper words of love.

Then my little bark, oh! swiftly glide.
    And bear me quickly on,
To where yon castle repels the tide,
    From its walls of dark grey stone.
Through the loop-holes of the turret there,
    Fair Edith's light I see;
And I come, I come, my maiden dear,
    To pledge my vows to thee!

Where was Father Augustine? could not his malignant smile destroy his happiness so pure? Since the departure of the baron, the monk had but seldom visited the castle; whether his own dark purposes entirely occupied his attention, or whether he could not endure the sight of a happiness which he could not participate in, however this might be, he seldom intruded his presence upon the fair friends. Cordelia rapidly regained her usual spirits, and in the society of Edith, seemed to have gained a new existence. Robert L'Espee was a valuable companion to his hostess: he was of middle age, valiant in the field, and gentle in a lady's bower. Edith had known him well from childhood; she esteemed his character, and almost rejoiced at the illness which made him her guest. L'Espee had been much pleased with the lively graces of Cordelia. Her wit soothed his pain, and her vivacity lightened many a gloomy hour. He had understood from the baron that she was an orphan —a dowerless, friendless orphan; and although he felt considerable curiosity to learn her parentage, his courtesy would not allow him to make the inquiry. At times, when in a serious mood, there was an expression of melancholy in her countenance, which recalled to him a vision of his early years; but so fleeting was the look, that he in vain endeavoured to fix either time or place for his remembrance, and at length he ceased to trouble his memory by the attempt.

One evening, while conversing with Edith upon the battle-scenes and tournaments of chivalry which he had witnessed in his youth, L'Espee was warmed by his subject into a description of the festivities which attended the bridals of Robert of Normandy and the beautiful Sybilla. Much did L'Espee descant upon the loveliness of the bride, upon her accomplishments and virtues, and indignantly did he repel the observations of the Norman prince, that the court of England could show no dames worthy to outvie her wimple.

"I could speak of my own lady, then a bride of a few weeks, but modesty forbids the vaunt," said the knight. "There were others, however, not unworthy to match with the beautiful Italian, need I name the Lady Adelina de Warrene, the Lady Mabel de Belesme, or the Lady Maud de Montgomery; or, more beautiful yet, the Lady Eleanor de Tunstall, then just betrothed to Robert de Hesling. Alas! how sad was her fate!"

The countenance of Cordelia was overcast at this speech, and trembling from head to foot, she made an ineffectual attempt to speak, but burst into a violent flood of tears.

Edith alarmed at the unusual emotion of her friend, eagerly inquired what was the matter.

"My mother! my own mother!" sobbed Cordelia.

Edith was thunderstruck. She knew not the history of her friend's unfortunate birth, and taking her hand, she said, "Compose yourself, dear Cordelia, our guest did not mean to vex thee."

"Vex her? no indeed!" replied the knight. "I knew Eleanor de Tunstall and, together with every one who knew her, I admired. Bright and bewitching as was her supereminent beauty, the charms of her wit, of her conversation, excelled her loveliness; and those who were taken captive by the lustre of her eyes, were held in willing thraldom by the fascinations of her mind. Indeed, my dear young friend, you may be proud of the memory of her beauty and wit; and well were they bestowed upon Robert de Hesling, a more gallant knight never reined a war-horse, a more courteous gentleman never deserved a fair lady. Shame on the caitiff who destroyed their happiness! unworthy the honourable name he bore, was the traitor De Dunstanville!"

Cordelia's tears flowed afresh, and with increased violence at these words; till after a silence of some minutes she roused her courage, and said, in a tone scarcely to be heard by her companions,—

"Oh, pity me! I am his child!"

"Pity thee!" exclaimed L'Espee, "woe betide me if I visit the parent's sins upon his innocent offspring. Poor maiden! I do indeed pity thee!" Then after a short pause, he said, "I have many times and oft endeavoured to trace in my memory the form of a vision of my early years, to whom thy sparkling eyes bear resemblance—it is now unravelled, the mystery which has bound my attention to thy lineaments; thou bearest the features of Eleanor de Tunstall, as she was in the day of her prime, in happiness, and in love. Oh! may thy fate be less disastrous!"

"We will retire, my Cordelia," said Edith; "solitude is necessary after this conversation."

Thus saying, the friends rose, and bidding L'Espee adieu, they left the hall. The knight courteously attended them to the gallery, and kissing the hand of Cordelia, he said,—

"Perhaps to-morrow I may be able to communicate something which may pour balm into the wounds I have so unintentionally opened."

The morrow came, and found Cordelia restored in spirits. She had told to Edith the principal circumstances relating to her history, and the pang which the acknowledgment of her mother's guilt had caused her to feel, was sweetly and effectually soothed by the kindness of her friend. While acknowledging how much less heavy those griefs were which had bowed down her spirit, than those which rent the heart of her friend, Edith was yet able to speak a few words of comfort and of hope; and towards noon of the following day, the hour at which she constantly visited her sick guest, she had prevailed on Cordelia to accompany her as usual, adding,—

"Remember, dearest Cordelia, L'Espee said he had some words of consolation for you; let us not neglect to seize them."

"Be it as you wish," replied the afflicted maiden. "Consolation can scarcely come to the nameless and disgraced orphan."

"Oh! say not so!" replied Edith tenderly, "L'Espee knows your family, he will entreat them for you."

"And would you have me leave you?" asked Cordelia, anxiously.

"Oh, no!" replied her friend, embracing her, "but I would keep thee here a the acknowledged and honoured heiress of De Tunstall; as my willing, not my enforced guest, and it may be so."

While thus saying, the friends sought the chamber of L'Espee. His address, always respectful, was deepened to reverence; as in a gentle tone he inquired after the health of Cordelia.

"I had some difficulty in persuading our friend to appear in your presence to-day," replied Edith; "she is dispirited and abashed; but Robert L'Espee is too true a knight to grieve a fair maiden willingly, and it is right that Cordelia should hear the words of consolation you promised her."

"I would not indeed grieve her—her mother's spirit sits enthroned upon her fair brow; and I would give my broad lands for the smile which has heretofore cheered me, though I knew not wherefore. And now, when I may recognise the admired of my youth, shall I not endeavour again to light that smile, and awaken the sweetness of its flashes?"

Cordelia bent her eyes to the ground at this discourse; the language of compliment was strange to her; she had never before been told she was beautiful, and even now the knowledge was accompanied with so much that was painful and perhaps humiliating, that it produced no exultation of spirit.

"Some words of consolation I can give, fair maiden," continued L'Espee, regarding her with emotion. "Your uncle, William de Tunstall, still lives; and lives, I trust, to be the guardian of his sister's child. In vain, since his return from Palestine, has he endeavoured to ascertain whether such a tie was in existence. The relatives of De Dunstanville have earnestly denied the fact, and have asserted that in his last days in this country the traitor—forgive me, maiden, but he was a traitor to those who loved thee best—declared that there was no heir to his unhappy wife's lands, and that she had bestowed them upon him. For himself, wrought upon by the persuasions of one of his former lawless companions, who had entered the monastic life, he left the whole of his possessions to the Church, in hope of her forgiveness."

Light now broke in upon the mind of Cordelia. "Father Augustine!" she exclaimed.

"Nay, I know not the name of the monk who persuaded him to do thee this wrong," replied the knight, "but is not Father Augustine the name of him whom I have so often seen in this castle?"

"It is. I know, by his own statement, that he confessed my poor mother just before her death," replied Cordelia, "and he constantly endeavours to persuade me to enter the holy life, alleging that it would be in vain to attempt to regain my dowry, and that poverty and shame are all that belong to me. But there is a paper (my aunt the abbess knew that there was) which would have proved me the undoubted heir to my mother."

"And where is that paper?" asked L'Espee, whose interest for the forlorn maiden was every minute becoming stronger.

"Alas! I know not. The abbess thought that it was contained in a casket which has been my mother's, and which was brought to the abbey of Thornbury by the same person who conveyed me, then a helpless infant, to that peaceful home," said Cordelia sighing.

"And can it not be recovered?" asked L'Espee.

"Who will exert themselves for me?" asked Cordelia, in a desponding tone.

"I will!" exclaimed the knight, "I will right the orphan!" then after a pause, during which he was deeply meditating, he added, "Perhaps this Father Augustine knows somewhat of the paper you mention?"

"I fear not," replied Cordelia, "indeed he not did know of its existence until the abbess acquainted him with it, and with its loss, upon her death-bed."

"It matters not," answered the knight, "I will see this monk when he next visits the castle; and although, if he be the man of whom I have heard, and albeit a rough-spoken soldier is but a sorry match for a smooth-shaven monk, I will yet endeavour to learn somewhat respecting it; and be assured, fair maiden, that Robert L'Espee never betrayed the trust reposed in him, whether it were to counsel a brave knight, or succour an afflicted damsel."

"Did I not tell thee," said Edith, "that hope and comfort might be found if we but seek them?"

"Oh, dearest Edith!" replied her friend, "comfort I have ever found with thee; but Hope—even now she appears like the shadowy rainbow to my sight, too bright and too fleeting. Alas! for the orphan!"

CHAPTER VI.

With beaker's clang, with harper's lay,
With all that olden times deem'd gay,
The island chieftain feasted high;
But there was in his troubled eye
A gloomy fire—and on his brow,
Now sudden flushed, and faded now,
Emotions such as draw their birth
From deeper source than festal mirth.
By fits he paused, and harper's strain
And jester's tale went round in vain,
Or fell but on his idle ear
Like distant sounds which dreamers hear.
Then would he rouse him, and employ
Each art to aid the clamorous joy;
   And call for pledge and lay,
And for brief space, of all the crowd,
As he was loudest of the loud,
    Seem gayest of the gay.—SCOTT.

THE brave L'Espee held his promise to Cordelia. At the next visit of Father Augustine to the castle, he was ushered into the apartment of the sick knight, and a long conversation ensued, unsatisfactory, however, to both parties. The monk positively denied any further knowledge or concern respecting Cordelia, except that he was acquainted with the last desires of De Dunstanville, that his property should be given to the Church in expiation of his sins ; and truly did L'Espee say that a plain-spoken warrior was no match for a smooth-tongued Churchman. The knight was considerably disappointed at the result of the interview, nor was the monk less annoyed. It did not at all agree with any of his schemes that the kindred of Cordelia should acknowledge her existence or relationship; still less that William de Tunstall, a highly renowned knight, should become her defender. The words, therefore, of L'Espee struck terror and mortification into the soul of Father Augustine.

Matters remained thus in Thornbury Castle, when one evening, about a fortnight after the departure of its master, a violent ringing and knocking was heard at the outer gate. It was the custom in those troubled times to let down the barricades, and raise the drawbridge at sunset ; it was considerably past this hour when the ringing was heard, and at the first moment the servants were unwilling to attend the summons. The warder, however, gave notice that the Baron de Fougeres it was who arrived at this late and unseasonable hour ; and immediately all was agitation and bustle within. Entrance to the little train was speedily given, and De Fougeres, with a few attendants, entered the hall.

Who can describe the joy of Edith at the unexpected return of her beloved father? She heeded not the crowd that surrounded him ; she remembered only his safety, and upon his bosom she wept forth tears of delight and thankfulness.

"Edith, I have brought a companion for you, my child, one whom I shall yield entirely to your care," said Ralph de Fougeres ; and Edith, for the first time, perceived a stranger standing by her father.

Her smile of welcome was saddened by the appearance of melancholy in the countenance of the stranger; she said something of welcome, but it was in a low tone, for the bearing of the young knight impressed her with sadness. The youth also whispered his thanks in a tone which went directly to Edith's heart, for it sounded of sorrow.

"Edith shall be your gaoler, young knight. You conducted yourself bravely, and deserve more than common attention. Edith," continued the chief to his daughter, "you must admit this youth to be the inhabitant of your tower ; he will not find the castl e uninteresting to him, and with you as a companion, I trust he will not find his residence with us very irksome."

A deep-drawn sigh from the youth was his only answer to De Fougeres ; Edith looked at her father for further explanation, for she felt, from the manner of both, that there was something yet untold ; but De Fougeres had left them together, and was in another part of the hall.   Edith turned towards the youth as he stood before her with folded arms and eyes bent upon the ground ; there was grace in his attitude, his light auburn locks curled upon his forehead, which seemed as yet but slightly tinged by the sun, and Edith imagined the dark fringes which shaded his eyes were moistened by a tear.   She did not speak ; but when the stranger raised his eyes to her countenance, he read in its speaking expression so much tender sympathy and interest, that taking her hand respectfully, he impressed a kiss, while the teardrop which had hung upon his eyelid fell upon it ; from that moment they were friends.

When an opportunity offered, Ralph de Fougeres drew his daughter aside, saying,—

"It is right, my Edith, that I explain to you that the rank and name of the young prisoner, whom I have this evening confided to your companionship, be not unworthy of your attention.   Your guest is Edward de Albini, the only son of Geoffrey de Albini, who, fighting in the cause of Matilda, became in a skirmish my prisoner."

At the name of Albini, Edith started ; but her father not noticing her agitation, continued,—

"I must again leave you in two days.   I should not now have returned to Thornbury, but this young knight is a prisoner of some importance to me, not only on account of the valour and power of his father in the cause to which we are adverse, but personally of importance to myself ; and I, therefore, chose to be his escort.   I need not now repeat my commands, that he be treated with due consideration and respect."

Edith assured her father that his orders should be strictly complied with in every respect; and was about to add some inquiry respecting the manner of the skirmish when De Fougeres added, in an under tone of considerable excitement,—

"Above all, remember that not a word escape you, which can lead him to think that you have ever heard the name of De Albini mentioned before.   I give this caution to your friend Cordelia, also.   I desire that she prattle not about anything that the sisters at the   convent may have told her, or let a syllable be heard by him, respecting the guardianship promised to her by the young knight's mother. Edith, hear me !   Your father's life depends upon this ; and what is dearer to him—his fame—his honour."

Edith readily promised obedience for herself and for her friend ; and the baron continued,—

"I would not trouble my child's ear with the history of war and carnage ; it suffices my Edith to know that I was in the midst of the battle, if indeed it can be called so, it was in fact only a skirmish ; our forces overtook a small party of the enemy—we fought, and were victorious.   This youth, who headed his father's vassals, fought bravely, but numbers were against him, and his bravery was vain. I respected his courage, and, myself, received his sword.   But, as I have before said, he is a prisoner of importance ; and must remain in this castle until the grand struggle, for which both parties are preparing, be over.   A valuable exchange has been offered for him by Geoffrey de Albini, but I cannot, I dare not accept it."

"Oh, my dear father !" said Edith, imploringly, "restore this youth to his parents, he is their only son ; take the exchange offered ; gratitude will prevent his bearing arms against you.   Pray, dearest father," continued Edith, but looking up, she found her father's dark, stern eyes fixed upon her, and although they beamed not in anger, there was that peculiar indescribable expression in them, which, from her earliest infancy, Edith had felt awe in encountering, and which she would not again call forth by an allusion to the subject.   Gently kissing her father, she left him without saying anything further.

The next morning the fair friends occupied themselves in rendering the Lady's Tower a fit abode for Edward de Albini. It needed but little to make it so, and the young knight was received there with kind consideration.

Edith had communicated the particulars of his capture to Cordelia, repeating to her the command of De Fougeres respecting any allusion to Cordelia's history. The latter, after Edith had finished her recital, asked her whether she did not trace in the prisoner a strong resemblance to the portrait in the western turret?

"Indeed," replied her friend, "I have not thought of it; De Albini is so melancholy, and has so much reason to be unhappy, that I scarcely dare to look at him. I wish my father would restore him to his parents."

"Oh, Edith, it is that very melancholy look which is so like the picture. I dare say our prisoner is very much like his mother. How I should love her!" said Cordelia.

"And so should I, if she resembles the portrait," replied Edith; "but we must prepare for the banquet-hall—you know that my father holds great rejoicing to-day."

The friends turned their steps towards the castle; but before they had reached it, the sound of rowers was heard upon the water and they hesitated a moment to ascertain whether it was Father Augustine who had arrived.

A deep blush of joy dyed Edith's cheek, as she recognised the barge of Eustace Mowbray, and stepping upon the bank of turf which edged the river, her arm was quickly locked in that of her lover, who said,—

"You see how I hasten to welcome the baron home, dearest Edith."

"Alas! he comes but for a day," replied Edith, sighing deeply.

"De Fougeres has brought us a prisoner," said Cordelia, gaily.

"A prisoner!" exclaimed Eustace.

"Yes," replied Edith. "It is Edward de Albini, who is to remain here until the great battle shall have taken place. He will be a companion to you, Eustace; my father says he is brave, and we know that he is noble."

"He is to reside in the Lady's Tower," said Cordelia, "and Edith is to be his goalor."

A sudden pang shot through the frame of Eustace—it was not jealousy, but it was something nearly approaching to it. He did not fear losing the affection of his beloved; he knew that it had been given to him unreservedly and spontaneously; but he did not like the thought of any knight being in her presence continually while he was absent.

"And are you then to be this young knight's companion, Edith?" he asked, gravely.

"Nay—nay—dearest Eustace, grudge him not the solace of our poor conversation," replied Edith: "he is very unhappy; he repines at being kept in a state of inactivity, while his presence and exertions are wanted elsewhere; and surely we may exert ourselves, to render his captivity tolerable. If you were unhappily to be taken prisoner, Eustace, would you not rejoice that I should bear you company?"

"The case is rather different now," said Eustace, smiling, and quite disarmed of his jealousy. "But you shall introduce me to your prisoner; perhaps his presence may keep Father Augustine from the castle; and if it does, you will find me a much more frequent visitor than I have lately been."

"Edward de Albini will, indeed, be a benefactor to us, if it be so," said Edith; "and I shall not regret the chance of war which brought him to us."

"I must seek De Fougeres," said De Mowbray; "there is much that I want to hear from him respecting the movements of the armies. Adieu, for the present, Edith! we shall meet at supper; let not your prisoner make you think less of him who truly and devotedly adores you. Adieu!"

Edith well knew, although she would not say it to her lover, that she would never change towards him. From childhood she had loved him, unconsciously, but not the less devotedly; and, however her pity and attention might be engaged by the misfortunes of the young knight, her heart was for Eustace de Mowbray only.

Not so Cordelia. In the first moment of meeting, an indescribable impulse seemed to draw her affection towards Edward; she pitied him as Edith did, but her pity was mixed with a warmer feeling. She thought, as she gazed upon him and traced his resemblance to the portrait in the western turret, that his likeness to his mother prompted her feelings towards him. Cordelia had heard of love—she saw its peaceful happiness in Edith and De Mowbray, but she had no suspicion that she was giving willing entrance to the stranger to her own heart. Time only could make this apparent to her.

The magnificent banquet was spread in the hall; the plenteous viands smoked upon the board; the numerous vassels gathered round their chief, conversing of war and strife, hearing tales of present warfare, and reckoning eagerly upon the glory to be gained in the forthcoming conflict. De Fougeres alone was reserved—nay, almost gloomy; and his retainers wondered that he, whose valour was universally acknowledged, felt no elation of mind as the future was talked of. They whispered among themselves upon this, till one said, " our master shall have mirth, by-and-by; we have a plot to amuse him, and raise his spirits; wait but till the dessert be served."

Those who were in the secret smiled, the others continued their conversation. The banquet was served. De Fougeres was seated upon the dais, at the upper end of the table; Edith, as usual, graced his right hand; on his left sat L'Espee, and near him Cordelia; while Eustace de Mowbray sat by the side of his Edith. The prisoner knight was in the Lady's Tower; the sounds of mirth and revelry sounded through the castle, but in the Lady's Tower they were but faintly heard and Edward, sunk in melancholy reverie, heeded them not.

"I see not our nighbour, Father Augustine," observed De Fougeres, as he sat at table; "he was not wont to shun our feasts even in peaceful times, and now his warlike spirit might have been stirred by the history of our late encounter."

" Father Augustine but seldom honours the castle with his presence while you are away," replied L'Espee; "and I have heard that lately he has secluded himself from society more closely than is usual with him."

" I am sorry," replied the baron; " I feel the father regrets that he exchanged the helmet for the cowl."

"It were, however," said L'Espee, " a fitting change; and if report speaks truly, not made too soon. But I wish not to say anything against Father Augustine."

The brow of De Fougeres became more and more cloudy, and his manner more and more constrained. Edith fancied that he liked not leaving home again so soon, and as his manner towards her was more tender than ever, she felt grateful to him even for his obvious gloominess.

When the viands were removed, the dessert made its appearance. In the middle was a large covered pasty, on seeing which De Fougeres exclaimed to the steward,—

" Why, Furnival, this dish is unseasonable, it should have come with the repast; we do not need any more of such substantial meats, let it be removed; I like not to see things out of their place."

" Please you, Sir Knight," replied the steward, " this dish is of a new kind, and one which we trust will give you amusement. Uncover the pasty," said the steward to his menials.

The pasty was uncovered, and the dwarf belonging to the castle stepped out of it upon the table, attired in a very gay suit of various colours, and adorned with the cap and bells which belonged to him as jester.

" Ha! Ronald!" cried De Fougeres, " I marvelled at missing thee from my side this evening. I thought thou oughtest to welcome thy master from battle."

"Is even a fool's welcome valuable?" replied Ronald; "then my master shall have it, and in rhyme too."

So saying, Ronald placed himself opposite to the baron and sang as follows:—

Hurrah! hurrah! our lord is come,
From the battle-field to his peaceful home,
   He hath ceas'd his foes to batter;

Of his knightly helm he a goblet hath made,
And a carving knife of his falchion blade,
   Of his shield a serving platter.
We will drink and sing right gloriously,
   For he hath returned victoriously!

And what brings our lord from the field of war?
A countenance marr'd with many a scar?
   Of a leg or an arm is he minus?

No. 6.

Had the foeman's sword such deadly power,
That in courtly hall or in lady's bower,
    Our lord may no longer outshine us?
We will drink and sing right gloriously,
For he hath returned victoriously !

Or comes the victor in flowing vest?
Does the diamond's blaze adorn his breast ?
    With gold is his war-horse laden ?
Doth he lead by his saddle a dusky child,
Of pliant limb, and temper mild,
    To attend on his high-born maiden ?
Let us drink and sing right gloriously,
For he hath returned victoriously !

Or nobler—doth the baron bring
The trophies of a vanquish'd king?
    Or the heads of unseemly giants ?
Oh ! well on old Thornbury's castle gate,
Might such ugly customers hold their state,
    And grin on our foes defiance,
While we drink and sing right gloriously,
There might they hang victoriously !

But no—nor giant, nor eastern slave,
Nor trophy of regal foe so brave,
    Hath our noble master brought us ;
But a stripling youth of modest air,
Of unscath'd cheek and unsunn'd air,
    As if children or women he thought us.
Let him drink and sing right gloriously,
Whom our lord hath won victoriously !

Then hurrah ! hurrah ! for our warlike knight,
And hurrah ! for the gentle youth so bright,
    The fame of our baron sharing ;
And ever and aye may the battle field,
To the war-loving knight a victim yield,
    So worthy his noble daring.
Then we'll drink and sing right gloriously,
While our master fights victoriously !

With difficulty had De Fougeres mastered his anger during this song ; twice had he arisen, and twice controlled himself, and again sat down, as if resolved to endure the satire of his jester, without betraying how nearly it touched him.   When the song was ended, he sharply inquired who made the verses.

"Who made them ?" replied the dwarf; "does not my noble master believe that a fool can make verses ? Ask Eustace de Mowbray, does he not make verses too ?" added the dwarf, with an impertinent leer at De Mowbray.

"Knave !" cried Eustace, touching his sword.

"There is yet another verse," said the dwarf, not heeding the anger either of De Fougeres or of De Mowbray. "Ye may some of you like it better."

He sang as follows :—

But change we the strain—let him beware,
Who hath prison'd the kid in his warlike lair,
    And stole the nestling away ;
The tempest shall roll—and the winds shall sweep—
The brave shall bleed—and the fair shall weep—
    But the waters must yield their prey :
And the robber who parts right gloriously,
May not return victoriously !

" Seize him," cried De Fougeres, in a fury, " darest thou threaten thy master, thou ungrateful varlet? Seize him ! take him to the dungeon ; there let him repent his audacity."

The guards sprang forth to obey the orders of their master, when the dwarf, evidently not aware of the purport of the last words which he had sung, flung himself at the feet of the baron, exclaiming,—

" Mercy—mercy—master ! dear master ! I knew not that I should offend."

" Knew not that thou shouldst offend ? Who then put those words into thy mouth ?" said De Fougeres, still in a paroxysm of rage.

The jester hung down his head, and spoke not.

" Nay, if thou wilt not acknowledge, thou must be treated as if they were thine own," said the baron. " Away with him to the dungeon !"

But the dwarf clung to his knees, so evidently in terror at what he had said, as well as of the fate which awaited him, that L'Espee ventured to interfere.

" I know not," he said to De Fougeres, " the meaning of the words which have so much excited your anger ; but it appears to me that this poor fool is but the retailer of the venom of a more subtle reptile, and that he intended that in jest which has concluded in earnest. Let me beg a little mercy for him." Then lowering his voice so that De Fougeres only could hear, " I have a suspicion upon this subject ; leave the fool for to-night under a safe guard, forbidding all access to him, and question him yourself more closely to-morrow evening."

De Fougeres pondered a while upon the advice of his friend and brother in arms ; at length speaking low to LE'spee only, he said, " Be it so, I too have secret thoughts upon the matter ; although how it could be, is a mystery to me. I am much ruffled to-night, and would break up this company." Then aloud to his guards, " See that Ronald be safely lodged to-night in the upper dungeon ; you," he said, pointing out four of his retainers, " are answerable for his appearance to-morrow. And hark ye, no tampering or questioning ; and on peril of your lives," continued De Fougeres, in a voice of thunder, " Let no one approach him, not even a monk."

At this word a glance escaped the fool, which was not lost either upon the baron or L'Espee, it spoke volumes to them. The guards removed the dwarf from the hall, and after a silence which every one seemed afraid to break, the baron said,—

" A parting cup, my friends, to-morrow I again plunge into scenes of warfare: let us drink 'Success to King Stephen !' "

The pledge went round duly honoured, and the baron and his friends left the hall.

CHAPTER VII.

They sin who tell us love can die,
With life all other passions fly :—
    All others are but vanity;
Earthly these passions of the earth,
They perish where they have their birth,
    But love is indestructible!
Its holy flame for ever burneth ;
From Heaven it came, to Heaven returneth ;
Too oft on earth a troubled guest,
At times deceiv'd, at times opprest;
Where it's tried and purified,
Then hath in Heaven its perfect rest ;
It soweth here with toil and care,
But the harvest time of love is there!—SOUTHEY.

ON the following morning early, De Fougeres ordered the dwarf to be brought before him. He desired to question him in private, lest circumstances should be brought to light which he would not have others made acquainted with. Having carefully secured the doors that no ear might pry into his secrets, he said,—

" Now, knave, for such name you well deserve, what can you say to excuse yourself for insulting your master and-benefactor ?"

The dwarf, who had from his appearance passed a sleepless and harassed night, replied, " My lord may believe me, I knew not that my words insulted him."

" Knew you not the meaning then of the last verse of your miserable song ? for I pass over the rest as unworthy my notice ?" asked the knight.

" No, truly," replied the dwarf.

" They were not then your own verses ?" asked De Fougeres.

The dwarf did not answer, but hung down his head.

" Tell me," said his master, in an angry tone, " remember there is a lower dungeon, and harder punishment—who made the verses ?"

Still the dwarf did not speak, but looking cautiously around, as if to ascertain that he was not observed, he put his hands to the back of his head, and then drew them thence forward over his temples and ears.

" Is it so, then ? From the monkish cowl was this insult engendered ?" cried De Fougeres ; " tell me, was it, was it ——"

The dwarf, trembling from head to foot, said, " I have sworn ; oh ! master, save me !"

" Poor fool !" answered the baron, " I would not have thee break thy oath ; but I must know."

" I have seen the war-horse start at the hiss of the viper ; I have seen the mailed knight bend before the monkish cowl," said the dwarf ; " I have seen the saintly hypocrite thwart the righteous designs of the noble-hearted warrior ; and I have seen the fool's motley coat upon the cold stone, where the hypocrite's knee ought to bend in penance. Ask L'Espee, who foiled the designs of the honourable, who cast a mist before the eyes of the orphan's deliverer ? Ask thyself, whose serpent guile affrighted the noble war-horse ? Whose monkish cowl hath lorded it over the knightly helmet ? Thou knowest whose villany gave the fool's motley garb to shame."

" I do know, and I will be revenged !" exclaimed the baron. Then, after musing a short time, he added, " But this war,—time presses—justice, revenge, must be delayed ; but the traitor shall not escape me. " And did the monk give you no idea of the meaning of these words ? Tell me the truth !"

" None, my lord," replied the dwarf.

" Then mark me. He will doubtless question you respecting their effect upon me. See that you give him such an answer as may prevent all knowledge of what has taken place between us," said De Fougeres.

" A fool's answer," said the dwarf sneeringly, and in an under tone.

" Right, or, in this case, a wise man's answer," answered his lord. " If but a syllable be breathed which can lead him to imagine that the song touched my feelings, or irritated my temper, there shall be no chance of further mischief from your tongue. I go to the war to-day, but I leave a trusty knight in my place. Robert L'Espee is your master."

Thus saying, De Fougeres left the room ; and the dwarf, liberated from his fears, ran out into the grove, bounding among the trees, as if he were anxious to ascertain that his freedom was not a dream, or that he had escaped with uninjured limbs from his captivity. While he was thus engaging himself, he saw Father Augustine approaching the castle in his boat—it was but the thought of a moment, and running towards the Lady's Bower, he hid himself behind the projection of a piece of a wall which joined it. Still fancying himself insecure, and hearing the father's dreaded voice inquiring for him, he contrived to mount the wall, and thus gain the casement of the upper room of the tower, now appropriated to the young prisoner's use as a bed-room.

Meanwhile, Father Augustine had landed ; and what was his dismay on inquiring for his victim, to learn that since his liberation from the dungeon no tidings could be heard of him. He had disappeared, no one knew whither. The account of what had taken place in the hall the preceding evening, told to Father Augustine with, of course, many exaggerations, and the fact of the imprisonment of the dwarf, convinced the monk that it would be unwise, if not dangerous, to meet Ralph de Fougeres; he therefore retreated again to his barge, exulting in the mischief he had occasioned, and the anger he had caused to the baron.

At noon, De Fougeres and his train left the castle. Edith's tears flowed freely as she beheld the train depart. Far other sensations moved the dwarf, who from the casement of the tower watched the disappearance of his dreaded master. As the last horseman vanished in the distance, his joy was so ungovernable, that Ronald made one of his uncouth jumps, and clapped his hands violently. The noise startled De Albini, who was sitting at the window which looked out upon the river, meditating on his unhappy captivity. At once he started from his seat, and listened attentively, but after some time, hearing no further movement, he concluded that the noise came from without the walls of the tower, and again he seated himself to watch the rippless of the stream, and mark the waving of the tall rushes as they gradually bent their heads to the water, and rose again to their farmer position.

Edward had remained thus about half an hour, when to his further amazement he distinctly heard a footstep descending the staircase, and presently the dwarf entered the apartment. De Albini on the first impulse put his hand to his side, but alas! he had no sword; and a full view of his supposed enemy assured him that he did not need one. The silence was broken by the fool, who taking up the remains of Edward's morning meal, exclaimed,—

"Good—good—a fasting body makes a witless mind; and I have need of all my wits to keep myself out of the duugeon."

"Who are you?" asked Edward in surprise, "and how came you here?"

"What! not know my lord's fool, Ronald!" answered the dwarf. "I thought everybody knew the fool."

"And how came you here?" said Albini; "what right have you to intrude upon me? Even a prisoner as I am has a claim to solitude."

"And how came you here?" retorted the dwarf. "By right of war. You perilled your life, and lost your liberty for one whom you know not, whom you have never seen."

"I lost my liberty in defence of the honour of my father's house," replied De Albini, sternly and proudly.

"Honour! What is honour? Will honour save a life? Will honour set a limb? Will honour throw down these walls and give thee room to escape? I pray thee, tell me what is honour? I am a poor, iguorant fool, and have never been taught the language of nobility."

"Leave me," said Edward, angrily, "I am in no humour for mockery."

"Leave thee? no, no, the fool will not run into the trap. Better be a prisoner here than in the dungeon of the castle, or the cell of the convent," answered Ronald.

"What do you mean? What have you done to deserve imprisonment?" asked Edward.

"Did I say that I deserved it? If I did, I said that which I do not believe to be true. I have fairly earned it, yet not deserved it; can the fool expect his deserts when the wise man does not get his?" said Ronald.

"I know not, and I care not; but, if indeed you are hiding yourself from undeserved injury, stay here until some of the menials from the castle come to bring me more food," replied De Albini; and seating himself at the window, he took no further notice of his strange companion.

The dwarf also seemed to forget that he was not alone; for after singing several snatches of songs, he at last repeated in an apparently careless tone, rather of speaking than singing,—

> " But change we the strain—let him beware,
> Who hath prison'd the kid in his warlike lair,
> And stole the nestling away ;
> The tempest shall roll—and the winds shall sweep—
> The brave shall bleed—and the fair shall weep—
> But the waters must yield their prey !"

Then looking earnestly at Edward, he sung,—

> " A stripling youth of modest air,
> Of unscath'd cheek, and unsunn'd hair,"—

"Truly the father painteth 'right; the kid is in the warlike lair, and it may be long ere he escape from it. But where is the nestling ? Ha!—I have it —the father would have prisoned the nestling in his cage of stone, and she preferred the courtly bower."

"But the waters must yield their prey! This a poor fool can never understand. It is that line which so angered my Lord de Fougeres," and again he sung the offensive stanza.

The attention of De Albini was at length aroused, and he asked sharply,—

"What nonsense is that?"

"Such as a fool may not sing, nor a baron hear," was the reply ; then in a lower tone, "but I should like to hear the monk utter it."

"Repeat it," said Edward.

"Do you at last take me for a wise man ? Did I not say a fool may not sing it? And it cost me a night's lodging in a dungeon too. Well, listen," and the dwarf repeated the last line.

Edward mused.

"What can that mean ?" said he.

"I know not," said Ronald ; "mischief, no doubt, or the monk would not have bade me sing it. Perhaps you are to be thrown into the river, to save the expense of feeing the kid," observed the dwarf, with a tone of derision.

"Nay, nay, Ralph de Fougeres dares not do that," cried Edward.

"But others may dare. De Fougeres is gone to the war, and has left Robert L'Espee guardian of the castle ; a brave knight, and, besides, one who loves not Father Augustine."

" Is that the monk who taught you the verses?" asked Edward.

" Yes," replied the dwarf; then looking cautiously round, he added in a tone of fear, "beware of him ! What he says, trust not ; what he counsels, act not ; what he forbids, fear not to do."

A long pause ensued, broken by the sighs of Edward, and the occasional singing of the dwarf. During this time, Edith and Cordelia had been engaged in the castle; they now came to pay a vist to the young prisoner. What was their surprise to findt he dwarf in the Lady's Tower ! Edith immediately dismissed him, but scarcely had left their presence, when he came running back, exclaiming,—

"Father Augustine! Father Augustine!" and shutting the door violently, hid himself behind Cordelia.

"We will go to meet the father," said Edith; "I am desired not to give him entrance here. Farewell, De Albini."

The fair friends found Father Augustine in the castle hall, walking up and down in gloomy silence. Seeing Edith, he made his usual salutation, adding,—

"You have a prisoner, I hear?"

"Yes," replied Edith ; "the son of Geoffrey de Albini, who was made captive in a skirmish, and my father brought him here for safe keeping."

"And does the youth know what castle this is ?" asked the monk.

"Undoubtedly," replied Edith, somewhat surprised at the question, "he knows this to be the residence of Ralph de Fougeres."

"And its name ?" asked Father Augustine.

"He has doubtless heard it called Thornbury," said Edith, "indeed I now remember that I myself have used the name."

"And did he betray no emotion at the mention ?" asked the monk.

"Indeed I know not, father," replied Edith; "I am not used to scrutinise the feelings of the unhappy."

"It is well that he is here, he is safe from the danger of battle. Lady Edith, receive my admonition. Cherish the stranger; love him, if thou canst; his fate is interwoven with thine; upon his welfare depends thy happiness. Nay, my child, thou needst not blush and look upon the ground, thou wilt cherish him; thou wilt love him; thou must do so—it is thy fate to do so, and thou canst not avoid it. I will see thee again to-morrow. Farewell."

Edith remained in speechless astonishment at the address of the father, long after he had entered his boat, and was again far on the river. She dreaded lest the arrival of this young knight taken prisoner while fighting for Matilda, whose cause the monk espoused, should awaken the utmost fury of his anger, and she was proportionably surprised at the amicable manner in which he received the intelligence. His injunction to herself was still more extraordinary; to cherish—to love,—did he not know of her betrothment to Eustace de Mowbray, her betrothment with her father's full consent and approbation? And the monk bade her love a stranger; one whose kindred she knew not; who was opposed to De Fougeres in the battle-field. What could it mean?

Not less disturbed was Cordelia at the monk's discourse. She had viewed the young knight with an eye of favour, if not of love; and to hear her friend, her only friend, urged to cherish and to love him, it gave her a pang more bitter than any she had yet known. Not even her own uncertain destiny, her mother's unhappy fate, or the knowledge of her father's villany, had given her so severe a blow. It, however, determined her to keep a more strict guard upon her own feelings; to present, if possible, any love for Edward de Albini from taking root in her heart.

Days passed away; Father Augustine came not. Edith's attention was divided between the companionship of L'Espee, and her endeavours to render the poor captive as happy as his unfortunate condition would allow him to be. While accounts of the various successes of the king's forces from time to time arrived at Thornbury, the sounds of mirth and revelry sounded through the castle; in the Lady's Tower they were scarcely to be heard; and Edith, with an instinctive kindness, forbore when in Edward's presence any reference to happiness or mirth, and almost restrained her sunny smiles.

She chose her sweetest and most plaintive songs to amuse him; she listened patiently to his grief at being separated from his family. To her willing ear Edward told his sorrows, and spoke in raptures of his mother; he was not ashamed to weep in the presence of his gentle companion, for he knew that she sympathised with him, and they loved each other—but it was with a love so pure, so holy, that Eustace de Mowbray could not, did not wish it less. He watched the kind attentions of his beautiful betrothed towards the interesting prisoner, and while he felt assured that her brightest smile and happiest feelings were his own, he envied not the sighs and tears which she gave to De Albini.

Were these the feelings of Cordelia? Alas! no. The deceitful poison had entered her soul, and destroyed her small store of happiness. Still loving Edith with the most devoted attachment, seeing her extreme beauty, and knowing all her advantages, Cordelia still felt that all was not quite right between them. She thought Edith much too free in speech with the young knight, and she wondered that Eustace would permit their intimacy; she sighed when she thought how well the Father Augustine's commands had been obeyed.

Ronald, the dwarf, also increased the uneasiness of Cordelia by his communications of the conversations held between himself and De Albini, with whom he passed the greater part of each day. He told how the prisoner talked of the beauty, of the sweetness, of the grace of Edith; and of his happiness who should win her for his bride; while he bestowed but a passing notice upon Cordelia. Upon what hope, then, could Cordelia build? Would that she were far away, or safe in th solitude of the convent! but no—it was some happiness to be near the object of her love, to hear his gentle voice, even although it spoke but to her whom she must consider her rival.   Upon this Cordelia lived ; and if by chance she found Edward's eye resting upon her countenance, if in the familiarity of conversation he addressed but one word to her, how was that look, that word, treasured in her heart, to be called forth in solitude and in sorrow.

And what were the feelings of the prisoner? Did he indeed love the betrothed Edith, and slight the gentle, and not less fair Cordelia? Oh, no !   True, that he but seldom addressed his discourse to her, who reigned in his inmost heart its sole mistress ; true, that his eye avoided hers ; that he hastened not to meet her when he heard her light step approaching ; but the beating of his heart told him, long before she appeared, whose gentle foot it was that pressed the green sward which surrounded his prison.   In solitude he dwelt upon the remembrance of her countenance ; in solitude, her sweet voice still sounded on his ear ; her lively smile still enlivened his hopes.   Alas! did he hope ? Yes,—because he loved.

Many, many hours did the captive pass in the society of his fair gaoless.   Edith and Eustace would sing to him ; while Cordelia, in place of the gaiety which had hitherto been the distinguishing feature of her character, would sit musing by the window, listening to every word he uttered, and at times stealing a glance at the countenance which gave light to her heart.

One morning as the young friends were thus met together, Edith and Cordelia engaged upon their embroidery, and De Albini meditating in hopeless sorrow upon his inactive and bereaved destiny, Edith handed her lute to him, asking if he would endeavour to divert his melancholy by a song.

"Fair lady," replied Edward, " I have forgotten the lays I sang while happy."

" Nay, nay," said Edith, " time has not been so treacherous.   Cordelia, join your prayers with mine : our young friend cannot refuse such a supplication."

Cordelia gave but one glance to the young knight ; he felt its power, and taking the lute from her hand, he swept its strings in mournful cadence, and after a few minutes he thus sang :—

> " And dost thou bid the captive sing,
> And must his fingers wake the string ?
> Alas ! a cloud is o'er me cast,
> I can but sing of freedom past;
> Nor joy nor hope to me belong,
> And love,—is that a captive's song ?
>
> I cannot sing of Nature's face ;
> The noble groves this mansion grace,
> Are not so fair as those which shade
> The turf on which my childhood play'd :
> These meadows green, tho' rich they be,
> Have not a charm of love for me.
>
> My lady mother weeps alone—
> My sire is to the battle gone—
> My war-steed frets within its stall—
> My dogs in vain await my call—
> My vassals at the castle board
> Speak sighing of their absent lord.
>
> Then Edith bid me not to sing,
> Lest sorrow so imbue the string,
> That when thou wak'st its altered tone,
> Thou find its joy and gladness gone,
> And its unhappy touch impart
> The captive's misery to thy heart."

Sadly did these lines express the wretchedness of the singer, and deeply did his auditors sympathise with him. But there was one to whom they brought the value of awakened hope. As Edward concluded the first verse of his song, his eyes sought those of Cordelia, and the expression which she read in them told her a secret which she had never suspected. It told her that Edward de Albini loved her. Shrinking within herself, Cordelia scarcely heard the rest of the song, and when it had been concluded, she was still sunk in a deep reverie.

The weather was hot, but delightful, and Eustace, seeing that Edith was much overcome by the expression of De Albini's feelings, and perhaps willing to remove her from an influence which he at times extremely dreaded, proposed that the barge

belonging to the castle should be ordered, and that she should accompany him to his father's castle for an hour or two.

Edith who was accustomed to such excursions with Eustace, readily agreed to the proposal, and asked Cordelia if she would accompany her. Cordelia however, excused herself, saying, that one of the boarders at the convent, who had been more than commonly friendly to her, was ill, and had that morning sent a message requesting her to call upon her.

No. 7.

Edith readily excused her friend, and left the tower with Eustace.

Cordelia was arranging her embroidery in order to go to the convent, when Edward said,—

"And will you too leave me, fair Cordelia?"

Cordelia trembled, but made no answer.

"Is the captain then unworthy of a word?" said Edward, in a tone of grief.

"Oh no!" replied Cordelia, not daring to turn her head. She felt that De Albini was approaching her, and she trembled still more violently.

"Cordelia," he said, "pity me!"

"I do!—indeed, 1 do!" replied Cordelia.

"You know not all," answered Edward. "You know not that the captive has dared to love."

A few hours ago Cordelia would have supposed that this confession alluded to Edith; but that one look had undeceived her. She answered not.

"Yes," continued Edward taking her hand, "the captive has indulged a dream, a selfish one,—but it has cheered his solitude, and made restraint tolerable; do not awaken him from it, in pity do not."

Still Cordelia made no answer.

"From the first moment that I beheld the Lady Edith," continued Edward, "I felt that my fate was linked with hers. Exquisitely beautiful as she is, it was not her beauty alone that touched me; I felt towards her a secret attraction which I cannot describe, still less oppose."

Who shall describe the despair, the misery of Cordelia at those words? She sunk upon a chair, utterly powerless to escape from a conversation which she felt was death to her newly awakened hopes; and yet well knowing that every succeeding word would be a stab to her deluded heart. Flight, however, was impossible, and she suffered Edward to go on.

"Oh, Cordelia, to you, whose affection for the lovely Edith is so strong and disinterested, I may pour out my whole soul in confidence. I have long sought for this moment, and impatiently have I awaited it; it is come, and my heart is almost too full to give utterance to my words. But to your friendly ear I may confide my sorrow."

Edward here paused, but in vain; Cordelia was incapable of speaking.

"When I first arrived here," continued De Albini, "anger against De Fougeres, and a vehement desire of revevge, were the feelings uppermost in my bosom. I burned again to rush upon the battle-field; and in the blood of De Fougeres to wash out the stain of captivity. But when Edith visited me—when her gentle voice bade me take comfort, all these violent feelings died away; and in the enchantment of her smile I forgot that I was a prisoner. Still my father's disappointment weighs heavily upon me. Brave and noble-minded as he is, he has clung to the fortunes of the injured empress, while his kindred have embraced the cause of Stephen, even although he feels in common with the rest of the Norman barons, that in the present unsettled state of the kingdom, a ruler is needed who should be able to head the troops in the field, as well as preside at the council table. But would Geoffrey de Albini desert an unsuccessful cause? Never! and he bade me, his only child, to follow him to the field of battle to fight for the betrayed and injured Matilda. My mother too—oh, Cordelia, if you knew her, you would indeed love her."

At these words Cordelia raised her head, and was about to speak, when the desire of the baron that she should give no intimation to Edward that the name of De Albini had ever before been heard by her, rushed across her mind; and she checked the expression of admiration and sympathy which had arisen to her lips.

De Albini resumed his discourse.

"Cordelia, my mother weeps for her only child. Gladly would she have seen me risk my life in the field of battle, honourably contending for an honourable cause; but pent up in captivity, debarred the common gift of liberty—oh! it is worse than death itself. The Lady Elfrida de Albini has now no solace, I had been to her a beloved and a loving child; I had succeeded to the love and the hope of one too early lost, and a double share of tenderness seemed to fall to my lot; and shall I not weep when I remember what she must now suffer? Yes, Cordelia, she is worthy your commiseration—your tears."

Cordelia did indeed weep—but wherefore? Were not all her lately cherished hopes overthrown? Well, indeed, might she weep—well might she feel the destitute situation of the unprotected orphan. Yet Cordelia still fondly clung to love, although she must dismiss all hope from her breast. She, however, resolved that Edward should never suspect her love; and how deeply did she rejoice that she had never suffered Edith to become acquainted with it. She almost scorned herself for having condescended to love unasked.

While these thoughts were passing in the mind of Cordelia, the scenes of home had arisen before De Albini, and he said,—

"You will not be surprised, Cordelia, that, loving and beloved by my mother as I have described, the only solace to my imprisonment arose from the society of the beautiful Edith. I was, besides, as I have said, irresistibly attached to her. My heart seemed to seek hers; her feelings, her opinions became, or rather already, by the unconscious power of love, they were mine; her tone spoke peace to me, even when her words were not addressed directly to myself; her graceful step brought happiness with it, when it approached my solitary tower; and when she left my presence, every hope, every joy seemed banished from me—grief and despondency alone remained."

As Edward thus spoke, a step approached along the grass walk. Cordelia started; too well did she know that tread: it was Father Augustine, and she felt like a guilty person, well knowing that the monk would not speak or think charitably of her presence with the interesting prisoner.

The door was but half closed, and Father Augustine, not condescending to give any announcement of his visit, entered.

De Albini was surprised, but his natural courtliness and grace of manner did not forsake him, and rising, he said,—

"Father Augustine, I presume?"

"Yes, my son; my visit to you, though long delayed, is not, I trust, too late."

"I have been taught, reverend father," replied the youth, "that it is never too late to do a good deed; and surely the visit to a forlorn and almost broken-hearted captive is a good deed."

"And what motive brought you here, my daughter?" asked the monk, turning to Cordelia; "you are alone, too. Is yours a good deed to yourself?"

"Nay, father, blame not the Lady Cordelia; she came here with her friends, Lady Edith and Eustace de Mowbray," said Edward.

"And why departed she not with them?" asked the monk.

"I am going, father," replied Cordelia, in a voice of extreme humility. "I am going to the convent to see Sister Agnes, who is ill."

"Then begone, child," said the monk, hastily; and Cordelia, not daring to raise her weeping eyes to Edward, left the tower.

Slowly and sadly the maiden took her way to the abbey. Hitherto, notwithstanding the melancholy remembrances called up by the scene of her infant nurture, and the sufferings of her after years, Cordelia always felt that the abbey was a place of holy rest and quiet. It was endeared to her by many associations. In one corner of the garden had been the little plot of ground allotted to her for her own amusement; this was now barren and uncultivated, her sweet flowers had died by neglect and premature decay. Thus had her sweetly budding hopes been ruthlessly destroyed—there, under that spreading yew, had she in childhood sought shelter from the heat of the noonday sun—under its baleful branches she had found rest when wearied by exercise. Alas! now the withering blight of disappointment had overcast her bright promise of the future. Heretofore Cordelia had entered the convent garden with a peaceful, although an oppressed heart; but now a tumult was within her—a tumult of fear, of dismay, of dread, which, in her darkest hours, she had never yet known.

With a heavy step did Cordelia cross the lawn of the convent, and with a hesitating hand did she pull the door-bell.

She was readily and willingly admitted; for the gay and lively Cordelia had been, and still was, a great favourite there. Upon inquiring for Sister Agnes, she was informed that her friend was much better, and Cordelia repaired to her cell.

"I could not think it was my friend Cordelia," said the the nun, "the touch of the bell was heavy, and the footstep which just crossed the lawn was not elastic as usual. Are you ill or—unhappy?" said Sister Agnes, as she looked at the woe-worn countenance of Cordelia.

"Ill, my sister," replied Cordelia.

"No—no, I know the lines of that countenance too well," replied the nun. "Tell me, dearest Cordelia, hath Edith been unkind?"

"Oh no, that cannot be!" replied Cordelia.

"Then the interesting prisoner, is it aught that concerns him?" asked Agnes.

Cordelia spoke not, but throwing herself upon the bosom of the nun she burst into a torrent of tears.

"Tell me all, my friend, and let me comfort you," answered the nun, in a tone of commisseration. "Here, in this peaceful retreat we have no troubles, no sorrows, let us then endeavour to console and soothe those that the stormy world engenders."

But notwithstanding the kindness of her friend's address, Cordelia could not find words for her sorrow, till Sister Agnes asked,—

"Is the young knight gone?"

"No—but," hesitated Cordelia.

"But what? Has De Fougeres at last relented, and accepted the ransom offered?" asked the nun.

"No—no," sobbed her unhappy friend, "but he loves Edith."

"Loves Lady Edith—impossible!" exclaimed Sister Agnes; "you must be mistaken."

"Oh, it is too true—he told me so himself;" cried Cordelia.

"Told you so; was he so cruel? and Eustace, what says he to this?" asked the nun.

"I know not," said Cordelia, "we were alone, and he told me all."

"My poor friend," said the nun tenderly; "but he knows of the betrothment between Edith and Eustace, does he not?"

"I know not; yes, he must be acquainted with it," replied Cordelia.

"And how then can he love her?" said Sister Agnes; "the traitor! would that he had died upon the field of battle, rather than be brought here. Tell me all, dearest Cordelia."

"I will, I will," sobbed the unhappy girl. "Edith and Eustace had left us, and I was going to follow them, when De Albini implored me to remain; and he then acquainted me with his love for Edith from the first moment that he saw her; that he thought her most beautiful, and that she was his only solace in his imprisonment."

' Now, dearest Cordelia," said Sister Agnes, gravely, " I have for some time seen that this young knight was gradually obtaining a place in your heart, which a stranger ought not to possess; and I have wished to speak to you about him; but although I trust that you know my love for you well enough to prevent your thinking me impertinent, yet I was unwilling to allude to a subject, the consideration of which is, you know, forbidden to us professed sisters. I have long known that you loved Edward de Albini, with an over-weening and sinful love."

' Oh, do not say that!" exclaimed Cordelia, "I never said that I loved him; I did not know it till this unhappy morning."

"You never said it," answered the nun, "you scarcely talked of him; but have I not seen that your daily visits to the Lady's Tower formed the happiness of your life? that you reckoned all the moments of the day lost, except those which you passed with the prisoner? have I not seen your avoidance of my eye when you mentioned him? and how could I doubt that you had unhappily suffered yourself to love him."

"I knew it not, I knew it not," cried Cordelia, earnestly; "I never knew it till this morning; and then one look when he was singing, told me that he loved me."

"Indeed, poor child, and he told you he loved Edith?" said Sister Agnes.

"He did," replied Cordelia.

"Then you must love him no longer," said Sister Agnes, in a tone of admonition.

Cordelia wept, but spoke not.

"And what but misery could attend your love, even were it returned," continued the sister. "Would Geoffry de Albini allow his son to wed you, unknown, and unprotected by powerful kindred. Or if your relations were to claim you, would they allow you to marry a knight who has fought against Stephen? Be assured, however, that the Baron de Fougeres will never let the victim slip from his hold; he has taken the prey, he will not let him loose again; he dares not for the sake of Stephen's cause."

"I know all that you say is true," said Cordelia, "I know that I am friendless and poor; but the Lady de Albini once promised me her protection whenever I should need it."

"And did my poor friend build upon that," said the nun. "Alas! little as I know of the world, by what I have heard of it, I can tell you, that although the Lady de Albini may be ready to befriend the poor Cordelia, by giving her protection and countenance as a dependant or menial, she would scorn as an insult the supposition that she would receive her as her son's bride. No, Cordelia! your hopes are rudely crushed ere they are budded; believe me, even had they gone on to blossoming, they would have been as surely destroyed, and with a greater cost of misery and shame."

"Nay, say not shame!" cried Cordelia, proudly; "my mother's house is as noble as that of De Albini; and, trust me, never would her child sue to any one for the protection due to a menial. No, Edward de Albini should never wed me as an inferior."

"But what else could be hoped?" asked the nun.

"I will be acknowledged by my kindred," replied Cordelia, disdainfully; "then I am indeed the equal of Edward de Albini. But tell me, Sister Agnes," she continued after a pause, "is the Lady Elfrida de Albini so very haughty?"

"I know her not," replied Sister Agnes; "I have but heard of her from our regretted mother abbess; she is said to be beautiful and kind-hearted. But why this question, Cordelia, and so earnestly too?"

"I cannot stay here if Edward wed Edith," answered Cordelia, "and I would go to my only friend."

"No, Cordelia, there is a safer refuge from disappointment and despair," said Sister Agnes.

"What mean you?" asked Cordelia.

"These convents walls," answered the nun, earnestly. "Oh neglect not the holy call!"

Cordelia shook her head.

"And can you, my sister, hesitate between the miseries, the heart-burnings of the world, and the peace and happiness of this retreat!" asked the nun.

"It cannot be—it must not be. I pray you urge it not, if you love me, Agnes," said the agitated Cordelia.

"I do love you," replied Sister Agnes, tenderly, "and I would see you happy. But you will not be so until you leave a world which brings but trouble to those who dwell in it. Nay, Cordelia, you may shake your head, but ere long you will come again to Sister Agnes, and acknowledge that she is right. Wait but till Edith marries Edward de Albini."

"Oh, speak not of it, if you would not break my heart!" cried Cordelia, convulsively.

Sister Agnes kissed her tenderly, saying, "Poor dove!" thou flutterest in the net of the fowler—one struggle will burst the meshes and free thee."

Cordelia shook her head mournfully. "No," she said, "although he loves me not, I may still love him. Oh, Agnes! I have dwelt upon his smile till it rose before me wherever I turned my eye; I have studied his features till every scene presented them to my view; I have listened to his voice till the breeze murmured it, and the hoarse wind thundered it in my ear; and must I give him up? They have become a part of my life; they are necessary to me as the air I breathe. Bid me not dismiss them."

"Weakness! weakness!" said the nun, in a tone of reprehension. "Is it possible that Cordelia can be so feeble-minded? No! cast this young knight at once from your heart. But what says Eustace de Mowbray to this matter? He is not of a race to endure being supplanted without avenging himself."

"Eustace knows nothing of De Albini's love," replied Cordelia.

"Then, await quietly until it comes to his knowledge," said the nun; "and remember, Cordelia, the convent offers you a safe asylum from all the troubles of the world."

Cordelia took an affectionate leave of her friend, and prepared to return to the castle, with a heavy step and an oppressed heart. She dreaded seeing Edith after the disclosure De Albini had made; she doubted whether she ought not to acquaint her friend with what had passed; but she felt how painful such a conversation must be, and she determined to keep the secret of the prisoner from her whom it most intimately concerned.

On reaching the castle, Cordelia found that Edith had not yet returned. She rejoiced at this, as it gave her a short time longer to prepare for the meeting, which she much dreaded. She therefore retired to her room in order to consider her situation, and recover in solitude that composure which had in the last few hours been so painfully disturbed.

CHAPTER VIII.

Dark and unearthly is the scowl
That glares beneath his dusky cowl:
The flash of that dilating eye
Reveals too much of times gone by;
Though varying, indistinct its hue,
Oft will his glance the gazer rue.
For in it lurks that nameless spell
Which speaks itself unspeakable,
A spirit yet unquelled and high,
That claims and keeps ascendancy;
And like the bird whose pinions quake,
But cannot fly the gazing snake,
While others quail beneath his look,
Nor 'scape the glance they scarce can brook.—BYRON.

During Cordelia's visit to the cell of Sister Agnes, an extraordinary scene took place in the Lady's Tower. The visit of Father Augustine surprised Edward, as the monk had but once before intruded himself upon the prisoner, and then but for a few minutes.

The holy Father Augustine had, almost unconsciously, made a deep and powerful impression upon the mind of De Albini; who almost hoped, although he feared to cultivate further acquaintance with the monk. He came not, however, to the tower until the day of which we are speaking, and in the meanwhile the sweets and cares of a concealed affection had so completely filled the mind and heart of Edward that the sudden appearance of the monk was to him rather as a half forgotten vision than as a reality.

De Albini was however extremely annoyed at the entrance of Father Augustine at that moment. He had long sought for an opportunity of declaring his affection to Cordelia, or at least of endeavouring to interest her in his situation; for he would have considered it dishonourable to endeavour to gain the affection of her whom he loved, while he was a hopeless prisoner to De Fougeres, considering him, rightly, a hard and vindictive enemy. But he might, without any dereliction of honour, awaken, if possible, a feeling of pity for his misfortune, and interest for those whom he tenderly loved, and who were so grievously afflicted by his detention.

Father Augustine saluted De Albini most courteously; he could veil his pride and moroseness under the appearance of affability whenever it suited his purpose to do so, or his own interest was at stake; and on this occasion he exerted his utmost condescension.

"I am a strange visitor, my son," said the monk, "and perhaps it may be difficult for me to excuse myself for not paying earlier attention to the captive and the unhappy. Our holy vocation enjoins us to succour the afflicted."

Edward made no answer, not knowing to what this address was intended to lead.

"But, my son," continued Father Augustine, after a short pause, "I believe my negligence has been amply atoned for by the repeated visits of more youthful, probably more welcome, visitors. The Lady Edith and the youth, Eustace de Mowbray, I understand, have passed much of their time with you."

Edward bowed; he could make no other answer.

"And the unhappy girl who has just left us," asked the monk in an inquisitive tone, "has she, too, been the companion of your solitude?"

De Albini was startled at the manner in which the father spoke of Cordelia, and was on the point of making an indignant reply, when the monk continued,—

"Are you aware that Cordelia is about to become the bride of the Church? And is it right to induce her to forget her religious vows in the light society of worldly youth?"

"I know not, father, the condition or fate of the lovely Cordelia. I but know that she is the chosen friend of the Lady Edith, and the guest of the Baron de Fougeres. I do not seek to interfere in the household of my jailor," said Edward, proudly.

"Jailor!" cried the monk, "and can a child of De Albini acknowledge a jailor?'

"Truly, it is a melancholy word," replied Edward.

"And can you, descended from a house as honourable as it is ancient, brave in the battle-field, loyal and true in the council chamber, can you be content here? tied like a bird in a cage, while your companions in arms fight for the most glorious, the most chivalric, cause that ever called knight to conquer or to die—the cause of the injured Matilda!"

The monk said this with an eager voice, and with a countenance in which scorn struggled for mastery with enthusiasm.

"But, father," said Edward, "I am a prisoner."

"So you are told; but it is your own mind that enslaves you,' said the father.

"Nay, I am not a willing captive," replied Edward, gloomily, fearing lest the monk intended to allude to his attachment to Cordelia.

"Then why not away to the battle field?" asked Father Agustine.

"I have sworn to abide here the return of De Fougeres," replied the youth. "Would you, father, counsel me to break my oath? Oh no!"

"And know you not, my son," said the monk, "that an oath taken under pressure of danger or bodily fear is not to be regarded?"

"A convenient resource," replied De Albini, "but one of which I cannot avail myself."

"And know you not, also, that the Church has power to free you from an oath taken against her holy welfare, and detrimental to her prosperity?" asked the monk, cautiously.

"Foolish, rash, unthinking youth! see you not that if Stephen be allowed to govern this realm, the Church must be sacrificed. Oh! it is a holy cause, the cause of Matilda; and everlasting glory awaits those who fall in her defence!" exclaimed the monk, warmly. "For those who shelter their cowardice under the plea of constraint, and dare not enter the lists for the crown of martyrdom, infamy shall be their portion; for them no wreaths of glory are woven; but their names shall be held up to scorn and ignominy."

"Who dares to use the word cowardice to De Albini?" cried Edward, angrily. "It is well that he wears the monkish cowl, and not the knightly helmet; or he should rue the day when such a word escaped his lying lips."

"Thou callest me a liar, and thou talkest of the monkish cowl; it shall not protect thee long; it shall speedily be doffed, and the plumed helmet take its place," said Father Augustine.

De Albini looked at the monk in amazement. After a short pause the latter said,—

"Hear me, boy! I come to offer thee liberty and fame, if thou darest to seize it. I can no longer endure this inactive life; my country—my queen demand my services, and they shall have them. I depart for the field of contention, and I come to offer thee my assistance to escape from this thraldom, and accompany me to glory. Hast thou courage?"

"No, father! I have not courage to dishonour my word," replied Edward, firmly.

"And wilt thou linger here, a helpless captive, while thy kindred, while thy sire, are boldly meeting danger, it may be death, in the rightful cause?" exclaimed the monk.

"Father, tempt me not!" said Edward.

"Canst thou then know that thy sire is seeking glory, and thou art touching the lute? Canst thou picture him to thyself wounded, dying in the arms of menials, it may be of foes, and his child—his only child is living in luxurious idleness?" cried the monk.

"Father! father! I cannot bear such a picture!" replied De Albini.

"Then reverse it," said the monk. "Paint the son, long mourned, long despaired of; paint him returning to the hall of his fathers; paint him wiping the tears from his lady mother's eyes; let him tell her that her sorrow has not been in vain—that the kid hath escaped from the lair of the wild beasts—and, that though the waters have not yet given up their prey, that yet she is not childless; paint him leading his father's vassals to glory and conquest; paint this—realise it!"

The figure of the monk seemed to dilate with the earnestness with which he said this. He assumed a tone of authority which awed the young knight, and his allusion to the words of the dwarf's song astonished Edward.

De Albini held silence for a short time. Many and painful were the thoughts which arose in his mind, and the feelings which chased each other through his breast. Ambition—the thirst for military glory—the love of action—love to his parents, all combined to shake his resolution; but he remembered his oath, and a gentler form stood before him, as he said to Father Augustine,—

"No more, father, my oath is sacred."

"But my son, I can—I do absolve thee," replied the monk.

Edward shook his head. "Can you absolve my conscience?" he asked.

"Yes, proud boy," he answered; "it were glorious to absolve an oath in the cause of Matilda! Say but the word, and my rowers shall bear you far from these proud and doomed towers.''

"I cannot say it. No, father; I must give up all to honour," said Edward firmly.

"Honour!" repeated the monk, sneeringly.

"Yes, father! could De Albini welcome his son, even in the hour of death upon the battle field, if his presence placed a blot upon his shield, never to be erased

from it. No," continued the young knight, "rather would I meet an inglorious death here, by the hand of my foe, than earn miscalled glory by the sacrifice of honour. Thou knowest me not to tempt me thus."

"Do I not know thee? Do I not know that it is not thy oath that withholds thee; that were a fetter easily broken; there are softer fetters, bright eyes hold thee here in shame and captivity," said the monk, stealing a glance at Edward's disturbed countenance.

No. 8.

"I know not your meaning, father," said the youth.

"Yes, thou dost know it, and hear me. She whom thou lovest with an unholy love, is, as I have told thee, the spouse of the Church. I am her fate, and I will it so. But were she free to wed a child of the world, she could never be thy bride. She is nameless, friendless, the child of shame and of poverty ; disowned by her kindred as a plague-spot upon their fair fame, and dependant upon the charity of strangers for the bread she eats. Can such an one be the bride of a De Albini ? No, shame on his meanness who would stoop to such an alliance !"

Edward was thunderstruck at this denunciation. He knew not the birth of her whom he dared to love, almost without being aware of it ; and this disclosure of her unhappy state was a dreadful blow to him. Well, indeed, did he feel that such an one was not worthy to match with one of his noble lineage ; but did he really love her ? Was it not a mere transient liking, brought forth by his own melancholy circumstances of seclusion and depression ?"

"Father," said he, "you have touched a chord which I thought that no human hand could awaken. True, I have liked the company of Cordelia ; she has, in the presence of the Lady Edith, consoled me with her sprightly conversation. A captive, father, has but few pleasures ; surely he may enliven his spirits by the kindness of those who condescend to visit him."

"And is it kindness to them to win the heart of one predestined to the veil ?" asked the monk.

"I knew not this. The Lady Edith treats Cordelia as a sister—nay, they talk together of plans for their future years ; I have never heard the veil hinted at. Besides, father," said the young knight, earnestly, "I have never spoken to Cordelia of love ; how can I, a captive, and hopeless of release seek to entangle another, and one I love, in the mesh which renders me miserable ? No, father, never have I breathed of love to the maiden."

"It is well thou hast not, thy days might have been short had it been so," said Father Augustine.

"Nay, threaten me not," said De Albini. "Neither thou nor such as thou shall dictate to me of what I shall do. I now aver to thee, I love Cordelia—and as soon as I can with honour solicit a return of affection from her, I will do so."

"Rash, foolish boy !" exclaimed the monk, "and here in this tower thou darest to tell me so. Thy fate be upon thine own head."

"I am content," replied De Albini. "Never will I swerve from honour, and in a rightful cause I fear no man."

"Well—wed Cordelia—a disgraced, a dependant orphan ; disgraced by the crimes of her parents, and ensuring her own misery by a refusal to enter the holy order. Wed her, and be happy," said the monk, sneeringly.

"You say, disgraced by the crimes of her parents. Tell me, then, who is Cordelia ?" asked the young knight.

"The wretched daughter of Eleanor de Tunstall, and her paramour De Dunstanville," replied the father. "Her mother fled from her rightful husband and died in seclusion."

De Albini mused for a few moments ; he could have borne that the lady of his love should be friendless, dowerless ; he saw that she was beautiful, and the grace of her movements told that she was of noble birth ; he could thus have married her. But the daughter of a woman who had so disgraced herself, he was cut to the heart at the thought.

Father Augustine, who had watched his companion's countenance, saw its agitation, and read the thought of Edward's mind. An advantage was gained, and the monk hastened to make use of it.

"And such a bride would you introduce to the Lady Elfrida de Albini ; well you know how she would receive such an one. And thus," said the monk, "would you supply to her the daughter of whom she was cruelly deprived. Hear me once more, young knight, pollute not the halls of your fathers by such an insult. Well do I know your lady mother would scorn you as the dupe of a designing girl."

" Do you then know my mother?" asked Edward.

" Yes," replied the monk

" How? where? oh, tell me!" cried Edward, hastily.

" Here, in this tower," answered the father, " ere sorrow had blighted her cheek, or dimmed the brightness of her eye."

Edward's amazement was extreme. "Oh, tell me," he cried, " speak not to me obscurely! How came the Lady de Albini here at Thornbury?"

" Poor boy! and know you not the history of your parent's misery?" asked Father Augustine.

" I knew of nought but happiness," replied the young knight, " until my sad captivity.

" Has thy lady mother then forgotten the child of her first affections? Is even a mother's love but a mockery?" asked the monk, in a tone of derision.

" Oh! speak not to me thus!" implored De Albini.

" I will tell thee, then, what thou oughtest to know," said the monk. " Here, in the noble castle of Thornbury, dwelt Geoffrey de Albini and the Lady Elfrida, his wife. In peace and happiness they dwelt, for he was brave, and she was fair. But alas! how fleeting is happiness! One only child blessed their union, but this treasure was suddenly snatched from them; the infant was lost, and from the circumstance of its bonnet being found in the stream, it was supposed to be drowned. Geoffrey de Albini and his lady left Thornbury for ever."

" And is this the scene of my parents' bereavement?" asked Edward, in a tone of grief.

" It is," replied Father Augustine, " and of their son's unhappy love."

" Oh, father! speak not of it; how could I ever have a thought of anything but my dear mother's grief," cried De Albini.

" Thou knewest not of it," said the monk.

" How many solitary hours have I sat by this window, watching the shadows stealing over forest and brake, unconscious that my lady mother had ever trod those grassy paths, or sheltered herself under these lofty trees. Oh! how much dearer now to me is this tower," cried Edward. " I may believe that her spirit is beside me."

" Here, in this tower, was the Lady Elfrida seated, when tidings were brought to her of the death of her child," said Father Augustine. " This was her favourite retreat from the bustle and company of the castle."

" And how came the Baron de Fougeres to hold this castle?" asked Edward.

" Geoffrey de Albini cared not who should dwell here after the misfortune which made it a scene of misery to him; and De Fougeres asked it," replied the monk.

" And did De Fougeres know of that misfortune?" asked the young knight.

" But too well," replied Father Augustine, in a tone of bitterness; " and therefore he loved the place."

" Were they then foes?" asked Edward.

" Are they not now foes? Is not one the valiant defender of his rightful sovereign?—does not De Fougeres uphold the usurper? and thy sire, does he not honourably support Matilda? They are foes, and they shall remain so," said the monk.

" Oh, father! you have indeed made me feel the bitterness of captivity," cried De Albini.

" Then why not escape from it?" asked the monk.

" It is impossible," replied Edward, " for though he be foe to me, and to my sire, my word is given; and here I must await a better fortune."

" A better fortune truly! and what will that be? De Fougeres will never give liberty to his foeman's child; rather will he see thee dashed upon the rocks which hem in yonder brawling stream," said the monk.

" And even that fate, father," replied Edward, indignantly, " inglorious as it would be, were more fitting to the heir of the house of De Albini, than a glorious death upon the battle-field won by the forfeit of his word of honour."

"Rash boy, you know not what you say; that stream hath already been fatal enough to the happiness of your much vaunted house," said Father Augustine. "But the waters may yet yield their prey."

"What do you mean?" asked Edward, eagerly.

"It matters not," answered the monk.

"Nay—but, father, tell me, I pray thee," cried the young knight.

"Never; I love thee not," said his persecutor.

"I know it—but those words—I have already heard them, and in vain have scanned their import," said Edward.

"Heard them already," cried Father Augustine, in a tone of amazement. Then after a pause, "Yes, I said them myself."

"But I have heard them from other lips than yours," remarked the captive.

"Whose? Where?" asked the monk, impatiently.

"Here," replied Edward, the conduct of the dwarf respecting Father Augustine recurring to his memory.

"Trifle not with me," cried the father, angrily; "tell me how you heard those words."

"I heard them from one who sought my protection from injury and injustice, and therefore the name you will not hear from me," said Edward, firmly.

"And what protection has a prisoner to give?" asked the monk; "an unarmed prisoner—even I could crush him," cried the monk.

"I gave what was asked of me. Even I can protect the innocent and helpless; and I would do it at the hazard of my life," said De Albini, proudly.

"But tell me," cried the monk.

"Never!" replied the knight.

After a pause of a few minutes, the monk cried, "Ha! I have it. The dwarf has been here."

Edward was silent.

"Thou wilt not answer me," cried the monk in a rage; "then farewell. There are other means of gaining the information I require."

"But the meaning of the words, father?" asked Edward.

"No," replied the monk, still angry; "courtesy for courtesy. He who denies me shall be refused himself."

Edward was annoyed; yet he could not consistently with his honour give up the dwarf to the certain displeasure of the monk.

"Farewell, young man; when you want a friend, reckon not upon Father Augustine," said the monk, in a tone of defiance. "And I may tell Geoffrey de Albini that his son prefers the Lady's Tower to the tented field."

"Oh, father! father! be not the bearer of such a message," said the prisoner, in a tone of extreme distress.

"Nay, I have given him his choice, and he has preferred it. But once more," continued the monk, "not for love of yourself, but for hatred to De Fougeres, wilt thou escape?"

"No!" firmly replied Edward.

"Then farewell for ever," cried Father Augustine, muttering as he left the tower— "coward and fool; and I am foiled in my revenge—foiled by a stripling, by a love-sick boy. But he shall never wed Cordelia. No; if she cannot be the monk's bride, the blood-red sword may win her, and it shall do so, shortly too."

Saying this, the father took his way to the castle, intending to seek the dwarf and punish him for his intrusion upon Edward.

CHAPTER IX.

Few are the hearts that have proved the truth
  Of their early affections' vow,
And let those 'ew, the beloved of youth,
  Be dear in their absence now,
Oh! vivid long in the faith'ul breast,
  Shall the gleam of remembrance play,
Like the lingering light on the crimson west,
  When the sunbeam has pass'd away!——II. Twiss.

With angry feelings did the monk proceed to the castle. Like all those who condescend to employ an agent in their malicious designs, he feared continually that the dwarf had betrayed him. It did not suit the plans of Father Augustine at once to break off all intercourse with the family of De Fougeres; but he had absented himself lately from an undefined dread of some exposure, and by whose means could this take place but from Ronald?

Despising yet dreading this unhappy being, the monk had in his cell eagerly received every rumour respecting the proceedings of De Fougeres. He thus heard of the scene in the banquet-hall—a perhaps exaggerated account, and his anger against the dwarf was vehement for having, as he concluded, betrayed him. But his anger was increased tenfold on finding that Ronald had visited the prisoner in the Lady's Tower, and had to him repeated the obnoxious verses.

It was not that he cared that Edward should know the mastery which he held over the mind of De Fougeres, but there was a hidden meaning in those lines—a meaning which, if discovered, would place his own safety, as well as that of the baron, in jeopardy. That this meaning should be discovered by any one except by him, for whose ears it was especially intended—still more that it should be discovered by Edward de Albina, a stranger, and a captive—seemed very improbable; nevertheless the guilt of Father Augustine rendered him fearful, and he almost wished that there were means to silence the babbling of the dwarf by death.

Means there were, had the monk opportunity to use them; courage he wanted not, but he dare not run the risk of exposure; particularly just at this moment, when a reputation for extreme sanctity would so much aid and advance his purposes. He was therefore restricted to a milder punishment, and this, severe enough in itself, he resolved should be inflicted upon the unhappy dwarf whenever he could meet with him.

Towards De Albini, Father Augustine was constrained to feel admiration His resolute adherence to his word of honour, notwithstanding every blandishment of ambition, affection, and love, was used to seduce him, won even from the hard heart of the monk, something like approval; and had he loved any but Cordelia, he might have rejoiced.

With these mixed feeling he entered the castle, in the hall of which he met L'Espee. The knight and the monk regarded each other with distrust, almost with abhorrence, and at first each seemed willing to pass by without salutation; but just as they met each other, a thought appeared to dart across the mind of L'Espee, and he said,—

"Good morning. father; a goodly day for those mewed up in castle and convent."

"A fairer day, my son," replied the monk, "for those at large upon the battle-field. Have you had any news lately of the usurper?"

"Nay," said Robert L'Espee, "not that word to me, I have a sword to avenge it, even upon the shaven crown."

"Well, well, why so fiery? I did not think the spirit chafed so hotly in you," returned the monk. "What news then from the combatants?"

"Glorious news! A general muster has taken place, and both parties are preparing for the fight," cried L'Espee, exultingly. "Robert, Earl of Gloucester, is the viper who has raised the insurrection."

It was now the monk's turn to be angry.

"Viper!" he cried, "well viper, not traitor."

"Both, both," cried L'Espee. "He has broken his oath to Stephen, and has gathered together the discontented nobles; but, dastard as he is, he dares not meet his injured sovereign, and has withdrawn himself beyond sea."

"Robert of Gloucester is no dastard," exclaimed the monk.

"Vainly have the barons of the south withstood their sovereign," continued the knight; "they have fled from his side, but Stephen has brought down their pride to submission. Still more futile has been the attempt of king the of Scotland. Thurstan, archbishop of York, has stayed his progress."

"Shame on the old dotard!" cried the monk. "Was he not pledged to Matilda?"

At this moment a noise was heard in the outer court, and the attention of L'Espee and the monk was strongly excited. The former was about to leave the hall in order to ascertain the cause of the tumult, when the dwarf entered hastily, crying,—

"News! news! room for our lord's herald!" then, seeing the father, he ran and hid himself behind the oaken screen which skirted the upper end of the hall.

The monk was however too much engrossed by the arrival of the herald to attend to Ronald, upon whom internally he vowed bitter vengeance; and he joined the group who had gathered round Robert L'Espee, to whom the herald was delivering a packet from De Fougeres.

Robert L'Espee opened the packet, and read over its contents to himself, uttering, from time to time, exclamations of astonishment at the intelligence which it contained. Father Augustine, who was earnestly regarding the knight's countenance, could with difficulty restrain his impatience and anxiety; twice he attempted to ask a question, but the knight regarded him not. Totally absorbed in the intelligence which the packet contained, he saw not the impatient gestures of Father Augustine, till at length, having read through the whole packet, he exclaimed,—

"Brave news, by St. George! and I am here an unfortunate cripple. Shame upon this leg of mine," cried the knight, "that keeps me from the fight."

"How go the affairs of the kingdom?" asked Father Augustine, in a tone of repressed anxiety.

"And my father, my dear father," cried Edith, who had entered the hall unobserved during the period in which Robert L'Espee had been reading the letter.

The news of a herald from De Fougeres had quickly flown through all parts of the castle. The dwarf had carried it to Edith and Cordelia, to the latter of whom he had lately become much attached; probably because he observed that Father Augustine, whom he regarded as his own enemy, seemed also to be unfriendly to Cordelia; and the latter liked his company because he talked to her of Edward.

"Is my dear father returning home?" asked Edith.

"Not yet, I fear," replied De L'Espee; "the crisis approaches which shall tell to England whether Stephen or Matilda shall be our sovereign."

Then turning to the monk, he said, "This messenger brings intelligence that Robert of Gloucester and the Empress Matilda have landed in England, and have been joined by a few Norman knights."

"A few? and are there but a few who would aid their lawful queen?" cried the monk.

"Treason! treason!" resounded through the hall; and a general rush took place towards the spot where the monk was standing.

But Robert L'Espee desired the crowd to forbear, saying,—

"We may call it treason, but remember the sacred habit of the wearer; let not this castle hall become the scene of insult towards a helpless, if not an unoffending, man."

At these words from one whom they much respected as the representative of their master, the menials held back, but there were many among them who showed by countenance and gesture, their forbearance was forced, and that they only delayed revenge.

Far different was the effect of the words of L'Espee upon Father Augustine. The anger of the monk seemed to be much more highly raised by the allusion to his monkish habit and his defenceless condition, than by the threats of the menials, armed as they were, and he turned to L'Espee, saying, in a voice of the utmost rage,—

"Thou and I may not meet again. I leave thee with the kid in yonder tower, to touch the lute, and sing lays of peace and love; the battle-field were unworthy of thee; but I go to uphold the cause of my rightful but injured sovereign, Matilda; this arm, although defenceless here, shall be dreaded by her foes; and even in this retreat of idleness, the name of him whom you have insulted shall be heard with terror and dread."

Thus' saying, he turned to leave the hall. The domestics showed a great disposition to oppose his passage, but L'Espee checked them, saying,—

"Let Father Augustine pass quietly, we war not against monks. But first let him hear a word from me of intelligence just received. Robert de Hesling has arrived from the Holy Land, and has joined the army of Stephen."

"And what concerneth such intelligence to me?" asked the monk, in a tone of affected tranquillity.

"He brings with him William de Tunstall," replied L'Espee; "and the orphan shall have her right," he added, in a significant manner.

"Shall have? truly!" cried Father Augustine, rushing out of the castle; and taking the path to the river side, he entered his barge, and desired his rowers to make all speed towards the convent.

We shall not follow him. His fate seemed to have reached a crisis, as far as his plots and conspiracies were concerned; and he felt that it was time for him to do that which he had long meditated, namely to exchange the gown for the cuirass, the cowl for the helmet.

But let us return to the castle hall.

Upon hearing the announcement of L'Espee, that her kindred were indeed in England, Cordelia threw herself at the feet of the knight, crying,—

"And will you indeed save me?"

"Yes, lovely Cordelia, if it be possible; but this is not the place for such conversation; let us repair to another chamber," said the knight.

Edith led the way to a room which she had appropriated to herself and her friend, as a sitting room, and inviting L'Espee to enter, she said,—

"May I be present at your conference?"

"Dearest Edith! can you ask?" said Cordelia, affectionately embracing her friend; "are not my hopes and fears well known to you? would that I had no fears to overshadow your own bright happiness."

"Alas!" replied Edith, "my dear father is among scenes of danger, and how can I be happy?"

"Shall I tell you the contents of this packet?" asked L'Espee; "that violent monk has disturbed me much, and withdrawn my thoughts from more urgent affairs."

The fair friends having given an assent to the proposal of the knight, he said,— "These letters are more important than I chose to avow in the hall. De Fougeres is perfectly safe. Hitherto there has been no decisive battle; but the forces on each side are preparing for the blow which shall decide the fate of England. I grieve to say that Stephen has made himself unpopular by his conduct towards the clergy, and that Alexander, bishop of Lincoln, and Nigel, bishop of Ely, have openly joined Matilda. Still De Fougeres fears not. A battle must be hazarded, and may the rightful cause prosper."

Edith trembled as she thought of a battle. Images arose before her of danger and of death to her beloved parent, and a still deeper feeling was in her heart—

fear for Eustace de Mowbray, fear lest he should be called upon to give his aid to the cause.

Cordelia thought not of war; her hopes of recognition by her kindred had been called forth, and she asked L'Espee if indeed his intelligence respecting her uncle were true.

"De Fougeres mentions the arrival of De Hesling as a circumstance which has inspired hope into all Stephen's party," replied the knight. "He is known as a valiant and experienced soldier, and such are much wanted by the king's party."

"And my uncle?" asked Cordelia.

"De Tunstall also is with the king's army," replied the knight. "De Fougeres adds a postscript merely to say, 'Cordelia's interests are not forgotten.'"

"Then, dearest Cordelia," said Edith, affectionately, "you may hope for better times."

Cordelia shook her head doubtingly. "Alas!" she said, "it is kind of the Baron de Fougeres to remember the helpless orphan in the midst of the stirring scenes of war."

"And lest those scenes should interpose, and prevent my fulfilling my pledge to you, fair maiden, I purpose transmitting by a safe messenger to De Tunstall the little history of your life, with my own request that he at once, or at least as early as circumstances will permit, will take steps towards claiming your mother's dowry. I await only," continued L'Espee, "such a messenger as may be safe and trusty."

Cordelia poured out her thanks to the knight, and Edith said,—

"A monk surely would be the fittest person for such an embassy."

"No, no," replied L'Espee; "I like not the cowl—it hides treachery as securely as honesty. And the monks of the neighbouring convent are the creatures of Father Augustine: they would scarce serve one truly."

"My father has many trusty servants," said Edith.

"The messenger must not be known as belonging to Thornbury Castle," observed L'Espee. "I must think awhile upon this matter. We have more subtle foes to encounter than the soldiers of Matilda."

"What mean you?" asked Edith.

"Father Augustine," replied L'Espee.

Cordelia almost shuddered, as she reflected with dread that she must indeed regard the father as her enemy.

The friends left Robert L'Espee and bent their steps towards the grove adjoining the Lady's Tower. Edith proposed paying a visit to their prisoner, and Cordelia with a beating heart consenting, they proceeded along the grassy path together, when Cordelia felt that something touched her garment. She turned round, but saw no one, and concluding that it was the branch of a tree, she walked on by the side of Edith in silence, when, just as they reached the entrance to the tower, a stronger pull made her turn hastily round, and behind her stood, or rather crouched, the dwarf Ronald.

"What would you have, Ronald?" she asked.

"A word with a fair lady," was the reply.

"Stay, Edith," said Cordelia, "Ronald wants you."

"Is there no fair lady but the Lady Edith?" cried the dwarf. "Nay, there is one still fairer in the eyes of some than the Lady Edith, beauteous though she be. It is the Lady Cordelia that I seek."

"Nay, Ronald, if it be any favour of Lady Edith that you want, ask yourself; she will hear you graciously—fear her not," said Cordelia.

"I do not fear her; I have no favour to ask. If Lady Cordelia knew what I can tell, she would bestow her sweetest smiles to win me to speak," said the dwarf, in an ambiguous manner.

"And what can you tell, Ronald?" asked Cordelia. "If you have any secrets of the kitchen, carry them to the seneschal. See you not that the Lady Edith is engaged?"

"Well, I know I am but a fool," replied the dwarf, in a melancholy tone; "were I a knight, even a captive knight, Lady Cordelia would listen to me."

"And she will listen now, Ronald," blushing at his illusion, "but speak quickly."

"Then walk this way," said the dwarf, "my secrets are not for every one's ear."

Cordelia was started at Ronald's importunity, and at his boldness, as he pointed to a secluded walk, which led in a direction opposite to the Lady's Tower,

and which wound by degrees to the summit of the hill, upon the slope of which the castle stood. The walk was fenced by lofty trees, and completely shut out from the remainder of the ground by a thick growth of underwood, carefully platted in with creeping plants which grew wild. There, the white convolvulus reared its stately head, and the spindle-tree spread its rich scarlet berries. The yony and the vetchling gave their bright green leaves, and the orchis and the St. Johns wort made a varied and brilliant carpet.

No. 9.

Hither the dwarf led the Lady Cordelia. Unwilling was she to follow him, as she grudged the loss of her visit to the tower, and she was now more than ever jealous that Edith should visit the prisoner alone, as she feared that he only awaited such an opportunity to confess his love to her. But the words and manner of Ronald had excited her curiosity; therefore, stepping forward, she requested Edith, who was waiting for her at the entrance of the tower, to relinquish her company for the present, promising to join her in a short time.

Edith, who concluded that Ronald had some request to prefer to herself, in which he was willing to make Cordelia the mediator, gave her assent; and entered the prisoner's chamber alone, leaving her friend to accompany the dwarf.

CHAPTER X.

Oh! why should we seek to anticipate sorrow,
  By throwing the flower of the present away,
And gather the black rolling clouds of to-morrow,
  To darken the generous sun of to-day?
How often we brood over misery madly,
  Till we murder the hope that was sent to inspire;
And pleasure grown old, and decrepit, turns sadly
  To shake his grey looks o'er the tomb of his sire.
Cherish hope, and though life by affliction be shaded,
  Still his ray shall shine lovely, and gild the scene o'er;
Like the dew-drop that glistens the leaves when they're faded,
  As bright and as clear as it glisten'd before.—NEALE.

CORDELIA followed the dwarf for some distance in silence, till they arrived at an open glade, which was shut in by trees on every side but one, where an opening in the wood showed the river winding through the meadows, and Mowbray Castle in the distance. This was a favourite place of retirement with Edith, and it was worthy of her choice. A rude bench had been placed there at her request, and she passed many hours in the seclusion of this spot.

When the dwarf and Cordelia reached this glade, Ronald made a movement to his companion to seat herself. He then carefully examined the brushwood which surrounded the glade, and having ascertained that no one was near, he seated himself at Cordelia's feet, saying,—

"There are more prying ears than those which the round cap covers."

"What do you mean, Ronald?" said Cordelia, somewhat terrified.

"Fear not, lady," answered the dwarf, "It is I who ought to fear."

"Then tell me at once, what you have to say," repeated Cordelia.

"Nay, well do I guess that your heart is in yonder prison tower," said Ronald. "Truly it is but an exchange of hearts, the captive's is with you."

"What?" cried Cordelia.

"The captive knight loves Cordelia," said Ronald.

"No, no," cried his companion, blushing, "it is the Lady Edith whom he loves."

"Are not my ears true to me?" said the dwarf. "Did I not hear him say it?"

"When, and to whom?" asked Cordelia.

"To one I scarcely dare name," replied Ronald.

"I beseech you tell me all, Ronald; I pray, I [beg [you to] speak," cried Cordelia.

"Know you the serpent whose venom gave me to the dungeon? He it was," replied the dwarf. "The captive was kind to me; he saved me from his fangs, he deigned to converse with the dwarf—the fool—and the fool is grateful. Truly this is a proof of his folly; but it is so. When the monk," continued Ronald, looking round and speaking in a low tone, "came to the tower, I was near; I saw the glance which he cast upon the Lady Cordelia, and I heard the words he said as she left the presence of the young knight."

"Where were you?" interrupted Cordelia.

"It matters not," replied the dwarf. "I heard, and I saw; but I was not seen. I know his looks, and I feared mischance from such an unwonted visit. I therefore placed myself so as to hear all, in order afterwards to counteract his wiles. Canst thou guess his holy errand?" asked Ronaldo, with a sneer of malice.

"How can I?" answered Cordelia. "Probably to confess a penitent."

"Nay, nay; the young knight hath few sins, except one great one," said the dwarf, "and that he did not willingly confess to the father. A sweeter voice than Father Augustine's must give him absolution for that."

Cordelia blushed, and said, "Go on with the story."

"No, the wily monk offered him liberty," cried Ronald.

"Liberty?" exclaimed Cordelia, starting.

"Yes, liberty—to fight for Matilda," answered the dwarf.

"And his answer?" asked Cordelia.

"It was worthy of his name; he refused to break his word to the baron," replied Ronald.

"Noble—brave Edward! L'Espee must know this," cried Cordelia

"Stay, stay—hear all. The monk placed before him all the temptations that could be held out. His love to his lady mother—duty to his father, to his queen —ambition—glory—but all failed; he swerved not. The father declared his oath to De Fougeres cancelled; and said that his rowers only awaited his command to waft him far from Thornbury. Further, he told of the loss of his infant sister in the stream which flows by the Lady's Tower of the Lady Elfrida's misery, and he threatened—mark me—he threatened the same fate to the young knight if he consented not to escape."

Cordelia burst into tears, and hiding her face in her hands, she said,—

"Go on—I too have suffered the father's persecution."

"All was of no avail," continued the dwarf, "the knight was firm. The history of his lady mother's woes touched him, but fear for himself he knows not. Finding all his persuasions ineffectual, the monk then touched a different object," said Ronald in a hesitating manner.

"What?" asked Cordelia, timidly.

"Love," replied the dwarf.

"Love! and to whom? to Edith—he loves Edith," cried Cordelia hurriedly but in a tone which spoke that she dreaded lest her assertion should be confirmed."

"He loves you," whispered Ronald.

"No—no—say not so," cried his agitated companion.

"But it is so," replied the dwarf. "The young knight confessed to Father Augustine, and moreover avowed his determination to make you his bride as soon as his liberation should allow him with honour to gain your love."

How can the feelings of Cordelia be described at this intelligence? Hope, hitherto clouded, nay almost destroyed, again shed her light upon the heart of the fair girl; she recalled the look which De Albini had cast upon her, and indulged the hope of the truth of the captive's love. This remembrance confirmed what Ronald said; and despite the uncertainty, the hopelessness of her situation and prospects, a gleam of happiness shot across her.

Ronald, who had watched the changes in the countenance of his companion saw the effects of his words, and rejoiced. He liked Cordelia; she was more lively than Edith, and her position in the castle of De Fougeres made her more companionable to the dwarf than the Lady Edith was. Besides he pitied Cordelia; she was a fellow-sufferer with him from the tyranny of Father Augustine.

After a pause of a few minutes, in which new-born happiness seemed to strive with doubt and fear in the bosom of Cordelia, she said,—

"And the monk—tell me Ronald, did he not threaten me with his vengeance?"

"He did," replied the dwarf, "but glory is now Father Augustine's passion. He will depart for the field of contention, and, lady, he will there forget Thornbury and its inhabitants; or if he remember them for a moment, it will be but to scorn them."

"And has the young knight no hope of liberation?" asked Cordelia, anxiously.

"None. The monk foretold his death under the roof of his goaler, if he refused to escape," said Ronald.

Cordelia sighed deeply.

"Yet I would not have him escape in dishonour," she said, "that were indeed unworthy of his race and name. Oh, Ronald! if I were the acknowledged child of my kindred, he should at once be liberated."

Ronald shook his head.

"What do you mean?" asked Cordelia.

"There is some hidden motive for his captivity," replied her companion. "It is not merely the hostility of party animosity which makes De Fougeres so tenacious of the safe-guard of his prisoner; nor is it fear of De Albini's arms alone which keeps him far from the field of action. There is a deeper cause."

"What cause?" asked Cordelia, eagerly.

"I know not," answered Ronald, "but it is so. The Father Augustine hinted at it, and his words are never spoken at random, each is aimed at a particular mark."

Cordelia vainly endeavoured to trace a motive which she thought might actuate De Fougeres; at last, turning to the dwarf she said,—

"Ronald you are my friend."

The dwarf professed his readiness to serve her in any way which lay in his power, and she added—

"He must never know my parentage, he would scorn me."

"He does know it; Father Augustine told him all," replied Ronald.

"Then I am lost and scorned," cried Cordelia, bursting into a passionate flood of tears; "the name of De Albini must never be joined to one so degraded as mine. Cruel Father Augustine! Well have you declared that there is no refuge for me except in the convent."

The dwarf was appalled at the wretchedness of his companion, and he could say nothing to alleviate it. Until the conversation which he overheard between the monk and Edward, he had known nothing of the family circumstances of Cordelia; and he now sincerely pitied her. After a short period of silence he rose to leave her, but Cordelia said,—

"Oh, do not leave me, Ronald! wait but a short time till I have somewhat composed my spirits, and I will accompany you back to the castle. I cannot visit the tower now."

Cordelia at length having in some degree regained her composure, the couple walked slowly back to the castle. How much had Cordelia's views been changed within the last hour. Hope had brightly dawned upon her, but only again to be overcast, and to plunge her into deeper despair. She saw too plainly the disadvantages of her situation to place much reliance upon the affection of Edward de Albini, even were it to survive the disclosures of Father Augustine; and more bitterly than all, she reflected that it was now impossible to ask the protection of the Lady Elfrida. Still, amidst all her troubles, there was one happy thought—she was beloved, and by the only person for whose love she had ever sighed. Would he ever tell her he loved her? No—how could he do so? She dreaded, yet longed again to be in his presence; again to hear his voice; dear to her, even in words which bore no relation to her feelings, nor to his own. In these reflections Cordelia was absorbed as she walked home. When she bade adieu to the dwarf at the portal of the castle-hall, the latter made some observation respecting Father Augustine, which, although but partly heard or understood by his companion, aroused her notice, and she said,

"Ronald, it will not be advisable to divulge the conversation which you overheard; let it remain secret for my sake."—

The dwarf promised that it should be so, and they parted; Cordelia to her own apartment, and Ronald to the chamber of L'Espee, who had desired a messenger to seek him on important business.

"Ronald," said the knight, as he entered the apartment, "can you undertake, and will you execute a commission of some importance to the army?"

The dwarf was surprised, and fearing that the business was to convey intelligence to De Fougeres, whose anger against him he well remembered, he hesitated a moment.

"Nay, if you doubt," said L'Espee, "I must seek some more trusty messenger."

"I am willing," replied the dwarf, "but——"

"But what?" asked L'Espee.

"The baron likes me not," replied Ronald.

"It is not to the Baron de Fougeres," said L'Espee, "that I wish to send you as a faithful messenger, but to William de Tunstall. I have papers of importance which I wish to have conveyed to him, and I think you may, if you be prudent and courageous, perform the journey in safety. But circumspection is required."

The dwarf assured the knight of his willingness to undertake the journey, adding,

"You shall have no reason to charge me with cowardice; I can fight well, even, although I am but a dwarf."

"It is not want of courage that I so much fear," replied L'Espee, "as want of prudence. You will be less liable to assault or impertinence than one of the baron's household retainers, and you must not suffer any one to suspect that you bear any papers. Pursue your journey quietly; deliver the packet; and after receiving the orders of the Baron de Tunstall, return quickly to Thornbury; and you shall be handsomely rewarded."

"The dwarf promised obedience, and inquired when he was to depart.

"To-night," replied the knight. "I have especial reasons for wishing your departure to be a secret to all but ourselves; therefore take heed that no hint of it be given in the hall. Come to me at eight o'clock this evening, when all the rest of the household will be engaged, and I will deliver this packet to you with further instructions."

"May I not take leave of the young knight in the tower?" asked the dwarf.

"Why should you wish that particularly?" said L'Espee.

"It is but a word that I would say," replied Ronald.

"Father Augustine visits the captive, and I would not have that monk acquainted with my purposes," said L'Espee.

"The monk will not be at the tower again," said the dwarf, significantly.

"What do you mean?" asked L'Espee.

"I owe him no kindness for a night's lodging in the dungeon," replied the dwarf, moving towards the door of the room.

L'Espee was at first inclined to detain him, but remembering it was useless to question him upon a subject which he evidently intended to avoid, he suffered him to leave the chamber.

"A pretty business, truly," said Ronald to himself, after he had left L'Espee, "and I am to go to the army with papers instead of arms; a safe defence for so noble a warrior as myself! And not to know my errand too! Well, I shall have sport by the way. Master Warden cannot refuse me the roan palfrey, now, to ride upon his lord's business; I told him I would have it one day. It is a long journey though, and what if I be murdered on the road—who will care for the dwarf? The Lady Cordelia will; for her sake I wish I were neither dwarf nor fool, but a noble knight. And the young captive, I may not tell him that she loves him—he will soon find it out. It is well that I go to-night; I shall not cross the path of Father Augustine."

As the dwarf was thus ruminating, he met the Lady Edith, who inquired for Cordelia. Ronald told her that her friend was in the castle, and Edith immediately sought her.

She found Cordelia in an attitude of abstraction and meditation, from which the entrance of Edith scarcely aroused her.

"Cordelia," said her friend, taking her hand, "our friend in the tower is jealous."

The startled girl uttered an exclamation of surprise.

"I do not ask the meaning of your absence with Ronald," said Edith, "but our poor prisoner feels keenly the slightest disappointment, and he was grieved that you did not accompany me to-day."

"Can Cordelia be missed when Edith is present?" asked her friend.

"Be not unjust, dearest Cordelia," replied Edith, "De Albini seeks you only, you are his solace, his beloved, if I may say so much."

Cordelia hid her face in her hands for a moment, then looking up to Edith, she said,—

"Oh Edith! deceive me not."

"I would not deceive thee for the wealth of worlds," said Edith, "but I must tell thee the truth; it may be a bright spot in a dark picture, that De Albini loves thee."

"Has he then said so?" asked Cordelia.

"Not exactly," replied her friend, "but he has begged me to use my influence to prevent Father Augustine from obtaining any promise from you to enter the convent. Edward de Albini is too honourable to ask for the affection of her whom he loves, while he thus remains in captivity; but when my dear father returns, he will be set at liberty."

"And forget me," said Cordelia, weeping.

"Fear not," replied Edith, "that can hardly be. Oh, Cordelia! how happy we shall be; you and I, and De Albini and Eustace. I am sure my dear father will be happy in making us so. And if these wars should end in the establishment of Stephen upon the throne, we will go to court, and partake in all the gay pleasures which our friend L'Espee describes with so much vividness. Nay, sigh not, dearest, all will be well yet."

Cordelia could not help sighing. The unhappiness of her birth seemed to place an invincible obstacle to her enjoyment, or even endurance of public life; and the picture which her friend had drawn almost made her resolve to seek the shelter of the convent. But there were deeper feelings in her heart. Love and hope asserted their sway over her youthful breast—she longed to hear more of the conversation of De Albini, but she dared not ask Edith any further; and she looked forward with apprehensive joy to her next visit to the tower.

In the evening the dwarf repaired to the chamber of L'Espee, as he had been commanded to do, and having received his packet and instructions, he departed from the castle, mounted upon the roan palfrey. L'Espee had given him orders to several persons whose habitations lay in his way to afford him food, lodging, or anything he might require; and he was straitly charged to avoid all scenes of military preparation, or peaceful festivity, but to select the most quiet and least frequented places of rest.

CHAPTER XI.

But war had silenced rural trade,
And the deserted mine was made
The banquet-hall and fortress, too,
Of Denzil and his desperate crew.
There guilt his anxious revel kept;
There, on his sordid pallet, slept
Guilt-born excess, the goblet drain'd
Still in his slumbering grasp retain'd;
Regret was there, his eye still cast
With voice repining on the past;
Among the features waited near
Sorrow, and unrepentant Fear,
And Blasphemy, to frenzy driven,
With his own crimes reproaching Heaven.—SCOTT.

ON the morning which succeeded Ronald's departure, the castle presented a scene of consternation and confusion. Intelligence was brought thither early that Father Augustine had not returned to the convent on the preceding evening; and fears were entertained lest, in this period of military licence, some harm should have happened to the monk. A messenger was despatched to Thornbury, to inquire whether the father had been there on the day preceding, but no tidings could be given of him by the inhabitants of the castle—he had not been there for many days. So great was the reputation for holiness which Father Augustine had contrived to acquire, that some of the younger monks hinted at a miraculous exit from this world of trouble; while the more worldly-minded expressed their fears openly, that the money which the father had been supposed lately to have amassed, and which it was said he carried constantly about his person had tempted the banditti who infested the country.

One singular circumstance was, that the robe of the father was found in his cell together with his breviary and rosary; a fact which somewhat scandalised those who considered Father Augustine as a pattern of piety and virtue.

Among the inhabitants of the castle, Cordelia was the least amazed at the sudden disappearance of her persecutor; and perhaps she was the only person who unfeignedly rejoiced at it. She told her conjectures to Edith, and Edith made known to L'Espee the probability that Father Augustine had indeed betaken himself to the battle-field, there to fight for Matilda. L'Espee could scarcely believe this information; he did not know the character of the monk well enough to understand such an action; but when Cordelia hinted the young captive could confirm the tale, L'Espee determined to visit the Lady's Tower, for the purpose of conversing with Edward.

L'Espee found the young captive gazing upon the green meadows which he was forbidden to tread, and listening to the rush of the gentle river beneath his prison walls. He knew not L'Espee, for the indisposition of the aged knight had hitherto prevented him from visiting the Lady's Tower, and De Albini was surprised and somewhat alarmed at the intrusion. His thoughts at once flew to his own home, and to his beloved parents, and he dreaded lest his stranger visitor should announce some misfortune respecting them. His fear was allayed by the courteous tone in which L'Espee announced himself, adding that the departure of Father Augustine in secret from his convent was the occasion of his visit to De Albini.

Edward immediately acknowledged his acquaintance with the schemes of the monk, and related that part of their recent conversation which had reference to his departure.

L'Espee expressed his astonishment at the conduct of the monk, and by his observations and questions, he at length drew from Edward the proposal of escape which had been made to him.

"Noble young man!" he exclaimed, "worthy of the name you bear; such truth must not be unrewarded. Await but the return of the Baron de Fougeres, and I will promise liberty."

A long conversation ensued, in the course of which L'Espee expressed his wish that he had known of the conduct of Father Augustine, in tampering with the captive, on the previous day.

"I have last night despatched a messenger to the court of Stephen, with papers of importance to William de Tunstall; I would have warned De Fougeres of the enterprise of the monk. I much fear lest my messenger be molested on his way by the monk or his confederates. I should be grieved were Ronald to be harmed."

"Is the dwarf then your emissary? I marvelled why he came not to my solitary meal this morning, as has been his wont," said Edward.

"Yes," I thought him the safest messenger in these boisterous times; few will imagine that a dwarf and a fool is charged with matters of importance, no less than the summons to right an orphan maiden," said L'Espee.

"Oh! may I ask is that orphan maiden the fair Cordelia?" cried Edward.

The knight smiled at the vehemence of his companion, and replied,—

"Know you her history?"

"Alas, yes!" answered Edward. "Father Augustine told me that she is intended for the cloister, her only safe refuge from the disgrace and misery entailed upon her by her parents."

"The cloister!" cried L'Espee, in astonishment.

"Yes," replied De Albini, "the monk repeated it to me more than once or twice, affirming that he alone could control the fate of Cordelia, and that he *willed* her taking the veil."

"And what led to this strange conversation?" asked L'Espee.

Edward looked down, and was silent.

"Speak, young man, I know the fame and honour of your sire, and I feel an interest in the fate of his son. We have embraced opposite sides in this unhappy war, but such a misfortune as thine demands pity. I am also the friend of Cordelia," added the knight, "and am interested in the monk's conduct towards her."

Edward still hesitated. At last he said in a low tone,—

"Father Augustine charged me with being averse to embrace his offer on account of the Lady Cordelia."

"And is it so?" asked L'Espee.

"Can you think so ill of the son of Geoffry de Albini," replied the youth, "as to suppose that I would forfeit my word, and betray the confidence reposed in me by the Baron de Fougeres? No, the noble race from which I spring, shall never have cause to disclaim me. I may be—I am unhappy, but I will never purchase liberty at the expense of honour. I have received much solace from the visits of Lady Edith and her friend, and I am interested in the welfare of both."

"You will then be much gratified to hear that I have great hope of the Lady Cordelia being again received by her kindred. William de Tunstall is an influential knight at the court of Stephen, and to him I have applied," said L'Espee. "I have sent to him proofs of her identity, urging him to place her at once in the rank which she is entitled to hold."

"But the monk said that she had no rank," said Edward, "that she is illegitimate—unworthy of love, of respect in the guilty circumstances of her birth."

"False liar!" cried L'Espee, in a rage. "Dares he, the friend, the companion of the treacherous father, thus traduce the unhappy child? Hear me, young man. Proofs still exist of the marriage of De Dunstanville with Eleanor de Tunstall, and such proofs shall be found. I have pledged my knightly word to reinstate the orphan in the rights of which she has been deprived, and my word was never yet given in vain."

The heart of Edward beat quickly at these words, and visions of love floated before his eyes. " Is there then any hope that she may be saved from the cloister?" he asked.

" She has never been intended for the cloister," replied L'Espee.

" Then I may hope," exclaimed Edward, in a low voice.

" Hope—what?" asked the knight.

" I am ashamed to acknowledge my weakness," said Edward, "and yet, you, who are her friend, may pity me—I love Cordelia."

" I guessed your secret, nor can I wonder at the confession," said L'Espee. "I too have loved—I loved her mother. Alas, how unsuccessfully! but may your suit be more propitious than mine was. There is but one obstacle."

" I know it; these wretched wars. Oh! that some agreement could be made to bring back peace and happiness to the land," cried Edward.

" It cannot be, while Matilda is misguided by Robert of Gloucester," replied L'Espee. "But, my young friend, you have a life before you, despair not of happiness. Is Cordelia aware of your affection?"

No. 10.

"I have never spoken of love to her—I dared not to do it. The malediction of Father Augustine hangs over me. But may I speak?" cried De Albini.

"Nay," said L'Espee, smiling, "I am too old to counsel upon this matter. The maiden can scarcely be blind to your feelings."

"I have ventured to hint them to the Lady Edith, and to bespeak her favour," said Edward.

"I will be your friend," replied L'Espee. "These wars will not last long, and it will be the best policy of Stephen to concert the union of his nobles by the bonds of marriage. I have some influence, and will exert it in your favour; your long captivity will be some atonement for the crime of your rebellion."

After mutual professions of regard, the knight left the Lady's Tower. De Albini was grateful for his attention, and he sat down to muse upon the future in a less disconsolate strain.

Meanwhile, how had Ronald sped on his errand? Although, of late, for some months his life had been circumscribed within the walls which bounded the domain of the Castle of Thornbury, yet the dwarf had, in his earlier days, been no inconsiderable traveller. He had accompanied a former master from the southern part of England, on a pilgrimage to the famous shrine of St. Cuthbert at Durham, and he had gained much experience by these journeyings; he had learned, not merely how to track his footsteps through the uncultivated wilds o the country, but he had learned to understand, and perhaps overreach his fellow-creatures; and the experience thus gained was of considerable service to him on this occasion. In fact, L'Espee could not have chosen a better messenger, nor one more likely to execute his commission with dexterity and secrecy.

Ronald parted from the towers of Thornbury at nightfall; the packet was safely lodged in concealment in his bosom, and his dress and accoutrements were so arranged as neither to attract attention by their superior quality, nor to raise suspicion by their shabbiness. He passed along the road for some distance alone till his palfrey appearing to be fatigued, he bethought himself that it was time to seek some place of rest for an hour or two. His appetite told him that his supper hour was far past; and although he had levied considerable contributions on the buttery and wine-stores of Thornbury Castle, he began to wish for a more substantial meal. While he was exerting his memory to think of the most secure and quiet place for the purpose of securing this, the step of a horse behind him made him start. He turned round, and a faint gleam of moonlight showed to him a horseman fully armed, emerging from a low thicket of brushwood, which skirted one side of the road.

Ronald finding that the stranger was fast gaining upon him, thought it the best policy to speak to him in a civil tone; he therefore said,

"Good morrow, friend."

"It is not morrow yet," replied the stranger, who had now come alongside of the dwarf, "and in these times, a wise man says friend to no one."

The dwarf looked at his surly companion with as much terror as his little person, which contained more than its proportion of courage, could feel.

"Good night were a churlish salutation," said Ronald, "but methinks we might each be glad to say the word over a blazing fire."

"It might be so for you," returned the stranger, "for me night is the time o action and engagement. But if you be so sluggishly inclined, there is a house a mile or two farther on, where rest may be had to your heart's content."

Ronald still thought it well to speak civilly to his unpleasant companion, and he thanked him for the intelligence he had given him.

"Are you for the true cause?" asked the soldier. "If you are not I warn you to continue your journey, rather than enter the house I have spoken of."

"I am for no cause," replied the dwarf.

"Why then travelling in these disturbed times? who is thy master?" asked his companion.

"I have no master, or many masters," said the dwarf.

" Speak," cried the soldier, " dost thou follow the usurper, or fight under the banner of the empress ?'

" Fight, truly ! a dwarf and a fool fight ! No, the cap and bells is my helmet ; the parti-coloured robe my armour ; and as to a master, give me him whose buttery is the richest, and whose wine is the strongest."

" A jolly fellow !" cried the soldier, " then come with me, I will bring you to choice spirits ; our lord the Baron de Bohun wants a page, and if good cheer be all the pay you require, fear not for your wages."

The dwarf knew not what to reply ; he dreaded lest his acquiescence should lead him into difficulty, and he also feared to hazard a refusal, unarmed as he was, and powerless compared to the fully-accoutred soldier by his side. He therefore gave his thanks, and they rode on in silence for some time.

After passing over about three miles of barren, lonely country, a twinkling light at a distance showed that they approached the house which the soldier had spoken of. When they came near it, Ronald discovered a mean and dilapidated hut, standing entirely alone, and surrounded by an impassable marsh, except at the spot where it was entered from the road. Lights beamed from an upper window, and through their bewildering gleam across the narrow road, and from a lower casement, partially obscured by a rough shutter, came sounds of revelry and military disturbance.

The stranger reined in his horse at the door, and knocking violently, demanded admittance. This was readily answered ; a man made his appearance whose dress and manner bespoke him to be the host of the cottage, and a half-naked boy coming forward for the horses, the two travellers entered the inn, if so it might be called.

The scene which greeted Ronald's view was by no means a pleasing one to him. Around a large fire was seated about a dozen wild and ferocious looking soldiers, their arms partially laid aside; but by the side of each was a heavy and powerful pike. There was perhaps among them more the appearance of banditti than of regular soldiers ; and certain signs in the room and upon their dress told Ronald that he was in the company of a band of those adventurers, half thieves, half soldiers, whom one of the lesser barons had gathered together to grace the cause of Matilda.

As the travellers entered, a moment's pause ensued in the boisterous conversation, till a cry arose of,—

Ho! Ferraud! thou art late, and what bundle of humanity hast brought with thee ?'

" A fellow traveller," answered the soldier, " of noble bearing, of courtly mien, as thou may'st see. The fellow wants food, and our lord wants a page ; it were a good exchange."

" Nay, Ferraud, jest not, our lord is in no humour for it." said one of the men.

" What has happened ?" asked Ferraud ; " any bad news from the camp ?"

" We move hence by daybreak," was the reply. " Geoffri de Albini deigns not to attend upon our master here, and he has vowed to tame the haughty baron's pride, ere he draw a lance for Matilda."

" And well will he keep his word," replied Ferraud, " our master is no boaster. I must see him directly. Boy or fool, whichever name delights thee most, attend me to the Baron de Bohun."

" Nay, nay," interposed several voices, " this is not a fitting time ; the baron is chafed with pride and rage against De Albini. Better do thy message quietly and quickly. The roof may tumble over our heads else."

Ferraud left the room to seek his master's presence, and while he was gone, the soldiers questioned the dwarf in various ways respecting his errand, and the place whence he came. He skilfully evaded their inquiries, but with considerable difficulty, and at great expense of the truth, however ; he held all matters light compared with his master's business ; and his own safety appeared in too much danger to allow him to hesitate between truth and present security. He found, as he suspected, that the party were determined followers of Matilda, and his greatest difficulty was in concealing his own predilections in favour of Stephen. Happily for his self-control, one of the party called for a song soon after the departure of Ferraud. A slight and pale youth answered the call, and began to tune his harp in compliance with the desire of his comrades. His appearance betokened gentle birth and delicate nurture; but vice had set her seal upon his brow, and the eye which ought to have beamed with intelligence and good-will, burned with the fire of inebriety and hardihood. Ronald amidst all his own disquiets and fears, pitied the youth, who, after a short prelude, thus sang :—

Brave men we be,
Joyous and free,
What careth we
    For our country's cause ?
To know no fear,
Wield sword and spear,
And secure good cheer,—
    These are our laws.
Then heg, heg, for a soldier's life,
His heart is in war, his home is in strife.

The belted knight
For fame may fight,
Or for fancied right
    His blood may shed.
But chill and cold
Is the earth-worm's fold,
And the blood-stained mould
    Is honour's bed.
Then heg, heg, for the soldier's trade,
Whose sword is less bright than the gold he's paid.

With wiser eyes,
Our honour lies
In the golden prize
    Which pays our score.
Our fame can't fail,
For 'tis nut-brown ale,
And a merry tale,—
    What would we more ?
Then heg, heg, the tankard bring,
While gold is afloat, the soldier's a king !

Long and vehement applause followed this uncouth song; it found an echo in every heart but one; the minstrel seemed to loathe while he poured forth his verses, and Ronald gazed sadly on the countenance which spoke disdain of the praises of his companions. The eye of the young singer for a moment rested on Ronald's face; he might read there pity and interest, and, for a moment, a better spirit came over him, but as he brushed away the tear-drop which hung upon his eyelid, his hardened mood returned, and under pretence of fatigue, he withdrew to a corner of the room, and feigned sleep.

"Poor lad," said one of the soldiers, "he is not yet able to bear us company."

"I marvel," said another, "that our lord does not leave him in some safe care until our return from battle. He is an incumbrance to us only."

"Till to-night we have scarcely had a cheerful song from him. Our lord cares little for him," observed a third soldier. "Let him sleep, and if we march without him, he will be a rare prize for the usurper."

At this moment Ferraud entered, with a lowering scowl upon his brow.

"You said well," he cried, "my lord is indeed angry with this audacious baron who refuses to hold converse with him."

"Why does my lord care for the pride of Geoffri de Albini ?" said one of the men. "Let him show him in the field that he is his equal."

"There is some hidden feud between them," said Ferraud. "My lord hath known him in early days."

"While he himself was but Father Augustine, perhaps," said one of the soldiers, scornfully.

Ronald started as if a spectre had risen before him ; indeed, he would rather have encountered the most fearful visitant from the grave, than have thus found himself in the dreaded vicinity of the monk. The start was not unobserved. One of the men asked Ronald if he knew Father Augustine.

"I have heard of him," was the reply. "The reputation of Father Augustine' sancity was spread far and near."

"Sanctity, forsooth !" said the soldier who had before spoken slightly of his lord.

"Nay, I know not of myself, I speak but as I have heard," replied the dwarf.

"Truly he hath outwitted the simple monks of Thornbury ; and he is a brave master, or I would never serve under him. Even as it is, Ralph the Rover will not bend to the monkish cowl, or follow the bidding of the crosier."

"Except it lead on to plunder a peaceful village, and drive away honest folks' kine," said one of the men.

"Would that it never led to worse !" murmured the young harper, loud enough for Ronald only to hear. "Know'st thou Thornbury ?"

"I am bound by an oath, gentle sir," replied the dwarf, "to hold no communings of my coming or my going."

The youth sighed. "It is a peaceful home to those worthy of peace," he said. Ronald turned sharply to him. "Would'st thou seek Thornbury ?" he asked.

"I know not," replied the boy, "yes,—I am tired of travel—and of vice," he added, in a significant whisper.

"Then why not fly from it ?" asked the dwarf.

"Can I—can the prisoned dove regain her native copse?" said the youth.

"I have had no song to-night," said Ferraud. "Edmund take the harp."

The youth hesitated. "Nay, no delay," said Ferraud, "thy voice is ready at m will."

Edmund took the harp, and sighing deeply, he thus sang :—

> The captive bird for freedom pines,
>   And beats his wiry cage :
> The glittering gold that round him shines,
>   Cannot his wrath assuage.
> The lamb that's led to sacrifice,
>   In flow'ry wreaths array'd,
> Turns to the plain her wishful eyes,
>   In which her young ones stray'd.
> Alas ! nor gold nor flowers atone,
> For freedom's priceless treasure gone.
>
> The soldier waves his bloody sword,
>   Upon the battle plain,
> Yet quails beneath the tyrant's word,
>   Who holds him in his chain.
> But stronger still the tyrant Love,
>   His rosy chains can bind ;
> And death's sharp pangs alone remove
>   The fetters of the mind.
> What hope then for the traitor's slave,
> Who yields, yet dreads, the love he gave !

"A mornful and miserable ditty," said Ferraud ; "I love not such. Give me the merry song that tells of adventures in the forest glade, or of the glory of the battle field. Try again, Edmund, but beware of a love ditty."

"He is sleepy, poor boy," said one of the men, "let him rest ; he will be trouble enough in our next long march."

"Well, well," replied Ferraud, "one verse only, to drive those melancholy sounds which he lately sung, from my head."

Edmund complied as follows :—

> The captive bird
>   His cage shall leave ;
> The trembling lamb
>   Shall cease to grieve ;
> The helmed cowl
>   Shall bite the sand ;
> The Church shall yield,
>   The orphan's land.
>
> True love shall reign,
>   All sorrow past ;
> And knightly faith
>   Be blest at last.
> But the father's hope
>   Must pass away,
> Ere the waters wild
>   Can yield their prey.

"Enough, enough," cried Ferraud, "some evil spirit must possess thee, Edmund ; it is well our master hear not thy song. Go to sleep."

Edmund followed, or seemed to follow the advice of Ferraud; and the rest of the soldiers stretched themselves upon the benches, and, wraped in their cloaks, were speedily asleep. Ronald said boldly that he must attend to his palfrey, and left the room ; his companions being too much overcome with fatigue, and the copious libations in which they had indulged, to take any notice of his retreat.

CHAPTER XII.

> Once I was blithe as bird on tree,
>   No lighter heart on earth did sing;
> Now I am wed to miseries,
>   And thou the cause from which they spring.
>
> Oh! had ye ne'er looked kind on me,
>   With your two fair but treacherous eyne,
> I ne'er had thought of loving thee,
>   My passion had but wonder been.—OLD BALLAD.

RONALD left the company, and repaired to the stable, less to attend to the wants of his palfrey, than to consider the course which it was best for him to pursue. The events of the night considerably alarmed him. To find himself thus suddenly and, as it appeared, irretrievably in the power of one whom he must regard as his enemy, shook the nerves of the dwarf; and there were collateral circumstances which added to his embarrassment. He understood from the few words of Ferraud, that Geoffri de Albini refused to hold any communion privately with the monk, or Baron de Bohun, as Father Augustine now styled himself.

What could possibly lead the baron to wish for such communication? It must relate to the young prisoner at Thornbury; and remembering that Bohun and De Albini had each embraced the cause of Matilda, the dwarf hoped that it boded liberation, or at least some good, to Edward.

But the most extraordinary occurrence of the night was the song which the young harper had sung. The concluding words had involuntarily impressed themselves upon his memory, as referring to the song which had so much raised the anger of De Fougeres ; and he felt a burning curiosity to know the meaning of the prophecy, which he now regarded as affecting in some hidden manner the fame and honour both of De Fougeres and the monk. Ronald was leaning over his palfrey, thinking about the difficulties that seemed to environ him, and revolving in his mind the best means of making his escape, when a light step approaching the stable attracted his attention. He turned round and in the faint glimmer which the coming daybreak gave, he recognised the young harper, stealing warily along to the stable. Ronald was at first afraid of some hostile design, but reflection told him that he was at any rate a match for the youth; and stepping to the door, he said,—

"What brings you here, my lad?"

"Hush, hush! my life, perhaps your own, hangs upon secrecy," answered the youth.

"Explain," cried Ronald, alarmed.

"You do not love the Baron de Bohun," said Edmund.

"I have no reason to like Father Augustine," replied the dwarf.

"Hush! breathe not that name. What do you purpose to do?" asked Edmund.

"To leave this place instantly," answered Ronald. "I am even now preparing my palfrey. I would not willingly encounter your companions again."

"Oh! call them not my companions," cried Edmund, "let me be the companion of your journey. I am tired of my life among these lawless men."

Ronald hesitated. He feared collision with the band of De Bohun, and he could not be certain that the young minstrel was not sent by them to entrap him. He expressed these fears to his companion, who cried,—

"Whatever may be your risk, believe me that mine is tenfold greater. No, no, however guilty I may have been, I would not willingly betray a fellow-creature to ruin. Take me but to the confines of the camp, I entreat you!" cried Edmund.

The heart of Ronald was softened. "And to whom wouldst thou go?" he asked.

"To Geoffri de Albini," was the answer.

"He fights for Matilda," answered the dwarf. "I am bound to the court of Stephen."

"I know it. I guessed it. I know from whom you come," said the youth.

"You know?" cried Ronald, in surprise; "how do you guess my business?"

"It matters not now. Will you take me, or must I roam alone and unprotected, through this wild land?" asked the harper.

"Unprotected, forsooth! Thou art more able to protect me than I thee," replied Ronald; "but thou art a gentle youth, and thy harp may perchance win for us courtesy in our journey."

The matter was soon settled. Edmund took a small nag, which he said had been given to him by his master, solely for his use, and which he therefore had a right to appropriate, and the strange, and apparently ill-assorted couple unceremoniously left the little inn, and striking into a by-road endeavoured to proceed in the direction ordered to Ronald. The grey light of dawn was just beginning to streak the horizon when they left the inn, but every pace increased the light, and before they had ridden a couple of miles every object was discernible to the eye.

Ronald and his companion at first rode on in silence, they seemed to fear lest their voices should betray them to pursuit, and no sound disturbed the quiet of the way. After proceeding for some distance along the narrow lanes, they found that they were again approaching the high road; and Ronald requested the youth to hold his palfrey while he ascended a small hillock to reconnoitre the surrounding country. It was well that he did so; for a few yards' further progress would have brought them to the high road, and to his inexpressible dismay on a rising ground, at half a mile distance, he beheld the company of his dreaded enemy approaching along this very road. The dwarf now blessed his diminutive stature, and cowering down amidst some bushes, he crept along the low ground to the spot where Edmund awaited him with the palfreys.

"What is the matter?" asked the youth, alarmed.

"See, yonder are the band," replied Ronald. "The saints save us, we are caught."

"No, no!" cried the youth, in reality as much alarmed as Ronald, but possessing more presence of mind.

" I tell thee we are lost," repeated the dwarf.

" There is yet time," replied Edmund " hold my horse ; surely I can find some nook, in yonder mountain, where we may hide till these men be passed."

He dismounted ; and winding round a rugged hill which was near, disappeared from the sight of his companion.

Every minute that he was gone seemed an age to the dwarf ; fears began to steal over him that he had indeed thrown himself into the power of De Bohun, and that the harper youth was merely a spy of the party. Blaming his evil fortune, and foreswearing for the future the company of all smooth-faced youths, the dwarf was upon the point of letting go the bridle of his companion's horse, when he saw Edmund carefully advancing towards him, and making signs to him to approach the side of the hill. The dwarf did so, and the youth informed him that on the other side of the hill there was a cave in which they might lay securely hidden till the danger was over.

Gladly did Ronald follow the youth ; and they found a dark cave, which had, in more peaceful times, been a mine, but had been neglected when the civil wars put an end to all kinds of industrious occupations. The entrance was narrow and low, and almost concealed by bushes; but once passed, a spacious chamber opened to the view, dimly lighted from the entrance. It was with considerable difficulty that the palfreys were made to enter this dismal place; and no time must be lost ; the troop was fast approaching. At last, however, Ronald had the happiness to feel that all was secure, when a fresh subject of apprehension took possession of his mind.

" Is this cave well known to you ?" he asked his companion. " I marvel much how you found it so readily, if, indeed, you have not been here often before."

" I have never seen it till now," replied the youth ; " till yesternight I heard some of the soldiers describing it as a place where treasure may be securely stored."

" They will come here then," cried Ronald, in a tone of despair. " Fool that I was to trust to thee."

" Fear not," replied Edmund ;" our master will not readily allow his followers to part company ; and they were lamenting that it would be impossible for them to visit this cave as they journeyed near it to-day."

This explanation in some degree re-assured Ronald, and he began to converse with his companion with more freedom.

" It is well that thou canst explain thy knowledge," he said, " my sword should have paid the penalty of thy treachery, hadst thou been faithless."

" I have said that your risk were little to mine," said Edmund. " If I dared to tell you by what unholy bonds I have hitherto been bound to De Bohun, and what I have sacrificed to follow him, you would understand that my life, in case of discovery, were not worth an hour's purchase."

" What then is your history ?" asked the dwarf.

" Hast never heard of Rosamond Beverley, of Thornbury ?" asked the youth.

" Often," replied the dwarf; " she disappeared most unaccountably, just before I went to reside at the castle."

" Unaccountably !" exclaimed his companion.

" Yes ; no one knew why she left the neighbourhood, nor whither she went," said Ronald ; " people supposed that she had fled to the Lady Albini. But what of her ?"

" She never left Thornbury ; would that she had," said Edmund, sighing. " No, the traitor held her tightly in his thrall, and she lingered in his prison without the power to free herself."

" What dost mean ?" asked the dwarf.

" He whom you dread was the traitor. He it was who persuaded the damsel to leave her lowly cot—to forsake her beloved parents—to sacrifice fame and happiness for his sake. And in his dismal prison the victim impatiently submitted to be immured. But the bird has flown," cried Edmund, in a tone of exultation; "the net of the fowler shall never inclose it more."

Ronald looked at the youth in amazement. Recollection of the tales which he had heard respecting Rosamond Beverley was mingled with curiosity concerning his companion, and he asked,—" Didst thou know her ?"

"No," replied the youth, "I knew not Rosamond. I believed her to be good, virtuous, dutiful—she was vain, weak, and, oh, worse than all, she brought her aged parents to the grave! Ask me not of that hour—it was ample punishment; and he refused to let me see their poor remains laid in earth ; but I disobeyed him —I saw it."

"Thou!" exclaimed the dwarf, " art thou Rosamond ?"

The youth looked down, and burst into tears.

No. 11.

Ronald felt for his companion, and suffered him to weep undisturbed. After a pause, Edmund, or Rosamond, as we must now call the harper, said,—

"I have not wept since that dreadful day, when the turf was laid upon my dear mother; that moment, my eyes were dried by the thirst for escape and vengeance. I have escaped—I may yet be revenged."

"Poor Rosamond! and what do you propose by going to the army?" asked Ronald.

"To see the Baron de Albini, and tell him my tale," said the minstrel.

"And will he do thee justice?" asked the dwarf.

"I believe he will," replied Rosamond. "Little as I saw of the world after my disgrace. I heard much during the two years in which I was secluded in the priory of St. Benedict. I learned to know my tyrant, to judge his motives by his actions, and to connect the events of which I occasionally heard with his intrigues. Besides this, he was sometimes off his guard, when thwarted in his wicked designs, and hatred and jealousy quickened my apprehension."

"Jealousy! Well," said the dwarf, "there was no need of jealousy."

"You are mistaken," said his companion, "the priestly cowl hides many vices. But all this cannot interest you. Only promise me your protection and secrecy till we arrive near the camp of Matilda's barons, and I ask no more."

"Poor maiden, you shall have my protection, were it but for hatred to that monk," said Ronald. "I owe him payment for my night's lodging in the dungeon."

"I heard of that. Oh, how the wily hypocrite exulted in the mischief he had made!" exclaimed Rosamond.

"You can explain to me why De Fougeres was so angry at my song," said the dwarf. "Your song, last evening, almost repeated the offensive word."

Rosamond shook her head.

"Oh, tell me! I am so curious," cried the dwarf.

"I dare not," replied the harper.

"The secret shall be safe with me; do tell me what bondage of fear there is between the baron and the monk," said Ronald.

"I dare not betray the confessional, at present," replied Rosamond.

"The confessional!" exclaimed the dwarf.

"Yes. The secret was betrayed to me by accident, in the ravings of fever," answered Rosamond; "but, when consciousness returned, I was solemnly swore not to reveal it."

"There is then a secret. Is it a tale of life and death?" asked Ronald.

"Question me no further. I have sworn," said Rosamond.

"But one word. Does it affect the life of the young captive in the Lady's Tower?" asked the dwarf, pertinaciously.

"No," replied Rosamond.

"Nor the life and happiness of the Lady ——"

Rosamond interrupted the dwarf.

"I will say no more. Gladly would I unburden my mind of this sad secret, but, until I can tell Geoffri de Albini the shameful history of my own sufferings, vain would be my accusation."

The dwarf was silent. He feared from the hasty manner in which his companion had interrupted him, that some danger impended over Cordelia; and respecting her as he did, he was extremely uneasy about it. He determined, however, in a less direct manner to obtain the information he desired.

"The poor young knight," he said, "knows no solace but the company of Lady Edith and Cordelia; and truly I do not wonder that he loves Cordelia."

"Loves Cordelia?" exclaimed Rosamond; "who loves Cordelia?"

"Edward de Albini," replied the dwarf.

"Sayest thou truly?" cried Rosamond, clasping his arm.

"He confessed it in my hearing to Father Augustine," cried Ronald.

"I see it all," cried his companion, "but he shall be unshrouded. Let us hasten from this cave."

"Not yet, surely; the band can hardly have descended into the valley," replied the dwarf, "and until they have passed yon hill, we are not safe."

"Right,—right, but revenge is impatient," answered Rosamond.

"I will aid your revenge, if you will but explain to me," said the dwarf.

"I may tell thee this, it will show the subtle hypocrisy of him whose arts I was a victim. The Baron de Bohun loves Cordelia, as dearly as Father Augustine loved her, and almost as passionately as he covets her dowry. He has resolved to thwart the young De Albini's love, as much through hatred to the young knight, as because he loves Cordelia; and he has departed for the war, determined, by some stratagem, to obtain the maiden's hand."

An exclamation of surprise burst from Ronald.

"How many words of deep meaning are unfolded to me," he said; "words which appeared of but little consequence when spoken."

"Does Cordelia know of the young knight's love?" asked Rosamond.

"Only as I told her," replied Ronald.

"And what favour will she give his suit?" asked the harper.

"All that an orphan, portionless and friendless, may give," replied the dwarf.

"Then she is safe. Thou saidst just now that I could not know jealousy. I do know it; even although that which I fancied was love for him, for that monk, is now turned to hatred. But he praised Cordelia to me; he talked of her grace, her high-born grace, and he compared it with the awkwardness of a country maid; he boasted of her accomplishments: he painted her as gracing the court of Matilda as his wife."

"His wife?—the monk's wife?" cried Ronald, amazed.

"Yes, the father never took the vows; the cowl and robe were assumed but in a short-lived fit of disgust at the world, or in furtherance of his wicked designs. They were lightly taken, they are yet more lightly shaken off," said Rosamond. "He loves Cordelia; and he thinks that she would aid his ambitious views, but he shall be disappointed."

"And is it not to Cordelia that the hated song refers?" asked Ronald, looking inquisitively in the face of his companion.

"Alas!—no," she replied.

"Then I am easy," answered the dwarf. "I would not that harm should befal her."

"Harm will not befal the innocent; but the guilty may dread the exposure which those words betoken," said Rosamond. "But now," she continued, as if willing to change the topic of conversation, "if you have not sworn secrecy, tell me, I pray you, what errand carries you to the battle-field."

"I must see the Baron de Tunstall, the near kinsman of Cordelia. The worthy knight, Robert L'Espee, sends me upon business which influences her welfare," answered the dwarf.

"Then Cordelia has a friend," cried Rosamond.

"She has; and one that hates the monk, and will protect her from him," said Ronald.

"And is that friend aware that Cordelia is not portionless?" asked Rosamond.

"Nay, I know not," replied Ronald; "doubtless he will protect the orphan's fortune."

"I guessed, nay, rather I knew, your errand; the talk of the brothers at the convent had prepared me for it," observed Rosamond. "I must hasten to Geoffri de Albini."

"But will you seek his presence alone?" asked Ronald; "you will meet your former comrades."

"It is well said," replied Rosamond. "When we part, I will seek some obscure place where I may resume my feminine attire. I need but little change, and under a close bonnet and ample cloak, they will not recognise the minstrel who has so often sung to them a lay of boisterous gladness, when his heart was almost breaking."

Ronald now ventured to look out ; and ascending the hill, he descried the Baron de Bohun's company at a great distance, having passed through the valley and ascended a hill which lay in their road. He therefore announced to his companion that they might safely continue their journey ; and re-mounting their palfreys, they proceeded on their way.

The conversation which had taken place in the cave had removed all Ronald's suspicion, and considerably softened his churlishness towards his unhappy companion. He felt his dignity increased by having somebody dependent upon him for assistance and protection ; and being naturally of a generous and benevolent disposition, he was glad to exert those qualities. The story of the disappearance of Rosamond Beverley had been often told to him at Thornbury ; he had arrived at the castle, just after the death of her father, and he had, with many others, watched the gradual decay and lingering death of her mother. One of the most worthy retainers of the Baron de Fougeres had been attached to Rosamnod, who was extremely pretty ; and it was supposed that they would shortly be married, when she was suddenly missed, and no endeavours could discover her retreat. She had appeared to be attached to her lover, who was wretched at her loss ; and Father Augustine moved, as it seemed by his unhappiness, offered to search among the neighbouring hamlets for the maiden. His search was of course in vain ; Rosamond was at the very moment concealed in his own monastery. By degrees she was remembered only as the object of a mystery, which it was useless to endeavour to penetrate ; and Father Augustine quieted the rumours about her, by suggesting that she had probably taken up the service of the Lady de Albini. Thus the matter ended ; and therefore the astonishment of Ronald was great, when he heard the true story. His anger and hatred to the monk was doubled by the knowledge of his atrocious conduct towards Rosamond ; and the hope that she would aid his revenge made him her willing protector.

The couple passed along the high road for some time silently, till Ronald said,—

" Methinks, the hall at Thornbury is not empty of good cheer at this moment ; and I should be glad if we had as fair a prospect before us as the baron's lazy retainers. What say you, companion ?"

Rosamond, who had been carefully provided for during the period that she had been in the band of the Baron de Bohun, began to be extremely faint for want of food ; and gladly assented to the proposition of the dwarf, that they should endeavour to procure refreshment at the first house at which it should appear safe to stop. The palfreys also needed better provender than the scanty herbage afforded.

The road of the travellers lay now across a wide and barren moor, enlivened only by the purple heath which tufted it. On the other side of the heath stood a lone cottage, and thither Ronald and his companion proceeded.

" What account shall we give of ourselves, if asked ?" said Ronald.

" Merely that we are journeying to the camp to rejoin my father and your master," answered Rosamond.

"And who is to be my master ?" asked the dwarf.

" The name of the Baron de Tunstall will serve us well enough," replied his companion. " It will be well not to say too much."

To this Ronald assented, and they proceeded to the cottage, where fresh troubles awaited them.

CHAPTER XIII.

Oh, blame her not !—when zephyrs wake,
The aspen's trembling leaves must shake ;
When beams the sun through April's shower,
It needs must bloom, the violet flower ;
And Love, howe'er the maiden strive,
Must with reviving hope revive !—SCOTT.

LET us return to the Castle of Thornbury, where the sudden absence of the dwarf raised considerable wonder. As he was not generally beloved, this wonder was almost unmixed with regret. Not that Ronald had enemies ; he could not have, for he was always ready to perform a kindness to any of those around him ; but he was a favourite, and a favourite has no friends. He was trusted by De Fougeres until that unhappy night when he allowed himself to be made the tool of Father Augustine ; and the Lady Edith liked his conversation, it enlivened the monotony of her life.

Many jests went round among the retainers ; some asserted that the dwarf had gone to the battle-field as page to Father Augustine : while others affirmed that he had been thrown into the dungeon for assisting the young captive knight to escape from the Lady's Tower.

" I heard him myself talk of the prisoner's escaping," said one of the men ; " he told the Lady Cordelia that it might be done."

" Ay, I heard him talking to her in the grove ; and they both agreed to help him," said another.

" And the young knight was to take Lady Cordelia with him," said a third, " and Father Augustine was to marry them."

" A pretty story, truly !" said the first speaker. " I warrant you Father Augustine is in love with Cordelia himself."

" What ! what !" exclaimed many voices.

" I know what I say," replied the man, with a mysterious air. " Father Augustine will marry the Lady Cordelia."

" But he is a monk," they called out.

" Never mind ; he has a dispensation ready, which he carries always about him, fastened into the bosom of his dress," said the man ; " I know it, for I have seen it."

" How ?" burst from them all.

" Why, you shall hear. Last year, when the father was ill, I was sent to the monastery, to carry him some wine from the castle. You know that wine is forbidden, so I was forced to hide it under my cloak ; and as I must deliver it to no one but the father, I was taken into his cell. I shall not forget the day, it was so pinching cold ; it was that very day when Jerney's two children were frozen, poor little hearts ; and as I went, I met Simon, the carter, and he said to me——"

" Never mind,—never mind,—tell us what you saw in the father's cell," said one of the men.

" Give me time," replied the narrator. " I tell you it was a cold day, and I dared not run to keep myself warm, for fear of the bottles ; so I sat down, and made a fire with some dead twigs, and I thought my lame foot was perished : you remember, Gervase, how I hurt that foot when the old apple-tree was thrown down."

" Well, never mind the apple-tree ; we want to hear about the father," cried Gervase, together with one or two others.

" How can I go on, when you interrupt me so ? What was I saying," asked Barnaby, for that was the narrator's name.

" You went into the father's cell, and there you saw——" said one of the listeners.

"No, no I did not see it till I was coming out again," said the relater.

"Well, only tell us what it was like," cried the men.

"Like, why, do not you all know the look of a woman's kerchief said Barnaby.

"A woman's kerchief!" exclaimed all voices at once, "and do you say you saw that in the Fathe· Augustine's cell?"

"As certainly as I now see your gerkins," said Barnaby, in a tone of authority.

Looks of incredulous astonishment passed round the company, and whispers were interchanged

"How came it there?" asked one.

"Satan himself!" said another.

"Nonsense! it was the father's nightcap," said another, in a tone of ridicule.

But Barnaby insisted seriously upon the extraordinary sight which he had seen, adding that he had heard a very extraordinary noise as he entered the cell, like a woman's cough.

"And was there not a strong smell of brimstone?" asked the man who before ridiculed the story.

"There was a strong smell of something very good," replied Barnaby; "and well there might be, for on a table by the father's couch, was some delicious trout, cooked as our master likes it."

"It was that which Satan came for, I warrant," said one of the men.

"Well, I suppose he does like good living, for those monks always preach against it," said Barnaby; "and I reckon he likes good drinking too; at least I know who does, for when I poured out a glass of the wine for the father, he drank it off, and did not leave enough in the glass to wet his majesty's hoofs with."

"And did he give *you* none?" asked a man.

"Me? no—but I was before hand with him," answered Barnaby.

"How?" asked two or three voices.

"Why, you see, as I told you, it was very cold; and when I sat down by the way to warm myself, I thought it was of no use warming myself outside only; and if the wine I carried was so good for Father Augustine, it must be good for me too, so I ——"

"So you just tasted it," cried one of the listeners.

"Why, if I did drink something like a bottle," said Barnaby, "did not I confess it afterwards?"

"Not to Father Augustine, I'll answer for it," said one, slily.

"No, no—but I did to Father Paul; and did not I make all right when I persuaded Judy to let me give his reverence the pig we fatted at Christmas? Sure the taste of the wine I brought home for her was worth the pig anyhow. Oh! it was rare drinking!" said Barnaby.

"Then I know," said one of the men, "the woman's kerchief that you say you saw, was only the father's hood after all, the wine made it into a kerchief."

"Be quiet," cried Barnaby, in a tone that showed how much he was affronted at his veracity being questioned; it was a kerchief, and a delicate one too, fit for our Lady Edith to wear."

"A love token from the Lady Cordelia," cried one.

"No, no," said another, "her love tokens light not at the monastery : they rest nearer home."

"Any one may see that," said Barnaby; "besides, the Lady Cordelia does not carry her embroidery to the monastery."

"Was it an embroidered kerchief?" they asked.

"Aye, with the needle upon it," replied Barnaby.

"Nay, then we must believe you," said the man who had so much attempted to discredit the story of Barnaby, "for I never heard of Satan's embroidery."

The last touch seemed satisfactory to Barnaby's audience and they made various sage remarks on the subject.

"But the dispensation," said one of the men, "how did you see that?"

"I did not say I saw it," said Barnaby.

"Yes, yes, you did, " cried all the voices.

"Well, I did and I did not," answered Barnaby.

"Now tell us the truth, good fellow," said one of the men.

"I will if you give me time," replied Barnaby, "where was I?"

"Why, when you saw the woman's kerchief," said one.

"No, no," cried Barnaby, "I did not see the kerchief till I was coming out again.

"Well, begin at your going in," said his auditor.

"I was shown the father's cell, and I tapped gently at the door, as in honour bound not to disturb his reverence suddenly," continued Barnaby. "Well, he made me no answer, so I waited a minute, and I heard a woman's cough."

"How you know it was a woman's voice?" said one.

"Why, do I not hear Judy cough every winter, as if every breath was her last?" asked Barnaby

"Nonsense ; it was the father, he was very ill, I dare say," said his tormentor.

"Well, let me go on. I know the difference, as you will hear," said Barnaby, "I said the father did not hear me, and so I knocked again, after a minute the father said, 'come in.' I went in, frightened enough at the woman's cough, you may be sure."

"And how did Father Augustine look ? Did he say anything about the cough?" asked one of the men.

"Not he, to be sure," said another. "Perhaps he did not hear the cough ; and it could not frighten him, you know, because he knows how to drive somebody away."

"Well, the father looked bad enough," continued Barnaby, "he was so angry with me for intruding upon him, till I told my errand ; and then he took a bottle, and bid me open it, and pour out a goblet ; and I did."

"And then he drank it, did he ? Did he not drink health to the cough and the kerchief?" said one of the men, jeeringly.

"Fie ! fie !" said Barnaby.

"And now tell us how you saw the dispensation?" asked one.

"Why, did not he cough when he had done drinking, as if he would die?" said Barnaby. "And pretty well frightened I was ; he was as black as his gown, so I went to undo his throat, and there I saw the dispensation."

"Where ? where?" they asked.

"Sewed in the front of his robe," replied Barnaby, "ay, and sewed neatly too—no bungling friar's work."

"With the same needle that sewed the kerchief, aye, Barnaby," said his opponent.

"May be so," answered Barnaby, quietly.

"But did you read the paper ?" was asked.

"I read ? I cannot read, you know," answered Barnaby.

"Then how do you know what was written on the paper?" cried one.

"I do not know!—what difficulties you make," said Barnaby.

"Then after all it might not have been a dispensation," said the man who had before shown himself so incredulous.

"Why now ! what should Father Augustine carry so carefully sewn up in his robe, but a dispensation to marry Lady Cordelia?" asked Barnaby, "We all know he loves her ; and how can he marry her without a dispensation?"

"How can he marry her at all ? Is not he a monk?" cried some of the men.

"And are you sure she will have him?" asked Barnaby.

"Why, she must," said one of the men.

"'Tis better than going into a convent, at any rate," said another.

"Well, I shall look for the kerchief, I assure you," said a third, "if I am sent to Father Augustine. Why did not you steal it, Barnaby?"

"How do I know what it really was ?" answered Barnaby ; "besides, what would Judy have said ?"

"It would have made the old crone young again," said Barnaby's tormentor.

"Nonsense, nonsense," said Barnaby. "I did not even confess it to Father Paul."

"Best not, I should think," said one ; "we are forbidden to bring scandal upon the Church, you know."

"Scandal or not," said Barnaby, angrily, "'tis true, and I will always say so. You are a set of unbelievers, what is the use of confession to you."

"Nothing without a pig, Barnaby," said the man who had teased him so. But Barnaby was out of hearing, having left the company in great disdain of their dulness of comprehension.

Robert L'Espee, who had watched Cordelia with the eye of a benevolent friend, became convinced that her heart was deeply attached to the young Edward de Albini ; and having heard from the dwarf that the captive entertained a similar predilection, he resolved to be the means of imparting as much happiness to the lovers as in their present uncertain state they could feel.

One day, therefore, when the Lady Edith was at Mowbray Castle, L'Espee asked Cordelia to accompany him to the Lady's Tower. Cordelia reluctantly agreed ; she dreaded seeing Edward, and feared lest she should betray her affection.

"I am not the less welcome, young man, I trust," said L'Espee, as they entered, "because I bring with me this fair excuse for my intrusion."

Edward arose, and received the knight with courtesy, and Cordelia with ill-restrained joy.

"As the representative of the Baron de Fougeres," he replied, "you are welcome ; and as one who has been pleased to express some interest in the captive, you are entitled to my gratitude."

"And do you say not one word of courtesy to my companion ?" said L'Espee.

"The Lady Cordelia knows the pleasure which her society bestows too well to doubt my welcome," replied Edward.

Cordelia blushed deeply, and seated herself behind L'Espee, as if fearing the scrutiny of his eye.

"I am a plain soldier, young knight," said L'Espee, after a short pause, "but I have known other feelings besides those of the battle-field—I have loved."

Edward looked astonished at this address, but spoke not.

"I loved the mother of this maiden, but she returned not my affection," continued the knight; "her heart was otherwise fixed. Till lately, I knew not that her child lived ; she does, and I have promised to befriend her in her difficulties. She is dear to me as a daughter, but I have not the authority of a parent. I have, however, taken measures to apprise her nearest kinsman of her existence and residence at the Castle of Thornbury ; and, I hope, ere long, to receive assurance of his willing reception of her. You have heard much from Father Augustine of the claims of the Church upon Cordelia. Believe him not, he is himself interested in her not assuming the rank to which she is entitled ; and he is, I grieve to say it for the sake of the Church, not one whom you should take as counsellor. However, he will not visit you again."

"How ?" asked De Albini.

"Father Augustine is now the Baron de Bohun, and has joined the army of the empress," said L'Espee.

Edward felt no surprise at this, he had expected the event.

"I leave you a fairer and a more sincere counsellor," said L'Espee, rising ; "may I hope that your deliberations will be amicable ?" he added, smiling, as he left the tower.

Cordelia knew not what to do or to say ; her suspense was ended by Edward, who said, "Fair maiden, I feared you had deserted me."

"Oh no !" she replied.

"If I could tell how delightful your presence is to the captive, how the remembrance of your smile cheers his loneliness, and how the sweet melody of your voice rings in his ear, you would not begrudge him such a solace."

"It is due to the unhappy," replied Cordelia.

"And yet, fairest Cordelia, one word from you would make the captive the happiest of beings. He has dared to love you," said Edward, "grant him but forgiveness."

Cordelia could scarcely breathe. The assurance of the dwarf had been received

by her with doubt; and trembling she dared not wholly believe it; but the words of De Albini were not to be mistaken. She could not answer him, and Edward said,—

"Only tell me that my presumption shall not deprive me of your presence. That would, indeed, be death to me."

Still Cordelia spoke not.

No. 12,

" I have hinted to the Lady Edith the state of my affections," continued Edward, " she did not bid me despair ; but you only, dearest Cordelia, can bid me hope."

" Alas!" said Cordelia, " what hope can I give ?"

" I know that I must be a prisoner until these unhappy wars are over, but I am not a culprit. De Fougeres will not, cannot refuse to liberate me after the next battle shall have decided the fate of the kingdom. Then may I hope that Cordelia will listen to my suit ?"

Cordelia sighed, and was silent—but the glance which she turned upon the young knight told that his discourse was not unpleasing to her.

Edward took courage from it, and proceeded thus :—

" I well know, also, that our kindred have embraced opposite sides on this occasion ; that my father upholds the cause of Matilda, while your relations are in arms with Stephen ; but, dearest lady, may not love heal all these feuds ? My sire is noble-minded and just, deeply attached to me, his only child ; and did he but know the virtues and perfections of Cordelia, gladly would he receive from Thornbury the fair daughter whom he here lost. But tell me that you love no other, that the heart which I should consider the greatest treasure of my existence is not otherwise engaged."

" Oh no !" cried Cordelia.

" And may I hope that time and sincere affection will give me some interest in your heart ?" asked Edward.

" I must await the return of the messenger whom L'Espee has sent to my uncle," said Cordelia ; " I dare not pledge myself."

" But say you do not despise me," cried Edward, eagerly.

" Oh no—despise !" exclaimed Cordelia.

" And can you love me then, fair Cordelia ?" said the youth.

Cordelia murmured a gentle affirmative, and Edward, throwing himself on his knees before her, exclaimed,—

" Thanks ! thanks ! beloved maiden ! now is the captive indeed happy. Nor restraint nor separation from those whom he loves, can trouble him now that Cordelia has given him her love."

" Rise, Edward !" said Cordelia, " that position ill becomes a youth bearing the name of De Albini."

" Not till you have promised me, that when released from this captivity, you will bestow upon me that gentle hand," said the youth.

" Nay," replied Cordelia, " I dare not give such a promise."

" Wilt thou influence thy kindred in my favour ?" urged Edward.

" I will say all that a maiden may say," answered Cordelia.

" Thanks ! deepest thanks," said Edward rising, from his knees.

Hours passed in delightful converse between the lovers, and neither were aware how quickly the moments had flown, till a messenger from the castle announced the return of the Lady Edith, and that she requested Cordelia's immediate presence.

" And must we part ?" said Edward. " How dreary are the hours in which I sit alone, and ruminate upon my inactive life. But Cordelia has given me happier thoughts, she has inspired me with new feelings of life and hope."

" Adieu, Edward !" said Cordelia.

" Adieu, my beloved !" said the youth, " say, when shall we meet again ?"

" Perhaps to-morrow, if it be Edith's wish," replied the maiden.

" And if Edith come not, may not Cordelia come ?" replied Edward.

" Perhaps so," replied Cordelia.

" Adieu, then !" cried Edward, " remember him who adores you."

They parted ; Edward to enjoy the bright hope which dawned upon him, and Cordelia to claim the sympathy of her friend in her prospect of happiness.

CHAPTER XIV.

Now by the rising sun I view'd,
  In tears my lady's face :
She gave me many a token good,
  And many a soft embrace.
Our parting bitterly we mourn'd ;
The hearts which erst with rapture burn'd,
  Were cold with woe and care.

A ring with glittering ruby red,
  Gave me that lady sheen ;
And with me from the castle sped,
  Along the meadow green :
And whilst I saw my lady bright,
  She wav'd on high her kerchief white:
"Courage ! to arms," she cried.—GERMAN SONG.

WHEN Cordelia returned to the castle, she inquired for Lady Edith; and, told that her friend had retired to her own apartment, she sought her there, eager to communicate the happiness which filled her heart. But alas! how shall we describe her agitation, when, upon entering the room, she found Edith lying upon a couch sobbing violently.

"What is the matter, dearest Edith ? are you ill ?" asked Cordelia.

Edith attempted to speak, but sobs choked her utterance.

Cordelia seated herself by her, and taking her friend's hand, awaited her recovery. After some time Edith said with considerable effort,—

"Oh, Cordelia ! what I have long dreaded has arrived."

"What dearest ?" asked her friend.

"Eustace !" sobbed Edith.

"Is Eustace ill ?" asked Cordelia.

"He goes to-morrow !" cried Edith, redoubling her tears.

"To the war ?" asked her friend.

"Alas ! yes !" cried Edith.

"Poor lady !" said Cordelia deeply grieved, "how comes this ?"

"The Baron de Mowbray, his father, has sent for him to lead on his retainers," said Edith.

"I fear, then, the chances of victory are desperate," said Cordelia.

"No," replied Edith; "but it is desirable for the party of the king to muster all their strength. A battle is daily expected."

Here a fresh torrent of tears burst from Edith's eyes, which her friend in vain urged her to control.

"Oh, Cordelia !" she said, "what a happy life mine has been hitherto, and now——"

"Nay, dearest Edith ! all may be well," replied her friend.

"My dear father in danger, and Eustace going to leave me, perhaps, never to return," cried Edith.

Cordelia could give but little comfort to her unhappy friend; the scene burst which had brightened her own hopes, made the grief of Edith appear more overwhelming. Fain would she have uttered some sentence of resignation or hope, she could not ; and the two friends passed the remainder of the day in mourning.

Cordelia would not intrude her own circumstances of hope upon her friend, therefore she said nothing about her interesting interview with the young knight ; but when she descended alone into the hall to give the customary evening salutation to L'Espee, she said to him,—

"The Lady Edith's misery damps my happiness, but it cannot damp my gratitude."

" What dost mean, my child ?" asked the knight.

" You have heard that Eustace de Mowbray departs for the camp to-morrow ?" she asked.

" I heard such a rumour," replied L'Espee, " and I sought the Lady Edith to inquire the truth of the report, but I found her not."

" She is weeping in her chamber," replied Cordelia, " the rumour is too true."

" Alas ! poor damsel," returned the knight, " I fear then there is danger of defeat."

" I know not ; and if you have such fear, it would be cruel to express it," said Cordelia, " my poor friend is sufficiently dejected already."

" Would that I could join my comrades," cried L'Espee, " this inglorious life is unsuited to me.   But, fair Cordelia, how speeds it with the captive knight ?"

Cordelia looked upon the ground, and made no answer.

" Nay, my child, be not afraid to speak to a friend," said L'Espee, " has he pleaded his suit to thee ?"

" He has," replied Cordelia.

" And what said Cordelia? Did she bid him despair?" asked the knight, kindly.

" She could not," answered Cordelia. " But what avails her word? Oh, tell me, have I done wrong?"

" No, no ! my messenger will soon return with tidings of thy kinsmen. If he receive thee as I expect he will, I will speak in favour of De Albini. If he discard thee, I will be thy parent," cried L'Espee, embracing her.

" And I could be happy so, were it not that I should be nameless and portionless.   Would the Baron de Albini receive a portionless bride for his son?" asked Cordelia, in a melancholy tone.

" The adopted child of Robert L'Espee will not be portionless. I loved thy mother, Cordelia, dearly loved her ; and although her place in my heart was afterwards filled by another, her kindred claim nothing from me.   They are rich and want nothing ; the orphan of my adoption shall be my heiress," said the knight.

Cordelia gratefully poured out her warmest thanks, and with a heart somewhat cheered, she acknowledged to her kind friend her affection for Edward de Albini.

On the following morning at daybreak, Eustace de Mowbray, heading the troop of soldiers belonging to the Mowbray domain, arrived at Thornbury Castle. He had promised to pass that way, in order to bid a last adieu to Edith ; and he brought with him a request that she would take up her residence with his lady mother, at Mowbray Castle, during the first week of his absence.

Edith and Cordelia, already risen, met Eustace in the hall of the castle.

" Beloved Edith," said he, " my mother is alone, and nought but your sweet company can console her for the absence of her son.   Wilt thou be a daughter to her, while I am far away upon the battle-field ?"

" Willingly would I give my poor company," said Edith, " to lighten the passing hours of the Lady de Mowbray ; but what does Cordelia say ?"

" May not the Lady Cordelia accompany you ?" asked Eustace.

" What sayest thou, Cordelia ?" said her friend.

" I will remain at Thornbury," replied Cordelia. " Robert L'Espee will be my companion ; he will entertain me with his stories of days gone by."

" And the young captive, what will he tell thee ?" said Edith, archly.

" Nay—nay—dearest Edith ?" replied Cordelia, blushing deeply, " mention him not now."

Edith's heart was too full of her own sorrow to wound that of her friend ; and turning to Eustace, she told him she would repair to Mowbray Castle in the course of the morning.

" And now, dearest Edith," said her lover, " have you no love token to bestow upon your knight, whereby it may be known that he serves a noble and beauteous lady ?"

" Need you such a token of remembrance ?" asked Edith, fondly.

" I need it not," replied Eustace ; " memory will fail me but with life. But this is my first field, and I would fain bear some token of Edith's love."

Edith took a knot of ribbon from her robe, and giving it to her lover, he fastened it upon his cap.

"Now am I fully armed, fair Edith," he said. "If victory determine for us, this knot shall be returned to the spotless from shame, and unfaded by cowardice:—if I fall——"

"Hush! hush! Eustace," cried Edith, sobbing.

"Dearest Edith! you unman me, 'twere time we part," said Eustace. "Adieu!"

"Adieu!" cried Edith, bursting into tears.

Cordelia too wept, and the lovers parted, amidst mutual words of endearment.

The maidens watched the band of De Mowbray from the walls of the castle, as they wound along the vale; and when the rising hid the last horseman from their view, they retired to their chamber.

"And how will Cordelia employ her time during my absence?" asked Edith.

"With Robert L'Espee, as I have said," replied Cordelia; "he needs a friend to aid his unsteady steps."

"And hast thou no other reason for declining to accompany me to Mowbray Castle?" said Edith.

"Robert L'Espee has sent a trusty messenger to my kinsman, De Tunstall," replied her friend, "and I would here await the result."

"And hast thou no other reason? Alas! then, poor Edward!" said Edith.

Cordelia looked down, and gaining resolution, said, "I would not intrude upon your grief, dearest Edith, by speaking of myself; but I have that to say which may give you pleasure for your friend."

"Speak then, Cordelia; think me not so selfish as to grudge happiness to others, even although I have parted with mine," said her friend.

"The young knight loves me!" said Cordelia.

"I know it, my friend, and I rejoice at it," answered Edith. "May this war soon cease, for the sake of both of us, we shall then be happy. You will seek the protection of the Lady de Albini, as a daughter, and I am sure you will love her."

"If she be like the picture in the western turret, I shall indeed," said Cordelia.

"Have you ever mentioned that picture to the prisoner?" asked Edith.

"Certainly not;" replied Cordelia. "It was, you know, the strict desire of the baron that no hint should be given to the knight, that the name of De Albini had ever been heard of in the Castle of Thornbnry."

"True, and you are very prudent, Cordelia," said Edith; "but surely you might now inform him that the Lady Abbess, your aunt, desired you on her death-bed to claim performance of the promise given in your infancy by the Lady de Albini, in case you ever required it."

"Perhaps I may do so," answered Cordelia; "the knowledge of such a promise may incline the Lady Elfrida to a kind reception of her son's attachment."

"And you will visit the Lady's Tower in my absence, dearest Cordelia. Bear my best and kindest greeting to Edward. Tell him he has my warmest wishes for his happy restoration to liberty and home. I have, from the day of his arrival here felt an interest in him,—nay, an attachment, most unaccountable. Be not jealous, dear Cordelia," continued Edith, "it is not love, thou knowest."

"I once feared——" said Cordelia, hesitating.

"What didst fear?" asked Edith.

"That Edward de Albini loved Edith," returned Cordelia.

"Oh no! that could not be. Such a thought never came near me," said Edith.

"Ah! dearest Edith, you were too happy then to have any fear," cried Cordelia.

"And we shall be happy again," replied Edith, "let us not imagine evil. Remember, Cordelia, I shall be obliged to exert myself to enliven Lady de Mowbray's spirits as well as my own. Now adieu. Love your Edith!"

"Adieu, my kindest, best friend!" said Cordelia.

The friends parted with tears and embraces; Edith leaving strict charge that in the event of any news arriving from the baron, she should be informed of it. She departed for Mowbray Castle, where she found the Lady de Mowbray sadly dispirited and unhappy; but she received Edith with the affection of a mother to a daughter. The virtues of Eustace were a never-failing subject of tender conversation between them; and Edith found that by endeavouring to cheer the spirits of the lady, she insensibly soothed her own.

Cordelia repaired soon after her friend's departure to the Lady's Tower, where she was greeted with expressions of ardent love by Edward de Albini. Many vows of unchanging affection were breathed between them; many bright prospects of happiness were talked of. Cordelia related to her lover some of the events of her early life; the almost motherly affection of the abbess, her peaceful and quiet home at the convent, the sad loss of her protectress, and the harsh conduct of Father Augustine. She also expressed her certain conviction of the document of marriage between her mother and De Dunstanville, and her fear that the monk was in some way connected with the loss of it.

Edward listened with pleased interest to the fair narrator; he entered into her feelings of respectful affection for the lost friend of her early years, and her description of the conduct of the monk made a deep impression upon him.

"A singular fate has brought us together," said Cordelia. "The abbess told me that when the Lady de Albini left Thornbury, in grief for the loss of her beloved and only child, she wished very much to take me with her, but the abbess dared not give her consent."

"Indeed!" cried Edward, "would that it had been so!"

"Upon the abbess refusing this request, the Lady de Albini gave a promise," continued Cordelia, "that if I ever wanted a friend and protectress, she would, upon my application, be such an one to me."

"How like my revered mother!" said Edward; "she is always the friend of the unhappy and unfortunate."

"I have been many times inclined to throw myself upon the kindness of the lady," said Cordelia, "once when the abbess died and I was homeless, and, as I thought, friendless."

"You would have been received with a deep remembrance of a very painful event," said the knight, "which I fear my mother will never recover."

"Again," said Cordelia, "I wished to seek her protection when my heart first told me——"

"What? sweetest Cordelia," cried Edward.

"That I have loved her son," murmured the maiden.

"And wouldst thou fly me then?" asked the young knight.

"I thought it was my duty," answered Cordelia.

"Together, we will seek my lady mother," said Edward. "Believe me, she will welcome my lovely Cordelia with true affection. But, Cordelia, I have been much disturbed by the dwarf Ronald."

"How?" asked Cordelia.

"He often sought my tower;—once, after having angered the Baron de Fougeres by a foolish song," said Edward, "I could not understand how it was."

"I know not," answered the maiden. "The baron, although kind without change towards Lady Edith, is often morose and angry with others, apparently without cause. This was the case on the evening which you mention," said Cordelia.

"I have not seen Ronald for many days," observed the knight.

"He has departed for the camp of the king, on a message from L'Espee," said Cordelia. "His summons was short, and he probably had no time to warn you of his departure.

"I have missed Ronald much," said Edward, "his remarks amused me. But now, fair Cordelia, I need no other company than thine."

Again the time passed quickly to the lovers; again they exchanged vows of unshaken fidelity; and again they parted in the hope and promise of meeting on the morrow.

CHAPTER XV.

Oh! the sight entrancing
When morning's beam is glancing,
O'er fields array'd
With helm and blade,
And plumes in the gay wind dancing,
When hearts are all high beating,
And the trumpet's voice repeating
That song, whose breath
May lead to death,
But never to retreating.—MOORE.

WHEN Ronald and his companion arrived at the cottage they were extremely fatigued, and much wanting food; they knocked, but for some time no one answered the summons. Ronald became impatient, and after repeated knocks, a man put forth his head from a window above, and bid the travellers begone about their business.

"We want food for ourselves and our palfreys," said Ronald, angrily.

"You will get neither here," answered the man.

"But is not this a hostelry?" asked Ronald, "why then deny us?"

"Oh, my fine fellow! hast thou as much impudence as trump?" exclaimed the man.

"I pray you, let us have some rest; we are honest folks," said Rosamond.

"So all knaves call themselves. No, no—I want no honest folks here, beside myself," returned the churl. "So begone, Mr. Fair-face."

At this appellation being applied to the young harper, a female face made its appearance for a moment at the window. The glance was apparently satisfactory, for she was heard to say,—

"They look honest enough, Gregory, suppose we let them in!"

"I suppose no such thing, dame," answered Gregory, "is not one loss enough?"

"That youth seems hardly able to carry his harp," said the woman. "I wonder if he can really play it. Ask him, husband."

"Nay, I want none of his jingle. I shall not ask him," said Gregory.

"Then I will," replied the woman, and putting her head out of the window, she said,—

"Canst thou make music, young sir?"

"That I can; wilt hear it?" asked Rosamond, adding aside to Ronald, "Patience! I have hope that a song may soften their hearts."

She then sang as follows:—

I have song of war for knight,
Lay of love for lady bright,
Carol blithe for huntsman's ear,
Song of hope the sad to cheer;
I have wandered all the day,
Do not bid me farther stray.

Hunger's pang is hard to prove,
Let my case your pity move,

> Ope your hospitable door,
> Charity will bless your store,
> And your kindness I'll repay,
> With the harper's sweetest lay.
>
> I can bid the past appear,
> I can bring the distant near,
> The hidden future I can shew,
> And lost treasure bring to view,
> If you would your fortune see,
> Give the harper entrance free.

"Well sung, by my troth!" said Gregory.

"Let them come in," cried his dame; "he says he can tell my fortune."

"Better let him tell where the silver tankard is gone to. Hark ye, young sir, if thou canst give any tidings of our silver tankard, thou shalt have food and rest," said Gregory to the harper.

"I can," said the harper, "but not here. My noble art cannot be exercised in the open air; I must have appliances for it."

"I know not what those are, but we have a rare rasher of bacon," said the dame, "and the baron's soldiers have left us a few eggs."

"Come, dame," said Gregory, "unlock the door; let us see what stories the conjuror will tell us."

The man and woman disappeared from the window, and Ronald turned hastily to his companion, saying,—

"I know not what black arts you may have learned from the soldier monk, but much I fear we shall be in a scrape here."

"Fear not," replied Rosamond. "Did you not hear that the baron's soldiers have been here? No doubt it was they who stole the tankard¶ need be no conjuror to guess that. Leave it to me."

"Thou art ready-witted enough," said the dwarf. "I marvel where thou hast learned thy trade."

"If thou meanest the trade of deceit, I learned it where it is best taught— in the monk's cell," said Rosamond.

"And thou wert an apt scholar," returned Ronald.

"Here is the churl," said his companion. "Now, Ronald, only do as I desire you, and swear to do what I affirm, and we will have the rasher of bacon, ay, and intelligence to guide our steps by too. But mind, no word of the baron."

The dwarf promised obedience, and they alighted from their palfreys, which Gregory took to a small stable, and Ronald and the harper followed the dame into the house.

It was a rude dwelling, consisting only of a large kitchen, or hall, below, and a couple of chambers above. In the hall stood a solid and cumbrous screen, lined with benches, and before it was a round table covered with scraps of food and empty mugs. It was evident that no weak carousers had recently been there.

"Dame," said Rosamond, "thou hast had company lately."

"Truth, we have, and rough company too," answered the woman, who was occupied in clearing away some of the dirt.

Ronald had drawn nigh to the fire, and the dame had been so intent upon examining the good looks of the harper, that she had not yet noticed the dwarf. Her attention was drawn to him by his saying,—

"Rough customers are better than none, dame."

"Who art thou?" cried the woman in horror.

"What dost take me for?" asked Ronald.

"The saints bless us and keep us!" she cried.

"Woman, what do you mean?" cried Ronald, angrily.

"Did you never see a dwarf before?" asked Rosamond.

"A dwarf! and is that what they call a dwarf?" said the dame.

"Truly so; and at your service," answered Ronald, "to dance, sing, tumble, or jump."

"Canst tell fortunes?" asked the dame.

"My companion can," replied the dwarf.

The dame had by this time overcome her fear of Ronald's mis-shapen figure, and busied herself in preparing the fire to give them some food. At Ronald's last words, however, she turned round to the harper, saying,—

"If you can give any tidings of our lost tankard, I pray thee, do it quickly; you may eke lack a vessel to drink your ale from."

"Such a proceeding requires preparation," said the harper, "and it cannot be done fasting; the spirit whom I must bring will not come to a hungry man."

Here Ronald gave the harper a look expressive of the most ardent admiration and satisfaction.

No. 13.

"I fear also," said the harper, after appearing to think solemnly for some minutes, "I fear that we must wait until nightfall before I can get such an answer to my inquiries as may really bring back your tankard to your hand."

"Till nightfall?" cried the dame, sighing.

"Yes," replied Rosamond; "it were easy to learn where the tankard is, but that is not sufficient, and would hardly satisfy you: it is much more difficult to obtain it, and requires days of preparation."

"Only let me see it again," cried the dame.

"Well, although my journey is one of the utmost importance, I will oblige you by delaying it till after nightfall, and I will exert the art which I profess to learn the fate of your treasure. I must now see to my palfrey; and, good dame, I charge you, entice my familiar here, by your best cookery and most plentiful dishes."

Thus saying, Rosamond left the kitchen, giving Ronald an intimation to follow her, which he did, and they entered the little shed where their palfreys were.

"What are you after?" asked the dwarf, in a tone of alarm; "we shall be stopped, or taken to a justice, and perhaps flogged. Mischievous creature that thou art!"

"Be not alarmed, good Ronald; have I not been for two years apprenticed to jugglers?" cried Rosamond, laughing; "I must have been stupid, indeed, not to have learned my trade from the masters of it."

"But what do you mean by staying here?" asked Ronald.

"To secure ourselves from any interruption by the baron's party; for, you see, if we tread so closely upon their heels as we have hitherto done, we may stumble unawares upon some stragglers belonging to the band," replied Rosamond.

"But how can I afford to lose the time?" cried Ronald.

"There will be little time really lost," said his companion; "our noble steeds want rest and food, and if you are so sublime as to do without these necessary comforts, I am not."

"Well, be it so," replied the dwarf. "I own that side of bacon which hangs in the kitchen, hath very attractive qualities. But as to the tankard?"

"Trust to me; do not I tell you I have not lost my two years in the cell?" said Rosamond. "The dame's fear of you shall be turned to good account."

The travellers returned to the kitchen, where they found the fire blazing, the table cleared, and their hostess busily preparing their repast.

"In the hope that you will bring back my tankard," she said, "I have prevailed upon Gregory to kill the only chicken that those ravenous soldiers spared us; and he is now making it ready for your dinner."

"Soldiers are bad customers, dame," said the harper.

"Truth, they are indeed," she replied, "even if they take no more than they pay for."

"And where were these travelling to!" asked Rosamond.

"Where the carrion is, will not the crows gather? Where should they be going to, but to the camp?" asked the dame.

"When do they expect to reach it;" asked Rosamond.

"In two days," replied the woman, "but why dost ask?"

"Only because I wanted to know whether we were far from those horrid scenes," replied the harper, "I would not willingly go near them."

"I suppose, dame," said Ronald, "you admired the brave captain more than you did the soldiers. Or he admired you more perhaps! How many fine speeches did he make you, dame?"

"He make fine speeches forsooth!" cried the dame, indignantly; "I scarcely saw his face."

"Why was that?" asked Rosamond.

He alighted from his horse, and marched straight up stairs to the chamber, without even saying good day to me," cried the dame. "The men said he was angry that one of the band had left them suddenly. And now I recollect it was a harper youth that ran away from them. Was it you?" said the woman, turning suddenly round to Rosamond.

"Me?—no; I never was one of the soldiers." Then turning to Ronald, who was in an agony of trepidation at this fancied discovery, she said—

"Doubtless this harper was that poor unhappy youth whom we met in the valley, and who wanted to join our company."

"Yes," said Ronald; "I think he said he had left his party."

"And why did not you let him join you?" asked the woman.

"What, two harpers together?" asked Rosamond. "No, good dame, that might spoil my trade."

"And may I ask where you are travelling to," said the woman.

"We know not," answered the harper. "Wherever we find good cheer, there we stay; and when we find bad cheer we pass somewhere else. We are rovers."

"Then you are not going to the camp," asked the dame.

"If there be no clashing but the jingling of ale-mugs at present, perhaps we may seek the outskirts. Such a scene suits my trade," said the harper.

The dinner was now ready; and the dame, having called her husband to draw the ale, sets the dishes before the hungry traveller. Ronald and his companion did full justice to their homely fare, and having drank their ale as freely as if it had been presented to them in the silver tankard, they reclined upon the benches which surrounded the fire-place.

"Now," said Gregory, "desire the tankard to appear."

"Desire!" cried the harper, "dost think that it is thus that I pursue my art? Know that the slightest information respecting the utensil, must be gained with the utmost labour by me, and perhaps at the risk of my life."

'Make haste, and work hard, or, by the saints, my oaken stick shall rouse thee," cried the man.

"Ronald looked aghast, but Rosamond answered calmly, "Patience! patience! friend; procure for me such things as I require, and thou shalt speedily see the effect. I do not fear labour or danger to repay you for your hospitality."

"What dost require!" asked the dame.

"Only a dark room and a candle," answered Rosamond.

"The woman left the kitchen for a short time, and when she returned, she said to the harper, "Follow me up stairs."

Rosamond followed her to the chamber, which she found completely darkened; and desiring that she might not be disturbed while making her preparations she dismissed her hostess.

CHAPTER XVI.

> Mortal! to thy bidding bow'd,
> From my mansion in the cloud,
> Which the breath of twilight builds,
> And the summer's sun-set gilds
> With the azure and vermilion,
> Which is mix'd for my pavilion,
> Though thy quest may be forbidden,
> On a star-beam I have ridden;
> To thine adjuration bow'd,
> Mortal——be thy wish avow'd!—BYRON.

WHILE Rosamond was making her preparations in the upper chamber, Ronald had composed himself comfortably to rest by the kitchen fire. He was not entirely in the secret of his companion's plan, as he had not had an opportunity of hearing them; therefore he thought that the safest place for him would be to go to sleep; or at least to feign to do so. He therefore stretched himself upon a bench and covering his head, and shading his face with his cloak, he pretended to be asleep having first impressed it upon the minds of his hosts that they must admit no one into the house during the period that the harper was engaged above.

Gregory left the kitchen, and the dame sat down to her spinning-wheel. An hour had thus passed, when a knocking above, announced that the conjurer desired the presence of the dame. She was not at all willing to encounter her alone, and awakened Ronald from a real sleep into which he had fallen, requesting him to accompany her, which he readily agreed to do, as he was curinatto see his comrade's tricks, and more than a little anxious about the term ion of them.

When they opened the door of the chamber they could perceive nothing, in consequence of a dense white smoke which filled the room, accompanied with an unpleasant smell, not however of brimstone. The dame drew back coughing, but Ronald ventured in.

"My spells have hitherto been successful," said the harper, "and I have with some difficulty, learned where your treasure is; your own impatience in not allowing me to wait till dusk, before I tried my art, prevents it being restored to you at once."

"Have you seen it?" asked the dame eagerly.

"A shadowy representation of the tankard was accompanied by a clear portraiture of the person who stole it," answered Rosamond.

"And who was it?" asked the dame.

"In a quarter of an hour you shall know," replied the harper; "go down stairs, and in that time I will follow you."

The woman and Ronald descended the stairs, Rosamond unfastened the curtains, opened the window, put by in her bag the herbs which she had used, and the room being restored to its usual condition, the conjurer went down to the kitchen where she found Gregory and his wife anxiously expecting her. Taking her harp, he sang the following lines :—

> Dark his beard, and scarr'd his cheek,
> Who hath your treasure ta'en ;
> His jerkin mark'd with a yellow streak,
> And the wild-brooms spray o'er his bonnet-peak,
> And his bridle-front doth the cause bespeak,
> For which he draws the rein.
>
> Seek ye him o'er hill and dale.
> And the tankard shall be found,
> Crown'd with the foaming nut-brown ale,
> Where the warriors for the fight regale,
> And the helmed monk from the cloister's pale,
> Frowns o'er his followers round.

"Thou art a wonderful youth," said the dame; "that is exactly the picture of one of the men who were here, and a bad looking fellow he was, sure enough."

"Yes," cried Gregory, "and there was only one of them who had a sprig of broom in his bridle-band. If that's the thief I should know him among a hundred."

"You hear it is," said the dame; "so take Sorrel, and set off directly for the camp, and bring back my tankard."

"Fair and softly, good dame," cried Ronald, "how knows your master where to go to?"

"How indeed?" said Gregory.

"Why, you can find out the man by inquiring, surely," said the dame."

"And how should I inquire when I do not know the name of their captain, said Gregory.

"The men called him 'my lord,' and if you ask for those that came last from the east, will not that do?" asked the dame.

Ronald and Rosamond thought it would do much too well, and must be prevented.

"Let me try my skill once more," said the conjuror, "the spell will be stronger at midnight; and perhaps by particular conjuration I can compel the spirit to bring back your tankard. But one thing is absolutely necessary."

"What is that?" asked the dame.

"Faith," replied Rosamond.

"I shall have no faith," answered Gregory, "till I see my tankard."

"Hush! hush!" said Rosamond, "even such a word as that weakens the charm."

"Well, well! dame seems to have faith, and to like you; therefore stay here till midnight, and mind ye, if I have no tidings of my tankard then, off you go, instantly," said the man, in a threatening tone.

"Content," replied Ronald; "but, master, to show you that we are well able to pay our reckoning, only tell us the cost of to-day's fare, and you shall have the money."

The man seemed amazed and softened at this speech, and Rosamond sang,—

"Wandering harpers though we be,
We pay our way right cheerily;
And when we have spent our gold,
We seek for more by fortunes told."

"A gay life!" said the dame.

"Would'st join us?" asked Rosamond.

The dame looked rather inclined to follow the fortunes of the youth, she however answered, "Nay, nay, I will stay with Gregory."

During the evening the dwarf and the harper had many snatches of conversation. The harper told Ronald her plan of promising a restoration of the tankard, and if this should render Gregory troublesome, it were easy to leave the cottage immediately. Their safety could scarcely be compromised by this.

"Besides," said Rosamond, "I really mean to restore the tankard."

"Thou restore it?" cried Ronald.

"Yes, I have means of intimidation over Ferraud and his comrades," said Rosamond. "Let me but once place myself under the protection of Geoffrey de Albini, and I will deliver the tankard into your hands to be restored."

"Pardon my want of faith, comrade," replied Ronald.

"Well—judge me by my arts," said Rosamond.

As night drew near, the dame was evidently alarmed at the prospect of the spiritual encounter which was about to take place under her roof; she became restless and uneasy, and the conjurer took every means to increase her fears. At length the period for repose arrived, and Rosamond dismissed Gregory and his wife to their rest. Ronald had determined to take his night's sleep where he had taken it by day—on the bench by the kitchen fire. Rosamond was thus left, as she desired, in undisturbed possession of the chamber which she had already used.

Well and effectually did she weave her spells. From the moment that midnight had passed, till within an hour of daylight, a succession of noises of all unaccountable kinds, disturbed Gregory and his wife. Groans, yells, the hissing of serpents, and the croaking of ravens were continually heard, intermingled with shouts of what appeared to be unearthly laughter. The dame was so much alarmed that nothing less than the hope of recovering her treasure prevented her from beseeching the conjurer to give over his incantations. At last towards daylight all was quiet and the pair sunk into profound sleep.

While Gregory and his wife were taking the repose which their unusual state of excitement rendered so necessary to them, the conjurer and his comrade were very differently engaged.

The palfreys were well fed, bridled, and led sut, and the travellers left the cottage, long ere their entertainers had begun to dream. It was a lovely morning, and the fresh air seemed to invigorate every nerve of Rosamond, whose magical works had fatigued her considerably. She left a purse of gold in a conspicuous place in the kitchen, much more than sufficient to repay doubly the attentions of the dame and Gregory.

"We have nothing to fear," said the harper; "trust me, they will be amply satisfied."

"Without the tankard?" asked Ronald, doubtingly.

"Ay, without the tankard; but they shall have that too, ere long," she replied. "I only wish I were present when they discovered our flight."

"Save us!" cried Ronald, urging on his palfrey, "thou may'st like such jugglery; but for me."—

"And didst thou never like jugglery, Ronald?" asked his companion. "No, no, thou art too sober-minded. Thou hast never enticed a comely dame into the wood to have her fortune told, and eaten up her fowl and bacon while she was gone. No, no!" cried Rosamond, laughing.

"Art thou really a conjurer, or where didst hear that?" asked Ronald, in a tone of pleased vanity.

"Did I not tell you I served an apprenticeship to deceit and villany?" asked the harper, in a grave tone.

"Well, well, there was no harm done; better an honest man like me should have the capon, than thy masters the monks, and it was for one of them that the dame robbed her husband's hen-roost," said the dwarf.

"I know it. Father Paul did not thank you for that turn," said Rosamond.

While the travellers are journeying onward to the camp, let us return to Gregory and his dame.

Having overslept themselves by several hours, they arose, and were equally surprised at the height of the sun, and the stillness of the house. Gregory's heart misgave him, as he descended to the kitchen. "Sure they have not stripped us of everything," he said. Then seeing the purse, he exclaimed,—

"Dame, dame, these were true fairies, and good ones too."

The woman came hastily down stairs at her husband's call, and seizing the purse, emptied its contents upon the table. The gold rolled in all directions, and Gregory was one minute scolding his wife for her carelessness, and the next thanking his good fortune for having brought him such guests.

"You may thank me," said his wife; "if I had not had more discernment than you, they would have been turned away, and then bad luck to us."

"If you had not been struck with a smooth face you mean," said Gregory.

"Well, be it so," replied the wife.

"Have you looked into the conjurer's room?" said the man; "perhaps the tankard is there."

"No; I came down the instant that I heard you call," answered the dame; "but let us go up stairs together. I am not fond of conjurer's rooms."

"Although you are of conjurers, eh, dame?" said Gregory, good humouredly. "Well, well, we will go together."

They went up stairs, and, what was their surprise to see on the wall of the room, which Rosamond had effectually darkened, the following lines written in letters of fire :—

"When seven days are come and gone,
The lost treasure shall be won;
But seek it not, or to your cost
The tankard is for ever lost:"

"A poor promise, dame," said Gregory.

"Even this promise is better than none," answered his wife. "We cannot to look for our tankard, so we may as well hope for seven days, at least,"

"True," replied Gregory.

With this resolution to hope, the simple couple went about their ordinary occupations; the well-filled purse which they had found upon the kitchen table conduced not a little to the equanimity of their minds; and their principal care now was to hide the money securely, in case the events of the civil war should bring robbers to their dwelling, who would be less scrupulous in their gains than even the lawless soldiers of De Bohun.

CHAPTER XVII.

By the hope within us springing,
　Herald of to-morrow's strife,
By that sun whose light is tringing,
　Chains or freedom, death or life—
Oh! remember life can be
　No charms for him who lives not free!—MOORE.

As Ronald and his companion approached the outskirts of the camp, the spirits of each underwent some change. Hitherto, whatever had been their troubles, and perils, they had joyfully looked forward to the termination of their journey as setting them free from them; but, as the period drew near which was to separate them, and leave each to his and her own resources, a gloom gradually overspread them. In addition to this gloominess, and, as if purposely to increase it, the day had become overcast, and before noon the clouds had gathered all around them, and poured forth an incessant and heavy rain.

"How unfortunate this is," said Ronald, as they seated themselves under a large tree, to divide their last meal.

"Not so," said his companion. "It is unpleasant, certainly; but I rather rejoice in this weather, as it will enable me, with the less observation, to gain the tent of Geoffrey de Albini."

"And do you mean to attempt that alone?" asked Ronald.

"Certainly," replied Rosamond. "I know exactly its position, from the conversations which I have overheard between De Bohun and his followers."

"And the tankard?" asked the dwarf.

"Meet me in this spot to-morrow at sunset," said his companion, "and it shall be put into your hands, to be restored to the good people from whom it was stolen."

"Agreed," said Ronald, "and here we part for the present,"

"Adieu!" replied Rosamond, "till to-morrow at sunset. If you find me not here, you must conclude that I am a prisoner; but I expect no such misfortune."

The travellers took a melancholy farewell of each other; Rosamond bending her steps slowly toward that quarter of Matilda's camp in which was situated the tents of De Albini and his followers; and Ronald proceeding across the country to the army of Stephen. We must accompany the latter.

As he journeyed, everything wore the aspect of an approaching conflict. On account of the rain, which still poured down in torrents, which seemed to increase rather than diminish in violence, but few stragglers were to be seen; and those whom he did meet, scarcely vouchsafed to Ronald the passing compliments of courtesy. Apprehension, even dread, seemed to lie upon every brow; every step was heavy and hurried, every countenance care-worn. As the dwarf drew nearer to the camp, rather more bustle prevailed; perhaps in consequence of the preparations making to receive a large body of allies, who were seen at a considerable distance passing over a high mountain. Still everything appeared gloomy, and every person dispirited.

The first sentinel whom Ronald attempted to pass, questioned him closely as to his errand, and the place whence he came; but upon producing the passport which had been given to him by L'Espee, the dwarf was allowed to proceed. The succeeding sentinel was less civil; he pretended to doubt the authenticity of the passport, and Ronald was obliged to endure some cutting remarks upon his personal appearance, before he was freed from delay.

" A pretty errand," he said to himself, " it seems that my adventures in yonder cottage were but the beginning of my misfortunes. However, once in Tunstall's tent, I care for nothing, my intelligence will secure me civility, at least there."

At length the dwarf reached the tent he was in search of, and was challenged by the sentinel on duty.

" Well, my fine fellow," cried the soldier, " what dost want? to enlist, eh? our lord will be truly glad of such a comely knight."

" Peace, fellow," replied Ronald; " I seek your lord upon private business."

" And of course you expect that my lord will be ready to attend to you," said the soldier, jeeringly.

" Yes, I do," said Ronald; " and I desire to be conducted to him without delay."

" A modest request," cried the soldier, " in these times. Why, man, or whatever you are, we are every day expecting to fight for our king and country, and confusion to our enemies! Hurrah !"

Ronald joined in the shout, and by his fervent exclamations in favour of King Stephen, he in a short time so won upon the soldier, that the latter offered to conduct him to the presence of Tunstall.

Upon entering the tent, which was of rich materials, evidently of eastern manufacture, and profusely decorated with oriental ornaments, Ronald was completely astonished and bewildered. The sides of the tent were hung with arms of all kinds, various in their sizes and uses, but all of the most gorgeous materials and the most elaborate workmanship, evidently chosen for their beauty as well as their usefulness. Upon a sofa of eastern construction, lay a warrior of middle age, fully accoutred for battle; his polished and highly-ornamented armour strongly contrasting with the embroidered satin couch on which he reclined. The first glance of all around would have impressed the beholder with the idea that he saw before him a mere carpet knight,—and not one of the stanchest supporters and most valorous defenders of Stephen. But a more minute observation would convince the spectators that De Tunstall was in every respect a hardy and brave soldier; his sword, of the best Damascus steel, and curiously inlaid with gold, had done ample service in the plains of Palestine; and his baldric, although embroidered with gems of great value, had faced many valiant and persevering foes.

Upon the entrance of Ronald the knight raised himself from his couch, and in a stern voice demanded why he was disturbed.

" This person insisted upon an entrance," said the soldier.

" I cannot and will not speak to him now," said the knight.

" My errand is of importance, I beseech you to hear me," cried Ronald.

" Whence come you?" asked Tunstall, " from Stephen our king ?

" No," replied the dwarf; then looking at the guard, he added, " mine is a secret mission, from one who ought to be dearer to you even than your king."

" What mean you ?" asked the knight, impatiently.

" These letters will tell you." answered Ronald, presenting the papers. " They are from a brave and trusty knight, although now disabled from battle, Robert L'Espee."

" You say truly, L'Espee is a valiant knight, and much do we feel his absence. Retire, friend, until I have read the letters he sends," said Tunstall.

Ronald made an obeisance, and left the tent. The guard took him to an adjoining one, where there were several soldiers carousing, apparently forgetful that a few days, even hours, might lay them breathless upon the field of battle. The entrance of Ronald seemed to be a signal for their renewed festivity; an attack was immediately made upon him, and he was required to join in their noisy mirth. This was by no means agreeable to the dwarf, who was under considerable apprehension as to the issue of the interview with De Tunstall. He, however, gladly partook of the fare which was set before him, undisturbed by the jeers of his companions at his uncouth figure and appearance.

While the dwarf was busily engaged in devouring the remains of a piece of beef, and solacing his thirst with copious draughts of ale, he listened, with a curious ear, to the conversation (if so it might be called,) that was passing around

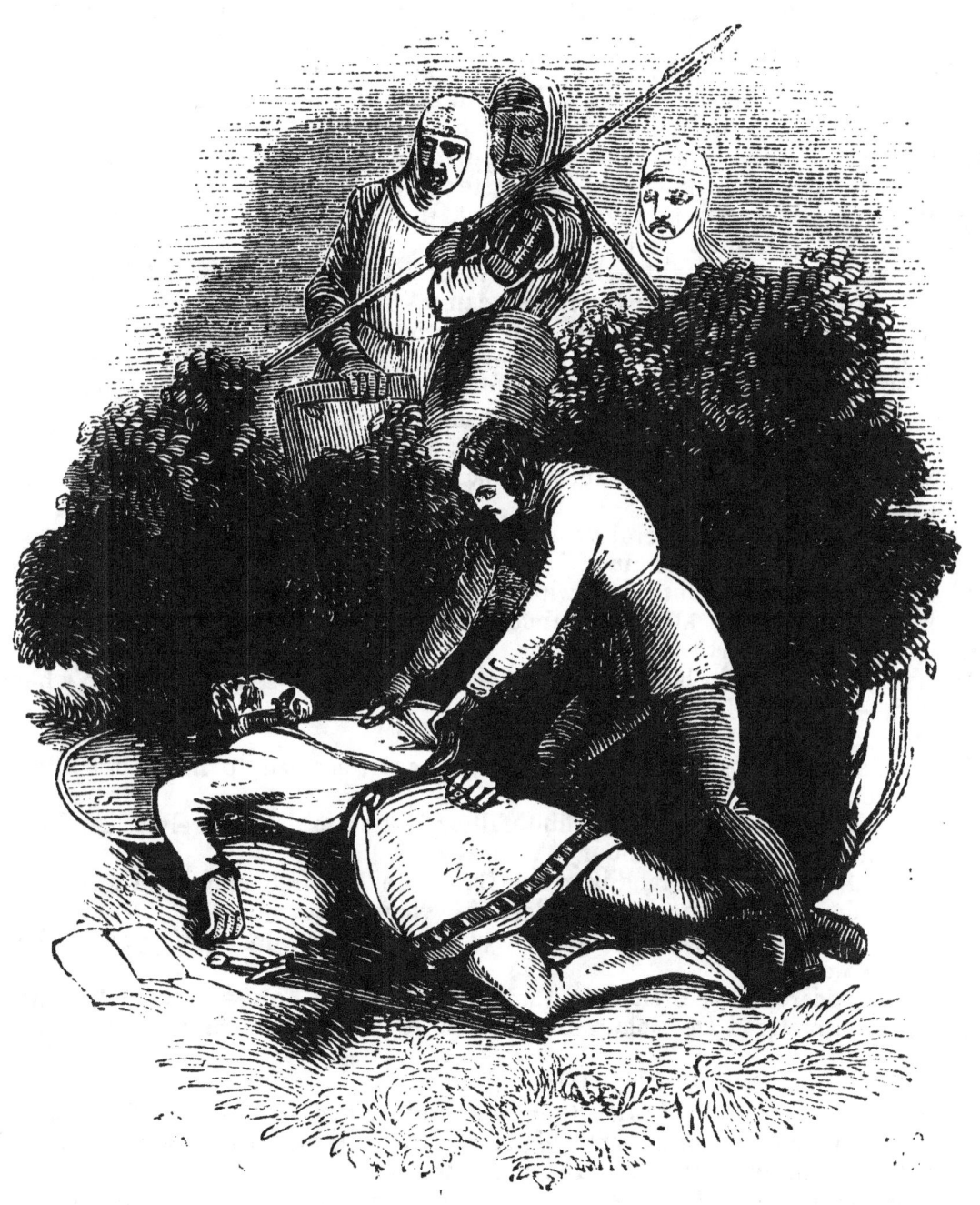

him. Every one seemed eager to speak, none willing to hear; and the confused jabber of tongues could not lead Ronald to any conclusion upon the subject upn which he was the most anxious namely; the probability of an immediate engagement, when his ear caught the name of his master, the Baron de Fougeres.

"Shame!" cried one of the men, "that the baron should desert us at the last moment; I did not think De Fougeres was a coward."

"Nor any one else, till now," cried another.

"He is no coward," said one of the soldiers, coming forward ; "I would stake my life upon the Baron de Fougeres' courage,"

"Why, then, run home to his own castle at this moment when we are not sure of safety for an hour ?" asked the first speaker.

"Is there no motive but cowardice, think you ?" said the man who had defended the baron. "Has he not left a gentle and lovely daughter in his castle, and may he not wish to take leave of her at the last minute ?"

"Nonsense,—nonsense,—who thinks of daughters now ?" cried a soldier

"I believe he is gone to Matilda's camp," said the first speaker.

"What ! desert his king ? No,—no !" cried many voices.

Ronald had some difficulty in restraining himself at this insinuation. Although he did not leave the Baron de Fougeres, he knew him to be honourable and valiant, and he burned to say so. His unjust imprisonment ever seemed to be forgotten, in his wish to exculpate his master from the possibility of treachery to Stephen. His advocacy, however, was not needed ; the absurdity of such a supposition being soon apparent to the talkers.

"It would be a pretty thing, truly, for the baron to go over to Matilda, and leave his son-in-law, that is to be, in our camp," said a man."

"What the young Mowbray ?—a brave youth, that," said another.

"He is likely to do good service to our cause," said the defender of the baron. "Depend upon it, De Fougeres is merely gone to make some arrangements, it case he should fall in battle, and to persuade the old Lady de Mowbray to le her son marry the girl as soon as he comes from the war.

"Hold your peace," cried a soldier who had just entered, "and do not talk of wha you do not understand."

"It is Bertram," cried several voices. "Now, Bertram, tell us, is your master, the baron, going to desert his king ?"

"I do not presume to interfere with my lord's intentions," replied Bertram ; "but of this I warn you all, that whoever dares to breathe a word against his honour, must answer for it to me."

At these words Ronald burst forth into the crowd, and seizing Bertram's hand exclaimed,—

"Well spoken, brave Bertram !"

The soldier started back at the apparition, for so it seemed to him ; but after a moment, recollecting himself, he said,—

"And what brings you here, my fine fellow ?—not to fight surely ? And how are all the home birds at Thornbury ?"

"Well and safe. My errand is to the Baron de Tunstall, and I am waiting to be summoned to his presence. But, Bertram, where is our master ?"

"Gone, as you have heard, to Thornbury," replied Bertram. "Did you not meet him on your way ?"

Ronald shuddered at the reflection that had he and De Fougeres met, the latter would have encountered De Bohun also, and he replied in a triumphant tone,—

"No, happily."

"Art in disgrace then ?" asked Bertram.

"Oh no !" answered the dwarf ; then in a whisper to Bertram, "Father Augustine, now the Baron de Bohun, with his band, overtook me on my way. I would not that the Baron de Fougeres had met that man."

Bertram made a sign of acquiescence. "Our young Lady Edith, how bears she her knight's absence ?" he asked.

"She is at Mowbray Castle," replied Ronald. "I could tell of one dearer and nearer to you, Bertram ; but I would not have these people hear me."

Bertram led the dwarf to an inner closet, saying,—

"Nearer and dearer ? there is not—there never was but one—poor Rose."

"And if I can tell you tidings of your niece, Bertram ?" said the dwarf.

"Speak, man," cried Bertram, "is she alive ?"

"She is," replied Ronald. "It is a sad tale of villany ; but those whom we suspect are innocent,—it is monkish villany. Father Augustine," added the dwarf, in a whisper.

Bertram's hand was on his sword in an instant. "Vengeance—vengeance—for my poor Rosamond!" he cried. "But where is she?"

"Here," replied Ronald; "at least in the camp of Matilda. She journeyed with me in the disguise of a harper, and having business of importance to communicate to Geoffry de Albini, she immediately repaired to his camp."

Bertram mused for a few moments. "Geoffrey de Albini," he said, "does it concern the young captive Edward?"

"I believe so," replied the dwarf; "but Rosamand said she dared not betray the secrets of the confessional. However, I am to meet her to-morow evening at a certain spot where we parted, and you may accompany me."

At this minute the dwarf being summoned to the presence of De Tunstall, no more could be said. Bertram, however, desired him to return to the guard-room, as soon as the interview should be over.

Many emotions chased each other through the breast of Bertram, while he reflected upon what he had just heard.

The sudden disappearance of Rosamond had caused much uneasiness in the neighbourhood of Thornbury Castle, independently of the wretchedness of those more immediately interested in her fate. The absence at the same time of the Baron de Fougeres, who left the castle without imparting the cause of his journey to any one, or even telling Edith where he was going, had tended to fix the stigma of her disgrace upon him, and his subsequent silence as to his journey caused the few who disliked him to conclude upon his guilt.

Father Augustine, too, not indeed by words, but by well-applied insinuations suffered it to be supposed that he, as the baron's confessor and spiritual adviser, was aware of De Fougeres having taken the girl away; and in consequence, her relations incessantly entreated him to discover her retreat. Well might he refuse this; and their importunities at times worked upon him so strongly, as to lead him to wish that there were some safe means at hand for ridding himself of his victim. But there were no safe means; the river would betray him; poison would betray him; it was not merely necessary to avoid the suspicion of being concerned in her death, but it must not be known that she had resided in the monastery; and although Father Augustine was well aware that such deeds had been done, and the perpetrator had escaped with impunity, yet he as well knew that in his case detection would most probably follow the commission of the further crime of murder. There were some among his monks who regarded Father Augustine with a suspicious eye—wickedness cannot always be hidden; and the mysterious thraldom in which he held De Fougeres raised the envy of those who were as ambitious as himself, while the virtuous shook their heads, and muttered something of "companionship in wickedness."

Thus was poor Rosamond's life preserved only through the fear of detection in her seducer; and thus the ignominy of a crime of which he was not only innocent but ignorant was fastened upon De Fougeres. Bertram alone, of all the baron's household, disbelieved his master's guilt. Favoured and esteemed by the baron, the honest retainer saw his character with clearer eye; and in spite of appearances and allegations, he acquitted him of his niece's misfortune. Still whom could he accuse? It were a crime against the Church to doubt the virtue of Father Augustine; and Bertram at last concluded that Rosamond—the Rosamond, who from childhood had been his delight and admiration, for her goodness and her gentleness, as well as her beauty, was in heart corrupt, and in manners a hypocrite. Gradually his mind had hardened against her, till the intelligence that she was alive brought back his better feelings; but even now he felt assured that if she had so forgotten her duty as to love the monk, he must cast her off from him, however penitent and miserable she might be.

One feeling occupied his mind which was utterly incapable of alleviation,—this was hatred of Father Augustine; and deeply did he swear that the monk should rue the day when he had destroyed the happiness of an innocent family. He would seek him on the battle plain; and if denied an equal combat with the proud Baron de Bohun, he would secretly rid the world of one who was unworthy to live in it.

For this he knew that he should receive the thanks of De Fougeres, whose subjugation of mind to the monk, Bertram had seen and lamented.

But as to Rosamond herself, what was to be done? That Bertram could not decide. He would meet her, and if she willingly renounced the monk, he would receive and protect her as his sister's daughter, until he could safely send her back to Thornbury.

With these reflections Bertram continued to occupy himself without being aware of the lapse of time, till a summons to supper informed him that more than two hours had elapsed since Ronald had been admitted to the presence of De Tunstall. Bertram was surprised at this, and inquired of his companions whether the dwarf had not been seen by them.

They answered that no one had seen him, and that he was still in the tent of De Tunstall, who had especially desired that he should not be intruded upon by any one. Bertram therefore was obliged to be content, although wondering at the long interview between the dwarf and the baron. This we will now describe.

CHAPTER XVIII.

The child may weep a bramble's smart,
The maid to see her lover part,
The stripling for a woman's heart;
But woe awaits a country, when
She sees the tears of bearded men;
Then oh! what omen dark and high,
When Douglas wets his manly eye.—SCOTT.

WHEN Ronald entered the tent of De Tunstall, he found the baron absorbed in deep and, it seemed, troubled meditation. Letters and papers lay scattered upon the couch beside him; and he held in his hand a small locket upon which he was intently gazing. Upon Ronald's entrance, he raised his head, and displayed to the dwarf a countenance upon which the traces of recent tears were visible. Tunstall, however, speedily recovered himself, and resumed his usual demeanour; then turning to Ronald, he said, " You have brought me unexpected tidings. Know you the purport of the letters of which you were the bearer?"

" In part, my lord," replied the dwarf.

" You are a retainer, it seems, of the Baron de Fougeres," said Tunstall.

" I am," answered Ronald.

" Are you aware that the baron has left our camp for a few days, on some domestic errand?" asked the baron.

" I knew it not till to-day," replied Ronald, " and I would it were not so; he could tell you much that you ought to know."

" You have seen my child, probably?" asked the baron.

Ronald bowed his head in token of assent.

" Tell me, then, is she like this picture?" asked De Tunstall, drawing out a small painting of a lady.

" As like as if it were herself," exclaimed Ronald. Then, after looking at it for a minute, he added, " No, Miss Cordelia is more lively than that face."

" She has not yet known unhappiness," said the baron, sighing.

" Not known unhappiness!" exclaimed the dwarf. " Is she not a dependent in a stranger's halls? is she not fatherless, motherless, portionless, nay, almost friendless? and even were she not all these, has not death removed her best friend? and does not he who ought to befriend her, become her remorseless persecutor?"

Ronald spoke these words in a tone of considerable warmth, and while he was speaking, a variety of emotions agitated De Tunstall.

"Blame not me," he replied; "I knew not till to-day of her existence; I had been informed by one who was acquainted with her mother, and attended upon her dying-bed, that the infant had died."

"Father Augustine?" cried Ronald.

"Yes; that was the name of the monk. I know him not; but the proofs which he gave were so strong, that nothing less than the letters of Robert L'Espee and this locket would have undeceived me. The monk was mistaken probably," added the baron, carelessly.

"Mistaken? Father Augustine mistaken?" cried Ronald; "not he!"

"Do you know him?" asked Tunstall.

"Too well," replied the dwarf.

"What mean you?" cried Tunstall.

"He has resided near Thornbury," replied Ronald, "and his endeavours to force the Lady Cordelia to enter a convent have made a great part of the wretchedness of her life."

"What motive could he have?" asked the baron.

"Rumour tells us of a stong one," replied Ronald.

"Explain," cried Tunstall.

"It is said that the father holds some gift of the lands of Eleanor de Dunstanville, which the friends of the Lady Cordelia might easily dispute," said Ronald, with a scrutinising glance at the baron.

"By our saints, these letters hint at such an instrument," cried Tunstall. "What character does this monk bear?"

Ronald did not answer, but looked round hesitatingly.

"Speak, man! of what art thou afraid?"

"Of him—of Father Augustine," whispered the dwarf.

"Fool, he is not here; tell me all," demanded the baron, angrily.

"I owe father now a night's lodging in a dungeon; my next offence might be more speedily punished," said the dwarf. "But I have heard the name of De Tunstall, and I esteem the Lady Cordelia, and I would fain do service to both."

"Speak, then; on the word of a knight, thou shalt not be harmed for the truth of thy tongue," said the baron.

"Know you the Baron de Bohun of Matilda's camp?" asked Ronald.

"I heard, yesterday, of the arrival of such an one, with a small band of retainers; men, it is said, of desperate character and fortune," replied Tunstall.

"True enough. He, their leader, is Father Augustine; and a more wily priest, or a more licentious soldier, never disgraced either name," said Ronald. "Of the dealings of the father in Thornbury Castle, I may suspect much that I dare not speak; of his conduct to the Lady Cordelia I may speak. She is all that the proudest knight can admire, thanks to her friend, our late Lady Abbess, who has given her all the accomplishments due to her station. It were a pity indeed that so gay and brilliant a bird should be immured in a nunnery."

"It shall not be; I will immediately claim her dowry; and as soon as these wars are over, I will seek among the young knights of Stephen's court, a fitting husband for my niece," said the baron.

Ronald shook his head; which Tunstall observing, said,—

"Dost think then she would not wed?"

"She has seen nothing beyond the convent walls," replied Ronald, "and she is young."

"Well, that must await for peace. Meanwhile I would have you return to Thornbury, carrying my acknowledgments and tender affection to your lady, and assuring her that I will myself claim her as soon as the event of this battle allows me to do so. And to Robert L'Espee," added the baron, "I desire you to deliver the letters which I shall make ready for you. One word more. Does the Father Augustine, or whatever he calls himself, know of this matter?"

"Certainly not," replied the dwárf, "would I were a soldier, and he should pay the penalty of his numerous sins; I would avenge the orphan and the betrayed."

In answer to the inquiry of the baron, Ronald related the history of Rosamond, dwelling warmly upon the various crimes of the father. Tunstall was astonished, and declared his intention of revealing the whole to the Baron de Fougeres, as soon as the latter should return to the camp. Then dismissing the dwarf, he bade him be in readiness to depart on the following day.

Ronald retired from the tent somewhat happier than he had entered it; he had given vent to his anger against Father Augustine, and he hoped he had said enough to ensure the vengeance of De Tunstall against him. His thoughts now turned to his meeting with Rosamond, of whom we must give some account.

After parting with the dwarf, Rosamond proceeded quietly on her journey to the camp of Matilda. Much caution was necessary, to avoid the stragglers from the camp, particularly any who might belong to De Bohun's party; these difficulties, however, her prudence successfully overcame, and at length she found herself near the tent of Geoffrey de Albini. Now her courage failed her; she was about to present herself to a noble baron, who, except by reputation, was an entire stranger to her, and Rosamond's heart sunk within her, when she remembered how much of her own story was necessary to be revealed, and the shame which such a disclosure must bring upon her. The desire of revenge was, however, stronger than even shame.

Upon application to the guard she was immediately admitted to the presence of De Albini.

"Will you give audience to one who brings tidings of your son?" asked Rosamond, still disguised as a harper.

"My son! my Edward?" exclaimed the bereaved father.

"He is well, compose yourself; he is in captivity, but in honourable, in respected captivity," said Rosamond.

"Alas!" said Albini, "how must his noble spirit pine for action."

"It pines for action, and for the society of those he loves," replied Rosamond. "Well may the heart of Edward de Albini be sad, but it shall speedily be gladdened."

"How!" cried the baron, "will his unrelenting gaoler set him free? Oh, tell me that you bear such blessed tidings."

"Alas! I have no such glad commission," answered Rosamond. "De Fougeres fights zealously for his king; and until the cause which now distracts our unhappy country be determined, he will not, by giving liberty to his young prisoner, add another arm to those which fight for Matilda."

"Would, indeed, that this disastrous war were terminated," said De Albini. "Might I then hope to behold my only son, my only child, once more?"

"Your only son, but would I dared to say not your only child," said Rosamond.

"What meanest thou? Dost thou not know the sad fate of my infant daughter?" asked De Albini.

"I do know it; the melancholy history is not forgotten at Thornbury," replied Rosamond; "but you know not positively that she was drowned."

"There was, at least, every reason to suppose it," said the baron. "Speak plainly, good youth, knowest thou aught which may contradict this?"

"Be patient! I can but give a slight hope; time must bring the hidden things to light," answered Rosamond. "Methinks I have brought tidings already well worth hearing, of the health and peace of your son."

"True—true!" cried de Albini.

"I must speedily return, unless the Baron de Albini will consent to rescue from misery and shame one who has brought happiness to him," said Rosamond.

"What dost mean? who art thou?" cried the baron.

"One more weak than wicked," answered Rosamond; "a victim to priestly villany, but not the participator in crime. Dost know the Baron de Bohun?"

"By name only," replied the baron.

"He was the Father Augustine of the monastery of Thornbury," said Rosamond.

De Albini started. He at once remembered that, when called to the council board, the Baron de Bohun had especially shunned the presence of Geoffrey de Albini, and that various comments had been made upon this conduct. In the only passing glimpse which he had caught of De Bohun's countenance, it had struck De Albini as familiar to his memory, although he had vainly endeavoured to recal to his mind where he had met with such a person. All this mystery was now cleared up ; Father Augustine had been the trusted inmate of Thornbury Castle, in those days of early happiness ; and when misfortune came, his exhortations to peace and resignation had been a means of strengthening the minds of the bereaved parents.

"To this man," continued Rosamond, "does the unhappy being before you owe the loss of family, station, and respectability. I am the daughter of one of the most devoted followers of Geoffry de Albini! but alas! my conduct has brought my parents to the grave. This wily monk, I know not how, gained upon my confidence, and by his arts and promises induced me to leave my happy home. For three years I was a prisoner in the monastery of Thornbury, while my friends were vainly seeking me from home. How I endured this, I know not ; a spell was over me, until that man unveiled his wicked purposes, and I found that my eyes were opened.

"Circumstances had given Father Augustine some control over an orphan, who resides with the Lady Edith, the daughter of Ralph de Fougeres ———"

A deep groan from her auditor here interrupted Rosamond. She cast a pitying glance at the baron, and proceeded.

"I would not have named that name, it is painful now, but the daughter of De Fougeres is worthy to bear it."

"Go on, go on," cried the baron ; "tell me of yourself."

"The Lady Cordelia de Dunstanville had withstood every endeavour of Father Augustine to persuade her to enter the monastic life ; in vain had he employed threats ; the kindness of De Fougeres and his lovely daughter rendered such resource unnecessary. The father then formed another scheme. Tired of a monastic life, ambitious, and avaricious, he rejoiced in the wars which distract our country, and resolved to embark anew in the turmoil of the world. Deeply was his plan laid. He sought to win wealth, command renown ; and the further reward of his toil is to be the hand of Cordelia. But it will never be—it shall never be— he who betrayed Rosamond, shall not marry Cordelia."

Albini had listened with interested attention to the narration of Rosamond; he now asked how it in any way affected him ?

"Vitally," replied Rosamond. "An attachment has sprung up between the Lady Cordelia and your beloved son."

"An attachment!" exclaimed De Albini ; "Oh! woe—woe to his father's house !"

"Say not so," replied Rosamond. "Cordelia de Dunstanville is worthy of his love."

"Is she not the daughter, ay, and the illegitimate daughter of the worthless Eleanor de Tunstall? Well do I remember her in her husband's house, ere she left it for the society of a villain. No!" cried De Albini, "never shall my son ally himself to the child of that lost woman."

"Hear me!" said Rosamond. "The Lady Cordelia is not illegitimate ; he knows she is not. Father Augustine, now the Baron de Bohun, knows that she is not. He has in his possession a paper declaring the marriage of her parents, and bequeathing to her the dowry of her mother."

"Then, what claim has the baron himself upon her property?" asked De Albini.

"Merely a gift from De Dunstanville on his death-bed of that which he had no right to dispose of," replied his companion. "But I alone know that the monk possesses this paper ; I learned it during my residence in the monastery ; vainly did the Lady Cordelia seek it among her mother's papers ; and now, although fully convinced that such a document has existed, she gives up all hope of recovering it."

"But wherefore not tell her of its existence? What motive have you for keeping this secret?" asked the baron.

"The strongest of all motives—fear," replied Rosamond. "Therefore did I come hither. The purpose of the Baron de Bohun is to obtain the settlement of her mother's lands upon the Lady Cordelia ; and then, by the threat of illigetimacy and poverty, to force her to marry him, the land being settled under that condition."

"Villain! but I am not deceived in him!" cried De Albini.

"He even intends to use your influence with Matilda to accomplish this," added Rosamond.

"My influence!" exclaimed the baron, "that cannot be. Never will I ask even a personal favour of Matilda, and for him, impossible!"

"Should the Lady Cordelia be proved the lawful daughter and heiress of De Dunstanville, and should you find her worthy to supply the place of your lost child, will you give her to her lover?" asked Rosamond.

De Albini was silent. He knew that the family of Cordelia were of the adherents of Stephen, and his own honour was engaged to the empress; still he felt that his heart was not in the cause which he had espoused. Disgusted by the rapacity which the barons who followed Matilda displayed, and having become aware of the character of the empress herself, De Albini saw, in the event of her success, but a long train of disasters at home, and disgrace abroad. Sincerely did he regret having embarked in such a cause; and his regret at the detention of his son arose more from personal motives than from any wish to entangle Edward in what he felt was a wrong cause. This secret feeling had made him hold himself, as it were, aloof from the council board, and the presence of his soveriegn; and although honour forbade him to desert the cause which he knew to be hopeless, he resolved to involve himself as little as possible in it. Hence the anger f De Albini upon being told that his influence was to be made use of by De Bohun to furthur his nefarious purposes; and firmly did he resolve to disappoint such schemes as much as lay in his power.

With respect to his own son, the baron was less decided. Unwilling to thwart his only son, he yet dreaded this unlooked-for attachment, and he was certain that the high propriety of the Lady Elfrida would never consent to such an union. These thoughts cast an additional cloud over his brow, and imposed upon him a melancholy silence.

Rosamond observed and guessed the cause of De Albini's melancholy musing.

"At least," she said, "you will give no aid to the machinations of my enemy."

"Certainly not," he replied. "I would willingly engage in any assistance to compel the Baron de Bohun to make you the only reparation in his power—marriage."

"Never, never! Have I been the inmate of his cell for so long, and not learned to hate him?" exclaimed Rosamond. "No; but I await the result of this battle, and my doom will be determined."

"How—what do you mean?" asked the baron.

"Should he fall, I only know where the paper is secreted," she answered, "and for that I await."

"But he may conquer and live, and then, surely ——"

"Then I would present myself before the empress, and declare his villany, cried Rosamond, proudly.

"Unhappy girl!" said De Albini.

"Well mayst thou apply that word to me," said Rosamond; "but I am not yet despicable. While I live, I will endeavour to repair the wrong I have in part caused by my weakness."

"How?" asked the baron.

"At the moment when I discovered the concealed paper, the monk [obliged me toswear that I would never discover it to the Lady Cordelia, or any one at Thornbury," replied Rosamond. 'I have painfully kept my oath till this day. nor do I think it is now broken. I suspect that Father Augustine has deeper, blacker, secrets in his keeping, but of them I can only guess. Will you receive me under your protection till the event of the coming conflict shall determine my fate, and that of the Lady Cordelia?"

"I will," replied De Albini; "fear not my protection and assistance for my son' sake."

Rosamond left the tent with expressions of gratitude, and sought the guard-room, where she intimated to one of the soldiers her wish to see Farraud, the principal follower of the Baron de Bohun. One of the men went directly to seek him, and Rosamond retired to meditate upon what had passed between herself and the Baron de Albini.

CHAPTER XIX.

By the perfection of thine art
Which pass'd for human, thine own heart,
By thy delight in others' pain,
And by thy brotherhood of Cain,
I call upon thee! and compel
Thyself to be thy proper Hell.—BYRON.

WHAT was Ferraud's astonishment at beholding Rosamond. A few words told him all of the past that she wished him to be acquainted with; but on mention o the tankard, his countenance was overcast.   He acknowledged that he knew of the theft, and had been much alarmed in consequence ; not that the conscience or feeling of a mercenary soldier could be made uneasy by such an occurrence, but he feared lest it should be known by the baron, who, however unscrupulous himself as to any gains which could with any appearance of propriety be made available to his luxury, was, at this time especially, in such a state of irritation, that anything which could tarnish the fame of his followers was sure of being severely punished by him.

A bad report of his company had, it seems, preceded the Baron de Bohun to the camp ; and the wily monk feared lest this should mar his ambitious projects. He was therefore unusually strict, and had desired Ferraud to keep a careful eye over the disobedient spirits under his command.

"Do not fancy our master grown honest," said Ferraud, "he is only wary ; and so morose and harsh, that I shall be truly glad to get rid of this foolish tankard."

" Then bring it to me at sunset, and I have means to restore it to the owner," said Rosamond.

'Truly thou art a witch," said Ferraud ; "how didst hear who is the thief?"

" It matters not," replied his companion.   " I have deeper matters to discuss now.   You know your master's temper ; I would not meet him at present, but if any harm happen to him upon the field of battle, send immediately for me ; even in case of death, let no one touch him till I am near."

Ferraud looked astonished at this discourse, and Rosamond continue :—

" It is for your own safety that I urge this.   Our master's compact with one whom I may not name, requires that none should he near him at his last hour, but one who is a party to that compact.   Dreadful would be the consequences of disobedience—death probably to all around him.   If you wish to save yourself from a horrible fate, promise me that should your master be wounded or killed, you will immediately send for me."

Ferraud was just about to give the required promise, when a bustle at the entrance of the tent attracted their attention.   The soldier went out to ascertain the cause, and came hastily back, exclaiming,—

"My master, the Baron De Bohun !'

Rosamond was in despair ; she had but just time to hide herself behind the hangings of the tent, when De Bohun entered, saying,—

" Tell the Baron de Albini that I, the Baron de Bohun, request an audience with him."

De Bohun was immediately admitted to the tent of De Albini, and Rosamond accompanied by Ferraud, escaped ; and the latter having procured the tankard, they repaired to the spot appointed for the rendezvous with Ronald, whom they found awaiting his companion.

" Restore the treasure to its owners," said Rosamond, giving him the tankard ; " and peace go with you, I am sure peace is not here !"

" Then why not return with me yourself?" said Ronald.

" No," replied Rosamond, " my duty is not done.   Tell the Lady Cordelia that I, humble as I am, may watch over the interests of the orphan.   And tell Edward de Albini that his father is safe.   Now adieu."

Ronald bade her farewell, and went on his way.   Rosamond looked after him for a few minutes ; then sighing, she said,—

" There goes as brave and true a heart as ever beat beneath a knight's corselet."

"A likely specimen of knighthood truly," replied Ferraud ; " methinks our master even were more comely."

" Peace !" cried Rosamond ; " can I not distinguish friend from foe, thinkest thou ? I have had experience of both.   Mind Ferraud, not a word must escape you of my being here, or thou knowest I can do that which cannot be undone," added she, with a gesture which her companion well understood.

Ferraud had been guilty of some offence towards his lord with which Rosamond was acquainted, and he knew that a single word from her might cause his death. He therefore gave in fear the promise she required.

Meanwhile on De Bohun's entrance into the baron's tent, he was received by the latter with a studied and stately air of courtesy.

"To what do I owe the honour of this visit?" said De Albini.

"The honour lies in paying it," replied De Bohun, graciously. "I wish to consult one of the most valliant and respected of our queen's barons upon the best means of forwarding a suit which I have much at heart."

De Albini made no answer.

"I have a ward, an orphan, young and beautiful, to whom I wish to secure her lands, in the event of our being conquerors. Her kinsmen are on the side of the usurper, valiant and powerful, and her patrimony will be confiscated and lost, if I do not make interest to prevent it."

Still the baron spoke not; and De Bohun, somewhat disconcerted, was obliged to continue.

"I would apply to the queen for a gift to me of those lands; in case that, by the rebellion and resistance of my ward's kindred to the rightful sovereign, they be lost to her."

"I comprehend not in what manner my little interest can avail," replied Geoffrey de Albini; "if our foes conquer, and Stephen of Blois be acknowledged sovereign of England, your ward's fortune is safe by the interest of her kindred; if Matilda's party be the victors, surely the interest of the Baron de Bohun is sufficient to secure her rights."

"Not so," replied the baron; "I am but lately returned from foreign lands, and consequently am almost a stranger to Matilda."

"But lately returned," exclaimed De Albini, "methinks—yet—"and he checked his speech; but enough had been said to alarm De Bohun, who answered carelessly,—

"However tardily I may have embraced her cause, the empress has not a more devoted follower than myself."

De Albini bowed, but made no answer.

"In short," continued his companion, "I would, if it were possible, have the dowry of my ward placed under my care; a woman, feeble and ignorant, is but a poor guardian of her rights in these troubled times; it needs a strong arm to repel aggression."

De Albini looked up in mute surprise. Prepared as he had been for almost any degree of moral turpitude in his visitor, this bold avowal of intended robbery astonished him. He made no answer, thinking it best to let De Bohun unveil himself completely.

"In case of Stephen's success, my ward would be utterly despoiled of her patrimony, as no doubt her uncle, who has entirely disowned her from her birth, would claim it; and the orphan would be left destitute."

"And therefore you would relieve her of the trouble of defending her possessions?" said De Albini, sneeringly; "a worthy charity, truly! and disinterested also."

"Not perhaps wholly disinterested," replied De Bohun; "as this unhappy war alone prevents our nuptials."

"In that case," said his companion, "Matilda will gladly confirm the possessions of your ward; and most truly shall I rejoice to see Cordelia de Dunstanville united in her marriage to one able and willing to reclaim her patrimony from the unworthy hands into which it has fallen."

How shall we describe the astonishment of the baron at these words? Dread, lest he himself should be discovered; amazement, at the information of De Albini at his knowledge of what seemed completely out of his reach to obtain; curiosity to learn whence that knowledge was derived—all struggled for mastery in the breast of De Bohun. The remembrance of the young captive at Thornbury Castle for a moment seemed to give a clue to the mystery; but well did De Bohun know that all communication between Edward and his family had been sedulously guarded against, and the idea was discarded.

"How know you the name of my ward?"

"It matters not," replied De Albini. "Not, however, from my son, who is unhappily a prisoner in the Castle of Thornbury, where the Lady Cordelia resides."

"You know not then of your son's unhappy attachment?" asked De Bohun.

"My Edward is too honourable, too good, to do anything which can anger me," replied De Albini. "You came hither unasked, uninvited, to speak upon your own affairs, not to interfere with mine. Have you anything further to purpose to me?"

Baffled and disconcerted, the Baron de Bohun feared to trust himself longer in the presence of one whom he felt to be his superior. He therefore took a hasty leave of De Albini, and left the tent. His meditations on what had passed were by no means satisfactory, except that it was evident to him that De Albini had no idea of his being the Father Augustine of the monastery of Thornbury. Not a look had escaped the baron which could raise a fear of such a recognition. Indeed, when he considered the number of years which had passed by since the father and Geoffrey de Albini had met, and when he remembered his total change of dress and manner, he felt entire security upon that point. But as to Cordelia, he feared his hopes were overthrown. He had hinted at the attachment of Edward, thinking that the anger of De Albini would be thereby excited against him; but seeing how calmly the unhappy father received the intelligence, De Bohun regretted having acknowledged Cordelia's right to her inheritance. He judged Geoffrey by himself; and supposing that Cordelia's fortune made him overlook the cloud upon her birth and situation, he concluded that De Albini would endeavour to gain her for his son's bride.

Thus do the wicked attribute to others their own motives and passions; and thus do they fancy themselves betrayed when they are merely conscience-struck. Still De Bohun did not give up his scheme, but resolved to carry it on more secretly; and vowing vengeance against De Albini, he returned to his tent to prepare for the combat which was expected to take place on the ensuing day.

Nor was the Baron de Bohun the only one whose heart was troubled. Throughout the camp all was silent bustle; the soldier was preparing his arms, the commander was arranging his method of attack. Many a lingering thought was cast upon the past, upon the peaceful hamlet, and the lordly hall; many an ambitious glance was cast upon the future, upon the gilded spurs, and the knightly sword.

The Baron de Albini had perhaps more reason to be thoughtful than many of those whose fate was soon to be decided; he had many misgivings as to the event of the battle; and in any case, he saw that between himself and the Baron de Bohun the torch of discord was kindled.

Far diffferent were the feelings that prevailed in the camp of Stephen. His troops, far superior in numbers to those of the empress, had the urther advantage of a commanding position. Between the two armies flowed the silver Thames, gently gliding along, unconscious of the scenes of carnage which might soon sully its banks. But it was not to be so. On the second evening, the Earl of Arundel happening, as it were by chance, to say that it was an unreasonable thing to prolong the calamities of a whole nation on account of the ambition of two princes, to many lords who were of the same opinion, overtures were made towards an amicable arrangement.

Prince Henry who commanded the troops of Matilda, and Stephen met each other on a narrow part of the Thames, and a truce was concluded between them, in order to give time to negotiate a lasting peace. Joy spread through both camps but there were two upon whose feelings the news acted vividly but indifferently.

Rosamond, whose dread of a battle grew more and more harassing during every hour of the night, beheld the sunrise with feelings of extreme misery; her woman's heart was full of wretchedness; she could act with spirit and promptitude, but she could not calmly await misfortune; and when, on leaving her resting-place, she was greeted by the joyful intelligence that the rivals were in conference together, and that there was every prospect of peace, a burst of tears relieved her full heart. Fortunately, the soldier who had communicated this glad intelligence, was too much occupied to observe her emotion; and speedily recovering herself, she sought her solitude, to indulge in reflection undisturbed.

Far different were the sensations of De Bohun. He saw his schemes of aggrandisement at once destroyed; his character probably unveiled, and where should he find a home? Cordelia would now probably be received by her kindred, that dream must be dismissed—her lands might be retained, but with difficulty; and the ambitious Baron de Bohun must sink into a poor courtier, if, indeed, he were allowed to attend upon the court of Stephen. Even a retreat to foreign lands was cut off from him; what then would be his fate? These thoughts, wretched as they were, occupied the Baron de Bohun, while all around him were rejoicing; one resource only presented itself. He knew that he held a heavy chain upon the Baron de Fougeres; he might claim, nay, even demand, whatever he required; were it even his daughter, his Edith, it could not be refused. Such a hint would he give as should secure to him the baron's countenance; but it must be done in secret, or he should betray himself. Ralph de Fougeres alone must know that Father Augustine still lived in the Baron de Bohun; the secrets of the confessional might be used as a threat, but they must not be revealed.

Yet for a moment De Bohun wavered. His fear, however, of De Albini decided him, and he awaited with trembling anticipation the effect of the impending peace. That it would unite friends now severed, heal feuds now sorely rankling, bind relatives now sundered, must be expected; but that there would be a sound, a lasting piece, De Bohun doubted. Fiery spirits were abroad, not easily to be subdued; and of these Prince Eustace, Stephen's eldest son, was the most turbulent. From him De Bohun expected disquiet, nor was he disappointed.

Before the conference between the two rival princes had terminated, the news arrived in Matilda's camp, that Prince Eustace, suspecting that the first act of amnesty would be his exclusion from the throne of England, had, after a violent quarrel with his father, left the camp of Stephen in extreme anger; and that, gathering together a band of desperate men, whose prospects did not accord with peace, he had marched northward, with the intention of spreading discontent and dissention.

This intelligence at once decided De Bohun's plans. Having nothing to lose, but everything to gain by war of any kind, he determined to embrace the side of Prince Eustace, and ordering his band to be ready for a march, he equipped himself, and at the head of his disorderly followers endeavoured to overtake the prince.

In vain did his followers inquire of each other whither they were destined. At first, they hoped that their master, with his usual caution or cunning, was leading them to the camp of Stephen; but a few words, dropped thoughtlessly from De Bohun, opened their eyes. A consultation was held, and Ferraud was deputed to inquire the destination intended.

Although Ferraud approached his lord with more than his usual deference, the brow of the baron became black as night, ere a sentence had passed his lips.

"It ill becomes the serf to ask the master's purpose," he said, in a haughty tone; "obey my orders, and trouble not your foolish heads for reasons."

"We are willing to obey as heretofore," replied Ferraud, mildly; "but when it seems that peace is at last about to be proclaimed, we think we have a right to know why we are withdrawn from its benefits."

"Coward! fool! art so fond of peace? go then, doff the badge of the Baron de Bohun, and take the monkish habit," cried the baron, in a rage.

'The self-styled Baron de Bohun may bestow upon me that which he has cast off,' said Ferraud, tauntingly.

"Ha! dost brave me thus, base slave?" cried the baron, striking him, "ho, there—seize the traitor!—bind him!"

Not a soldier came forward ; and the baron, losing prudence as his rage increased, drew his dagger, and made a thrust at Ferraud. The latter, however, sprung upon his master, and being less encumbered with armour, and more youthful, he held the baron in such a manner as to render his passion harmless. Meanwhile others of the band had come up, and seemed disposed to take their comrade's part.

"Villains ! slaves ! am I thus to be treated by those whom my word can give to death ? Unhand me, or your lives shall answer for it."

"Thou hast called me coward," cried Ferraud, "blood only can wash out the insult. Wilt meet me here, hand to hand for life or death ?"

"Meet thee, slave ? the Baron de Bohun meet a slave ?" cried De Bohun.

"Thou wilt not ! then thus do I remove the stain," said Ferraud, giving him a cut with his sword.

"Take this for Rosamond !" said one of the men, wounding the baron.

At that word a dreadful groan escaped De Bohun. He endeavoured in vain to defend himself ; all hated him, and all endeavoured to revenge themselves till overpowered by wounds and numbers, the proud Baron de Bohun sunk lifeless upon the earth.

For a few minutes the exasperated soldiers gazed upon the corpse without speaking ; they scarcely knew what they had done ; but the question as to what was now to ensue, struck all of them. Ferraud was the first to speak, and he suggested an immediate return to the camp. This was assented to, but the body —how should that be disposed of ?

Some, indeed the greater number, were for immediately and secretly interring it in a neighbouring wood ; and they were proceeding to strip it with this intention, when one of the men exclaimed, on opening the inner vest,—

"Ah ! what have we here ? our noble lord's patent of nobility ?"

"That lay in his sword, I fancy," said another.

Other jeering remarks were made, till Ferraud, understanding the subject of their conversation, came hastily up, exclaiming,—

"On your lives, touch it not !"

"What, Master Ferraud ! may we not read our lord's last love-letter ?"

"Hold ! I say, touch it not ! 'tis his compact with the evil one !" cried Ferraud, pushing his comrades away from the body ; Rosamond's words flashing upon his memory.

His words were enough ; all stood horror-struck and appalled.

"There is but one who may touch this paper," said Ferraud ; "we must bear the body as it is to the camp ; Robert, the harper alone may touch him."

"How knowest thou this ?" asked a man.

"It was told to me yester-even," replied Ferraud ; "we must do as I have said."

"But we shall be discovered," said one.

"Those who fear discovery may leave me," said Ferraud ; "I here declare that I will never disclose their part in this good deed, who care not to proceed to the camp."

Several declared their wish to go with Ferraud, but the greater part refused ; and Ferraud placing the body on the baron's horse, retook the road which they had before traversed.

"I would go to Geoffrey de Albini," said Ferraud ; "he was the only baron to whom our master was known ; he is honourable, and I suspect has cause of complaint against De Bohun. Besides, Robert, the harper, is in the train of De Albini, and to him I must straight repair."

CHAPTER XX.

They turned him on his back; his breast
And brow were stained with gore and dust,
And through his lips the life-blood oozed,
From its deep veins lately loosed;
But in his pulse there was no throb,
Nor on his lips one dying sob;
Sigh, nor word, nor struggling breath,
Heralded his way to death,
Ere his very thought could pray,
Unannealed he passed away,
Without a hope from mercy's aid—
To the last a renegade.—BYRON.

ALTHOUGH Ferraud adopted the plan of taking De Bohun's corpse to the camp, as the least of all the evils following the rash deed which he and his followers had committed, he dreaded the exposure of the murder. As he drew near the tent of De Albini, he felt more and more uneasy, till he resolved to halt at a short distance, and send to Rosamond the tidings of the baron's death. He therefore despatched the most trusty of his companions to her, urging her immediately to join him.

The soldier found, upon entering the precincts of De Albini's tent, that there was a general bustle. A truce had been concluded between Stephen and Prince Henry, with the understanding that the latter was to give up all claim to the crown of England during Stephen's life, and that he was to succeed upon Stephen's death. The partisans of Matilda were therefore left to make their own terms with the successful prince; and from the excellence of his disposition, this was supposed to be no difficult matter. Geoffrey de Albini had, however, a nearer and more interesting duty to fulfil, that of claiming his beloved son, and he was now preparing to depart for his own house, intending to send a messenger thence to De Fougeres reminding him that he must release the captive.

Rosamond had declared to De Albini that she would never again visit Thornbury, the scene of her misery and disgrace; and she had earnestly entreated him to let her accompany him to his castle, to reside there as an attendant upon the Lady Elfrida. De Albini objected to her disguise; but, at length, moved by her entreaties, he consented that she should resume her female dress when within a mile of the castle, and, on that condition, he would permit her to join his train.

Rosamond was sitting disconsolately listening to the old and warlike tales of one of De Albini's aged and trusty followers, when the messenger sent by Ferraud drew near.

"I am sent to Robert, the harper," said the man, "to request the lad to go with me to Master Ferraud, of the Baron de Bohun's company, that was."

"I am Robert, the harper," replied Rosamond; "what does Ferraud want with me?"

"I was desired not to answer questions," said the man, "but to request you to go directly with me."

This man had joined De Bohun's party after Rosamond had parted from it, and therefore she did not know him, and she felt a little unwilling to trust herself, as she thought it might be merely a scheme to get her into the power of her enemy; she, therefore, still hesitated.

"I am desired to hasten you," added the man, seeing her hesitation.

"I am no friend to the Baron de Bohun," said Rosamond, "and I fear him."

"His worst enemy need not fear him now; good and evil are not in his power," said the man, exultingly.

"What mean you?" cried Rosamond, astonished.

"He is dead," said the man, in a whisper.

Rosamond started up, and, rushing past the old man, to whom she had been listening, cried,—

"Where—which way?"

"Follow me," said her conductor; and he led her away from the camp, to a small glen, through which ran a brawling brook, by the side of which she saw Ferraud and his companions.

This glen was about half a mile from the camp. On her way thither, not a word passed between Rosamond and her guide. Her heart was full, too full for speech, and she was overwhelmed with the suddenness of the intelligence. Not the least feeling of love, however, pervaded her bosom. He whom she had once loved, and who had flung away her love, was no more; and yet Rosamond scarcely felt pity. Horror, at his being at last cut off in the midst of intended crime, was the prevailing emotion of her heart, as she walked on in silence.

Upon descending the slope of the glen, she beheld several horses tied to the trees, and Ferraud and his companions seated upon a green knoll, at whose foot lay something wrapped in a warrior's cloak. It was the lifeless body of the Baron de Bohun.

Ferraud arose, and meeting Rosamond, said,—

"Your presence is necessary here to release our master's soul."

"Tell me," said Rosamond, "how did he die, and where?"

"He fell by my sword," answered Ferraud. "Believe I was bitterly wronged, or never would I have harmed him; villain though I know he be!"

"A quarrel then?" asked Rosamond.

"He called me coward, and bade me put off my armour, and take the monkish habit. I retorted sharply, and he struck me. Could I bear that, and from him? He denied our equality, and refused the combat; then, I know not how it was, we fought; they," continued Ferraud, pointing to his comrades, "hated him, and they aided me; he fell.'

"Have you removed his armour?" asked Rosamond.

"They had done so, intending to bury him in the spot where he fell; bu es found a paper sewn within his inner vest, and I at once remembered that it mu be his compact with the evil one; and therefore replacing the paper, I sent for you."

"Right," said Rosamond, only smiling at her companion's superstition, "But in my presence you may unloose the paper."

"Not I," cried Ferraud; "I will not touch his wicked compact; and my companions are so horror-struck at the discovery, that they will not one of them approach the body."

"What can be done then?" asked Rosamond, in dismay.

"You witnessed the agreement," replied Ferraud, "you must unloose it; I have no objection to stand by at the time; and perhaps when this terrible paper is destroyed, I can persuade my comrades to assist me to bury the body."

Rosamond dreaded again seeing the face of De Bohun, particularly in death; but she remembered the importance of securing the paper, and requesting Ferraud's aid, she approached the body.

Ferraud drew aside the cloak, and revealed to Rosamond, the corpse of her enemy, awful in death; Rosamond started, and for a moment drew back appalled; but summoning courage, she said,—

"Unloose his baldric and vest."

Ferraud did so, and the paper was disclosed.

Rosamond, with a trembling hand, took a knife, and cutting the threads which confined it firmly to the vest, she snatched the precious paper, and retreated from the body.

The men crowded round her. "Burn it at once," said they. One of them immediately began to search for a flint, and another gathered some sticks for a fire.

"No," said Rosamond, "not here; not on the beautiful earth, which he was so unworthy to tread; not under the blue heavens, too pure to canopy him; no in light which was shamed by his dark deeds, must this be done. In darkness, in solitude, this paper must be destroyed. *I* alone must bear witness to its destruction. Leave it to me ; and let us at once give the body decent burial."

Ferraud agreed to this ; and his comrades having no objection to touch it, the corpse was speedily stripped of its outer garments, while Rosamond retreated into the thicket to secure the precious paper.

A grave was dug upon the border of the stream, and the body being laid in it, Ferraud covered it with the baron's cloak, and requested Rosamond to join the little band, and see the turf laid upon all that now remained of that ambitious spirit.

Bending over the grave, Rosamond in a low voice chanted the following dirge :—

> Sleep—thine earthly race is run,
> Sleep the sleep that knows no ending ;
> Dream not of the crimes thou'st done,
> Nor the guilt thou wast intending.

No. 16,

In thy dark and bloody pall,
　　Hands unloo'd thy couch are strewing;
No fair strains of music fall,
　　No sad tears thy grave bedewing.
Soldier rest—thy race is o'er,
Dream of glory's field no more.
Churchman rest—a quiet grave
Is all the realm thou now canst have.

By the monkish cowl and word,
　　Lur'd the victim to thy scheming;
By the knightly crest and sword,
　　Which thou hop'st would hide thy seeming;
By the friends for ever fled,
　　By the hate with which they shun thee,
By the life thy youth hath led,
　　By the death thy crimes have won thee;—
Soldier rest—thy race is o'er,
Glory's field thou'lt tread no more;
Churchman rest—a quiet grave
Is all the realm thy pride can have.

The task being over, Ferraud and his party prepared to return to the camp. Rosamond accompanied them.

As they were slowly walking onwards, one of the men having lingered behind, approached Rosamond, saying, "Dost remember me?"

Rosamond looked earnestly at him, and recognised one whom she had known in her happy days, but whose love she had then slighted.

"Norman?" she said. "Ah! how much of misery does that name recal to me. But why here? art thou too a friend of him whom we have just laid under the sod?"

"A friend but till time arrived for vengeance," replied the soldier. "It is over now, and I return to my peaceful home."

"To Thornbury, dear Thornbury!" cried Rosamond; "but wherefore vengeance?"

"For Rosamond's sake," replied Norman.

"How! did you—did all know of my disgrace?" asked his companion, anxiously.

"No—after Father Augustine left the convent, there were strange rumours of an inmate there; and fearing, yet hoping, that Rosamond might be the subject of them, I left my home, and endeavoured to overtake the baron's company, hoping thereby to ascertain the truth."

"But Norman was not with them while the poor harper was kept in thraldom by her enemy?" asked Rosamond.

"No; I overtook the party the very day after your escape," replied the man; "but from the description of the harper, and a forced confession from Ferraud, that there was mystery about him, I had no doubt of your being the person; and from that moment I was resolved on vengeance—I have had it!"

Rosamond sighed deeply.

"Nay, Rosamond," said Norman, "sigh not; but could I believe thou couldst for one moment regret the deed that has this day been done, I should be willing to cut off this right hand for assisting in its completion."

"You mistake me, Norman," said Rosamond, "I never loved him; I feared him, but I soon learned to hate him; and believe me, that although the deed of this morning may give love, wealth, happiness to some whom he would have wronged, it gives to the poor degraded Rosamond, a dearer treasure—peace and safety."

"Then why not return to Thornbury?" Norman asked.

"Alas! I cannot!" murmured Rosamond. "The Baron de Albini has promised me an asylum with the Lady Elfrida, and we depart to-morrow morning."

"Rosamond," said Norman, seriously, "hear me. Thou dost not know—I cannot tell, how I have loved thee. *He* never loved thee as I have done—as I now do. Why then a second time throw away a heart devoted to you, and you alone?"

Again Rosamond sighed.

"The Lady Edith de Fougeres—" said Norman.

Rosamond started, and exclaimed, "Would that I could speak to her, but——"

"Fear not," replied Norman ; " she will receive you, and pity you. She is ever ready to assist the unhappy, and she liked not Father Augustine ; he continually endeavoured to prejudice her parent's mind against her, happily without success."

"Ah!" said Rosamond, "she little knows Father Augustine."

"Indeed she will receive thee ; and the Lady Cordelia too; she has known sorrow."

"I will be the bearer of joy to her," cried Rosamond, in a town of exultation. "I will go to Thornbury." Then after a pause, she added, "But my kindred, Norman, are almost all gone ; who will receive the sinner ?"

"I will," answered Norman ; "my kindred will be your kindred, my home shall be your home. Speak, Rosamond, will you be my wife ?"

"No," replied his companion ; "my path lies in darkness and solitude ; I may not carry my sorrow into your dwelling."

"You will bring gladness to it," answered Norman ; "sorrow has dwelt there for many years ; with Rosamond, all would be brightness and joy. Refuse me not ! be my wife before we journey to Thornbury !"

"I fear," said Rosamond, hesitating.

"Fear nothing ; mine is not a love of yesterday. Let us be united to-morrow morning ; let me carry back with me the treasure in search of which I left my home."

With such pleadings did Norman urge his suit to the unhappy girl, and at length she consented to be his wife on the morrow.

"Meanwhile," she said, " I have much to communicate to Geoffrey de Albini ; let us part now; to-morrow I will accompany you to the priest of yonder abbey."

"And your apparel, Rosamond ?" asked Norman.

" I will doff my harper's dress to-morrow ; it has carried me well through many troubles," said Rosamond, "but I willingly lay it aside. Now, Norman, adieu."

"Farewell," said Norman, and they parted ; Rosamond seeking the tent of De Albini, and Norman pursuing the way to the abbey, in order to engage the priest to be in readiness on the following morning.

CHAPTER XXI.

To worth I would give honour,
  I'd dry the mourner's tears,
And to the pallid lip recal
  The smile of former years.
And hearts that had been long estrang'd
  And friends that had grown cold,
Should meet again like parted streams
  And mingle as of old.

And hearts that has been mourning
O'er vanished dreams of love,
Should find them all returning,
Like Noah's faithful dove.
And hope should launch her blessed bark
On Sorrow's darkening sea.
And Misery's children have an ark,
And saved from sinking be.—LOVER.

ROSAMOND immediately requested an interview with Geoffrey de Albini, which was granted. She briefly recounted to him the event of the morning, and related the discovery of the packet.

A variety of emotions agitated the breast of the baron. He could not forget that the unhappy victim had been his trusted and, apparently, sincere friend, for a short time, indeed, as De Albini had left Thornbury about two years after Father Augustine came to reside at the monastery; but even in that time he had gained some ascendancy over the mind of De Albini. Subsequent events had unveiled the dark shadows of the monk's character and conduct, and in the Baron de Bohun, De Albini could not, and would not, recognise his former associate. Now, upon hearing of his disastrous death, the feelings of former days returned in all their vigour, and deeply did the baron lament the wretched career of De Bohun. But for his death he could scarcely grieve, the manner of it was awful and appalling; but even De Albini saw that good must result from his removal from the scene of his crimes.

"What do you propose doing with the paper?" he asked Rosamond.

"I will restore it to Cordelia de Dunstanville," she replied.

"But you will not return to Thornbury?" said the baron.

"Yes, I will. My plans are somewhat changed; I have met with a friend of my youth in the company of the baron, and with him I will return. You also will visit Thornbury," added Rosamond. "You will yourself claim your child, your son?"

"Never—never—can I again visit that spot where my happiness was blasted," said De Albini.

"Not if that visit would restore the happiness which you lost?" asked Rosamond.

"It cannot," said the baron, "it is gone for ever. But my Edward remains to me; and if indeed Cordelia de Dunstanville be what you describe, I may yet have a daughter."

"You *shall* have a daughter," cried Rosamond; "I would but hasten the gift; it may be that the death of this man may give her to you at once, or it may delay the step; but I have some influence at Thornbury, and, humble as I seem, I may be of service to you. Meanwhile, prepare the Lady Elfrida to receive Cordelia de Dunstanville as a daughter."

"I must be assured of my son's attachment," said the baron.

"It cannot be doubted," replied Rosamond, "her company is his chief solace when she visits the Lady's Tower, accompanied by the Lady Edith, who alone excels her in beauty and grace."

"What can I care for the daughter of De Fougeres, except to rejoice that my son did not fix his affections upon *her*?" said De Albini, bitterly.

"They are nevertheless truly attached to each other; but the Lady Edith is betrothed to the young Eustace de Mowbray," said Rosamond; "and they await only his return from the war to be united."

"What, the son of my old and valued friend, the Baron de Mowbray?" asked De Albini.

"Yes," replied Rosamond; "the worthy son of a worthy father. It has been an attachment from childhood."

"Alas!" said the baron, sighing deeply, "how often did the Lady Elfrida and I promise ourselves that our own lovely child should, by marriage with De Mobray's young heir, cement the friendship of our houses. But it was not to be"

"Wait awhile," replied Rosamond, "and rejoice that your son has fixed his affections so worthily. I depart to-morrow morning; may I ask the Baron de Albini for his blessing upon my humble nuptials?"

"Willingly will I bestow it," answered De Albini. "I shall have letters for Thornbury; let me see you before your departure."

Thus saying, De Albini put some money into the hand of Rosamond, and she left the tent.

On the following morning Norman was in due attendance upon Rosamond, and they proceeded together to the chapel of the neighbouring monastery, where they were united. De Albini met them on their return, and giving them his blessing, and wishes for their happiness, they departed for Thornbury.

Rosamond had, as she promised, laid aside her harper's dress, and resumed that of her sex. She had carefully secured the important paper, together with the letters with which she was entrusted by De Albini, and she parted from the camp with feelings very different to those with which she entered it. Nor was hers the only light heart; all were rejoicing at the prospect of a lasting peace, and the manners and extreme personal beauty of Stephen, (perhaps the handsomest monarch who ever sat on the throne of England,) these qualifications, together with the wearisomeness of a protracted war, made all parties wish for a more settled state of affairs. Consequently every voice spoke of anticipated happiness; even the most determined of Matilda's followers saw the prudence of yielding to the ruling power, and the barons of the empress's camp were already preparing to swear allegiance to her successful rival. We must leave the camp, and follow Norman and his bride.

On their way Rosamond related to her husband her adventures at the little inn, and expressed her curiosity to see whether Gregory and his dame would recognise the magician and harper in his novel attire.

"I hope they will," said Norman; "they owe you some thanks for the recovery of the silver tankard."

"Yes" replied Rosamond, "I dare say they paid that debt to Ronald, who would be very willing to drink 'health to the magician' out of it. But there is the cottage. Now we shall see. Who shall speak?"

"I will," said Norman; "do not you speak till we ascertain whether they know you."

Upon knocking at the cottage door, Gregory came from the little enclosure by the side of it, and asked what they wanted.

"Food for ourselves and our nag," replied Norman.

Gregory started at the speaker, and at last said, "We cannot give it you."

"Oh yes, good fellow," replied Norman, "we will pay you well."

"You belong to that baron—I know by your cap; and his band are thieves," said Gregory.

"The baron is dead, peace is made, and we are peacefully travelling to our home," said Norman; "but we want rest and food."

"Dame, dame!" cried Gregory, "that robber baron is dead, and peace is come. Come here directly, and hear the news!"

The dame obeyed the call, and when she saw Norman and his wife, [she said sharply to her husband,—

"For shame, to let that nice young lady sit there waiting upon your temper. Come in, come in, we will give you the best we have."

"Well, I don't know," said Gregory, "but I do not like any of his folks."

"Peace, man; remember if they stole the tankard, it was my luck to get it again," said the dame.

"Yes; and you have never forgotton that smooth-faced young harper. For my part, I wish he had taken you to the war with him," muttered Gregory, as he entered the house.

Having seen that his palfrey was properly housed and fed, Norman joined the party in the kitchen, where he found the dame busy, preparing a savoury meal for their dinner; but every now and then stealing a look at Rosamond, who was quietly seated by the open window.

"Dost admire my bride, eh, dame?" said Norman.

"She is like some dream of mine," replied the woman; "there is a merry look in her eyes, that I am almost certain I have seen before; but ladies so seldom come here, that it cannot be."

"But harpers come sometimes, do they not?" asked Rosamond, turning round.

The woman started. The voice at once touched her heart, and she exclaimed, "The young harper, I declare!"

"Yes, dame; but no harper now, a young damsel, at your service," said Rosamond, making her a low curtsey.

"And my wife, dame," said Norman. "We must have a draught from the tankard to drink her health, must we not?"

"That is if the tankard be in safe keeping," said Rosamond.

"Oh, yes, my lady," cried the dame; "that queer man that was with you here brought it honestly back, and it has never been used since that day. Gregory keeps it safe hidden up."

"That is right," said Rosamond.

"If I might be so bold," said the woman, "may I ask how all this came about?"

"It is a long story, and not worth telling," answered Rosamond. "My purpose is answered, and you have your tankard; so we will ask no questions of the past, but enjoy a rasher of that bacon which I know is so good."

"I wonder what Gregory will say; I fancy it will be my turn to be jealous now," cried the dame, significantly.

When the repast was ready, the dame called her husband, saying on his entrance,

"Here is the young harper come again."

"Where?" asked Gregory.

"Here I am," said Rosamond.

"Sure enough 'tis his voice; how is this?" cried Gregory.

A few words sufficed to tell the state and relationship of his guests, and all sat down to dinner in high good humour. Norman and his wife did full justice to the cookery of the hostess, nor was the tankard seldom replenished. At length it was time to depart, when Gregory asked Rosamond if she still gave a song in payment for her cheer.

"With all my heart," she replied, "if you will take it without my harp."

This being agreed upon, she sang as follows :—

> "A wand'ring harper now no more,
>   At others' will I roam;
> But led by friendship and by love,
>   I seek my childhood's home;
> Where, all my toils and sorrows past,
> My footsteps shall find rest at last.
>
> "The bonnet with its broomy spray,
>   The nest of Lincoln green,
> The silken belt so proudly tied,
>   The jaunty air and mien,
> I've laid for aye aside, and now
> The modest wimple shades my brow.
>
> "Yet tho' my harp no more I bear,
>   Nor act the sorcerer's part,
> I still can sing a tender lay,
>   Or song to cheer the heart;
> Then give me, as I homeward stray,
> A kindly word to cheer my way.
>
> "The baron seeks his castle halls,
>   The knight his lady's bower,
> And peace broods, with her gentle wing,
>   O'er hamlet, town, and tower;
> Then let us drink King Stephen's health,
>   And to the nation, peace and wealth."

Rosamond's song was received with great applause, and three cheers having been given for the new king, Norman and his wife liberally paid for their entertainment, and departed on the road to Thornbury. It was dusk when they approached the village, and Rosamond rejoiced at this, as she dreaded meeting her former companions. With considerable trepidation she accompanied her husband to the dwelling of his parents; she dreaded her reception by them, fearing they would scorn the unhappy dupe of monkish villany. But Norman reassured her on this point, telling her that they were well aware that his only motive for seeking the field of battle was to discover the fate of her whom he had never ceased to love; and that he had always expressed his intention of marrying her, should he discover her.

Such assurances rendered Rosamond less uneasy; and the meeting between her and the parents of Norman was such as to make her happy. Gladly did they welcome their son's early love, and warmly did they promise that no endeavour should be wanting, on their part, to render the remainder of her life as happy as the former part had been miserable.

Many tales were related by Norman of the events of the battle field and the council; his heart had, like those of the inhabitants of Thornbury, always been with Stephen; he merely joined De Bohun the more surely to find Rosamond; and now that peace was established, by means of the recognition of him whom they considered their rightful monarch, every heart was light and gladsome. Perhaps in the whole of that monarch's dominions there was not a more happy and contented circle than the one gathered round the fire in an obscure and humble cottage in the village of Thornbury.

The inhabitants of the castle were less untroubled; De Fougeres had not yet returned, but he was daily expected, and the Lady Edith had returned from her residence at Mowbray Castle in order to be ready to welcome her father. Eustace, too, might soon arrive, it was well known that both were safe, and joyful anticipations were indulged in.

CHAPTER XXII.

Had I a heart for falsehood fram'd
 I ne'er could injure you,
For tho' your tongue no promise claim'd,
 Your charms would make me true.
To you no soul shall bear deceit,
 No stranger offer wrong,
But friends in all the old you'll meet,
 And lovers in the young.

But when they learn that you have blest
 Another with your heart,
They'll bid aspiring passion rest,
 And act a brother's part.
Then, lady! dread not here deceit,
 Nor fear to suffer wrong,
For friends in all the old you'll meet.
 And lovers in the young.—SHERIDAN.

On the following morning, Rosamond went to the castle, and, inquiring for the Lady Cordelia de Dunstauville, requested to be admitted to her presence. She was shown into a room especially appropriated to Lady Edith, and she found there her friends engaged at their embroidery. As Rosamond had not mentioned her name errand, the ladies were in perfect ignorance respecting her, till Edith exclaimed " Surely you are Rosamond of the valley farm ?"

Rosamond assented, and added a short history of her life, concluding with an account of the death of Father Augustine.

" I cannot grieve," said Edith, " he made my dear father so unhappy."

" No one can grieve," said Cordelia, " except at the manner of his death."

" We thank you for bringing us this intelligence. The Baron de Fougeres is expected home every day, and it will interest him to learn the fate of our former neighbour," said Edith.

" I have also tidings of the Baron de Albini," continued Rosamond; " and would be glad to deliver these letters to his son."

" The Lady Cordelia will accompany you to the Lady's Tower, where Edward de Albini resides," said Edith.

Cordelia blushed rosy red at her friend's words, and murmured her acquiescence when Rosamond said,—

" But my principal business is with the Lady Cordelia de Dunstanville; to her I bring precious tidings of happiness."

" What !" exclaimed Cordelia, " happiness to me ?"

" It has been my good fortune to recover the lost document of the Lady Eleanor's marriage," said Rosamond, drawing forth the packet.

. Cordelia uttered one cry, and fell senseless from her seat. Alarmed to the utmost, Edith knew not how to assist the poor girl, but Rosamond had more presence of mind happily, and she at once took every means of recovering Cordelia At length the patient opened her eyes, and becoming by degrees aware of what had passed, she said,—

" Oh ! let me see it !"

Rosamond handed the packet to her.

" This is indeed the paper, the loss of which cost the revered abbess so much unhappiness. Would she were alive at this moment !" exclaimed Cordelia, bursting into a flood of tears.

Edith tried to console her friend; but Rosamond, who knew that weeping would tend to relieve her full heart, advised her to give way to her tears.

After a few moments of silence, Edith said,—

" But are we certain that this is indeed the document which was lost? It is sealed; but Cordelia you have a right to break the seal, and thereby ascertain its truth."

" I need not do it," answered her friend. " I remember, as if it were but yesterday, the appearance of this packet, which I saw when the abbess opened the casket to present to me my mother's chain."

" And were the Lady Cordelia doubtful," answered Rosamond, " I could answer for its authenticity. I know it but too well."

" How ?" exclaimed both friends at once.

Rosamond blushed, and looking upon the ground, she said,—

" I was present when Father Augustine brought to his cell this paper, which he had purloined from the abbess, then upon her death-bed. He related to me the manner in which, when she requested him to search in the casket for the packet, which she described as being so precious to her child's welfare, he slipped it hastily into the sleeve of his robe, and then showed the abbess that the casket contained no such paper."

" Dreadful !" cried Edith, " and this man my father respected."

" Father Augustine, however, did not succeed in persuading my dear aunt that no such paper had existed," said Cordelia. " Her last words exhorted me to make every inquiry possible for it; and not only have I done so, but my kind friend Robert L'Espee has caused examination to be made at the convent near the place where my poor mother died; we heard that a box had most unaccountably disappeared some years ago; and from the copy of this document not being to be found, it was supposed to be in that box."

"The father again!" observed Rosamond, "I remember his journey into Cumberland."

"And how did you persuade him at last to yield this treasure?" asked Edith.

"He yielded but with life," replied Rosamond. "I knew of its existence, and of

the place where it was deposited; and, upon being informed of his death, I immediately repaired to the spot and secured the packet,"

"How shall I express my gratitude?" exclaimed Cordelia. "I am no longer an outcast; poor and despised."

"Alas!" said Edith, "will this separate us, Cordelia?"

"No," replied Cordelia; "never can I find a home so dear to me as this has been?"

No. 17.

"But your kindred, your uncle De Hesling?" asked Edith.

"He will be my friend," replied Cordelia; "but Edith has been my comforter in sorrow, my help in hope; she is dearer to me than any one else in the world."

Edith gave an inquiring look at her friend.

"Yes, Edith, I speak sincerely," said Cordelia, "I know not what my fate may be in that respect; but if I am doomed to disappointment, and if the cloister must at last be my refuge, even there, when every other love is stifled by duty, my affection for Edith will survive."

"Nay, nay!" cried Edith; "let us not look forward gloomily, you shall be happy."

"It would be presumption in me to offer consolation or hope, but there is one," said Rosamond, "who feels a lively interest in the Lady Cordelia de Dunstanville; one who has power to make her happy. I speak of the Baron de Albini."

Cordelia's agitation was extreme; trembling, and in tears, she said, "How does the baron know my name?"

"He knows your history, and remembers the infant of the convent with interest," replied Rosamond. "I would now see his son, and deliver to him the messages with which I am charged. Farewell, Lady Cordelia!"

Thus saying, Rosamond was going to leave the room, when Cordelia said,

"I cannot now accompany you to the Lady's Tower; my spirits are too much agitated."

"Compose yourself, Cordelia, I will be Rosamond's conductress," said her friend.

"Thanks!" replied Cordelia; "I will meanwhile seek my good friend Robert L'Espee, with him I will examine this important document."

Edith accompanied Rosamond to the tower, where she found the young prisoner more dejected than usual. The news of peace had reached him, and he trusted that now De Fougeres would restore him to his family. But could he leave Thornbury with an unrepining heart? Alas! no! feelings more tender, more enthralling, than those which were due to his parents, held him in their chain, and he felt that in gaining liberty, he lost happiness.

When Edith entered, she found Edward in melancholy musing in his accustomed place; but when she introduced Rosamond as one just arrived from the camp of Matilda, he started up, exclaiming,

"Oh! have you seen my dear father?"

"Yes," replied Rosamond, "and it is to bring you tidings of him that I now intrude upon you."

"Call it not intrusion;" cried Edward, "tell me is he safe?"

"He is!" replied Rosamond, "and he trusts that circumstances will soon enable him to claim and to receive his son."

"I know it," said Edward; "the kind dwarf has told me that there is at last peace. But does not the Baron de Albini grieve at this inglorious termination of our struggle? would he not rather lay down his life for the Empress, than give allegiance to Stephen?"

"I know not the secret feelings of the noble baron," answered Rosamond; "but his words to me were, 'Tell my son that I will be one of the first of England's barons to swear fealty to Stephen, and I shall do it willingly. I like his character, it promises well for England, and I trust he will earn his right to the throne by justice and mercy.' It was rumoured that the Baron de Albini had long held these sentiments," added Rosamond.

Edward was surprised; he knew his father's dread of war and love of peace; but he thought him devoted to Matilda, and he could not account for the change in his opinions. But Edward saw that his father's adherence to Stephen would remove one obstruction to his union with Cordelia, and having been accustomed to hear from Edith continued praises of Stephen's person and character, he had himself wavered in his partiality for the cause of Matilda. Still the idea that his father was aiding, with his person and his estate, her attempt to gain the throne prevented his entirely deserting her cause. He now expressed to Edith his joy at this intelligence, and avowed himself a convert to Stephen's popularity.

"But where is Cordelia?" asked Edward; "will she not rejoice with us for this happy peace?"

"The Lady Cordelia has received tidings which have somewhat agitated her," replied Edith. "Father Augustine, lately the Baron de Bohun, is dead; and his decease influences her situation in a most happy manner. I am not at liberty to explain exactly."

"Suffice it to me, that she is happy," said the knight. "But tell me of the father, how did he die?"

Rosamond narrated as much as it was necessary for Edward to hear, respecting De Bohun; interrupted many times by the exclamations of Edward, whose joy at being released from the persecutions of this bad man, was but slightly damped by the manner of his death.

"A glorious death on the field of battle would have been too honourable a fate," he observed; "he was a traitor and deserved to die like one. What will my friend Ronald say to this?" cried Edward.

"Ronald owes it from me that I should be the bearer of the news," said Rosamond; and if my lord will allow me, I will seek him at once for that purpose."

The young knight bade her farewell, with many heartfelt thanks for the tidings which she had brought him; and Rosamond sought Ronald, whom she found in the ward room of the castle eagerly discoursing with the domestics respecting the news from the camp.

When he saw Rosamond, the dwarf was struck dumb with astonishment.

"What! my young harper?" he cried.

"Hush," said Rosamond; "now, the wife of Norman, the carpenter, if you please."

"A pretty change, indeed, it may be said; why dame, the wimple is as becoming as the harper's cap," said Ronald.

"Nonsense! I have that to tell thee that will change thy mood," said Rosamond.

"Tell it then," said the dwarf.

"Our *friend*, the baron, is gone where neither thou nor I should wish to follow him," said Rosamond, mysteriously.

"Gone! how?" asked Ronald, scarcely understanding her.

"Cold steel, and a few resolute hands," said Rosamond.

The dwarf now understood what she meant, and jumping up and clapping his hands, he shouted, rather than sang,—

> Oh! weep for the Lord de Bohun!
> Sing a dirge for his knightly head!
> Our grief we will steep,
> In the goblet deep,
> And *thus* we will wail for the dead.
>
> Oh! weep for the holy friar!
> Let the muffled bell for him toll!
> Let his grave be made,
> And mass be said,
> And he whom he serv'd take his soul!

Rosamond begged the dwarf to moderate his transports, but in vain; he jumped, he danced, and uttered various strange sounds of outrageous joy; then breaking out into song, he shouted,

> Ho! master friar! art thou low?
> The dwarf a rare frolic will have;
> No more will I sleep,
> In the dungeon deep,
> But gladly dance o'er thy grave.

"What! hast not yet forgotten that?" said Rosamond.

"Nor ever will," said Ronald.

"Thou may'st have more reason to remember that song by and by," observed Rosamond.

'The saints forbid!" cried Ronald.

"Will you sing it again?" asked Rosamond.

"Not for a kingdom!" cried the dwarf.

"But if the Baron de Fougeres bid thee?" said his companion.

"I may safely say that," replied Ronald.

"We shall see," cried Rosamond; "the time is not yet come for the waters to give up their treasure, but it may be so one day."

Rosamond and the dwarf had then some conversation upon the scenes which they had witnessed together, and the adventures in which they had participated. Rosamond related her last visit to the cottage of Gregory, and Ronald described the joy of the dame on recovering her tankard. Rosamond desired the dwarf to accompany her home, as Norman wished to see him, and they proceeded to the carpenter's cottage.

CHAPTER XXIII.

Come o'er the stream, Charlie; brave Charlie, dear Charlie!
Come o'er the stream, Charlie, and dine with Maclean,
    And tho' you be weary, we'll make your heart cheery
And welcome our Charlie, and his loyal men.
        We'll bring down the black steer,
        We'll bring down the track deer,
The lamb from the breches, and doe from the glen;
        The salt seas we'll harry,
        And bring to our Charlie,
The cream from the bothy, and curd from the pen.—OLD SONG.

INTELLIGENCE arrived on the following day at Thornbury Castle that the Baron de Fougéres might be hourly expected, and in the afternoon he arrived, accompanied by Eustace de Mowbray. Who shall describe the joy of Edith! She welcomed her father with smiles and with tears of gladness, as if he had indeed been in danger on the battle-field. To Eustace she gave the hand of friendship and what was dearer to him—the blush of love. Cordelia, too, rejoiced in the joy of her friend, and almost forgot that the return of De Fougeres might be the signal for the release of Edward de Albini.

In order to do honour to their lord's return, and to shew rejoicing at the happy termination of the war, the vassals of De Fougeres had prepared something like a rural fete, to the arrangements for which the Ladies Edith and Cordelia had willingly lent their assistance. A tent was spread upon the turf, and various amusements provided for the villagers, while it was intended to lay the tables out for supper upon the terrace near the river. Upon being made acquainted with these arrangements, De Fougeres courteously entered into all the plans of his daughter, and persuaded Eustace de Mowbray to remain at Thornbury till the following day.

This, the youth would have been ready to accede to under any circumstances; and he now agreed the more willingly to it, because he had parted from the baron, his father, at a short distance only from the castle. He came to Thornbury with his father's permission at once to declare his affection for Edith, and to request of the Baron de Fougeres his sanction to their immediate nuptials.

In the evening, the villagers being assembled, Thornbury wore a face of mirth and happiness. Rosamond once more acted the part of a harper, and the dance was commenced by De Fougeres and Cordelia.

"I am but an unworthy partner for so fair a damsel," said the baron; "but thy kinsman, Robert de Hesling, will soon find thee a better."

Rosamond sighed. The thought that De Fougeres could provide her with a knightly companion to whom she would not object; but the sigh was in secret, she would not cloud the happiness of her friends.

The Lady Edith was led out by Eustace de Mowbray, and as they gracefully moved through the mazes of the dance, a murmur arose among the bystanders, that never had been seen a more lovely couple. The murmur reached the ears of the lovers; Edith blushed, and cast down her beautiful eyes, while Eustace looked round with delighted affection upon the gazers, and then whispered a few words to Edith that deepened her blushes tenfold.

Nor was De Fougeres an uninterested spectator of this little drama. Devoted as he was to his child, he acknowledged to himself, that, but for one little pang, he would willingly consign her happiness to the care of Eustace de Mowbray. What was that pang? However, he was cheerful and courteous; he had accompanied the court of Stephen to London, and there he had eagerly and with fervour sworn allegiance to him, as his rightful sovereign. There, too, he had met Geoffry de Albini; and surprised was De Fougeres at seeing his rival among the most honoured and favoured of Stephen's followers. A few brief words had passed between them respecting the young captive, but De Fougeres would give no distinct pledge upon the subject, and had speedily departed for Thornbury; while De Albini remained at court, with the intention of interesting the king in the liberation of the prisoner.

After the dance, the repast was served up, and at the close of it, De Fougeres desired Ronald to sing a song.

Various unpleasant feelings assailed the dwarf at this command; he remembered too well his last attempt in the presence of his master, and these feelings were increased by a most significant look from Rosamond. There could, however, be no refusal, and determined to keep strictly to the text afforded by the state of public affairs, Ronald sung as follows:

It was all for our rightful king,
  We left our peaceful home;
It was all for our rightful king,
  We went abroad to roam, my dear,
  We went abroad to roam.

Now all is done that men can do,
  And nought is done in vain;
Matilda, bid this land farewell,
  For thou must cross the main, my dear,
  For thou must cross the main.

She turn'd her right and round about,
  Upon the English shore,
And gave her bridle-reins a shake,
  With " adieu for evermore, false land,
  Adieu for evermore."

The soldier from the war returns,
  The sailor from the main,
The knight is come to claim his love,
  Never to part again, my dear,
  Never to part again.

The war is gone, and peace is come
  And all folk soundly sleep;
We'll dream no more of the thund'ring drum,
  And thou no more shalt weep, my dear,
  And thou no more shalt weep.

Loud applause followed Ronald's song, which might be expected, as all felt its beauty and truth. The dwarf himself, glad to have escaped so well, made his way at once from the company, lest he should be requested again to sing. But this was not probable; De Fougeres was anxious to have some conversation with Robert L'Espee, who acquainted him with the death of Father Augustine.

This intelligence seemed to relieve De Fougeres of some hidden pain; his spirits rose, and he laid various plans of aggrandisement for Edith. He declared to the good knight his intention of at once taking her up to London, and presenting her at court, where he was certain that her beauty and grace would be admired.

"And the Lady Cordelia," said Robert L'Espee, "remember that she is now the equal, not the dependant, of the Lady Edith; her beauty will secure her favour."

"She shall accompany us," replied De Fougeres. "Robert de Hesling is at this moment unable to come in person to claim his kinswoman, but he will receive her in London as well as at Thornbury. We will depart in a few days."

"Methinks," replied L'Espee, "it were cruel to the young knights of the court to take the Lady Edith there before her bridal, she will be much sought, doubtless."

"I would have Queen Maud herself grace my child's nuptials," answered De Fougeres; "it were a favour of some importance to me."

"Doubtless it will be granted," said L'Espee, "I will accompany you; I need the intercession of a friend to procure pardon for my long absence from court."

"I shall be happy to serve you," said the Baron; "you have kept watch and ward well during my absence."

While the above conversation was passing in the hall, one of a more tender nature took place in Edith's saloon. Eustace was there, pleading for an immediate betrothment, and a speedy marriage; to which Edith listened, nothing loth, but she knew that there was one, whose will had been her law from infancy, and whose pleasure now, must, as usual, guide her's. She therefore referred Eustace to her father, and the young lover declared his resolution to make the appeal early on the following morning, before his departure for Mowbray Castle.

"How sweet, my Edith!" he said, "to pass our lives together amid the scenes which we both love so dearly; to enjoy the shade of these groves, and the freshness of this stream, undisturbed by even a dream of separation."

"Ah, Eustace! but such may not be our lot. My dear father talks to me of the duty which a noble owes to his king; and he hinted this evening that I must accompany him to the court of Stephen. I like it not," added Edith, mournfully.

"Nor I," said Eustace. "I do not doubt my Edith's constancy, but I fear lest the gay scenes of the court, and admiring courtiers, should make my love less satisfied with her choice."

"Shame! shame! Eustace," said Edith, playfully; "have I never seen a gay cavalier, thinkest thou? or heard the language of admiration from any but thyself? and wilt thou not trust me?"

"Yes, yes, forgive me, dearest Edith! I do trust thee; but I have strange misgivings sometimes. I overheard a word from one of the villagers this evening which alarmed me."

"What was it?" asked Edith.

"Nay, it was but a word, and I know not why it vexed me. Norman's bride said to him as you passed, talking smilingly to the baron, 'He loves her too well; he will sacrifice his duty, and her happiness will be lost.' What could these words mean, my Edith!"

"I cannot guess; that young woman is more shrewd and knows more of every thing than she choses to say. I fancy she learned much of Father Agustine," replied Edith.

"The words made me uneasy," said Eustace, "although I comprehend them not; and this scheme of De Fougeres of taking you to court seems to give them truth. Will my dearest Edith, join me in beseeching that our bridal may take place before our removal to London?" said Eustace tenderly.

Edith looked down, and then giving her hand to her lover said, " Be it as you wish, if my dear father will consent."

" And may I find Edith here to-morrow morning, if I bring the baron hither to ask her consent to fix a day in the approaching week?" said Eustace.

" I am usually here in the morning," replied Edith,

" Then to-morrow morning, dearest Edith," replied Eustace, " will seal my fate,"

" Farewell, Eustace," said Edith.

" Farewell, deare t," replied her lover.

De Fougeres retired to rest with visions of ambition and grandeur floating in his brain. He fell asleep, and the thoughts which had fascinated his waking hours influenced his dreams. He fancied that he was at the court of Stephen, attending a court ball; courtiers and high-born ladies, were around him, the saloon was lighted by a hundred lamps, the walls were splendidly adorned with pictures and tapestry; bright eyes were glancing, and fair forms moving in every direction; but the fairest, the brightest of the brilliant assemblage was his own Edith. He thought that he was leading up to her a young knight, who had requested her hand as a partner in the dance, when, just as he had placed the hand of his child in that of the young knight, a monkish robe seemed to be flung around Edith. The countenance of the knight assumed the features of Edward de Albini, and a voice, which De Fougeres recognised but too well as that of Father Augustine, cried in a loud tone, " BEWARE!"

De Fougeres started with horror from his couch; he knew not the exact purport of his appalling dream, but it touched a secret chord in his breast, and aroused, feelings which he in vain endeavoured to appease. Had Edith given her affections to Edward de Albini? He ought to have foreseen such a circumstance, and have provided against it. He had done so; he had encouraged the hopes and the devoted love of Eustace de Mowbray, and his awakened reason assured him that Edith was equally devoted to Eustace. Every occurrence of the past evening, every circumstance of many past years, proved this, and should a dream, however frightful, prevent his uniting the lovers? No—and yet the tone, the words, the gesture, of the dreaded monk, bewildered him. But was it a dream, only a dream, and should a brave knight be driven from his purpose by a dream? He would give his consent to the immediate nuptials of Eustace and his beloved daughter, and forget his shadowy persecutor.

Again De Fougeres sought rest upon his couch. He had, as he thought, calmed his mind by reason and reflection, and fatigued his body by pacing with a hurried step forwards and backwards in his room, and he hoped that a refreshing and dreamless sleep would be the consequence.

But De Fougeres was deceived; conscience once roused is not so easily lulled. The scene of his dream was indeed changed, but its purport remained the same. He stood in the chapel of his castle; before the altar kneeled Edith and Eustace. when a form, assuming at one moment the likeness of De Hesling, and at another, of Geoffery de Albini, gradually withdrew Edith from the embrace of her lover, who, in vain endeavoured to rescue her; while the form of Edith changed to that of one dearly but vainly beloved in the days of youth by De Fougeres. Springing forward to claim and save his daughter, a strong arm, clothed in a monk's habit, held him back, while the same terrible voice which had disturbed his former slumbers again cried out, "Beware!" Immediately the scene was changed, and De Fougeres found himself in a barren desert, lying naked on the burning sand; beside him stood the dreaded Father Agustine, pointing with triumphant gesture to a castle brilliantly illuminated in the distance, whence arose the sounds of mirth and feasting. A name uttered in a whisper by the monk—the name of her whom De Fougeres had loved early and fondly, awoke the wretched dreamer, and it was some considerable time before he could persuade himself that he was indeed in his own castle, and in his own apartment. Vainly did he again endeavour to compose his spirits, sleep was now impossible, and the interval till daylight broke over the distant hills, was intolerably tedious to the harrassed baron.

The thoughts of De Fougeres ranged over the occurrences of past years with a scrutinizing glance; hatred, fear, shame passed before him; but all was brightened by parental love. His Edith had never disobliged him, and might he not look to her for the happiness of his later years? Alas! that conscience should be constrained to answer—"no!"

In the morning De Fougeres descended to the hall at his accustomed hour; there he met Robert L'Espee, who immediately exclaimed,—

"What ails my friend and host?"

"Nothing," answered the baron. "Why dost ask?"

"The paleness of death is on your brow," said L'Espee; "let me prevail on you to send to the monastery for Father Clement, he is skilful in herbs to cure all illness."

"No, no," replied the baron, "the festivities of yesternight fatigued me; this is all my ailment, it will quickly pass away."

"I grieve that any ailment should darken the happiness of your return to Thornbury," said L'Espee: "and besides, if I mistake not, festivities of a still more joyful nature, will take place here, and at Mowbray Castle ere long."

"I know not," said De Fougeres, sighing, "I sometimes fear——"

"Fear!—what?" exclaimed his friend,

"I fear that I have done unwisely in allowing such unrestrained communication between Edith and the young De Albini. But I thought not of love."

"Nor need you fear it now," replied L'Espee; "Edith indeed esteems him, but——"

"But what! oh speak, and relieve my worst fears," cried De Fougeres, eagerly.

"Edward de Albini's heart is otherwise engaged," said his friend.

"Tell me to whom?" cried De Fougeres.

"I dare not say at present," replied the knight.

"Then you know it not," exclaimed the baron, again remembering his dreams. "Oh, if you have any mercy for the unhappy in your bosom, tell me that my Edith loves not that youth; tell me that he loves not her. Their union never shall, never can take place; but an attachment between them would indeed render me an object of pity to my deadliest enemy, even to him who last night persecuted me."

"What mean you?" asked 'L'Espee.

"I have had wretched dreams. Methought that the shade of Father Augustine twice forbade the marraige of my Edith to Eustace de Mowbray, and the young Edward de Albini was mysteriously implicated in this declaration.

"It is strange," said L'Espae, "but it is only a dream."

"Yes. it is more than a dream; I feel that it is," exclaimed the baron. "The father was so frequently here, that he must have become acquainted with the most secret heart of my Edith, and I fear that it is from some of these observations that he has come from his grave to give me this warning."

Robert L'Espee mused for some time in silence. Consonant with the superstition of the times, his mind was impressed with the truth of such a vision as that by which his friend had been so much disturbed, and he revolved in his mind all that he knew respecting the attachment of Edward to Cordelia, without being able to reconcile it with the mysterious warning.

"You know her habits," said De Fougeres; tell me, did my child ofen visit the tower alone?"

"Certainly she did," replied L'Espee.

"And may not an unhappy attachment have sprung up?" asked De Fougeres.

"It may, but indeed—indeed my friend, it is not so," said the baron. Edward is attached deeply attached, to another, and he awaits but freedom to avow it.

"He shall be free then," exclaimed de Fougeres. "But beware that I am not deceived; the moment which brings the avowal of love from the son of Geoffrey De Albini to my daughter, that very moment shall be my last. Rather would live an outcast in a desert land, than see their union.

"I understand not the violence of your antipathy," said the baron, "but if you still fear their love, surely it would be well to question your Edith upon it."

"It shall be so" answered his friend, "your counsel is wise."

Thus saying, De Fougeres joined the assembled family at their morning's meal. Every other brow was open and happy, his alone was troubled. The affectionate heart of Edith was pained to see her father unhappy, and even her smile was saddened, she knew not why. Eustace too augured ill, from the demeanour of the baron; and when, in answer to his request of a private audience, De Fougeres gave a melancholy and somewhat morose acquiesence, the youth felt his hopes sink, and his heart grow cold.

No. 18.

CHAPTER XXIV,

What equal torments to the grief of mind,
And pining anguish hid in gentle heart,
That only feeds itself with thoughts unkind,
And nourisheth its own consuming smart,
And will to none its malady impart.—SPENSER.

EUSTACE followed De Fougeres silently from the hall to a chamber in that part of the castle which was appropriated to the residence of the family. The baron pointing to a chair bade Eustace seat himself, adding,—

" Had you not sought this interview, my young friend, I should have repuested it myself ; I need some explanation from you."

" Explanation!" cried De Mowbray.

" Well—call it by what name you will," replied the baron.

"My motive for thus seeking you," said Eustace, " is to request your accordance to the union of the Lady Edith with one who, however unworthy of her, will think it his greatest happiness to contribute to her's."

" Are you secure of my daughter's affection ?" asked the baron.

" Believe me, I would not have made this request had I not received Edith's consent," replied the youth   " From childhood I have loved her—tenderly loved her ; and if her tongue has not yet confessed so early an attachment, I must remain content with the assurance that I am now the chosen of her heart."

" And has absence made no change in my child"s sentiments?" asked the baron.

" Why should you suspect it ?" cried Eustace, alarmed.

" I feared," said De Fougeres.

" Oh, tell me not of fear," exclaimed Eustace ; " Edith says she loves me, and I cannot doubt her."

" No—no—believe her, she does love you ; I know it," replied De Fougeres. " I was wrong, suspicious ; she must love you, and yet——"

" Yet what ?" cried Eustace ! " do not torture me thus, I pray you."

" I feared that the young knight in the Lady's Tower might have withdrawn my Edith's affection ; she has, I understand, passed much of her time with him during my absence," said the baron.

" Fear not that," replied Eustace, " Your Edith feels deeply the misfortune of Edward de Albini ; her tender heart pities his captivity, but it is the pity of a friend only."

" The saints be praised," ejaculated the baron.

" If I might presume to speak," said Eustace, hesitating.

" What ? say !" cried De Fougeres.

" I would ask that the captive might be free," said the youth. " I promised Edith to make this request.   The war has happily terminated, the partizans of Matilda are now the adherents of Stephen, even Geoffrey de Albini has renounced the cause of the Empress, why then retain this youth ?"

De Fourges remained silent, but his countenance shewed that his feelings were not unmoved by the appeal of Eustace.

" Oh, think," continued the latter, " of the anguish of his father when he returns from the war, and finds his only son, his sole child detained in captivity. What would be your misery to lose your Edith ? think of this, and pity the father and the still more wretched mother."

De Fougeres started, " Hush, young man, beware !" he cried.

" I must speak," exclaimed Eustace. " Can I, can you, Edith, give way to the happiness of our souls, while we know that the prisoner languishes in his cage ? Oh—release Edward de Albini, and your child will join her thanks to mine !"

" I had thought—I did intend," said De Fougeres, " to dismiss the young De Albini, but I feared his influence over my Edith."

" If you still fear that, I can convince you that your alarm is entirely groundlesss," replied the youth. "No other occasion should have drawn the secret from my bosom, but if his release depend upon its removal, I may venture to reveal that Edward de Albini loves hopelessly, but fervently, the Lady Cordelia de Dunstanville."

The baron started forward, and seizing the hand of Mowbray, he exclaimed, " do you tell me, indeed, truly what you know, or is it the mere fancy of your brain ?"

" It is true," replied Eustace.

" And Cordelia, does she return his love?" asked De Fougeres.

" Nay, nay," said Eustace smiling, " ask me not of that. Edith believes that her young friend is not wholly indifferent to the accomplishments and virtues of the interesting captive. But her lot is clouded, she knows not where her home may be, nor how her relations may dispose of her."

" Young man, you have given a pulse of joy and hope to my heart to which it has long been a stranger," cried De Fougeres. "All will yet be well, and my Edith shall be happy."

" May I then claim my bride as soon as my father returns to Mowbray ?" said Eustace.

The baron hesitated.

" Oh ! promise me but this," cried the youth, " Edith will never leave you, we will reside at Thornbury, we will cheer you, we will tend you."

" Nay," said the baron, "the bride of Eustace de Mowbray must not be immured at Thornbury. The court will claim your attendance."

" I do not love the court, and my Edith prefers the quiet of Thornbury to the bustle of the metropolis. No ! here let us live," said Eustace ; " here, where every object recals to our minds the innocence and happiness of childhood. Although not born at Thornbury, Edith knows no other home; if not here her infant steps first pressed the greensward, yet here she gambolled in childhood; if not here her infant tongue first lisped the name of 'father,' yet here her gentle tones have cheered your solitude, or enlivened your gaiety ; *here* must be our home, oh, refuse us not ! you would not surely part with your Edith willingly."

" Part with Edith ?" cried De Fougeres vehemently, " part with her whom I have risked my soul to obtain, and keep? No, boy—the sacrifice which the wily monk failed to obtain from me, I will never yield to Eustace Mowbray. Part with Edith ! beware, beware young man, your hand is on a lion's mane."

Eustace was astonished at the vehemence of the baron ; he could not comprehend how his words should have given rise to such a demonstration of passion, he therefore answered mildly, " I await, then, the return of my father to Mowbray Castle, when I may claim my bride, and your paternal blessing."

De Fougeres answered not, and Eustace retired, perplexed, but somewhat satisfied that the baron consented to his union with Edith, whom he sought in her chamber to recount the conversation which has just been recorded.

Edith, who was aware of the baron's ambitious views for her, was less surprised than her lover had been at his wish of exhibiting her at court, and she calmed his uneasiness by reminding him that the baron had given his decided and willing consent to their union.

" My father will be satisfied to let us remain here, I am sure," she added, " he does not love the court himself; and it was but this morning that he expressed to our guest, L'Espée, his apprehension that Stephen, in order to render his position on the throne perfectly secure, would be obliged to collect around his person the friends of Matilda , and both feared that interest would have more weight with the king than gratitude."

" Indeed," said Eustace.

" My father seems particularly to dread the presence of Geoffrey de Albini at Stephen's court," continued Edith, " he is brave, and an able counsellor, and it is expected that he will speedily gain the favor of the king. I know not why the baron should fear him while he holds his son in custody."

"There is hope of Edward's release," replied Eustace; and he recounted to Edith all that had passed between him and the baron upon this subject. Edith expressed her pleasure at hearing that there was a chance of the young captive's being restored to his family. "How must his lady mother have sorrowed," she added, "she looks as if she could indeed love her son."

"Have you then ever seen the Lady de Albini?" asked Eustace.

"Never; but there is a picture of her in the turret chamber, and I used to love to look at the gentle face; of late the baron has kept the key of the chamber himself, and has forbidden all access to it."

"Is the portrait like Edward?" asked Eustace.

"A little," replied Edith; "but what is very strange, Cordelia says that of late, since I have been anxious, and, perhaps, a little melancholy, I sometimes resemble that picture. I wonder if I am related to the Lady de Albini?"

"Has the baron never named your mother to you?" asked the youth.

"Never—he has told me that she was beautiful, virtuous, and beloved; but of her family and rank I am perfectly ignorant," answered Edith. "It always gave my father pain to speak of her, and therefore I have never questioned of her since I learned to read his feelings."

"Probably she was related to the Lady Elfrida," said Eustace; "a sister or a near kindred, and some domestic uneasiness may have early occurred to dissever the ties of relationship."

"It may be so," said Edith. "The Baron de Albini fought for Matilda, my dear father sided with Stephen; alas! that such a trifle should disunite kindred and bring misery to our hearths. Now all is peaceful, long may it continue so."

While the lovers were thus imparting to each other their hopes and fears for the future, the Baron de Fougeres was wrapt in meditation upon the past. Unhappy, he dared not to tell why—fearful of that which he dared not to express, he felt that hope which comes to all, came not to him. Many hours did he pass alone in deep meditation; at first in gloomy sullenness, and at last in the resolve which duty and a sense of honour inspired. He determined to release Edward, even before the day which should give his Edith to another protector. What led to this resolution? We will not attempt to unveil his thoughts, it suffices to us that we read them in his deeds: he sought the castle hall an altered man; still reserved as usual, but neither morose nor vehement; his smile again kindled at the voice of his child, again he returned the gentle glance which sought his favour, and to Eustace his manner was friendly and cheerful. Such power has virtuous resolve.

But De Fougéres was weak and irresolute; although not wavering in purpose he was dilatory in action; he had determined to release Edward as soon as he should hear of the arrival of the Baron de Mowbray at his castle; this arrival was unexpectedly and unavoidably delayed, and the Baron de Fougéres was not sorry that he was thus enabled to defer his dreaded task.

Edith and Eustace paid a daily visit to the prisoner; Cordelia but rarely accompanied them, she dared not trust herself in Edward's presence, and feeling that her lot must be shortly decided by the conduct which De Tunstall should adopt towards her, she thought that prudence dictated her absence from the Lady's Tower.

In vain did Edward de Albini hope that each succeeding day would bring his liberty, or give him the society once more of her, whose presence had cheered his long imprisonment; vainly did he listen for that footstep which, light as the southern breeze, was yet music to his ear; for that voice which alone spoke peace to his heart. She came not; and his days were gloomy, his nights sleepless. Youth might for a time sustain the harrassed spirit, but time and anxiety can overcome even the buoyancy of youth, and Edward became wasted and ill.

One morning L'Espée accompanied Edith to the tower, and on entering was struck with the alteration in the appearance of the young knight. In answer to the inquiries after his health, Edward shook his head, and answered,

"Ronald sings his song in vain to me; the kid still pines in the fox's lair. It may not be long ere this stream, already fatal to one of our house, may bathe the turf beneath which I sleep. Alas! for my dear mother!

L'Espee's worthy heart was deeply touched by this despondency, and he attempted to cheer the young knight by the intelligence that as soon as the Baron de Mowbray should return to his castle, De Fougeres intended to release his captive.

"It will be too late," said Edward, mournfully.

"Oh, say not so," cried Edith, weeping.

"It shall not be too late; I will intercede for you with my friend," said L'Espee; "he will not refuse the suit of an old brother-in-arms."

Edward expressed his gratitude, but avowed his despair at the success of the suit.

"You judge, my dear father, harshly," said Edith; he is unhappy, and therefore appears unkind."

"May I presume to ask why the Lady Cordelia so seldom visits the prisoner?" asked Edward. "Methinks it is many weeks since she honoured this humble abode with her presence."

"Cordelia is in daily expectation of the arrival of her kinsman, the Baron de Tunstall," replied Edith; "she charged me to give you her good wishes, but she is too anxious respecting the issue of the meeting, to visit her friend."

"And will the Lady Cordelia then leave Thornbury?" asked Edward.

"I trust not," replied Edith; "but her kinsman is noble, and has but Cordelia to love, and I fear he may repine at giving up the treasure so lately gained. However, I must persuade him to leave my friend with me for a time."

Edward sighed heavily. "What right have I," he said, "to think of the free and happy?"

"Be of good cheer," said L'Espee, "I will seek the baron immediately. But hark! what sounds are those?"

A horn at this moment was heard sounding at the outer gate of the castle; the party listened a moment, when Ronald burst in, exclaiming,

> "Room, room, ye gentles all,
> In castle, bower and hall,—"

But my song will not do here, I must away to the castle."

"What news, Ronald?" cried L'Espee.

"A pursuivant of the Baron de Tunstall," answered the dwarf, "to announce the speedy arrival of his noble master."

"Indeed," cried L'Espee—"then adieu, young knight, I will not forget the pledge I have given you."

Thus saying, the knight and his companion left the tower; and on their arrival at the castle, found that the intelligence brought by Ronald was true.

CHAPTER XXV.

> I have a silent sorrow here,
>   A grief I'll ne'er impart,
> It breathes no sigh, it sheds no tear,
>   But it consumes my heart.
> This cherish'd woe, this lov'd despair,
>   My lot for ever be,
> So my soul's lord the pangs I bear,
>   Be never known by thee.—SHERIDAN.

WHEN L'Espee reached the castle gate, he found a number of retainers belonging to the Baron de Fougeres, crowding round a stranger, eagerly asking a variety of hasty questions concerning his journey; at the approach of the knight they drew aside, and at the command of the latter ushered the stranger into the hall of the castle.   L'Espee sought his friend, De Fougeres, whom he found absorbed in the perusal of a paper, which, after some minutes, he handed to L'Espee, saying,

"A herald from the Baron de Tunstall, to warn me of his approach. The baron writes most courteously, and I shall rejoice to receive so valiant and noble a warrior within my castle, although I can scarcely comprehend his errand."

"I well understand it," replied L'Espee, "and truly I am glad to have been instrumental in restoring the orphan to her kindred."

"My Edith will grieve to relinquish her friend," replied De Fougeres, "and what course shall I pursue, respecting the young De Albini? The Baron de Tunstall ought to be informed of his kinswoman's attachment."

"If I may offer my advice, leave that subject to the discretion and feeling of the maiden herself," said L'Espee. "When may we expect our guest?"

"This evening, or to-morrow morning early," answered the baron; "orders must be given for a fitting reception to him."

Thus saying, De Fougeres was about to retire, when, remembering that Edith had been absent from the castle, he inquired for her.

"She left me in the castle hall, probably to seek her friend Cordelia, in order to prepare her for the meeting with her kinsman."

L'Espee was right; Edith had sought the chamber of Cordelia, whom she found wrapt in melancholy musings, which told Edith that the news of the messenger's arrival, had reached the chamber in which the friends were accustomed to abide.   Taking the hand of her friend, Edith said,

"My beloved Cordelia, your kinsman must not meet you thus."

"How can I be otherwise?" mournfully replied the maiden; "am I not to leave you and this my home?"

"I am eager to hope not," answered Edith; "I must not relinquish you yet; remember our promise to Eustace de Mowbray, that you should be as a sister to me."

"Well do I trust my Edith's kindness," cried Cordelia; "but do not marvel if I feel somewhat perplexed when I reflect, that for the first time, I am about to meet the eye of one to whom I am bound by natural, although hitherto unacknowledged ties. Oh, that he may be disposed favourably to regard the orphan of his sister?"

"Fear it not," said Edith; "and calm your spirits, dear Cordelia, for surely I see the train approaching over yonder hill."

Cordelia looked out, and beheld a body of horsemen, richly dressed, and well mounted on handsomely caparisoned horses; in the midst was borne aloft, the snow-white banner of De Tunstall. The sun was just setting like a globe of fire behind the oak-crowned hill which separated the domain of Thornbury from that of Mowbray; the valley, with its quiet river, already lay in deep shadow, but a rosy light tinged the towers of Mowbray Castle, whose lattices reflected the ruddy gleam. The distant horsemen were shrouded in darkness when Edith first beheld them, but as they wound round the side of the hill, the warm light flashed upon them, their spears and shields sparkled, and the stainless banner appeared as if no longer deserving of its acknowledged appellation.

"Alas!" said Edith, as she gazed, "that so brave an array, should be too often the accompaniment of war and misery. Let us descend my Cordelia; it is fit that I be in the hall to welcome your noble kinsman, and surely Cordelia will not now desert my side."

Cordelia would have excused herself, but upon Edith's hinting to her that De Fougeres might be displeased at her absence, she reluctantly accompanied her friend.

The ladies found De Fougeres and L'Espee in the castle hall, the retainers were marshalled in the court to receive the expected guest, with the proper demonstrations of welcome and respect. The gunner was ready with his band to fire the salute; the trumpeters were prepared to give their most melodious blast; the minstrels were not backward in recalling to their auditors the rank and achievements of De Tunstall. In the foremost rank of these, stood Ronald, waiting with eager impatience, for the baron's arrival. Not long was his patience tried, for the tramp of horses rapidly approaching announced the guest. The train entered the castle yard, heralded by a flourish of trumpets, and a salvo of artillery, the noise of which ving died away, Ronald chaunted, rather than sung, the following stanzas :—

> " Room, room, ye gentles all,
> In castle, bower, and hall;
>   Room for the stainless knight!
> Who come from lands afar,
> From bloody scenes of war,
>   The orphans cause to right.
>
> Let heralds loud proclaim
> De Tunstall's rank and fame,
>   Proclam his deeds in arms;
> While fair Cordelia's praise,
> Invokes our gentler lays.
>   To celebrate her charms."

Ronald's effusion was not in vain; De Tunstall recognised the dwarf, and on alighting from his steed, threw down to him a valuable silver chain, which, Ronald received well pleased, crying, " Good, my master,—a brave knight, and a liberal one to boot. This will be rare news for my travelling mate, Rosamund."

At the entrance of the castle-hall De Tunstall was met by his host and L'Espee, to whom De Fougeres introduced him. The marshal led De Tunstall to the dais at the upper end of the hall, where was placed a table spread with every suitable refreshment for a weary traveller ; and, in this case, it was much needed, as the guest had performed a long and hurried journey in order to reach Thornbury before nightfall.

When the servitors had retired, De Tunstall turned to L'Espee, saying,—

" My thanks are due, brave knight, for the intelligence given me of a relative, of whose existence I was scarcely conscious. Would that every one bearing the golden spurs, were as disinterested and active in the cause of the unfriended."

L'Espee sighed deeply. " I love the Lady Cordelia," he said, " she reminds me of days of happiness and hope, gone, never to return."

" What mean you ?" asked De Tunstall.

" I loved her mother," said L'Espee, " but she slighted my affection."

" You are dearly avenged, and she was deeply punished," said De Tunstall.

" I grieved for her punishment," replied the knight.

" Rather say that you exulted," observed De Fougeres.

" No, never—even had Eleanor de Tunstall broken a plighted vow, I could not have exulted," replied L'Espee. " My heart would have bled for her wrongs."

" Can such be your weakness ?" exclaimed De Fougeres. " Know you not the rapture of seeing an enemy humbled, a betrayer betrayed ?"

" I know it not," answered the knight. " I could meet my enemy face to face upon the battle-field ; I could fight, and if it so chance, I could conquer and slay ; but a woman—and one too whom I had loved, could I wish harm to her ? No— a man who can so far forget the dignity of manhood, must be a coward to his own sex."

" Callest thou me a coward ?" cried De Fougeres, starting up.

" You ? Ralph de Fougeres, a coward ? No, never were those word joined," said L'Espee seizing his friend's arm.

" Leave me—you know not—I know not—" cried De Fougeres.

" My friend," said L'Espee, " you are ill, I pray you retire, let me entertain our guest according to my humble powers."

But De Fougeres again seated himself, and leaning his head upon his hand, seemed for a time to be lost in abstraction. Many significant glances were interchanged between L'Espee and De Tunstall, but neither ventured to interrupt the silence, till De Fougeres, raising his head, said,—

" Forgive me, my friends, strange thoughts sometimes cross my brain, you know," added he, turning to L'Espee, " that family business, at this time, presses hardly upon me."

A silent pressure of the hand testified the friendship of the knight, who then endeavoured to turn the conversation towards the immediate object of De Tunstall's visit.

" The Lady Cordelia," he said, " is worthy of your care, she is like her mother in person, and would be an ornament to any lineage."

" And when may I be introduced to your fair guest?" asked the baron.

" To-morrow she will wait on you. Past recollections crowd upon her, and she entreats this small delay," replied De Fougeres.

" To-morrow, then, must determine my actions with regard to her," replied De Tunstall. " That she is my sister's child, gives her a claim upon my compassion, while the memory of the other parent, will, I fear, render her presence painful to me."

" Let not that distress you," replied De Fougeres, " my daughter will not willingly part with her friend. As long as the Lady Edith owns Thornbury Castle for her home, the fair Cordelia shall leave it only by her own wish."

De Tunstall expressed his obligations to both his companions, assuring De Fougeres that he had his warmest thanks for all his kindness to his niece. Towards midnight the companions separated, and shortly after all was silent in the castle; the wearied had sunk to repose, the domestic had rested from his labour, and the menial from his toil; one only had watched the slowly pacing hours upon the couch of care. De Fougeres slept not. The words of L'Espee had sunk deeply into his heart, and rankled there; not with the burning of anger towards the knight, but with a pang of secret guilt. All seemed to conspire against his peace. His child—his friend—his guest—and he whom he guarded with a jealous eye.

" I can bear it no longer," he exclaimed " he shall know all'"

" Taking up his taper De Fougeres sought for the keys of the castle gates, and descended to the hall. All was silent there, and as the baron crossed the scene of last night's events his mind gathered fresh courage to do that which he thought was right. But when the light flashed upon the rude pictures of the ancestors of De Albini, with which the hall was decorated, and shewed their grim features, denouncing vengeance on the oppressor of their house, the baron was obliged to summon all his courage to hold his course undaunted. At length he reached the outer gate, and gently unlocking it and drawing the bolts with which it was secured, he passed into the open air. The gentle breeze of morning played among the trees; the lark had already begun her sweet matin song; the dew scented by the wild flowers of the adjoining grove, gave forth those sweets which were denied to the gaudy day—De Fougeres felt the influence of the time and scene, yet he was about to do that which might for ever shut that scene from his eyes. But he persevered, and gaining the Lady's Tower, he unlocked the gate and entered the chamber of his prisoner.

Before him on a rude and humble bed lay the heir of the noble house of De Albini, the sleep of innocence closed his eyes, but a slight contraction of his brow shewed that there was heaviness of heart even in innocence. De Fougeres gazed intently; the delicate features recalled to him the bright dreams of former days, and a deep sigh esaaped him.

The sound reached the ear of the sleeper, for he stretched out his hand, murmuring, " my mother !"

De Fougeres could bear it no longer, and setting down the lamp, he cried, " Edward de Albini !"

" The young man started from the bed, exclaiming, " Who are you ? why come you here ?"

" 1 am Ralph de Fougeres, follow me," answered the baron.

" Whither ? to death? oh, my mother !" cried Edward.

" Ask no questions; but quickly follow me," replied De Fougeres; and taking up the now useless lamp, he descended the stairs.

Edward arose, and dressed himself, more asleep than awake. He doubted no that his gaoler was come to end at once his imprisonment and his life, but he determined to sell the latter dearly.

Upon rejoining De Fougeres, he made another effort to move his compassion.

"Is there aught upon this earth that would lead thee to release me?" he asked

"Nought that thou canst give," was the stern reply.

"Gold, lands, all would be cheap to De Albini to reclaim his only child," cried Edward. "Already have these castle walls echoed with the groan of misery; already has this gale borne with it the sigh of the bereaved mother; oh! pity her first misfortune, and give back her son."

"Ha!" exclaimed De Fougeres, "hast thou too heard that tale? Then follow me; nay, no expostulation, your life is safe whatever may be the consequence."

No. 19.

De Fougeres led the way back to the castle, and entering the hall, he ascended a narrow staircase, which, after many windings, led into a small and neglected chamber.   Here he desired Edward to remain while he was absent.   Some time elapsed, and Edward thought that he had merely changed his prison; for De Fougeres had carefully locked and bolted the door by which they had entered; he endeavoured, by looking from the window, to ascertain the possibility of escape, but he found it would be unavailing, the chamber being at a great height from the ground, and utterly dismantled of furniture.   No hope appeared possible, and he sat down to mourn his fate, when the baron returned.

"Follow me!" he said.

Edward did so, and ascended another staircase to a chamber, which, although evidently disused, yet bore some tokens that it was occasionally visited.

"Look there," said De Fougeres, pointing to a picture which hung in a small recess.

Edward uttered a scream of surprise and joy on beholding a resemblance of his mother.   Long and mournfully he gazed upon the picture, and would have continued to do so for some time longer, had he not been roused by a smothered sigh which burst from his companion.   He turned round hastily, and De Fougeres finding himself observed, said, " It is a beautiful picture!"

"Yes," returned Edward, " but oh! not so beautiful as the dear original.   Would that it could speak to your hard heart, and plead for her only child.   Look on it, ruffian! and think what she must suffer in losing one she so doated on.   Think of the trouble and the watching I have caused her; think of the love such a tender being must feel for her child; and judge, if you can, what must be her sufferings when she mourns over the loss of her son, lost to her by worse than death.   But your heart is hardened, you can form no idea of a mother's love."

De Fougeres stood before him with folded arms, his countenance wearing the mournful expression which so often crossed its sternness; then assuming his accustomed haughtiness and coldness, and drawing up his figure to its full height, he said,—

"You have called me ' Ruffian;' has my conduct towards you warranted such an appellation?   You have said that my heart is hard—alas! you know it not.   You have said that I cannot form an idea of a mother's love—but I had once a mother who loved me with a tenderness which is not surpassed by that of the Lady Elfrida for her only son."

"If then," said Edward, almost kneeling, and with clasped hands stretched towards his companion, "if then you have ever experienced a mother's love, let the recollection of it move your heart to pity; and if ever you delighted to give joy to your parent, oh! in mercy release me, that I may again call a smile upon the face of that dear being who from that spot seems to join me in my prayer."

De Fougeres shook his head.   " Edward, I cannot restore you to your parents without making a disclosure of circumstances which have been buried in my bosom for many long years; nor without relinquishing my Edith, which would be much more dreadful to me.   You know not the love with which I have cherished that beautiful girl, Edward," he continued, earnestly, laying his hand upon the arm of the youth, and with the other pointing to the picture, " she is as beautiful, as virtuous, as tender, as the original of that picture."

Edward was touched by the solemn and mournful manner of De Fougeres, and he asked, " Why should my release demand such a sacrifice ?"

A big tear stood on the cheek of the baron as he replied,—

"You said that my heart was hard—does this moment prove it so?   I have told you how deeply I feel the affection of a parent.   Believe me, Edward, I pity the sufferings of your mother, deeply do I pity them; but I cannot relinquish her who has been the pride and the joy of my wounded heart."

"Then if I plead in vain for a parent's peace, know that the happiness of a young and lovely woman hangs upon my release.   If you have ever loved, De Fougeres, I conjure you to think of her sufferings with pity."

"If I have ever loved," replied De Fougeres with a smile of bitter anguish, " I tell you, young man, that dearly as you love your betrothed, the love I once felt far, very far, surpassed it. Hard as my heart may seem, it once doated upon a lovely woman, fondly and devotedly, and I believe that I was also beloved. But I was deceived, and woman's treachery has made me what you know me. I was deceived," he continued, in a mournful voice, " deceived too, after vows had been breathed as fervently as ever woman breathed to man. Then it was that I was driven to madness. The woman I loved married another. But she has suffered for her treachery, deeply suffered ; and through me she has had her punishment."

As he said this, his whole frame became convulsed, and a few minutes of uncontrollable agitation ensued ; after the agony of feeling had passed away, De Fougeres said in tone of scorn, " But why should I unbosom myself to you—to one who from the moment that he leaves my castle must be as an alien, a stranger to me?"

" Nay," said Edward, somewhat moved with pity for him whom he had hitherto regarded with dread almost amounting to hatred, " nay, it cannot, it will not be so. My father is honourable, and I will be grateful for my release."

" I have already told you more of my history than I have ever yet told to any man, save one—and he—but he is gone to his account. What has prompted me I can but guess," said De Fougeres, looking earnestly and tenderly at the portrait. "The hour which he foretold is come, and I can no further pursue my vengeance. I have already suffered too much in punishing others. Edward, you are honourable, I know it ; you have been tempted by one but too well skilled in such arts, and you resisted his inducements to sully your fair fame."

Edward started: " Father Augustine ?" he asked.

" Name not the traitor, I know the whole !" cried the baron ; " I would, if possible, claim from you a promise not to hate me, ere I farther disclose my tale."

" Edward was about to speak when De Fougeres interrupted him, saying,—

" Yet make no promise, but listen to me attentively ; villain as I may appear to you, even you must acknowledge that I have faithfully fulfilled the obligation I took upon myself. My Edith is indeed all that a parent can wish."

" May I presume to praise the Lady Edith ?" said Edward.

" Praise her—admire her—love her," cried De Fougeres.

" Alas," said Edward, " that may not be ; he whom I dare not name to you would have urged me to love her, but my heart was not my own to give : I love another."

" Then are my fears at rest. Nay, think me not inconsistent, but hear me," said the baron. He paused and fixing his eyes upon the portrait, " It is like, very like," he at last said, as if speaking to himself alone, " but there was no sadness upon the brow when I knew her. Oh ! she was beautiful and joyous, as the flowers and birds of spring. Edward, I loved your mother."

The youth started, but dared not give utterance to the question, " Could she betray or deceve?"

" I loved her," said De Fougeres, " when she was young. I was betrothed to her ; but she took alarm at my passionate temper, and broke her faith. Yet, Edward, her gentleness would have tamed me ; under her guidance I should have learned to curb my temper, but she refused to make the trial. She broke with me, and I was miserable. I vowed vengeance, and I have had it. Yet when I have most worked upon her feelings, I have myself suffered deeply, for I never forgot how dear she had been to me. A recollection of her virtues at this moment induces me to communicate actions and thoughts to you which, I believed, would have gone to the grave in secrecy with me."

De Fougeres saw that his auditor was deeply touched, and after a pause of some minutes, during which he seemed to be gathering strength and composure for the subsequent disclosure, he added,—

" The Lady Elfrida married and forgot her first love : it was unwisely done—I did not forget her. Edward, you have heard that you had a sister, your parents mourned her loss. Nay, speak not," he said, seeing that Edward appeared impatient, " but attend, she was not drowned. It was the first punishment which I inflicted on your mother, and I suffered scarcely less than she did. Be calm and interrupt me not.   It was I who stole the child; it was I who sent the little bonne to land itself at the foot of Elfrida's favourite retirement ; and no lover ever watched so anxiously the voyage of his love-wreath, as I watched the progress of that bonnet down the river, which was to bear to Elfrida the tidings of the supposed fate of her little one.   But Edith so much resembled her mother that she won my love.   I brought her up as my own child, and have cherished her as my dearest treasure.   I have drunk enough of vengeance.   I will restore you both to the Lady Elfrida, and nthe virtues of her daughter, she will learn how devotedly my heart has beat to its first and fondest affections."

Who shall describe the feelngs of Edward as this disclosure was made to him? Did anger towards him who had nearly brought his mother to the grave, counterbalance the strange joy he felt at learning that he had a sister, and such a sister? No—he scarcely recollected the agency of De Fougeres in the delicious emotions of affection, which agitated his awakened heart.   How could he ever have said that he did not love Edith ?   He did love her, he had loved from the first moment that he beheld her.   But would she love him ?   How would she receive the announcement of relationship?   She loved Eustace—true—but she could love a brother also ; and when Edward remembered the gentleness she had always shown towards him, the pity, almost amounting to affection, which she had expressed for his misfortune—he felt assured that she would not withdraw her esteem.   For the Lady Elfrida de Albini also, Edith had expressed commiseration,—how dearly she must love her as a mother.

These thoughts chased each other rapidly through the mind and heart of Fdward, while his companion remained silent and melancholy.   A glance at De Fougeres recalled the youth to a remembrance of what his sufferings must be, and falling upon his knees, Edward expressed in the most heartfelt tones his gratitude for the change in his sentiments towards his captive.

" Nay, kneel not to me, Edward," said the baron ; " I deserve not your thanks. Your sister is worthy of your love ; I have brought her up in her father's house, and she has loved that portrait, without knowing it to be that of her mother, while she has loved me, supposing me to be her parent.   How she will feel when she knows this tale I durst not think ; but," he said, and brushed a tear from his eye, " I shall lose my happiness in losing her.   The only ransom I require of De Albini shall be, his renouncing all connection with the enemies of his country— this, I believe, he has already done.   All that I will ask of Elfrida shall be, forgiveness ; from her children I claim pity."

De Fougeres seated himself upon a chair, and his head sunk upon his breast ; thus he remained for some time, and at last turning to Edward, he said,—

" The morning wears on, and the inmates of the castle will soon be stirring.   I have much before me of anxiety and difficulty, but my conscience is relieved, and I would new seek a short repose before I enter into the scene of action.   The Baron de Tunstall arrived last night, to claim the guardianship of the Lady Cordelia, and to him I must give an account of her history."

Edward expressed his surprise at this intelligence, and, sighing deeply, he added, "the Lady Cordelia will then leave Thornbury ?"

" Probably so," replied De Fougeres, " how are my projects disappointed !   but I had no right to form them.   May but my dearest Edith be happy, and I care for nought else.   I pray you, Edward, give me a few hours, return to your tower, and I will soon visit you, and receive you as a guest at the castle.   But I have much to undergo."

Thus saying, De Fougeres gave one long look at the picture, and led the way down from the chamber.   Edward followed in silence ; both were too much agitated by what had passed, to hold further converse ; De Albini returned to his lonely abode, while the baron sought his chamber to recruit, in some measure, his shattered spirits, by a more peaceful sleep than he had of late enjoyed.

He thought over all the events of his life ; there was little in the past to yield him comfort ; and the future—what was it ?   The dim and doubtful point in the scene regarded his child, his Edith ; would De Albini sanction her union with

Eustace? The baron hoped he would; it was an alliance which would have reflected lustre upon a higher name than that of Albini, and in a worldly point of view, was extremely advantageous. But to De Albini, to one who had held arms against Stephen, such an alliance was especially desirable, as it would guarantee to Stephen the fidelity which De Albini had tendered, and it would give to the baron an importance in the eyes of the king and his nobles which would soothe the wounded pride of the follower of the empress. De Fougeres thought of all this, and his anxiety was alleviated; and he sunk to a short repose in the feeling of hope tempered by uncertainty.

And what were Edward's thoughts? May it not be forgiven him, if the first sweet emotions of newly-found affection having passed away, he dwelt with a lover's fear upon a situation as respected Cordelia. He dreaded, yet hoped, for an interview with her kinsman, but what could he offer her? No—he must return to his father ere he dared to declare to De Tunstall his affection. And he feared his father's pride, his mother's stern ideas of female propriety. Nevertheless Edward could not disguise from himself that the situation of De Albini at the court of Stephen was one of difficulty, if not of danger.

Many of the adherents of Matilda had given in their tardy adherence to Stephen. Geoffry de Albini had been among the earliest of these, and had been most graciously received; but still he was in a doubtful position, more dstressing to an active mind than open disagreement. Edward saw that an alliance with De Tunstall would heal many of the discomforts to which his father might be subjected; and he hoped, faintly hoped, that such reflections might pave the way to his union with Cordelia. But he knew his stainless lineage, and he again feared. De Tunstall also might have other views for his niece. How embarrassing were these thoughts! the bright morning sun shone in upon De Albini's humble meal ere he had calmed his mind.

The same morning sun awoke Cordelia to the consciousness of her difficulties. She could no longer delay to meet her kinsman, and, accordingly, after a toilet more than usually careful, she descended to the hall. She there found her good friends L'Espee and De Tunstall. The latter approached her kindly, and took her hand, saying,—

"My Cordelia! I do indeed trace in these features the child of my beloved but unfortunate sister. May'st thou inherit her grace and beauty, untarnished by her faults."

Thus saying, De Tunstall kissed the forehead of the maiden, who, bursting into tears, sunk on her knees before him.

"My poor child!" said her kinsman; "it shall be the first aim of my life to make thee happy. Thou shalt accompany me to the court of Stephen, there to claim thy rights, and to be acknowledged the lawful child of Eleanor de Duntauville."

"I am happy here," sighed Cordelia.

"But it is necessary to clear thy mother's fame," said De Tunstall, "I would not part thee from thy friend the Lady Edith, and hither thou shalt speedily return."

Cordelia expressed her gratitude, and her willingness to be guided by the advice of her kinsman. A conversation then ensued respecting the lost document which De Tunstall showed to his niece, and related the singular manner in which it had been restored to him.

"Oh, my dear aunt," cried Cordelia, "would that you were now alive to embrace your child."

"The Lady Abbess was so much older than myself, and led so recluse a life, that she was scarcely a sister to me," said De Tunstall; "but I owe her my gratitude that she did not desert the orphan."

At this moment De Fougeres entered, looking harassed and pale. He scarcely noticed Cordelia or Edith, and apologised to De Tunstall for his apparent inhospitality by alleging illness as its cause. Edith looked anxiously at her father as he spoke, and gave him her usual morning embrace, which he returned with more warmth than common. The meal passed away, and De Fougeres left the hall. The rest of the party were occupied in earnest conversation, and they were not aware of the departure of Edith, who left them to seek her father.

CHAPTER XXVI.

The rose is fairest when 'tis budding new,
     And hope is brightest when it dawns from fears;
The rose is sweetest wash'd with morning dew,
     And love is loveliest when embalm'd in tears.—SCOTT.

The Lady Edith found the baron in his private sitting-room, in an attitude of deep abstraction, from which her gentle step did not rouse him. For a few minutes he stood regarding her father with a look of that affection which was the strongest feeling of her heart; then fearing that his meditations were painful to himself, and hoping that she should be able to cheer and gladden him.

"Father," said the maiden, "I come to seek you, and Eustace awaits his promised audience,"

"Call me not *Father*," cried Ralph de Fougeres with an intensity of feeling scarcely controlled.

The bewildered girl looked alarmed; she approached him, and placing one hand gently on his shoulder, she looked tenderly in his face, saying,—

"Wherefore may I not call you father?"

"Edith, I am no longer your father."

"What mean you? not my father! Oh! what have I done that you should renounce me?" then kneeling to him, she said, weeping,—"I have loved you too dearly to be expressed, and if I have offended you, oh! forgive me, for it has not been done wilfully. Forgive me, and do not renounce me, for that would kill me. I will be more guarded in future."

De Fougeres turned from her in agony.

"Nay, now I know," she continued, "that I have indeed offended, when my father thus turns from me. I must seek Eustace; he must kneel with me and assist me to implore forgiveness."

"Edith, Edith, you unman me!" cried the baron. "But seek not Eustace, I cannot yet converse with him; I must tell *you* all, must tell you of my sins. Ay, of my sins, dearest child."

De Fougeres then, in as few words as possible, told his tale. During the recital Edith continued on her knees before him, her eyes fixed intently upon his face, and her countenance varying with every emotion. When the tale was ended, the spirit of De Fougeres seemed to be completely broken he fell upon the bosom of the kneeling maiden and wept; she clasped her arms around him, and whispered words of endearment.

"Father," she said, "you still must be to me; how can I at once love a stranger as I love you? Have you not been to me ever indulgent and orbearing? And now——"

"Edith you know not the pang which this renouncement gives me; but in the Lady Elfrida de Albini," said De Fougeres, deeply sighing, "you will find a kinder mother, whom you will love, as you have loved me."

"Her countenance bespeaks gentleness," said Edith musing.

"Have you then ever visited the chamber in the western tower," asked the baron.

"Yes," replied Edith.

"And who told you whom the picture represents?"

"Father Augustine," replied Edith. "Oh! my dear father, how I disliked that monk for making you unhappy! But we shall all be happy now."

"Alas!" said De Fougeres, "I would not cloud your hopes, but I must remind my Edith that she has a father now, whose consent is necessary to an union with Eustace de Mowbray. Nay, my child," he exclaimed, seeing a deadly paleness spread itself over the face of Edith, "fear not that such consent will be denied. Policy, as well as humanity, will induce Geoffrey de Albini to rejoice in such an alliance."

"There is another of whom I must ask. Does the young knight know of our relationship?" asked Edith.

"He does; and longs to embrace his sister," replied De Fougeres.

"May I then go to the tower?" asked Edith.

"Go, my child," replied the baron; "while I explain to Eustace de Mowbray the new situation in which he stands to me. But, my Edith, remember that you are still my child in the presence of our guests. I would not unfold this tale to them until Edward de Albini shall have revealed it to his parents."

Edith tenderly embraced her father, for so she still called him, and with a palpitating heart and faltering footstep she bent her graceful way towards the Lady's Tower. Her first summons at the door was answered by Ronald, who seemed to be lurking about as he had used to do in former days; for since his journey to the camp, he had very seldom visited the young knight. Now, however, emerging from the thicket of shrubs, which almost surrounded the tower, he exclaimed, as he opened the door to Edith, "The fool may sing his song now, and the wise man will echo it."

Edith, not comprehending his meaning, waited a minute ere she entered, saying, —

"Ronald, we have not seen you at the castle lately."

"Where the carrion is, there will be the eagles, and perchance a less noble bird may be found among them. There will be feasting and revelry at the castle ere long, Lady Edith; the prisoned kid will be released before this day's sun has sunk beyond yonder grove; and the waters have yielded their prey," added Ronald, significantly; "but there is yet one unhappy one."

"Oh stay me not, Ronald," said Edith; "we shall meet again."

"Yes," cried the dwarf, "but the bride of Eustace de Mowbray will not recognise the fool."

Edith blushed and sighed. "A dark cloud still hides the feature," she said, "but I go to claim a brother: oh, happy word!"

"My blessing be upon thee, sweet bird," said Ronald, as Edith left him, and entered the tower.

Who shall describe the meeting of the brother and sister? A considerable time elapsed ere either could speak; Edith wept as she looked upon Edward, and felt that he was indeed her brother, and that she might pour out to him all the feelings of her heart. Deeply attached as she was to De Fougeres, fear was mingled with her love; and her affection for Eustace was a repressed and secret feeling; but towards her brother there was neither fear nor secrecy; she did not hesitate to tell him that she had loved him from the moment of his arrival at Thornbury.

"Oh! that bitter day," said Edward; "how little did I then think that I should here find that lost one, whom I have since heard was the cause of my dearest mother's unhappiness."

"Did you not know then of the cause of your parents leaving Thornbury?" asked Edith.

"No, it was told to me by that monk, by Father Augustine."

"Oh, Edward! tell me of your mother," said Edith. "Will she love me?"

"Love thee?" replied the youth, embracing her. "Will not all love thee?"

"And what are the designs of the baron as to my brother's release?" asked the maiden

"De Fougeres has requested me but to remain here for an hour or two, until he visits me to set me free."

"Edward, we shall miss you," said Edith, sighing.

"Would you accompany me, dearest?"

"Oh how willingly——to my mother, my own mother—but no," said Edith, after a pause. "The baron is unhappy. You know not what I owe to his love: never will I desert him."

"And there is still a dearer tie, Edith," said Edward, whisperingly.

"Not dearer," answered his sister; "and oh, Edward, that tie may soon be broken for ever; I dare not think upon it."

"What mean you?"

"Will the Baron de Albini approve Eustace de Mowbray?"

"Why shouldst thou fear it?"

"He has opposed him in battle," replied Edith.

"Fear not; I will be his advocate; and you know not my father if you think that he can for a moment risk the happiness of one but just reclaimed to him, from what he considered certain death. My father has rendered fealty to Stephen, and his allegiance was graciously accepted; believe me he will not for that refuse De Mowbray's alliance. Would that my prospect was equally clear."

"What do you mean, Edward?" asked Edith.

"You surely have not been blind to my attachment to your friend Cordelia?"

"I have hoped suspected," said Edith, hesitating.

"It has been in vain that I have endeavoured to subdue my unhappy passion," replied De Albini; "the efforts of my reason, and the denunciations of Father Augustine, have alike failed in eradicating from my heart a passion which neither time nor disappointment can quench, and which death alone can destroy."

"And wherefore, dear brother, shouldst thou love my friend?"

"You know Cordelia's history?" asked Edward.

"Yes, I do know that at present she is portionless and, apparently, friendless."

"And you not know the circumstances of her birth?"

"Alas! yes—they are painful. But her kinsman, De Tunstal, has fully recognised in her, the child of his sister and the heiress of De Dunstanville."

"How! is Cordelia not illegitimate?"

"No; she is the lawful acknowledged child of De Dunstanville. The document so long lost was recovered and conveyed to De Hesling, and it needs only the interference of the king to obtain for Cordelia the rank and lands which are her due. The conference which, as I expect, ere this, taken place in the castle, must end by placing my dearest Cordelia in that station which she is so qualified to ornament."

Edward listened to these words in silent amazement. A bright beam of joy irritated his fine features, and, seizing the hand of Edith, he exclaimed,—

"Oh, my sister! am I to receive a double happiness from you?"

Then, after a pause, he added, "I still fear that De Tunstall may have other and more lofty views for his niece. She has beauty to grace a court, and he may choose to introduce her there; how can I then hope for favour?"

"May you not rely upon Cordelia's favour?" asked Edith.

"I have never mentioned my love," replied Edward; "I knew Cordelia's birth, and I knew that it would be an insurmountable barrier to my dear mother's consent. I therefore forebore to press my suit; besides, what could I, a prisoner, offer her?"

"I may not betray secrets which I have discovered," answered the maiden, "but be assured, dear Edward, that you are cherished by one, who, perhaps, has involuntarily allowed me to read that in her heart which she scarcely dares acknowledge to herself."

"Oh, Edith! you give me life and hope; I shall leave Thornbury with a heart lightened of half its cares. I will proceed to my father, relate the tale of De Fougeres, declare my love to Cordelia, and return to claim my sister and my bride."

"Will you not remember that your sister cannot leave Thornbury in happiness, unless——"

"I will remember," said Edward, tenderly embracing her.

A knock at the door at this moment preceded the entrance of De Fougeres; his countenance wore an expression of happiness to which it had long been a stranger, as he said, "My children!"

"Yes, father," replied Edith, throwing herself upon his neck, "still your child."

"I have just left our friend, Eustace de Mowbray, while I fulfil the promise which I made to you, De Albini, that I would give you the liberty of which, believe me, I reluctantly deprived you. From this time you are my guest only."

Edward poured forth his gratitude, and Edith joined her tears.

No. 20.

"This packet," said De Fougeres to Edward, "will acquaint Geoffrey de Albini with the wrong he has received at my hands ; I but delay restitution of th e precious treasure until he claims it in person ; then it shall be yielded, even at the expense of my happiness—perhaps my life."

"No ! no ! dear father, we will all be happy," said Edith, affectionately.

"You will depart immediately," continued the baron, "my retainers shall escort you. Fancy not that I am unwilling to receive you in the castle, but there are many hearts whose pains your journey may heal, and perhaps it were better not at present to unfold the whole to my guests in the castle. But may I ask a favour for one friend ?"

"Speak," said Edward ; "command me in any way which does not interfere with my duty."

"Eustace de Mowbray wishes to accompany you."

Edith started, and a glance at the baron brought deep blushes into her cheek, hitherto so pale.

"Nay Edith," said the baron, "fear not for Eustace, we have held a long conference, and by my advice he goes to ask my child's hand of him who alone has a right to bestow it. Doubt not, dearest, that Eustace will soon return in happiness and hope."

Edith sighed mournfully. "I know not how to understand all this, my father," she said, "but I cling to your love, oh ! do not desert me !"

"Desert thee, child ?" cried De Fougeres, embracing her, "desert the only light which blesses my life? Dearest Edith !" Then turning to De Albini he said, will you accept of the young De Mowbray as your companion ?"

"Joyfully," replied Edward, "and I would depart at once."

"Eustace only awaits your summons," said the baron, "I will send him to you."

De Fougeres left the tower, and shortly Eustace de Mowbray approached.

"My Edith," he said, "it will be but a short absence, and on a peaceful errand. To you, Edward, he continued, holding out his hand, "I but offer friendship now. I trust soon to be allowed to offer the the esteem of a brother. Adieu, Edith ! may we meet in happiness. I dare not touch upon what I have been told."

Edith suffered Eustace to embrace her, then turning to Edward, and throwing her arms round him, she exclaimed,—

"My brother ! my dear brother ! speak for me to our parents, tell them that although a stranger to their love, their child knows the duty that she owes, and that her love waits upon her duty."

"Believe me, Edith, we shall be fair ambassadors," said Edward. "Adieu."

So saying, the young men left the tower, and Eustace led his companion to the gate in the outer wall of the castle, where they found horses and all needful attendants awaiting them. Ere the noonday sun penetrated the valley of Thornbury, they were far beyond its neighbourhood ; many times had each looked back upon the towers which held the beloved of their hearts ; the lessening turrets were at last lost to their sight, and they entered into conversation upon the strange events of the last few hours.

Gently and delicately did each speak of De Fougeres, and with warm hope did each look forward to the future for happiness. The journey was lightened of its wearisomeness to Edward by the company of his friend, and at the end of three days, he saw, with a beating heart, the walls wherein his infancy and his youth had been made happy by maternal care. But before we enter the presence of Lady de Albini, we must ask what had meanwhile been passing at the Castle of Thornbury.

Upon Cordelia's introduction to De Tunstall the latter had been struck with her resemblance to his deceased sister ; he was pleased with her manners and her graceful behaviour, and being childless himself, he felt that he had found a child who would render the remainder of his life happy.

"Cordelia," he said, when they were alone, "vainly have I endeavoured to ascertain whether any representative of my poor Eleanor were in existence : I wa constantly assured that there was no such a being as thyself in the world.   How was your birth made known to you?"

"My revered aunt, or rather mother," replied Cordelia, "acquainted me with my sad history, just before she died, giving me a casket which contains a picture of my mother, a locket with her hair, and some papers."

"Have you that casket still? Methinks it would be a melancholy pleasure again to look upon the representation of features imprinted on my memory."

Cordelia left the room, and soon returned with the valued casket.   De Tunstall opened it, and taking out the picture, pressed it to his lips, saying,—

"It is like, but it has not the soul of my poor Eleanor.   And this locket, these are fair locks, but with whose are they intertwined?"

Cordelia hesitated.

"I can but too well guess," said De Tunstall. "Well! he is gone ! perished by the hand of the man whom he had injured so deeply.   These proofs are sufficient, they will support my claim in the orphan's behalf, and our king will befriend me. What says my Cordelia to a journey to London?"

"Is it necessary that I should appear?" she asked timidly.   "Surely the knowledge of my unhappy circumstances might draw down upon me observations painful to be borne."

"Nay, fear not, my child ; I will shield thee from aught that can alarm thy timid nature.   But so fair a suppliant can hardly be denied, and we have a mighty opponent in the Church. Know you anything of the monk who obtained from De Dunstanville the gift of the lands which by right are yours?"

"He will not dispute them with me," replied Cordelia—"he is dead."

"You knew him then?" asked her uncle.

"But too well ; he was the terror of my youth, the tyrant of my life," answered the maiden.   "His treachery respecting the paper restored to you has unmasked him, but he can no more trouble you."

"Who was he?" asked De Tunstall.

"He was called Father Augustine during his residence at Thornbury, but he died the Baron de Bohun," replied Cordelia.

"The Baron de Bohun!" exclaimed De Tunstall ; "then our task is comparatively easy.   This baron went to the camp of Matilda with a train of hired followers, men who knew no rule of honour, mere bravos, and by some strange occurrences it was ascertained among those whom he joined, that he was no other than the Lord of Scrivelby, who in his youth had been obliged to leave his native land for presumed murder."

Cordelia started, and exclaimed in a voice of terror, "Can this be?"

"It is so,   replied her kinsman ; "his guilt is well known, and I now bethink me that in youth he was a friend and companion of De Dunstauville. Well, indeed, poor child, might he be thy tyrant, and well might he endeavour to force thee to enter into that Church which he so deeply disgraced."

Cordelia answered not ; she was busied in tracing within her own mind all that she had known of Father Augustine, there was not a single bright spot in the retrospection.

"We must repair to the court my child," said De Tunstall, "it will not be difficult to assert thy rights.   Will not Cordelia rejoice to view the gaities of a court?"

"Oh do not fancy me ungrateful, but Thornbury has been a happy home to me. I know not the manners of courtly maidens, my ignorance would disgrace my kind friend," said Cordelia.

"Disgrace me? oh no, Cordelia.   I shall have pride in exhibiting my little rustic niece among the ladies of the court—and among the nobles too," added De Tunstall, looking archly at the maiden,

Codelia blushed deeply, and her blush was accompanied by a heavy sigh.

"Why that sigh, fair girl? Has some rural swain touched thy young heart believe me, thou needest but to enter the lists of beauty, and lovers more becoming of thy lineage will be at thy feet ; thou wilt speedily forget Thornbury."

Again Cordelia sighed.

"Thus is it with youth," said De Tunstall, half to himself, and sighing in his turn. "The first affection is ever the deepest. But," said he, turning to Cordelia, "I must protest against my child leaving her heart at Thornbury. I did but jest ; there surely is no rustic squire ?"

"No, no," cried Cordelia ; "fear not that the daughter of Eleanor de Dunstanville will ever feel or act in any way derogatory to her birth. I only grieve to quit my beloved Edith."

"It may not be necessary," replied the baron ; "I will proceed to London to-night, as time is precious in this case. I will immediately require an udience of the king, I have a claim upon his favour ; then should I find it necessary for you to repair to court, I will engage some trusty person to conduct you thither. But I do not expect this ; Stephen is just and generous, and as it is probable that these lands have never really been affixed to the Church, but have been privately appropriated by the Baron de Bohun, or whatever he may be called, to his own use, it will, I think not be difficult to have them restored. Now, farewell, fair kinswoman, and remember that the Baron de Tunstall allows no rustic knight to ensnare his lovely niece."

Cordelia again blushingly assured De Tunstall that her heart was worthy of the race whence she sprang, and expressing her deep gratitude to her kinsman, she bade him farewell.

Upon leaving the hall, Cordelia sought Edith in the chamber particularly appropriated to their use ; but she was not there, nor was there any appearance of her usual occupations ; after considerable hesitation therefore Cordelia resolved to seek her friend in the Lady's Tower, and she descended for that purpose.

On passing through the castle's inner gate, Ronald crossed the path. He made salutation to the lady, but in a manner so unlike that which was usual to him, that Cordelia involuntarily slackened her pace, gazing earnestly upon the dwarf, whose dark and generally forbidding countenance was now absolutely radiant with joy.

"A good day to you, Ronald," said Cordelia to him.

"A good day to me ? and to whom else ?" answered the dwarf.

"I hope to many," replied the maiden, "but your face belies your words, Ronald ; you look merry, and you speak sneeringly."

"Then I am no fool at last. Is it not the wise man's virtue, that his face belies his heart?"

"Well, good morning, Ronald, I seek the Lady Edith ; can you give me tidings of her?" asked Cordelia.

"I saw her enter the Lady's Tower two hours since," replied the dwarf, significantly ; "and she has not yet departed. The fetters bound by love are strong, and time passes quickly if love aid his flight."

"What can you mean ?" cried Cordelia, alarmed.

"That the young knight and the Lady Edith may well forget the flight of time," replied Ronald ; "such love as theirs, so long crossed, so suddenly set free, knows nought of time. Alas! that they should so soon be again separated."

"Love! separated ! What can you mean ? Oh, tell me—tell me !" cried the lady.

"Tell thee ? No, although Father Augustine be safe under the sod—that is, if the grass will grow over so rank a grave—though there may be no more fear of his chastising the dwarf, yet the Baron de Fougeres lives, and the fool may tell more than the baron may choose should be told."

"Is the Lady Edith still with Edward de Albini at the tower ?" asked Cordelia.

"She is still at the tower, but he whom you would still more gladly see, he whose image is in your heart, is no longer there. The kid has escaped from the hunter's toils, he seeks the fold of his birth."

"Gone ? Edward de Albini gone ?"

"Even a, I say."

"And has his noble spirit at last yielded to temptation ? Alas, Edward, deeply do I grieve for thee."

"Grieve not, no honour is compromised, no fame tarnished; Edward de Albini has left Thornbury with the full consent of its owner," replied Ronald.

"Has De Fougeres then at last relented?" asked Cordelia.

"He has; but, lady, you have deeper tidings to learn, tidings which will overcome all the feelings of your heart," said the dwarf.

"And who shall tell them to me?" exclaimed Cordelia.

"Sne who, half in tears and half in smiles, sits in yonder tower," answered Ronald.

Cordelia entered the tower, and found Edith sitting in the chair which Edward usually occupied.

"Oh, Cordelia, dearest Cordelia," she exclaimed, "my brother!"

"Brother!" cried her friend. "What mean you, Edith?"

"Edward de Albini is my brother," said Edith.

"How; oh, tell me; Edward the son of De Fougeres?"

"No, no, I could almost say would it were so," answered her friend. "Listen to me, Cordelia, and hear a relation of the events of the last few hours."

Edith then told Cordelia all that had passed in the castle, the total change in her views and hopes, and the departure of Edward and Eustace.

"Oh, Edith! how you will love the Lady de Albini. Do you remember how Father Augustine spoke when you mentioned her?"

"But too well," replied Edith: "his voice has rung in my ears ever since."

"Do you think the monk knew all this?" asked Cordelia.

"Doubtless he did, and it is the only good act of the father which I can recollect, that he did not betray it," replied her friend.

"He dared not betray the secrets of the confessional," said Cordelia.

Many hours were passed by the friends in unreserved and affectionate converse; their hearts seemed the more closely united by the cloud of uncertainty which hung over both; all little fears and jealousies were past, and fervently did they hope for each other's happiness. When they returned to the castle, they found De Fougeres alone, L'Espee having departed for London with De Tunstall. L'Espee had interest at court, and he intended to use it in favour of Cordelia. The young friends therefore were some days in seclusion and repose, and thus their shattered spirits regained strength to endure the fresh excitements which were in store for them.

———

CHAPTER XXVII.

Ah! happy hills, ah! pleasing shades,
 Ah! fields beloved in vain;
Where once my careless childhood stray'd.
 A stranger yet to pain.
I feel the gales that from ye blow,
A momentary bliss bestow,
As waving fresh with gladsome wing,
 My weary soul ye seem to soothe,
And redolent of joy and youth,
 To breathe a second spring.—GRAY.

PERCIVAL CASTLE, the residence of Geoffry de Albini, was an ancient baronial residence, situated upon the top of a mountain, whose sides, bare and rugged, owed nothing to the hand of art, and had been but little favoured by nature. It commanded a wide, but barren landscape, the view extended over many moors, bounded by rugged hills, and valleys dark and deep, cloven by brawling streams, which leapt over the rocks, hurled down from the mountains which barred their course.

The castle was a fortress of unusual strength; its long bare walls spanned the summit of the mountain, and its tall towers stood out in bold relief, flinging their deep shadow across the ravine at the bottom. Scarcely a tree ornamented the scene; a few stunted bushes clothed the lower part of the mountain, and grew, or tried to grow, upon the edge of the river. But even these did not relieve the monotonous dreariness of the scene; they rather seemed to add to it, by showing what might have been under more favourable circumstances.

The path to the castle was cut out of the solid rock, and was precipituos and rude! it wound around the hill, at each turn bringing the traveller within range of cannon planted upon the battlement. Thus secured against assault, Percival Castle frowned defiance upon the neighbouring country.

As Edward and his companion began to ascend the steep path, the thought of the former reverted to Thornbury. How different was the present landscape to that presented by the peaceful and highly ornamented beauty of the latter place! Edward had never before thought the place of his birth otherwise than delightful; he now found it dreary and barren. He endeavoured to believe that the place was changed; but no, there was the brown heath, which, more than once in his childhood, he had seen a prey to the devouring flame; there was the thicket in which he had roused the wolf, when come depredation more daring than usual urged the herdsman to invade the domain of the wild beast of the forest; there was the precipice to whose edge having one day strayed in infancy, the scream of the Lady de Albini brought the truant back to her arms; and there was the circumscribed bit of greensward, where his first feats of horsemanship had been essayed; all was as he left it—but how was he changed.

Sadness stole over the heart of Edward; not even the thought of again meeting his beloved mother could chase it. And of that mother what might he not hear. He had left her pensive and melancholy, even his most lively sallies of childhood had failed to cheer her brow; even his presence seemed to give no balm to her wounded heart. And had she survived his loss? He dared scarcely think of the possibility of her gentle nature having sunk under his protracted imprisonment.

His father too—brave, courteous, in former days, was he still the same? Well, indeed, might Edward's spirits be oppressed by apprehension, and Eustace de Mowbray, guessing in some degree the feelings of his friend, forbore to interrupt his meditations. Thus did they pass on in silence.

The setting sun threw his golden beams aslant the horizon, tinging the tops of the mountains with a ruddy gleam, and casting the valleys into deep shade; the silver brocks leaping, dashing, and foaming, vainly endeavoured to catch a ray of that light which had marked their noon-day course; the tall pine bent his stately head in homage to the departing luminary; and the songsters of the grove who nestled among the boughs of the sturdy and weather-beaten oak, sung their evening song, their glossy wings touched with gold.

As Edward and Eustace approached the outer fortifications of the castle, the sentinel advanced, and immediately recognising the young knight, he burst into an exclamation of surprise and joy. The news of Edward's arrival was speedily proclaimed, and before he reached the castle gate, he was surrounded by his father's retainers, eager to welcome the heir of the house of Albini to the halls of his ancestors. Fearful lest the tumult should reach the ears of his parents and cause too sudden a surprise of joy, Edward requested his friend Eustace to prepare the way for him, by announcing himself as the bearer of tidings from the absent son to his anxious parents.

Eustace de Mowbray was ushered into the aparment where the Lady Elfrida and her maidens were engaged at their usual occupation of embroidery—in those days the almost sole employment alike of lady and of menial. Eustace advanced with reverence; for besides that he had from childhood been accustomed to hear the Lady de Albini mentioned in terms of the highest respect, as one of the most accomplished but retiring women of her age, her appearance at once impressed him with the feeling of nobility and refinement. The Lady Elfrida was of a commanding and dignified appearance, taller than most of her sex; she was still graceful, and if misfortune had not planted grief upon her brow, she might still have been considered eminently handsome. But the premature furrow, the dim eye, told of years passed in mental suffering, and perhaps a minute examination of her countenance would impress upon the heart of the spectator a feeling of pity rather than of admiration. She rose from her seat upon the entrance of Eustace, saying,—

"If the tidings which you bear of one still dear to the mother, although lost to her hope, be of good import, you are indeed welcome, nor shall the rights of hospitality be denied even to the messenger of evil."

"Were mine tidings of evil," replied De Mowbray, "I should reluctantly present myself to the Lady de Albini, but I come to cheer her maternal heart with the tidings of the release of her beloved son, and his speedy arrival at the castle of his parents."

"What do I hear?" exclaimed the lady. "Is it no dream?"

"It is true—I but left the youth to prepare his mother for his arrival," answered De Mowbray.

"Oh, more than hoped for happiness!" cried the lady. "And his unfeeling gaoler, how has he been worked upon to consent to release his prey?"

"Edward de Albini will himself explain the cause and manner of his release," replied Eustace; "the Lady Elfrida has much to hear; may she be enabled to bear with fortitude the interesting recital."

"Oh, tell me! is my Edward safe? Your words are ominous; tell me that my beloved son is indeed well, and at liberty."

At this moment the door of the apartment was burst hastily open, and Edward threw himself into the arms of the Lady Elfrida, exclaiming, "My mother, my dear mother!"

The lady moved not.

"Oh, speak to your son! to your Edward!" cried the young man; "I scarcely hoped ever to see this day."

Still the lady spoke not; and on relaxing from his embrace, she would have fallen to the ground, had not Eustace stepped forward, and caught her insensible form in his arms.

"My mother," cried Edward, "oh! I have killed her!"

The maidens who were present assisted to bear the lady to a couch, and all busied themselves in applying restoratives to their beloved mistress. Edward was distracted with grief, accusing himself as her murderer, and needing the attention of others to himself, he was utterly incapable either of exertion or self-control, and Eustace in vain advised his removal from the apartment. Kneeling by the couch of his mother, he persisted in giving that assistance which was in fact a hindrance, until after more than four hours, during which time the Lady Elfrida passed through a succession of fainting fits, unrelieved by any interval of consciousness. Edward sank in exhaustion upon the floor, and fell into a deep slumber.

It was now nearly midnight, and the domestics wished to remove Edward to bed but Eustace fancying that the lady was in some degree regaining her consciousness, and knowing that her first inquiry would be for her son, would not allow his friend to be disturbed, well aware that a relapse would be inevitable should the lady not immediately see Edward, and that such a relapse would probably be fatal.

Geoffry de Albini was from home, and was not expected to return for some days. Eustace therefore hoped that the weakened frame of his friend would be in some degree restored to composure ere he had to undergo that meeting. In silence did Eustace watch the sufferers; Edward's sleep was apparently easy, and the Lady Elfrida was gradually recovering from her swoon. At length she murmured, "My son!"

"He is here," said Eustace,

"Where?" exclaimed the lady. "Oh, Edward! speak to me, let me hear that angel voice."

"He sleeps, madam; exhausted by the agitation of his spirits, he has sunk into a peaceful slumber," replied Eustace; "it were best not to disturb him."

"Let me but see my child, my only child," said the lady, raising herself on her couch. "Oh, remove him not, he needs repose."

"And the Lady Elfrida also needs it," said De Mowbray.

"No—no—joy is repose to me," replied the lady.

Her maidens however persuaded their lady to retire to her chamber, and a short time after Edward awoke, and having spoken to the steward respecting the accommodation of De Mowbray, the youth retired to rest in the chamber of his infancy. He retired to rest, but not to slumber; hopes and fears crowded upon him, and not till the sun had dawned upon his couch did he close his eyes in sleep.

Morning came, and with it came the sober certainty of waking bliss to the inmates of Percival Castle. The Lady Elfrida summoned the domestics and retainers in the castle hall, and presenting her son to them, claimed for him the recognition due to his father's heir. Joy lighted up every countenance, although tears dimmed many an aged eye, when they beheld him whose absence had been so heavily deplored.

After the first emotion of maternal affection had subsided, the Lady de Albini questioned her son respecting his residence at Thornbury, his amusements and occupations; and upon his mention of Cordelia and Edith, she asked if those ladies were the daughters of the Baron de Fougeres.

The friends hesitated, and at last Edward finding his mother's eye fixed upon him with a look of anxious inquiry, said, hesitatingly, "No, mother, they are not."

"Do I not remember the name of Cordelia at Thornbury? Surely the infant who was so mysteriously brought to the convent, and placed under the care of the abbess was so named?" asked the lady.

"She is the same," replied Eustace, pitying his friend's embarrassment. "I have known her from childhood till she has grown up a beautiful and fascinating woman."

"Has it ever been discovered to whom she owes her parentage?" asked the lady.

"A concurrence of circumstances have brought the whole to light," answered Eustace; "and Cordelia is now claimed by her uncle De Tunstall; she only remains for a time a beloved inmate of Thornbury Castle."

"De Tunstall!" exclaimed the lady. "Whose child then is she?"

"The child of Eleanor de Tunstall by her second marriage with the Baron de Dunstanville," replied Eustace.

"Marriage! it was no marriage," cried Lady Elfrida proudly. "The unhappy woman forfeited her place in society by her ill-conduct; and I much wonder that the Baron de Fougeres should suffer his daughter to hold such companionship; contamination is sure. But you said, Edward," continued the lady, after a pause, "that neither of these maidens were the daughters of your tyrant, who then is the other whom you named?"

"Edith; your own—your lost Edith!" exclaimed Edward, embracing his mother.

The Lady Elfrida started. "Name not that name, Edward, it is now eighteen years since it met my ear."

"But, my mother, I speak in truth. Your Edith was rescued by the Barond Fougeres, and has been brought up by him with the utmost care," said Edward.

"My child! my Edith! why has she not flown to her mother's arms?" cried the lady. "No—it cannot be—the child whose loss I have for so many years unceasingly wept, cannot be restored to me."

"She can—she will," exclaimed both the friends.

"And wherefore does the Baron de Fougeres detain my treasure? No Edward, you are deceiving me; this Edith is some low-born child, not my noble girl," said the lady, despondingly.

"Hear me, my dearest mother," said Edward, gravely. "You know well that your son has never deceived you in the slightest manner, and can you imagine that in this blissful moment of renewed affection, he would give you a pang either through wantonness or deceit?"

"No—no—you have ever been the soul of truth to me, speak on" replied the lady.

"The Baron de Fougeres," said Edward, "was by some means, not now necessary to explain, enabled to save your and my Edith. He educated her as his own child; he engaged Thornbury Castle in order that she might be reared in her native halls; he intended to restore her; but when her advancing years brought increasing beauty and attraction he had not resolution to part with his treasure. Now,

No. 21.

however, he has confided the whole of her history to my sister's ear, and she is impatient to be welcomed to her mother's arms."

"It shall be so—I will immediately return with you to Thornbury, and reclaim my darling child. But, Edward, answer me ; know you the circumstances which attend her loss ?"

"I do," replied De Albini.

" And know you by what means the Baron de Fougeres saved my child ?"

Edward hesitated; he feared to acquaint his mother with all the truth.

"There was an old acquaintance," continued the lady, " and to the anger of the baron at its discontinuance I attribute his vindictive conduct towards you, in refusing even the ransom of a prince which your father has repeatedly and imploringly tendered to him. How then is it that he rescued my other child from her watery grave?".

" Mother, I know the whole," replied Edward, looking down. "The Baron de Fougeres has passed a life of misery ; Edith alone has been his comfort ; she it is who has softened his temper and ameliorated his disposition; he is a broken spirited, but no longer a vindictive man, and although his injuries towards you have been indeed guilty and dreadful, he is ready to make all the amends now in his power, by giving back to you the child of whom he deprived you, as beautiful, as affectionate, and as graceful, as she could have become under your maternal care.

"Deprived me, Edward? Then I do not judge him too hardly," cried the lady.

" I promised you that I would tell the whole truth. The Baron de Fougeres stole your infant, under the influence of feelings which I cannot mention, but which you may comprehend, and surely can forgive ; he has taught her to love and revere you, although till lately she knew not that she was your child."

"Edward," said the lady, in a tone of serious determination, " I can never see that man, I can never enter Thornbury while he is there ; but my Edith must be reclaimed, and immediately.—She is in society unworthy of her purity."

Eustace had left the room at the beginning of this conversation, and Edward answered, " I know to whom you allude ; but mother, is it just to condemn the child for the faults of the parent ?"

" I know not whether it be justice, Edward ; but never was my house dishonoured by contact with such an offender, and I have the honour of the race of De Albini in my keeping."

" True, mother ; and no one can be more anxious to preserve that honour unsullied than your son, as others can tell you what it would be vain-glorious in me to speak. But this poor orphan has never seen her mother since she was brought to Thornbury and placed under the care of her aunt, the abbess. Eleanor de Dunstanville died a few months after this, and in the seclusion of the convent Cordelia only learned the ways of innocence and religion. How then could she be contaminated ?"

" But Edward, this girl is illegitimate, and therefore unworthy the companionship of my child," said the lady Elfrida, proudly.

"Forgive me, mother," replied Edward. "Circumstances have recently brought to light a contract of marriage between Eleanor de Tunstall and the Baron de Dunstanville, and her worst enemy must acknowledge that the stain is thereby removed from her name. My dearest mother, I beseech you, be generous."

" I will be generous my son ; but happily this question concerns not us; this maiden's acquaintance with my child will not be continued under this roof."

Edward fell at the feet of the Lady Elfrida, exclaiming,—

"Mother, forgive me—I love Cordelia."

The lady started as if a serpent had crossed her path.

' Edward it can never be—say not such a word again."

" And will you sacrifice your son's happiness to a mere prejudice ?"

' To a proper rule of propriety, Edward ; never has such an alliance disgraced our house, and my son shall not be the first to introduce the degradation."

"Then you again banish your only son; for, mark me, mother, never will I wed any but Cordelia de Dunstanville."

The Lady Elfrida hesitated.

"Edward, let us leave this subject; the intelligence respecting my Edith has disturbed me. Let us defer any further mention of your unhappy love till your father's arrival, I would not cloud his joy at your return.

Edward embraced his mother affectionately, saying, "I only ask you to see her and hear her story, and you will readily love her."

· Of Edith all were willing to speak. Edward described her person and accomplishments, and the Lady de Albini was never weary of hearing the most minute details respecting the manners and habits of her long lost daughter. While receiving from Edward assurances of the perfections of Edith, her feelings towards De Fougeres were gradually softened, and her repugnance to returning to Thornbury so much lessened, that she almost promised Edward she would endeavour to persuade the Baron de Albini to accompany her there, in order the sooner to embrace her daughter.

And where was Eustace de Mowbray during these hours? Silently did he listen to the praises of his beloved Edith, and if occasionally his uncontrollable feelings led him to join in the eulogy of his friend, he again shrunk back as if ashamed of his interference. The Lady Elfrida became daily more affable towards her guest; it seemed indeed, that she was becoming attached to the youth, to whom she frequently spoke of his parents, especially of the Lady Mowbray, his mother, who had married about the same time with herself.

One evening, while thus conversing, the Lady Elfrida dropped a hint of some agreement between herself and her early friend as to an alliance between their children.

Eustace eagerly begged for an explanation of her words.

"It was more than mere friendly gossip," answered the lady; "had my poor Edith been spared to me, the Baron de Mowbray and Geoffrey de Albini had promised us that they would not thwart our wishes."

."And may I not now claim the performance of that promise?" asked Eustace.

"I know not, circumstances are altered," replied the lady. "I know not my Edith's wishes, and I would not in the first moment of our meeting ask them."

"But if I tell you that Edith is not averse to such a union," asked Edward, "will you then claim the performance of your early intention?"

The lady did not answer, and De Albini continued. "My friend Eustace de Mowbray loves Edith; he has been her playmate in childhood, her companion in youth, and a strong affection has grown up between them. De Mowbray accompanied me here in order to make known his attachment, and to request my father's consent."

"I will readily give mine," said the lady; "but what says the Baron de Fougeres to this attachment? Has it had his encouragement?"

"It has," said Edward, "but with the reservation of its being subject to your approbation."

This conversation rendered Eustace Mowbray the happiest of beings; he was from this day lively and vivacious, and the hours and days flew rapidly by, till the day approached on which the return of the Baron de Albini was expected. On that day the retainers of the baron sent a deputation, headed by the seneschal to the Lady de Albini, requesting her permission to light the beacon fire upon the tower, and to make other signals of rejoicing to welcome their lord.

The lady Elfrida complied with this request, and the beacon fire was duly lighted in the evening, and the bells of the village church rang merrily. Edward awaited with anxiety and impatience his parent's return; he felt deeply how much depended upon his word respecting the future happiness of his life, and he dreaded his denial. Eustace also lost the buoyancy of his spirits as the time arrived which was to seal his destiny.'

After sun-set a violent ringing at the outer gate of the castle was heard, and presently, the voice of the Baron de Albini, exclaiming, "Where is he? where is he ?" The door opened, and Edward was the next moment in his father's arms. After a few mutual exclamations of joy, the baron inquired into the circumstances of his son's escape from the guardianship of the Baron de Fougeres, scarcely believing that the baron could have willingly dismissed him. Edward explained all to his father, except what respected Edith and Cordelia ; this he left the Lady Elfrida to communicate. Upon Geoffrey de Albini requesting an introduction to Eustace, the lady announced him as the only son of Lord de Mowbray, and as the infant whose birth had been the cause of so much rejoicing during her residence at Thornbury castle. De Albini, who had never heard his lady allude in the slightest degree to the events of their early married life, looked at her with astonishment, and his surprise was too great to be controlled when she added, —

" My lord, I have that to tell you which would startle the dull, cold ear of death. You are surprised at my mentioning Thornbury with calmness, retire with me, and learn a tale which will bring back to us that happiness which I thought was gone for ever."

So saying, she led the way to an inner apartment, where she unfolded the whole circumstances to her astonished husband.

De Albini had not been aware of the early engagement of his wife to De Fougeres ; this she was obliged to mention to him, and his pity for the disappointment of his rival, lessened his indignation and horror at his crime. His anxiety respecting Edith was even greater than that of the Lady Elfrida, but to her infinite surprise he was well acquainted with Cordelia's history, and looked favourably upon his son's attachment.

" I have heard of this matter at the court of Stephen, whence I am but now returned," he said. " The wrongs and misfortunes of Cordelia de Dunstanville, have raised her friends among the highest in the land; the king himself has commanded her attendance at court, in order to receive the assurance of the lands and honors of her parents, and it is rumoured that she is the richest heiress in the kingdom of England."

" But riches will not wipe out the stain of illegitimacy," said the lady.

" She is not regarded as illegitimate," replied the baron ; " the paper which was found upon the person of the Baron de Bohun, when he died, is considered sufficient claim to legal inheritance. It is even said that the king intends to marry her to one of the young nobles of the highest rank."

" My poor Edward ! " exclaimed the lady ; " how will he bear to lose her ? "

" He shall not lose her ; my claims upon Stephen are, it is true, not great, nor are they founded upon services rendered in the field ; but I am honored at the council board, and I have reasons to think that what Geoffrey de Albini condescends to ask, will not be lightly refused."

" You gladden my heart," said the Lady Elfrida. " Did you hear anything of the Lady Cordelia's personal deportment ? "

" I heard that she is beautiful, extremely beautiful, like her unhappy mother, and that she inherits that genius and wit which rendered Eleanor de Tunstall the ornament of the court, and of society"

" I trust she does not inherit her mother's volatility of principle," said the lady.

" I made that inquiry merely through curiosity," replied the baron ; " little thinking that I should ever be personally interested in the answer, and I was told by an ancient knight who had been a resident at Thornbury, that Cordelia has been educated with great care, and that under circumstances of peculiar difficulty she has conducted herself with a prudence and reserve remarkable in one so young, and so secluded."

" Our Edward may then be happy," exclaimed the lady.

" I also heard the daughter of the Baron de Fougeres mentioned in terms of the warmest praise,—praise which would almost seem exaggerated, but that they were used by one who knew her well."

" And you knew not that they spoke of your own Edith ? " said the lady.

" No, but an inexplicable feeling of curiosity took possession of me ; and hearing that the Baron de Fougeres had at last reluctantly yielded to the desire of his monarch, that he should bring his beautiful daughter to the court, I delayed my return home for some days, in order to behold this paragon of loveliness."

"And did you—oh, did you see her?" asked the Lady Elfrida impetuously.

"I did not. I heard that the maiden herself was averse to appearing in public; that mysterious circumstances had taken place at Thornbury, and that the lady claimed the fulfilment of her father's promise, that she should not leave her retirement until the return of a young prisoner who had escaped from the castle, and to whom she was said to be attached,"

"This is all now explained to us," said the lady; "and I am impatient to see my child."

"The aged knight whom I have alluded to, shook his head when questioned about the mysteries of Thornbury, but it now strikes me that he made my acquaintance chiefly with a view of talking to me of my child."

"Did he then know her history?" asked the lady.

"A part of it I imagine. I thought his advances to me rude and impertinent, and I endeavoured to repel them, but I could not succeed. I now give him full credit for kindness of intention."

"And when shall we claim our dear Edith?" asked the lady.

"I am most ready to depart for Thornbury directly; I will give orders for our journey to-morrow morning," replied De Albini.

"Most gladly shall I set out, answered Lady Elfrida. Now let us rejoin our guest and son."

A few words sufficed to explain to Edward his father's concurrence in his attachment for Cordelia. De Albini saw that such an alliance would assure to Stephen his son's fealty, and he felt certain that this idea would have sufficient weight with the king to render his acquiescence certain, notwithstanding that Stephen had planned a marriage between the orphan heiress and the son of the Baron Mouthermer.

De Albini received Eustace de Mowbray with kindness sufficient to subdue any alarm, and, in a subsequent interview, when Eustace pleaded for the baron's consent to his marriage with Edith, De Albini unhesitatingly complied; merely requiring that Eustace should not consider him finally pledged to give him his daughter, until De Albini had embraced his long-lost Edith.

On the following day a happy, but anxious party, left Percival Castle to cross the country to Thornbury. The journey appeared long to all, and when, at the end of the third day, the well-remembered towers struck the view of the Lady Elfrida, she uttered a cry of joy, and sunk back in her litter dissolved in tears. Her lord, understanding her feelings, forbore to interrupt her, and the cavalcade passed on in silence, Edward and Eustace being too much absorbed in their feelings to enter into conversation. There was, however, one of the party, who, whether in joy or in sorrow, kept her woman's privilege of talking. This was old Ursula; who, by dint of earnest entreaties, had prevailed on Lady Elfrida to permit her to make one of the party to claim her young lady. Ursula seemed still to regard Edith as a child; the lapse of years had been lost to the sorrowing domestic; and, although she often busied herself in imagining what a beautiful young lady Miss Edith would have been had she lived, she could not now be brought to regard her except as an helpless infant. Ursula amused her hearers with absurd suppositions respecting her young lady; she loved Edward, but he was in her heart but second to the memory of her lost infant; and when he told her of Edith's grace and beauty, she scarcely listened to him; it was the lost babe whom she loved to talk of.

There was, besides Lady Edith, another subject of interest to Ursula at Thornbury. She had known father Augustine in his younger days, when he first took up his residence at the monastery. She knew him at first, as he was known to his other companions, only as a handsome man and pious monk; but had not the melancholy event of Edith's supposed death intervened, there was every probability that Ursula would have fallen into the snares of the villain. Ursula was now anxious to hear some tidings of her former lover; and after having in vain inquired of her fellow attendants, none of whom, of course, could give her the information she desired, she applied to her young lord, and heard from Edward a tale of the father's career, by no means gently coloured.

With the true instinct of women, Ursula would not credit all that Edward told her to the disadvantage of Father Augustine; she could not believe that he who had flattered her beauty, and spoke with honied words of her fascinations, could be what Edward described him, and even when the latter related the story of Rosamond, his auditor blamed the simple girl, and almost exonerated her betrayer. His death, however, gave a necessary close to the story. She still grieved for her lover, till Edward, half jestingly, and half in earnest, reminded her that the years which had changed her beauty into age, would have destroyed he comeliness of Father Augustine, had he been still alive.

CHAPTER XXVIII.

Some feelings are to mortals given,
With less of earth in them than heaven;
And if there be a human tear,
From passion's dross refin'd and clear,
A tear so limpid and so meek,
It might not stain an angel's cheek,
'Tis that which pious fathers shed,
Upon a duteous daughter's head.—SCOTT.

THE anxious party reached Thornbury, about sunset; Edward and Eustace rode on to prepare the inhabitants for the visit which awaited them. After having acquainted the Baron de Fougeres with the approach of his parents, Edward requested to be admitted to the presence of his sister, Edith, whom he found in her chamber with Cordelia. After the first greetings, Edith enquired whose was the cavalcade which she saw at a considerable distance, slowly approaching.

"It is that of your father, dearest Edith," replied Edward. "The Baron de Albini comes to claim his daughter."

Edith sighed deeply.

"Why dost sigh my sister? The Lady Elfrida also comes," said Edward.

"My mother? and does she take this long journey for my sake?" said Edith.

"She does," replied her brother; "they but wait until I have announced their approach to the Baron de Fougeres."

At this moment the baron entered, and Edith embracing him, exclaimed, "My dear father! oh, let me not leave you."

De Fougeres trembled from head to foot; he seemed to be contending against some strong emotion, and unable to speak, he sunk into a chair.

Edith was alarmed. Although accustomed to the various changes in the mood of the baron she had never seen him thus violently affected.

"You are ill, my dearest father," she cried.

"Not father, Edith," cried De Fougeres.

"Yes, father!—always father!" replied Edith, sobbing.

After a struggle De Fougeres said, "Edith, I have known that this day must come, yet am I not the more prepared to meet it; the thought of resigning you who have been a comfort and solace to me, from your tenderest years, is of itself sufficient to unman me; but there are other causes for my agitation. I am this evening to meet her for whom I would have sacrificed my early life; her for whose happiness I would have died; and I meet her, how?—as a robber, a deceiver; as having embittered her solitary hours, and turned her happiness into sorrow."

"Oh!" cried Edith, "the Lady Elfrida will not feel thus."

"Believe me," said Edward; "my father and mother can forgive. They rejoice too sincerely in the prospect of again living in the society of their children, to show resentment or unkindness."

"But Edith," said the baron; "we must part.

"I will be your frequent guest," replied Edith, tenderly. "I can never neglect the protector and friend of my infancy."

Presently the castle bell rung loudly, and De Fougeres reluctantly descended to receive his guests. The meeting between him and Geoffrey de Albini was cordial, but ceremonious; that with the Lady Elfrida was more embarrassed. The guests were ushered into the saloon of the castle, and in a moment Edith threw herself into her mother's arms.

Releasing herself from her embrace, the Lady Elfrida gazed on the beautiful girl for some minutes, without speaking; while Edith, somewhat alarmed, whispered, "Will my mother love me?"

"Is it indeed my own child, my Edith whom I behold?" cried Lady Elfrida. "Yes! even now, I trace the features of the infant I lost, but how much more lovely than even a mother's imagination pictured." Edith turned blushing to her father, and Geoffrey de Albini taking her hand and placing it in that of Eustace de Mowbray, said,—

"May my child be happy!"

Eustace surprised, warmly thanked De Albini on his knee, and Edith hastened to her mother, to beg her to ratify her father's consent.

"Freely, my child, do I receive Eustace de Mowbray as my betrothed son," said the Lady Elfrida; "our old friendship thereby shall be renewed." Then turning to De Fougeres, she added, "our Edith has had the consent of him whose will has hitherto guided her."

"Yes," replied the baron. "I know and value the youth; I have seen the attachment which has grown between them, and feeling that the day must come when I must surrender my charge, I have encouraged that attachment which I knew was intended between the infants."

"Did you then know of the compact between our family and that of the Baron de Mowbray?" asked Geoffrey de Albini.

"Yes," replied De Fougeres. "The Lady de Mowbray has repeatedly alluded to it, and although she is devotedly attached to Edith, she has never ceased to wish that the compact which was so unexpectedly broken could be renewed."

During this conversation, Edward was gloomily stationed at the further end of the apartment. Cordelia was not present, and he dreaded to mention her destiny.

At length De Albini said,—

"I have heard much of a lady companion of my Edith's, the Lady Cordelia de Dunstanville, if she be still at Thornbury, may I beg that she will favour our evening repast with her presence?'

"Cheerfully she will," said Edith, "I will seek her."

So saying, Edith left the room, followed by Edward. When the former had delivered her message, Edward said,—

"Will you not speak to me, Cordelia? Have these few short days sufficed to make you forget your Edward?"

"Oh, no—no! not forget. But alas! I know not if I may speak," cried Cordelia.

"What do you mean?" asked Edward.

"I have this day received intelligence from my kinsman that the king has demanded me in marriage for the young Baron de Mouthermer," replied the maiden.

"And can Cordelia forget her vows of love, for one whom she has never seen?" asked Edward.

"Never," replied Cordelia. "But the king is powerful, he may command my compliance."

"Does De Tunstall know of our attachment?" asked Edward.

"He has some surmise of it. He is ambitious for his niece, and I much fear he will not regard her wishes," answered Cordelia.

" Fear not," said Edward ; " my father has influence with Stephen ; he approves my choice, and he will exert himself to procure his son's happiness. May I hope that my Cordelia will attend the summons which she has received."

" I dread meeting Geoffrey de Albini," replied the lady.

" Why should my Cordelia dread it ? Her graces and her beauty will plead her cause more effectually than any words of mine can do," cried Edward.

Cordelia reluctantly consented to descend into the saloon. During Edward's absence, his parents had conquered the awkwardness of their situation ; the Lady Elfrida gazed with interest upon the spot where her first happy days had been passed, she ceased to regret having undertaken this harrassing journey ; and allusion having been made to the Lady's Tower, she expressed her wish to visit that once beloved retreat.

Soon after supper one of the domestics approached Edith, saying,—

" There is one of the followers of the Baron de Albini who wishes to see the Lady Edith."

" It is, doubtless, old Ursula," said the Lady Elfrida ; " she talks much of her nursling."

" Let her be admitted instantly," said De Fougeres.

Ursula was accordingly introduced into the hall, and Edith rose to receive her. Ursula made a humble curtsey, but looked round without speaking.

" You wish to see the Lady Edith," said the Baron de Fougeres.

" Yes, please your honour ; they told me she was here," replied Ursula.

" And do you not know me, Ursula ?" asked Edith.

" Why you cannot be my sweet babe," said Ursula, in a tone of wonder.

" I am Edith," replied the maiden.

" Nay, nay, my Edith was a sweet infant, a babe," said Ursula, in a tone of wonder.

" Indeed I am Edith," said the maiden.

After some conversation Ursula was satisfied that the lovely creature whom she beheld was her own babe ; but she seemed to regret that years had rendered unnecessary those cares and attentions which she had reckoned upon bestowing on the young Edith as in early years. Now she saw that those attentions would be entirely misplaced, Ursula felt vexed and disappointed, and betraying in her manner and countenance the emotions of her mind, she was about to leave the hall, when Edith, who saw that something had displeased her, although she could not guess what it could be, took her hand, saying,—

" My good Ursula, you shall still be my nurse and attendant ; desire to be conducted to my chamber iu the morning, and you shall again preside over the toilet of your child."

Ursula expressed her pleasure at Edith's kind condescension, and returned to the servants' hall, declaring that her young lady was as beautiful as could be expected, considering what a lovely infant she had been.

On the ensuing morning the Lady Elfrida, Edith, and Edward, prepared after breakfast to visit the Lady's Tower. Not without many a pang had the Lady Elfrida formed the resolution, and not without much difficulty and pain did she adhere to it. Everything conspired to remind her of the fatal evening on which she had last enjoyed her loved retreat ; the time of the year was the same, autumn spread his golden tinge over the face of the country, the corn had bowed before the sickle of the industrious husbandman, and the fields were bare with stubble, the stately oak and the steady birch, told that the day was approaching which should rob them of their beauty, the dark pine still waved high in its unchanging gloominess, nor spring nor autumn robbed it of its feathery foliage, and smmer failed to enliven its dark tresses. The lady looked around.

" Is nought then changed?" said she, musingly. " Nor is the heart of woman changed. Time has blanched her locks, sorrow has furrowed her cheek, but the heart of the mother still burns with the summer sun of love. My children," she continued, turning to the fair young forms which reverentially waited on her footsteps, " nature may change and decay, but love survives."

They entered the tower, all was exactly as Edward had left it. His chair by the window where he used to muse upon the river's flow ere he learnt the sad history of his mother's bereavement; the lute which Edith used to waken to ac-

company her voice when she exerted the power of music to soothe his imprisonment—the few books wherewith his solitary hours were hastened in their course—all were there—and all spoke powerfully to the heart of the Lady Elfrida. She gazed alternately upon her children, and the tear-drop hung upon her eyelid.

" And this was your prison, Edward," she said.

" Call it not prison, mother," replied the youth, " it was here that I learned to love a sister, and——"

No. 22.

Edward stopped, but his companions guessed his thoughts.

"Fear not," my son," said the lady. "You will find a friend in your father, let the orphan's claim to her parentage be established, and your love will be prosperous."

"Does my father, then, indeed consent?" asked Edward.

"He does. He has heard of the intention of the king, but he has confidence in the goodness of Stephen, that he will not commence his reign by rendering any of his subjects miserable; and De Albini is so much pleased with the person and demeanour of the Lady Cordelia, that it will be more than a matter of mere cold justice with him to promote her welfare, and accomplish a union so honourable and advantageous to our house."

Edward expressed his joy and gratitude to his father, and asked his mother her opinion of his Cordelia.

"She reminds me of her mother," replied the lady; "but her bearing is modest and maidenly. My deceased friend, the abbess, has done her duty towards her niece, in keeping her free from the contamination of the world. But admidst the troubles which followed upon the death of her protectress, how was it that the young Cordelia did not seek the asylum which I had promised the abbess would always be open to her?"

"I believe," said Edith, "that Father Augustine discouraged that idea. He told Cordelia that the Lady de Albini would scorn the nameless and dowerless orphan, while he unceasingly endeavoured to persuade her to profess herself as a nun."

"Wily to the last, as at the first," exclaimed the lady. "Well do I remember his mean arts on many occasions, and I left Thornbury with the less regret, because I should be released from that man. How had the Lady Cordelia resolution to withstand him?"

"I interceded, and obtained permission for Cordelia to reside with me," said Edith. "She has been a dear and true friend, and I shall ever consider that a happy day which bestowed her affection upon me."

"I trust ere long Cordelia will have ceased to consider the Lady de Albini the unbending and harsh person the monk depicted to her. I would not sully the unblemished honour of my race by an alliance with illegitimacy or vice, but it seems that this will not apply to Cordelia de Dunstanville. The paper found upon the Baron de Bohun sufficiently proves that she may be considered the lawful heiress of her father; and if our monarch, in his superior wisdom, allow her claim to her lands and fortune, it would ill become a dutiful subject, as I hope Geoffery de Albini will always prove himself, to dispute her title to respect and honour."

While the lady was speaking, strange noises were heard without the tower. Edward listened for a few minutes, and then opening the door, Ronald entered with many contortions and grimaces. Lady Elfrida started, and made a sign to Edward to dismiss the intruder, but he said, "What cheer, Ronald?"

"The waters have given up their dead," said Ronald "The kid is restored to the fold of the dam, and Ronald only is left cheerless.",

"Not entirely cheerless," said Edward. "I am not so ungrateful."

"Who is this, my son?" asked the lady.

"A being rude enough in appearance, but ready-witted in mind," replied Edward. "One who cheered my solitude, kept up my hope, and foretold my release. Ronald," he added, turning to the dwarf, "This is the Lady Elfrida de Albini."

"I know it," replied Ronald.

"How dost know me?" asked the lady.

"By force of benefits conferred and not forgotten," answered the dwarf.

"Explain your meaning," said the lady.

"Does not the Lady Elfrida remember the infant of Ralph, the huntsman? whose life she saved?" asked Ronald.

"Well," replied the lady.

"I am that infant. The life preserved by the Lady Elfrida's charity and care is tough, and has lasted through difficulty and danger; the casket which contained it was injured, but it has not yielded to pain and sickness. In return I have tended the young heir in his captivity, and if I was enabled to foretel his release it was well to raise his spirits. But I never tempted him to dishonour, as I have heard him tempted."

Edward was uneasy at this hint; and, in answer to his mother's inquiry as to Ronald's meaning, he would have turned the subject, had not the dwarf added,—

"It is fit that Geoffery de Albini should know how worthy his son is of the race whence he sprang."

"How?" asked the lady.

"The tempter sought him, and beseeched, nay commanded him, to barter honour for liberty. But the spirit of his race was in him, and he refused," said Ronald.

"Who was this? who was the tempter?" asked the lady.

"The monk," answered the dwarf.

"Father Augustine would have released me to fight by the side of my father," said Edward.

"My noble-hearted son !" exclaimed the lady.

"That cause could not prosper whose adherents embraced it by means of dishonour," answered Edward; "and my father would not have welcomed his son to his side, had he betrayed his word."

"Truly may this person say that the spirit of thy race is in thee, my Edward," said the lady, tenderly embracing him. "But how could he foretel thy release?"

"Does not the looker-on at a game see more than the movers?" asked the dwarf. "And did I not know that the baron, my master, had promised to release his prey as soon as peace should be concluded between those who struggled for that bauble—the crown? And what did I learn when sent to the camp, but that peace must soon be concluded? I have been called a fool. Am I so?"

"No," said Edward. "But how could you foresee the change in the fortunes of the Lady Edith?"

"I did not foresee them," answered Ronald. "But it may be that others knew that the waters must yield their prey, and Ronald was no fool to profit by the intelligence accidentally gained. But I have done with being a fool now. I must sit down in sober sadness, and think of what has been."

"Will you go with me, Ronald?" asked Edward.

"I was born at Thornbury, and where the shoot was raised the tree must be felled," replied the dwarf.

"We shall at least meet again," observed Edward.

The dwarf made an uncouth obeisance, and departed. A conversation ensued between the Lady Elfrida and her son, as they returned to the castle, and Edward related the interview with the monk, and the pertinacious attempts of the latter to induce him to escape.

Upon reaching the castle, Lady Elfrida found her lord in secret conference with De Fougeres ; and when, afer some hours, De Albini joined his wife, he informed her that it was his intention to proceed to London directly, in order to ascertain in what position the affairs of Cordelia were placed, to demand her hand of De Tunstall, and to request the king's ratification of the engagement.

"It is necessary that Edward should accompany me; and the Baron de Fougeres desires that if you are so inclined, you will consider Thornbury as your home during my absence. He is himself called to another part of the kingdom, and he will join me in London a short time hence."

"I can make no objection to that arrangement; it will give me time to enjoy my dearest Edith's company. You know not, De Albini, the treasure we have so uuexpectedly discovered in that charming girl ; her education has been entirely befitting the daughter of our house, nor could I have succeeded more completely in rendering her all that a mother can wish."

"Your observation gives me great pleasure ; but we shall speedily be called to relinquish her. The Baron de Fougeres tells me that our ancient friend, De Mowbray, expects the nuptials to be no longer delayed than is absolutely necessary under the altered circumstances in which Edith is placed."

"I shall, during your absence, renew my friendship with the Lady de Mowbray," replied the lady, "and shall hear her wishes upon the subject."

"De Fougeres hinted to me this morning, that if you are inclined to make Thornbury again your residence, he should gladly retire to the west, as this place cannot be a very happy home to him after what has taken place."

Lady de Albini expressed her joyful assent. "This absence of yours," she added, "will give me opportunities of learning the character and accomplishments of her who will soon be our daughter—the Lady Cordelia. I am anxious for Edward's happiness, and shall watch her narrowly."

"I have heard such favourable accounts of the fair Cordelia," answered Geoffrey de Albini, "that I do not fear your scrutiny. Should happily my embasy to court prove successful, the double nuptials shall be celebrated at Thornbury with a splendour befitting our station and power."

"Such has been my day-dream," exclaimed the lady; "but I feared that our host would scarcely allow it to be realised."

"Oh! yes. De Fougeres will always be a kind friend to our Edith; and I see plainly that the sooner she is relieved from her present awkward position towards him and me, and given to the love of Eustace Mowbray, the more happy De Fougeres will be— he has such acute feelings, and they pain him."

On the following day Geoffrey de Albini and his son departed for London. De Fougeres remained behind for a few hours in order to give proper instructions for the accomodation of his guest! and then, after a respectful adieu to the Lady Elfrida, aud a tender emorace to his beloved Edith, he pursued his journey into Wales.

Thus relieved from the presence of one who could not but remind her of the misery of many long years, the Lady de Albini recovered in a great degree her health and spirits. The Lady de Mowbray renewed her habits of intimacy at Thornbury Castle, und many other families in the neighbourhood sought the acquaintance of the Lady de Albini. Although professing to live in a retired manner, the lady could not resist the supplications of those whom she had early known, to join in their society; and Edith who had hitherto mixed not at all in the world, and had no companion, save Cordelia, was rejoiced to make friends among her young equals. Everywhere that she went, she was admired. Hitherto she had been regarded as the rich, but recluse heiress of Ralph de Fougeres, and her engagement with Eustace Mowbray being well known she had rather been shunned than courted by the female nobility of the neighbourhood. She was known to be good and charitable, but she was supposed to be haughty. Now her true character appeared, and as the daughter af one so highly respected as the Lady Elfrida de Albini, Edith found welcome and admiration.

Nor was the mother's heart ungrateful. Indeed, how could that be, when she saw her Edith the leading star of every eye, the admired of every heart. The ladies copied her manners and dress, and the first nobles in the land were withheld only by her known engagement and evident attachment to De Mowbray, from laying their titles and fortune at her feet.

"I must hasten your father's return, Edith," said Eustace to her one day, as they returned from an archery meeting where Edith's beauty had shone pre-eminently conspicuous. "I shall be afraid of the dagger or the bowl, if you continue thus admired. The young Duke of Norfolk seemed much inclined to put me out of his way."

"Oh! Eustace, do not laugh at me because these young courtiers like to look at a new face. Remember how I have been mewed up at Thornbury, and I have no doubt that (thanks to Father Augustine) most appalling stories have gone forth of the terrible secrets of the castle."

"Oh! yes," replied her lover, "I have detected absurdities which I should not like to repeat to you."

"It is the fear of this which makes me so willing to show myself to the gossiping world, during the absence of De Fougeres. When it is once generally known that I am neither a sorceress, nor a mermaid, living half my hours in the river, I shall sink again into oblivion."

" Not while beauty is admired and gracefulness felt," replied Eustace tenderly. "But it is in some degree as you say. I have heard both the stories to which you allude, with various embellishments. They all, however, emanate from the monastery."

" How much mischief that bad man has done ! " cried Edith; " and how much more might he have done, had he not departed to the fight, and met with the death he so well merited. But, indeed, Eustace, I am tired of this gay life, and were it not for my dear mother's sake, I would willingly draw back into my shell again."

" I fancy that will not be allowed," replied De Mowbray. " The Lady Elfrida expects that we shall be called upon to attend the court immediately after our nuptials, if indeed the king do not require the ceremony to take place at London."

" Oh, Eustace ! pray do not let it be so," exclaimed Edith.

" I am deeply interested in avoiding it," replied her lover; " not only for your sake, dearest, but because my mother's infirm health prevents all thought of her visiting London, and she is anxious to be present."

" The baron's return will decide it, I suppose," said Edith; " I almost dread the intelligence he will bring respecting Cordelia."

" Why, will she not join in our amusements ?" asked Eustace.

" Cordelia has very delicate feelings, and until she knows that her position in society is established, she will not subject herself to observations which might be mortifying to her pride. I think she is right, although I regret her absence in scenes which I enjoy."

" Surely, under the protection of the Lady de Albini, no wounding remarks could reach her," answered De Mowbray, " but I like her for her self-denial."

Thus the time passed at Thornbury Castle, during the absence of De Albini, to whom we must now attend.

CHAPTER XXIX.

Oh, for the swords of former time !
Oh, for the men who bore them !
When arm'd for right, they stood sublime
And tyrants crouch'd before them !
When pure yet, 'ere courts began
With honours to enslave him,
The best honours worn by man,
Were those that virtue gave him.—MOORE.

DE ALBINI and his son reached London, after three days travelling, and proceeding to their city house in Blackfriars, they endeavoured to gain intelligence of the movements of the court of Stephen. De Albini learned that the king was hunting at Windsor, for a few days, and well knowing that it would be of no use to request an audience at such a time, he determined to await the return of Stephen to London. In the meantime he sought de Tunstall, and by a trusty messenger requested him to name a time to receive him.

At the appointed time De Albini waited on De Tunstall, by whom he was received courteously, but coldly.

" To what am I indebted for the honour of this interview ? " asked Tunstall.

" My visit respects your niece, the Lady Cordelia de Dunstanville, my lord," replied De Albini.

"Indeed! I trust no harm has befallen the daughter of my sister?" inquired De Tunstall. "The maiden's own obstinate wish prevailed on me to leave her a Thornbury Castle."

"No harm has befallen the lady," replied his companion; "I left her at Thornbury, three days ago, in health and beauty."

"Indeed, the latter may well be said," observed De Tunstall; "as my heiress, and the possessor of so much beauty and wit, the Lady Cordelia de Dunstanville is a fit match for the highest noble in our monarch's dominions, and for such an one is she destined."

"Then my errand is sped," replied De Albini.

"You have not named your errand," said De Tunstall.

"Nor shall I do it," cried De Albini, haughtily, "I am not accustomed to refusal."

"Then adieu, my time is precious," said De Tunstall, "you may leave me."

"I do leave you, proud man, and with this warning," cried De Albini. "The daughter of a divorced and corrupt woman, be her beauty and riches what they may, is not a mate for an honest man's son. Illegitimacy may be gilded, but it cannot be disguised."

"What do I hear? and did you dare to ask the niece of De Tunstall for your son?" cried the baron.

"I have not asked it, nor shall I do so," answered De Albini coldly. "I leave the Baron de Tunstall, proud as he is, to ask my son for his niece."

"What! No! never shall Cordelia de Dunstanville sue for a husband. Did I not tell you, proud upstart, that she is already engaged to the young Mouthermer. The king himself commands the nuptials."

"Upstart!" cried De Albini. "But it matters not now; were it not that I have seen, and liked the fair Cordelia, her uncle should rue such a word to me. But I appeal to Stephen, he will not command two young and loving hearts to be severed."

"Love! and is it then true that my niece loves a low-born beggar?" cried De Tunstall, in a rage. "I must to Thornbury directly."

Thus saying, De Tunstall left the room, and De Albini returned with a heavy heart, to recount to his son the strange conversation related above.

"I know not what it can mean," said De Albini. "Were my birth less noble, my rank less dignified, or my name less honoured, I would challenge this proud baron; but surely there must be some mistake. Upstart to Albini! impossible!"

"Impossible indeed, my father!" replied Edward; "De Tunstall must have committed some great mistake towards you; but how, I cannot guess."

"Let it be as it may," answered De Albini, "I will await the king's return, and lay the whole matter before him. I grieve for you, Edward, as I know the hold which a first love has upon the heart; but we must hold the honour of our house above all other considerations."

Edward acquiesced with his father in a tone of despondency, and withdrew to his chamber, to lament over the change which had so strangely taken place in his prospects.

On the following day, Edward was sauntering in the Mall with some young noblemen, when they were joined by an extremely handsome youth about his own age, whose graceful manner, and the respect evinced towards him by Edward's companions, would alone have fixed the attention of the young De Albini, had not the name by which the young nobleman was addressed, raised that attention to extreme interest.

"You are not then gone, Mouthermer," cried one, "how did you escape?"

"By obstinate self-will," replied the youth.

"Obstinate indeed! and rash too," said another; "I wonder you dared to disobey the king."

"Although the king is my guardian, and controls my lands, he cannot control my heart," said Mouthermer, gloomily.

"And is De Tunstall really gone after this niece of his?" asked a young man.

"He is gone to Thornbury," said Mouthermer; "that is, I believe, the name of the place where she is secluded."

"And he will bring her back to be married to you directly?" said one.

"Well, I would not marry an illegitimate girl, half nun, half dairy-maid," said one of the gallants proudly.

Edward's agitation was uncontrollable; but he saw from the jeering tone in which the young nobles spoke, that it would only be absurd to interfere, and there was something in the tone and words of Mouthermer, which told him he was not a willing rival. He therefore determined not at present to make himself known, but to listen to the conversation, from which he hoped to gather hints for his future conduct.

"And what does De Tunstall mean to do with his rival?" asked one.

"Do? why cut his throat to be sure," said another.

"Nay," said the first, "hanging were more fit for the churl."

"I care not," cried Mouthermer, "so that I be rid of the damsel and her kinsman."

Edward could be silent no longer.

"Do you know me?" he asked.

"Yes, the son of the noble Geoffrey de Albini," they replied.

"And am I a churl, for whom the dagger is too good?" cried Edward.

"You!" they all exclaimed.

"I am that rival so much misrepresented to you," said Edward to Mouthermer; "if you will allow me a few minutes private conversation, perhaps it will be well for both of us."

To describe the consternation and surprise of Edward's associates was impossible; they regarded each other in silence—none dared to speak; and they were breaking off from him and seemed inclined to leave him, when he again said to Mouthermer,—

"Will your lordship grant me the audience which I ask?"

One of the youths now interfered.

"Do not go, Mouthermer; how should you know who he was, or that he was in love with this country beauty. I advise you to have nothing to say on the matter."

"I know what is due to my own character and the pretensions of others, without your interference," said Mouthermer. Then turning to Edward, he proposed a turn in the further walk of the park.

Thither accordingly the two young men went in silence, neither of them knowing in what manner to begin the conversation; at length Edward said,—

"You have never, my lord, beheld the Lady Cordelia de Dunstanville?"

"I have not," replied Mouthermer. "She was mentioned at court as beautiful; it is well known that she will be rich; but I care for neither of these things. The king proposed a union between us, and that hot-headed fellow, De Tunstall, grasped at it, but I cannot—I will not marry the girl."

"Speak not discourteously of her," said Edward; "that were unworthy of you as well as of herself."

"I do not mean to do so," replied the youth; "but I have been so tormented on her account, that I scarcely know how I speak."

"Why have you been so tormented?" asked Edward.

"My gay, boisterous companions laugh at me for being obliged to marry a country girl who has been brought up in ignorance and seclusion; they know that I am deeply attached to another, and they laugh at my perplexity."

"If it be, indeed, true that you are attached to another, I may tell you that an engagement has existed between myself and the Lady Cordelia for some time, and my father, Geoffrey de Albini, yesterday waited on her kinsman, in order to request her hand," said Edward.

"And what answer did he obtain?" asked Mouthermer.

"The behaviour of the Baron de Tunstall was so extraordinary," replied Edward "that my father left him abruptly, after an assurance that the Lady Cordelia was to be married to a young nobleman much my father's superior."

"Did any one dare to say this to Geoffrey de Albini?" asked Mouthermer, in a tone of extreme surprise.

"It was so, indeed," replied his companion; "and were it not that I believe the happiness of the fair Cordelia to be bound up in mine, I would sue no more for her hand."

"This explains Tunstall's sudden journey to Thornbury; he wished me to go also, but I excused myself," said the young man. "I willingly give up to you all claim in the favour of the Lady Cordelia de Dunstanville, and will lend all my influence to secure her to you. I have power with Stephen, and will exert it."

Edward expressed his gratitude to his new friend, and returned home to tell his father what had occurred. He found De Albini still disturbed by his interview with Tunstall, and s ill more discomposed by having heard that the king had unexpectedly returned to London, and that he would remain but a few days in town before he should go down to Winchester. De Albini resolved to lose no time in seeking an audience of Stephen; and determined to attend at court on the following day, and that his son should accompany him.

Edward would have excused himself, but his father insisted on his attendance, and advised his seeing Mouthermer and acquainting him with their purpose. Edward did so; receiving an assurance from the young nobleman that he would befriend him, if possible.

On the following morning Geoffrey de Albini and his son embarked on board their barge and proceeded to the Tower, where Stephen was lodged. They found the king's apartments thronged with persons waiting for an audience of his majesty, for Stephen was by nature of an affable disposition, and he felt the political necessity of complaisance and civility towards his new subjects.

However, as soon as the name of the Baron de Albini was announced to the king, he desired that he should be admitted to an audience. The Baron and Edward, therefore, were introduced to Stephen, who received them with condescension. Geoffrey de Albini stated his business, that he requested his majesty's permission to affiance the orphan Lady Cordelia de Dunstanville, to his only son Edward de Albini.

"We have heard much of the circumstances of the Lady Cordelia," said the king; "and it had been our intention to affiance her to our ward, the Baron de Mouthermer, according to the wish of her kinsman, De Tunstall. Knows he of this application?"

"He does not," replied De Albini. "He has behaved churlishly in the matter, and is now gone down to Thornbury castle, where the damsel resides, for the purpose, probably, of extorting her compliance with the addresses of the Baron Mouthermer."

"And why should she not accept the husband pointed out to her by her kinsman?" asked Stephen.

"She loves him not," replied De Albini.

"Pshaw! pshaw! I have heard that she was brought up in a convent," observed the king. "Love is not among the conventual duties."

"But, please your majesty, she loves another person," replied Geoffrey.

"How is that?" exclaimed Stephen, surprised; "that is not conventual. Who is he?"

"My son," replied De Albini; and he briefly recapitulated the events of Edward's capture and release.

"We hold ourselves deeply indebted to the Baron de Fougeres for the safe custody of the young knight," said the king. "We know the valour of his father, and of his race, and we think that he was far more safe to us in Thornbury Castle than in the army of the empress. Would that more of our opponents had been cared for in the same way."

De Albini looked somewhat displeased, and the king added, "We trust, however, we shall never have cause to wish him again in the dungeon. So there have been love tokens exchanged between the prisoner and the maiden?"

"Yes, your majesty," replied De Albini.

"Then De Tunstall must give his consent," said Stephen. "But what says the Baron de Mouthermer to this?"

The young nobleman stepped forward, saying, "I relinquish all claim to the hand of Cordelia de Dunstanville, if your majesty please to bestow her elsewhere."

"So, so, indeed. Lightly won and lightly lost," said the king to himself. "Well," he continued aloud, "I give my full and free permission to the young

No. 23.

De Albini to marry the heiress of De Dunstanville, and I hope he will become a true and stanch supporter of our throne."

De Albini and his son professed their allegiance to the king, and retired from his presence, followed by Mouthermer, who congratulated Edward heartily upon the prospect of a successful issue to his journey.

"So much is gained," said De Albini, "but I scarcely know how to proceed; whether to await the return of Tunstall, or proceed at once to Thornbury."

"Await the return of Tunstall by all means," replied Mouthermer. "I know him well; he is hasty and impetuous, but he will not be deaf to reason. He will probably bring the Lady Cordelia back with him."

Edward would have returned immediately to Thornbury to claim his bride in spite of her kinsman but he was obliged to yield; and the next few days hung heavily upon his hands, while he made frequent inquiries respecting the return of Tunstall.

Meanwhile how had the latter been received at Thornbury?"

As the Lady Elfrida and her young companions were sitting at their embroidery one morning, they were startled by the announcement of the Baron de Tunstall. Cordelia started, surprised and scarcely pleased, and Edith arose for the purpose of descending to the castle hall to receive her unexpected guest.

"What does it mean?" exclaimed Cordelia.

"You shall soon know," replied her friend, leaving the room.

Upon Edith's entering the hall, De Tunstall advanced towards her, saying, "I see the Lady Edith de Fougeres, I believe."

Edith curtsied in some perplexity.

"My errand is to claim my kinswoman, the Lady Cordelia de Dunstanville," said Tunstall.

"The Lady Cordelia will willingly attend your summons," replied Edith; "but I trust you will leave her to my company for a short time longer; a dear friend is at present residing in the castle, and the Baron de Fougeres is from home."

The brow of the baron was instantly clouded. "A dear friend," he said proudly. "The Lady Cordelia de Dunstanville must have no friends but those of her family and house."

Edith left the room, and with some difficulty prevailed upon her friend to attend the summons of her kinsman, but Cordelia insisted upon Edith's accompanying her.

De Tunstall received Cordelia very kindly, saying, "Prepare, my child, to accompany me back to London, with as little delay as possible. Your presence is required there."

"Oh! my uncle, not yet!" cried Cordelia. "I cannot yet leave Thornbury."

"It must be so; it were time that some decided step were taken for assuming your rank, and it were also time to give you a protector who shall defend your rights."

"What mean you?" asked Cordelia, in a tone of alarm.

"The young Baron de Mouthermer expects with impatience my return. He is noble, valiant, handsome, accomplished; and he will assert the rights of my Cordelia better as her husband than I can as her kinsman."

"Oh no!" cried Cordelia, "that cannot be."

"How! do you dispute my will?" cried Tunstall.

"Command me in anything else and I will obey you," replied the maiden; "but in this I cannot!"

"Is it so then? Does my niece, the child of Eleanor de Tunstall, dare to love a rustic?" cried her uncle.

Edith stepped forward, and modestly begging De Tunstall to pardon her intrusion, she said, "the Lady Cordelia may have offended her kinsman by bestowing her affections while she had no relations to love and cherish her, but he whom she loves is no rustic: *my* brother is a worthy match for the heiress of De Tunstall."

"*Your brother*, Lady Edith? Pardon me, but I knew not that the

Baron de Fougeres had any child besides yourself?" said the baron in a tone of surprise.

"The Baron de Fougeres has no child," replied Edith; "the youth to whom I allude is Edward, the only son of Geoffrey de Albini."

De Tunstall seemed more and more perplexed. "And you?" he asked, turning to Edith.

"I am Edith Albini. It does not benefit me to unfold the history of my life, nor does it concern the present question. Edward de Albini loves your niece, and his love is returned."

"Then I discard her for ever," cried De Tunstall, violently. "I have given my word to the king that Cordelia, the heiress to my wealth, shall marry the Baron de Mouthermer, and I command her compliance."

During this conversation Cordelia had been weeping bitterly. The threats and denunciations of Father Augustine recurred to her mind, and she dreaded lest in refusing to enter into the cloistered life, she should indeed draw down upon herself unceasing misfortunes.

"Oh, my dear aunt, my protectress!" she exclaimed, "here am I left in a heartless world!"

"Say not so, my Cordelia," cried Edith, "I will never desert you, we have been friends from chilhood; and you shall never want a home."

Still Cordelia's tears continued to flow, till De Tunstall seemed to be somewhat moved at her grief and he said,—

"I know not the condition in which you stand here, therefore you must prepare to accompany me, and perhaps when the Baron de Mouthermer shall be introduced to you, you will not be so averse as you now are to the destiny chosen for you."

"May I not await the return of the Baron de Albini?" asked Cordelia.

"Return! where then is he gone?" asked Tunstall.

"My father and brother are gone to London, to solicit from you the hand of the Lady Cordelia," replied Edith. "I much wonder that you have not seen them."

"A man who gave no name visited me, and desired my consent to my niece's marriage with his son," replied Tunstall; "but I am sure it was not Geoffrey de Albini."

"It must have been my father," said Edith; and she described his person and dress in such a manner, that Tunstall began to think that the stranger whom he had so rudely dismissed, was indeed the influential Baron de Albini. Still resolved to marry his heiress to the man who had been chosen for her by the king himself, he did not regret the answer he had given, although he feared that, should his conduct become known, he might suffer some inconvenience from the ill-will of one to whom Stephen was known to be so friendly as he was to the Baron de Albini.

"You must return with me," he said at length, mildly to Cordelia, "perhaps after a time you may revisit Thornbury, but you must be ready to accompany me to-morrow morning."

Cordelia could not recover her spirits after this conversation; she retired to prepare for her journey, and Edith acquainted her mother with what had passed. Edith's heart was oppressed; she dreaded losing Cordelia, and for the first time she had been made to feel the extreme delicacy of her situation towards De Fougeres. At Thornbury all was smooth to her, she was still the Lady Edith, the mistress of the castle, the beloved child of the Baron de Fougeres, and she had not been aware how much her relative position in society was changed; but the questions and surprise of De Tunstall had opened her eyes, and she began to regard her union with Eustace de Mowbray as the only means of escape from a situation of pain and difficulty.

When Edith acquainted her mother with the expressions of De Tunstall towards herself, the latter immediately said,—

"The tale must be told, my child, and it were well that it were told at once.

This baron will talk of it at court, and thus smoothe the way for your appearance in your real character."

"Oh, my mother, let it not be talked of!" cried Edith. "And who shall tell him? I cannot do it."

"No," replied the Lady Elfrida, "we must entrust the delicate task to your friend Cordelia; she will have the opportunity, and will execute it well."

"Will you prepare her for it, madam?" asked Edith.

"Certainly," answered the lady; "let Cordelia attend me this evening in my closet."

Cordelia accordingly visited the Lady Elfrida, who, after much talk respecting the situation of Edith, began to speak upon her own prospects.

"My child," said the lady, "be not discouraged; remember that I promised to your earliest friend, the abbess, that I would give you a home should you ever require it; I now repeat that promise, and whether you ever become more nearly connected with me than by friendship, or not, still I will never forsake nor slight you."

Cordelia expressed her thanks, and the lady continued,—

"Of course the happiness of my Edward is the dearest wish of my heart, and I believe that will be secured but by this union with you; if, therefore, your own affection be firmly fixed, I will support you against the persecution which seems to threaten you; but I charge you, Cordelia, to be honest towards me; and if, after being introduced to the Baron de Mouthermer, you feel any diminution of your love towards Edward, acquaint me with the change in your affection."

Cordelia protested that such a change was impossible.

"Say not so, my child; we know not how wayward the heart is till we have been tried," replied the lady, sighing deeply. "Give me but the promise I require, that in this point you will have no reserve with me, and my blessing attends you."

Cordelia threw herself into the arms of the Lady Elfrida, and promised obedience; then bidding her a tender adieu, she retired to take leave of her friend Edith.

Bitter was the parting on both sides, and many were the plans laid for future meeting. Edith assured her friend that as soon as her marriage had been solemnised, she would accompany her father to London, and she would then seek out her friend. "But," she added, "I think Edward will not delay so long as this to reclaim his love."

"Alas!" said Cordelia, "I hope I shall not be the means of embroiling Edward with De Tunstall. I will never marry the Baron de Mouthermer; tell Edward so, and we must wait patiently for brighter days."

"I trust they will speedily arrive," said Edith.

Cordelia shook her head mournfully. "Have my days ever been bright?" she said. "Oh, why did I not enter the convent?"

"Nay, nay, Cordelia, say not so; we have been happy, and we shall be happy again," answered her friend, tenderly. "You must now retire to rest; you will need all your strength for this journey."

On the following morning De Tunstall and Cordelia left Thornbury. During the first few hours, but little conversation passed between the travellers, but after a time Tunstall's brow became more smooth, and he attempted to engage his niece in discourse upon the court and the various topics relating to it. Cordelia answered as well as she could; her heart, it is true, was in London with Edward de Albini, but she could not forget her peaceful home at Thornbury. To the great astonishment of Tunstall, Cordelia expressed no curiosity respecting London. The only question which she asked was, whether her uncle's residence was near the Strand, where she knew was situated the house of the Albinis; and upon Tunstall asking her the reason of the question, she hesitated, and relapsed into silence.

After some time the baron again approached Cordelia, and made an allusion to what had taken place the day preceding, respecting Edith's parentage. Cordelia gave him a short sketch of her history, as she had been instructed to do by the

Lady Elfrida, at which Tunstall expressed his surprise, and the recital seemed to soften his resentment towards De Albini.

"I cannot imagine that he who called upon me, nameless and unintroduced, on your account, could be the Baron de Albini. I will see the baron and inquire of him the truth of this ; he is favoured by the king, who places great reliance upon his judgment and experience, and I must not make myself enemies among those who are influential and powerful. I shall need all their assistance to make good your claim to the dower of Eleanor de Dunstanville."

Cordelia sighed. "I care nought for riches," she said, "let me be but happy."

"Nevertheless, riches are valuable ; and although the Baron de Mouthermer be one of the most wealthy young noblemen in England, I would not have my child go dowerless into his family."

Cordelia turned from the hated name, and rode on in silence ; till on the third day of their journey, towards evening, the servants who preceded them suddenly stopped in confusion ; and one of them turning back, rode up to Cordelia, exclaiming, "Robbers ! robbers ! save yourself, lady."

It was too late, the robbers had overpowered the servants, and as Tunstall came up with them, two were already lying lifeless upon the road. Tunstall, who was a man of considerable valour, boldly attacked the assailants, assisted by the remaining domestics ; but his numbers were unequal to those of the robbers, and the latter were speedily gaining the ascendancy, when four horsemen rode up and turned the fortune of the strife. The succour was most timely, as Tunstall lay disarmed and in the power of a robber, who was just about to plunge his dagger into his victim, when his arm was arrested by a sword blow from a young man, one of those who now rode up. Another of the new comers attacked the same robber, and he was soon despatched. The rest seeing the rescue of the travellers, and the overthrow and death of their leader, rode off as quickly as they could.

The first word spoken by Tunstall, was, "Cordelia ! Save her !"

"The Baron de Tunstall !" exclaimed Mouthermer, who now came up to him.

The deliverer of the baron did not wait to hear more, but turning in the direction pointed out by the servants, he rode off as fast as he possibly could, and was speedily out of sight.

"A fortunate meeting, Mouthermer," said Tunstall. "To your gallant companion do I owe my life, which was at its last gasp, under the dagger of that villain."

"De Albini is valiant. He first saw your situation," answered the nobleman.

"De Albini !" exclaimed Tunstall.

"Yes, the son of Geoffrey de Albini, of whom you must have heard," replied Mouthermer.

"And do I owe my life to him ? Unlucky chance !" cried Tunstall. "Where is he ?"

The followers informed their master that the young knight had ridden off towards the place where the Lady Cordelia had been left, but that she was gone, and Edward after her.

"Worse and worse !" cried Tunstall. "You should have followed your betrothed."

"That is a subject upon which I cannot now enter," said the young man.

"What mean you ?" asked Tunstall.

"Let us first think of saving the Lady Cordelia. Edward de Albini will not give up the pursuit, but it would be advisable to send servants in all directions, lest she should fall into the hands of the robbers."

Mouthermer accordingly sent servants in every direction ; but after a long search, no tidings could be heard of Cordelia. Night came ; still Tunstall hoped she might be found. He would not stir from the spot where he had parted from her, and Mouthermer remained with him. When day broke, to their great surprise, they saw the horse which Cordelia had ridden, quietly grazing near them. The animal was covered with dirt and foam, and seemed to have travelled some distance. The saddle showed that its rider had been thrown from it, as it was displaced, and a fragment of the unfortunate girl's dress hanging to it.

De Tunstall was in despair at the sight. He wrung his hands, lamenting his own rashness in commanding his niece to accompany him to town. Willingly would he have given all his riches to know her safe in Thornbury Castle.

One consolation the sight of the horse suggested; she had not fallen into the hands of the robbers, they would not have suffered the animal to return to his master; but this was but meagre consolation, she might be dead. Tunstall was sure she would die; she had been so tenderly nourished, and the journey which had been thus disastrously interrupted had considerably fatigued her; she had been ill and in low spirits during the whole day, and had repeatedly expressed a wish that they had arrived at the termination of their toilsome journey. All this now recurred to Tunstall, and he accused himself as the murderer of his niece.

Mouthermer endeavoured to comfort the baron, but in vain. "You do not love her," replied Tunstall; "or you could not think so calmly."

The young man made no answer to this, it was not the time for explanation; and he calmly suffered De Tunstall to heap reproaches upon him for his insensibility.

Shortly after the return of the horse, just as Mouthermer had with extreme difficulty persuaded Tunstall to proceed to London, the servant who had accompanied Edward de Albini rode up.

"Have you found my child?" cried Tunstall.

The man shook his head mournfully.

"Tell me, have you seen my child?" again cried the baron.

"We rode on for a considerable time, following the new-made track of a horse's feet," answered the man; "till near the bottom of a hill we saw the horse which the lady rode standing still grazing, but no trace of his rider could we find. Upon our approach the horse galloped off, and I suppose returned to this place."

"Could you not find my child? Oh, you did not search! Let me go! I will find her," exclaimed Tunstall.

"Indeed we searched everywhere; my master ran in all directions, calling her name, but no one answered. When it grew dark, we lighted a fire, and my master took a lighted branch of a tree, and carrying it high above his head passed the whole night in searching, but in vain."

"Where is your master?" asked Mouthermer.

"He is at last gone to London," replied the man; "he is like a distracted person, and but that he fears the Baron de Albini will be alarmed at his unwonted absence, he would search the country round himself."

"That shall be done at once," replied Tunstall; "I will apply to the king, and engage proper persons to proceed in all directions likely to discover my child."

With a heavy heart Tunstall and Mouthermer proceeded to London; the latter was too much vexed with the distress of his friend to give him farther cause of unhappiness; he therefore forebore to mention his own wishes with regard to Cordelia. Upon their arrival in town, Tunstall made known in the proper quarter the accident which had occurred, and he had the satisfaction of receiving assurances that the haunts of the robbers should be found out, and his niece if possible found. But Tunstall knew too well the unsettled state of the kingdom, to place any reliance upon the promises that were given him.

On the following morning the Baron de Mouthermer called upon Tunstall, when the latter began to lament the sad mischance of Cordelia, and ended by saying,—

"Much as I lament the loss of my child, I grieve more for you than for myself. I must soon have relinquished her society to a husband, but your heart must be broken indeed; I am surprised that you have the fortitude you display."

"Do not praise me," replied Mouthermer, "I desire it not. This blow is not so heavy to me as you imagine."

"What mean you?" cried Tunstall.

"That Cordelia de Dunstanville possessed not my heart," replied the youth.

"Dare you to scorn my child?" exclaimed Tunstall.

"I did not say so; I only said that she was not the choice of my heart, which has long been fixed upon another," replied Mouthermer.

"And does the king know of this perverseness?" cried Tunstall. "I much think that Stephen will not brook the disobedience of his favourite."

"Do not alarm yourself on that account," answered Mouthermer; in a private audience with the king yesterday evening, I informed him of my repugnance to a marriage with the Lady Cordelia, and requested his permission to offer my suit elsewhere."

"What said the monarch?" asked Tunstall.

"He graciously gave me the full permission to follow my inclination," replied the young man; "and the more readily, he said, because the Baron de Albini has asked his influence with you in favour of his son."

"A pretty tale truly," cried Tunstall; "and so my child is to be disposed of as you and the king please, without my word. Well," added he sighing, "she is lost now—dead."

"We must hope not," replied Mouthermer; "and you should remember who it was that saved your life; my assistance would have been useless, but for the aid of Edward de Albini."

"True—true—I *am* grateful," answered the baron, "but it does not follow that I must give him my niece."

"They are attached to each other, and have been so for some time," urged the youth.

"But the Baron de Albini fought against the king," said Tunstall.

"He did; but he has given allegiance to Stephen," replied Mouthermer; "and you may soon learn at court in what high estimation he is held."

"Indeed! I knew not that," said Tunstall, in a tone of surprise.

"Our new master knows how to choose wise counsellors," said De Mouthermer; "and surely Geoffrey de Albini is among these. His son would not be slighted by any family in the kingdon, believe me."

Tunstall remained silent and musing during a considerable time; at last he burst out,—

"But she is dead! It is all in vain to talk of it."

"No, it is not in vain," cried Mouthermer. "Say but that you will give the Lady Cordelia to my friend Edward de Albini, and every effort shall be made to discover her retreat—not unsuccessfully, I trust."

"I will do anything, only bring me my child," exclaimed Tunstall. "Tell me, do you know where she is?"

"I would not raise fallen hopes; but from some dark intelligence received by Edward de Albini, we have hope of regaining her," replied Mouthermer.

Tunstall seized his hand, exclaiming,—

"Oh, bring her to me! bring her to me!"

"Be patient," replied Mouthermer, "it may be but a false hope."

Tunstall was now as much elevated as he had before been depressed. He seemed to forget that his niece's return was extremely doubtful, and so sanguine and elated was he, that when, at the end of some days, it was found that the information which had been given to De Albini was entirely without a shadow of foundation, Mouthermer was almost afraid to acquaint the baron with the disappointment. He was obliged to do so, however, and Tunstall was again cast down.

Thus passed days, weeks, until all the friends of Cordelia mourned her as dead. At Thornbury Castle, the sad occurrence had spread a deep gloom. Edith mourned for her dear friend, nor would she listen to the entreaties of Eustace Mowbray for their union, until a certain period should have elapsed, of seclusion, due to the memory of the friend and companion of her childhood. Edward was inconsolable, and the once happy family was overcast with mourning and affliction. All remained at Thornbury; De Fougeres had become reconciled to his Edith's new situation, and, in his turn, he endeavoured to comfort her in this heavy grief.

CHAPTER XXX.

.A light broke in upon my brain,
　　It was the carol of a bird ;
It ceased, and then it came again,
　　The sweetest song ear ever heard !
And mine was thankful till my eyes
Ran over with the glad surprise,
And they that moment could not see,
I was the mate of misery;
But then by dull degrees came back
My senses to their wonted track.—BYRON.

LET us return to Cordelia, who had, as the attendants supposed, been unable to manage her palfrey, which, alarmed by the noise, had started off at full gallop. For some miles this continued, until, in descending a steep hill, the horse's foot stumbled, and the poor girl was thrown with violence on the ground. She fell upon her head, and lay insensible upon the ground, while her palfrey returned, as we have seen, to the place where the party had been interrupted by the robbers.

Cordelia lay in a state of insensibility till evening, when a peasant passing by from his labour beheld her. At first he hesitated as to approaching her, but at length, with some caution, he ventured near. What was his alarm and consternation at beholding a beautiful young female, richly dressed, apparently dead? Her luxuriant tresses hung over her face, hiding it, in part, from the gazer. One arm was bent under her, and her position evidently showed that she had not moved since her fall. The man thought she had been murdered, and was afraid to touch her, lest the crime should be attributed to him ; he therefore left her, and proceeded home. When he acquainted his dame with the scene he had witnessed, she exclaimed at his cruelty in leaving a young lady to die in the wood.

"But she is dead, I tell you," said the man.

" Well, then, so much the worse, not to give her Christian burial," replied the dame.

" But what can I do? It is almost dark now, dame, and I cannot bring her home alone," said her husband.

" Let us take the palfrey, and I will go with you. Remember what luck a chance customer brought us before," answered the woman.

" What the smooth-faced youth and the hunchback? Ay, dame, you will never forget that youth."

" Nonsense, nonsense, Gregory ! Come, let us go."

Gregory, who had always been accustomed to yield his opinion to that of his dame, and, since the adventure of the smooth-faced youth, had been implicitly guided by her, went into the little stable to saddle his palfrey; while Margery, having made up a blazing fire, rightly judging that either the dead person or herself might be glad of a little artificial warmth when she returned, prepared to accompany her husband to the wood.

Our readers may have recognised the worthy couple at whose cottage Ronald and Rosamond had met some time ago. It was so. These were the persons who were now going to the assistance of Cordelia.

When Gregory and his dame arrived at the spot where he had left the murdered lady, as he called her, he found her just awaking from the fainting fit into which she had fallen. She had vainly endeavoured to raise herself, but had with considerable difficulty dragged herself to a tree which stood near, and she was now recalled to a consciousness of what had befallen her, by seeing the state of her dress, and feeling the pain of her wounded limbs. Tears began to flow in abundance, which somewhat relieved the poor girl's mental misery ; and as Gregory approached, they were redoubled from the dread of further misfortune. The appearance of Margery, however, gave her courage to speak.

"Oh! whoever you may be," cried Cordelia, "I implore you to befriend an unfortunate creature."

"You see she is not dead. I told you she was not," said Margery to her husband.

"We are come on purpose to help you," said Gregory. "Raise yourself, and mount the palfrey, and we will give you a night's lodging at our cottage."

"How came you here?" asked the dame, approaching.

"We were attacked by robbers, and my horse, I suppose, threw me," replied Cordelia. "Oh, find my friends, I pray you! My dear uncle cannot be far off."

"We must attend to you first, I fancy," cried Margery, endeavouring to raise

Cordelia. But the attempt was vain; the poor girl could not in the least degree help herself. She was so much bruised that she could scarcely bear to be touched, and a deep wound on her right shoulder, from a stone upon which she had fallen, began to bleed afresh as soon as she moved.

"Poor thing!" said Gregory; "I must lift her, dame; bring the palfrey quite close, and I will place her on its back."

"Be gentle," replied the wife; "I must think she is used to nicer hands than ours."

Gregory, by degrees, lifted Cordelia in his arms, and with his wife's help placed her gently on the palfrey; then each supporting her, they proceeded homeward. The poor sufferer had nearly fainted away during the removal; but the breeze fanned her face as she was carried onward, and recovered her. They proceeded at a slow pace to the cottage, and Margery having prepared her best bed, laid Cordelia in it, and proceeded to ascertain what injury she had received. Although her limbs were uninjured, she was violently bruised, and the wound on her shoulder was a bad one; nevertheless, the dame was certain she could cure all her ailments, and she immediately applied such remedies as her simple knowledge suggested. While she was doing this, the patient seemed in a state of stupor, and the dame left her for a short time, hoping that she would fall into an easy sleep.

"Well, dame," said Gregory, on his wife's return to the kitchen, "and have you found out who she is?"

"Not I! Why, should you have me ask such impertinent questions of the poor creature, when she was all but dead?" cried Margery indignantly.

"But will she die?" asked Gregory.

"I hope not," replied the dame. "There is an ugly cut on her shoulder and some bad bruises, but you know how I cured you when you cut your arm with the hook, and I'll be bound I can cure her delicate flesh."

"She is a pretty damsel, dame," said Gregory, musingly.

"Yes; she is none of your common people," replied his wife; "she is some great lord's daughter, I'll be bound."

"We'll cure her, and mayhap he will reward us handsomely," said the man.

"That's it; always thinking of the purse, man," cried Margery.

"And all for your sake, Margery," said her husband.

"Well, I won't say but you're industrious, and now that peaceable times are come, we are not so badly off," said Margery. "That hump-back has done us many a good turn."

"And may do many more," observed Gregory.

"Nay, I do not know what can have become of him," said the dame, "he has not been here for many months."

"Perhaps he is settled somewhere far off," said Gregory. "But hark! what noise is that? a groan!"

The dame listened, and presently the sound of a deep groan made her start from her seat, and returning to Cordelia's chamber, she found her restless, and tossing about as if in extreme pain. The dame approached the bed, and tenderly inquired what was the matter.

"My shoulder! oh, my shoulder!" was the answer.

Margery immediately applied the same balsam which she had before used, and the wound became less painful; but it was evident that the sufferer was in a high state of fever, and this increased so rapidly that Margery determined to sit up by her bedside during the night. It was well that she did so, for delirium came on, and poor Cordelia called for Edward and Edith. Sometimes her thoughts went further back, and she would beg to be saved from Father Augustine. During this the dame attended her tenderly, assiduously providing such refreshment as she hoped would alleviate the fever, and with good effect. Towards morning Cordelia was more quiet, and at last she fell into an easy slumber, which lasted till late the day.

Margery and her husband had been extremely anxious during the period of her fever; but the former was certain that it arose more from fright than injury, and she was correct, as it returned on the following night but in a slight degree; and in a few days Cordelia was better, although extremely weak, and suffering much from her wound and bruises.

As soon as she was able, Cordelia related to her nurse the history of her accident, and all relating to it. Margery was extremely gratified to find that her guest was indeed of noble birth; nor was Gregory less delighted when Cordelia gave him a handsome sum of money from her purse, assuring him that he would be amply recompensed by her kinsman De Tunstall. Every day made her more anxious to rejoin her friends, and upon hearing in what part of the country she was, she determined to travel to Thornbury as soon as her strength should permit her to do so.

One day as she was sitting alone in her chamber, thinking over the late events, and wondering when her strangely varied life should subside into quiet, her ear caught the tone of a voice which seemed familiar to her, in the following dialogue between Margery and the stranger, the latter speaking so low that she could with difficulty catch his words.

"We thought you had forgotton us," said Margery.

"Strange events have happened," replied the stranger, "and unhappy one too."

"How now?" asked the dame.

"It were a story," replied Ronald, "and you could not understand it."

"Strange things have happened here, too," said Margery.

"What another tankard stolen?" asked Ronald, jestingly.

"No, no, master," answered the dame, laughing; "but a young lady almost murdered."

"A young lady?" cried Ronald.

"Yes, a real lady, I warrant," said Margery, "and I saved her life."

"Where and how?" cried the dwarf.

"Gregory found her by the road, dead, and I tell you I have cured her."

"And where is she now?" asked Ronald eagerly.

"Here, in my house; as soon as she is well enough, Gregory is going to take her home," said the woman.

"Oh! let me see her!" cried Ronald. "But it cannot be, it cannot be!"

"What do you mean?" asked Margery.

"We have lost our Lady Cordelia; the robbers have taken her," said Ronald.

When Cordelia heard this, she ran into the room exclaiming, "Who names me?"

Ronald was too much startled to speak, but kneeling to his lady, burst into tears.

Cordelia also was much affected, till after some time, she said,—

"My friends Ronald! How are they?"

"Miserable for the loss of you," sobbed Ronald.

"Oh, let me go to Thornbury! And De Tunstall too?" cried Cordelia.

"He is in London," replied Ronald. "When all search was unavailing, we heard that a band of robbers from this neighbourhood had left England and sailed beyond sea, carrying with them a beautiful lady as their captive; and concluding it to be you, the Baron de Tunstall has despatched messengers in pursuit of the robbers, and he remains in London to gather the first tidings which may come.

"And Edith—Edward, where are they?" asked Cordelia.

"At Thornbury," answered Ronald. "The Lady Edith will not consent to become the wife of the young De Mowbray, until some period of mourning has elapsed for you."

"And Edward?" asked Cordelia, timidly.

"Nay, lady, I cannot describe his grief, he passes whole days in the Lady's Tower, refusing all society," answered Ronald.

"Oh! let me go directly!" cried Cordelia.

"Can your ladyship bear the journey?" asked Ronald.

"Oh, yes!" was the reply.

But Ronald looked sadly upon the wan figure of Cordelia, and doubted whether her strength would suffice to reach Thornbury. He offered to return immediately to the castle, and acquaint the party there with her safety, and they would send a proper conveyance for her.

Still Cordelia persisted that she was quite able to travel, and while she was arranging this, the dame entered, having been to assure Gregory that Cordelia was a great lady indeed.

"May I not go to Thornbury directly, dame?" asked Cordelia.

The woman hesitated, and at last said,—

"I am afraid you cannot ride yet, my lady; you will faint as you did yesterday when you only walked down to the brook."

Ronald looked alarmed, and said,—

"If my lady will permit me, I will set off at once to Thornbury, and tell the baron where she is: they will soon fetch her."

"Do so then, Ronald; and tell my dear Edith I long to embrace her again," said Cordelia.

"I carry joy with me to Thornbury," answered Ronald; "and truly it is needed, there has been sorrow enough there."

Ronald departed, leaving Cordelia lonely but happy. Some days must elapse before she could receive any tidings from Thornbury, and the poor girl knew not how she should pass those days. However, her hostess did not allow her to be much alone, and she amused Cordelia extremely by giving her an account of the manner in which her first acquaintance with Ronald had begun, little thinking how deeply the young lady was interested in the result of that journey. The description of Father Augustine, as the Baron de Bohun, made Cordelia shudder; sufficient hints of his views had come to light to show her that he intended, by marrying her, to claim those lands which he could not by any other means secure, and she felt as if she had escaped from an imminent danger. Cordelia told the dame a part of the history of Rosamond; Margery's penetration had discovered some of her adventures, and Cordelia gladdened her heart by informing her that Rosamond was now a happy wife.

Thus the days passed, but we must look back to Thornbury.

As Ronald journeyed along, his old habits returned upon him: joy brought back to his memory the snatches of old songs which he used to sing, and he burst into the following strain :—

"Long have we pined for thee,
Fairest of maidens free,
Now we'll rejoice with thee,
    Lady of love!
Gladly will Ronald tell
Him whom thou lov'st so well,
How this glad chance befel,
    Grief to remove.

"Not as the robber's bride,
O'er the salt ocean tide,
Roaming both far and wide,
    Hast thou been borne;
But tended by homely skill,
Curing each pain and ill,
In peaceful cottage still,
    'Neath sheltering thorn.

> "Now in our castle grand,
> Famed throughout all the land,
> Young Edward claims thy hand,
> Richer than gold!
> While Lady Edith bright,
> And Mowbray's noble knight,
> Their long-tried troth do plight,
> With hearts never cold."

Thus did Ronald cheat the time away, as he rode along. His arrival at the castle caused great surprise among his comrades, who knew that he had been to Gregory's cottage where he generally made a pretty long stay.

"What ho! Ronald," cried one, "is Dame Margery less loving than usual?"

"Or Gregory more jealous?" cried another.

"No—no," said a third, "I know how it is; the larder is empty, and Gregory has no more fat capons to kill."

"Peace! peace!" answered Ronald, "you know nothing of the matter. Take my palfrey, fellows,"

"Heyday, indeed!" cried one of the men; "Gregory's humour has infected you; has he sent home any writing on your back, Ronald?"

This was too much for Ronald; and with a powerful arm he dealt such a blow as laid the man at his feet.

"I'll teach you to insult your betters," he cried.

But Ronald was instantly attacked by two or three of the domestics, and he would soon have suffered severely for his irritability, had not De Fougeres come up attracted by the sound of quarrelling; and desiring the men to desist, inquired what had occasioned the disturbance.

"My lord," said Ronald, "I have returned sooner than was expected from a visit I made, and therefore these fellows chose to insult me."

"My lord, he knocked me down," said the man.

"And well did you deserve it," answered Ronald.

"Let me have have no more disturbance," said De Fougeres.

"My lord, I bring you good news," said Ronald; "and I believe that made me angry."

"Well, it is the first time I have heard of good news making any one angry," observed De Fougeres; "does your good news concern me, Ronald?"

"Yes, my lord. I have found the Lady Cordelia," replied the dwarf.

"Found her! Where?" exclaimed the baron.

"She is in a cottage at some distance," replied Ronald. "I have promised to return for her, as she has been very ill, and is still too weak to ride."

"Good tidings indeed! Come with me to the Lady Edith directly," said De Fougeres.

Ronald followed his lord, and acquainted the Lady de Albini and Lady Edith with all the particulars which he knew respecting the accident and illness of her friend, and most rejoicingly was the information received. But Ronald saw not the person to whom he most wished to disclose Cordelia's safety; Edward de Albini was not present, and Ronald, as he was retiring, asked where he was most likely to find him.

"No doubt at the Lady's Tower," replied Edith; "but I will seek him myself, and acquaint him with the happy intelligence."

Edith repaired to the Lady's Tower, where she found Edward in a state of melancholy, as usual; he had taken up his guitar, and as Edith approached, she heard him sing the following song:—

> "Oh! who will dry the dropping tear
> I shed alone;
> Or who my heavy heart will cheer,
> Since she is gone?

" Cordelia was to be my bride,
     One gladsome day,
Now she I love, oh! woe betide!
     Is far away.
" Her wedding dress was well nigh made,

     It ne'er was on ;
The pearls that should have decked her head
     Look pale and wan.
The bloom has faded from my cheek
     In youthful prime,
And Sorrow's with'ring hand has done
     The work of Time."

Edith's tears flowed fast as she listened to this melancholy song; it told too plainly of a broken heart, and she paused lest the tidings which she brought, happy though they were, should be too overpowering for his weakened spirit.   She knocked quietly at the door, and entering, said, " Dear Edward! you must change your strain to one of joy."

" Alas, Edith!" he replied, " there is no joy for me."

" Yes, Edward; I bring joy and good news," said Edith.

" Good news ?   Is it of her?   Oh, tell me," cried Edward.

" Compose yourself, we have heard of her," replied the lady.

" Is she safe—is she mine ?" cried Edward.

" She is safe.   She has been ill, but with care may be removed to Thornbury." answered Edith.

" Tell me where, and I will go directly !   Nay, stay me not, if you love me;" exclaimed Edward, rushing out of the apartment.

" Edward! Edward! dearest brother! hear me ?" cried Edith.

But Edward heeded not ; and hastening to the castle, he commanded his horse to be saddled immediately ; then running into his mother's apartment, he threw himself into her arms, crying out—

" She is found, dear mother, she is found !"

" I know it, Edward," replied the Lady Elfrida, embracing him.   " I have just been making arrangements for her journey to Thornbury."

" I go this instant !" cried Edward.

" No, my son," said the Lady de Albini, laying her hand upon his arm to detain him.   " Hear what I say.   Cordelia is weak; we must consider her situation.   I have ordered my own litter to be made ready, and my servant will go with it, under Ronald's guidance, to bring Cordelia safely to Thornbury."

" And I will go with you," cried Edward.

" My son, it will be wiser not.   Your presence would excite Cordelia's spirits too much ; and in the state of weakness in which she is, might prevent her travelling in safety.   Trust to Ronald and Mabel, who will attend upon her carefully."

Edward was not convinced ; he reminded his mother of her former accident, and strongly urged that Cordelia ought to have a better escort than mere servants.

The lady admitted that it might be prudent, and proposed asking their worthy friend L' Espee to accompany Ronald.   The knight had been passing some time at Thornbury ; he too seemed to have lost a daughter in losing Cordelia, and he could not force himself from a spot which so forcibly and incessantly recalled her to his memory.   L' Espee gladly undertook the commission, and by his persuasion and advice, Edward at last consented to remain at home.   But with an aching heart he saw the party depart, and it required all Edith's skill and kindness to sooth his spirits.   Much did Edward blame himself for having neglected more closely to examine the country, when he heard where Cordelia had found refuge ; the false report of her having been carried off by the robbers had damped all hope of finding her ; and the search was speedily abandoned as fruitless.   For this Edward now severely repented, although reflection told him that it was scarcely likely that any search would have found her in the secluded cottage of Gregory and his dame. By degrees Edward recovered his serenity, and messengers were despatched to London to summon De Tunstall to meet his lost niece at Thornbury without delay. This baron had become reconciled to the union of Cordelia with Edward de Albini; grief had softened his heart and temper, and the Baron de Mouthermer having married the lady to whom he was attached, Tunstall yielded to his sovereign's desire, that, in case Cordelia should be returned to him, he would bestow her upon Edward de Albini.

De Tunstall had given his consent in the full persuasion that he should never behold his child again; when, therefore, the messenger from Thornbury gave him a letter from Fougeres acquainting him with her speedy arrival being expected, and requesting his presence at the castle, Tunstall was almost overcome with joy. He wrote to De Fougeres declaring his intention of taking the journey immediately, and his resolution that the lovers should be married without delay at Thornbury, as he would not again undertake a journey with so precious a trust under his care.

This letter produced fresh joy at Thornbury; Edward looked forward with redoubled impatience to the arrival of L'Espee and his beloved charge, while De Fougeres and Geoffrey de Albini united in ordering due preparations to be made for the double nuptials.

CHAPTER XXXI.

Where now is gone my morning star ?
　Where now my sun his beams are fled,
Though high at noon it held afar,
　Its course above my humble head.
Yet gentle evening came, and then
　It stooped from high to comfort me,
And I forgot its late disdain,
　In transport living joyfully.—MORANGE.

L'ESPEE and his attendants arrived in due time at the cottage, but what was the astonishment and despair of the faithful knight at the reception which awaited him. On seeing him approach, Margery ran from her door, and hid herself in her kitchen, where she was found by Ronald, cowering down in a corner, crying bitterly.

"What ails you, mistress?" asked the dwarf. "See you not the noble knight at your door? Come, bestir yourself, and tell us where is the Lady Cordelia."

These words only redoubled Margery's sobs, and in vain did Ronald endeavour to bring her to a state of reason. The only answer he could get, was, "Oh, pray don't kill me! I could not help it!"

"Help what?" asked Ronald.

"Her going away," answered the dame.

Ronald was now considerably alarmed. "Going away! what do you mean?" he exclaimed. "Tell me instantly, where is the lady?"

Margery shook her head, and cried still more.

By this time L'Espee had dismounted, and entered the house. "Where is the lady, good woman?" he asked; but getting no answer, he repeated the same question to Gregory, who now entered the kitchen.

"She was taken away three days ago," replied the man.

"Taken away, by whom?" exclaimed both Ronald and the knight.

"I do not know who they were," said the man; "but they came and carried her away, and bitterly did she cry."

"What is to be done?" cried L'Espee, in dismay at this intelligence. "Which way did they go, and have you any idea who they were? Tell us the whole, man."

"It was just before dinner, and the lady was resting herself in the porch of the cottage, when four horsemen rode up; they said not a word, but one of them seizing the lady, put her on one of the horses before one of the men, and in spite of her screams, rode off with her."

"How strange," cried L'Espee, "did you not try to save her?"

"It was of no use, they were into the forest in a moment," said the man.

"What sort of men were they?" asked Ronald.

"Black enough, if you want to know that," answered Gregory.

'Were they soldiers?" asked L'Espee.

"Not to my thinking," said Gregory, "robbers, more likely."

"Three days ago! then it is of no use following them now," said L'Espee. "We must return to Thornbury, and raise a general alarm."

"My dame has been crying ever since," said Gregory. "She was sure you would kill her."

"Silly fool!" said Ronald angrily. "What would be the use of that? Would it bring back th e poor Lady Cordelia?"

"Alas, and alas!" cried Margery, now for the first time beginning to comprehend that her life was safe, "that ever I should see this day."

"It is indeed a wretched one," said L'Espee. "I know not what the consequences will be to the Lady Cordelia's friends: it will, I fear, be death almost to some."

"Oh, the beautiful lady," cried the dame; "and such wicked-looking men too, and no clothes with her, nor any food."

L'Espee having concerted with Ronald as to their proceedings, they remunerated the cottagers for their reception of Cordelia, and having got together the remainder of her clothes, they departed to return to that home which their intelligence would again render the scene of misery..

Let us draw a veil over the arrival of L'Espee at Thornbury; indeed it would be in vain to attempt a description of the dismay his intelligence created. Edith swooned away upon hearing the fatal tidings, and it was many days before her life was pronounced to be out of danger. Edward's sufferings were equally great; but it was upon De Tunstall that the blow fell the most heavily. He neither wept nor lamented, but fell into a state of stupor, from which it was impossible to rouse him; he refused to take any nourishment, and thus declining, in less than a week from L'Espee's arrival, he sunk under this last and bitterest misfortune and was buried in the cloister of the adjoining monastery. In the meanwhile, no pains had been spared to gain intelligence of the robbers; spies were sent all over the country in every direction, the king having giving orders for immediately scouring the country—but in vain.

One morning as Edith was sitting at the window of her apartment, absorbed in melancholy reflection upon the sad fate of her beloved friend, she saw a man riding towards the castle at full speed. Her heart beat quickly with fear and expectation, and summoning the Lady Elfrida to the window, they agreed to descend to the castle hall at once, to learn his errand, for his haste made them hope that he brought intelligence of their beloved lost one. Rushing into the hall at the moment of the horseman's arrival, the Lady Edith found her conjecture verified; the traveller was a retainer of De Fougeres, who had been employed in the search after the robbers, and he now came to inform the baron that a lady answering the description of Cordelia was secreted in a cottage in the forest of which we have already spoken.

Upon hearing this welcome intelligence, Edward resolved to undertake her rescue himself, and he immediately set out on the expedition, armed, and followed by a number of the servants of De Albini. He resolved to encounter all hazards, and to take the most desperate measures, rather than fail in the object of his enterprise; and his followers were equally determined. They departed from Thornbury the day after the decease of De Tunstall, bearing with them the blessings and prayers of the assembled household.

The forest lay several leagues from the castle of Thornbury, and the day was closing when the band of resolute men entered upon its borders. The thick foliage of the trees spread a deeper shade around, and they were obliged to proceed cautiously, as none were acquainted with the country. Darkness had long

spread her sable, but salutary, veil upon the earth, when they reached the cottage, to which they were directed by a feeble flashing light, that glimmered from afar, among the lofty pines and thick umbrageous oaks. Edward left his people at a short distance; and dismounting, accompanied only by one servant, he approached the cottage. Upon approaching, the window whence the light issued, he behe a man and woman, in the dress of peasants, sitting at their supper. They we

No. 25.

conversing with considerable earnestness; and Edward hoped to gain some intelligence respecting the object of his search. The peasants were speaking of a lady for whom they seemed much interested, they praised her beauty, and said it was a pity she was in such a state, wondering how far she had at that time proceeded on her journey.

"I am sure she is some great lady," said the woman, "she is so beautiful."

"Ah, poor thing! it is a sad misfortune to her family," replied the man.

Edward knocked at the door, and it being opened by the man, he inquired concerning the lady who was concealed in his cottage.

"The saints bless us!" said the man, "we cannot conceal any lady; we have only one room, and there is only my wife and I in it."

"But you have a lady concealed, I know; she was brought here by some robbers," said Edward.

The man persisted that there were no other persons in the cottage than those whom he saw.

Edward gave the signal, and his men approached, and surrounded the hut, which terrified the man, who then confessed that a lady had been there, but was gone.

"Tell me truly, when was she here? and where is she gone?" asked Edward. The man hesitated.

"Upon your life tell me all you know, and quickly," cried Edward.

"A lady was brought here yesterday," answered the man. "She had run away from her husband, and was being conveyed back to him."

"Scoundrel! Liar!" cried Edward, "dare you tell me such a falsehood?"

"Nay," replied the man, extremely, alarmed, "that was the tale told to me by her husband's servants. They were concealed here all night, and at daybreak they set off for the coast."

Edward paused. "What sort of men were they?" he asked.

"Why not very civil," said the man. "But the lady had given them a great deal of trouble, she had run away several times from her lord, and now he intended to take her beyond sea for safety."

Edward's heart died within him at these words. Could this indeed be his Cordelia? and was this a story made up by her persecutors to impose upon those who might be inclined to rescue her from them? or was it a true story, and was it some unhappy wife whom he was then pursuing in mistake? He could not decide—he dared not hope. Upon describing as nearly as he could the person of Cordelia, Edward became assured from the answers given him, that the lady was indeed his beloved Cordelia; especially as the man admitted that the lady repeatedly affirmed the story told by her conductors to be false, and that she had no husband. She had mentioned a castle and a name, but one of them held a pistol to her, threatening instant death if she repeated it.

"What was the name?" asked Edward.

"I cannot tell your honour, I am sure," answered the man.

"Should you know it were you to hear it?" asked Edward.

"Perhaps I might," said the man.

"Was it Albini?" cried Edward.

"No," said the man.

"De Fougeres? Tunstall?" said Edward.

"No, no, none of those."

"Thornbury?" cried Edward.

"That was the word she said, and one more," answered the man.

"Edward or Edith?" asked the knight.

"Yes, yes, the last; she called that name often," replied the man.

Edward was now convinced that it was his Cordelia who had been thus cruelly torn away by the ruffians who but a few hours earlier had stood upon the very spot where he now was; but those fews hours made all hope of overtaking them impossible; still he resolved to persevere, and having inquired concerning the course which it was supposed that the robbers had taken, he remounted his horse, and set forward in pursuit, not without many attemps at dissuasion by the peasant, who represented the forest as the resort of a formidable band of robbers. But this information only made Edward the more resolute, as he the more hoped to regain the treasure thus torn from him.

The road lay for several leagues through the forest, and the darkness and uncertain nature of the road made the journey dangerous. About the break of day the party quitted the forest, and entered on a wild and mountainous country, in which they travelled some miles without perceiving a hut, or a human being. No symptom of cultivation appeared, and no sounds reached them but those of their horses' feet, and the roaring of the winds through the deep forests that overhung the mountains. The pursuit was uncertain, but Edward resolved to persevere.

They came at length to a cottage, where having repeated his inquiries, he learned to his great delight that a party of four horsemen, bearing a lady with them, had stopped there for refreshment about two hours before. He now found it necessary to stop for the same purpose, and a scanty allowance of bread and milk, all the place afforded, was set before him. The attendants could hardly satisfy their hunger upon this meagre fare; their master was too much agitated to partake of it, and having despatched a hearty meal, they set out again in the way pointed out to them, as that which the horsemen had taken.

The country soon assumed a more civilised aspect. Corn-fields, orchards, and groves adorned the landscape; the valleys, luxuriant in shade, were frequently embellished by the windings of a lucid stream, and diversified by clusters of half seen cottages. Here the rising turrets of a monastery appeared above the thick trees with which they were surrounded; and there the savage wilds which the travellers had passed, formed a bold and picturesque back ground to the scene.

To the questions put by Edward to the several persons whom he met, he received answers that encouraged him to proceed. At noon he again halted to refresh his people and horses. He could gain no distinct intelligence of the fugitives, who had probably avoided the villages, and kept upon a more secluded track, and he was perplexed which way to choose; however, at last he determined to keep the way he was in, as it led directly to the seashore. After travelling several miles, the lengthened shadows of the mountains, and the fading light, gave tokens of declining day; when, having gained the summit of a high hill, he observed some persons on horseback crossing the plain below. The light was not sufficient for distinguishing exactly the particulars of this party, but it might be discerned that one of the men carried a person before him, and this was enough to convince Edward that at least he was in the right track. While he stood attentively surveying them, it seemed that they looked towards the hill, and descried their pursuers, for, as if urged by a sudden impulse of terror, they set off at full speed across the plain.

Edward immediately gave orders for rapid pursuit, and pushed his horse into a gallop; but his horses were jaded and fatigued, and the utmost efforts of the men could not force them to rapid speed. Before they reached the plain, the horsemen winding round an abrupt hill were lost to view, and when Edward and his men reached the hill behind which the robbers had disappeared, not a trace of them was to be seen. The shades of evening fell thick, and the country was soon enveloped in darkness, except where illumined by the flitting and uncertain light of a young moon. The prospect was gloomy and vast, and not a human habitation met their eye, and the attendants, alarmed at the prospect before them, endeavoured to dissuade their master from continuing his journey. But what alternative was there; even if they turned back, the night would be far advanced before they could regain the cottage they had last visited, and it therefore seemed the most prudent course to endeavour to reach some other habitation. At every step they listened with anxious attention for some sound that might discover to them the haunts of men, but in vain; the wind moaning through the defiles of the mountains was the only sound that met the ear.

At length, as they proceeded with silent caution, they perceived a light break from among the rocks at some distance, and in a vague hope of finding some place of shelter, the party pushed on as quickly as their fatigued horses would allow. They soon perceived that the light issued not from the window of a friendly cottage or humble monastery, but from a cavern, the entrance to which seemed to lie half way up the mountain, and to be covered with tangled shrubs. Edward and his attendants immediately comprehended that they had fallen in with the stronghold of some of those robbers of whom he had been warned, and great caution was necessary to be observed on the occasion. Edward dismounted, and with one trusty attendant moved with careful steps towards the cave. As they drew near, many voices in high carousal struck upon them ; and the uproar closing the following song was sung by a clear and manly voice.

> Fill the sparkling wine cup high,
>   'Tis to Bacchus that we fill,
> His joys can brighten sorrow's eye,
>   And bid the aching heart be still.
>
> As his magic raptures steal
>   Through the warm and kindling brain,
> A happiness more great we feel,
>   Than dull poets ever feign.
>
> Visions float before our sight,
>   Fancy free our spirits flow.
> Bacchus gives us true delight,
>   Every joy to wine we owe.

A long uproar of applause followed this song, which both in manner and words seemed to contradict the supposition that it could be a band of robbers who were thus carousing, and Edward felt rather inclined boldly to ask the occupants of the cave for shelter to himself and his band. But on mentioning this idea to his attendant, the latter in terror strongly remonstrated against running into the lion's mouth, as he called it, and while they were thus whispering, a strain broke forth from the cave which convinced Edward of the imprudence of such a step. A vulgar voice sung as follows :—

> Oh ! talk not to me of the pleasure of day,
>   The bright sun gives no warmth to my soul ;
> My pleasures approach as his splendours decay,
> And the woods in brown horror shut out every ray
>   Of the moon, and the planets that roll.
>
> My sun is the juice blaze that flashes so bright,
>   O'er the booty brought in from the plain ;
> We have earned by our swords which are red from the fight,
> The cheer and the revel which startle dull night,
>   While triumphantly king-like we reign.
>
> Then, my boys, for night ! let us drink and forget.
>   That the hand which now pledges the bowl,
> With the blood of aught else than the kidling is wet
> And if we can keep from the law's fatal net,
>   We will live and die free from control.

The last verse of this song was conclusive, and Edward was about to retire, but observing that the robbers seemed still to linger over their repast, he determined to listen a while, hoping to gain from their discourse some useful intelligence by which his conduct might be guided. They talked for some time in a high strain of conviviality, recounting in exultation many of their exploits. They described the behaviour of many persons whom they had robbed, with highly ridiculous allusions, and with much rude humour, while the cave re-echoed with loud bursts of laughter and applause.

"A pretty business those fellows are upon," said one.

"Pretty indeed! Where did you meet them?" said another.

"Just at the corner of the rock, by the blasted oak," said the first speaker. "The woman was decently quiet there, but her conductor said that she had been so violent that he thought starvation was the best cure for her noise."

"Well, 'tis a queer business. I should not like the job," said another.

"But 'tis fine pay," replied his comrade.

"Why don't they still her at once? We could teach them how," said a ruffian.

"What would her ransom be worth then, pray?" cried another, sneeringly.

"Ransom! Why, I thought 'twas a runaway wife."

"No, no! 'tis a rich heiress, and there is another claimant for her lands; so as two cannot live on one crust, it is thought best to put this beyond the sea."

Edward's astonishment at this disclosure may be imagined. Here then was the motive for the outrage, but who could be the instigator? He had heard of no opposition to Cordelia's claim; and even if there were such, it was strange that these measures should be resorted to. He listened almost breathless, to the continuation of the conversation.

"And where do they mean to put the girl?" asked one of the robbers.

"I know not; but beyond sea in some monastery," answered his comrade.

"The fittest place for such squeakers," replied another.

"They are almost at their post by this time; observed the first speaker; "but they were in great alarm on yonder plain; they thought they were pursued."

"Indeed!" cried one who had not yet spoken; "it must be a strong band that dare come near this spot; what say you to looking for them, comrades?"

Edward did not stay to hear more; but beckoning to his attendant, he gently crept away from the cave, and speedily rejoined his party; they took the road which they had been told led to the seashore.

Upon his arrival at the village upon the sea coast, Edward was informed that a party of four men and a woman had a few hours before embarked in a small boat, and had been taken on board a vessel which had been riding at anchor a short distance from the shore during some days, apparently waiting for the party. The vessel immediately sailed, and the villagers neither knew her name nor destination. Words cannot describe the despair and misery of Edward, baffled thus where he had the strongest reason to hope for success. He had not calculated upon the preconcerted plan of having a vessel in readiness, and the circumstance not only made him wretched in his present disappointment, but convinced him that there was throughout the whole business a regular plan for the secretion of Cordelia. He remembered what the robber had said respecting another claimant to her estates, and he resolved to act upon this information by proceeding at once to London, in order to ascertain who the claimant was, and by his or her means to learn the fate of his bethrothed.

With reluctant steps, Edward prepared to retrace the road to Thornbury, but before he had proceeded far, the anxiety and fatigue he had undergone threw him into a violent fever, and for some days his bewildered attendants despaired of his life. A naturally good constitution, however, triumphed over the disease, and by slow degrees he was enabled to pursue his journey.

On his arrival at the castle, his parents were so shocked at the alteration in his appearance, that they determined at once to leave Thornbury, and return to their former residence at a considerable distance. Before their departure, however, Edith was united to Eustace Mowbray, and it was agreed that she should reside by turns with her parents and the Baron de Mowbray. Thornbury was deserted; no one of the family could endure to reside there after the last sad event, and De Fougeres departed for his castle in Scotland, where he had resided in early youth.

CHAPTER XXXII.

Far on the rocky shore the surges sound,
The lashing whirlwinds cleave the vast profound:
While high in air, amid the rising storm,
Driving the blast, sits Danger's black'ning form.—CAMPBELL.

IT is needless to attempt to describe the agony of Cordelia during her forced journey. Vainly did she endeavour to soften the hearts or awaken the fears of her conductors ; vainly did she implore them to tell her why and where they were thus tearing her from her home and friends. No answer did she get, except a threat, or a hint that she would be well taken care of, if she were quiet. Nature gave way under the struggle, and weakness overcame despair. She became quiet, but not resigned ; and when she reached the coast, she was so exhausted as to be unable to speak, she remained passive in the hand of her persecutors.

The vessel set sail with a fresh breeze, which towards night increased to a storm ; a tempest came on, and the captain vainly sounded for anchorage ; it was deep sea, and the vessel drove furiously before the wind. The darkness was interrupted only at intervals by the broad expanse of vivid lightnings, which quivered upon the waters, and disclosing the horrible gaspings of the waves, served to render the darkness which succeeded more awful.

Cordelia lay fainting with terror and weakness in the cabin ; almost hoping that the storm might put an end to her misery and life ; but when she remembered the dear ones who were doubtless mourning her loss, the love of life, natural to every creature, infused new hope into her breast. She knew that every effort would be made to find and release her, and she was not entirely hopeless that those efforts would succeed.

By degrees the storm somewhat abated, although the sea remained rough, and the wind boisterous. After two days and nights thus passed, Cordelia was put into a small boat, and conveyed ashore. The coast was bold and rocky, and totally destitute of any sign of human habitation ; except that on a crag, which over-hung the ocean, stood the half-dilapidated remains of an old castle. To this was Cordelia conveyed.

The castle of Duncraig was situated in the Highlands of Scotland. It had been the abode of various feudal chiefs, and had formerly been strongly fortified, but its defences were now broken down, its walls dismantled. No chief now hung his shield on its walls : the rolling surge, and the howling wind as it burst through the desolate courts, were alone heard by the stranger, whom curiosity led to explore its ruins. One part, however, was in some degree saved from decay, and appeared to have been recently repaired in order to render it fit for habitation. To this Cordelia was borne by the men who had hitherto guarded her, and at the entrance hey were met by one who seemed to be their superior, between whom and the others the following conversation took place.

"You have arrived at last," said the cavalier ; "I expected you last night."
"It is well that we are here at last," replied one ; "the tempest was awful."
"'Tis well we had a good ship," said another ; "she rode it bravely."
"And your charge ?" asked the cavalier.
"More dead than alive," was the reply. "Methinks we might have spared her the voyage—it would but have shortened her life a few days."
"Hush, hush," said the cavalier.

Cordelia was taken into a small room, cheerless, and yet exhibiting some symptoms of occupation ; she was received by an old woman, whom the men called Bridget ; this creature, ugly, dirty, and morose-looking, roughly desired Cordelia to eat of the viands set before her, a command which it was impossible for the unhappy girl to obey, and after a violent flood of tears,—

"Oh, tell me," she cried, "why am I thus torn from family and home? Oh, if you have any of the pity belonging to your sex, save me from misery."

"I can do nothing and say nothing," replied the woman sharply.

"You can pity and assist me," cried Cordelia.

"Assist you to what?" said Bridget.

"To escape," replied Cordelia.

The woman looked astonished. "Foolish girl," she said, "can you believe that I would assist a runaway wife to escape from her lawful husband?"

"I am no wife," cried Cordelia. "Oh! believe not the cruel falsehood."

"Nonsense, nonsense," said Bridget. "Be easy, you are well taken care of."

Cordelia gave herself up to her misery; and after a violent flood of tears, she approached the window of her prison in order to endeavour to ascertain whether there could be any possibility of escape thence. But all hope was shut out by the situation of the part of the castle in which she was confined. The window from which she gazed was at the height at least of thirty feet from the base of the castle wall, and the face of the edifice was apparently built in continuation of the perpendicular cliff upon which it stood. At the foot of this cliff the everlasting ocean beat in hollow surges, which scattering their spray on high were yet as toys when viewed from the dizzy height at which Cordelia stood. No living object met her gaze, the wild sea-mew flew with fluttering wing and shrill scream over the bosom of the wave, now dipping its pinion in the white foam, now soaring aloft into the clouds above; but the sea-mew approached not the window of Cordelia.

Afar off rode the vessel in which the forlorn maiden had been conveyed to her prison; as it met her eye, a chill came over her, and she sunk down upon her seat. She saw that she was alone, and this gave a little relief to her spirit; she therefore took the opportunity of examining her apartment. She found it decently furnished with all that might be wanted for her accommodation, but throughout the whole there appeared an obvious intention to prevent any possibility of escaping. Besides the window looking out upon the ocean, there was a small casement in the opposite direction; but this was so high that Cordelia attempted in vain to reach it even with a chair. A low door led to a large closet in which was placed a bed, evidently intended for her use.

Cordelia's spirits sunk within her as she surveyed her prison, and overcome by fatigue, abstinence, and grief, she sunk into a state of reverie almost approaching to sleep. While in this state the past seemed vividly present to her; even her childhood seemed to be before her, and every incident of her life struck her memory with an intensity which made her feel alarmed lest her reason should be departing. Prominent in the picture stood the figure of Father Augustine; he seemed to delight in her misery, and pointing to the venerable walls of Thornbury Abbey, appeared to intimate that in leaving that holy sanctuary she had forfeited safety and happiness.

But there was another and a dearer vision. Her beloved Edward stood before her as she had last seen him at Thornbury, full of love and hope; alas! the vision faded into the likeness of a wan and faded youth, heart-broken and apparently dying.

"Is it so, my Edward?" murmured Cordelia, "am I indeed so dear that life itself fades away because I am gone? Oh, my friends, my dear friends! if I am doomed to end my days in this dreary prison, oh! cherish the memory of your lost Cordelia! Death is not far from me. I feel his icy chill, my mother's spirit beckons me and I come!"

"Death or life is in your own choice," said a voice close to her. The prisoner startled from her trance, and beheld at her side a man of stern look and dark complexion. Cordelia trembled violently, and could not speak.

"You may be free this instant," said the man.

At these words she startled up, crying, "Oh, let me begone!"

"Nay, not in such haste, my bird, the cage cannot be loosed but under certain conditions," said the man.

"Oh! tell me then! any reward, what reward? only restore me to my friends," cried Cordelia, clasping her hands.

"The mere resignation of a bit of paper will liberate you," said the man.

"What? How?"

"Hear me. You hold the marriage contract of Eleanor de Tunstall with De Dunstanville; give it up, and you are instantly free."

The astonishment of Cordelia was so great that she was bereft of speech.

"You do not answer me," said the man.

"I know you not," cried Cordelia. "I cannot judge whether you have any right to demand this of me."

"Might sometimes give right," he answered; "and might I have and will exercise."

The tone of these words recalled Cordelia's presence of mind; they seemed to strike upon her memory, and to bring back the remembrance of some painful scene of her youth. The form of her aunt the abbess rose up before her, and with a beseeching look warned her to be firm.

"No," she replied; "my mother's honour is in my hands, and never will I betray it."

"Foolish girl," said her companion, sneeringly; "that were an easy trust truly; say rather that the lands of De Dunstanville are coveted by you."

"I care not for lands," cried the maiden.

"And is Edward de Albini as disinterested?" said the man.

Cordelia burst into tears at the name of her beloved Edward, and there was a pause for a few moments.

"But if the youth were so generous, his noble father——"

"Say not a word of insult," interrupted Cordelia. "I am your prisoner, why I know not, but surely common courtesy might lead you to avoid insult. You are unworthy to speak the noble name."

"Know you who I am?" cried the man haughtily. "You may repent your pride. The outcast child of Eleanor de Hestin may be glad of this retreat ere long."

"Never! outcast, as you call me, I am the true and lawful daughter of Eleanor de Dunstanville; of my father it becomes me not to speak as truth would command."

"Deliver to me that forged paper and you are free," said the man.

"If it be forged, of what value is it to any one?" asked Cordelia.

"Give it to me," said her companion.

"I have it not," answered the maiden.

"Give me directions where to find it."

"I know not; and even did I know, never will I part from that paper."

"Obstinate girl! then this room is your prison until I obtain it."

As he said these words, the man left the room, carefully locking the door, and Cordelia sat some time in suspense whether what had just taken place were not a continuation of her previous dream. Indeed there was a strange connection in her mind between the present and the past, which she vainly endeavoured to analyse.

The person who had thus intruded upon the forlorn girl was a man of middle age, or perhaps rather beyond it; he was tall, extremely dark, and had an air of command about him which to unprejudiced observers might betoken noble blood. His features had been handsome, and were still striking, although by no means attractive, and his dress was in the style of a foreign land, handsome, even expensive.

Cordelia pondered long upon the person and manners of him who appeared to be her gaoler. His tone had awakened early recollections, and there was something in his features which seemed familiar to her, and this remembrance was associated with Father Augustine. She had always been assured that her father was dead, that he had died in the Holy Land by the sword of the injured De Hesling; had she not felt certain of this, the thought might have remained with her that this stern man was her parent. But she trusted the word of the abbess as well as of Father Augustine upon this point.

After long communing with herself, bringing before her memory every event of her convent life which could bear any relation to her present situation, she

remembered that when quite a child, she had been spoken to by a strange man at the grate of the convent, and that she had immediately been snatched away by the abbess, who seemed to be considerably alarmed at the apparently unwelcome visitor. This was impressed upon her mind by the fact of her having in some slight manner offended the abbess on that day; that Father Augustine had been sent for in great haste, she thought in order to chide her; and that he had threatened to send for this strange man to take her away if she ever again behaved unbecomingly. All this now returned upon her memory, and she decided that the person who had just left her was the man by whose look she had been so much terrified on the day in question.

But this conviction was far from consolatory to the forlorn maiden. She saw that there was some mysterious chain which linked her to him; but let this chain be what it will, she resolved to die rather than part with the document which attested that which was far dearer than life to her—the fame of her unhappy mother.

Night came, and the old woman brought Cordelia her supper, and attended her as waiting woman, but she refused to speak or to give any answer to what Cordelia said. She left a watch-light in the room, and locking the doors, retired. It may be imagined that Cordelia slept but little; towards daylight weariness overcame her, and she had just fallen into a slumber when the noise of horses in the court-yard underneath awakened her. Hoping for a moment that it might betoken her deliverance, she instantly dressed herself in order to be in readiness to obey the wished-for summons; but, alas! no step approached her apartment, and the noise below continuing, she determined by some means to climb up to the little window whence the sounds proceeded. By removing a large press, she at length succeeded, and found that window looked into the court-yard, and that it was not by many feet so distant from the ground as the other window.

In the court-yard was assembled a handsome retinue of horsemen splendidly accoutred, and mounted on noble steeds; they were evidently preparing for a long journey, and seemed awaiting the arrival of their leader. Presently from a little porch opposite to the grand arched entrance to the court, two persons came forth: one was the old woman Bridget, and the other Cordelia, after a few moments, recognised to be her gaoler. His dress was changed, and seemed adapted for convenience in travelling; a splendid sword hung by his side—this weapon alone agreed with the English costume. After a few words to Bridget, he mounted the horse which was brought to him, and heading the train, they passed out of the court-yard.

While the horses' footsteps were dying away in the distance, Cordelia noted the appearance of the court-yard. It was indeed a dreary place; in many parts the walls were shattered and broken down, crumbling with their own weight; no part of the building seemed to be a fit habitation for a person of the rank and wealth that her gaoler appeared to possess. Not daring to remain long at the casement, Cordelia descended, replaced the press, and again sought her little couch, somewhat relieved by having seen her persecutor depart. From the observations she had made, she concluded that it was upon her account alone that he had come to the castle; and comparing its apparently comfortless condition with the style and number of his followers, she hoped that it would be long ere he revisited a place evidently uncongenial to his habits.

In the morning Bridget brought Cordelia her breakfast, but nothing was said respecting the departure of the man. Towards the middle of the day Bridget made an observation which obliged her to mention this person, and she spoke of him by the title of count.

"To whom then does this castle belong?" asked Cordelia.

"To my master, the Count Mancini," replied the woman; "you know that well enough."

"I never heard the name before," said the lady.

"Not hear the name before? a good joke," said Bridget.

"By all the saints," replied Cordelia, "I never did. Who, or what, do you think I am?"

"Why, the count's runaway daughter, to be sure," replied the woman.

"It is false! I never saw him that I am aware of till yesterday. My parents, alas! are dead, and I am a helpless orphan."

"Well, the count had better have told me the truth," murmured Bridget.

"Why then are you here?" she asked aloud.

"I know not; I was torn from home and friends, apparently without any reason," answered Cordelia, bursting into tears.

"He need not have deceived me," said Bridget to herself. "No matter, though, runaway daughter or wife, I cannot betray him."

"Oh! if you have any pity——" Cordelia began.

"If I had, it would be of no avail," interrupted the woman, "you are closely guarded and watched, not by me alone; so say no more, or I may be dumb again."

So saying, she left the room, leaving the prisoner as much in the dark as ever, as to the history of her seizure. Some days passed thus, till one morning Cordelia was surprised by a young girl entering with her breakfast instead of the old woman. Steadfastly regarding her, the wretched lady thought she could discern a ray of good nature in her countenance, which deepened into sympathy, as she observed the wan looks of Cordelia. "You had better eat something," said the girl, "you look ill."

"Can a prisoner be well?" said Cordelia.

The girl shook her head mornfully. "There are strange things even abroad enough to make a stout heart afraid."

"What mean you?" asked the lady.

"Hush! not so loud," said Kate, for that was the girl's name. "Vincent is at the door; but if you speak low, I will tell you, for I want some one to tell it to."

Cordelia promised to be prudent, and Kate continued.

"You must know, that last night as Sandie was passing the western turret, he heard a strange low moaning; he stopped and listened, and he heard some one say, "Oh, I am dying! forgive me. It was not you, was it, madam?"

"No," replied Cordelia, "I know nothing of it, probably it was merely fancy."

"No, indeed, it was not, for he concealed himself behind the wall, and he saw a figure come out of the turret, and as it got near the old tree at the corner, it vanished."

"Some person had hurt himself, no doubt."

"No, it was nothing earthly. All night there were such noises in the castle that no one could sleep, and even my mother wishes the count were here."

"Is Bridget then your mother?" asked Cordelia.

"Yes," replied the girl. "She is busy now, and cannot wait upon you; therefore, I am sent."

"You do not like to see people unhappy, I am sure, and you cannot imagine how miserable I must be shut up in this place."

"Oh! I would not be shut up so," said the girl.

"Would you then assist me to escape?" cried Cordelia.

The girl shook her head, saying that was impossible.

"Will you endeavour then to get a letter conveyed for me to my friends to tell them where I am? Surely you know some one who would convey it safely, and he should be handsomely rewarded."

Still Kate shook her head.

"Think what it is," cried the lady, "to be taken away from every one you love, and shut up in a dismal castle for no reason whatever."

"Not for no reason?" said Kate.

Cordelia found that this girl thought that she had done something very wicked, and that the count had a right to detain her. She therefore told her part of her history, explaining the situation in which her friends were, and endeavouring to interest her feelings in her behalf.

Kate seemed touched, and especially when Cordelia told her that she had been near being married with the consent of all her friends. The girl then alluded to an attachment of her own to Sandie, and acknowledged that on account of her mother's opposition, she was obliged to meet him by stealth in the evening, and that in a short time she was to run away with him and, be married. But she said that her mother was grown so cross since Cordelia came, on account of the increase of household trouble, that she was more afraid than ever lest she should discover her intentions.

This conversation, trivial as it was, gave Cordelia a little hope ; she began to lay a plan for escaping in the disguise of this girl, and only hoped that the count would not return before she had persuaded Kate to assist her.

For some days there seemed to be some confusion in the castle, her meals were not brought regularly, and Kate refused to answer any questions. She had been scolded, she said, for staying so long in the room on the first day, and Vincent was more suspicious than ever. She found means, however, to tell Cordelia that the groans and noises were still heard at night, and that her mother was extremely angry when the subject was mentioned in her presence. Kate was directed to keep her room all day, except when expressly employed by her mother, whose temper became worse and worse.

Cordelia dreaded least all this should portend some fresh misfortune to herself, but she had no one to whom she could communicate her thoughts. She now frequently ascended to the little casement in the hope of being able to see some one to whom she might appeal. One day, hearing a noise in the court-yard, she climbed up, and to her horror and dismay, she beheld the count arrive with but one attendant. The state of dread in which the poor girl passed the succeeding hours is beyond description, momentarily expecting a visit from him, and fearing lest this day would be her last. However, he came not ; Kate brought her meals as usual, but she dared not say more than, " The count is come at last, and I am to remain here with you ; Vincent will bring our food. I come to night."

Even this was a relief to Cordelia, although she could gain no information as to the cause of the evident disturbance in the castle ; which she sometimes thought might arise from the dreaded attack of an enemy ; but she learned from Kate that the place of her confinement was situated on the coast of Scotland, in a rude and unfrequented part of the country ; she therefore gave up reluctantly the hope of any help from without.

On the day following that on which Kate became the inmate of her chamber, this girl was looking out of the little window when she exclaimed,

" Save us ! What means this ? a priest with his eyes bound !"

" What say you ?" asked Cordelia, starting up.

" Hush ! hush !" answered Kate ; " it is the count, and the father who came to confess my mother when they thought she was dying. I wonder why he is bound. They go into the western Tower."

" Perhaps in order to ascertain the cause of the noises you mentioned," said Cordelia.

" I suppose so, but I dare not stay here lest the count see me."

The remainder of the day was passed in apprehension : Vincent brought the food as usual and seemed more cross than ever. At night Cordelia could not sleep ; the moon shone brightly, and gently rising, she sat down by the window which overhung the sea, and watched the billows as they rose and fell in the silver moonbeam. About midnight she heard a slight noise in the court-yard, and the stealthy tread of two or more persons passing under the gateway. At this moment a door fell to, and awakened Kate, who, starting up in her bed, beheld Cordelia sitting by the window.

" The saints save me !" she cried in alarm. " A ghost ! a ghost !"

" Hush, silly girl, it is me," said Cordelia.

" You ! my lady ! oh speak to me in your own voice !" cried Kate."

" Be quiet then, there are persons stirring in the castle," said the lady.

" Oh we shall be murdered ! we shall be murdered !" cried the girl.

" Get up, and assist me to move the bed to the door, we shall not be easily overcome ;" said Cordelia, whose fears took their colour from her companion's words.

Kate did as she was desired, and with some difficulty they succeeded in barricading the door with such articles of furniture as could be moved without making a noise. When they had done this, Cordelia asked Kate to sit down by her at the window, which she did. A short time had elapsed when Kate pointing to a smal. object on the shore, exclaimed in an under tone of great fear,

" Look there ! what is it ?"

Cordelia looked in the direction pointed out, and saw a small boat with one man in it endeavour to put off from shore. They watched it attentively, the bright moonlight allowing them to observe all its movements. Presently two men, carrying an apparently heavy burden, appeared from the castle; they descended the rock, and were lost sight of for a short time; a cloud obscured the moon for some minutes, and Cordelia was almost breathless with expectation and anxiety, when, by a bright flash of moonlight she caught a glimpse of the two men on the strand raising their burden over into the boat. She shuddered as Kate whispered, " 'Tis a dead body by the saints !"

Cordelia's own observation had likewise suggested this horrible thought, which she dared not breathe to her companion, till the words of the latter confirmed her suspicions. She watched still more intently, the boat left the shore, it floated on the waves, after rowing off to a little distance it was stationary for a short time, it then returned quickly to the shore, and the men landed. But where was their burden ?

Neither Kate nor her companion dared to speak as the same thought crossed both their minds at one moment; Cordelia hid her face in her hand, and leaning back in her chair endeavoured to shut out the remembrance of what she had witnessed, but Kate kept her eyes fixed upon the men, who, ascending the rock, stood for a moment under the window, and Kate, drawing Cordelia forward, pointed. What was Cordelia's horror at beholding the count and Vincent. She could not be mistaken, his dress was too peculiar, and his foreign air marked him as strongly as his dress. She saw the men re-enter the gateway, heard their steps for a few minutes in the court-yard, a gentle noise of shutting a door, and all was again still.

Cordelia felt that it was safer again to return to her bed, and she advised her companion to do the same; not in hope of sleeping—that both felt to be impossible ; but they feared lest their footsteps or even whispers should be heard. The night passed slowly, but too fast for the wretched prisoner; she now knew that her jailer was capable of dark deeds, perhaps he was a murderer, and for a moment she feared lest Edward had discovered her retreat and that his was the corse which she had seen consigned to the waves. Reflection happily showed the improbability of this, but it did not lessen the certainty of some deed of guilt having been committed in the castle. How awful was the light of the morning sun as it broke into her chamber !

Vincent's astonishment was great, when, at a much earlier hour than usual in the morning, he endeavoured to enter the chamber.

" What means all this ? girl ! open the door," he cried.

Cordelia made a sign to her companion to be silent, and answered,

" We did not expect you so early, and I chose to protect myself as long as I am able."

" Nay," said Vincent, " you have never done this before, why do it last night ?"

" I chose it," replied Cordelia as carlessly as she could take courage to speak.

" I shall inform the count," observed Vincent.

" I beseech you, I pray you, on my knees I pray you, do not !" cried Cordelia, throwing herself before him.

" Then tell me truly why you did this last night," said Vincent ; " has anything alarmed you more than usual."

" I thought I heard the count's horses yesterday," said Cordelia hesitating, " and I feared he was arrived."

" Is that all ?" asked Vincent.

" Is not that enough to alarm one !" said the lady.

Vincent appeared satisfied with this, but he desired the girl to go down to her mother, as soon as she had finished her attendance upon Cordelia. When the man was gone, Cordelia spoke earnestly to Kate upon the necessity of keeping what they had witnessed strictly secret ; she found the girl so much alarmed that she dared not hint it to any one, and so great was the fear which she entertained of her mother, that Cordelia was tolerably easy upon the matter. The companions parted with mutual regret ; Cordelia felt that her solitude would now be doubly irksome, she also saw that Kate had been placed as a prisoner in her room in order to keep her in ignorance of what had been going on in the castle, and in which it was but too probable old Bridget participated ; and the girl dreaded her return to the society of her crabbed and unfeeling mother.

About noon Cordelia was distured by the entrance of Bridget, who announced the intended visit of the count. Although this was expected, it was no less, alarming, and the scenes of the past night coming forcibly to her remembrance she could scarcely retain tolerable composure.

The count entered, and at once asked whether she still resolved to withhold the paper which he demanded.

"It was given to me a sacred deposit by one now gone," she replied, "and my duty demands that I keep it as such."

"You know the consequences of your refusal," replied her visitor ; "perpetual and solitary imprisonment."

"You may imprison me for a time, but discovery and vengeance must overtake you at last," said Cordelia gently.

"I can well provide against that," replied the count with a peculiar smile, which Cordelia too truly referred to the event of the past-night, and she shuddered.

Pehaps her tormentor saw the shudder, .for he said, "My interest is not to harm you, and as a proof of that, I make you one more proposal. Be my wife and you are free."

"Your wife? base man ! never! even were I not already betrothed to one who I trust will speedily avenge my wrongs, never will I marry a——"

"What?" cried the count.

"A murderer!" replied Cordelia. But scarcely had the words escaped her lips ere she repented her imprudence, for the count seizing her arm exclaimed,—

"Woman ! what mean you?"

Cordelia spoke not, but trembling awaited the doom which she expected must overtake her.

"I again ask, what mean you ? has any one dared to hint,—" cried the count.

"I see no one," at length replied Cordeliea. "You take good care that I should receive no communications from abroad."

"Why then call me what I am not," asked her tormentor.

"Is it wonderful that this cruel imprisonment has disturbed my faculties?" replied the lady.

"You are your own enemy only. Give me the paper and you are free," exclaimed the count.

"I cannot give up that which I do not possess," replied Cordelia.

"But you know where it is deposited?" asked the count.

"I know only that it was in the safe keeping of my kinsman when I was so cruelly torn from those who love me," answered the the lady.

"De Tunstall cannot now be called upon for it, or I would insist upon your authorising me to claim it," observed the count.

"I do not understand your meaning, but I will die rather than ask it of my beloved uncle," replied Cordesia.

"You need not do it. De Tunstall is dead," said her enemy sneeringly.

Cordelia heard no more, she fell senseless upon the floor. The count, alarmed, endeavoured to raise his victim, but finding that the cruel blow which his information had inflicted had entirely bereft her of sensibility, he hastily left the room and summoned Kate to Cordelia's apartment.

What was the terror of the poor girl at the sight which presented itself. Her master had merely told her that the lady was ill, and she beheld her to all appearance dead. However, Kate retained her presence of mind under her surprise and dismay, or rather her attachment and respect for the unhappy prisoner, and fetching some water she knelt down and bathed the face of the unconscious girl, until, after a considerable time had elapsed, Cordelia shewed symptoms of returning sensation. A deep groan testified that conscious misery was the first feeling of her heart, it was followed by a sob, and the words, "Oh, my uncle, my dear uncle!" relieved Kate's worst apprehension. The tender-hearted girl asked no questions, but assisting her mistress to her little bed, she sat herself down by its side, not knowing what consolation to offer.

A slight tap at the door drew forth an exclamation from Cordelia—

"Oh, do not let him come again, it will kill me at once."

Kate went to the door and found it was old Bridget, who merely requested to know how the lady was.

"Say that I feel that my heart is breaking, I shall not long remain here," cried the wretched maiden. "Tell my cruel persecutor that as he values his own soul I charge him to let me see a priest; it is my only, my last request; I shall soon be beyond his power."

The old woman disappeared for a few minutes, and then returned with a person who appeared to be a kind of esquire to the count, superior to a common menial.

"My lord has desired me to see the lady in order that I may suggest the proper restoratives for her case," said the person advancing to the bed upon which the poor victim was lying.

Cordelia made no answer except by a motion of her hand commanding him to leave the room. But the person advanced to the bedside, and taking the hand of his patient carefully examined her pulse, looked steadily in her face, and making a sign to Kate that he wished to speak with her, she retreated to the outer chamber,

"Oh, whoever you may be," cried Cordelia, "have mercy upon a wretched orphan."

"My errand is done," was the reply.

"Oh, do not leave me thus! if you cannot release me, you can tell me how my dear kinsman died; oh! have some pity for one bereft of kindred and friends!"

"I may say this only," answered the man. "De Tunstall died at Thornbury."

"I dare not ask whether of grief for his lost Cordelia," said the lady.

"It was so," said the man.

"And my friends; are they safe? are they well?" cried Cordelia.

"I know not who your friends are, and I dare say no more," said the man, hastily leaving the room.

Kate returned to the bedside and found Cordelia weeping bitterly; these were the first tears which she had shed, and Kate rejoiced that nature had found this relief. She informed the lady that the man had ordered her all strengthening meats and food, anything which she wished was to be procured for her, however great the trouble might be; a few religious books were to be allowed her; and an old harp, almost as antiquated as the castle itself, was to be brought to her for her amusement.

"From something that Frazer said," continued Kate, "I fancy that the count is going away directly; he hinted that if you became worse, father Ambrose is to be sent for."

"I am dying, Kate," replied the lady.

"Oh, say not so!" said the attendant. "Frazer said that you might live to be married yet."

A shudder ran through the poor girl as she heard these words. "Never to that man," she cried, "a murderer!"

"The count had a wife when he first came here," said Kate; "and I never heard of her death, therefore Frazer cannot mean him."

Cordelia made no answer, but closing her eyes, her thoughts reverted to Thornbury and its inmates. After some time, her reverie gave way to sleep, and for some hours she lay composedly slumbering. During this time Vincent and old Bridget brought into the chamber the harp of which Kate had spoken, a large but commodious easy chair, and some articles of furniture of a better kind than those which were already in the room. They also brought a few religious books.

But the intelligence that awaited Cordelia's awaking was more agreeable than any personal accommodation could be ; Kate had heard the count depart, and it was the first word that she spoke when Cordelia opened her eyes. The poor girl felt that, wretched as her confinement was, it could yet be made worse by the presence of her enemy, and she yielded to a glimmering of hope upon hearing of his departure. Kate urged her to rise, which with some reluctance she yielded to, and in tolerable composure she sat down by the window, and taking up one of the books, attempted to read.

CHAPTER XXXIII.

Silent nymph with curious eye,
    Who the purple evening lie,
On the mountain's lonely van,
    Beyond the voice of busy man ;
Painting fair the forms of things,
    While the yellow linnet sings,
Or the tuneful nightingale,
    Charms the forest with her tale.—DYER.

LET us now return to Thornbury, deserted of its inhabitants, its fair grassy walks neglected, its thickets overgrown, its halls gloomy and tenantless. The retainers who had been used to make the walls ring with laughter at the jest, or with the shout of welcome to their lord, were far away ; they had followed de Fougeres to Scotland ; Ronald only remained, and it was his delight to roam through the deserted apartments, indulging his faithful memory with the remembrance of the fair and splendid visions of happier days. Edward de Albini had endeavoured to persuade the dwarf to accompany him to Percival Castle, but Ronald seemed to have a vague hope that by remaining at Thornbury he might in some unexpected way be instrumental in learning the fate of Cordelia, and under this idea he pertinaciously refused to change his residence. Listless and unemployed, Ronald was the pity and commiseration of his companions, and at the same time his advice was sought under every difficulty, as the dwarf was acquainted with every thing of interest which occurred in the neighbourhood.

One autumnal evening two strangers alighted at the little inn of the village of Thornbury, for the purpose of inquiring the road to the monastery. Their appearance was singular, betokening high breeding and foreign habits ; with considerable haughtiness the one who seemed to be the superior received the information required, and desiring that the horses might be properly tended, the strangers took the road to the monastery. Ronald, who had been as usual lounging about the village, witnessed the new arrival, and in his true spirit of curiosity followed the gentlemen at a distance.

Upon arriving at the monastery, and enquiring for the superior, the strangers were admitted into the parlour, where father Lewis received them courteously.

The elder stranger, whom we may as well at once announce as the Count Mancini, spoke upon the subject which brought him to Thornbury. "I was acquainted," he said, "with the family of the late baron De Tunstall, and I am anxious to learn some particulars respecting his decease."

"Sad, indeed, "replied the father, "have been the events which connect the name of De Tunstall with our village, and of all those circumstances the most dreadful is the one which broke the heart of the bereaved baron. I allude to the mysterious disappearance of the Lady Cordelia de Dunstanville."

"I heard of it," observed the count. Beloved as she was, nay, adored by our villagers, as well as by her friends and kinsman, every heart beats high with revenge against her murderer," continued the priest. "The day may soon come which shall disclose the author of the foul deed, and I trust that he will not pass to the grave unpunished."

"Know you who is the heir to the lands claimed by the lady de Dunstanville?" asked the stranger.

"Not I," replied the father? "heraldry and pedigrees befit not our peaceful convent. But no one would dare to claim them while the fate of the lady remains doubtful."

"Certainly not," replied the count. "Besides which, they are, I believe, dependent upon a mere thread, a forged document of marriage."

No. 27.

"Forged?" exclaimed the priest in a tone of astonishment.

"Yes, I have heard that the paper was forged by the baron de Fougeres," observed the count carelessly.

"It is false!" cried father Lewis with warmth.

"It matters not," said the count.

"It matters to my master's honour, however," replied the priest, "that such a report be contradicted ; he who spreads it must answer to me, whose anger is not to be carelessly treated. Your name, sir ?"

"An unknown one, not worth mentioning," said the count. "I merely mentioned the report, as one prevalent in the world. But is that paper in existence ?"

The father hesitated ; he was suspicious of the integrity of the guest, and he was not willing to give the information he required.

"I scarcely can answer you ; I have heard various extraordinary tales," he said. "You say that you know the family of the Baron de Tunstall, therefore probably you can *give* me information instead of asking it."

"I am lately returned from abroad, and I was anxious respecting the welfare of an old acquaintance. But what are the extraordinary tales to which you alluded ?" asked the count.

"It is said that the Baron de Tunstall, apprehensive of some distant relative of the Lady Cordelia, left especial orders on his death-bed, that the paper securing her rights should be buried with him in his coffin," said the father.

"And was this strange order followed ?" asked the count anxiously.

"It was. Even did the person whom he feared dare to disturb the sanctuary of the tomb, the spirit of the Baron de Tunstall would prevent it, as nightly he walks in the chapel of Thornbury Castle in order to protect the precious document."

The count was intimidated, and had almost resolved to make no more enquiries, when the priest added,—

"All that friendship can do to honour the dead will be done ; even now are the servants of the Baron de Albini engaged in erecting a noble monument, setting forth the lineage and virtues of him who sleeps in peace below."

A significant glance here passed between the count and his companion ; and the former hastily took leave of the father with many courtly thanks for the information he had given to them.

"What think you now, Frazer?" said the count, as they left the monastery. "I shall foil the puling girl yet. The paper shall be mine, and then away with the girl, I will not ask her to be my bride."

Ronald, who, in his usual capacity of listener, had heard this speech, drew back among the bushes, and stealthily creeping along, he contrived to gain the road a little in advance of the strangers.

Meanwhile Frazer asked his master how he intended to proceed.

"Open the coffin, to be sure," was the reply.

"But—" said Frazer, hesitating.

"Art afraid ?" cried the count.

Frazer made no answer.

"Nay, if you are afraid of this old baron, I will do it alone ; but the paper I will have, and this night, too," exclaimed Mancini.

"If you are so decided," said his companion. "I will not shrink from you."

"We will repair to the chapel at midnight," said the count ; "the tools with which the workmen are erecting the monument will serve us well, and we can immediately escape with our treasure."

"But the horses?" asked Frazer.

"The paper will furnish us with better ones ; besides, our having left them behind will assist in turning away suspicion from us should our theft be discovered."

"Still I like not the encounter," said Fraser.

"Of the dead knight? Well, I prefer a battle with flesh and blood myself, but this may be a mere idle tale. Shall we question yonder mis-shapen being," asked Mancini, "he may know somewhat of the ghost's haunts."

Thus saying, the strangers approached Ronald, who was trudging on, apparently unconscious of everything, save the song, which he was singing as follows :—

> "And the knight he bore that lady fair,
>   To his castle by the sea,
> And he said, ' Uutil you are my bride,
>   This place your cage shall be.
> But from the south with arm of strength,
>   A noble knight there came ;
> And the traitor he gave to the gibbet high,
>   And the castle to the flame."

The count did not much enjoy Ronald's song, and he stopped it by saying,— "Fellow! a word with thee."

"Hilloa, there ! room for Lord Ronald !" cried the dwarf, as with a step of mock dignity he approached Mancini.

"Whose castle is that ?" asked the count.

"A better man's than thou or I," replied Ronald.

"Poor courtesy, truly," observed the count. "We are travellers, and like to know where we are."

"Then why not have asked at the monastery ?" said the dwarf.

"Wilt tell us or not ?" cried Frazer, angrily.

"Oh yes, willingly ; the whole history of the castle, true and untrue," said Ronald. "How the noble Lady Edith married the noble Eustace de Mowbray ; how the beautiful Lady Cordelia de Dunstanville married—no—stop—she did not marry Edward de Albini—how the baron, my master, went away over yonder hill —and how there was mourning for the Baron de Tunstall. And I will tell you what a tomb is erecting in the chapel for him, with angels all round it to scare away the evil one ; and how the baron himself carries away at night the dirt which the men dig up in the day."

"The baron ! 1 thought he was dead ?" asked Mancini,

"So he is ; but don't the dead work at night sometimes ?" cried the dwarf.

"Lead us to the chapel, fellow, I would fain see this grand monument," said the count.

Ronald led the way to the chapel, where they found the workmen busy with their task ; the pavement was broken up, and the count observed with satisfaction that the coffin of De Tunstall was covered only by a few feet of rough earth. A look of congratulation passed between the strangers and they left the chapel. At the inn they desired to have refreshment served to them, and they shut themselves up in their room during the remaider of the day.

In the meanwhile Ronald had not been idle ; he had resolved to counteract, or at any rate to hinder, the plans of the strangers, and after some consideration, he determined on effecting this secretly and without assistance from any one. Having procured from Rosamond a long white garment, he hid himself in the church towards midnight, in expectation of the count and his companion. Rosamond had been very solicitous to know for what purpose the dwarf wanted the disguise, and he was obliged to tell her the history of the strangers. Although now a staid matron, Rosalind still loved adventure, and after many denials she persuaded Ronald to let her accompany him to the chapel. Accordingly, as we have said, they repaired thither just before midnight, and concealed themselves behind an arch near the burial place of the Baron de Tunstall.

Soon after twelve o'clock the Count and Frazer prepared for their unholy expedition, saying to their landlord, that as they must reach a neighbouring town by noon on the following day, they would ride to the next village by moonlight ; they therefore paid their reckoning and departed. This plan was proposed by Frazer, who was fearful of discovery if they attempted to escape on foot. Having mounted their horses the strangers took their way to the castle, which, frowning black over the river which sparkled in the moonlight, seemed to endeavour to forbid their intrusion. But no slight obstacle could debar the Count from his unhallowed enterprise ; he was too well practised in guilt, and too well accustomed to think lightly of the means by which he might accomplish his wishes, to hesitate at fancied hindrances. His companion, having less at stake, several times expressed his awe of the scene before them, and on reaching the little wood which skirted the castle on the side next the chapel, he earnestly implored the Count to desist.

But it was vain, and the strangers passed through the wood and gained the entrance to the chapel, which was a small but handsome structure, lighted only by an oriel window of stained glass, through which the moonbeams fell upon the pavement in streaks of various hues. The Count stood still a moment in admiration of the hallowed scene upon which he had obtruded himself, but speedily recovering, he proposed to commence their operations, and going to the spot where the workmen's tools were deposited, he selected a spade whish he gave to his companion. Frazer unwillingly received the implement, and the Count preparing preparing to break up the ground which covered the remains of De Tunstall, bade Frazer clear away the soil.

For some minutes they proceeded in their work without speaking, till Frazer exclaimed in a half whisper, "Hark! my lord, did you hear it ?"

"Hear what ?" cried the count.

"A groan, a dreadful groan," replied his companion.

"Nonsense ! have I not ears as well as yourself?" said Mancini ; "it was only the wind among the tall fir-trees."

They continued their work for a few minutes, till a second groan startled them both, and the count raising himself, looked round to the part of the chapel whence the sound proceeded.

"Nor ghost nor devil shall prevent my obtaining this paper," he cried in a tone of defiance, "that, once accomplished, a whole legion may be set loose upon me and I will defy them all—the lands of De Dunstanville shall be my protection."

A louder groan, accompanied by a sudden flash of light, here startled even Mancini, while his companion, flinging down the spade, declared he would do no more of the unholy work.

"Remember our compact," cried Mancini, "assist me to obtain this paper and third of the spoil is yours ; refuse, and your fate be on your own head."

"Nay, for that matter," replied Frazier, "a hempen rope may await us both. I engaged to assist you against the girl herself, or even against her friends, but truly know not how to fight against ghosts."

"See," said the count, "a few more shovels full and you will touch the coffin."

"And what then ?" asked Frazer.

"Seek a tool for me," replied his master ; "I will finish the work."

Frazer accordingly went towards the spot where the tools were deposited, but instantly running back he cried,—

"He is there ! he is there !" and a deep groan seemed to corroborate his assertion.

"Who is there ?" demanded the count.

"The dead knight !" replied his companion, in a tone of horror.

"Where ?" asked Mancini.

"Beyond yonder arch," cried, Frazer pointing to a dark corner of the chapel, and at the same instant a flash of blue light discovered a white figure standing motionless in the recess. Even the count was appalled, and laying down the axe, he stood in mute astonishment, gazing upon the figure, which had in the darkness faded to mere outline.

Presently another flash of light shewed the spectre again plainly, its right hand was held up in warning, and a deep voice groaned rather than spoke "Beware !"

Still the Count hesitated, he was not accustomed to fear, and unwilling to loss the treasure for which he had risked so much, but the apparition dismayed him.

"Invade not the repose of the dead ! even now the orphan's rights are guarded securely," said the unearthly figure raising its arms.

The count waited no longer, but hastening out of the chapel, he and his companion remounted their horses which they had fastened to a tree near the entrance, and rode off as quickly as possible. For some miles neither ventured to speak, till the count exclaimed,—

"Bad luck to my stars to-night, I know not how to obtain this precious paper. But I will proceed to court directly, and gain from the king what I hoped to obtain with less trouble."

"Will you proceed alone, my lord ?" asked Frazer.

"No," replied Mancini ; "my usual attendants await me in London."

After the strangers had left the chapel, Ronald and Rosamond congratulated each other on the complete success of their scheme; but the dwarf was by no means satisfied with having merely prevented present mischief, his curiosity was roused respecting the strangers, and he was determined not to lose sight of them.

"I have a strange suspicion that these men know something about our poor Lady Cordelia," he said; "but I fear I cannot do much towards discovering them, although I am sure I should know the elder one anywhere should I see him again."

"He appears to be a foreigner," replied Rosamond.

"Yes, that villanous look does not belong to merry England," replied the dwarf.

"He must be a villain indeed that could harm our sweet lady," said Rosamond. "And the Lady Edith de Mowbray too, she often comes to the castle and sits in the saloon weeping for hours together over the happy days that are gone."

"I am much inclined, Rosamond, to journey to Percival Castle and acquaint the young knight with the visit of these queer strangers, perhaps, after all, we may be able to get some tidings of the poor Lady Cordelia," said Ronald.

"Oh, she cannot be alive, else why should this man want to get that paper ?" observed Rosamond.

"I do not understand anything about it, but have long wished to go to Percival Castle, and this occurrence decides me," replied the dwarf, "will you accompany me to Mowbray to-morrow ? I would see the Lady Edith before I go."

"Willingly," replied Rosamond ; and it was arranged that these companions should go over to Mowbray Castle on the following day. When, however, Ronald announced the cause of the visit at Mowbray, he learned that the Lady Edith and her lord had been sent for upon the illness of Geoffrey de Albini, and that they had not yet returned from Percival.

Ronald therefore determined to proceed thither, and enter the service of Edward de Albini. It was not, however, without many bitter pangs that the faithful dwarf bid adieu to Thornbury Castle; it was the house of his youth, among its glades his childhood had played, and in its walls the best years of his life had been passed ; and if De Fougeres had been a stern master, the fair Edith had softened his sternness towards all around him. Melancholy thoughts of the past, and gloomy anticipations for the future, crowded upon Ronald's mind and heart as he passed the castle walls, and his feelings found their relief as was his wont in the following lines, which he chaunted to a mournful dirge as he went along.

Farewell, old towers ! farewell, my home !
Tho' from your sheltering walls I roam,
Yet memory oft, to childhood true,
Shall bring back Thornbury to my view.

How chang'd the scene ! the hall no more
Re-echoes to the wassail roar ;
No more beside you half-closed gate,
The baron's stately steed may wait.

No more the noise of merry sport,
From happy menials fills the court;
The warder's voice no more is heard,
To give De Fougeres' battle word.

All silent! destiny's dark doom,
Hath turn'd our happiness to gloom;
And sorrow o'er these tow'rs and hall
Relentless spreads her dark'ning pall.

Yet nature mourns not—yon fair stream,
Sparkles beneath the morning beam,
Brightly as when its placid face,
Reflected noble Edith's grace.

The lark his carol bears on high,
Blithely as if the mortal eye,
Which marks his progress thro' the air,
Ne'er droop'd 'neath misery or despair.

Then when misfortune's touch we mourn,
To nature let us gladly turn,
Secure, that tho' of joy bereft,
Friendless, deprest, *hope* still is left.

With these thoughts in his mind Ronald journeyed on, amusing himself with observations upon the country through which he passed, and laying up a store of facts and anecdotes for future use. Ronald had gone through life with his eyes open, and had thereby acquired a character for something beyond common knowledge, and many times this reputation had assisted him in working out the truth of his own predictions. The change of affairs at Thornbury had rendered his life much too dull for his taste; he loved bustle and occupation, and he would have left the deserted castle long before this period, had not the society of Rosamond held him in some degree to his old home. Now the late occurrence had decided him to leave Thornbury.

Ronald travelled on to Percival, but as he approached the castle he thought it would be better to seek in the village adjoining some rest and refreshment, and also to make inquiries respecting the family of De Albini. He, therefore, rode up to the village inn, and alighting from his horse called for the master of the house, who speedily appeared and offered the stranger refreshment.

"I have journeyed far to-day, and shall be glad of food," said Ronald.

"It is a melancholy cause which has brought your honour here," said the landlord.

"It is; but how know you that it is so?" asked the dwarf, astonished.

"You are doubtless from Thornbury to attend our lord," replied the man.

"I am," he answered.

"Our young master has given especial orders that any traveller from Thornbury should be well attended to, and liberally treated."

"Did he expect any of the Thornbury retainers, then?" asked Ronald.

"I believe he hoped some would pay their last respects to-night," said the landlord.

"Last respects—to-night! What do you mean? Surely Edward de Albini is not about to be married!" cried Ronald.

"Would that he were!" answered the man. "But know you not that the good Baron de Albini is dead, and is to be interred to-night?"

"Dead! Oh, my poor young master!" exclaimed the dwarf.

"He died three days since," answered the man.

"And the Lady Edith de Mowbray, is she here?" asked Ronald.

"She is; she arrived just in time to close her father's eyes, and I fear she will remain to follow the Lady Elfrida to the grave."

"Woe still awaits this house, then," cried Ronald.

"May a stranger attend at the chapel?"

"Certainly," replied the landlord.

Ronald therefore resolved to take up his residence for the day at the little inn, and in the evening to attend unseen at the funeral of Geoffrey de Albini. At the appointed time he took the road to the castle, accompanied by the landlord, and they stationed themselves near the entrance to the chapel. It was a solemn and imposing scene, and the number of spectators evinced how much the deceased baron had been respected and beloved.

Percival Castle stood frowning over the valley below in solemn grandeur, a hundred torches threw their lurid glare over the walls, casting into deep shadow the recesses of the bowers; the castle bell tolled loudly in the midnight air, and a solemn procession issued from the gate, and, winding round a point of the building, slowly proceeded to the chapel.

A band of retainers headed the procession, and were followed by heralds, bearing the arms of the deceased, decorated with mourning tokens. Then came the favourite steed of the baron, fully caparisoned, and immediately behind, the principal object in the procession. The pall was held by six barons of equal rank with the deceased, attended by their squires.

Ronald's heart was touched by the sight of this melancholy array, but his whole attention was speedily absorbed by the figure who followed as chief mourner. It was Edward de Albini, but so changed that the faithful dwarf could scarcely recognise him, and at first he could not believe that so short a period could have worked such a change as that which he now beheld. Woe-worn, emaciated, drooping, Edward de Albini bore testimony to the sorrows which had afflicted his youth. How different was he now to the buoyant and active knight who had won and received the love of Cordelia de Dunstanville! His steps were supported by a youth of noble appearance and singularly handsome countenance, whom Ronald recognised as the Baron Mouthermer.

A numerous band of noblemen and gentlemen followed in the mournful train, which reached from the castle gate to the entrance of the chapel. Ronald was fortunate enough, with some difficulty, to obtain admission to the sacred edifice, and he was deeply affected as the ceremony proceeded. After all was over, he returned to the little inn, resolving on the following morning to present himself to De Albini.

Ronald accordingly presented himself at the castle, requesting an audience of the young baron. The warder expressed his reluctance to introduce a stranger into the castle at such a melancholy period, and alleged that the baron was in such wretched spirits, that it was not at all probable that he would see the dwarf.

"Tell the baron that I come from Thornbury, and that I bring tidings of importance to him," said Ronald.

"From Thornbury!" exclaimed the warder, in a more complying tone, "then, perhaps, my lord may see you; but I trust that you bring no bad news from Thornbruy."

"None," replied the dwarf. Is not lady Edith here?"

"She is, and may she long remain to solace her widowed mother, for I much fear our lord's life is but an uncertain one," said the warder.

"I do not ask whether he still grieve for the lost lady Cordelia;" replied the dwarf, "his appearance speaks too plainly of his broken heart."

"It is indeed broken, I fear," said the warder, "but one word of hope might revive it."

"I trust I bring that word of hope," answered Ronald, at least, I think I have found a clue to the lost treasure."

"The saints grant it!" cried the warder.

At this moment the servant who had announced Ronald returned with a message from his master, that Ronald was to be admitted. The dwarf was accordingly ushered into an apartment o the castle, where he found Edward de Albini seated at a writing table, apparently deeply engaged. He raised his eyes upon Ronald's entrance, and what was his astonishment at perceiving his old companion! De Albini started from his chair, and advancing towards th dwarf, held out his hand to him in silence. Ronald took it respectfully, an bowed low while the young baron wrung his hand convulsively, and burst int tears. He continued to weep for a few minutes, then recovering himself, h said,

"Ronald! this last blow has unmanned me, or I would not have me an old friend thus."

"I am grieved indeed, my lord," replied Ronald; "had I known that yo were thus sorrowing, I would not have intruded upon you at present, but was anxious to see your lordship."

"Wherefore, Ronald?" exclaimed Edward; "but no! I have ceased to hop for a termination to my unhappiness."

"I am tired of Thornbury," replied Ronald, fearing to speak upon the real sub ject of his journey, lest it should too deeply affect the baron.

"Alas! the name but awakens regret," said De Albini, sighing.

"I would humbly beg to be admitted to your lordship's service, and therefore have left the house of my birth," replied the dwarf.

"You are welcome, Ronald," said the baron, "atthough your presence forcibl recals to me the remembrance of days of happiness now gone for ever; yet, methink it will be soothing to me sometimes to speak of her whom I shall never again behold but to whom my heart will remain devoted to the last period of my existence."

"Perhaps, my lord—" said Ronald, hesitating.

But Edward heard him not; he had sunk into a mournful reverie, and appeared t forget the presence of the dwarf, who remained silent for some time, and at last sum moning all his courage, said,

"Methinks, my lord, I could tell you something which might interest you."

"Never, Ronald! nothing more can interest me, now she is no more," crie Edward.

"Are you certain of her death!" asked Ronald.

"There can be no doubt of it," replied Edward.

"Unless you know it, I would still hope," said the dwarf; "and if I dared t mention such a subject, I would tell of a circumstance that might give some clue—

"To what! oh tell me!" cried Edward, eagerly.

"I fear to raise hopes which I cannot satisfy," said Ronald.

"Oh, in mercy tell me!" exclaimed the Baron.

"There have been strangers at Thornbury," said Ronald, "whose proceeding were extraordinary, and of them I wish to tell your lordship."

"Speak! say on!" cried De Albini.

"A few days since two travellers of rather uncommon appearance came to Thorn bury, and alighted at the little village inn. I was loitering as usual in the roa and heard them inquire the way to the monastery. I followed them, and from what I heard of their conversation, on their return, I understood that they intende to search the coffin of the Baron de Tunstall for some hidden paper."

"Can it be!" exclaimed De Albini. "They must know my Cordelia. Go on.

"I remembered father Augustine," continued Ronald, "and consulted my frien Rosamond upon the subject. We concealed ourselves in the castle chapel at mid night, and when these robbers came we frightened them so much, that they wen away without having accomplished their purpose."

"Thanks, thanks, Ronald!" cried Edward; "but they would not have foun the object of their search. In what direction did they escape?"

"Towards London, their horses were on the outside of the chapel, and they were off directly," answered the dwarf.

"Describe these men to me," said the baron.

"One who was the older of the two, and appeared to be the superior, looked like a foreigner; he wore a very rich embroidered cloak, and had a sword like those which my master brought from over sea. He was dark, and his black hair curled round his head. The other—"

"Tell me more about the foreigner," interrupted De Albini.

"He looked extremely proud and tyrannical and had certainly seen much fighting, both from his manner and a scar on his face," replied Ronald.

"A scar?" cried Edward hastily.

"Yes, there was a very singular mark on his mouth as if both lips had been cut through."

"Ha!" cried Edward.

"This scar caught my eye as I saw the man, and the landlord of the inn mentioned it to me afterwards," said the dwarf. "It was a very singular mark."

"Did this person walk a little lame?" asked Edward.

"I once or twice thought that he did," replied the dwarf, "but it was very slightly."

"It is—it must be the same!" cried De Albini.

No. 28.

"Do you then know him, my lord?" asked the dwarf.

"Perhaps I do," replied the baron,

"And was I right in preventing his attempt upon the dead?" asked Ronald.

"Perfectly, he could have no right to the paper. Know you the object of his visit to the monastery?" asked De Albini.

"I fancy to gain tidings of the treasure," said the dwarf. "But, my lord—"

"What, Ronald? speak your wishes," said Edward.

"I would not be impertinent, but I respected the lady, and—" said the dwarf, again hesitating.

"Speak," said the baron.

"Is there any hope of learning her fate by this stranger," asked Ronald.

"Alas, I fear not," replied Edward.

"But if you know the man," observed Ronald.

"I have seen him at court only," replied the baron.

"Can I seek him there, and learn his history?" asked the dwarf.

"I must deliberate upon this matter; but my friend Monthermer may assist me in my enquiries," said the baron; "but, Ronald, you will remain here?"

"If your lordship will permit me," replied the dwarf.

"I may have occasion for your services," replied De Albini; "but I would not have a word escape you of this business."

Ronald promised secrecy, and retired into the castle hall where he found many who had visited Thornbury with their late master, and to whom he was extremely welcome.

The Baron de Albini had controlled his feelings during the presence of his faithful dwarf, but the intelligence which he had just received had awakened both interest and curiosity. To understand this we must resume the history of the bereaved family at Thornbury, from the time of Cordelia's disappearance.

CHAPTER XXXIV.

" As time glides on in silent flow,
  To-day yields to to-morrow;
To-morrow's expectations grow,
  To-day's own bliss or sorrow.
Still as to-morrow's sun appears,
  It shines upon to-day;
Lo, realised, our hopes and fears
  For ever melt away."

AFTER the marriage of Edith the Baron de Albini and his lady returned to their residence at Percival castle, dispirited and lonely. Edward at first declared that he could not leave the scene of his happiness and his misery, but he was persuaded to do so, and he resided with his father at Percival. By degrees his spirits became more composed, and in renewed companionship with his beloved mother his health appeared to regain its accustomed strength.

Meanwhile the aspect of public affairs was by no means unclouded. The health of Stephen was rapidly declining, and the thoughtful men of the nation looked forward with considerable apprehension to the accession of his successor. Among these was Geoffrey de Albini. Formerly attached to the cause of Matilda, more because he thought her right to the crown greater than that of her competitor than because he wished to see England under the dominion of a woman, de Albini had been nevertheless one of the principal supports of the throne of Stephen; he was trusted in the cabinet and consulted at the council board ; and his former prejudices had gradually given way before the wise and equitable government of him whom he now ceased to consider as an usurper.

Vainly had the noble Baron de Albini endeavoured to induce his son to seek in public business a relief from the melancholy which evidently preyed upon his spirits and enfeebled his health. Edward performed his duty to his sovereign by suffering himself to be presented at court, but he respectfully declined accepting any office, which should require his residence in London. Such an one had been repeatedly offered to him, and de Albini was disappointed at his son's rejection of them, but Edward's happiness, if we may so term it, was comprised in his mother's society ; with her he might again talk over the failure of his cherished hopes, and in her beloved society lament his sad bereavement, secure of sympathy and support. Edward therefore, unless when the importunity of his friend Mouthermer forced him to pay a short visit to the metropolis, resided at Percival, where he was beloved and respected by all around him.

It was on one of these occasions that Edward de Albini had seen the Count Mancini, and although the interview was a hurried one, and unmarked by any event of more than ordinary interest, the foreigner was not a person easily to be forgotten.

It chanced that the young Baron Mouthermer one day entering the shop of his jeweller, saw upon the counter a small miniature of a young man of very prepossessing appearance. The picture was evidently by a foreign artist, and it was most gorgeously set in very valuable diamonds. The brilliancy of the jewels attracted the attention of Mouthermer and his friend De Albini, and the latter, taking up the miniature carefully, remarked that it bore some resemblance to his friend's wife. Mouthermer then looked at it also, and exclaimed.

" By the saints, it must be so !"

" How ?" asked Edward,

" This must be a portrait of Lady Mouthermer's father, Count Rosenberg," exclaimed Mouthermer.

" Indeed !" replied Edward.

" I wonder who brought it here." said Mouthermer ? " my wife would pay any price for the possession of it."

" You can easily ascertain ; perhaps the jeweller may be commissioned to sell it," observed Edward.

Upon the entrance of the master of the shop, Mouthermer asked him how he became possessed of the miniature, and whether it was for sale.

" No," replied the man ; " a gentleman left it here just now, to have the diamonds taken out and reset. I remonstrated, as the diamonds are remarkably valuable ones, and I am sorry to touch them, but I am ordered to do it."

" Who was the gentleman ?" asked Mouthermer,

" I do not know, my Lord," replied the man.

" Do you not then know for whom you are to do this work ? it seems strange that you did not enquire his name," observed Edward.

" I do not know the name of the gentleman who left the picture," said the man, " he said he was not the owner of it, but he wrote a name here in my book, as that of the person who would pay me for it."

" Let me see the name," said Mouthermer, " perhaps he would be willing to part with the picture."

" I do not think he values the painting very highly," replied the man, " as when I told him that I must injure it a little in taking the border to pieces, he said that was no consequence, but that I must be careful of the jewels."

" Then I may be able to negociate with him," said Mouthermer,

" Here is the name, my lord," said the man, pointing to his book ; " it is a foreign name, but I am sure that the gentleman who brought the picture is an Englishman."

The baron looked at the book and read, " The Count Mancini."

" Who is he ? Do you know him ?" asked De Albini.

"I see him frequently at court," replied his friend.

"I am glad to hear that you know him, my lord," said the jeweller; "for although I cannot lose any thing by such a job, to tell you the truth the diamonds are such valuable ones, that I have been uneasy at being thus trusted by a stranger and evidently a person very suspicious and particular."

"You may be quite easy respecting the riches of your employer," answered Mouthermer; "but who or what he is, I cannot tell you. He comes to court with a numerous retinue, and from his style and appearance seems to be wealthy, but he knows no one."

"He is a foreigner," observed Edward, "an Italian, I suppose, who came over with King Stephen?"

"No, he has not been long in England, I believe; but I know nothing of him, except that he is more lavish of money than smiles, for the latter he seldom bestows upon us, he seems to have left them all in his own sunny land," said the baron.

"Shall you try to obtain the picture?" asked Edward."

"Certainly, but I cannot imagine how the count came by it; had he been acquainted with Count Rosenberg, he would surely have gained an introduction to me,' said the baron.

"Can I be of any use to you, my lord?" said the jeweller.

"No," replied Mouthermer; "I shall call upon the Count Mancini myself, respecting it. Edward, will you accompany me?"

"Willingly," replied his friend.

The two young men left the shop, Mouthermer desiring the jeweller not to touch the picture until he heard from him, which he assured him should be on the following daw.

"This is a singular circumstance," said Mouthermer walking along; "I shall say nothing to my lady of it, lest she should be disappointed, but if I can obtain the picture it will be an agreeable present to her upon her ensuing birthday."

"As the count does not seem to value the painting, there is great hope of your obtaining it," observed De Albini.

"But how did he get it? that is my subject of curiosity," said the baron.

"Probably by some strange means abroad," said Edward. "Is he not some very distant relative to the Count Rosenberg?"

"God forbid!" exclaimed Mouthermer;" "I like neither the man nor his character well enough to acknowledge him as such, however distant."

Well might the young baron thus express himself. Mancini was regarded as a singular person, at the least, by the high bred nobility of Stephen's court; he had made his appearance there unknown to every one; nobody could tell his parentage or connexions; he had certainly served in the holy wars as they were called, but no one recognised his name in the armies of Palestine; his apppearance, however, bore testimony to the truth of his tale in this respect. He said that the recent death of a beloved wife had drawn him from his country, and that he visited England in order to dissipate his grief; but neither the habits nor the occupations of English noblemen seemed to suit his taste, and he secluded himself from society under the plea of his unequal spirits. When he did appear abroad, a studied magnificence and display attended all his proceedings; his servants were numerous and splendidly attired; and his own dress extravagantly decorated. The populace wondered and admired, but his equals shunned him as an equivocal personage. The king, had, however, received him when presented, but he made no frequent appearance at court. The idle gossip of the day had invested count Mancini with the power of using the philosopher's stone, and turning all baser metals into gold, while, at the same time, stories were whispered which alleged that his riches were not wholly inexhaustible.

Such was the man upon whom the Baron Mouthermer and De Albini were about to call.

Upon their arrival at the hotel where Mancini lived, the baron announced him-

Mouthermer began to think with his friend, that the count was rather a suspicious person, but he saw him noticed by the grandees of the land, and therefore said nothing of his doubts, nor did he tell his lady the history of the miniature, but merely observed that he had picked it up at a jeweller's.

The illness of his father withdrew Edward's thoughts from the Count Mancini; he was deeply attached to him, and nursed him with true filial affection. It was probable from the beginning of his illness that the Baron de Albini would not recover, and he was quite aware of this himself. Many an hour did he pass in conversing with his son respecting the past and future, both of his private and public life. He urged Edward not to neglect his duty to his king, now the more urgent, as Stephen was evidently declining in health, and upon the accession of Henry Fitz-Empress, Edward de Albini might command a prominent station on account of his father's services to Matilda. But Edward expressed himself, as usual disinclined to the bustle of a court. "Life is dark to me," he said, " she for whom honours and wealth might have been sought by me, is lost, gone, and I care only for peace, such peace as unavailing and endless sorrow can afford me."

The baron endeavoured to combat this idea. "It is said that the near approach of death sometimes reveals the future," he said. "It is so now. Mark me, my son, you will not always mourn, Cordelia will be found, and you will be happy."

But Edward shook his head mournfully, and changed the subject of conversation.

There was mourning in Percival Castle, for the noble and respected Geoffry de Albini was no more. All mourned, for all had lost a support—a friend, and although Edward was deservedly esteemed, yet the dependants mourned for the baron. The lady Elfrida felt that she must soon follow her beloved lord, and most willingly did she listen to her son, when he declared that he would never leave the roof under which she resided, except indeed intelligence should arrive of his betrothed. Of this he despaired, and he gave up his whole heart to his mother to cheer and solace her. Such was the state of affairs when Ronald arrived at the castle.

CHAPTER XXXV.

Fade, day dreams sweet, from memory fade!
   The perish'd bliss of youth's first prime,
That once so bright on fancy play'd,
   Revives no more in after time.
   Far from my sacred natal clime,
I haste to an untimely grave ;
   The daring thoughts that soar'd sublime,
Are sunk in ocean's changeful wave.—LEYDEN.

WHILE the above events were passing in the world, Cordelia was pining in her prison. Her health had been much affected by the circumstances attending her last interview with her enemy, as we have related, but a naturally good constitution struggled against her misfortunes, and her new acquisition of books and music, although neither numerous nor intrinsically valuable, were of infinite service to her health and spirits. Kate was allowed to attend her instead of old Bridget, indeed the well-meaning and simple girl had become extremely attached to the fair prisoner, and passed the greater part of her time in Cordelia's apartment. Although entirely uneducated, Kate possessed good sense and feeling, and her lively conversation cheered many a gloomy hour which would otherwise have hung heavily upon her. Kate had likewise seen the world, she was born abroad, and had resided there till the Count Mancini came to England two years previous, and she could tell of the dark forests of Italy and the sunny plains of France.

Often when sitting with her lady watching the gradual disappearance of the orb of day behind the distant mountains, she would describe his descent into the mediterranean, painting in homely but glowing language the rosy tints which he left upon the wave, and contrasting his southern splendour with the chilly evenings of Britain. Cordelia would listen to these descriptions till she half forgot her im. prisonment, and fancied herself in the country so vaunted by her companion—but short was the dream—reality broke in bitterly upon it, and then Kate would sing some simple Italian air, to which she had put English words, in praise of that which she loved as her native land.

Oh, Italy ! my native land !
Tho' far from thee I roam,
On Scotland's bleak and barren strand,
Thou art my home !

I'll not forget the olive grove,
To pierce whose darkning shade
The unclouded sunbeams vainly strove,
Where ence I stray'd.

I'll not forget the rippling wave,
Upon thy moonlit shore,
Where I was wont my limbs to lave,
When day was o'er.

I'll not forget how from the vine
We tore its clustering spoil,
While merry song and mirth combine
To lighten toil.

Forget ? oh no ! Tho' drear and chill,
This land of flood and storm,
Yet thy bright sunny skies shall still
My memory warm.

And while I watch the moon's cold rays,
Glance o'er yon heaving sea,
I'll think how bright in happier days,
She shone o'er thee.

Kate's songs always ended as they began, with a sigh for the loveliness of Italy and yet when closely questioned she admitted that even in those happy days she seasons of trouble and care. She spok of the count as a severe and unbending master, but liberal, and loving daiety.

" And his wife ! had he not one ?" asked Cordelia,

Kate shook her head, and did not anwer.

" I thought you said he had a wife," repeated Cordelia.

" Ah, poor lady !" sighed Kate, " but I ought not to pity her."

" Why ?" asked Cordelia.

" She was wrong, very wrong," said Kate.

" Oh, tell me her history, she could not have loved this man," said Cordelia.

" I dare not tell it, lady, She is never named in this castle," Kate replied; " and my mother might learn that I had spoken of her. Oh, the count is a severe man."

Cordelia sighingly assented to this. " But tell me of your going abroad," she said.

" Oh, it was a grand place, fit for a monarch, and truly, my lord was a monarch there," replied Kate, quite willing to talk upon this subject. " We had *fetes* almost every day, the castle was always full of visitors, when the count resided there in the summer time, and such fine noblemen and beautiful ladies. They usd to go upon the sea in grand pleasure boats, but once, oh, I shall never forget it."

"What was the matter," asked Cordelia.

"Such a storm, and a large party were out at sea, when a small black cloud arose and swept over the boat, and it was wrecked upon a rock which lay just out of the bay."

"Was any one drowned?" asked the lady.

"Yes, one young lady, her's was a sad story," replied Kate.

"How?" cried Cordelia.

"She was engaged to be married to the young count Vallombrosa, and he was of the party."

"Could he not save her?" asked Cordelia.

"Perhaps he did not try," whispered Kate mysteriously.

"Was he a coward then? oh cruel man," exclaimed Cordelia.

No. 29.

"He saved some one who it was said he loved better than he did the lady Hipolita," replied Kate.

"What do you mean?" asked Cordelia.

"He saved our lady Mancini," whispered Kate.

"And did she love him?" asked Cordelia.

"Nay, I know not. My lord left Italy and came to Scotland, but she was never happy afterwards," answered Kate. "But, lady, ask me no more, I dare not say what I know about her. I believe she is dead."

Cordelia was much interested by this little tale, but she saw that it would be wrong to ask her companion any farther particulars; she therefore changed the conversation, hoping that the curiosity which she could not help feeling might be satisfied at a future time.

One day, shortly after the above dialogue had taken place, Cordelia was alone in her room reading, or attempting to read, an old missal which had been brought with the other books to her. Rising suddenly the book fell, and one of the covers bursting open a sealed letter fell out of it. Cordelia, astonished, picked up the letter, and how shall we describe the amazement which seized her when she saw the superscription, "To my daughter, Lady Mouthermer." A tide of recollections rushed upon her memory and almost paralysed her mind; she stood holding the letter in her hand, gazing at it intently for many minutes before she could awaken her faculties to consider how to act with regard to it. But with recollection came questions of dismay and trouble.

Was Mancini indeed the father of the fair and noble bride, for whom Mouthermer had risked the displeasure of his sovereign and friend? It was impossible. She knew that there had been difficulties which opposed the marriage, but she had never heard their source mentioned: she recollected, however, having understood that lady Mouthermer was not of English birth, and this corroborated her fears—for fears they were, lest the wife of Edward de Albini's friend should prove to be the daughter of her most inveterate enemy. And the letter—what was to be done with it? She would not certainly betray it to old Bridget. She had after all no right to conclude that the missal had belonged to the Countess Mancini; in fact the only initials which it contained forbade this supposition. She searched it through carefully; no mark was in it which could identify its former owner except the letters D. R. written in a remarkably delicate foreign hand upon the corner of one of the leaves. These were not the initials of Mancini's wife, and Cordelia's first superstitious dread faded from her mind. She concluded that the missal had been stolen from some one, probably a stranger, and that the letter had been left in it by mistake.

Thus Cordelia endeavoured to calm her mind after this strange accident, and resolving to question Kate upon the history of the countess, she placed the letter where it could be secure, with the intention of conveying it to lady Mouthermer if she should ever be released from her present confinement.

The next time that Kate came to sit with her, she said:—

"Your account of the countess Mancini has much interested me, and excited my curiosity; has she been long dead?"

"I know not," replied Kate, "I only heard my mother say that she died."

"Did she not reside here with her husband?" asked Cordelia.

"Oh no," said Kate mournfully.

"Where then?" asked Cordelia.

"She retired to a convent," replied her companion.

"Had she a daughter?" said the lady.

"No," replied Kate, "she had no children, if she had it might have been better for her."

"What do you mean?" asked Cordelia.

"She might not have been so gay, but she was very beautiful," replied Kate.

"And are you sure she had no daughter?" asked Cordelia.

"Oh quite sure," answered her companion. "My mother was the countess

Mancini's own servant, and I was brought up to wait upon her also, till the goings on at the castle made my mother remove me."

"Why ?" asked Cordelia.

"The young count Vallombrosa was always with my lady, and my mother feared there would be trouble one day, and so there was sure enough," observed Kate.

"What happened then ?" said Cordelia.

"I will tell your ladyship all, if you will promise me not to betray me to my mother," replied Kate.

Cordelia gave the required promise, and Kate continued her tale.

"While we were in Italy the countess, who was extremely beautiful, was admired and courted by every nobleman who came to the castle, but by none among them all so much as by the count Vallombrosa. Oh, he was a handsome cavalier! He was engaged to marry the lady Hipolita, who lived with her parents so near the castle that she was with our countess almost every day, and thus count Vallombrosa also became a constant guest there. Our lady was lively and gay, she loved dancing and mirth, while our master was generally gloomy and reserved. He liked grandeur and state, while she did not care for these, provided she could roam about the woods, or make excursions on the water with a train of young noblemen and ladies about her. I never saw any harm in all this, but my mother used to shake her head and say it would end badly. Well, at last our count became jealous. I do not know what made him so, but he grew more and more gloomy, while my lady continued as gay as usual. Well just at this time my lord must go to Naples, and said he should be absent some weeks. My lady, to enliven the time of his being away from the castle, invited a great many grand people, and one day was appointed to make an excursion on the sea, to a village a few miles distant. Every thing was prepared, but it was near being set aside by a sudden occurrence."

"What was that ?" asked Cordelia.

"The count arrived on the very morning," replied Kate. "He came in worse temper than usual, and it was whispered in the castle that he had met some one at Naples whom he did not wish to see, and had therefore returned home suddenly. When the count heard of the water party, he said he would go too; he could not put it off without offending the nobleman who had come on purpose for it, and accordingly the party set off. Oh how sadly did that day end."

"Was that the day of the storm which you told me of ?" asked Cordelia.

"Yes," replied her narrator. "The sun shone bright and clear, when they embarked. My mother had sent me down to the village on an errand, and I was so hot and tired with the scorching sun, that I went into a vineyard to beg a bunch of grapes to refresh me. I was going to sit down to eat them when the owner, who knew me, said I had better not wait but make haste home, as he was sure a storm was coming. I did not believe him, and said there was not a cloud to be seen. "What do you call that," he said, pointing over the mountain. There it was, sure enough; a dull dark cloud sweeping on, but it scarcely seemed large enough to harm me, and I said so. The man however insisted upon my going home directly, and I did so. I had scarcely reached the castle when I saw the river come roaring and foaming down its dry bed, which I had a few minutes before crossed without wetting my feet. On it came and the little cloud with it, but it was not a little cloud now, it grew bigger and bigger, till a flash of lightning, and a clap of thunder spoke too plainly its terrible strength.

"The boats," cried Cordelia, "you said they were wrecked, did you not?"

"I ran to my mother; the castle shook from top to bottom, while the wind and thunder seemed to rival each other in loudness. Every body in the castle was terror-struck, but in the midst of all every one thought of the danger o the count and the party with him. Frazer went up to the turret to endeavour to ascertain where they were, as they hoped they might have arranged at the little village before the storm came on, and that they would remain there safely. Oh how anxiously did we wait his news! At first the black darkness over the sea was so great that he could see nothing, but after a little while he cried out that he saw the boats by the flashes of lightning, and that one was near the shore. We were almo t breathless with anxiety. There came one, tossed up by the waves for one minute, then sunk below them and apparently lost, at last the storm cleared away from over the castle, and the boat gained the shore safely."

" What happiness! but where was the other boat ?" cried Cordelia.

" That was a question we all asked, and a sorrowful answer we had," replied Kate, Frazer exclaimed, " I cannot see her, she is gone." My mother cried, and I cried too ; we did not know which boat our lady was in, and we dreaded to hear. Presently, while we were all mourning thus, the persons who had landed came up to the castle wet through, and the ladies half-dead with fear."

"Was the countess one of them ?" asked Cordelia.

"Alas, no!" answered Kate, " These persons could tell us nothing of the other boat ; they had seen it beaten about, but had hoped it might have reached the shore at some other point, and they tried to make us hope also, but we could not. Frazer had watched too long and closely for us to have any hope. It was a sad day at the castle, and a still sadder night. The ladies who had landed we assisted to bed, and by care and proper restoratives they recovered ; but no one else went to bed, they dared not."

" Did the storm then continue ?" asked Cordelia.

" It did, at least so much that I could not have slept for that reason ; but we did not go to bed for other, reasons Frazer hung a lantern out from the high turret, and two of the men kept watch by turns through the night, hoping that the count and countess might yet be saved, and by that means find their way home to the castle. Alas, it was not so. Oh, that dreadful night. We wandered about the passages, listening to every noise, till our ears became so sharp that we heard distant sounds we could never hear before, and Frazer said he could see the village tower which he could not see by daylight. The gentlemen sat in the hall, refreshments of every kind were ready, and blazing fires kept up—all to no purpose, night passed away, and they were not come. Morning beamed, the storm was hushed, the wind was lulled, and the sea became calm. Towards noon, Frazer, who was watching in the bell turret, shouted out, " They are safe !" Oh, what joy was there throughout the castle ! We ran to the battlements and beheld the little boat gently making its way over the smooth water. Who that saw it now would have believed that but a few hours ago that same ocean threatened its destruction. It came to shore. the party landed, but what did we see ? There was one person less than when it went out."

Kate paused, overcome by the awe of her recollections. Cordelia too was horror-struck at the narrative of the artless but deeply-feeling girl, and she sat for some time silent.

" Forgive me, lady," said Kate, when she had a little recovered herself, " but the dreadful certainty of that moment I cannot think of without horror. Still we did not know who was missing, we but knew that it was a female. You may suppose all the inhabitants of the castle ran down to the beach immediately ; I went with the rest, and when I saw our countess safe I scarcely thought of all we feared. It was the poor lady Hypolita who came not with her companions.

" Was she indeed lost ?" asked Cordelia anxiously.

" She was," replied Kate. " Never shall I forget count Mancini's countenance when her fate was told ; you would have thought that it was he who had been betrothed to her, not Vallombroso.' And our lady, I cannot describe the expression of her countenance. As to count Vallombroso, he seemed more afraid of our master than sorrowing for his beloved, if indeed he were sorrowing at all. It being required that the inmates of the castle should give up for a time their gaieties and amusements ! with our master this appeared to be no difficult matter, he became more and more gloomy, while the countess was not in a much more comfortable state. My mother was her attendant and she used to be so vexed about her."

" What was the matter then?" asked Cordelia.

"My master at times appeared very jealous," replied Kate.

"Poor lady! there could be no reason surely," said Cordelia.

Kate shook her head mournfully.

"I do not ask for mere curiosity," replied Cordelia.

"I know not what impels it, but I have an inexplicable feeling of interest in the fate of the wife of my jailor; it seems as if my fortune were in some way interwoven with hers."

"The saints forbid," cried Kate.

"Why? How did she die?" asked the lady.

"I know not exactly," replied the girl. "She died in Scotland."

"Here? in this castle?" asked Cordelia.

"No," replied Kate.

"Continue your tale," said Cordelia. "I long to hear of her."

"The young Vallombroso it seems, had saved the life of the countess when the boat was driven upon the rock," continued Kate. "Our lady and the lady Hypolita were the only females in that vessel, and most unaccountably Vallombroso neglected his future bride, and seizing the countess bore her to the shore senseless. When, after a few minutes, she opened her eyes, and saw the young count hanging over her in an agony of sorrow, a few words sufficed to betray to Mancini the secret of their hearts, which I truly believe they had never till that moment acknowledged to each other. Upon their return to the castle, I believe Mancini forbade Vallombroso to visit there any more, for he came not again publicly, although I have fancied that my lady met him sometimes in private. But my mother always forbade any enquiries into the countess's engagements."

"Did your mother then know of the misconduct of her lady?" asked Cordelia.

"I believe my mother did not believe the countess wrong," said Kate. "However that might be, in a few months after the accident, notice was given in the castle that my lord would at once leave Italy and proceed to Scotland. He desired my mother and Frazer with one or two others only, to accompany him, and we all set off on our journey."

"How did the countess like this?" asked Cordelia.

"She did not appear to object to it, but if she had done so, it would have been of no use; my lord never consulted her wishes in any thing except parties of pleasure," replied Kate. "As for me, I cannot tell you how I disliked leaving dear Italy, to come to this cold miserable country."

"How did you know it was cold and miserable? I thought you were born in Italy," observed the lady.

"I knew from the descriptions which Fraser gave us sometimes of Scotland. He is a Scotchman, although he had lived with my lord so many years," answered Kate. "We journeyed on; and although I was young, and knew but little of my lady's history, I could not avoid remarking some occurrences which made me certain that the true reason of our leaving Italy, was jealousy of count Vallombroso, although our master said that a large estate had been left to him in Scotland, and that he must go there to claim it."

"What occurrences do you mean?" asked Cordelia.

"One stormy evening we arrived, tired and hungry, at a small inn among the mountains; it rained heavily, and we had travelled very far that day. The count himself was fatigued, the countess almost worn out, and we all reckoned upon a good supper and a long rest. Well, when we arrived at this inn we found there a courier belonging to some noble traveller, who had just bespoken three beds. The landlord said he could well accommodate us, and we were assisting the countess into the house when we met the strange courier in the passage. I remember it well, for the countess had my arm as a support. The man passed so quickly that I did not see his face, but I suppose my lady did, for she shrieked and fainted away, falling down in the passage. My mother came up to us, and was going to assist me in removing the countess, when she too caught a glimpse of the courier's countenance, who had drawn near in order to give me help) and calling out, "Balthazar !" she desired him to leave the place instantly, adding that she would meet him presently under the trees, in the front of the inn."

"How strange!" cried Cordelia.

"Yes," replied Kate. "At first I thought it might be Vallombroso in disguise, but I remembered that my mother must have addressed him by his right name, so I determined to wait till I could satisfy my curiosity, which, you may imagine, was much excited. When we had removed the countess to an inner room, and she had recovered from her fainting fit, she began to rave so wildly, that my mother seemed quite alarmed, and not daring to leave her, she desired me to go and meet the man who had been the cause of of all this, and to tell him that Bridget desired he would keep out of the way of the count for a short time, and that she would undertake that in half an hour, we should be on our road again. I was likewise to ask which road his master was going."

"And had you courage for this ?" exclaimed Cordelia.

"I hesitated at first ; but my mother told me that she knew the man, and that he was a civil sort of person, and would not hurt me when he heard her name. It was so. The man told me that his master was going to England, to be present at the marriage of his daughter to a young lord, who was very rich, and a great favourite with king Stephen.

Here Cordelia interrupted Kate. Her interest or her curiosity respecting the countess Mancini had been much excited, and she enquired whether Kate could remember the name of the young nobleman, or whether she heard the name of the master of the courier. But Kate knew neither, and Cordelia desired her to continue her tale.

"When I went back to my lady, my mother made a sign to me to say nothing, but the countess having become more quiet, that is, exhausted, I was left in charge of her by my mother, who presently returned with the intelligence that all was ready for our continuing our journey."

"On that stormy night, and without food and rest ?" exclaimed Cordelia.

"Yes,"replied Kate. "Your ladyship may imagine how wretched we all were at losing our intended supper and rest, but that did not seem to affect my lord, he appeared to care only for making as much speed as possible ; and truly we did hurry on. We hurried from the high road soon, and took that to a seaport, in the south of France, where we embarked for Scotland."

"And did you never find out who that man was ?" asked Cordella.

"Never," replied her companion.

"Would not your mother tell you ?" asked Cordelia.

"I never directly asked her," said Kate ; "but if I ever gave a hint about it, she always told me not to interfere in the count's business; and truly I was too much afraid of him to risk his anger for mere curiosity."

"Do you think the man belonged to the count Vallombroso ?" said the lady.

"That could not be, as the count was too young to have a daughter," said Kate.

"I had forgotten that circumstance," replied Cordelia. "How did your lady live when you arrived here ?"

"We did not come here then," replied the girl. "We went to a large grand castle, over yonder mountains, and there we led a very quiet life. My lady seldom went out : when she did, it was merely to hear mass at a convent near."

"Had she no friends or relations?" asked Cordelia.

"No, she could scarcely speak this barbarous language, and her greatest pleasure was to talk with me about sunny Italy in our own sweet tongue,'" replied Kate sighing, "My lord went away sometimes, and Frazer accompanied him. Ah! it would have been well for the countess had he never left her."

"Why ?" asked her auditor.

"I dare scarcely tell you," replied the girl.

"Oh pray do !" cried Cordelia. "I am so interested for the poor lady,"

"It is a sad tale," replied Kate. "While my master was away one fine summer's morning, as I was walking with the countess by the side of the lake, when we heard the low sound of a guitar apparently from the other sde of the water. We stopped and listened, and I recognised a tune which I had often heard in Italy, and I thought I remembered hearing it one evening after the accident on the sea. The countess exclaimed hastily, ''Tis he!' and upon my enquiring what she meant, she turned off my question, but appeared evidently agitated. Presently a small boat approached the shore, and who should jump out of it but the count Vallombrosa. He threw himself at the feet of the countess, and from the tender words which passed between them, I had no doubt that my lord had cause enough for jealousy, the count implored my lady to fly with him, and at first she seemed inclined to consent, but she soon remembered that they were both in a foreign country. knowing scarcely anything of the language, and they would certainly be discovered and overtaken.

"But did you remain to hear all this?" exclaimed Cordelia.

"I was compelled to it, my lady would not let me leave her, lest I should reveal what I had witnessed," replied Kate. "After some time, my lady agreed to meet Vallombroso again on the following evening, in the same place, if her lord did not return. Happily Mancini did come back next morning, and therefore the meeting did not take place."

"You told your mother all this of course?" observed Cordelia.

"Would that I had!" replied Kate. "But the countess beseeched me not to betray her, and when she found me hesitating what to do, she told me something which made me undutiful to my mother and to my master."

"What was that?" asked Cordelia.

"That she was not the count's wife," cried Kate.

"What can you mean?" exclaimed the lady.

"The countess merely told me this to quiet my conscience ; she likewise said that the Count Vallombrosa was related to her, and that he would convey her safely to her kindred in Italy. However," continued Kate, "although I reluctantly promised not to tell any one of what I had seen, I solemnly declared I would never assist in her elopement. This was, I acknowledge, more because I was afraid of Count Mancini than from a proper sense of my duty."

"You ought to have told your mother," said Cordelia.

"I know it," replied Kate; "if I had done so I should have saved myself much uneasiness."

"And how did matters go on after this?" asked Cordelia.

"I heard nothing more of the Count Vallambrosa or of the guitar," replied the girl, "till one fatal morning, when my lord having left the castle, with the intention of being absent for a week or two, my mother came to me in great dismay, exclaiming that my lady was nowhere to be found. You may imagine how much I was alarmed. I searched the room, the walks she was most fond of, I ran through the woods, but could not find her. Some of the men suggested that she might have destroyed herself, and proposed having the moat searched. Oh ! I cannot describe my feelings while this was being done. Fearing that it was vain, I should have rejoiced to see the body of my poor mistress brought from a watery grave ; but alas! conscience told me that it was not so."

"How did you control your feelings, poor girl?" asked Cordelia. "Did no one suspect your knowledge of your mistress's fate?"

"No, I nearly betrayed myself, by expressing my hope that the body would be found. One of the men called me an ungrateful girl, and said he supposed I expected to fill her place. Far enough from my wishes, sure enough," cried Kate.

"Did you not send to the count Mancini?" asked Cordelia.

"Oh yes," replied Kate, "messengers went to him, but he came soon enough."

"What do you mean," asked her auditor.

"In the evening a violent ringing at the castle announced our master's return ; we had expected it, and dreaded it, but what was our surprise to see that he had brought my lady with him. It appeared that he had known and watched Count Vallambroso for some time, and at last suspecting that an elopement would be intended, he pretended to leave home, and secreted himself among the moun-

tains, near, with only Frazer, who watched all the movements of the countess.
By these means he intercepted the lovers, and brought back my lady".

" And what became of Count Vallambroso ?" asked Cordelia.

" Alas, lady ! I may guess, but I cannot say," replied Kate.

" Then I was not wrong !" exclaimed Cordelia ; " he *is* a murderer !"

" I fear so, besides what we have seen," observed Kate, mournfully.

" Who could that be ?" said Cordelia.

" I cannot imagine," replied Kate.

" And what became of your lady ?" asked Cordelia.

" After a few days she was sent to a convent at a short distance," answered
Kate. " My mother went with her, and then we removed here, as they said my
lord could not bear the other place, because it reminded him of her."

" Was he then so much attached to her ?" asked the lady.

" I know not," replied Kate. " You know my lord is not a sort of person to
let his domestics know his feelings.'

" Did you not say that your lady is dead ?" asked Cordelia.

" Yes, my mother told me so the other day, when I inquired whether she had
been to the convent lately. But I do not know what to think ; my mother certainly loved the countess, and desired me to love her too, and yet she said strange
things to her sometimes," said Kate, musingly.

" Did your mother know that she was not married to Mancini, or was that a fab-
rication of your lady ?" asked Cordelia.

" I once hinted it to my mother," replied Kate ; " but she said it was nonsense
and that she herself had been present at her wedding."

" This is, indeed, a sad story," cried Cordelia ; " poor lady ! I must pity her."

" Oh, never let the count persuade you to marry him !" exclaimed Kate. " He
is a cruel man and a tyrant.'

Cordelia assured her humble adviser that she never would be forced to such a
marriage, and dismissing her for a awhile, she sat down to meditate upon what she
had just heard.   It was incomprehensible to her, how a man guilty of crime
should live as Mancini did, apparently without fear of detection ; she knew that
the unsettled state of the country had rendered crime comparatively fearless, and
the unhappy victim Vallambroso being a foreigner, concealment was not so
difficult ; but still there was a mystery in the matter which Cordelia could not
solve.

One only circumstance was apparent, and Cordelia hailed it joyfully—the Lady
Mouthermer could not be the daughter of Mancini, and the letter which had so
strangely fallen into her hands, must have belonged to some other person.   Then
came the consideration whether she had not better give the packet to old Bridget
in order to have it forwarded to its destination.   This she was unwilling to do,
both because she doubted whether the right end would be thereby gained, and
because it seemed almost to be given to her as a future means of making her place
of confinement known to her friends.   After mature deliberation, Cordelia determined to keep the packet secret and safe for the present, and taking up the harp,
she endeavoured to enliven her solitude by singing the following song, which
Edward de Albini had in happier days often sung while resting at her feet in the
bower :—

> Go, lovely rose !
> Tell her that wastes her time, and me,
>   That now she knows,
> When I resemble her to thee,
> How sweet and fair she seems to be.
>
>
> Tell her that's young,
> And shuns to have her graces spied,
>   That had'st thou sprung
> In deserts, where no men abide,
> Thou must have uncommended died.

Small is the worth
Of beauty, from the light retir'd;
  Bid her come forth,
Suffer herself to be desir'd,
And not blush so to be admir'd.

Then die! that she
The common fate of all things rare,
  May read in thee;
How small a part of time they share,
That are so wondrous sweet and fair.

Alas! not the concord of sweet sounds, nor music married to immortal verse, can soothe the aching heart for more than the passing moment. This Cordelia felt, and she resolved to make some attempt to free herself from her thraldom
No. 30.

before her enemy should again visit the castle of Duncraig. But how was she to accomplish this? She knew that she was closely guarded and watched by those who were devoted to their master for evil as well as good, and she almost feared the attempt.

CHAPTER XXXVI.

Know, on the stealing wing of time shall flee
  Some few, some short-lived years, and all is past ;
A future bard these awful domes may see,
  Muse o'er the present age, as I the last ;
Who smouldering in the grave, yet once like you
  The various maze of life were seen to tread,
Each bent their own peculiar to pursue,
  As custom urg'd, or wilful nature led ;
Mix'd with the various crowd's inglorious clay,
  The nobler virtues undistinguish'd lie ;
No more to melt with beauty's heaven-born ray,
  No more to wet compassion's tearful eye,
Catch from the poet raptures not their own,
  And feel the thrilling melody of sweet renown.—EMILY.

DURING several days Cordelia meditated deeply upon the possibility of escape from her prison, without being able to think of any means by which she could secretly accomplish her purpose. One day, when almost wearied out with laying useless plans, the unhappy prisoner sat by her window, listlessly gazing on the ever-changing element, which lay spread out far below her abode, she was interrupted by the unwelcome entrance of old Bridget, who bore in her hand a sealed letter without any superscription, which she held out to Cordelia. The unhappy maiden seized the paper, almost frantic at the instantaneous thought that it might contain tidings of release, and breaking the seal she saw the following lines :—

"I make the offer once more, infatuated girl ; consent to become my wife, and I will return and release you—persevere in your obstinacy and you shall perish. I can succeed in all my wishes without your aid—fortune befriends me in my attempt to obtain that from which your selfishness debars me. Your friends believe you dead. De Albini has followed you to an early tomb, and none are left who care for you. Give me your decision speedily ; Bridget will forward it to me.
                                "MANCINI."

Words cannot describe the agony of Cordelia as she read this cruel letter. Disappointment, anger, grief—all strove for mastery. Edward, too, gone, why then should she care for life? In terror she wrung her hands, and pacing the apartment, bewailed her bitter destiny. Bridget in vain attempted to soothe her, and finding her efforts ineffectual she retired and sent Kate to the prisoner. But even Kate, gentle and compassionating as she was, could offer no consolation to a grief which seemed to defy her power of soothing.

"My Edward! my beloved boy!" was the only sentence that Cordelia spoke. By degrees the violence of her agony subsided, Kate ventured to give her advice, counselling her to return a vague answer to the letter, and in the meanwhile perhaps something might occur to give her liberty.

"Frazer brings word," added the girl, "that the king is certainly dying, and he hinted that perhaps his master might return to Italy. In that case—"

"Talk not to me of kings," interrupted Cordelia impatiently. "What care I for a court? Are not my kindred, my friends all dead? and am not I left in this bleak world alone? Oh, I feel that I shall soon be gone too."

"Nay, dear lady, speak not so," replied Kate. "I think from what Frazer said, that some danger hangs over the count connected with the new king that is to be ; and Frazer does not seem so well contented with his master as usual."

Oh! let me see him? Will gold to any amount induce him to pity me ?" cried the lady.

Kate shook her head mournfully.

"Oh! I pray you let me see him !" again cried Cordelia.

"I will ask my mother," replied Kate, "but I fear it will be useless. He remains here but till tomorrow."

Kate left the room, and the fair prisoner threw herself on her bed to weep. She remained thus till night, resolutely refusing any nourshment, and Bridget's refusal to let Fraser visit her seemed scarcely noticed by her. Kate, who had but little experience in mental illness, hoped that her mistress was becoming more resigned what was her alarm then at being awakened at midnight by the ravings of Cordelia who was in a state of violent fever. The girl immediately summoned her mother who was almost as much alarmed as herself; cooling applications were administered and after a few hours the patient was more composed. But this excitement was followed by a corresponding exhaustion, and day-break found the poor victim in a state which seemed to presage approaching dissolution. Although scarcely able to speak, Cordelia signified her earnest wish to see a priest ; she hoped she was dying, but she could not die unconfessed. Bridget seemed extremely averse to the thought of such a thing, but the mute prayers of Cordelia and the beseechings of Kate made her at last consent to speak to Frazer upon the subject.

"A confessor! what can she have to confess?" was his answer. Then after a few minutes deliberation he said, "I do not think the count would care much in she were to die, providing she did it quietly; he is vexed enough now, and I shall not teaze him about a puling girl."

"Who then shall I send for?" asked Bridget.

"It must be father Anselm, he is bound to our lord's interests, and if she be as bad as you say, there can be no danger," said Frazer. "I will stay a few hours longer, and hear what the father says about her state; you know he is skilful at such cases."

Accordingly father Anselm was summoned from the neighbouring monastry to attend the dying girl. Father Anselm was a man far past middle age, of mild and prepossessing appearance, and charitable in his disposition, he was beloved by all who knew him. His uniform kindness to those in distress caused him to be the favourite of the poor, and if he sometimes gave the sinner hope, when perhaps a sterner justice would have forbidden it, the fault must be imputed to the innae benevolence which would not add a pang to those already consuming their victims. Father Anselm had known the countess Mancini, his voice had waked her to a sense of her errors, and he had thereby become somewhat acquainted with the character of the count.

When the monk entered the chamber of Cordelia, he was both shocked and surprised at the object which met his view. Stretched upon the bed lay a female apparantly dead—except that her breathing forbade the supposition—so still she was, so pale, so fair. Notwithstanding her death-like appearance there was evidence that the object before him was of high birth and education; the delicacy of her features and g aceful turn of her emaciated limbs, told the tale of partrician breeding. As the father approached the bed, Cordelia opened her eyes, and a ray of pleasure shot through her countenance. Taking her hand gently, the monk said in a tone of kindness ; "You are very ill my child."

Cordelia shook her head. "I am dying," she said.

"Nay, my daughter, my experience tells me not that ; but it were well to make thy peace with the church lest it should be so."

Then, feeling her pulse, the good monk ordered Kate to bring some spiced wine and cake, which he insisted upon the patient's swallowing. After this she felt somewhat revived ; and the father, desiring Kate to leave the room until he called for her, commenced his professional duty. But the answer to his first question completely astounded him. "Cordelia de Dunstanville?" he exclaimed, "What! the daughter of de Dunstanville and Eleanor De Tunstall ?"

"Even so," sighed Cordelia.

"And what brought thee to this lonely place, my child, the court or palace were your fitting house?" asked the monk.

Cordelia gave the monk a history of the principle events of her life, 'ending with her unaccountable capture by the Count de Mancini, at which her auditor expressed extreme surprise.

"Poor lamb!" he said, "thou art indeed in the fangs of a wolf powerful and ruthless; but knowest thou any cause why he should thus imprison thee?"

"He threatens that unles I will consent to become his wife immediately he will keep me imprisoned till my death, in this horrible place. I feel that the time will not be long," sighed Cordelia.

"Patience, my daughter," said the monk; "deliverance may yet even now be nigh in the depth of thy despair. What can move Mancini to marry thee? it cannot be love ?"

"Love? oh no! father," replied the maiden. "He covets my lands, poor as they are, and requires of me a paper which would give him possession of them."

"And where is this paper?" asked the father.

"Alas! I know not; my good kinsman De Tunstall held it, but he"——

Cordelia, overcome by the violence of her emotions, could not finish the sentence, but sunk back upon her pillow in a fainting fit. Father Anselm immediately summoned Kate to his wretched patient, and with her assistance the poor lady was at length brought back to life and recollection.

"My daughter," said the monk, "thou art too weak to renew thy confession at present; in the evening I will again visit thee. Farewell."

Cordelia extended her hand in silence, and by an expressive look and gesture she implored the father not to break the promise which he had just given her. He repeated his words, and recommending perfect quiet and frequent restoratives, left the room.

With a heavy heart father Anslem descended the staircase; under any circumstances he would have grieved to see the young and beautiful laid upon the bed of sickness, perhaps of death; but there was in the case before him circumstances which gave the sufferer a more than ordinary interest in his heart; and during the few minutes which intervened between his leaving her, and meeting with old Bridget in his hall, father Anselm had resolved upon saving, if possible, one so oppressed and so helpless. The monk liked not Mancini, but he feared his power; he knew but too well how unscrupulous he was in the means which he employed in furtherance of his designs, and although the monastery ought to be sacred as an asylum for innocence and weakness, yet he dared not to remove Cordelia by open means. He knew at present too little of her history and connections completely to understand the line of action which it would be best for her interests that he should pursue; he therefore determined to avoid giving an explicit answer to any interrogatories which might be put to him respecting the probability of her recovery. He saw no mortal symptoms, but he knew not how far the agony of the mind might destroy the body, and he had very serious doubts as to the end of the conflict which was going on.

In answer to Bridget's inquiry respecting the lady, father Anselm declared her to be in a most precarious state, and that her recovery must entirely depend upon the degree of quiet repose in which she was kept. While he was speaking Frazer came up to him; and repeating the inquiry which Bridget had made, expressed his impatience to rejoin his master, which this unfortunate illness prevented. Father Anslem assured him that the patient should be as well attended to in his absence from the castle as if he were still there, but Frazer exclaimed :

"I care not for the girl, her death were perhaps best for my lord, but I do care for being detained here while the world is stirring abroad, and bold spirits may make their fortunes."

"What mean you?" asked the monk.

"Know you not the death of Stephen is daily expected, and that Henry Fitz Empress promises to be a generous master?" asked Frazer.

"We holy men know not of court changes," replied the father, "and your lord, will he return to Duncraig upon the death of Stephen?"

"My lord has a deeper stake," replied the man. "He is upon the point of obtaining that which will place him among the foremost of England's barons in wealth and influence. The lands of this sick girl shall be ours."

The monk started at the last words which he had heard; they unveiled to him much of the mystery annexed to Cordelia's situation; and giving him a clue to Mancini's motives, inspired him with fresh determination to destroy his machinations. He made no answer to Frazer's remark, but repeated his question as to the return of the count to Duncraig.

"Return? no truly," repeated the man, "I shall tell him that the girl is dying or dead, and you may bury her where you will; only mind this, at your peril let a syllable get abroad about the matter."

Father Anselm gladly promised secrecy, and departed to his monastery lightened in spirit, and ruminating upon the means for effecting the deliverance of Cordelia, who in the meanwhile felt herself relieved in mind by her conversation with the monk. She sunk into a placid slumber, from which she awoke considerably refreshed; indeed, she was so much better that Kate was certain that a few days would restore her to her accustomed health. In the afternoon, Kate brought the joyful intelligence of the departure of Frazer, and the castle of Duncraig sunk back into its accustomed silence.

Gladly did Cordelia hail the entrance of father Anselm after the hour of vespers. She was sitting by the window, gazing as usual upon the ever-changing but wearying ocean, thinking over all that occurred since she was first brought to her prison, and more especially reflecting upon the mysterious circumstances of that night when she had seen the corpse of a fellow creature consigned to those waves which perhaps were to roll over her wretched form when life should have sunk beneath her misery. Such were her thoughts when the father was announced, and Kate by his command left the room.

"My daughter," he said, "I rejoice to see thee sitting up; let us hope that health may yet be restored to thee."

"Alas, father! what is health to the forlorn and friendless ophan?" cried Cordelia.

"The child of De Dunstanville ought not to be friendless?" said the monk.

"Did you then know my parents?" asked Cordelia.

"Yes," replied the father.

"Did you know my mother? Oh speak of her!" cried the lady.

"My child, it was but in misery, and I must add guilt, that I knew the once lovely Eleanor de Tunstall," answered the father. "Death had laid his finger on her; but she moved my compassion. Art thou, my daughter, that helpless infant whowas secretly conveyed to the abbess of Thornbury?"

"I am. Oh, holy father! if you indeed knew and pitied my mother, save her unhappy child!" cried the maiden, falling at Father Anselm's feet.

"Rise, my daughter, I will save thee if it be possible," replied the monk, lifting the lady from the ground. "Would that the convent of Edendale had never sheltered one more an enemy to Eleanor de Tunstall than the humble father Anslem!"

"Edendale!" exclaimed Cordelia.

"Yes, my child, it was during my residence in that lovely spot that chance brought me to the acquaintance of thy unhappy mother," answered the father.

"What change, father?" asked the maiden.

"In the accidental absence of him to whose charge the papers relating to that monastery were confided, it devolved upon me to receive and secretly treasure paper belonging to Eleanor de Dunstanville," replied father Anselm. "That paper was afterwards stolen from Edendale by agency, which I well know but dare not name."

"Oh! I know all!" exclaimed the astonished girl. "That paper, or at least the copy of it which the abbess possessed, has been the cause of much of my misery; and is the pretence for my present imprisonment. The count Mancini requires me to deliver it to him, and I know not where it is. The baron de Tunstall had it in his keeping, and alas! a broken heart has carried him to the tomb since my misfortunes. But never will I give up that which declares my mother's marriage and my own honourable birth."

"In those words spoke with the spirit of a Tunstall, stainless in honour as their snow white standard in the battle field," exclaimed the father with a degree of warmth little according with the monkish habit. "I will save thee at the risk even of my life!"

Again Cordelia embraced the knees of the holy man, weeping tears of gratitude and joy.

"But, my daughter," he continued, "what friends will receive thee? where wilt thou find shelter if I can succeed in removing thee from these hated walls?"

The lady paused for a few minutes. "Thornbury," she at last said, "was my dearest home, but I know not where its beloved inmates are now. I am indeed a houseless orphan."

"Perchance I may assist thy determination if thy wishes point to Thornbury," replied the father. "Dost thou know that Geoffrey de Albini is now gathered to his fathers, and that his son, the young baron, resides not there?"

Blushes of modesty and joy overspread the face of Cordelia. "Is the young baron de Albini yet alive then?" she asked eagerly.

"He is, and resides at Percival castle with his widowed mother," replied the father. "The baron de Fougeres arrived at our convent but a few days ago, and he informed me of this."

"The baron de Fougeres?" exclaimed the maiden clasping her hands. "Oh! had he but known the unhappy Cordelia was so near him, he would have flown to her release."

"Be calm, my daughter, he shall again embrace thee," replied the monk. "But we must be cautious, we must be secret; there have been deeds done in these walls which they dare not re-echo, and we must beware that we awaken not the suspicion which would be satisfied but with blood."

"I know, father—I saw—" cried Cordelia shuddering.

"Thou knowest?—what?" asked father Anselm.

"I saw the body committed to yonder deep," replied the lady. "Kate and I were watching the moon as she glanced through the pale midnight, when the deed was finished!"

"I suspected this, poor lady!" said the monk.

"Who then was the victim? Oh tell me!" cried Cordelia.

"I dare scarcely whisper it to thee, but our fates are bound together and I do not fear thy betraying me," replied the father.

"You need not fear it," said the maiden. "Never since that awful night has a word of what I beheld crossed my lips. Who was it?"

"His wife," answered Anselm; "at least his reputed wife."

Cordelia started. "And she was murdered," she exclaimed, "in order that I might become his bride; alas! he would not have murdered me, grief would speedily have done the work of the dagger and the bowl."

"I say not that the countess Mancini died by either," replied the father. "Remorse—grief—these can kill as surely as the assassin's hand, and by these perhaps she died. Her death was not necessary to his schemes."

"Kate told me that the countess secluded herself upon the death of her lover and her own disgrace, and that she resided and died in a neighbouring convent, where old Bridget used occasionally to visit her. Is not this true?" asked the lady.

"Entirely false. For many years the countess was confined in a part of the castle which was not supposed to be habitable, adjoining the eastern gateway," replied the father. "There I came in her dying illness, and received her penitent confession."

Cordelia now remembered the evening on which she and Kate had seen father Anselm so mysteriously cross the castle yard, and she acquainted him with her having observed him. "I little thought then," she added, "that I should so soon need such a comforter myself. I suppose then that these books, this harp, belonged to the unhappy countess; a strange circumstance has lately occurred in consequence of their being brought here."

"What was that, my daughter?" asked the monk.

"One day while reading one of the books, a letter dropped from the cover, addressed, "To my daughter, lady Mouthermer." But Kate informs me that the countess had no children; is it so? and by whom can the letter have been written?"

"The Countess Mancini had no children, at least I never heard of any," said the father. "It is true I know little of her early life, she came here a stranger and a foreigner, not understanding our language or following our manners. But, my daughter, let us not talk of her; a thought has struck me by which we may securely accomplish thy release; but it needs courage and resolution. Dost remember the stratagem by which the empress escaped form Wallingford?,'

Cordelia turned pale as ashes, and in a tone of dismay said. "A coffin?"

"Even so, my daughter," replied the father. "Hast thou courage?"

After a moment's thought the maiden exclaimed,—

"Yes, father, I trust to thee."

"It is well. I have told Bridget that thy recovery was unlikely, and I have orders from Frazer to see thee decently and quietly buried; his lord is detained in London, and is not likely to return to this place until Henry be firmly seated on the throne. But we must not delay; may I depend upon thy firmness?"

"Perfectly," replied Cordelia. "I am awed, but not afraid."

"Thou wilt need assistance; canst thou depend upon thy attendant?" asked the father. "Her mother must be deceived, I dare not trust her."

"I can answer for Kate's secrecy," replied Cordelia. "She is attached to me, and I believe would not be sorry to leave this dismal place."

"Nay, she need not be implicated so far as that. Thus shall it be; I will bring thee a composing draught, which shall throw thee into a healthy sleep for a few hours, and then thou shalt be removed as Matilda was. I shall tell Bridget to-night that thou art worse, but that Kate only must approach thee. Bridget is old, and loves rest, she will not interfere with our plan. In the morning I will come and remain here till thy supposed death; nay, I will visit thee frequently till thy removal."

Cordelia expressed her gratitude to the father, and her resolution to go through the trial unflinchingly. She proposed telling Kate that night, and giving her instructions as to the conduct which she should pursue towards her mother. The monk proposed her immediately travelling under some disguise to Percival castle, in order to place herself under the protection of the lady Elfrida; that place being at a considerable less distance than Mowbray, whither Cordelia had with maidenly delicacy wished to go. But it seemed imperative that she should be in safety with her friends before the return of Mancini; who, however, if Kate proved faithful, could have no reason to suspect the stratagem by which his intended victim had escaped. After a long conversation upon these matters, father Anselm bade a kind adieu to Cordelia, who threw herself at his feet expressing her gratitude in tears and broken sentences.

CHAPTER XXXVII.

Come away, come away, death;
    And in sad cypress let me be laid;
Fly away, fly away, breath,
    Alas! for me, hapless maid.
My shroud of white stuck all with yew,
    Oh, prepare it;
My part of death no one so true,
    Did share it.

Not a flower, not a flower sweet,
    On my black coffin let there be strewn;
Not a friend, not a friend greet,
    My poor corpse where my bones shall be thrown;
A thousand, thousand sighs to save,
    Lay me, oh! where
Sad true lover ne'er find my grave,
    To weep there.—SHAKSPERE.

WHEN father Anselm descended the stairs, he found, as he had ancipated, old Bridget waiting to see him. In answer to her anxious enquiries respecting Cordelia, he told her that he feared recovery was hopeless while she remained in her prison, and to the monk's surprise, the old woman testified sincere sorrow and concern for the damsel, at the same time giving hints of anger towards her lord. This was not lost upon the monk, who led her on unconsciously, when she betrayed her inmost feelings. Bridget seemed to have learned for the first time that day from Frazer, the true history of Cordelia's detention, and an accidental cause of anger towards Mancini, had made the old woman take the part of the fair prisoner, who she declared should never be teased or starved to death as her own beloved mistress had been. Father Anselm let her talk on for some time, and then he suddenly asked her whether she would be willing to aid in the escape of Cordelia.

"Aye truly, I would," was the reply, "but there are more careful watchers than I am. Dennis and Bennett, what will you do with them?"

"Say only that you will aid me," cried the monk, "and I will provide against all discovery."

Bridget avowed her fixed intention of leaving the castle, from the moment Frazer had told her that Mancini would certainly leave England for Italy as soon as Henry ascended the throne; but she said she grieved to leave the poor lady Cordelia to certain destruction; and besides, upon hinting the matter to Kate, that devoted girl had absolutely refused to leave Cordelia.

When the monk heard this, he unhesitatingly confided the plot to Bridget, desiring her to see the lady Cordelia and arrange with her all minor points necessary to its success. After enjoining the strictest secrecy and caution, father Anselm departed, promising to revisit Duncraig early in the morning.

Bridget then went up to the lady's apartment; where she found her daughter, and acquainted Cordelia with the conversation which had taken place with father Anselm; she offered her advice upon the subject, in a manner and tone very different to any that she had hitherto used towards her prisoner. Bridget was not devoid of feeling; she had been attached to the countess from her childhood, having been brought up by her, and although she never willingly adverted to any of the occurrences of her early years, and when questioned upon them always evaded any distinct answer, yet it was evident from her manner and the hints which she occasionally let fall, that she had resided in scenes of a higher character than those in which she now moved. To Kate she was a strict and stern mother; but this might perhaps be somewhat accounted for by the kind society in which they lived; men only, besides themselves, residing at the castle, and Count Mancini being but seldom there. Bridget loved her daughter as much as she loved any one, except her mistress, and since the last misfortune of the latter, she had become extremely uneasy respecting Kate's position in the castle. This uneasiness unfortunately took the complexion of ill temper, which Cordelia's arrival had materially increased. Bridget also saw a dark prospect before her as to the fair prisoner. Mancini had, in the first instance, deceived her

'specting Cordelia's history; and now that the truth was made clear to her, he felt indignant at the imposition which her master had practised upon her. Above all, the news of his intended journey to Italy alarmed and exasperated the ld woman, who saw before her only poverty and neglect, perhaps danger. There were points on which it would not have been agreeable to Bridget to be questioned, and she began to think that the castle of Duncraig might not be the very safest place for her when her master should be gone.

No. 31.

With all these thoughts and feelings in her mind, Bridget entered the poor prisoner's room. A long conversation ensued, in which the following pla of proceedings was determined upon.

As Bridget was to be a party to the escape, it was not necessary that Cordelia should be literally concealed in a coffin. The report of her alarming illness was to be spread through the castle immediately, and father Anslem sent for early in the morning; he was to announce her decease, and a coffin was to be procured in order that she might be conveyed to the monastery, in the cemetery of which she was to be buried. In the meanwhile, Bridget was to procure a suit of clothes such as a country woman might wear, and on the following evening Cordelia was to accompany Bridget to the monastery; should any one meet them on their way she was to be announced as a kinswoman of Bridget, who had just arrived from a distance to see her. Kate was to be sent out of the castle the next day, on pretence of change of scene being necessary to her. Thus everything being arranged for her escape, Cordelia expressed her thanks to the old woman for her unexpected acquiescence in the affair.

"Give me no thanks," replied Bridget, "This castle would prove but a sorry abode for either thee or me, should the count leave England. Woe betide him! wherever he goes he carries with him the malediction of the husband and the father."

When Bridget left the prisoner, she sat down by the window to watch, for the last time she hoped, the sun sink beneath the wave, and after an hour of placid contemplation, Cordelia retired to rest, in a happier mood than she had felt for many months. Hope gilded the future; and although a long and dreary journey lay before her, yet that journey was to lead her to love and happiness. A sweet sleep closed her eyes, and she awoke in the morning refreshed and invigorated.

When father Anslem arrived at the castle the first news which greeted him, was an exclamation from Dennis upon the increased illness of Cordelia, which at first the monk did not know whether to believe or not; so precarious had he really thought the condition of his patient. When, however, he entered her apartment, and saw her sitting by the table eating her humble morning's meal, and looking almost healthy, he could not control an exclamation of joy. The intended plan was revealed to him, and he entirely agreed with all its details, assuring Cordelia that he would meet her on the outside of the castle gates in the evening.

"But you must be careful," he continued; "Dennis is very suspicious of my visits, and had they not been openly allowed by Frazer, I have no doubt he would forbid them."

Cordelia promised circumspection, and the father left her.

When he reached the court-yard, Dennis met him with an inquiry respecting Cordelia.

"Poor lady!" replied the monk, "I trust she will soon be beyond the power of the Count Mancini to harrass her. A most happy release her's will be."

"Is she then so near her end?" asked the man.

"I believe so," was the answer.

"Why then do you leave her?" asked Dennis.

"I shall return a few hours' hence," replied the father. "In the meanwhile, I charge you that the castle be kept as still as possible; and that if anything particular occur, you send for me immediately. Had I not other important visits to make, I would not leave the castle at this time."

"Will not Bridget wish me to watch close to the chamber door?" asked the man. "I would fain do all that I can for the poor maiden."

"No—by no means. If indeed you pity her, show it by keeping everything quiet throughout the castle," replied the father; and bidding Dennis adieu, he returned to his convent to make preparations for receiving his strange guest.

This was an important and not easy matter; and the father, simple in the ways of the world, almost repented having promised an asylum to so unwonted a pilgrim. However, he determined to acquaint the prior with the undertaking in which he had engaged, and to ask his assistance towards its completion. With this intent he entered the parlour of the convent.

" What aileth you, my son?" said the prior. "Is the damsel at the castle no more?"

Father Anselm hesitated, and the prior added, " I like not the tales I hear."

" Well may'st thou not like them, father," replied the monk, " and I have that to tell which will vex and astonish thee."

"Speak on freely," said the prior.

Father Anselm then acquainted the prior with as much as he himself knew of the past history of Cordelia, and endeavoured to excite his pity and commiseration for her present situation.

"Truly and deeply do I pity the poor maiden," said the prior, " but what can I do? The Count Mancini is powerful and I fear ruthless; accustomed to control those around him without question or reproof, and I much surmise with too little respect for our holy church, to allow of her interference in his private affairs."

" But if the damsel should by any happy chance escape?" asked Anselm.

"I would not betray her to him," replied the prior.

"Would you not give her refuge from her persecutor?" asked the monk.

" Where?—how?" exclaimed the prior.

" Here, in this monastery," said Anselm.

"A woman here?" cried the prior.

"Nay, start not—you have said you would not betray her," urged Father Anslem.

" Nor would I, but our rules are strict," said the prior.

"I know it, nor would I infringe them, except in behalf of oppressed innocence," said Anselm. " It is but for a few hours that I ask it. Kate will accompany her, and I but beg for this parlour for their use until daylight shall allow them to set forth on their journey."

" You are urgent, my son," observed the prior.

"I acknowledge it," returned Anselm. "I knew Eleanor de Tunstall, the mother of his damsel, and——"

" Eleanor de Tunstall?" exclaimed the prior.

"Yes; did you too know that ill-faaed women?" asked the monk surprised.

" Well," answered the prior. " I knew her the wife of De Hesling. And is this unhappy one her child?"

"She is; and without our assistance she is lost!" replied Anselm.

" We will save her! it shall be as you have asked," said the prior.

"Thank! thanks! good father; I once did unintentional harm to the Lady de Dunstanville, and I would now repair it, in extending the hand of succour to her unhappy daughter," answered Anselm.

" I have received strange advices from London," observed the prior.

" Is our monarch yet alive?" asked Anselm.

"Yes; my intelligence relates not to him, but to the Count Mancini," replied the prior. " It is whispered at court that he bears not his real name; and he has laid claim to the inheritance of this very Cordelia de Dunstanville, on the ground of her death, and his next relationship to her."

" Relationship! how can that be?" exclaimed the monk.

"I know not," replied the prior. "My letters tell no more than that Mancini is hurrying on the decision, fearing least the decease of Stephen should take place before he has obtained what he calls his right."

" There is then no time to be lost," cried father Anselm. " She must be removed this very evening, at any risk."

" Whither does she go?" asked the prior.

" To Perceval Castle; to the protection of the Baron de Albini, her affianced lover," replied the monk.

" My advices say that the Baron de Albini resists this appropriation of the lands De Dunstanville, upon the ground that there is no proof of the lady's death, observed the prior, "and the young baron Mouthermer has given his friend the weight of his interest with the king on the same side."

"Mouthermer?" said the monk musingly. "Surely I know that name."

"Most probably you have heard it as the name of a young nobleman, a ward and especial favourity of Stephen," replied the prior. "The count has promised to bring forward certain evidence of the death of Cordelia de Dunstanville in a week's time, and has endeavoured to bind the king to decide his claims at the end of that period."

"What an escape for the lady! the count will make sure work no doubt if he come to Duncraig and find her there," exclaimed the monk. "But we will circumvent him."

The monk then told his superior the particulars of the scheme, and the latter readily promised him all the assistance that lay in his power.

The day passed anxiously to all parties ; Cordelia busied herself in preparing for her departure, and in packing up her scanty wardrobe. With Bridget's leave, and indeed at her suggestion, the prisoner packed up a few books which had belonged to the late countess, particularly the one in which she discovered the mysterious packet. Of the latter she said nothing to Bridget, but she took the opportunity while talking with the old woman to mention the name of Mouthermer. Bridget started, and sighed deeply. "Do you know the baron?" asked Cordelia, steadfastly regarding her.

"No," replied Bridget.

"I thought the name seemed familiar to you," observed Cordelia.

"Do you know him?" asked Bridget.

"Yes," replied Cordelia.

"And his lady?" asked the woman eagerly.

"I have never seen her ; but I have heard of her beauty," was the reply.

With a still deeper sigh than before, Bridget turned to the window, and seemed for a time lost in thought. At last she said, "I will go with you, lady, if you will accept my services ; I may meet with friends among your friends."

"With all my heart," said Cordelia cheerfully. "I shall not then fear travelling my long and weary way to Thornbury. Father Anselm too will accompany me."

"But what will the count say, mother?" asked Kate.

"Leave that to me ; he has no claim upon me now," replied the old woman.

Towards evening, Bridget brought the promised dress to Cordelia, and informed her that she had spread the report of her death through the castle, and that Dennis himself had suggested that the sooner every thing was over the better it would be, as he had a presentiment that Mancini would soon revisit Duncraig. "This very evening I told him all should be ready for removal to the monastery," continued Bridget; "therefore make haste, lady, and I will take Dennis out of the way while Kate conducts you across the court-yard, and at the western gate you will find father Anselm awaiting you."

Bridget having ascertained that Cordelia was ready, left the room, and under pretence of asking the advice of Dennis respecting the funeral, she drew the man into one of the remote rooms of the castle, and detained him there for a sufficient time to allow Cordelia to escape.

With a beating heart and trembling step did the maiden descend those stairs which she had never even seen since her arrival at Duncraig, but the sound of which she had so often listened to, sometimes in hope but more frequently in dread. She passed hastily through the hall, and an exclamation of joy smothered by fear burst from her as she set her foot upon the grass-grown pavement of the court-yard. The sun had not yet set, and his red light gleamed through the ruined arches and broken windows of the southern side of the castle. All bespoke neglect, decay,—yet even decay shewed that Duncraig had been at no very remote period a building of considerable strength, and even of beauty. As Cordelia passed through the court she looked round upon the low arched door through which father Anselm had passed on that memorable night, and a shudder ran through her frame when she remembered what she had probably escaped

Kate, whose arm supported her, remarked the shudder, and attributing it to the chilly air, to which the fair fugitive was not accustomed, made a movement to draw her cloak closer round her. Cordelia, grateful to the kind hearted girl, gently pressed her arm, and they passed on through the gateway, where they met father Anselm.

"Oh! my preserver!" exclaimed Cordelia in a tone of rapture, "do I indeed again behold the lovely face of nature? am I again free!"

"Gently, my daughter!" said the monk, "moderate thy feelings, thou hast much to go through with; much that requires strength and prudence."

"I am prudent, I am strong, father," cried Cordelia.

They reached the monastery, and at the gate they were met by the prior, who said to the lady, "In thus receiving a female I am doing an unwonted act, but one which I trust is not unbecoming me. My child, may our saints preserve thee and me!"

Cordelia and her attendant were then ushered into the parlour of the convent, where they found preparations made for their repose, and a neat and simple repast set out ready for them. Cordelia threw herself into a chair, and tears of joy relieved her overcharged heart. Long she wept, till Kate, fearful lest she should again be ill, warned her not to exhaust her strength.

"I am better," replied the lady; "but oh, Kate! if I could describe the blessed feelings of this moment you would not wonder at my weeping. They are tears of joy which I shed; tears of gratitude for the dangers which I have escaped."

Father Anselm and the good prior having persuaded their guests to partake of the refreshments prepared for them, bade them adieu for the night; and Cordelia threw herself on her pallet bed unmindful of its monkish hardness. She and Kate had agreed that they would not take off any of their clothes. Although the prior had not informed Cordelia of the intelligence which he had received from London, yet the lady had great fear that Mancini might unexpectedly return to the castle, and discovering her escape make search for her; she therefore thought it most prudent to hold herself in readiness to seek some place of more secure concealment at any moment, even should it be in the middle of the night.

No such alarm took place, and a quiet night's rest gave Cordelia and her attendant fresh strength and spirits to begin their journey as soon as Bridget should join them.

In the meanwhile the old woman was not idle at the castle. Having procured a coffin by the aid of Dennis, she had it conveyed into the outer room a few hours after the departure of the lady; and by daybreak she summoned Dennis to fasten it down and assist some of the menials to convey it to the monastery. This was done before Cordelia was awake, and it was secretly placed in an empty cell of the convent. Thus far all was right; but there was another more difficult matter, which was to inform Dennis of her own resolution to leave the castle. Upon her hinting this the man exclaimed vehemently that it was impossible.

"I cannot remain here," replied Bridget; "my poor lady is gone, and I can never be happy again in this place; and now this young creature, so innocent and lovely; there is a doom hangs over these towers to destroy all that is good."

"'Tis well my lord hears you not, old woman," replied the man. "And what am I to tell of the girl?" he asked.

"Tell!" replied Bridget, "the truth to be sure. She died and was buried."

"Well, it is very strange. I do not know that she is dead," said Dennis carelessly.

"Not know that she is dead?" cried Bridget, alarmed.

"No, you would not let me see her, remember," replied the man.

"Father Anselm knows she is gone," answered Bridget.

"And to be sure, I have Frazer's order for everything," observed Dennis.

"Indeed I should not much wonder if it be good news for my lord, from what I have just heard."

"What then?" asked the old woman somewhat relieved of her fears.

"Why, they say that our count is to have all her money if he can prove she is dead, and do you not think he would soon make us prove it, if he were to come here and find her alive?" said the man in a sort of a whisper.

"'Tis well," cried Bridget, "she has spared him some trouble and you a crime, Dennis. Will you not vouch for her death?"

"I think I will. I do not like such jobs as I had to do, you know, a short time ago : though, to be sure, the sea may be a safer bed than the church-yard;" replied the man. "But it is the manner of the thing; I shall never forget putting her into the boat."

"Hush, hush," said Bridget, "she had been an angel till she knew him. You will spare me then. Good bye."

Dennis took the offered hand, saying, "Well, I have half a mind to be off, too ; only I do expect some good from my lord's good fortune; and Frazer owes me a turn, I shall make him pay it me, yet."

So saying the man turned away, and Bridget took the road to the monastery. Upon her arrival there a consultation was held which terminated in Cordelia's immediate departure. Bridget and her daughter accompanied her, and they were escorted by father Anselm, who intended to proceed with them to Percival Castle.

CHAPTER XXXVIII.

"Oft morning dreams presage approaching fate,
    And morning dreams, as poets tell, are true.
Led by pale ghosts, I enter death's dark gate,
    And bid the realms of light and life adieu!

"I hear the helpless wail, the shriek of woe;
    I see the muddy wave, the dreary shore,
The sluggish streams that slowly creep below,
    Which mortals visit, and return no more."

LET us now return to Mancini, who, daunted, but not discouraged, by the failure of his atrocious attempt at Thornbury, determined boldly to claim as heir to Cordelia de Dunstanville, the lands which he could not otherwise obtain from her. He proceeded to London with Frazer, and, as a preliminary step, he spread abroad the report of Cordelia's death, and of his claim as her next heir. These reports soon reached the Baron Mouthermer, who, without waiting to communicate with Edward de Albini, called at once upon Mancini, and requested to know the grounds upon which he affirmed that Cordelia was dead.

Mancini uncourteously asked what right Mouthermer had to make the inquiry.

"The right of friendship," he replied. "There must be very clear proof to induce her friends to believe Cordelia de Dunstanville no more."

"I care not what proof her friends require," replied Mancini ; "It is sufficient for me to produce legal proof."

"May I ask in what relationship you pretend to stand to the unhappy maiden ? Her friends know no relative," observed Mouthermer.

"Probably not," replied the count, "but my claim is clear, nevertheless, as the cousin to her deceased father, De Dunstanville."

"That must be proved," said Mouthermer.

"I have ample proof of my identity, and I can assure your lordship that you need not trouble yourself in the matter," replied Mancini, scornfully.

"I shall trouble myself," replied the young man.

"As you please, my lord; but perhaps it were wiser not to do it," said the count in a menacing tone.

"I know not what you mean; I fear no one; and I give the Count Mancini notice that I will use every effort to resist his assumed right; and to induce the king to require unquestionable evidence of the death of Cordelia de Dunstanville, before he allows a stranger to claim her lands," exclaimed Mouthermer in a decided tone.

So saying the baron took his leave, and departed for the palace, where, notwithstanding the illness of the king, he was at once admitted to an audience. Mouthermer told the whole story of Cordelia's disappearance, and the intention of Mancini to claim her rights on proving her death. The first remark of Stephen was, that if Mancini could so positively prove her decease, he must have been a party to her disappearance, and on this account alone he was a suspected person. But Stephen had heard of this strange foreigner in other ways, and he did not feel inclined to favour his claims. He therefore suggested to Mouthermer that, as the first most material point was to ascertain who had taken Cordelia away, and where she had been concealed, the best plan to effect this purpose would be to let Mancini prosecute his claim, in the expectation that he would by some inadvertency betray the very secret that Cordelia's friends wished to discover. This advice appeared reasonable to the young baron, although delay was not a part of his character; and he determined to summon Edward de Albini to London, in order to take advantage of anything which might occur.

Upon the return of Frazer to his master, after having left Cordelia so ill, he found Mancini in a state of great agitation. In answer to his inquiry as to the cause,—

"Frazer," cried the count, "know you that he, my arch enemy, is expected in England?"

"Is it possible!" exclaimed Frazer, "What brings him my lord?"

"He comes with Henry Fitz Empress, or rather he is expected to precede him —I scarcely know how to act," replied the count.

"It is a common saying, my lord, that misfortunes never come single," replied Frazer, "but, perhaps, the intelligence which I bring may be scarcely accounted a misfortune."

"What mean you?" cried Mancini, impatiently.

"Your fair prisoner is dying or dead!" said the man.

"Dead, really dead? and by fair means?" asked the count.

"I should not have dared without your orders," replied Frazer. "Grief has forestalled us; I left her dying."

"And why leave her? why not have sent for me?" asked his master.

"Old Bridget is trustworthy, and I left orders for her interment in the abbey yard," replied Frazer.

"It is well. But she was not really dead?" asked Mancini.

"No. Father Anselm, who has confessed her, declared to me that she could not live an hour," said the man.

"Confessed her! stupid dolts!" exclaimed the count. "Then I am ruined!"

"Not so, my lord; the father is simple and unsuspicious, he knows nothing and can betray nothing," expostulated Frazer, alarmed at his lord's vehemence.

"He knows her name, and that is sufficient to ruin me!" cried Mancini.

"Surely in so remote a spot, there can be no fear, my lord," replied the man.

But Mancini made no answer; he walked forwards and backwards in the room, in a state of extreme perturbation. "Confess her! the fools!" he muttered. "What had she to confess except my sins?" In vain Frazer attempted to deprecate his anger by suggesting that her death was the happiest event that could, happen to his lord; he was not to be soothed, till at last he declared his intention of going down to Duncraig instantly. His companion, astonished, inquired whether he was to attend him.

"No," replied Mancini. "You must remain here to watch over my interests. I will go to the castle and see what has become of the foolish girl. But what caused her illness?"

"I believe the letter which I took from you to her; she fainted, and never recovered it," answered Frazer.

"Nonsense! I have only one command to give, and that I expect will be strictly attended to; not a word must be breathed of this affair, and if the hot-headed Baron de Mouthermer or his friend make any inquiries about me you are to reply that I am merely gone to a short distance from London, and that I shall return in a few days. Mind this command, on your peril disobey it!" commanded Mancini authoritatively.

Frazer promised obedience, and hinted an inquiry respecting the other matter which troubled his lord.

"Should he come, I shall either go to Italy directly or remain at Duncraig till I have obtained the lands," he replied; "but I dare not risk discovery. As to the old woman, I am in her power, and I must not quarrel with her."

The morning of the above conversation Mancini left London, giving out that he was merely going a few miles into the country in order to procure evidence respecting his suit.

In a few days Mouthermer and Edward called, as the count had expected, and not meeting with Mancini, left a message with Frazer that they should call again shortly.

"To-morrow," added Mouthermer, "I go to meet the Baron Rosenberg in the west of England, but I shall speedily return."

At the name of Rosenberg, Frazer turned as pale as death.

"What ails you, man?" asked Edward.

"Nothing, my lord, I am subject to illness; I beg you to excuse me," stammered out the man.

Mouthermer and Edward hurried away.

"There is guilt of some kind in that paleness," exclaimed the latter; "what can it mean? I must see that man again."

"I like not his face," replied his friend; but what can he or his master have in common with my father-in-law, who is not an Englishman?"

"Nay, I know not," answered de Albini; "but the change in his countenance was so great, that I am certain he knows more than he cares to tell?"

"Of whom? do you think he knows anything of the fate of the Lady de Dunstanville, or knowing would he tell?" asked Mouthermer.

"Alas! I know not; my mind has dwelt upon the subject until I am almost bewildered; but the appearance of this man accords with the description of one of the two strangers who endeavoured to search the tomb of Tunstall at Thornbury; the other I am certain was the Count Mancini."

"Methinks it were well if Ronald the dwarf were here to identify them both," observed Mouthermer.

"I will summon him to town immediately," replied Edward. "He would have accompanied me, but my Lady Elfrida, begged me to allow him to remain at Percival."

With a desponding heart the Count Mancini left London, on his road to Scotland. His horizon was darkly overcast, and he knew not to what point to guide his hopes. Should Stephen die before his return, certain ruin must ensue; and yet it would have been madness to neglect the present opportunity of ascertaining the real death of Cordelia. If she were indeed dead, he would immediately place proper evidence of it before the king, and then obtain the coveted possessions, which would give him a rank and consequence that not even his most dreaded enemy would dare to assail. Autumn was spreading its bright tints over the landscape as Mancini journeyed along, solitary and gloomy; he might have admired the variegated colours of hill and dale had his thoughts been disengaged from darker subjects, but Mancini regarded them not; nature had no charms, no beauties for a mind so ill at ease as his was: and, absorbed in gloomy meditations, he rode on, scarcely giving himself or beast the necessary rest and food, till he found himself upon the English border. Here his journey was disagreeably delayed by an accident.

Mancini had ridden his horse with all the speed of which he was capable, and the poor animal was almost worn out, when one day, just after crossing the border, the count was descending a steep hill, when his horse made a false step,

and falling, threw his rider. At the first moment Mancini was not aware of being hurt, and was going to remount, when a sharp pain in his side warned him that he might be severely injured. Not alarmed for his life, but dreading lest delay should destroy his schemes, Mancini slowly led his horse along to the bottom of the hill, where having ascertained that the creature had merely broken the skin of one of his knees, the count again attempted to mount, and was again obliged to refrain,

No. 32.

the agony arising from his injury being so acute that he could scarcely avoid fainting. He sat down by the road-side to decide what to do, when a monk passed him, and looking compassionately at him, inquired if he were ill. Mancini related the accident which he had met with, and the monk invited him to accompany him to a neighbouring monastery, where his hurt would be properly and kindly attended to.

Mancini gladly accepted the offered kindness, and leaning upon the monk, who held his horse by the bridle, he endeavoured to walk onwards. With considerable pain he made towards the abbey, which lay about a quarter of a mile off, and at last reached its hospitable gates, where he was received with kindness and pity by the superior, who assisted him into his parlour. His horse meanwhile was carefully led to the stable and supplied with provender.

One of the brothers, who was skilled in pharmacy, then examined Mancini, and proclaimed that one of his ribs was broken, but that with rest he might be able to resume his journey in a week or two.

"So long must I wait?" said the count impatiently.

"Be thankful, my son, that thy hurt is no more; that is an awkward hill, and many a limb has been irrecoverably injured by falling there," replied the monk.

"I am on hasty business, and I like not to be delayed," observed Mancini.

"If you tease thyself, fever will come on, and then I cannot answer for thy life," said the monk.

"I care not for my life," said Mancini pettishly.

"Is thy business then dearer to thee than thy life?" asked the monk. "Alas, for the children of the world, occupied in vanity and wickedness, and not reflecting that the mere false step of a brute animal may put an end to all their schemes."

Mancini was in no humour to hear the moralising of the monk, and bidding him apply what he thought necessary for his cure, he signified a desire to be left alone. The monk accordingly did as he was bid, and left him, carrying to his brethren no very favourable account of the temper of their guest.

A small, but neatly furnished room was appropriated to the count, and he was laid on a small bed, with strict injunctions not to move, or the bone would be displaced, and his time of seclusion materially protracted. Some religous books were brought to him, and he was informed that whenever he required it, one of the brothers would bear him company. But reading was never palatable to Mancini, and now above all he was not in a humour to have recourse to it; he lay gloomily thinking upon the past and the future till evening brought, as the monk had anticipated, a slight degree of fever with it. Troubled sleep succeeded to the chill of fever, and Mancini dreamed of the days that were gone, and the faces which were no more.

Before him arose the form of one whom he had once loved—his Dorothea. She appeared to warn him of some hidden danger, pointed with her bony and attenuated hand to an empty grave. The scene was familiar to him, it was the cemetery belonging to the priory of St. Agnes near Duncraig ; he seemed to be standing near the grave, a long train of monks were winding round the cloisters of the abbey chaunting the mass for the dead, while by the side of the dreamer stood the figure of his deceased wife clad as she had been when he consigned her to her watery grave. Her arm was raised, and she muttered the words, "Lost, lost, lost."

Mancini endeavoured to seize her arm, but the movement which he made gave him a sharp pain in his wounded side, and he awoke. But the influence of his dream remained, and it was some time before he could collect his scattered senses, and remember where he was. Even when he had quite succeeded in awakening himself, the effect upon his feelings was overpowering; he had seen before him her whom he had once loved, although not with the love which he ought to have borne towards her ; she seemed to reproach him with her unhallowed and watery grave, and to intimate that, however guilty she was towards him, he was not the person to punish her for sins which he had perhaps first led her to commit. He feared that his dream was intended to intimate to him that by her means his crimes were to be discovered; and although he felt certain that she herself could not accuse him of murder, yet there had been one towards whom his conscience was not so clear. Remorse, Mancini could not feel; but he was alive to terror, and he trembled.

After lying awake for a considerable time, sleep again overcame the count; he would have resisted its influence, fearing lest it should renew the former harassing dream; but the opiate which he had taken in order to relieve his pain gained the mastery over him, and again he slept. Again did he dream—but his dream was not now of his dead wife, it was of a more awful personage—Vallambrosa.

He was standing before the throne of Stephen, who had just presented him with the grant of the lands of De Dunstanville, when the murdered Vallambrosa stepped forward, and holding out to him a headsman's axe, pointed to spots of blood upon the paper which he held. As he gazed, the figure of Vallambrosa seemed to change to one known in earlier life, on whose arm hung a female figure resembling Cordelia de Dunstanville. The man struck him, and Mancini awoke with a groan. He resolved to sleep no more, and by a resolute effort he kept himself awake till daybreak, when the voices of the monks chaunting their matins came upon his ear with a soothing influence. The count listened attentively; he had always regarded religious exercises as mere hypocrasy, but he now felt that they might sometimes effect a beneficial influence upon the mind.

At the usual time of the morning meal, one of the brothers attended upon him, bringing him the refreshment he needed; his better feelings had subsided, and when the monk who was his physician visited him, he found him irritable and discontented. In vain did the monk tell him that peace of mind was as necessary to his restoration as quiet of body; Mancini could not or did not endeavour to conquer his restless disposition.

Thus several days passed, during which, however, the count was gradually recovering, and his medical friend assured him that a very few days longer of rest would enable him to pursue his journey with safety. Gladly was this intelligence accepted, and the guest was removed during the day to the parlour of the monastery, where the abbot and several of the monks passed the day with him.

One morning, being willing to make trial of his strength, Mancini rambled into the garden belonging to the monastery, where the brotherhood cultivated the vegetables used at table, and such flowers as pleased their fancy. The ground was portioned out in small patches belonging to each monk, and presented a pleasing variety of scene. The count was attended by one of the monks who conversed with him respecting the various plants. Mancini's attention was attracted by a small patch of ground entirely cultivated with artichokes, then a vegetable unknown in England; a young monk was breaking the ground around the plants, and was so intent upon his employment that he did not notice the approach of the stranger. Mancini had made some observation as they approached upon his astonishment at seeing that vegetable in so flourishing a condition, when the monk who was walking by his side answered, —

"Brother Hypolitus is very careful of his garden, and his care is well rewarded; his artichokes thrive, and they give him trouble enough; we wonder that he should cultivate them, as no one likes them at table but himself."

"They are the natives of my own dear country," said the young monk without raising his head, "and the remind me of happier days."

"Of Italy I suppose?" asked Mancini.

The young monk started, raised his head, fixed his eyes for a moment upon the face of the count, and throwing down his spade, walked quickly away.

"Your companion is shy," observed the count, "he seems alarmed at me."

"He is shy, but amiable and good," replied the monk; "he is we fear rapidly sinking into the grave; indeed father Benedict says nothing but the smell of the newly-turned earth keeps him alive."

"He appears young," remarked Mancini.

" I fancy he has passed through much of sin and danger, although he is young; he often talks of Italy and her sunny shores," replied the monk.

" Why does he not return thither ?" asked the count.

" I know not ; perhaps his relatives are dead," said the brother.

While thus speaking, Mancini and his attendant re-entered the convent, and the former retired to the parlour to rest himself.   He found the abbot reading, but at the entrance of his guest the latter laid down his book, and commenced a conversation, which was interrupted by a gentle tap at the door. Admission being granted, the young monk whom Mancini had seen in the garden entered, and advancing to the abbot, begged for the loan of a certain book which had been promised him. While he was speaking, he fixed his eyes upon Mancini with an expression of curiosity, and the latter said,—

" I too have visited Italy, young man, and feel like you an affection for its unclouded skies and fertile lands.   I shall probably return thither ere long."

The young monk sighed deeply.

" Can I convey any intelligence of your welfare ?" asked Mancini.

" None, there is but one who cares for me, and she——"

A look from his superior stayed his tongue and prevented his saying more.   These few words had been uttered in a low, hollow tone, so unlike that natural to youth, that Mancini could scarcely imagine they proceeded from the slight, fragile form before him.   He gazed with pity upon the youth, and his gaze was returned by one of contempt ; at least so it appeared to Mancini.   The monk left the room with an obeisance to the abbot, who gave him a friendly smile, and advised him to return to his labours in the garden.

There was something in the countenance of the young man that raised the count's curiosity, and he was proceeding to make inquiries of the abbot respecting him, when the latter stopped him by remarking that it was against the rules of the abbey to answer any question respecting the character of any of its residents ; the family name was carefully concealed from all but the abbot, who alone knew the causes and misfortunes or sins which had brought each brother under his roof. Mancini therefore said no more of the young monk, and the remembrance of him faded, as he thought, from his memory.

On the ensuing morning the abbot received Mancini in the parlour with a face more grave than usual, and bearing traces of suffering and sleeplessness.   He at once accounted for this by saying that he had gone through a painful duty since they had parted the night before.

" I have now," he continued, " a favour to request for the younger brother whom you saw yesterday.   He demands a few minutes private conversation with you upon family matters."

Mancini looked surprised, and the abbot continued,—

" He has confessed the whole to me, and I have, perhaps weakly, consented to the interview ; but his days are numbered, his soul is penitent, and I do not fear any renewal of the worldly feelings which led him to crime and misery."

" I can refuse nothing where I am so deeply indebted," answered Mancini.

" When will you receive the brother ?" asked the abbot.

" Now, at this moment," replied the count.

" Excuse me, we are all weak and frail—can you answer for yourself if any question touch your own family ?" asked the abbot.

" No one has a right to question me, and should such occur, I shall give no answer, but I know too well what is due to my host and to myself to suffer my temper to be ruffled by such impertinence," replied the count proudly.

" Then I will send brother Hypolitus to you," replied the abbot.

In a few minutes the young man entered the room, and advancing to the count stood opposite to him, when throwing back his cowl he exclaimed,—

" Mancini! do you not know me ?"

Startled at hearing his own name, but not recognising the speaker, the count was silent.

"Have disease and sickness so changed me then?" cried the monk. "Ten years have passed since we met, and hast thou already forgotten thy victim, Vallambrosa?"

Had a tiger crossed his path, the count would have been less appalled. It was not fear—it was not remorse—it was awe,—awe of the almost unearthly being who stood before him—one who he believed his sword had sent to the grave, to the punishment which he merited. The count spoke not, but gazed as if his soul was in his eyes.

"Our interview must be brief," resumed the monk, "I demanded it not to reproach you, I am no longer blind to the enormity of my sin; I have suffered and repented; but neither suffering, nor repentance, nor religion itself, forbid or can quench the desire, I have to ask one question. You may guess. Does she live?"

Mancini shook his head mournfully.

"I feared it; but tell me that thou wert not her murderer," cried Hypolitus.

"I am clear from that crime," replied Mancini.

"Once more—was she too penitent?" asked the monk.

"She was; at least father Anselm assured me so," replied Mancini.

"And when—how—oh! tell me!" cried the monk.

"A few months ago at Duncraig; Bridget attended her," replied the count.

"I am content, death now is welcome. Oh! blessed chance! which in bringing thee here has satisfied my soul upon its dearest doubt. Adieu! Mancini; I do not offer forgiveness, nor do I ask it," said Hypolitus; and he was about to leave the room when Mancini exclaimed,—

"Stop! it is now my turn to question. Is aught known here of my name or——"

"Nothing through me," replied the monk; "your name has not been mentioned by me, nor hers either. I am no babbler about others."

"It is well; had it been otherwise," exclaimed the count, "these walls, that dress of mummery—nay, not your mitred abbot should have protected you; this arm can yet make sure work."

"Threats ill become the Count Mancini," replied the monk; "but I forgive them, however I may despise the fear that makes such caution necessary."

"Despise! and dost thou, a prisoned monk, dare to despise the Count Mancini? Beware of my wrath, it may yet touch thee effectually," cried the count, laying his hand upon his sword.

But the monk was gone ere he could draw it. As he left the room, Hypolitus threw one hasty glance of pity and contempt upon his adversary, and presently his retreating step was heard along the corridor.

Mancini threw himself back in his chair overcome with contending emotions; surprise, rage, fear, all struggled for mastery, but the latter was at last triumphant. He determined to ascertain from the abbot whether it were indeed true that Vallambrosa had not betrayed his name or history; he knew that of the darkest part of his life the youth was the only one, except Bridget, who was acquainted with it, and at this moment, especially, it was necessary that it should be hidden in obscurity. Upon the return of the abbot, therefore, he led to the subject, and was considerably relieved to find that the monk had not indeed betrayed his name or history.

"I know only," said the abbot, "of the injury and guilt which our brother inflicted upon you, and this was not fully revealed to me till last night; I trust you have amply forgiven him whom the Church has received into her regenerating community?"

"We are at peace with one another, father," replied Mancini, "which is perhaps all that can be expected. But I cannot remain longer under the same roof that shelters him, I must depart to-morrow; already have I too long delayed my journey, and to-morrow's dawn sees me on my way."

Mancini retired to rest, but not to sleep; he remembered his former strange dreams, he saw that one of these had been in some degree realised, and he dreaded lest the other also should be verified; he thought of the young Count Vallambrosa thus hovering near the treasure for whom he had nearly lost his life, and now that she was no more, Mancini felt rejoiced that he had failed in his intended vengeance. But how Vallambrosa had escaped he could not imagine; he had left him for dead far away from any succour, and it seemed scarcely credible that he should have survived his many and dangerous wounds. Mancini feared that, although Vallambrosa had not betrayed him at his present place of refuge, yet that he must have done so to those who had at first succoured and healed him; and he regretted extremely not having inquired of the young man a little of the history of his recovery. He almost determined to ask an interview on the following morning, for the purpose of ascertaining the degree of publicity which had been given to his private history. Not that he much feared the personal consequences of such an attack; the count well knew that such was the unsettled state of the kingdom, especially in that remote part, offences like his were seldom punished; besides the provocation given would be considered as ample excuse for such a revenge. But Mancini had no superabundance of character to lose, and this he was well aware of.

Towards midnight the count fell asleep, but he was speedily awakened by the deep dull toll of the bell. At first he imagined it might portend an alarm of fire, but he listened a little while, and hearing no bustle nor noise in the convent he was satisfied that such was not the case. The bell continued its mournful sound, breaking upon the dull cold ear of night with an unearthly voice, its reverberations through the vaulted passages and arched corridors prolonged the sound, producing a solemnity almost appalling. Mancini listened; it evidently announced the departure of some soul from its earthly tenement, perhaps of one of those monks with whom he had conversed on the preceding day.

This idea Mancini dismissed as absurd; the young man, although declining in health, might yet live many years in that peaceful and healthy spot; and Mancini turned himself to sleep again, with a selfish feeling that he was not interested in the event which had happened, let it be to whom it might.

Early in the morning he arose, and prepared himself to resume his journey. In the parlour he found the morning repast ready for him, and the abbot awaiting his appearance.

"My lord," he said, "a mournful event has taken place in our house; heard you not the death-bell in the silence of the night?"

"I did," replied the count.

"The Count Vallambrosa is no more!" said the abbot, solemnly.

Mancini started, and turned upon the abbot a look of inquiry.

"We thought not that his death was so near, but he was prepared for it, and we cannot regret it," observed the father.

"Said he aught in his last moments?" asked Mancini.

"He desired me to acquaint you with the existence of this miniature," was the reply of the abbot, at the same time displaying to the count a small painting of his late wife.

Mancini would have taken it, but the abbot drew it back, saying,—

"I am desired to keep it until a fitting opportunity occurs for delivering it according to the direction here given," observed the abbot, pointing to an address upon the back of the picture.

"Traitress! villain, how knew he——" cried Mancini.

"It becomes not me to pry into your lordship's secrets," replied the abbot; "but the last wishes of the dead must be complied with."

"I care not for the bauble!" exclaimed the count, contemptuously. "But beware, dark monk, how by any secret dealing you raise the anger of Count Mancini."

"My vocation is peace," replied the abbot.

"Then fulfil it by delivering that which of right belongs to me into my own hand," said Mancini.

"I shall deliver it safely according to this address; and if Count Mancini will design to accept my advice, he will avoid agitating a subject which cannot redound to his honour."

"Know you to whom you are speaking?" asked Mancini, angrily.

"Better perhaps than he would like me to declare," replied the abbot calmly. "But, as I have said, my vocation is peace, and I will not break it. Adieu, my lord; your steed awaits you, and may your end be as peaceful as his was who is just gone."

So saying, the abbot left the room, and Mancini, little inclined to partake of the repast before him, repaired to the outer gate, and repaying by a considerable sum of money the hospitality which he had received, mounted his horse and rode at a rapid pace away from the monastery.

CHAPTER XXXIX.

'Twas but an instant he restrained
That fiery steed so sternly reined;
'Twas but a moment that he stood,
Then sped as if by death pursued;
But in that instant o'er his soul
Winters of mem'ry seem'd to roll,
And gather in that drop of time
A life of pain, an age of crime.—BYRON.

MANCINI pursued his journey through the valley in which the convent was situated, till he approached Duncraig. When about a mile from the castle, a storm came on violently; thunder and wind seemed to strive for the mastery, while at frequent intervals broad red flashes of lightning streamed through the darkness. The rain poured in torrents, and before Mancini had ridden even the short distance which was to terminate his journey, he was completely wet to the skin.

When he arrived at the castle gate, he hastily gave notice of his arrival by violently pulling the bell, and finding that no one came, he rang still more furiously. Presently a voice from one of the windows exclaimed, "Hilloa! who rings so loud this awful night?"

"Fool! slave! let me in immediately, or ill betide thee," cried Mancini.

Dennis did not wait to hear more than the first words of this address, and almost before his master finished speaking, he had opened the gate and was leading the count's horse into the court.

"Shame on thy laziness! could not thou tell it was I?" cried Mancini.

"Please you, my lord," began Dennis.

"No excuses, knave," replied his master. "Tell Bridget to make me a good supper ready, and help me to put off these dripping garments."

"Bridget, my lord?" said Dennis hesitating.

"Yes—call up the old woman if she be in bed. Do you not suppose I want food, fellow?" asked the count.

"Bridget is gone, my lord," said Dennis in a blundering soanner, as if he were determined to tell the unwelcome news, but dared not.

"Bridget gone? and where?" asked his master.

"I don't know," replied Dennis.

"Trifle not with me," exclaimed Mancini.

"My lord, indeed I know not," was the earnest answer.

"Send Kate then," said his master.

"She is gone too," said the man.

Mancini rose in a rage, and seizing Dennis by the arm, said, " Fellow, I will bear no jugglery nor deceit, tell me what has happened."

"Does not your lordship know"—began the frightened menial.

[" I know nothing," was the furious reply.

" The lady is dead and buried, and Bridget and Kate would not stop here," cried Dennis, trembling.

" When did she die ?" asked Mancini.

" More than a fortnight since," answered the man.

" And why did Bridget go ? asked the count.

" She said nothing good would stay here, and she would not," Dennis replied.

Mancini could not restrain a bitter smile. "Nothing good! and so the old hag would not attempt to break the charm. And why did not you go too ?"

. " I thought your lordship would be angry," said Dennis.

" Well, put the horse into the stable. Who is here besides you ?" asked Mancini.

" Andrew and Comyn ; they have taken the horse," answered Dennis.

" Then get me food, and let me hear how she died ; mind, no false tales, or thou knowest there are dungeons," said his lord.

Mancini seated himself by the fire, which Dennis had just replenished with well-blazing fuel, while the man brought in such materials for a meal as the scanty larder of the castle afforded. Tired, hungry, wet, and cold, and still more miserable in mind than in body, the count endeavoured to make a supper, and commanding Dennis to be seated, he inquired into the particulars of Cordelia's death. These Dennis related as circumstantially as he was able, endeavouring to excuse himself on many points respecting which his lord might be angry. But Mancini was relieved to learn that Cordelia was indeed removed from his path, and he gradually became more civil towards Dennis, as a cup of strong spiced wine did its kindly office in warming his benumbed frame.

" And what did you do with the maiden ?" as asked.

" She is buried in the cemetery belonging to the monastery of St. Agnes," replied the man.

" Buried ? and could you do no better than that, fool ?" exclaimed Mancini.

" Bridget would not hear of it, my lord ; she said she should never be happy after the other job. and you know I could not do it alone," observed Dennis.

" And so the girl's death has been gossiped over by the fat monk of St. Agnes," cried Mancini angrily.

" They knew 'twas all right," said the man in a low tone, " for father Anselm came and confessed her ; and he knew how she died."

" Was he with her when she died ?" asked Mancini.

" Not at the last moment, but a few hours before," was the answer.

" And you say he confessed her, how could Bridget suffer that ?" cried his master angrily.

" Why, my lord, you remember you suffered the father to come when——"

" Well ! well !" said Mancini interrupting Dennis. " I had my reason then, but this girl wanted no confession."

" Bridget thought it hard, my lord," said the man.

" And when did Bridget and her daughter go away ?" asked the count.

" The day after the lady died," was the reply.

" And you do not know where the old woman is gone to ? remember you tell me the truth," said Mancini.

" Indeed, my lord, I know not, by all the saints," answered the man.

" 'Tis well—prepare my room. In the morning I must see father Anselm. I hate those whining monks, but he must be sent for. I must know all about the burial of this silly girl."

Mancini sat over the hall-fire, while Dennis, most glad to get from his master's presence, made his chamber ready for him, and having lighted a fire there, he went down to the stable under pretence of looking to the horse, but in reality to avoid returning to the count.

In the morning Mancini desired Dennis to accompany him into the chamber which Cordelia had inhabited. He found every thing there in disorder; the harp was standing in a corner covered with dust, music and books were lying about th room, and everything betokened desolation and a hurried or forced relinquishmen

of the apartment. Mancini searched everywhere, hoping to discover some papers addressed to himself, but in vain; the only word of the unhappy prisoner which he found was the following sentence written upon the wall.

"Cordelia de Dunstanville confined here by the Count Mancini."

Another hand had written under this the date of her death, and an ejaculation of mercy.

No. 33.

Mancini immediately erased the words, picked up the books. and placing them in a corner of the room, hastily left it, locking it securely after him. He then descended the stairs and desired Dennis to go to the monastery of St. Agnes and desire that father Anselm should attend him at the castle without delay.

Dennis set out on his unwelcome errand, and ringing the bell of the convent, desired to speak to the father. A monk came to the gate and informed him that Father Anselm was gone on a mission of charity into England, and might not return for some months.

Dennis was extremely dismayed ; even he began to suspect that all was not right, but his fear was that the poor lady had been poisoned. All the strange circumstances which attended her death and funeral corroborated this suspicion, and Dennis resolved to reveal all that he knew to his master, and thus clear himself of any participation in the matter. In this mood he returned to the castle, and telling Mancini of Father Anselm's unwonted absence, he hinted that he feared all had not been right towards the lady.

Mancini asked him wherefore he now changed his opinion as to this, he having assured him the evening previous there had been no foul play.

"There were strange circumstances which did not strike me then," he observed.

"What were they?" asked the count.

"I was not allowed to see the body ; it was fastened down on the same day on which she died," replied Dennis.

"By whose orders?" asked the count.

"By those of Bridget," replied the man.

"I must know more concerning thi.," exclaimed the count ; "my name may be brought in question. Dennis, you attend me to the abbey, the prior must answer to me."

Most reluctantly did the man agree to this, and both then departed for the monastery.

The prior received Mancini courteously but coldly, and having ushered him into the convent parlour, inquired what had produced his visit.

"I wished to see Father Anselm, but I find that he is gone," said Mancini.

"He is gone on a mission of charity into England," was the reply.

"My castle also is deserted ; during my absence a most unpleasant event has taken place there and that it seems has frightened away my female servants. Know you anything of an old woman named Bridget Layton, and Kate her daughter?" asked the count.

"I know that such persons used occasionally to attend mass here," replied the monk ; "but of their history I know nothing."

"Much I fear," said the count, "that Bridget has been a party to some foul dealing towards the lady who was placed under my guardianship and care ; it seems that Father Anselm is in some degree implicated."

"I know not what fancied ground you may have for so dark an insinuation, but I repel it with indignation ; father Anselm is incapable of foul dealing towards any human being, more especially towards the child of his early friend Eleanor de Tunstall," said the prior, vehemently, and fixing his eyes upon the count.

"How know you the maiden's name and parentage?" asked Mancini.

"From her last confession to Father Anselm," was the reply.

"Whoever she may be, it is my duty to know that there was no unfair dealing with her ; and I require that the coffin be exhumed in order to ascertain the manner and cause of her death," said Mancini.

The prior looked aghast.

"Such a proceeding is entirely contrary to all laws and customs of our monastery," he said, "and I can give no such permission."

"It must and shall be done," said the count rising. "I take the responsibility upon myself."

"Hear me," exclaimed the monk. "Suppose the Lady de Dunstanville to have een murdered or poisoned, upon whom think you will the odium rest, if not upon who at this very moment makes application to the king for her inheritance, as him being the next heir to the unfortunate lady?"

Mancini seemed alarmed, and the friar proceeded.

"Were it not better then to let the matter remain in uncertainty than by a rash discovery to bring yourself into danger."

"I see the weight of what you say,' replied the count, "but feeling assured of my own innocence I would bring to punishment those whom I suspect to be guilty; and my suspicions point to Bridget and Father Anselm."

"I have said that I would stake my honour, nay, my life," cried the monk, " upon the innocence of Father Anselm; and if, as I cannot believe, Bridget have been guilty of so atrocious a deed, will not the blame of it lie upon you? as it is evident if she did it you were to reap the benefit."

The count seemed somewhat moved by this representation, but still unwilling to give up the point.

"I cannot imagine the monk's motive," said he, " and scarcely that of Bridget, but it is very strange that the old woman and her daughter should have gone away so suddenly."

To the latter observation the monk made no answer, and the count asked whether Cordelia had made any statement to Father Anselm respecting her property To this he received a negative, with the assurance that the particulars of any dying confession were never made known even to the superior. Mancini therefore took his leave of the prior, very little satisfied with the result of his mission. He saw no course before him but to repair again to London, and to take Dennis with him as evidence of the illness and burial of Cordelia. He hoped that when the unfortunate and accidental circumstance of his fall and illness should be made known to the king, the delay so occasioned would not be considered any impediment to his obtaining the suit he had undertaken, especially when he brought forward such ample proof of the death of Cordelia.

With these reflections Mancini desired Dennis to prepare to accompany him to London on the following day; orders which the man was extremely rejoiced to receive.

Let us revert to Cordelia and her companions, who had left the monastery with the blessing of the prior, and cheerfully began their journey to Percival Castle. As they proceeded, much conversation passed between the lady and the father, who was interested in hearing her history and the various adventures of her life. He listened to her account of Father Augustine with curiosity, having known him when he resided at Edendale, but he had never heard what had become of him, and had no idea that the freebooter Baron de Bohun was the same person with his old associate. He said that the same character had accompanied Father Augustine to the last, ambitious, rapacious, and vindictive.

Much was also said respecting the Count Mancini, and Kate used to burst forth in praise of her native Italy, while Bridget shook her head and wished she had never been there. No questions could draw from the old woman any account of her early life; she avowed her dislike and fear of the count, and her pity for his lady, but she would say nothing respecting her early history. With such discourse the travellers lightened the way, and Kate would sometimes warble her rustic songs when they reposed by some sparkling brook to rest and refresh themselves On one of these occasions Kate sang as follows.—:

> " Oh Italy! oh Italy!
> No home for me like Italy!
> The sun may rise
> In other skies,
> But nought like the sun of Italy!
> The grape is red in Italy,
> And the orange is ripe as e'er you'll see.

And the yellow corn
Where I was born,
Is the best in all fair Italy,
And the girls dance light in Italy!

And their eyes are bright where I would be,
And the morn they greet
With song so sweet,
Oh! life is gay in Italy!

Oh! there is no land like Italy!
Dear home of mine, I pine for thee;
When youth is e'er
I'll roam no more,
But dwell till I die in Italy!"

In this manner the time passed away, and the weary journey was accomplished; and at last the towers of Percival Castle arose before the travellers, frowning in solemn majesty over the valley below. Autumn had stripped the trees of their leafy honours, the tall dark pine alone retained its gloomy green hue, gloomy alike in the blaze of the summer sun, and in the chill of winter's snow. The river ran along its enlarged bed, bearing with it the tribute of many a mountain streamlet, which foaming and frothing in its winter's course, gave in summer a stony and sandy path to the herdsman.

Cordelia, fatigued and anxious, was struck with the gloominess of the scene, and would have hoped that this was not the Percival Castle which was to bring back to her happiness and joy. The party entered a small cottage at the foot of the hill, and requested a short rest before they proceeded. A blazing fire welcomed them into the kitchen, where several children were seated round a deal table eating their noon-day meal. A clean and good-looking young woman was serving out to each his portion, while a strong and healthy farmer was seated by the fire drying his clothes.

"You are welcome," said the woman: "you appear fatigued andcold; well it may be so, even my master here is glad to enjoy his hearth."

Thus speaking, she placed seats by the fire, while her husband arose, and was about to retire, when Cordelia requested that he would not disturb himself. "We have not much farther to go,'" she added, "but I am so cold and weary that I cannot undertake to mount the hill till I am rested."

"Are you then going to the castle?" asked the man.

"Yes," replied Cordelia, "is the Lady de Albini there?"

"She never leaves it, poor lady," replied the woman.

"The baron is dead, is he not?" asked Kate, pitying Cordelia's agitation.

"Yes," said the man, "and our young lord is in town."

Cordelia was rather rejoiced at this intelligence; she dreaded meeting her lover, almost fearing lest so long a period of uncertainty as to her fate should have rendered him unmindful of his former attachment. She knew the character of the Lady Elfrida too well to doubt being received kindly by her, and she longed to throw herself into her friendly arms.

As soon as the travellers had a little rested themselves, they left the cottage and began to ascend the hill-road. Cordelia's heart beat as she approached the noble gateway which formed the entrance, and when on requiring admittance to the Lady de Albini, the porter desired her to follow him, her agitation almost deprived her of the power of moving. Father Anslem with Bridget and her daughter remained in the inner hall.

CHAPTER XI.

"How long I've look'd from distant climes
 At evening on the west;
And dreamt in silence of the times
 That saw my soul at rest:
While from the margin of the tide
 I watch'd day's fading smile
And lov'd its glories, for they died
 Upon my own dear isle."

In the large and dreary saloon of Percival Castle sat the Lady Elfrida. Around her were the trophies of her ancestors; their war-spears and their swords glittered on the walls in the pale blaze of the embers, their figures frowned from their frames; here were the mail-clad knights of generations now long gathered to the silent tomb, each in his sable panoply arrayed, and looking defiance at the unseen foe; there the gentler scions of an illustrious house exhibited in their persons the grandeur and patrician order, less severe perhaps than their companions, but as proud of their long line of untarnished ancestry.

Beside the lady stood an embroidering frame, the usual occupation of females in her rank of life; it seemed to have been but just laid aside; as the red sun shed his last beams through the painted window, tinging the inlaid floor with colours more brilliant than those which had adorned it when it rose the pride of an eastern forest. The lady sat, or rather reclined, in a massive bigh-backed chair, her feet reposing upon a cushion covered with the skin of a leopard. Her dress was the deepest mourning, and her gaze was fixed in mournful remembrance upon the portrait of her deceased lord, which decorated the richly carved mantel-piece. She appeared buried in reverie, while her sole attendant, a young page, also attired in deep black, was vainly attempting to read a book which he held in his hand.

"Edgar," said the lady, "enough for the present of our friend Robert of Gloucester; thy young eyes may not be injured by the flickering light of these embers; leave me for a time. I would slumber."

The page was about to leave the room as he was desired to do, when the seneschal entered, and announced that a young maiden wished to be admitted to the Lady de Albini.

"I would be alone just now," replied the lady, "let the maiden attend tomorrow."

"May it please you, my lady," said the seneschel, "but the maiden desires admission without delay."

"Does she not tell her name?" asked the lady.

"No," said the servant.

"This is strange," said the lady. "Edgar, go and make inquiry, and if it be impossible to avoid it, usher her here."

The page followed the man into the inner hall, where Cordelia was waiting, but what was his surprise when she ran forward and clasping him in her arms, exclaimed,

"Edgar! dost not remember thy play-fellow?"

The page looked up in the lady's face in amazement, and at last said he did not remember her.

"Tell your lady that a stranger whom she loves wishes to see her," said Cordelia.

Cordelia was accordingly introduced by Edgar into the saloon, where by the dim fire-light, she beheld her early friend. Bursting into tears she flung herself at he lady's knees, and hiding her face in her robe wept convulsively.

"Who art thou?" cried the lady astonished.

"Cordelia—your own Cordelia," was the reply.

"Art thou come from the dead to visit her with whom the living hold but slight communion?" said the lady in a solemn tone.

"No—no! it is your own Cordelia!" exclaimed the maiden raising her head.

"Pale and unearthly as thou art, oh! tell me whence thou comest," exclaimed the lady in the same tone of awe.

"It is a long tale, oh! dearest lady, but, oh! receive your child," cried Cordelia.

"Receive her? oh! how gladly!" said the lady embracing her.

Cordelia arose and the lady did the same. After gazing for some minutes intently upon the tear-bedewed countenance of the stranger, the Lady Elfrida said,—

"It is indeed my child, my Cordelia, but how preserved to bless me?"

"Through danger and almost death, through treachery and persecution," replied the maiden, "but all is forgotten if the Lady Elfrida do but smile upon me."

"Alas, my child! a smile but seldom visits the face of her who, solitary and bereaved, sits here in loneliness," replied the lady. "But there is one to whom a smile is equally a stranger, but whose heart will glow with joy at thy return."

Cordelia blushed deeply, but answered not.

"My son Edward mourns thy supposed decease, how will it gladden his troubled heart again to behold the lost one," said the lady again, embracing Cordelia.

"May I ask where is the young baron?" asked the maiden.

"He is in London the Baron de Mouthermer, his friend. sent for him a short time ago on some particular occasion, and unwillingly did Edward obey the summons. It was but a few days since the dwarf Ronald followed his master."

"Ah! my faithful Ronald," cried Cordelia. "And Edith?"

"Edith de Mowbray resides at the castle; her lord is now master of that fair domain, and Edith is the queen of the country around," replied the lady.

"Is it not indeed a dream?" exclaimed Cordelia "do I once more talk with my earliest friend, my adopted mother?"

"Rest here my daughter; I will hasten Edwards return, and Percival Castle shall once again re-echo with the voice of happiness," said the lady.

"My weary pilgrimage is not yet over," said Cordelia; "I must see the Lady Mouthermer; there is justice yet to be done."

"Trust it to Edward, he will challenge the persecutor," said the lady, "But where hast thou been while we have been weeping thy loss?"

Cordelia gave the Lady Elfrida a short account of her detention at Duncraig, her sufferings and her escape. She told them how she had been befriended by Father Anselm, and how he had escorted her and her female attendants to Percival; of her mental sufferings she said little, and she did not mention the Countess Mancini or her history. The lady listened, absorbed in interest, and at last exclaimed,—

"The king must right you, my child."

"Alas!" said Cordelia, "much I fear that Mancini has already obtained my lands; he thinks me dead, but in what manner he claims them I know not. I owe him nothing, and willingly would I assist in his detection. Perhaps he may have been guilty of other crimes."

"What mean you, my child?" asked the Lady.

Cordelia then related the history of what she had witnessed, a burial in the sea, and told the lady of the packet which she found addressed to Lady Mouthermer. This she said she wished to deliver herself, and without delay.

"cannot imagine that packet to be of very great importance," said the lady; "Lday Mouthermer's mother died when she was a child, and certainly had never visited Scotland as she was an Italian by birth. But, my, child what wouldst thou do?"

"I would go to London," said Cordelia.

"But thou art tired and worn," replied the lady.

"A few days rest, lady, with you, and then I should be refreshed, and able to pursue my journey. Bridget has, I fancy, some purpose of her own to answer in London, she would attend me; and good father Anselm would protect me."

"Nay, my child, Edward would receive thee, oh! how gladly!" said the lady.

"Not so, dear lady; I feel a presentiment that a great purpose will be served by my going to London; but much as I wish to see Edward de Albini, it becomes not a Dunstanville to seek him," said the maiden in a dignified tone; "when my mission is accomplished, I will return and await him here."

The Lady Elfrida applauded Cordelia's resolve, although she could not fully understand all her motives. Cordelia asked permission to leave Kate at Percival castle during her absence, which was readily agreed to, and the lady having summoned the strangers to her presence bade them gladly welcome to the castle.

The evening passed in interesting conversation respecting the past; Cordelia brought to the recollection of Edgar the many occasions in which he had been the petted inmate of Thornbury during his childhood, and by condescending enquiries after his parents and her other friends at that the dear home of her youth, she gained his affectionate confidence. Kate too made already some progress in the esteem of the Lady Elfrida; her vivid descriptions of the beauties and romantic charms of her native country, her gentle gaiety of manner, and her skill in embroidery, which she had learned in a convent abroad, rendered her an acquisition to the Lady de Albini, whose amusements being circumscribed to the range of the castle and its garden, she felt at times a gloomy monotony of life from which it seemed that Kate would be able greatly to relieve her.

After a few days thus passed, Cordelia had made arrangements for proceeding to London, and most reluctantly did the lady consent to part with her. On the evening before the day which had been fixed for her departure, she was conversing with the Lady Elfrida upon the circumstances of her kinsman De Tunstalls death, when she expressed her anxiety to ascertain what had become of the paper which had been the cause of so much misery to her. The Lady Elfrida told her that D Tunstall had committed it to the care of Edward de Albini; "but," she continued "that paper is useless now."

"Wherefore, madam?" said Cordelia alarmed.

"The king has duly acknowledged your claim," replied the Lady Elfrida.

"Oh, happy news! then I am neither dowerless nor nameless!" cried the maiden.

"Neither, my child, and you may claim your rank and fortune; but I would counsel you to entrust the whole to Edward. I must acquaint him with your happy return," said the lady.

"A sacred duty must first be fulfilled," replied Cordelia; "that over, I will gladly return to this peaceful shelter."

"Be it as you will; but I dread lest this bad man again seize you," said the lady.

"Fear not, he thinks me dead," replied Cordelia.

Thus the evening wore away, enlivened by the song of Edgar the little page to the Lady Elfrida. His songs were generally of a melancholy cast; framed to suit the mood of his patroness, this evening he was gay, nor was he reproved for it.

> "Brown autumn of their leafy store
> Hath left yon stately trees;
> The ripe corn on the hill no more
> Rustles beneath the breeze;
> The nightengale hath ceased her lay,
> The lark's clear voice is still,
> The squirrel steals the last red nut
> Which hangs beside the rill,

'Tis cheerless in the open glade,
   'Tis cheerless in the grove,
And summer's self would cheerless be,
   Without my own true love.
But 'ere pale winter's dazzling garb
   Shall clothe each lawn and tree,
The halls of Percival shall ring
   With joy and revelry.

For Edward claims his own true love ;
   And all her sorrows past,
A bride she at the altar stands,
   So love is crowned at last.
Then oh ! when gladness cheers the heart
   And joys light up the eye,
We need no sultry summer's breeze
   To bid the moments fly.

The lady sighed, and Cordelia blushed at the conclusion of this song ; the former had been too much accustomed to sorrow to expect joy, and she dreaded Cordelia's journey to London, lest anything should occur to place her again in the power of Mancini.   The Lady de Albini knew not all that had occurred relating to this person ; her son had forborne to acquaint her with the visit of the stranger to Thornbury, for the purpose of searching the grave of De Tunstall ; well   known that the lady having now no stake in the world save himself, might well fear that such atrocious machinations portended evil towards him, nor had he told her of the adventure of Mouthermer respecting the mysterious miniature.   Had Cordelia known these circumstances, she would have been more enlightened as to the course which it would be prudent for her to take, and much of her anxiety respecting the manner in which she expected to be received by Lady Mouthermer would have been alleviated.   As it was, she set forth in ignorance of much that Edward or Roland could have have told her, but she resolved to avoid seeing the Baron de Albina or any one belonging to him until she had exposed the villany of Mancina.

On the following morning Cordelia departed from Percival Castle, and accompanied by Father Anslem and Bridget, took the road to London.   They arrived in the outskirts of the metropolis, and were astonished to hear the bells tolling a muffled peal.   Not being able to imagine what this could mean, they entered a small inn by the road side, and inquiring the cause of the dismal ounds, were informed that Stephen had died a few hours previously.   This intelligence caused Cordelia some dismay, as she feared that Henry might revoke th grant his predecessor had made.   However she did not alarm her companions by any fears that she felt, and the travellers entered London, determined to seek a quiet obscure lodging, where they might remain unnoticed and unsuspected.   They found one without difficulty ; their landlady was a respectable person, whose only failing was a ove of gossip, a failing which Father Anselm prophesied would prove of material service to them.

The metropolis was in a state of great excitement.   The death of Stephen had been long expected, and his successor was ready to ascend the vacant throne without any delay.   Henry was not yet in England, but a day or two must bring him to the kingdom which he had so long coveted, and grief for the late king was much alleviated by curiosity respecting the future sovereign.

Dame Alderton was among the most curious of Henry's future subjects ; the accession of a new king seemed to wholly fill her mind and thoughts ; she could speak of nothing but the grandeur which was expected to attend his entry into London ; and the feastings and merry-makings which would be held in his honour.   Upon this theme she discanted incessantly during the first days of Cordelia's arrival, and much she wondered that the latter took so little interest in her anticipations.   She said she did not expect Fthat ather Anselm should take pleasure in such proceedings, and she thought Bridget too old to do so, but a beautiful young lady like Cordelia ought to appear, and dame Alderton was certain that if she went to court, as she was surely entitled to do, half the young noblemen in the land would fall in love with her. But to all this the lady only listened in silence, occasionally making some inquiry in a careless manner, respecting the noble families of whom her voluble hostess delighted to converse.

After a couple of days rest, which were required by Cordelia, both on account of fatigue of body, and agitation of mind, she thought it necessary to acquaint Bridget with the business which had more immediately brought her to London, and she requested her to accompany her, to call upon the Baroness Mouthermer on the following day.

No. 34.

Bridget started at the name. "Mouthermer! what know you of her?" she asked.

"I have a packet to deliver, which must be given into her hands alone," replied Cordelia.

"From the Lady de Albini, I suppose?" asked Bridget.

"No," replied the maiden, "it came into my hands at Duncraig."

"Duncraig!" exclaimed the woman,

"Yes, it fell from one of the books which were brought to me after——" and she stopped short, remembering that Kate had warned her not to mention what they had seen on that terrible and mysterious night.

"After what? Speak, lady, I pray you," exclaimed Bridget in great agitation.

"I dare not, I cannot tell you, and yet I believe you are my friend," said Cordelia.

The woman made many protestations of sincerity, and at last won upon Cordelia to relate what she had seen.

"Oh, that wicked man!" cried Bridget, "he might have given her Christian burial at least; but she will not rest in her watery grave."

"You knew of it, then?" asked the maiden.

"I did; but believe me, lady, I never consented to it. Frazer and Dennis were the aiders of the count," replied Bridget. "I may revenge her yet!"

"Revenge! whom?" asked Cordelia.

"My lady, my dear lady," cried Bridget. "Oh! I knew her from childhood, and she was an angel till she knew him."

"But she was faithless to him," observed Cordelia.

"She never was his wife," observed Bridget.

Cordelia stared in amazement; she remembered what Kate had told her of her mother's aversion to allude to the earlier events of her life, and although she almost feared offending the old women, she was impelled by an impulse as unaccountable as it was resistless to ask her, "Who then was the countess Mancini?"

Bridget shook her head. "I will never betray my lady, nor wound the feelings of her survivors, unless it be to avenge her wrongs; they were many and bitter and I need not tell you, lady, that your own sufferings are connected with her. But let me see this packet."

Cordelia produced the packet, and shewed the address to Bridget, who exclaimed, "It is hers—it is her own hand-writing! Oh, how mysteriously do events work round!"

"And is the Baroness Mouthermer indeed the daughter of Mancini?" asked Cordelia.

"The daughter of Mancini? Oh, the saints forbid!" cried Bridget.

"Who then is she?" asked the maiden timidly.

Bridget made her no answer for a few minutes; but after a pause in which she seemed to be contending with some strong but secret feelings, she said in a low tone,—

"Lady, I will accompany you to Lady Mouthermer; this visit may be too much for you alone; I will see her myself."

To this Cordelia gladly assented, and it was agreed that they should, on the following day, together seek the residence of the Baron Mouthermer. Accordingly, having received full instructions from dame Alderton, whose gossiping propensity was in this case of great service to them, Cordelia and Bridget sallied forth. The latter had formerly visited London for a few hours, the former had never been there at all, and she was considerably alarmed at the idea of the crowd and bustle which she must encounter. They, however, reached the mansion of Lord Mouthermer in safety.

Upon ringing at the bell, and acquainting the porter with their wish to be admitted to Lady Mouthermer, the man replied that his lady was out of town for a few days. In answer to the inquiry when she was expected to return, the porter said, that he would ask his lordship, who was just going out with the Baron de Albini.

At this Cordelia trembled so much that she could scarcely stand. Was she then under the same roof with him who was dearer to her than her life—for whom she had suffered and wept—and whose continued affection every incident at Percival castle had assured to her? And must she not see him? Might she not tell him by one word, that she was alive and unchanged? For a few minutes her resolution wavered, but she speedily recovered herself, and retreating from the door, she told Bridget to receive the answer to their inquiry. It was fortunate that she had retreated, for the instant after, Ronald crossed the hall, and, seeing Bridget, inquired her business. The old woman told him, and he at once dismissed her, saying that Lady Mouthermer would return to town only in time to receive King Henry on the following day, but that after that time Bridget might see her. The old woman therefore departed, and joining the agitated Cordelia, they set out in return to their lodging.

When they had arrived within a short distance of their home, Bridget recollected that there some purchases which she wanted to make for her lady, and she asked the latter if she thought she could find her way alone to Dame Alderton's house. Cordelia answered in the affirmative, and they separated. In a very crowded street, Cordelia was walking slowly along, threading her way with difficulty through the numbers owh encompassed her, her thoughts dwelling upon scenes far off and days long gone by, when by the sudden dispersion of a small knot of persons who had gathered together, she found herself face to face with a gentleman in whom she instantly recognised the Count Mancini. He was at the first moment looking in another direction, but before she could make herself a passage to pass him, he turned his head, and giving a momentary glance at the lady turned as pale as death. A deep groan escaped him, he tottered, and would have fallen, had not a passer by supported him. Cordelia walked to a short distance out of the sight of Mancini, and awaited quietly the result of this unexpected meeting.

The crowd, ever watchful and curious upon such occasions, reported that the count was in a fit, and he was taken into a shop were every means was resorted to in order to restore him. For a considerable time all efforts were ineffectual, but at length he showed symptoms of returning animation. Gazing wildly around, as if in search of some dreaded object, he muttered, " Is she gone ?"

" Who does he mean ?" asked those who were tending him.

" It was her ghost ! she cannot hurt me !" he exclaimed again.

" Poor man ! he is mad," cried one.

" Hold him !" said another.

" Better call a constable, he is only drunk," said a third.

But Mancini shaking them all from him, rose up and looking round, asked where he was.

The master of the shop then came forward and offered to assist him to walk home, but the count was much too weak for this, and requested leave to wait till his strength was a little recruited. Meanwhile the report spread that the gentleman had beheld an apparition, of his deceased wife probably, whom he had perhaps murdered, and as this random guess passed from one to another, the fact became indisputable that it was so, and the crowed moved away, each enlarging upon the tale which he had heard.

While this was passing, Cordelia having ascertained by stealth that Mancini had nearly recovered, renewed her walk homewards; and reached her lodgings just as Bridget, alarmed at not finding her there when she returned, was about to set forth in order to meet her. Cordelia related her adventure, and expressed her horror at meeting with the count.

" He evidently believes you dead," observed Bridget.

" Yes, what he said when he first came to his senses shows that he does, and none of the persons around had any idea that I was concerned in his fit," replied Cordelia.

" Therefore he will not endeavour to trace you," said Bridget. " How fortunate that I was not with yon ; he would have known then that you were not a spirit."

" But I much fear," said the lady, " that the count will act upon the belief of my death, and endeavour to obtain my rights. However we shall hear of any such proceedings in time to stop them."

" Surely it would be well, lady, to consult the Baron de Albini," observed Bridget.

" By no means : never shall Edward know of my existence till I can present myself the lawful heiress and acknowledged child of De Dunstanville. Sooner would I go down to Thornbury, and there linger out the remainder of my days in seclusion and ignorance, than enter the house of De Albini unhonoured and unportioned."

" Will you not then tell the Lady Mouthermer who you are ?" asked the old woman.

" No—it concerns not her. The packet I will deliver safely, but I do no more," replied Cordelia.

" And what tale will you then tell her ?" asked Bridget.

" I have no tale ; I merely deliver the letter," replied the lady.

Bridget mused for a few minutes, and then said,—

" Nor shall my tongue betray to the knowledge of the innocent the crime of the guilty. Lady, you are right. The guilty must be punished at last, but not through the sufferings of the guiltless."

" I do not understand your thoughts, Bridget, and therefore forgive me if I ask you to promise that you will not by look or by word in any way betray your knowledge of my history, and above all that Count Mancini shall not be alluded to by you."

" Most willingly do I promise, lady, to be guided by you in all that I am to do or say; something holy attends your steps and guides you to the right path. Let me but attend you to the Lady Mouthermer—let me but look upon her face once more, and I will not even open my lips."

" Once more ! what do you mean, Bridget? Have you ever then seen the lady ?" asked Cordelia eagerly.

" I have, lady, and I would again behold her ; ask no more," replied Bridget.

In the evening dame Alderton entered the room as Cordelia was sitting by the fire, musing on her position and duties, saying in a tone of high joy,

" Great news, lady ! great news !"

" What mean you ?" asked Cordelia, almost hoping that the great news might be good news to her.

" Our new king enters London to-morrow," exclaimed the dame.

Cordelia was disappointed, and shewed her feelings in her looks so plainly that the good woman added,

" Is not that grand news, lady ?"

" I am glad to hear it," said Cordelia.

" But will you not go and see the grand procession ?" asked the dame.

" I know not where to go to see it ; and I am not inclined to encounter a crowd," she replied.

" You need not be uneasy about that," answered the dame ; " I have a friend who has a cousin who lives where the sight must pass, and if you and Mrs. Bridget like to go with me, we will ask her to take us."

At first Cordelia refused this, but considering that she could not be recognised in such a situation and in such company, she yielded to the temptation of seeing Edward de Albini, whom she had no doubt would be in the royal train. Her heart beat with joy at the thought of again beholding that beloved face, and of tracing in its well remembered lineaments the marks of sorrow for her supposed fate. But could she trust herself? could she submit patiently to see him pass without even a look of recognition ? Perhaps she would not have dared to encounter this had she been with companions who were acquainted with the Baron de Albini ; but in the present case she had hoped she might gaze on him without earing an other voice pronounce his name or notice his demeanour,

Under the influence of these thoughts Cordelia accepted the proposal of Dame Alderton, and Father Anselm having agreed to accompany them, they proceeded to the house mentioned by their hostess, in time to see the procession pass. Bridget loved sights and novelty, and she was rather curious to see Lord Mouthermer, who the dame assured her was certain to be the foremost in the array.

We have said nothing about the matter in which Father Auslem employed his time in London, but he had not been idle. He had, by desire of Cordelia, consulted a trustworthy advocate, who strongly advised that no public claim should be made by the lady until Mancini should have produced the required evidence of her death. In doing this the history of her imprisonment must be revealed by him, and he must convict himself of felony. The advocate then advised that Cordelia should appear and confront the count. In the meanwhile it was imperative that the lady should remain concealed, or at least unknown, till the proper moment should arrive for discovering herself. The advocate promised to watch the proceedings of the count, and in case of any unforeseen event to enter such a remonstrance as would at least compel a delay in the decision of the king.

On their arrival at the house they found it crowded with persons eager to see the sight, and at first Cordelia feared that it would be impossible for her to obtain a place near enough to the window to see him whose image filled her mind; but there was an air of nobility around her which at once convinced her beholders of her natural rank, although veiled in a plain dress of deep mourning. Her extreme beauty too won every heart, and the occupants of the window, without making any observation, drew back respectfully, and left her almost alone. This, however, Cordelia did not like, as it exposed her too much to the observation which she so much wished to avoid, and requesting Father Anselm to come near her, she retreated behind a young girl, over whose shoulder she might see the only one whom she cared for in the world.

After a considerable time had elapsed, the sound of the trumpets gave notice of the king's approach. Every eye was strained, every head bent forward, to catch the first view of their new monarch; every heart beat with anticipation—and one there was which beat almost to agony. At length the first horseman appeared, and soon after a fine band of music. Then followed a number of nobles richly dressed, and mounted on splendid horses, caparisoned and ornamented in as splendid a manner as their riders. Among the latter Cordelia looked in vain for her Edward; the persons around her named many of those who passed, and she found that they were the inferior nobility. Presently a loud shout of applause rent the and announced the approach of king Henry, who rode a magnificent charger, and looked well pleased with the acclamations which greeted him. Two young pages held his horse's rein, and others walked by his side. Immediately following the monarch rode two persons, the contrast, in whose dress irresistibly attracted the attention. The one was evidently an ecclesiastic, and was habited in the dress of a foreign order; he looked as if he had passed middle age, but war and time seemed to have done their work more completely than his age warranted. A martial air still pervaded his demeanour, while a stern and deep expression sat upon his brow which told of other conflicts than those of the field.

By his side was a gentleman also in a foreign costume, but it was the costume of a court; he too was advanced in years, but the glow of benevolence which overspread his yet handsome features, and exhilirating smile which animated them, as his sovereign, turning round, addressed to him some observation upon the scene, told that the spirit was still young.

As these noblemen passed, a single word escaped Bridget,

"My master!" she whispered; no one heard her, save Cordelia, all the rest of the party were loud in the inquiry as to the companion of De Rosenberg, for he it was whose smile spoke of a heart not hardened nor benumbed by worldy prosperity.

"Who is he?" was eagerly asked on all sides,

"I know not, I know not," was as universally repeated.

"What a splendid dress! What a noble air! What a martial bearing! How loldtlly his horse curves his neck, and how proudly his master checks him!"

All these expressions passed among her companions, but Cordelia heeded not the subject of them, till father Anselm spoke.

"He wears the dress of a Knight Templar," observed he.

"I have heard that king Henry has one of that order much with him," said a lady. "He is an Englishman, but has been much in the Holy Land. I have heard his name, but do not now remember it; I dare say this is he."

"Very probably," returned the father; "but can you not think of his name?"

"It was something like De Resley," replied the lady; "but that is not precisely the name."

The father looked at Cordelia anxiously, and seeing that she was too much absorbed in contemplation to notice the conversation which had taken place, he said quietly to the lady,—

"It is of no consequence, madam, but I dare say you are right."

Father Anselm knew well who it was that had just passed; the name which he had just heard recalled it to his memory; but he thought it advisable that Cordelia should not, in that place, hear of the return to England of Robert de Hesling. He therefore made some casual observation respecting the pageant, and the Knight Templar was immediately forgotten by all but himself.

Bridget had watched de Rosenberg till he was out of sight, and was still thinking of him when one of her neighbours exclaimed,—

"Oh! there is Lord Mouthermer, how handsome he is!"

Bridget and Cordelia were immediately recalled to the passing scene by this exclamation, and agreed with the speaker; but what was Cordelia's agitation when her eyes fell upon the pair of noblemen who immediately followed Mouthermer; they were the Baron de Mowbray and the Baron de Albini. Gazing with tearful eyes and a breaking heart, she drank in happiness at the sight, although in another, Edward might have been an object of pity. Both the young men were dressed in mourning; Eustace retained the happy aspect of careless youth, but Edward wore a brow of care."

"Who are those following Lord Mouthermer?" asked Bridget.

"One is the Baron de Mowbray," replied a lady; "but I do not know who his melancholy-looking companion is."

"It is the young Baron de Albini, his brother-in-law," observed another.

"I never saw him before, is he often at court?" asked the first speaker.

"No," was the reply. "His is a strange tale, too long to tell now; but his father is but just dead, and he resides with his widowed mother in the country. Some mystery hangs over him, and it is said that he has refused several noble offers on account of a lady who is dead."

"He looks melancholy indeed," replied the other lady.

"The Baron de Albini left a noble inheritance, but instead of spending it in equipages and splendour, as some do, the Count Mancini, for instance," continued the lady who had spoken of Edward, "the young lord gives it almost entirely away in charity; and he is, as you may imagine, adored by all the country round."

Cordelia listened with exquisite pleasure to this character of her lover, and she lost all pleasure in looking upon the scene before her. The mention of the count had raised her curiosity, and upon a hint to Bridget the latter asked what character Mancini bore about the court. The person whom she addressed shook her head, and said that the count was very eccentric and extravagant, that it had been reported that he had spent all his money, but that he was now come to a large fortune by the death of a relative, and that it was supposed that he would go back to Italy, as England did not agree with him.

"It is said, however," observed the lady, "that he does not bear his right name, and there are suspicious circumstances about him as to his wife. It is said too, that the new king knows something bad of him, however this may only idle talk."

When the procession had entirely passed, and the bustle was somwhat over Cordelia returned to her lodging, wearied in body but refreshed in mind. She had seen her lover.

CHAPTER XLI.

Yet now to sadness let me yield the hour—
Yes, let the tears of purest friendship shower.
I view, alas! what ne'er should die,
A form that wakes my deepest sigh,
A form that feels of death the leaden sleep,
Descending to the realms of shade,
I view a pale-eyed panting maid,
I see the virtues o'er their favourite weep.—PINDAR.

AFTER the procession had conducted the monarch to his palace, the nobles who had attended him separated to their residences, and Edward de Albini repaired to that of his friend Mouthermer, accompanied by Ronald, who had followed at the end of the procession with other attendants. When De Albini entered the house, his attendant requested to speak with him on business of importance. Edward hesitated, reminding Ronald that he was wished to join the company in the saloon in order to meet Count Rosenberg. But the dwarf was so importunate that Edward at last consented to be detained for a short time.

"What have you to say to me, Ronald?" asked Edward.

"I think I have seen a person who is extremely interesting to your lordship," replied the dwarf.

"Who do you mean?" asked his master impatiently.

"I saw a lady so like the Lady Cordelia that I think it must have been her spirit," observed Ronald.

"Nonsense, nonsense," replied the baron. "Tell me what thou meanest?"

"At a window which we passed there was one so like her, but paler and thinner in face; I scarce caught a glimpse of her, as she was in a crowd, but she was so like her that I was quite awe-struck, and if Lady Cordelia be not dead I am sure it was she," said Ronald.

"Alas!" cried Edward, "we know her fate too surely; for to-morrow this Count Mancini is to produce the evidence of her death before the king."

"The count may be mistaken," said Ronald, doubtingly.

"No, Ronald, it cannot be, deceive me not with false hopes which cannot be realised," said Edward, deeply sighing.

"I know more of this count than I like, and I may foil him yet," replied Ronald.

"I fear him, although I like him not. But who was this lady with!" asked Edward.

"I do not know but I can readily find the house at which I saw her. Shall I make inquiry there?" asked Ronald.

"It is useless," replied De Albini. "But you may do so if you please."

'I will go this very evening, my lord, and I trust I may bring you a good report of my success," said the dwarf as he left the room.

"Alas!" said Edward to himself, "what a strange life is mine! Doomed to this ever-gnawing grief for one whose fate must ever remain in mystery—one who has passed from the earth which she was so formed to adorn, and not even the solace allowed to me of weeping over her tomb. Could I but know where her pale ashes are laid, there would I take refuge—there would I pour forth the useless vows of a broken heart—there would I weep until my spirit should flee away and be at rest, seeking her in a purer atmosphere, in a brighter scene. But now—I have still one tie to earth, my mother! And Edith! No; she is happy in her Eustace—she shall never be troubled with my grief. Even now, I must disguise my feeling and join in scenes of revelry and joy, for I am but ill prepared but Mouthermer loves me, and understands me, and I may not in gratitude refuse to attend the ball given this evenng, in commemoration of our monarch's accession, by his lovely wife. Long may they enjoy their happiness nnclouded,

With these thoughts Edward de Albini repaired to the saloon of Lady Mouthermer, where was assembled much of the beauty and nobility of the land. The lady herself was the star of the surrounding throng. Exquisitely beautiful, and adorned with all that could enhance her beauty, she moved with a dignity and grace accorded only to patrician beauty. On this evening her costume was especially chosen to honour the beloved parent who was a stranger in the land! and she wore the dress of a German Baroness, her native dignity. Diamonds shone upon her fair tresses, diamonds studded her sleeves and glittered around her waist, while her fair throat was ornamented solely by a black ribbon, to which was appended an ornament which was hidden by the drapery of her vest. Every eye followed her, every heart admired her, every tongue praised her! even Edward was constrained to acknowledge to himself that he had seen but one more beautiful.

When Edward entered the saloon, he was immediately introduced to Count Rosenberg, and listened with amusement to an animated discussion which was carrying on between the count and some English nobleman upon political topics. When this was ended the count took Edward's arm, saying that he would saunter round the rooms with him, as there were many persons present whom he wished to have pointed out to him. Edward expressed his ignorance of the great world, and said that he feared he should prove but au useless pilot, but De Rosenberg evidently wishing to make his acquaintance, the youth led the way to the upper end of the room.

As they passed a low couch which was placed in a recess, partly shaded by a curtain, the silver voice of Lady Mouthermer arrested them by saying,—

" My father !"

" My child, what makes you here ?" asked the count.

"I am somewhat fatigued, and I retired for a few minutes of repose," she answered.

" I will not betray you," said De Rosenberg, moving on.

" Nay, stay here with me a few minutes, I must presently resume my place of state," observed the lady.

" We were moving round the rooms in order to see many persons of whom I have heard abroad, but whom I have never seen," replied her father.

" Sit here with me they will pass, and I shall have your company at the same time," said Lady Mouthermer.

The count sat down, and Edward was moving away when De Rosenberg expressed a wish that he should not leave them, and he took a seat accoringly Much conversation ensued upon the various guests ; characters and dresses were discussed, and the count expressed his admiration of the costume chosen by his daughter for that evening.

" I wear it to compliment my dear father," she replied tenderly,

" But I like not that black ribbon; why not have worn your diamond necklace ?"

" I wished also to compliment you even by this ribbon, no ornament can be so valuable in my eyes as the one which is attached to this band," said the lady, drawing out a miniure splendidly set in brilliants.

The count looked at it, and started back.

" My child ! where got you that picture ?" he cried in a tone of excitement.

" My lord met with it by chance," replied the lady, " and presented it to me but this morning. It must have been very like ; was it not ?"

The count made no answer, he seemed completely bewildered ; the ball room— the company—his daughter— all had faded before his eyes ; and memory painted to him years long gone by ; scenes long vanished from his mind. In this manner he sat for some minutes, looking about him with an abstracted air. till Lady Mouthermer said,—

"My dearest father, I have pained you ; and much I fear that this picture is linked with remembrances which I ought not to have awakened."

"It is, my child," replied the count, "but I ask only where did Mouthermer procure it ?"

"From a common jeweller's shop, I believe," she replied; "it was for sale there."

This was all that the lady knew about the miniature ; her lord had not told her of his visit to Mancini, as he feared hurting her feelings.

"I must trace it out directly," said De Rosenberg. "I will seek Mouthermer; you know not, my child, of how much interest this picture is to me ; it was my

No. 35.

first gift to your mother in the days of our happiness, and she promised to part with it but with life. Forgive my emotion, I will return shortly.

So saying, De Rosenberg was leaving the recess, when Edward said in a low voice, " I can tell you all, my lord, but not here ; let us seek a private room."

The count seemed astonished and incredulous, and still expressed his intention of asking an explanation of the Baron Mouthermer.

" I was with the baron when he negotiated for and purchased this picture," said Edward ; "Lord Mouthermer forbore to tell his lady the circumstances, lest it should hurt her feelings, to know in whose hands the picture had been."

" Do you—does he know then ? " exclaimed the count.

" We do," replied Edward, leading the way to a small room which Mouthermer had kindly appropriated solely to his use ; and shutting the door he invited the count to be seated. But the latter was in too much agitation to heed him and pacing up and down the room, he said in a tone of suppressed agony,—

" I had hoped that the secret had been buried with me ; but oh ! let not my child know it."

Edward could not answer, not knowing to what his companion alluded.

" Tell me ! where is the villian ? " cried the count.

" Mean you the person of whom we procured the picture ? " said Edward.

" Yes—the robber, the traitor," cried De Rosenberg.

" I believe he is in London," replied his companion.

" Let me seek him immediately," cried the count.

" Would it not be well to take certain steps to apprehend him as a felon ? " asked Edward. " He is powerful, and surrounded by his household : it were better to use the law."

" The law ? what mean you ? " asked the count.

" If you have any proof of the theft, it were best to be cautious," replied De Albini. " I am not surprised at the accusation, and my own hopes, or rather fears, are so bound up in his, that I would willingly aid in his detection."

" You ? " cried De Mowbray, stopping and gazing earnestly upon Edward.

" I know not what binds us," answered the youth, " but there are occurrences."

" What ! has the serpent crossed your path also ? " exclaimed the count. " But tell me by what accident you met with this trinket, and does she live ? "

" Lord Mouthermer purchased it of the Count Mancini, and if he stole it from you—as you intimate,——"

" Mancini ? I know not that name," interrupted the count.

" Then it must have come through other hands," observed Edward.

" It was obtained from her, let it have been in whose hands it may," said his companion. " But who is this Count Mancini, that you suspect him of theft ? "

" Nay, my lord, I repent me of that expression," replied De Albini ; " I was led to it by your remarks as to the picture being stolen from you."

" Not stolen by him," observed De Rosenberg.

" By whom then ? " asked Edward.

" You said you knew my history. Oh ! ask me not then," cried his agitated companion.

Edward now knew not what to answer ; he saw there was some mystery, some misunderstandrng between himself and De Rosenberg, and he could not clear it up.

" I would ascertain how this count became possessed of the picture," said the count.

" I would accompany you to his house, but—" and Edward hesitated.

" Nay, my young friend, I ask not that. Mouthermer will introduce me, I doubt not," observed his companion.

" Not to-night, will you ? " asked Edward.

" No ; I am unequal to the task to-night," replied De Rosenberg. " That picture has recalled to my heart days of happiness, of peace too bright for earth, and I am afraid I might act unworthily were I to attempt any exertion to-night."

" You will return to the saloon, I trust ? " asked Edward.

" I am almost unable," was the reply.

" Lady Mouthermer will be uneasy," observed De Albini.

" You must make an excuse for me," said the count.

" Excuse me, my lord, if it be but for a short time ; many surmises will be made as to the cause of your absence," said Edward respectfully.

" You are right, my young friend," said the count taking his arm. " I will control myself, and join the gay throng."

So saying the count and Edward proceeded to the saloon, where they found Lord Mouthermer inquiring of every one whether they had seen the absentees, but without success. He was therefore greatly relieved when he saw them enter the apartment, and going up to the count, he said,

" Lady Mouthermer told me you were seeking me, and the cause of it; I am truly sorry that any occurrence should have pained you to-night. But I hope the Baron de Albini has explained the matter to you."

" He has partly," replied De Rosenberg. " But I must request you to accompany me to the residence of this count to-morrow morning, that I may inquire the means by which he obtained the treasure."

" He told me that it fell by accident into his possession while in Italy," replied Mouthermer, " and that not knowing whose portrait it was, he did not value it."

" Then my hopes are vain, and inquiry is useless," said the count.

" Not so, I think," replied his son-in-law. " Our call may bring to his memory some facts relating to the picture which may lead to our enlightenment."

" It is scarcely likely that the Count Mancini or any other nobleman should possess a trinket of this kind without knowing how he came by it," said Edward.

" You must not judge hardly of Mancini in this case, Edward," said his friend, " although you may have personal vexation against him."

" Indeed, Mouthermer," said Edward as De Rosenberg left them. " I like not any of Mancini's proceedings ; he is not honest in any case."

" We shall see to-morrow. Believe me, the king will require very complete proof," observed Mouthermer.

Edward did not tell his friend of the assertion of Ronald ; he had confidence in it himself, and he gave way to the dwarf's humour, more from a wish not to appear to distrust him than from any expectation of good to arise from his inquiries.

When the Count de Rosenberg returned to his daughter, he found her in the place where he had left her, alone, and anxious. She arose to meet him with an expression of sympathy and sorrow for her incautiousness.

" Blame not yourself, my child," he replied ; " but treasure this portrait for my sake and hers, who was once beautiful and beloved as thyself."

" Have you seen Mouthermer ?" asked the lady.

" I have ; and from his account I do not think it worth while to prosecute any inquiries about the picture," replied De Rosenberg.

" Will you then escort me to the head of the room ; I am proud of my father ; and there are many here to whom I would introduce him," said the lady, leading him from the recess, and joining in the crowd.

The evening passed off brilliantly and gaily. The slight cloud on the brow of the hostess was attributed to fatigue of body, and her guests retired full of the praises of her beauty and grace, and of the noble mien and courtly manners of the baron. Edward had early left the gay assembly in order to hear the result of Ronald's expedition, and he found the faithful dwarf waiting for him in his room. In answer to the inquiries of the baron, Ronald shook his head.

" I feared this," said the baron; " have you heard no tidings ?"

" I went to the house where I saw the lady whom I mentioned, and I inquired who the lady was, but the person who belonged to the house could give me no information as to her name or station ; she merely knew that the lady came with an old woman and a monk ; but more she could not tell."

" Could she not tell the name of the woman who accompanied her ?" asked the baron.

"No," replied Ronald, "the party came with some other persons and nothing was said as to their names and rank.

"What was it? oh tell me!" cried Edward eagerly.

"As the Baron de Rosenberg passed, the old woman was heard to whisper, "My master!" replied the dwarf.

"What could that mean?" exclaimed De Albini. Then, after musing awhile, "There is an inexplicable link beeween the Count Mancini and the Count Rosenberg which I cannot understand, and which, I fear, is connected with some painful objects or remembrances. Time must unravel the mystery, and should it bring forth any tidings of my lost Cordelia, happiness may even yet be within my grasp."

"Oh! my lord, despair not," cried Ronald. "I have a strong feeling of hope."

"Meanwhile, Ronald," said his master, "let not a word escape you of this matter. We may keep our eyes and ears open, but our mouths must be shut. I would not vex my noble friend Mouthermer."

Ronald promised obedience and left his master, who, but little inclined to rest, sat by the fireside pondering upon the slight intelligence which his faithful emissary had brought him. Edward had long ago ceased to hope, and consequently was not disappointed at what he considered the failure of Ronald's attempt; still there was enough of interest in it to awaken his curiosity. The ensuing morning was to him one of peculiar anxiety; for then Mancini was to produce before the king the proofs of Cordelia's death, in order to be acknowledged the heir to her lands and title. Mouthermer earnestly desired that his friend should not be present on this occasion; and to ensure this he had engaged De Albini to accompany the Count Rosenberg to Windsor, for the purpose of passing a few days there.

For some hours Edward de Albini remained buried in thought till towards day-break, when the faithful Ronald having heard that his master had not retired to rest, gently tapped at the door, reminding De Albini that the horses were ordered to be in readiness early the next morning, ventured to remonstrate with him on the imprudence of not seeking the rest which was necessary to him.

Edward acknowledged the prudential advice of the faithful dwarf, and retired to his room to repose. Sleep soon visited his couch, and he awoke refreshed on the following morning. At the appointted time the Count Rosenberg and De Albini left London for Windsor.

CHAPTER XLII.

Man! that through the crowded city
   Passest in thy prime,
Doling forth superfluous pity
   To the sons of Time;
Thou, whose half of life is wasted,
   Unredeemed thy vow;
Religion's waters scarcely tasted,—
   Man! how old art thou?
And the man replied abstractedly,
In a voice that sounded remorsefully:—

"Oh! ask me not, the days are past,
That I vainly thought for aye would last!
The plans that I form'd in early years
Have brought to me only griefs and tears;
And those whom in youth I did most despise
Have been lifted up in the nation's eyes;
Whilst unimproved, the powerful sway
Of my forty summers hath passed away!"—Anon.

THE morning came, eventful to Cordelia, and she prepared for her intended visit to Lady Mouthermer. Bridget seemed to be in a state of restless, uneasy feverishness, and Cordelia proposed that she should remain at home instead of accompanying her to Mouthermer-house; but the old woman was almost angry at the suggestion, and prepared to accompany her lady. They accordingly set out, and on their arrival at Mouthermer-house were told that the lady had not yet risen, but that if they would wait for a short time they should be admitted to her presence as soon as she came down to breakfast. They were ushered into a small room where everything recalled to Cordelia the happy days gone by.

The first thing which struck her on entering was a favourite spaniel who lay fast asleep upon a mat. The noise made by the servant in stirring the fire and placing seats for the guests awakened the dog, who started up, and seeing Bridget begun to bark loudly. But in a moment his angry bark was changed to a joyful whine, for recognising Cordelia, he jumped upon her lap, licking her hands and giving every demonstration of glad recognition.

"Poor Diamond," said Cordelia, bending over him, while tears filled her eyes.

The servant who attended them stood at first in mute surprise, then looking earnestly at Cordelia, he said,—

"My lady, then, is a friend of the Baron de Albini?"

"I am slightly acquainted with him," was the reply.

"It is unfortunate that the baron has this very morning gone with Count Rosenberg to Windsor to pass a few days there," said the man.

"The baron is well, I hope?" said Bridget.

"Pretty well," replied the man; less in awe of the old woman than of her lady, and glad to have some one to whom he might display his importance. "But a cause is to be brought before the king to-day, which is somewhat interesting to his lordship, and my master thought it would agitate him too much were he to be present, he is therefore gone to Windsor, and the dwarf Ronald attends him."

Cordelia started at these words. Ronald then, her faithful, although humble friend was with her lover; she could not now doubt that her memory was cherished fondly if hopelessly by both, and she somewhat regretted that Edward would not be present at the impending inquiry.

As soon as the servant had left the apartment, Cordelia sought among the various articles before her for tokens of her Edward's presence, and she found many. There were books, writing materials, articles of fancy and ornament; and among the latter a small ivory paper knife which had belonged to her, and which she had many months, nay years, ago, given to the prisoner in the Lady's Tower. This she kissed fervently, and placing it in her bosom, declared that it should remain there until she could herself again present it to her lover. In its place she left a small seal which she had constantly used in her correspondence with him.

After waiting some time, Cordelia and her attendant were summoned to the presence of Lady Mouthermer, whom they found reclining upon a couch, evidently ill in body and harrassed in mind. Bridget was much shocked at her appearance, and an involuntary exclamation of, "Poor lady!" burst from her.

"I fear we have intruded upon your ladyship at an unseasonable moment," said Cordelia, "Your Ladyship appears ill."

"I am suffering this morning, I acknowledge," replied Lady Mouthermer; "and I trust that your business is not of so important a nature or of such length as to cause any increase to my ailment; if it be, I must beg that it may be deferred to another day."

Bridget and Cordelia looked at each other for a moment, and the latter whispered," What shall we do?"

"It must be finished now," replied Bridget; "but in mercy to her in as few words as possible."

Cordelia bowed her head in acquiescence, and stepping forward she drew forth her packet, which she respectfully presented to Lady Mouthermer. As the latter took it her eyes fell upon the superscription, and she exclaimed. "More mystery! How came this to your hand, lady?"

"By accident, lady," replied Cordelia.

" Then was it not given to you by her own blessed hand ?" asked Lady Mouthermer.

" Oh ! do you indeed love your mother's memory ?" cried Bridget unguardedly.

" I am not accustomed to speak of my family to strangers," replied Lady Mouthermer in a tone of rather haughty reserve. " But something tells me that I am speaking to friends at this moment. I never knew my mother, she died while I was yet an infant ; but my bereaved father taught me to revere her as a being almost too good for this earth. Judge then with what feelings I recognise her hand-writing."

" Cherish those feelings," exclaimed Bridget, " and may your fate be happier than hers."

" But," said the lady, " what am I to tell my father of this packet ? How came it to you ? and when ?"

" I entreat your ladyship to ask me no questions ; the answer would be even more painful to yourself than to me," said Cordelia. " Accident—mere accident—caused it to fall into my hands—it was not given to me by any one ; but having heard of Lady Mouthermer I resolved to deliver it myself."

" And to whom am I thus indebted ? You will not refuse me your name and address,'" said the lady.

With a respectful inclination of the head Cordelia answered, " It must be so at present. The time may speedily arrive when I may claim a name worthy of your ladyship's notice."

" Nay—nay—think me not so haughty as to refuse my gratitude because there may be a difference of rank between us," replied Lady Mouthermer.

Cordelia's brow was flushed with crimson at these words. " I said that I might shortly claim the notice of Lady Mouthermer ; when I do, it will be as an equal, at least," she said proudly.

Lady Mouthermer was astonished ; and vexed at having given pain, she said,—

" Believe me, lady, for such I am sure you are, I meant to give no offence. But I should be more satisfied did I know my benefactor."

" It cannot be at present," was all that Cordelia could reply. She would have sacrificed much to obtain the liberty of throwing herself into Lady Mouthermer's arms, and of confessing to her the whole history of her melancholy imprisonment. But a glance at Bridget recalled her to the remembrance of what the packet might contain, and she restrained her feelings, ardent though they were. She was about to take a respectful, but proud leave of the lady, when Bridget said, addressing Lady Mouthermer,—

" An aged woman like me, has seen much in a long and active life, and a word may save the young from misery. May I say that word, lady ?"

" Speak," was the rather impatient reply.

" I would counsel you not to mention that packet to any one, not even to your nearest and dearest, not even to Count Rosenberg or Baron Mouthermer, until in silence and seclusion you have read every word of that packet. Its contents may wound you, they must distress you, and I would not that my master—my lord count," said Bridget, correcting herself, " should know of its existence but with a caution, which you alone can exercise towards him."

Thus speaking, Bridget made a low obeisance to the lady, and the strangers left the apartment, leaving Lady Mouthermer overwhelmed with agitation and wonder.

She took up the mysterious packet, read the superscription again and again, attempted to break the seal, but her hand trembled so much that it was almost powerless to do its office, and she threw herself back on the couch exhausted. There was an instinctive dread on her mind which seemed to counterbalance her feeling of curiosity ; the words of Bridget rung in her ears, and the distressing scene of the previous evening was before her eyes. She dreaded to read the paper, yet she longed to know the worst, and she resolved to gather courage for the task. Upon ringing a small silver bell which lay by her side, a page, gaily apparelled in silver and green, entered the apartment.

" Bertie, I would be undisturbed, until I ring my bell," said the lady, " see that no one be admitted.'"

The page promised obedience and left the room ; while Lady Mouthermer with a trembling hand broke the seal of the packet. The first object which met her eye was a plain gold ring, which she at once guessed to have been her mother's wedding ring. There was also a very small locket containing a minute braid of hair, which the lady recognised as much resembling her own. Having laid them aside, she opened a letter directed to herself, the contents of which rivetted her attention. For upwards of an hour did she study this mysterious and mournful communication ; tears coursed each other down her pale face as Lady Mouthermer gazed upon the last words of her beloved parent. She read again and again the fatal words which wounded her very soul, and having almost learned them by rote, the thought struck her, " I have a husband !"

But the remembrance brought with it no joy to her bosom ; it was the first pang which her happy marriage had given to Lady Mouthermer, and she felt that it was almost overwhelming. Yet the mystery must be cleared up, and to apply to her father was entirely out of the question. She at length resolved to bury for the present in her own breast the contents of the awful packet, until some favourable opportunity should occur for disclosing them gradually to her beloved husband.

Meanwhile Cordelia and her attendant returned home, rejoiced that this important and much-dreaded interview was over. Bridget's tongue was voluble in praise of the beauty and elegance of Mouthermer, while Cordelia was absorbed in the remembrance of Edward.

Thus passed the day to the persons to whom our story relates. In the evening Lady Mouthermer became more composed, and received her lord most gladly on his return from the court, where he had been present at the intended decision of Mancini's claim to the estates of De Dunstanville. But the decision had been delayed by circumstances most unforeseen to all parties, and Lord Mouthermer returned home, agitated and anxious, by the events of the day. The events he at once recounted to his wife.

The new monarch, anxious to assume the duties of his station, and aware how much it was his policy to do so, had appointed the contending parties to meet in his presence, and accordingly Macini attended in the presence chamber accompanied by Frazer. It was not without considerable apprehension that the count appeared before his king ; there were feelings which he scarcely avowed to himself, and which he certainly would not have disclosed to any human being; these feelings were the stronger for having been so carefully controlled—to overcome these was impossible. Mancini knew there was one whose eye he dared not meet, and not until his trusty emissary, Frazer, had ascertained that there was no danger of such meeting, did the count overcome his reluctance to appear before the king in person. Armed as he was with what he considered incontestible evidence of the death of her who had stood between him and fortune, wealth and rank, he could not fear that the ultimate decision of the king would be given against him ; but there were queries, there were surmises, there were insinuations, which Mancini was well aware he could not and dared not to meet, and when Frazer reminded him that the dreaded hour had arrived, he turned to his attendant with an expression of apprehension which the latter was equally surprised and alarmed to behold.

" What mean you, my lord ?" asked Frazer.

" I know not what ails me, Frazer, but I own I dread this investigation," replied his master.

" Fear not, my lord," cried Frazer. " Have we not full and perfect proof which no one can deny ? Did 1 not see her myself, when father Anselm declared she had not an hour to live ?"

" True—true—it is mere weakness," repied Mancini. " Yet my presentiments of evil are rarely false."

" Rely upon my aid," answered Frazer.

"Let me but obtain these rich lands, and I bid adieu to England for ever;" said Mancini, as they proceeded to the palace.

In the audience chamber, upon a stately throne, was seated King Henry behind him were placed several peers of the realm, and some foreign noble men, and on the opposite side of the chamber were assembled many others, whom curiosity or interest had attracted to the scene.

Henry was of noble presence, and in person and general demeanour well calculated to awe and govern; the nobility were prepared to respect and uphold him, and the cause about to be tried was looked forward to with considerable interest by all ranks, as affording an opportunity of judging of the king's penetration of judgment.

As Mancini entered the hall every eye was turned upon him, and a whisper ran through the crowd assembled; while his own eye was anxiously scanning the nobles who surrounded King Henry. His rapid and searching glance speedily assumed more composure, as he saw that the object whom he dreaded was not in the presence, and he felt his mind relieved of one fear. Gradually his other fears became weaker, and faded beneath the certainty which Frazer had bound himself to demonstrate; so that by the time he was called upon to state his claim, he had acquired his usual self-possession.

The inquiry was made by order of the king,—

"Who is it that lays claim to the titles, lands, and other wealth of the Baron de Dunstanville?"

Mancini answered in a haughty and determined tone,—

"I, the Count Mancini, the nearest relative and next heir of the Lady Cordelia de Dunstanville, now deceased."

"How know you that the Lady Cordelia is no more?" asked a voice.

"Before I answer the question I must know who it is that asks it?" replied the count.

"The proofs must be produced," said the king.

"They are ready, may it please your majesty; and are so decisive that no one can gainsay them," answered Mancini.

"We will ourselves judge their sufficiency," said the king. "Produce them."

Upon this, Frazer stepping forward, said, "I was an attendant upon the Lady Cordelia de Dunstanville in her dying illness."

"And will you swear to her death?" asked the same voice that had before spoken.

Frazer hesitated, and the king, addressing Mancini, said

"To you, my lord, I appeal; will you swear to the lady's death."

"I was at a distance from home, please your majesty, when the lady was suddenly seized with a dangerous illness; this person," said Mancini, pointing to Frazer "immediately set out in quest of me, but I arrived not in time."

"Is this the proof of her death, your majesty?" asked the voice, while a murmur of approbation ran round the court.

"Peace—peace—" cried the king. "And you," asked he, turning to Frazer, "were you then not present at her death?"

Frazer bowed his head, adding, "By the lady's desire I summoned a confessor to her and he declared that she had not an hour to live."

"Is the confessor present? let him come forward," said the strange voice.

"Unfortunately the monk was obliged to leave his convent upon a mission of importance, immediately after the death and burial of Lady Cordelia," said Mancini, "or I would have brought him here. I visited the monastery, where she was by my order buried, and ascertained that the funeral had been conducted with due honour to her rank and descent, although in private."

"You visited her tomb?" asked the voice.

"I do not say that; the prior refused me admittance to the cemetery," replied Mancini in a tone of chagrin.

"Refused admittance! how is this!" cried the king, somewhat angrily. "I understand not your English customs—explain this."

"Did not you desire to re-open the grave, in order to ascertain whether the lady had died a natural death? And was not that the cause of the prior's refusal?" asked the voice.

"I acknowledge it; and surely as the nearest relative to the deceased I had a right to ascertain that there had been no foul play," replied Mancini.

"Doubtless you had; but it is difficult to conceive what motive any one could

have for injuring the lady, except him who was to inherit her lands. Whom did your lordship suspect!" asked the king.

"The very monk who confessed her," replied Mancini.

"His motive?" asked the king.

"Your majesty must excuse me," said Mancini. "I cannot answer for the motives of others."

No. 36.

"We are wandering from the point somewhat," said Henry. "Do I understan aright, that the proof offered by the Count Mancini of the death of the Lady Co delia de Dunstanville is that his servant left her in serious and dangerous illne and that the count himself was afterwards informed that she had been buried in neighbouring monastery. Am I correct.

Mancini bowed in acquiescence.

"But had the lady no female attendant?" asked the voice.

"She had," replied Mancini.

"Produce her," said the king.

"That I cannot do, your majesty. I know not where she is," replied thecoun

"There was a male attendant named Dennis," said the voice, deridingly.

"I answer not to anonymous interrogations," exclaimed Mancini angrily; bu Frazer, more on his guard, said,

"I have here the attestation of Dennis, that he assisted to bring the coffin t the Lady Cordelia's chamber, and also that he assisted in conveying it to th cemetery."

These words, and the exhibition of the document, produced a visible sensation i the court, and the king in a solemn tone said.

"This document is of considerable importance, and goes far to prove the validit of the Count Mancini's claim."

"May it please your majesty," cried the voice of the unknown, "the Lad Cordelia de Dunstanville yet lives."

"Lives!" cried Frazer. "I deny it, and defy the proof;" while Mancini stoo speechless with rage.

At this moment a monk stepped forward, and confronting the count, exclaimed "She lives!"

A tumult of applause was heard; but the king commanding instant silence, said "Proof—I must have proof."

"The countenance of the Count Mancini is my proof," cried father Anselm

"I know you not," faltered the count.

"Betray not yourself," whispered the monk.

"Oh! save me!" cried Mancini.

"Then cross not my path in the justice I demand," said the monk.

"I adjourn this court for three days further, at the end of which time you must either produce the Lady Cordelia de Dunstanville alive, or I shall adjudge the Count Mancini to be her heir," said the king; rising from his throne he imme diately left the hall.

Who shall describe the feelings of the various actors in this scene? Mancini, exhausted, irritated, unnerved; yet vindictive, and determined, left the court, and attended by Frazer, hastily sought his own abode, to ponder upon the course which it would be best for him to pursue. He spoke of immediate flight, but Frazer over ruled this, suggesting the impossiblity of Cordelia's being alive; till on Mancini's relating to him the meeting in the street between himself and intended victim, the man was alarmed beyond measure. "Surely," he said, "it was a vision!"

"I would fain believe it so," said his master, "but this monk's assertion makes me fear the worst."

"Did she recognise you?" asked Frazer.

"I think not," was the reply.

"I must find that monk, and endeavour to bend him to our purposes," said Frazer. "We have three days before us, and should he be stub born——"

"Nay—nay—we must not exasperate Father Anselm," interrupted the count.

"But we may tamper with him," said Frazer.

"And what then?" asked his master.

"He knows her retreat—the bowl or the dagger must do service even now?" said the man, in a low voice.

Mancini answered not, but by a significant motion of the head, gave to Frazer full intimation of power to pursue the course he had hinted at.

In the meanwhile there was one spectator of the eventful scene, who, though not personally interested, felt so much as to lead him at once to seek the monk, who had thus unexpectedly come forward. Descending from his station behind the monarch, Lord Mouthermer hastily passed into the crowd, and endeavoured to make his way to the spot where father Anselm had stood; but vain was his haste, the monk had already disappeared, and the bystanders could give no account of his retreat. Lord Mouthermer searched among the retreating crowd, but finding that no intelligence was to be gained, he returned home, where he found his lady extremely anxious to learn the events of the day.

Of these Mouthermer gave a faithful account, concluding with his own speculations upon the scene. "De Albini must be made acquainted with all this," he said; "it is important to his happiness, and he may be able to afford some clue to her discovery."

"Do you not think then," asked the lady, "that Lady Cordelia will herself claim her rights?"

"I cannot understand the matter at all," replied her husband; "it is evident that there is villany somewhere, and that Cordelia has been the victim; but how it has all been brought about I cannot imagine."

"Did you observe the countenance of Count Mancini, when it was announced that the Lady Cordelia was alive?" asked Lady Mouthermer.

"I did," replied her husband, "and the effect of those few words was almost miraculous. The count had hitherto spoken and looked with triumph on the certainty of success, but no sooner had those words escaped the stranger than his countenance fell, and a deathly paleness overspread his features, and an expression of horror took place of that of security. The change was so evident that one of my companions who was a perfect stranger to the affair under consideration, whispered to me, 'Whoever that man may be, he is a villain;' and I fear I must join in the opinion."

"How will your friend bear this news?" cried the lady.

"I almost fear the effect upon him," replied Mouthermer, "but I shall send off for him this evening, desiring him to return without delay."

"And my father also?" asked the lady in a faltering voice.

"Certainly; there is a mysterious link between him and this count, which I would fain see cleared up," replied Mouthermer.

"How? What can you mean?" cried the lady eagerly.

Mouthermer then related the true history of the miniature to his wife, at which the latter was extremely agitated and surprised. She wept for some time, and then throwing herself at her husband's feet, she cried,

"Oh Mouthermer! do not hate me!"

"Hate you, my love? What can you mean?" cried her husband in astonishment.

"Oh my mother! my mother!" cried the lady.

"What has happened? Tell me, dearest," said Mouthermer embracing her.

"I am the daughter of——" sobbed the lady.

"You are my wife—my beloved wife," said her husband.

"Alas! you married me under the supposition that my mother was then dead; that she had died in honour and respect," said the lady.

"And does she then still live?" cried Mouthermer. "Oh, tell me all, dearest!"

"I cannot tell you; read that packet—and I beseech you cast me not from you in disgrace,'" said the lady giving him the letter.

"Never—never—come what may; I married you in love, and you have never done anything to shake that love; fear not—no disclosure however unexpected and awful can estrange me from you," said Mouthermer; and tenderly embracing his wife he took the packet and left the room.

The following hour was one of anxiety to Lady Mouthermer; at the end of that time her husband entered the room, and said affectionately,

"This is indeed a melancholy tale; but, dearest, I can, and will support you under it."

"You will not desert me then?" asked the lady clasping her hands.

"Never—never—my beloved—this disclosure touches not your character—alas! would that it had never been revealed to you!" replied her beloved husband.

"Say not so, Mouthermer—if it rivet your affection to me, welcome any misery. But I can never hold up my head again in the world," said the lady sighing.

"The tale need not be proclaimed, dearest," replied Mouthermer, "Does it not account for the violent agitation of your father, and for other strange events?"

"It does indeed, but there is one point left in darkness," said the lady.

"What mean you?" asked Mouthermer.

"The name of the betrayer."

"And can you doubt who was the villain?" asked Mouthermer.

"I may fear, but I dare not guess," was the reply.

"It is he—it must be he—and your father—what can we do to prevent their meeting," said her husband.

Lady Mouthermer shuddered.

"Have you sent to Windsor?" she asked.

"I have."

"Then all is over, and I shall be the murderer of my father," cried the lady falling upon the floor.

Mouthermer raised his fainting wife with feelings not to be described, and laying her upon a couch endeavoured to revive her by rubbing her hands and applying such remedies as were within his reach. He was unwilling to summon an attendant, and after a considerable time he had the inexpressible delight of seeing her revive to restored consciousness. By tenderness and gentle expressions he at length succeeded in calming her perturbed spirit, and became able to converse with composure.

"De Rosenberg believes his lady to be alive, I suppose; but he must be informed of the truth" observed Mouthermer. "Oh would that he had been sincere with me at least, how much misery should we have been spared."

"I should not have been spared this," observed the lady.

"How then did you receive the packet?" asked her husband.

"In a most extraordinary manner," was the reply.

"Tell me, dearest, it may guide our actions."

"Two women requested admission to me this morning, and one of them delivered the packet to me," replied the lady.

"Who were they?"

"I know not; neither would tell their names, nor answer my questions."

"Of what rank in life were they?" asked Mouthermer.

"The younger one was extremely beautiful, but pale and melancholy; she was evidently of noble rank, while the elder appeared to be her attendant," was the reply.

Mouthermer paused a moment, then said,—

"It surely could not be Cordelia de Dunstanville!"

"Cordelia!" exclaimed the lady in a tone of astonishment.

"Nay—I merely suggest this."

"But how could the Lady Cordelia obtain this packet?" asked the lady.

"Did she give no account of this?"

'None—she said it was merely accident," replied the lady.

"And did nothing pass which would give you any idea respecting this," asked Mouthermer.

"Not the slightest word, but I remember that our friend's spaniel crept near the younger lady, and would not leave her."

"Then it is! oh—my happy friend!" exclaimed Mouthermer.

"And have I indeed seen this much lamented lady? Oh! that I had known her!" cried the Lady Mouthermer.

"I would not betray this tale to De Rosenberg," said Mouthermer. "It is very probable that the affair of the De Dunstanville estates may end in such a manner as to oblige Mancini at once to leave the kingdom, and thereby all exposure of our own affairs may be avoided."

"The saints grant that it may be so!" fervently exclaimed the lady. "Will you tell Edward of your suspicions?" she added.

"I must do so, and can very easily do it without betraying the contents of the packet," replied he.

Much conversation followed, and Lady Mouthermer was made more easy with respect to her mother's history; but it was a severe blow to her, and she dreaded meeting her beloved father, who was expected early on the ensuing day.

CHAPTER XLIII.

"Is sorrow on thy youthful brow?
Sadness in thy soul?
Heed them not who for thee now
Wreathe a midnight bowl.

There—there—you seek in vain,
For a joy to banish pain,
Nought your lips can drain,
Will grief controul."

WHAT were the feelings of Edward de Albini when the messenger sent by his friend delivered the letter with which he was charged. Surprise, joy, astonishment, all by turns agitated him, and well might Mouthermer fear the effect of this sudden revolution of feeling upon the sensitive mind of his friend. In a short time Edward stood in entranced amazement; then summoning Ronald, he acquainted him with the news he had just received.

"Did I not tell my lord I had seen her blessed face?" said the faithful dwarf.

"Alas! Ronald, forgive my unbelief—joy has been a stranger to me lately," replied his master.

"You will return to London immediately?" said Ronald.

"Instantly. Acquaint the Baron de Rosenberg with the arrival of this summons, and inquire whether he will accompany me."

This message brought De Rosenberg to Edward's apartment, and their return to London was immediately agreed upon.

"As Edward drew near the place which he sanguinely hoped might contain the beloved of his heart, new and contending emotions filled his mind, and rendered him averse to conversation, while his companion also rode on in silence. They were most warmly received by Lord Mouthermer, who congratulated Edward upon the change which appeared to have taken place in his prospects of happiness. Drawing Edward into the little room which was appropriated to his use, Lord Mouthermer commenced telling him of the events of the previous day, while his auditor sat entranced in surprise. When Mouthermer described the appearance of the monk who had declared the existence of Cordelia, Edward exclaimed,—

"Excuse me, my lord, but I know no such person as you describe. Could you not learn his name?"

"I endeavoured in vain to do so," replied his friend.

"Ronald told me that he had seen my Cordelia in company with such a monk, when the king made his entry into London," observed Edward, "but I distrusted his intelligence."

"You will attend the court on Thursday?" said Mouthermer.

"Doubtless," replied Edward. "I will now write to my mother, and claim her sympathy with me in the comparatively clear and cheerful prospect which thus unexpectedly opens before me."

"I will leave you, then," replied Mouthermer, as Edward seated himself at his writing-table; but before Mouthermer had closed the door, an exclamation from his friend caused him to turn round, and he beheld De Albini leaning back in his chair, his eyes fixed, and his countenance wearing an air of deep abstraction.

"What is the matter, Edward?" asked Mouthermer.

But Edward answered not.

"Edward! Edward!" cried his friend.

Still there was no answer.

Mouthermer advancing to the table, took his friend's hand and kindly said,—

"Speak to me, Edward, in mercy speak to me!"

Thus adjured, De Albini raised his head, and pointing to an object on the table, said,—

"It is hers—how came it here?"

"Hers?" cried Mouthermer.

"Yes—it was Edith's gift to her in happier days, and she promised never to part with it—but it is here," cried Edward.

"Then it was she herself; I thought it must be so," said Mouthermer.

"What mean you?" asked Edward.

"A lady yesterday called upon Lady Mouthermer in order to deliver to her a packet of importance, and I fancied from the description given that it must be the Lady Cordelia de Dunstanville."

"Oh! unhappy chance that I should have been absent," exclaimed Edward, in a tone of agony.

"Be of good cheer, my friend, a few hours must put an end to this mystery, as the Lady Cordelia will probably appear before the court to claim her rights."

"Where can she be?" asked Edward.

"I know not; the lady would neither give her name nor address to Lady Mouthermer," replied his friend.

"She has no friends in London," said Edward, musing.

"Is it probable that she may be under the care of Robert de Hesling?" asked Mouthermer.

"I know not, but I will make instant inquiry," said Edward, rising.

"Stay—stay—you know the circumstances of her birth; is it wise to recal them to his memory?" asked Mouthermer, in a tone of melancholy, which evinced his remembrance of the almost similar circumstances in which his own wife was placed.

"Oh! I fear nothing, I will see De Hesling myself," cried Edward.

"Shall I accompany you, my friend, or will you prefer going alone?" asked Mouthermer.

"Perhaps I had better be alone," replied Edward.

To this his friend agreed, and Edward set forth to the residence of Robert de Hesling. This nobleman had returned to England worn out and dissatisfied with the holy wars, in which he had borne a conspicuous share, and had reaped renown and glory. He had seen the man who had robbed him of his domestic happiness lie dead beneath his vindictive arm; his vengeance was satisfied, but his heart was not healed; and when age overtook him, he sighed once more for his native land. Henry the Second had gathered around him those Englishmen who in foreign lands had hoped for success to his claims, and among these the foremost in honour and in rank was Robert de Hesling. His adoption of the order of Knights Templars was a passport to courtly favour, and De Hesling became the trusted counseller of King Henry. Thus he returned to England under auspices most favourable to his advancement in wealth and fame.

But the worm was in his heart, and even on the shore of England De Hesling felt its pang. He had loved his wife, he had mourned her loss, he had avenged her her wrongs—but what availed this? Childless, almost friendless, De Hesling yearned for some one to love, and when in the gossip of the court, he heard the ending cause between Mancini and Cordelia mentioned, he almost felt that he ould have loved the helpless orphan, whom he had rendered fatherless.

Under these feelings, De Hesling was surprised by a call from Father Anselm The good monk was anxious and uneasy about Cordelia, and he wished to obtain for her some guardianship more likely to advance her interests than her present obscure residence. Under this feeling Father Anselm called upon De Hesling, and placing before him the misfortunes and merits of Lady Cordelia, he endeavoured to interest him in her favour. This was not entirely without success—the mind was softened, and the heart readily yielded. Robert de Hesling promised to give his testimony to the existence of Cordelia, and also proposed that she should visit the court on the day of trial, under his protection and guardianship.

Thus stood matters when Edward de Albini requested an audience of De Hesling; and being introduced to him, he, with considerable hesitation, mentined the purportof his visit.

"I am aware of the existence of the lady whom you mention, and shall be rejoiced when the time shall arrive at which I am to be made acquainted personally with her," replied De Hesling.

"You have not then seen her?" asked Edward.

"No," replied De Hesling.

"And know you not where she is ? Oh, if you ever loved; if you ever lost her whom——"

"Young man—young man—know you to whom you speak?" cried De Hesling.

"Forgive me, my lord," said Edward, respectfully; "every feeling of my heart, every hope of my life is bound up in this my only love, and I must find her."

"You shall find her, my friend," cried De Hesling. "Let but this hateful cause be settled in a manner favourable to the Lady Cordelia, and every effort upon my part shall be used to advance your views."

"Has your lordship any doubt respecting the issue of Count Mancini's claim?' asked De Albini.

"Not the least," replied De Hesling, "but I believe I know this Count Mancini, as he calls himself, too well; he is not so scrupulous as to the means which he employs to compass his ends. Know you aught of him?"

"No, my lord; nor can I imagine in what way he can be connected with the Lady Cordelia," replied de Albini.

"I know him but too well," said de Hesling, sighing.

"You can then perhaps explain what I want to know?" asked Edward.

"This Count Mancini is the nephew of one who was the bane of my peace, the destroyer of my domestic happiness; and if report speaks truly, this count follows in the steps of his hated relative."

"But the Lady Cordelia?" asked Edward.

"The count is decidedly the next heir to De Dunstanville after the Lady Cordelia, but while the latter lives, he can have no claim," replied De Hesling.

"And you assure me she does live, but will give me no further information?" asked Edward.

"I may tell you this. The Lady Cordelia, with a spirit worthy of a purer lineage, absolutely declines any introduction to her former friends, until she can claim their notice restored to her rank and wealth. To me this has been confided, and extraordinary as it may seem, I am chosen as the protector and stay of this persecuted orphan."

Edward saw that De Hesling was deeply affected, and he took his leave with many expressions of good will on each side. De Albini was surprised at the manner in which De Hesling had spoken of Mancini, avowing knowledge of his character, yet evidently unwilling to mention the particulars with which he was acquainted; and Edward felt an intense curiosity to tear away the mystery with which all concerning the count appeared to be shrouded. Time he trusted, and aa short time too, must bring the whole to light, and when he remembered that but a few hours were to elapse before he might hope again to behold his Cordelia, again press his beloved to his heart, Edward felt how weak, how wholly uninteresting were all other matters. He returned to his temporary home, and gazing fondly upon the little seal which Cordelia had left upon his writing table, he sat down in perturbation of spirit to impart his feelings to his beloved mother.

De Albini remained thus employed during a considerable time; he unfolded to the Lady Elfrida all his newly-born hopes, all his delicious anticipations; he claimed her congratulations, and asked a renewal of her former affection towards his betrothed love; and by doing this, his spirit became more calm, his mind more equable, more able to bear with the anxiety which must attend his present circumstances, more prepared for sorrow, more capable of happiness. Hours flew quickly by while Edward was thus employed, and when summoned to the evening meal, he joined his friends with a peaceful heart and an unclouded brow.

During the repast Ronald, who attended upon his master, seemed to have lost his accustomed readiness and alacrity. He made continual blunders, and was regarded with mingled surprise and scorn by his fellow servants; but this was perfectly unnoticed by the faithful dwarf, who seemed intent only upon making his master understand only by looks and signs that something of the utmost importance was upon his mind. Ronald had endeavoured in vain to obtain a few words with De Albini previous to his entrance into the supper hall; he had heard of the certainty of Cordelia's existence, and he burned to congratulate his master upon his own sagacity and penetration in recognising the lost one when no one suspected that she was alive.

Ronald's manner at supper was so extraordinary, that after the domestics had retired, Lady Mouthermer mentioned it, asking Edward if he knew the reason.

"I can answer that question," replied her husband. "The faithful fellow is so much rejoiced at the news which he has heard, that I am told he is scarcely in his senses with joy."

"What news?" asked Count Rosenberg.

"The intelligence that the Lady Cordelia de Dunstanville still lives," replied Mouthermer.

"De Dunstanville!" cried Rosenberg, turning as pale as ashes.

Mouthermer regarded him him with astonishment, and his lady with anxiety, and the former said,—

"You have heard us speak of her before, I think?"

"That hated name has not for many years met my ears, and I beseech you never again to obtrude it upon me. Tell me only, is she his child?" asked Rosenberg.

"The Lady Cordelia is an orphan," said Mouthermer; "her father died in Palestine by the hand of Robert de Hesling, whom he had grievously injured."

At this explanation, Count Rosenberg resumed his usual placid demeanour, the conversation took a general turn, and this little accident was forgotten by all save one. Who can trace the feelings of a daughter's heart. Lady Mouthermer adored her only parent; although parted from him during the short period which had elapsed since her happy marriage, her affection had suffered no diminution, and now that she was re-united to him under her husband's roof, he was second only to the latter in her cares and thoughts. The last few hours too had deepened her feelings towards her parent; she had learned how much he had suffered, and with how much resolution he had forborne to embitter her young years with a knowledge of those sufferings, and while her respect was increased tenfold, a sentiment of pity was mingled with it. Lady Mouthermer therefore saw and felt the agitation which her father betrayed at the name of Dunstanville, and she resolved to use every endeavour to prevent a recurrence of it. With this view she engaged him on the eventful morning to accompany her to visit a friend at a distance, but when the day arrived, she found herself too ill to take her intended drive. She therefore detained her father by the side of her couch till towards noon, when having fallen asleep, Count Rosenberg left her for a short time, as he wished to speak with Lord Mouthermer, and took his way to the palace.

We must now relate the proceedings which had taken place there.

Mancini entered the royal presence prepared for almost anything that might happen; he knew that he must renounce his claim upon the appearance of Cordelia, and he resolved to do so with a good grace. When he entered the court, there was a murmur of curiosity, and every eye was upon the count and Frazer who accompanied him. Mancini advanced boldly, again proclaiming his certain and absolute knowledge of the death of Cordelia de Dunstanville.

While he was speaking, Mouthermer and De Albini entered the court, and taking their seats near the king, attentively watched the proceedings. Among

the crowd Mouthermer observed the monk who had previously arrested his attention, and pointing him out to his friend inquired whether he knew him.

"His countenance is not familiar to me," replied Edward.

"That is strange," observed Mouthermer. "If he were really a friend of the Lady Cordelia, surely you would have known him at Thornbury."

To this Edward assented; when in a moment his attention was drawn towards

No. 37.

the entrance of the hall, where a movement was taking place among the crowd; and what was his agitation and delight when he saw De Hesling enter leading his beloved Cordelia. A cry of joy escaped him.

"Peace—peace, my friend," cried Mouthermer; "control yourself."

"Oh, my beloved Cordelia! why may I not embrace thee?" cried Edward.

Cordelia was habited in deep mourning; she looked pale, but beautiful; her eyes were cast upon the ground as she advanced, leaning for support upon De Hesling's arm, while Father Anselm had stepped forward and given her his aid on the other side.

Who shall describe the feelings of Mancini as the two advanced to the foot of the throne? Fear, rage, every villany was depicted upon his countenance, and he exclaimed in a tone hoarse and indistinct with anger,—

"Father Anselm, the traitorous monk! I will be revenged yet."

Frazer, too, was as one petrified; the whole of the successful plot burst upon him in an instant, and he directly remembered many suspicious circumstances which he wondered had not struck him before.

"Methinks," said the king, "we have here a fair answer to our inquiries. What say you, Count Mancini, do you acknowledge this lady to be your kinswoman, the lost Cordelia de Dunstanville?"

"I suppose I must admit it," replied the count; and as he said the words, a stranger bursting forwards cried out,—

"It is his voice! the villain! the traitor!" and springing upon the count, one hand of Rosenberg clasped the throat of Mancini, while the other drew his sword.

"Peace there," cried the king. "What means this?"

But neither could speak. Mancini seemed almost fainting as he shrunk under the grasp of the man whom he had injured, and Rosenberg seemed exhausted by the violence of his feelings. The crowd drew away from them, all but Frazer, who gazed upon Rosenberg as if his senses were bewildered.

Meanwhile Mouthermer, comprehending the meaning of the scene, came to the relief of his parent, and taking his arm endeavoured to lead him out. But Rosenberg resisted this, and after a minute he whispered rather than spoke,—

"Tell me but she lives?"

Mancini shook his head, but without looking up.

"Villain—murderer," cried the count, while again he laid his hand upon his sword.

The latter word seemed to arouse Mancini, for lifting up his head he gave one vindictive glance at Rosenberg, then scornfully smiling, he said,—

"I, too, have a sword."

"Leave the presence, or repress this quarrel," said King Henry.

"I declare this man a murderer and a traitor," cried Rosenberg, "and I call upon the guards to secure him,"

"Let no one leave the hall," said the king; and the doors were immediately closed; Mouthermer gently drew away Rosenberg, and Mancini stood alone.

While this was passing, Cordelia was at the foot of the throne, leaning downcast and agitated upon De Hesling; but a dearer arm now sustained her, for Edward gently coming from his station, had taken her other hand, and putting his arm round her waist whispered tenderly,—

"My own, at last!"

This was responded to only by a sigh of happiness, but that sigh was enough for her lover, and both were in an ecstasy of joy—quiet, but deep.

When peace was restored between Rosenberg and Mancini, the king, looking down upon Cordelia, exclaimed,—

"Why, what means this? Methought that just now the Lady Cordelia was supported by a holy father, now it is a gallant young knight who sustains her?"

"She is my affianced bride, your majesty," said Edward.

"Ho—ho—how is this, my Lord de Hesling?" asked the king.

"I cannot say nay," replied De Hesling,

' May I hope that your majesty will not forbid it ?" cried Edward.

"It would ill become me, on this my first public administration of justice, to make young hearts unhappy. We will talk of this matter at a future time," said the monarch; "I now declare the Lady Cordelia de Dunstanville the rightful heiress to the honours and estates of the late Baron de Dunstanville, and also of those of her mother Eleanor de Tunstal; and I command that she be re-instated in such honours and estates without delay."

"Amen," ejaculated De Hesling, while Edward and Cordelia bent in respectful reverence to the king.

They were about to leave the royal presence, when Henry, holding out his hand said,—

"My fair subject has not done me fitting homage."

Cordelia took the king's hand, and respectfully kissed it, when Henry rising, gently saluted her forehead, saying,—

"The fair Lady de Dunstanville must grace our court ere long. We command her presence there attended by our friend De Albini; a monarch's blessing may be fortunate."

Cordelia blushed, and Edward, delighted, made way for her and De Hesling to leave the hall. In the ante-room Bridget was waiting to receive her mistress, but it seemed that instead of thinking of Cordelia's triumph some other object absorbed her thoughts, for she said in a tone of disappointment,—

"I have seen him, my own master, but he knew not me."

"Who do you mean, Bridget?" asked Cordelia.

"My master, the Baron Rosenberg" answered the woman.

"You shall see him again," said Edward.

Bridget gazed bewildered on the speaker, then said, "I must see him."

"Follow me then to Mouthermer House," replied Edward.

Hitherto Cordelia and Edward had scarcely spoken to each other; it seemed to be sufficient to them to know that they were once more together, words were not needed. De Hesling's carriage drove up, and the three happy friends drove to Mouthermer House, where they found Lady Mouthermer in considerable alarm at the absence of her father. Edward introduced Cordelia, who was received with the warmest friendship, and the lady inquired if De Albini had seen or heard anything of Rosenberg.

"He will be here speedily, with Mouthermer," replied Edward.

"With my husband ? Oh ! then has he been to the trial ?" cried the lady, much agitated.

"He has, dear lady," answered Edward; "but be not alarmed ? all is right."

While De Albini was thus speaking, Mouthermer and Rosenberg entered the room, and the latter embracing his daughter, said,—

"Oh, my child ! my only tie now on earth !"

"She knows all," cried Mouthermer.

"How ! Knows she then her mother's disgrace and fate? Oh, my child, how have I carefully hidden this from you ?" exclaimed Rosenberg. "But now revenge is in my power, and the villain shall not go unpunished."

"It is as we feared then ?" asked Lady Mouthermer of her husband.

"The Count Mancini, the tyrant enemy of Cordelia de Dunstanville, was the man who destroyed the peace of Count Rosenberg," replied Mouthermer.

The lady gasped for breath. "And they have met ?" she said.

"We have—and shall meet again," said her father.

"Oh no—my father, beware of that man," cried Lady Mouthermer, clinging to him.

"Fear not, my child," replied Rosenberg, "the affair is in our monarch's hands. He is honourable and just, and will avenge me."

Lady Mouthermer was somewhat relieved by this assurance, and seating her parent by her side upon the couch, she took his hand in hers, and gazing fondly upon his face, leaned back exhausted with her agitation.

While this conversation had been going forward Edward had withdrawn Cordelia to the inner drawing room.

"Oh, my beloved!" cried De Albini embracing her, "do we indeed meet again? Are my miserable hours indeed for ever past, and shall we part no more?"

"Oh, Edward!" replied Cordelia, "we have indeed suffered."

"But, dearest, tell me, where have you been secreted from my searching inquiries? I have sought every part of our own land, and found you not."

Cordelia gave her lover a short history of what had befallen her since they last met. She told of her being carried off from the cottage; of her wretched and dangerous voyage—

"Oh, Edward!" she said, "how fervently did I hope that the waves would engulph me, and at once end my miseries!"

"The saints be thanked, you are preserved to me!" cried De Albini.

Of her imprisonment Cordelia spoke but slightly; she dwelt upon the goodness of Father Anselm and the fidelity of Kate; related the stratagem by which she had so almost miraculously escaped, and to Edward's intense surprise, recounted her visit to Percival Castle, and the kind reception she had received from the Lady Elfrida.

"My mother? and did you indeed go to Percival? Now I am jealous. Oh, that I had been there, how many weeks of misery should I have escaped."

"Nay, Edward, not so. I had ascertained that you were in London, or I would never have entered the walls of Percival Castle. I was resolved," she continued, "never again to see you until I were declared heiress of my father's and mother's rights; that has now taken place, and I shall re-visit Percival with happiness."

"My mother must be apprised of this," said Edward.

"She already knows that I am acknowledged by De Hesling," replied Cordelia; "I have written to her frequently, and have told her all."

"How she will rejoice, my Cordelia, to welcome her second daughter. But when may I promise that it shall be so?" asked her lover tenderly.

Cordelia sighed, but made no answer.

"Think me not importunate, but remember how long it is since you promised to be my wife; I am here but as a visitor, nor can I remain much longer from my mother; but oh, Cordelia! ask me not to return to Percival alone and cheerless as I left it," said Edward.

"I would not detain you, dear Edward," replied the maiden, "believe me, I need the peace and happiness of that blessed retreat; my spirits are broken, and the society of the Lady Elfrida would be my dearest means of restoration; but I have given myself into the hands of De Hesling, and to him I must refer you."

Edward gratefully and joyfully embraced his beloved; he well knew that he could persuade De Hesling to agree to a speedy union, and he at length left Cordelia, anxious that she would become intimately acquainted with those friends whom he himself so highly valued.

Lady Mouthermer treated Cordelia at once as a sister; she had been prepared by Edward to love her, and when in the undisguised conversation of domestic life Cordelia displayed the strength and eloquence of her mind, the enthusiasm of Lady Mouthermer knew no bounds. She declared that her house should be the scene of the ensuing bridal—that she would herself superintend all the arrangements which required a female's experience, and although she resolutely declared that no decorations nor jewels could add to the beauty of her friend, yet she persisted in being allowed a free choice of all that might be deemed desirable for the happy occasion.

Cordelia cared not for jewels nor splendour; she was daily, hourly, in the companionship of her Edward, and she felt almost vexed when any part of their conversation was given up to the consideration of matters which she considered of such trifling importance.

De Hesling had, as Edward expected, seen the propriety of an early marriage; he had unexpectedly offered to act as father to the bride; and had expressed his intention of making her his heiress, on condition that the young couple should pass a part of their time at his residence.

"I am old," he said; "I have no other child to love; and Cordelia has won upon me by her resemblance to her unfortunate mother, who, notwithstanding all her faults, was the only woman whom I ever loved. It will solace me to watch over the happiness of her child."

There was another being, who, cut off from the common sympathies of his fellows by his uncouth form and face, possessed as warm and faithful a heart as ever beat beneath the vest of a nobleman. The devotion of Ronald to Cordelia was unbounded, he watched every look, every gesture—he hung upon her words as if they were the sustenance of his being, and made every excuse which duty could allow to remain in her presence. Cordelia was grateful to the dwarf, his company reminded her of the happiness of former days; with him she could talk about Edith and Eustace, now the parents of a lovely child; she would speak of De Fougeres, of Thornbury, of all whom she had loved in childhood, and admired in youth; and many were the hours which she thus passed.

Bridget, too, had become domesticated at Lord Mouthermer's, but we must give her our more undivided attention, connected as she was with some of the darker pages of our history.

CHAPTER XLIV.

Friends depart, and memory takes them
To her caverns pure and deep;
And a forc'd smile only wakes them
From the shadows where they sleep.
Who shall school the heart's affection?
Who shall banish its regret?
If you blame my deep dejection,
Teach, oh! teach me to forget!

BAYLEY.

WHEN Bridget arrived according to Edward's desire at Mouthermer House, her first inquiry was for Count Rosenberg. On being introduced to his presence, her appearance did not recal her to his memory; and Bridget, who was not aware that time, who had laid his finger heavily upon the count, had likewise not spared her, was rather dismayed at what she termed a strange forgetfulness. As soon, however, as she mentioned her name, the memory of her old master returned, and he eagerly inquired of that which he dreaded, yet longed to hear.

"She is no more—but were you with her?" he cried.

"I was," replied the woman.

"Where?" asked the Count.

"Under the roof of him who betrayed you," said Bridget.

"Then she repented not," muttered the count.

"She did—deeply and bitterly,' said the woman.

"Then wherefore not seek other refuge?" asked Roseberg.

"What refuge is open to the sinner?" cried Bridget.

"The church extends her hospitable arms to her repentant children, and even I——"

"Alas! would that it could have been so," cried Bridget.

"Could! what mean you?" asked the count.

"She was a prisoner," said Bridget.

The count sighed deeply.

"I must tell all—it were injustice to you not to say it," said Bridget.

"Say on—I will hear it," replied Rosenberg.

"Jealousy prompted Mancini or De Dunstanville to keep my lady a prisoner. There was a young man, Count Vallombrosa——"

"Vallombrosa!" exclaimed Rosenberg. "He whose intended bride met with a watery grave while on a party of pleasure?"

"The same—it is a sad tale, but we must pass that. Mancini was jealous, and not without reason; he therefore came to Scotland, but the lover followed, my lady endeavoured to escape, but all was discovered, the Count Vallombrosa was slain, and my lady kept from that time in close confinement."

"Unhappy, misguided woman!" cried the count.

"She underwent some expiation in a long and rigorous imprisonment; I attended upon her, and when the hour of death approached, it found her repentant and resigned. Father Anselm confessed her, but he knows not your name."

"It is well; and wonderfully have events been brought round. But this Mancini, as he calls himself, he must not escape my vengeance," said Rosenberg.

"There are others, beside yourself, who long for revenge," observed Bridget.

"And did you see her laid in hallowed ground?" asked Rosenberg.

Bridget shook her head mournfully.

"What mean you, woman! Speak?" cried her master.

"It served not with her tyrant's views to inter her publicly," observed Bridget.

"How then?" cried Rosenberg.

"He gave her the same grave that she had given the Lady Hypolita."

"The ocean?" cried Rosenberg, with a shudder.

Bridget bowed her head.

"And could not you save her from this?" asked the count.

"Alas! my lord, you know not that man. Vain were tears to turn him from his unholy purpose."

"And wherefore did you remain there after her death?" asked Rosenberg.

"But to rescue the Lady Cordelia, and to make his exposure and vengeance certain," replied the woman.

"It is done, and the Count Mancini shall be exposed," cried Rosenberg.

As he said these words, the count left the room; and Bridget, glad to have made her conscience easy, repaired to the chamber of Cordelia.

Rosenberg sought an audience of the king, and declaring his ground of enmity to Mancini, requested permission to challenge him to single combat. The king endeavoured to dissuade his friend from this proceeding; he alleged the length of time which had elapsed since the injury was inflicted, the worthless character of the count, and the probability that after the exposure of his conduct towards Cordelia, he would at once retire to the continent.

But all these reasons failed to influence Rosenberg, and the king reluctantly consented to his request. Rosenberg accordingly sent a challenge to Mancini, requiring him either by himself or representative to do battle in the lists at Hampton Court, on a certain day, which he named.

When Mancini received this challenge, he was extremely enraged, and at first declared that he would pay no attention to the summons, but a little reflection decided him otherwise. He trusted in his prowess as a swordsman, he knew that his rival was much older than himself, and unaccustomed to fight, and he fancied that, should he overcome his adversary, his fame would be cleared up as respected all that had occurred. Under these thoughts Mancini accepted the challenge, and the day appointed was that which would succeed the day fixed for Edward's marriage to Cordelia.

Both De Albini and Cordelia wished their marriage to be privately solemnised, but in this they were over ruled by those around them. De Hesling especially urged that, considering the events which had taken place, the marriage ought to be publicly solemnised ; and King Henry himself condescended to give an opinion to the same effect. Edward and his bethrothed therefore yielded a reluctant assent, and extensive preparations were made for their nuptials.

But both the lovers had suffered too many trials to look forward to the event with overweening happiness, and they rejoiced in its approach principally because it would restore them to the domestic enjoyment of the society of the Lady Elfrida and the delightful seclusion of Percival Castle.

The day arrived ; the ceremony was performed by Father Anselm, in the presence of many assembled friends. De Hesling bestowed the bride upon her long-tried and faithful Edward, and immediately afterwards the happy pair departed for Percival Castle, where Eustace Mowbray and Edith were to meet them to enjoy together that re-union which a short time ago each had deemed to be impossible. The faithful dwarf and Bridget followed their master and mistress, and perhaps the former of these persons was the most uncontrollably happy of the party.

Upon their approach to the castle, they were met by a large body of the tenantry, who, notwithstanding the lateness of the season, had come in their holiday array to meet their lord. Ronald had hastened on, and joined the train ; indeed so generally were his talents known and appreciated, where anything like revelry was going forward, that the procession would not have been properly formed without his assistance.

First came a number of youths all wearing white favours, and singing the following welcome, which the dwarf had composed for them.

> Welcome to thy father's halls,
>   Long thou'st absent been,
> Many weary days have pass'd
>   Since thy face we've seen.
> Joy shall now each heart elate,
>   And every care beguile ;
> Shall make misfortune's eye grow bright,
>   And even sorrow smile.

> And welcome to the beauteous bride,
>   Who comes thy house to share,
> May she be blest with every good,
>   And happy as she's fair.
> May both beneath their own roof tree,
>   Pass many a gladsome day,
> While Time with iron hand regrets
>   To steal their joys away.

After these youths, appeared a band of the elder retainers, accompanied by a band of musicians. The whole as they wound round the side of the hill upon which the castle is situated, made a splendid appearance in their holiday attire, enlivened by their bright banners.

Edward was grateful for the feeling which had induced this display of attachment, and he responded to it by his accustomed liberality. He longed, however, to present Cordelia to his revered mother, and to meet again his sister Edith. The moment arrived—a moment agitating to all ; Cordelia was clasped in the arms of the Lady Elfrida, while Edith wept for joy.

"Oh my Cordelia! my first friend, do I again behold you ? and do I at last embrace you as my sister !" cried Edith.

"Little indeed have I hoped for this moment," replied Cordelia. "Oh, Edith, many a weary hour have I sat in almost heart-broken agony, recalling every event of our young days, and wondering whether Edith ever gave a thought to the memory of her friend."

"Could you doubt it ?" asked Edith tenderly. "We wept for you, and hoped while hope seemed possible; when the intelligence of your safety arrived, it appeared almost overwhelming."

"How did you learn my safety?" asked Cordelia.

"Edward wrote to me, and we should at once have come to London, but my mother prevented it, according to what she knew to be your wish."

While this short conversation was proceeding, Roland had prepared a band of young maidens, who with Kate at their head entered the hall. They were dressed in white, and decorated with such flowers as the season afforded. Kate approached Cordelia and sang as follows :—

> Peace be around thee wherever thou rovest,
> May life be for thee one summer's day,
> And all that thou wish'st and all that thou lov'st,
> Come smiling around thy sunny way.
> If sorrow e'er this calm should break,
> May e'en thy tears pass off so lightly,
> Like spring show'rs they'll only make
> The smiles which follow shine more brightly.

> May Time, who sheds his blight o'er all,
> And daily dooms some joy to death,
> O'er thee let years so gently fall,
> They shall not crush one flower beneath.
> As half in shade and half in sun,
> This world along its path advances,
> May that side the sun's upon,
> Be all that e'er shall meet thy glances.

Cordelia gratefully embraced her friend Kate at the conclusion of this song, and expressing her thanks to the other maidens her attendants, she passed on to the saloon, where there were friends awaiting her whom she dearly longed to behold, and the vividness of whose feelings would not allow them to undergo the meeting where there were other eyes to witness their emotion.

In her large chair by the fireside sat the venerable Lady Elfrida, her splendid form now bent by sorrow and anxiety, her once bright eye still beaming with affection through its tears, and her placid countenance showing that peace was at length restored to her heart. By her side stood he whom she had loved in youth, and who had loved her fervently, though hopelessly, through a long and agitated life. De Fougeres was at her side—all was forgiven which had cast disunion between them, friends they now were, friends according now in the one feeling of joy and gratitude for the happy termination of all their misery.

De Albini led his bride forward into the saloon; the lady rose to embrace her children, but throwing themselves at her feet, Edward exclaimed,—

"Mother! dear mother! bless our union!"

"I do, my children; may long years of happiness blot from your hearts the pangs of suspense and despair which you have endured," said the lady, as, sinking back into her couch, overcome by her emotions, she burst into a flood of tears. Edith and Cordelia flew to their parent.

"These are tears of joy, my children," she said. "Ah! how different is this meeting, my Cordelia, to that day on which you last implored my blessing!"

Cordelia shook her head mournfully; then looking up to the Lady Elfrida, and smiling through her tears, she said,—

"Have I not redeemed my pledge, dear lady?"

"Nobly—faithfully—my child. I was not deceived when, a poor deserted infant at the convent, I read in thy lineaments the traces of nobility of birth and elevation of soul," exclaimed the lady proudly. "The blood of De Tunstal tinged thy innocent cheek, and reposed upon thy brow; it spoke to my heart, and although years and events hid the persecuted child from my gaze, yet that heart responded to its early influences. How I have proved the truth of my presentiments, let this moment show!"

Cordelia, overcome by these praises, threw herself into her husband's arms, and hiding her face upon his shoulder, thus concealed the blushes and tears which struggled for mastery over her countenance.

"And I, too, dear mother," said Edith, "was I not always right in loving my sister Cordelia, notwithstanding the wicked arts of that monk who would have separatel us?"

"Name him not," cried De Fougeres. "He has no longer the power to harm us. Had I not listened to his counsels, how much misery should we all have been spared. You, Lady Elfrida, would have regained your lost treasure, and perhaps you, Cordelia, might have been saved your subsequent trials. Let this teach us

No. 38.

that to repair a fault is generally more difficult than to avoid one ; and that even the most wicked of mankind are able to see and correct the mistakes of others."

All present acknowledged the truth of this ; and their feelings towards Father Augustines memory were considerably softened by the words of Ralph de Fougeres. Turning to Cordelia, he said,—

"Thornbury has been deserted, but now that I have again seen you happy, I shall return to it, and I trust that in your visit to Mowbray Castle I shall not be forgotten."

Cordelia expressed how much happiness she should feel in revisiting the scenes of her youth ; while Edward declared that the Lady's Tower would always be dear to him, although associated with much that was painful in the retrospect.

In such conversation the time flew rapidly away ; thoughts long pent up in each breast were interchanged, feelings reciprocated, hopes enlivened, and even Cordelia forgot her long estrangement from happiness in the expectation of the future, or if she remembered it, did so only to throw a brighter light upon the present.

The Lady Elfrida informed Cordelia that she had known the Countess Rosenberg in her early days ; she spoke of her as one of those bright but fragile beings who seemed scarcely fitted for even the smoother paths of life ; and she was not surprised at the termination of her fate.

"I trust," she continued "that her daughter Lady Mouthermer will be saved from the perils which destroyed her mother ; she has a noble-minded husband who will guide as well as cherish her."

"Ah! my dear lady, when in my giddy days of happiness I scorned the proud noble who refused the hand of her whom he considered a rustic low-born girl, how little did I think that to that man I should be so much indebted for my return to wealth and station, as I am to Lord Mouthermer. Truly happy am I that I was the ignorant means of conveying to his lady a testimony of her lost mother's love, and of thus awakening in her heart renewed affection towards her remaining parent."

"It is ever thus, my child," replied the Lady Elfrida "a good action is retu rned upon the giver, while as surely does a bad one visit upon him who commits it."

A succession of merry-makings ensued upon the marriage of De Albini ; on the day after their lord's arrival a great feast was given to the tenants and dependants at Percival Castle ; sports of all kinds followed, such as the season would allow; the very poorest were made happy, and the sick were relieved. In all the scenes the Lady Elfrida took but a small share ; her spirits, although much better, were not equal to much excitement, and she preferred her fireside to the bustle of a crowd. Devoted to her son, in whom she saw the representation of her departed lord, she entered with interest into all that concerned his welfare ; and with joy she saw that Cordelia fully appreciated the virtues of her husband, and was as much devoted to him as a mother could desire.

Nor was the lovely Edith less happy ; she was the mother of a fine boy, who promised to inherit the virtues as well as the beauty of his parents. It had been the wish of Eustace, now the Baron de Mowbray, to present his charming wife at court, and at this period it appeared particularly desirable that every noble should rally round the monarch. Edward therefore proposed that that the newly married Baroness de Albini and the Baroness de Mowbray should make their appearance at the court of Henry at the same time, and as soon as the Lady Elfrida should be willing to part with them.

In the meanwhile what had become of Mancini? Let us return to London.

CHAPTER XLIV.

Oh ! breathe not his name, let it sleep in the shade,
  Where cold and unhallowed his ashes are laid ;
Sad, silent, and dark be the tears that we shed,
  As the night dew that falls on the turf o'er his head.
But the night dew that falls, tho' in darkness it weeps,
  Shall brighten with verdure the grave where he sleeps ;
And the tear that we shed tho' in silence it rolls,
  Shall long keep his memory green in our souls.—MOORE.

THE day which had been appointed by the king for the trial by single combat, according to the fashion of those days, drew near, and Mancini became more and more alarmed at the thought of its possible result. He felt that he had cast his all upon a throw, and he might lose it. In vain did he turn for comfort to Frazer ; that worthy person, now that he saw his master's fortunes falling, sought to withdraw himself from their influence, and gave the count notice that he should seek some other service. By persuasion, however, he was induced to remain with him until after the combat, as Mancini declared his intention of then retiring into Italy should he be the victor.

According to the rules of chivalry, a knight who was about to take the field, whether in public battle or private fight, after a cessation of warfare, was obliged for a certain number of hours to watch his armour on the night before he intended to wear it ; for this purpose the custom was for the armour to be exposed on the battlement or terrace of a castle, and the knight paraded the place alone from midnight till day break. This was supposed to make him invulnerable to his adversary's lance.

Mancini would fain have dispensed with this observance, but he felt that his cause was too weak to allow him to risk neglect of any means propiatory of success, and he reluctantly prepared to perform the customary service.

Upon a terrace-walk at the back of his residence, were deposited by Frazer the cuirass, breast-plate, corslet, lance, and other accoutrements which were to be used by the count on the ensuing day ; and a few minutes before midnight, Mancini himself stepped out upon the terrace. He had asked Frazer to watch with him, but the latter suggested that such companionship was contrary to the rules of chivalry, and that it might neutralise the good effect to be expected from the due observance of the regular custom. To this the count was obliged to submit, although he suspected, nay well knew, that the refusal of his follower arose from fear rather than from any reverential awe of the authority of chivalry.

It was a bright frosty night in November : the moon, which was just at the full, shone clearly, although occasionally obscured by the swiftly passing clouds which, edged with the light reflected from the beauteous planet, flitted about the heavens, now causing an almost palpable darkness, and now passing off, leaving almost the brightness of day. The stars shone out ; Orion with his splendid band, and Arcturus, scarcely less brilliant, disputed the palm of beauty with the moon.

As Mancini paced the terrace, with slow and solemn step, he looked up to the heavens, and Orion arrested his gaze. His thoughts in a moment reverted to his early days ; he remembered how, when but a stripling, he had followed his relative De Dunstanville to the plains of Syria ; he had there, under that unclouded sky, gazed upon the giant hero of the heavenly host, and had listened with delighted but awe-struck attention, to the tale related by the natives of that region of him whose existence was perpetuated in the dazzling orbs which he now again looked upon. From that remembrance his whole life passed in review before him ; he thought of his desertion of the sacred banners of Palestine in disgust at the little attention he was able to obtain from the leaders in that expedition; and a vision of beauty arrested his heart, as he remembered the next episode of his eventful life.

A magnificent castle in Germany appeared to his view; and there he beheld a happy group—a noble lord endowed with all that could endear life and render it honourable—a lady, beauteous as the day—an infant cherub—could the tempter prevail here? Alas! he did; mourning and misery succeeded to happiness; and Mancini next viewed himself tearing away the partner of his guilt from the scene of their treachery. Yet they loved, devotedly loved each other; she was unprincipled and vain; loving not her former lord, whom she had married when she had scarcely passed her girlhood, but as much attached to Mancini as a selfish person can love that one who ministers to her selfishness.

Then the scene changed to a castle on the shores of the Mediterranean; feelings of jealousy and distrust racked the memory of the count, and one event stood out painfully pre-eminent—that decisive day on which the lamentable shipwreck, and consequent death of the Lady Hypolita unveiled to all around the faithlessness of her, whom he had himself instructed in treachery. A burning pang shot through the heart of Mancini, and he hid his face in his hands for a few moments, till recovering himself by a violent effort, he recalled to his memory the latter events of his life.

Duncraig stood before him in its frowning desolation; he seemed to stand over a dying man, to whom a female was vainly clinging. Again he beheld the same female form in a lonely apartment, wretched, but resigned; could this be she whom he had borne away from her noble and happy home in Germany? Sorrow, more than time, had done its work upon her brow, which furrowed by grief and remorse, was shaded by premature grey hairs; her form was bent by penitence, her eye dimned by tears. A little while further, and she lay before him a corpse—his victim, and his accuser.

"Oh, Dorothea," he exclaimed, "would that I had never seen that beauteous face; then had this day been spared to me."

A faint groan startled Mancini as he said this.

"It was but the hollow wind in yonder fir-trees," cried the count after a pause.

But again the same faint groan startled his ear. He looked up, and concluding, as he had before done, that it was merely the wind, he again fell into a deep reverie, which turned upon the events in which Cordelia acted a prominent part. Mancini regretted that he had not compelled his prisoner to marry him while she was in his power; the tenderness which had filled his heart while thinking of his early days had passed away, and he felt nothing but disappointment and vexation at having neglected to grasp the prize while it was in his power to do so.

"Had I done so, I should now have been far away amid the mountains of Italy, secure from the pursuit of him whom I so deeply injured, and whom I fear is destined to avenge his wrongs upon my head to-morrow. But I never loved her pale face, no! Dorothea! through falsehood and murder, this heart has ever been true to thee; even in the day of death it will beat but for thee!" exclaimed Mancini, deeply sighing.

At this moment a gentle sigh was distinctly breathed at his side; looking up, he beheld a female figure clad in a flowing white robe, her dishevelled hair streaming over her shoulders, and apparently dripping with water. She fixed her eyes solemnly on Mancini, who exclaimed fearfully,—

"Dorothea!"

"I am here, as thou seest, Mancini," replied the phantom, in a tone which thrilled through the heart of her hearer.

"Wherefore troublest thou me?" cried the alarmed count.

"Askest thou wherefore? let these damp locks tell thee," she replied.

"It shall be done, begone!" commanded Mancini.

The phantom shook her head, and a faint smile passed for a moment across her face.

"What meanest thou?" asked Mancini.

"Does a spirit obey a mortal yet encumbered with its earthly tenement?"

"But I tell thee, it shall be done," replied the count.

Again the phantom shook her head.

"Time, time," she said.

"It is yet time," replied the count. "I will send for Father Anselm, and order masses for the repose of thy soul. Fear not."

"Fear? Can a spirit fear? No—Mancini—it is for thee to fear."

"I care not—death can come but once," said the count.

"But may it not be more bitter if it come by the hand of one whom we have injured? Do I not know this?" asked the phantom in a terrific tone.

"Peace—peace—I beseech thee to be gone, Dorothea; I have never failed in my love to thee," cried the agonised count.

"Was it love, then, that drugged the bitter potion, which sent me to my doom? Was this love?"

"It was mercy. What was life to thee, then?" asked Mancini.

"True; thy hand had everlastingly embittered it. But tell me—did he die?"

"Die! Whom dost thou mean?" asked the count.

"He whom thou taughtest me to seduce to my unhallowed love; he whom I dare not—may not now name."

"He fell under my blow, but he died not there; I saw him afterwards," replied Mancini.

"Where? How? Did he repent?" asked the phantom eagerly.

Mancini related the meeting with Vallombrosa in the monastery, his conversation with him, and his sudden, but unexpected decease.

The phantom gave a deep groan at the conclusion of this recital.

"I am happy—he was penitent," she exclaimed. "And my load of grief is lightened. But I must not stay longer. Hear me, Mancini—thy days, nay thine hours are numbered—Rosenberg will be avenged."

"Stay, Dorothea. One word. May nothing avail me to-morrow against my adversary?" cried the count in a tone of eager anxiety.

The phantom shook her head, and slowly vanished.

When he found himself alone, Mancini felt the whole force of the scene which had just passed. His personal fear, which had during the above conversation been overcome by awe, returned with double force upon him, and he trembled from head to foot. Had he indeed seen and conversed with his Dorothea? Had he again beheld her whom he had mercilessly consigned to a watery grave? Whom if he had not actually murdered, at least whom he had permitted to be murdered? Wholly unnerved by this rencounter Mancini's thoughts took a more gloomy turn; he almost resolved to avoid the risk of the next day's combat, but a feeling of vanity and self-confidence opposed this; he remembered his former prowess as a knight, and that he had youth and vigour on his side, and he still trusted in these qualifications to contradict the awful warning which he had so fearfully received.

At daybreak Mancini sought Frazer, who was to act as his esquire on this eventful day, and with him he closeted himself in his private room, in order to look over his papers, and settle his affairs; not only in case of his being mortally wounded, but in preparation for his immediate retreat from England should he be victorious.

This duty occupied him for some hours; he found papers of vital importance to his good name, if he indeed had one; these he destroyed, and with them several letters which had been written by Dorothea in the first years of their acquaintance. This occupation did not tend to calm the mind of Mancini, but he arose from it with a sort of dogged resolution of mind which he mistook for courage. The time wore away; both Frazer and his master were properly equipped, and proceeded to the spot appointed for the combat.

Let us now revert to his opponent Rosenberg, whose mind was in a very different temper.

The evening previous to the eventful day, Rosenberg passed in the bosom of his family by the happy fireside of Mouthermer. But a gloom now overspread the circle. Lady Mouthermer, whose disposition was somewhat inclined to be melancholy, looked forward with horror to the morrow, while her beloved husband, more hopeful, trusted in the rightfulness of the cause which led one so dear to them to risk his life and their happiness.

"My child," said Rosenberg, "should the event of to-morrow prove fatal to your parent, I pray you to remember him as one who, whatever his faults may have been, has been, deeply punished here, and may hope to be spared hereafter."

"Oh, my father!" cried Lady Mouthermer weeping.

"And my daughter," continued her parent, "I beseech you to remember your unhappy mother, as one more sinned against than sinning. She was a mere child when confided to my care ; beautiful beyond imagination, lovely and elegant, I worshipped her as a divinity, I forestalled every wish, and gave way to every caprice, till she became—not what I might and ought to have made her, a rational being, aware of her responsibility for her gifts—but a spoilt child of fortune, scarcely knowing her own heart, and utterly careless of the feelings of others. But the serpent whom I cherished taught her to feel, and I believe she loved him as she had never yet loved any one, not even the husband of her choice."

Here Rosenberg stopped, overcome by his feelings, nor could his auditors answer him ; but his daughter threw herself into his arms and sobbed upon his shoulder.

"I could be happy even now, were it not for the thought of her sufferings ; but it may soon be over," continued Rosenberg. "If I fall, Mouthermer, cherish your beloved wife ; not by a blind adherence to her wishes, not by ministering to her unreasonable caprices, but by leading her to acknowledge herself a responsible being, and by teaching her to act like one. Now, my beloved child, farewell; we shall meet in the morning."

With a flood of bitter tears, Lady Mouthermer received her father's blessing, and retired. Her husband sat up to arrange Rosenberg's worldly affairs, and prepare him to go through the knightly ceremonial which we have already described, in speaking of Mancini.

Count Rosenberg watched his armour that night upon a terrace which encircled the top of Mouthermer House, but how different were his thoughts to those which agitated his opponent upon this occasion. Serene as the sky above his head, trusting, hoping, did Rosenberg pace the terrace, and if for a moment the idea of approaching death came over his mind, it was met with that fortitude which is the certain offspring of a peaceful conscience. Rosenberg's life had been already a long and an eventful one ; he had faced death in the field, and he had seen the tyrant seize those whom he had dearly loved ; the contemplation of it therefore was not new to him. He felt too that he had done some good in the world ; he had been the counsellor of peace to his sovereign, when others had cried out for war ; and in this he had been successful ; he had never perverted the stream of justice, but had to the extent of his power relieved the oppressed, and comforted the miserable ; all this now returned to his memory with healing on its wings.

The great misfortune, perhaps we ought to say blot, in the life of Count Rosenberg, had been his conduct towards his wife ; he had never led her into the right path ; but of this he even now thought leniently, and while he grieved over her fate, he could scarcely accuse himself as the cause of it.

"Could I but be assured," he said to himself, "that she repented of her sins, and gave one kind thought to the husband who adored her, I could die happy."

"It is so," whispered a voice by his side ; and turning round he beheld the phantom of a woman.

"Speak! Who art thou? How comest thou here?" he cried eagerly.

"Know you me not?" asked the figure.

"No—begone ; nor endeavour to discompose my spirit in this awful hour, ;" replied the count.

"Rosenberg! Know you not your Dorothea?" cried the phantom.

"Dorothea? Thou my Dorothea?"

"I was that creature of sin and shame," said the figure. "I am now permitted for a few brief moments to visit thee, to urge upon thee that without which my spirit can never know repose."

"Speak! what meanest thou?"

The phantom pointed to her dripping hair and said, in a low tone,—

"Thou knowest my fate?"

"I do," replied her auditor.

"As thou hopest for an honest burial thyself, let not my spirit longer wander upon the earth."

"Will the ocean then give up its dead?" asked Rosenberg.

"Alas! that it might have been so, but my soul may be cared for; masses might propitiate my pardon."

"It shall be so. I will at daybreak take due measures to have masses said for thy soul. Would that I could do more," replied the count.

"It has been given to me to warn thee against thine adversary on the morrow; he is subtle and skilful; and even were I assured that thou wouldst be victorious, yet it is well not to neglect caution."

"Dorothea, the words coming from the dead are sacred in my eyes," said Rosenberg. "And hast thou indeed a thought for the man whom thou didst so grievously wrong?"

"I have been punished—deeply punished. Thou art even now avenged, and ere to-morrow's sun shall have sunk beneath the horizon, thou shalt be yet more signally avenged. He shall fall beneath thy arm."

Rosenberg regarded the phantom with amazement.

"Thou dost not love him then?" he cried.

"Talk not of love to me. But something is due to thee, and I will repay it. I left my house, my child, my husband; I followed the betrayer to a strange land, and for years I was happy with him. Nay, start not; I repeat it, I was happy, for I loved him, as I had never known how to love the father of my child."

"Then it was indeed true what I suspected," cried Rosenberg.

"Years passed on; a life of gaiety and dissipation hardened my heart to the call of duty; he became careless or indifferent; I saw that he no longer loved the toy which he had filched from a worthier hand, and I determined to be revenged. Fate too readily gave me the opportunity. The young Count Vallombrosa saw me, and loved me—madly loved me. He, the traitor, discovered it, and fled with me to his own native land, there he hoped to wean me from my lover. Again dissipation held her intoxicating cup to my lips, but it was now in vain."

"And did—" began the count, but the phantom stopped him.

"Hear me," she said. "I have told thee that my time is short and fleeting; thou hast yet to learn the wretched steps which led to my fate. Count Vallombrosa followed me—we met—repeatedly met. His suspicion was roused, and he followed me to the appointed place—they fought, and Vallombrosa fell. I thought him dead, but a more merciful doom was awarded him. He escaped, entered a convent, repented, and died. And ——— I"

Here the phantom shuddered, and stopping for a few minutes, made a gesture to Rosenberg to be silent. After a pause she continued,—

"But a moment more is allowed me, I see the red light of dawn break over yonder hills."

"Oh, tell me!" cried Rosenberg.

"The convent was denied to me; the bare and naked dungeon was at first allotted; but that was gradually smoothed to me till my cruel persecutor thought that he had given ample time for penitence, and the bowl was drugged for my death."

"Ha!" exclaimed Rosenberg eagerly, "wert thou indeed poisoned?"

"Thou hast said it, and my mission is ended. Farewell."

"The villain! If my arm fail me to-morrow in the fight, yet shall he answer for this."

As Rosenberg said these words, the phantom glided away. He followed her with his eyes till she melted into thin air, and was no longer visible. The count became impatient for day break, and when the first faint streak tinged the horizon, he descended to his room, where he immediately sat down, and wrote a letter of accusation against Mancini for the murder of Dorothea, Countess of Rosenberg.

He also wrote to Father Anselm, desiring that a certain number of masses should be said for the repose of the soul of the countess, and making ample provision that his desire should be attended to.

Rosenberg had scarcely finished this duty when Mouthermer entered the room, and acquainted the count that a strange monk wished to speak with him.

"I have, however," he added, "informed him that it is scarcely possible his wish should be complied with at this time; but he is so urgent that I could not refuse to mention his visit to you."

"His name?" asked Rosenberg.

"He calls himself Father Anselm, and says that he has travelled far to see you to-day," replied Mouthermer.

"Let me see him, my son," said the count. "Fear not, he will aid me in a sacred duty."

Mouthermer, extremely surprised, left the room for a short time, and returned leading in Father Anselm; when Mouthermer again retired.

"Count Rosenberg," said the monk, "my errrnd is this. Facts have lately come accidentally to my knowledge, which affix the crime of murder to him whom you are this day to meet in mortal combat. The murder was of one——"

"I know—I know—she has told me," cried the count.

"She!" cried the monk.

"Yes—hearken to my tale."

The count then related what had occurred on the preceding night, much to the astonishment of his auditor, who at first seemed to treat the account as the dream of a heated and over-excited imagination.

"I am past my youth," said the count, in reply to his doubts; "the dreams are gone which heretofore led me on; this is the sober conviction of a mind cooled by age and experience. I need not describe the effect of such an apparition upon me."

"It is strange, it is mysterious; but, my son, the warning is given for us to act upon," said the monk.

"And I have acted upon it," replied Rosenberg. "Here is a packet relating all the facts of my extraordinary revelation, and charging this Mancini, as he calls himself, with the deliberate murder of his unfortunate victim. If I survive, I will myself present it to the king—if I fall, the duty lies upon you; for to you have I directed it."

Thus saying, Rosenberg took up the two packets from the table; that to which he had just alluded, he gave to Father Anselm; the other he held out, saying.—

"This too is a melancholy bequest. It is to request that mass may be said at the chapel of the priory of St. Benedict at Duncraig, in Scotland, for the repose of the soul of Dorothea Rosenberg. I have herein directed that ample means be afforded from the revenues of my estates, for this holy purpose. That, too, I leave in your charge.

"Your desire shall be immediately complied with," replied Father Anselm; "I knew her in her brighter days, and will myself direct the required services."

"One other point," said the count. "I meet my deadliest enemy; I may fall, but I must not fall unabsolved."

"I will be upon the spot," replied the monk. "It was one purpose of my journey here. Farewell now, my son, and may right be might in the ensuing combat."

With these words, the monk retired, and Rosenberg prepared to take perhaps a last farewell of his beloved daughter.

Upon this interview we must drop a veil; we would not profane the feelings of either mourner, by exposing them to public gaze. The father and his child parted in sorow and tears; Lord Mouthermer accompanying the count to the place of meeting.

CHAPTER XLVI.

The lists are ope'd, the spacious area clear'd
  Thousands on thousands piled, are seated round
Long ere the first oud trumpet's note is heard,
  No vacant place for lated wight is found.—BYRON.

THE place which had been fixed upon by Henry for the trial by combat, was a piece of ground on the outside of the walls of London, beyond Clerkeny rell Here the lists had been arranged; a splendid stand had been erected for the king.
No. 39.

and his court, and other less magnificent but more capacious ones for the spectators. The latter, it was expected, would include almost all the nobility resident at that time in London, and many of the second rank, with a large concourse of the common people.

So great was the rage for shows and pageants at that time, that even a scene which was almost certain to terminate fatally on one side, if not both, was regarded as a subject for amusement and merry-making. The higher classes, accustomed to behold in war a means of self aggrandisement, had become callous to scenes of bloodshed; while the lower classes eagerly sought in pageantries and splendid processions, a relief from the burdens which the unsettled state of the kingdom for so long a time had entailed upon them. In this case they might almost be excused by the magnificent preparations which greeted their eyes.

The royal stand was elevated above the field; it was superbly decorated with gilded carving, and various devices, while the interior was fitted up with purple cloth worked in gold. The cumbrous draperies, the massy cornices, the richly wrought pillars which supported it, would rather lead one to think that it was a temple destined for the permanent habitation of the sovereign than a mere temporary building.

When Henry appeared, long and loud shouts rent the air: "God save King Henry!" "Long live King Henry!" burst from every lip, and was prompted by every heart. The king acknowledged this with repeated bows, and other tokens of gracious condescension, and by that means increased the acclamations of the multitude. With an air of kingly dignity Henry seated himself under a canopy in the centre of the stand appropriated to him and his court; and made a signal that he was ready to witness the combat.

The combatants rode forward into the ring; Rosenberg was mounted upon a white charger handsomely caparisoned; he wore silver plate armour, and bore for his crest a pair of wings with the motto, "Ready, aye, ready." His helmet was decorated with a splendid plume of white feathers.

Mancini was in a black chain armour, and wore black plumes in his helmet; his crest was a hand reaching out of a cloud, with the motto, "Courage in darkness." The two squires Lord Mouthermer and Frazer, attended on foot, equipped in a light armour.

A herald then came forward, and proclaimed as follows in a loud voice,

"By leave of King Henry, I hereby declare that Godfrey Count Rosenberg challenges to mortal combat Humphrey de Dunstanville, commonly called Count Mancini; accusing him of the murder of Dorothea Rosenberg, and of other matters traitorous to our sovereign lord the king. This challenge Count Mancini accepts, declaring himself innocent of the said murder."

The herald then blew three loud blasts upon his trumpet, and withdrew; while at a signal given by the king, the two foes burst upon each other. A dead silence prevailed among the spectators, nothing was heard but the heavy shock of the meeting; a cloud of dust was raised by the pawing and gallop of the impatient steeds.

Rosenberg received his adversary's furious onset upon his shield, while at the same time he darted his lance at Mancini. The second onset was more effective; each warrior being slightly wounded, but both the lances were broken in shivers. Then dismounted, their steeds were led away, and the combat continued on foot by swords.

At first Mancini had decidedly the advantage over his competitor, who was badly wounded in the side; but the former pressing too hard upon him, fell, and Rosenberg was for a moment supposed to be the victor.

"Confess thy guilt," cried Rosenberg, "and trust to my mercy."

"Never! while I have life," exclaimed his opponent, making a desperate thrust.

Rosenberg now saw that it must be no child's play; both were on their feet, and gazing on each other with furious eyes; a dreadful combat ensued; they closed in upon each other, and after a moment of breathless suspense, Mancini was stretched upon the ground mortally wounded, his sword broken, and his armour displaced.

The king immediately dropped his sceptre to intimate that the combat was over, and Frazer stepped forward to the assistance of his master, unclosed his helmet to give him air, and unlaced his armour. Rosenberg, too, approached his rival.

"If thou canst speak, adknowledge thy guilt, and a monk stands here ready to absolve thee in thy dying hour."

"I need no monk, she died not by my hand," replied Mancini.

"Liest thou with thy dying breath?" said father Anselm, stepping forward.

"What voice was that?" cried the count in a tone of agony.

"It is mine—too well dost thou know it, traitor and murderer," said the monk.

"Not murderer," replied Mancini.

"Do spirits then speak falsely?" asked Rosenberg. "She told me it was thy deed."

"She! hast thou too seen her then?" exclaimed Mancini.

"I have," replied Rosenberg.

"Where?" asked Mancini.

"Yesternight, when watching my armour according to the rules of knighthood," answered Rosenberg.

"I, too, have seen her, and she told me I should fall. But mine was not the deed," persisted Mancini.

"Unhappy man," cried Father Anselm. "Dost thou hope by a miserable, weak subterfuge, to evade the doom of thy crimes. It was by thy order that she died."

"Not even by my order," cried Mancini.

"Let us all leave the dying man; he has not many moments to live; I will endeavour to obtain from him a full confession."

It was as Father Anselm desired; he was left alone with Mancini, whose life was fast ebbing. After a short conversation in a low tone of exhortation by the monk, Mancini said,—

"Dennis was the guilty one; he knew that she prevented my forming a marriage with one whom you know; he was tired of the charge given into his hands, of her importunities and complaints; and it was he that mixed the fatal bowl."

"With thy knowledge," said Father Anselm.

Mancini made no answer.

"And where is the criminal?" asked the monk.

"I know not," was the reply of the dying man.

"False, hardened sinner, how darest thou trifle with me!" cried Father Anselm.

"I know not, father," ejaculated Mancini. "He left the country when I came last to London, and probably is in his native land."

"And dost thou repent?" asked the father.

"I repent that I have failed in my projects," replied Mancini.

"No more?" asked the monk.

"What avails repentance now? Will it bring back fame, honour, wealth, life? Say that it can, and I repent."

Father Anselm turned from the dying man, and was about to leave him, when in a weak voice Mancini requested his attention; the monk immediately returned to his side, and Mancini said,—

"One word—how did Cordelia de Dunstanville escape?"

"Let not that pure name be defiled by thy lips," returned the monk. "I was the humble instrument of her escape, and thy discomfiture."

"And the woman Bridget?" asked the count.

"She assisted me," answered the monk.

"Enough—enough——" The dying man turned his face from the monk, and made a sign to Frazer, who bending down to him received the last commands of him whom he had so long served. In a few minutes all was over, and a lifeless corpse was all that remained of the haughty Count Mancini.

The body was removed by Frazer to the house where he had resided, and was afterwards buried by Mancini's own directions, at a small church in a village in the vicinity of London.

In the meanwhile, Mouthermer had conveyed Rosenberg home, where he was received with rapture by his daughter; who, however, was considerably alarmed when she heard the nature and extent of his wound. A skilful surgeon was immediately sent for, and fitting remedies applied, which after some time happily proved successful, and Rosenberg was restored to health.

The first act of his convalescence was to send for Frazer, and to engage him to proceed to Duncraig, there to search for and obtain any relics of the property possessed by his deceased wife, especially certain papers and jewels which she had taken with her when she first left her happy home. The papers Frazer was able to recover, together with many others of a later date; but the jewels he could not discover, and he informed Rosenberg that he had no doubt they had been sold to supply, in part, the demands of Mancini's extravagance.

When the news of the combat, and of its fatal but fortunate issue, reached Percival Castle, it created a great sensation among the family assembled there. Cordelia, especially, was awe-struck at the sudden close of the life of him who had so deeply injured her; she felt, too, that she had lost the only link which bound her to her father's memory; and although that link was an unworthy one, yet she could not forget that he bore the name of the author of her being. Thus she felt, and Edward had too much respect for the heart whose goodness he fully appreciated, to blame her feelings.

To Bridget the loss of Mancini was a subject of heartfelt rejoicing; nor was it less so to Kate. Both had pined under his tyranny and mysterious proceedings at Duncraig, where nothing but affection for her old mistress would have induced Bridget so long to remain; and Kate, the child of a brighter land, hated the cloudy skies and chill atmosphere of the north.

There were others less closely interested, but who openly rejoiced at the downfall of Mancini; these were his equals, to whom he had been overbearing and proud, and who, not feeling the superiority to be founded on just grounds which he assumed towards them, felt only joy at his downfall and disastrous death. King Henry felt that he had but lost a doubtful subject, while he had in Rosenberg one of his most faithful and able counsellors, to whom he looked for aid in every crisis.

As soon after the fatal day of combat as Edward de Albini thought his wife would feel it to be decent, he proposed a journey to London, in order to present her in form at court

"I am happy here," replied Cordelia. "Why go to that hated place?"

"It is our duty to present ourselves there," said Edward.

"I cannot leave all my new friends this inclement weather; they need my care," said Cordelia.

"The Lady Elfrida will supply your place, my Cordelia, to your poor pensioners," answered Edward. "It is her proposal; and I am the more anxious to accede to it at once, as a letter which I have this morning received from Mouthermer informs me, that he and his wife intend accompanying the Count Rosenberg into Germany as soon as his health is sufficiently re-established, and, as they cannot leave him to come here, they wish us to go to London to take leave of them."

"If that be the case, I give up all opposition," replied Cordelia. "I wish above all things to have the benefit of Lady Mouthermer's countenance upon my first appearance in the courtly world."

"I have the same desire," said her husband; "therefore I may write to that effect?"

"Yes," said Cordelia. "And Edith?"

"She will join us in London."

Thus was the matter arranged; and Edward de Albini again travelled towards the metropolis. Upon their arrival at Mouthermer House they found Rosenberg quite able to travel, and all the family in excellent spirits.

Kate, who accompanied her mistress to town, no sooner heard of the contemplated journey than she begged earnestly to be allowed to accompany Lady Mouthermer abroad; she disliked England, and, as we have seen, had no reason for any very strong ties of affection towards her mother. Cordelia therefore granted her request.

The Baroness de Mowbray and the young Baroness de Albini were presented at court, where both were extremely admired. Edith's gentle but dignified demeanour gained her the respect and esteem of all whom she associated with; she was still somewhat timid, and this heightened and improved her beauty; while Cordelia had entirely recovered the spirits which were natural to her character, and her brilliant wit and graceful liveliness made her the theme of universal admiration.

De Hesling doated upon his adopted child; after the death of the Lady Elfrida, he resided at Percival Castle; and when he died, he left Cordelia heiress to immense wealth, which she bounteously distributed to all those who needed it.

With De Fougeres also a regular communication was kept up; although it was many years before Cordelia could summon courage enough to visit the scenes of her childhood and youth. At last, however, De Albini prevailed on her to accompany him thither, and together they roamed through the well-known woods, or lingered by the ever-flowing stream.

"How many feelings, contradictory and perplexing, does this call forth, my Edward," said Cordelia, as they entered the Lady's Bower.

"And yet how is the aspect of the place changed," replied her husband. "Decay's effacing fingers have left the marks of their labour in this wandering ivy, this obtrusive woodbine, which has found a way into the room. It was not here, Cordelia, when you——"

"Nay, Edward, be not ungenerous," replied Cordelia, gaily. "I must not be reminded of the follies of my youth on the very spot where they were committed."

"I was but going to mention that day when the faithful Ronald so mysteriously led you into yonder thicket, and there held a conversation so long and close, that surely a lover might be forgiven if he envied it."

"I too can tell of long and close conversation envied—oh! how deeply envied. When Edith followed so well the advice of Father Augustine, to love and cherish the captive knight. Oh, Edward," Cordelia added, "we have much to look back upon of misery——"

"And much to look forward to of happiness," interrupted her husband.

It was so. There was much of happiness to all.

THE END.

www.ingramcontent.com/pod-product-compliance
Lightning Source LLC
Chambersburg PA
CBHW081144020726
47504CB00009B/1999